THE
GODS
ARE
THIRSTY

THE GODS ARE THIRSTY

❖ ❖ ❖

TANITH LEE

THE OVERLOOK PRESS

WOODSTOCK • NEW YORK

First published in 1996 by
The Overlook Press
Lewis Hollow Road
Woodstock, New York 12498

Library of Congress Cataloging-in-Publication Data

Lee, Tanith
The gods are thirsty / Tanith Lee.
p. cm.
1. Desmoulins, Camille, 1760–1794 – Fiction.
2. France – History – Revolution, 1789–1799 – Fiction.
3. Revolutionaries – France – Fiction. 4. Journalists – France – Fiction.
I. Title. PR6062.E4163G63 1996
823'.914 – dc20 96-3583 CIP

Manufactured in The United States of America
ISBN: 0-87951-672-0
First Edition
1   3   5   7   9   10   8   6   4   2

For Lucile

O Fortuna!

✤ ✤ ✤

Author's Note

I HAVE, OF COURSE, leaned heavily on documents relating to the times and the people of the French Revolution, and my sources are many and various. Where – as often happens in these cases – accounts disagree, I have made my own deduction or, more relevantly perhaps, my own choice. I acknowledge with gratitude the help of my French translators, Mme. Malgarini and M. Simon; however, all translations used here are ultimately my own. Sometimes, obviously, I have resorted to précis. (This will be apparent in the reduction of a pamphlet over eighty pages long to only a few pages in the novel.) Sometimes I have annotated or developed the material slightly, juxtaposed passages, or incorporated elements from elsewhere, though never wantonly. Here and there I have tried to clarify points which might prove obscure to anyone unfamiliar with the terrain.

Of the songs, doggerel, and poetry, most (aside from such articles as patently could not be) are genuine, occasionally surprising, products of the era. My translations are in all instances what is normally termed "free." But with prose and poetry both, I have tried always to stay true to the heart, if not the flesh, of the matter, with actual material or with that affixed or invented.

So too with the anecdotes and jokes of the Revolution. I would comment that some of these that seem the least credible are the most likely to be real.

Because the historic past is the contemporary Now to those who are living it, I have no more attempted to write the book in an archaic vein than I would try to set it out in eighteenth-century French. The savage spirit of Year One is eternal and, I hope, recognizable. For such reasons, too, I have let the names of things, places, and persons flow in and out of French and English – in order to keep their intrinsic and evocative look and sound but also that they might come, as then they did, in a known vernacular.

On Guise. Camille was always edgy about his birthplace, but the picture one gets as a modern visitor is quite different. The kindness and help given a stray author, one bright March afternoon in 1983, is remembered by her with some pleasure. I think Camille, startled, might have smiled at the little caution I was also given: *He is thought well of, here.* I can only say to that, This is Camille's book and I could no more stop its course than a committed writer ever can with any work. I hope not to have offended. It was not my intention.

As to the solid facts that Guise has long since named a street for Camille Desmoulins, and put up to him a gallant handsome statue in the square, I am sure these things would have moved him, touched him. Like most of us, he was a mixture of opposites at war with himself. He was also possessed of a great intellectual talent and, like many creatures of the mind, found the world outside confusing. Basically self-questioning, his weakness sprang from his strength. And from his physical cowardice, if so it is even to be called, rose his final astonishing moral courage. As with Danton, it took a guillotine to silence him. And maybe even a guillotine did not succeed.

❧ ❧ ❧

Acknowledgments

The author wishes to thank the following places and institutions for their help:

The Public Library Services of Greenwich and Bromley
Guise Museum and Gendarmerie
The Musée de L'Ile de France
The French Embassy, London
Hachette Bookshop
Piccadilly Rare Books
Madame Tussaud's, Marylebone
Mary Evans Picture Library, Blackheath

And the following persons for their help, time, and insights:

Elizabeth Bell
Undine Concannon
Gerard Décotil
Diana and Helen Denney
Henk and Catherine Duval
Jean Noël Guiard
Christopher Hibbert
Anthony Higgins

Rosemary Hawley Jarman
Drusilla Koffman
Barbara La Rocca
Bernard Lee
Carol McShane
Elaine Malgarini
Eric Simon
Chelsea Quinn Yarbro

And a special thank you to Tracy Carns, and The Overlook Press of New York.

Principal Sources

The French Revolution, Thomas Carlyle
The French Revolution, Christopher Hibbert
Oeuvres de Camille Desmoulins (Kraus reprint)
Camille Desmoulins, Violet Methley
Love Is Revolution, John Hartcup
Mirabeau, Antonina Vallentin
Danton, Robert Christophe
Life of Danton, A. H. Beesly
Robespierre (The Tyranny of the Majority), Jean Matrat
Saint-Just, J. B. Morton
Marie Antoinette, Clara Tschudi
Madame Tussaud, Anita Leslie and Pauline Chapman

ONE

WHERE TO START. How to start. What to say and what to unsay. And where to draw the line between the heart's genuine loud crying and the justification of self.

There was no time, then. No space to do it. Not even anywhere, in that cramped little stone hole, to write. While they, and one in particular, had all the luxurious room in the world, and as much time as was needed, to make their accusations in the finest language, even—if he had wanted, the bastard—to put them into verse. In any case, they stopped our mouths. They wouldn't let us speak a word. And later again, too late, still trying, nobody listened. Except Danton, who said to me, Shut up, for God's sake shut up. Which seemed, in those final minutes, the last worst blow of all (though that was still to come). As if he had actually struck me across the face.

So now I mean to try to speak again. And already I see the fatal flaw. Since maybe it will all be lies, memory the slave bringing only the images it thinks I will like, and even those wrongly dressed for the occasion. Well. What else can I do? The thorn sears in my heel, or in my heart. I must attempt to pluck it out. And let the blood flow with the ink. As it did then, through all the gutters, till even the setting sun on the crimson river called Womb reminded us of blood.

Paris 1789: Summer

THE HORSE, as it came up the grass-stitched highway in the year seven hundred and eighty-nine of the second thousand A.D., was tired and beginning to labor. It had been ridden nearly flat out for twelve miles from that place known as Versailles. Also, though the rider who had hired the horse was light, he was consumed by nervous excitement and ire—and this the horse had felt through every mile and every equine bone. Now, trembling, heaving, and clattering, it was on the home straight. Not necessarily welcoming. For some distance, and some weeks, the wayside fields had changed contour into the anthill encampments of the king's foreign troops. Over the peaked tents the white Bourbon lily and the arms of the Allemande drooped in the heat, but figures kept moving in ominous clockwork maneuvers. Generally they spared no challenge for one man on a horse, though at Saint-Cloud there had been an altercation going on in the street which necessitated a diagonal gallop off the road and over a trio of hedges.

The effect of this army ringing Paris was depressing and baleful, as were the groups of lack-riddled itinerants washed up to the capital by bad harvests and now leaning at public cisterns and in the doors of hovels that sold wine. Here, on the final lap, men were sitting on the shoulder where houses untidily clustered. The cobbles were neatly pied with pats of dung from flocks driven through earlier in the day. You sensed bored morose hands quite ready to pick up a pat and throw it. But a couple of men called a question; that was all. He saw them, the rider, and heard, but only as part of the disquieting landscape he rushed through. Which is worth remembering in the light of what comes next.

Near where the old walls of the city were broken by a gate, he delivered the horse at the customs barrier. But they were edgy here, too, and wanted to make a joke out of his headlong ride. "Late for his wedding, I expect." That was one joke he could have done without. "Oh, she must be a rare catch, if she's taken on a pretty fellow like this." Which was, conversely, a joke he was used to. He fidgeted, waiting to be let through, biting his nails. "Cute, is she?" these official layabouts insisted. "Yes, gorgeous. Three eyes and one leg. A perfect match. Wish me joy." Which broke their tension and made them fall about laughing, hugging each other and him. And he was able then to shoulder by and escape.

He was twenty-nine, with all twenty-nine's impatience. Shabby, disheveled (I have two shirts, both worn to the sheerest gauze; laundresses mistake them for giant dead moths and scream with terror), and with a mass of black hair curling over his shoulders. In his teens he had had it powdered. You did that kind of thing then, bourgeois passing for aristo. But really he had only looked like a sort of diabolic sheep. His enemies always had and always would call him ugly. His friends grinned, slapped him on the back, and called him a fool.

(Then there were the other jokes about which way was the wind blowing today, or how was the corn? Not knowing his name, the customs oafs hadn't resorted to those.)

Look at his eyes, though, this thin wild young man hurrying into the city. Eyes bright black and curiously wide set, like those of some strange animal, some faun out of a pagan forest. Already, writing, he strains them. In a year or so there will be some reading spectacles. But they don't miss much, these eyes burning so bright in the mercurial ugliness of a face only the enemies say *is* ugly; but he will always have plenty of enemies.

The city, meanwhile, is beautiful. Yes, even though its edges degenerate into mighty slums, even though it stinks in parts with poverty, sewage, and all the filth bakings of summer.

Sorcerous Paris, Paris on the river which is the Fount of Life. As if to drink the water of the river, as do the buildings on its banks, would be to gain immortality. In fact, it would poison you. It is sometimes possible to catch fish from it and eat those, and this the poor now and then have done. Hunger is a poison too.

Because it will soon be hard to keep your distance, start by looking at the city from high up, as high as its tall summer hills. The city has, you perceive, its own definite color—which is dove-gray and faintest parchment-yellow—and one long vital artery of gray lead shot with gold, the river called Womb. (Poison apart, how many drowned there last night? Like any city worthy of the name, Paris has its murderous shadow life. It is only when shadows take on flesh that things get out of hand.)

Like a puzzle game the city's shape scatters in all directions, its interstices set with architecture. A slate-capped palace, gilded by early afternoon, and there a cathedral, asleep on its island with its paws tucked in, some great beast turned to stone, whose stained-glass eyes gaze only inward. And here the cluttered quays, and here the litter of winding, twining, plaiting streets, with all their own centerpieces that are towered churches, deep-spooned gardens white-flowered by statues, pillared theaters and arcades.

Down, now. No use trying to stay up in the air. That's the aristocratic ploy: powdered hair, and Paris besieged by her own troops because someone asked for bread. Down into the breathing sound, the scent and stench of it, the spilled wine, the sawn wood, the sewers, the sacred incense and the offal shops, and the perfume of trees in July leaf.

Juillet: Prime of summer, month of green uprisings

The garden of the Palais-Royal was held in by the linked arms of mildly yellow arcades, in which a cave work of jewelers, booksellers, glovemakers, astrologers, perfumers—and ubiquitous coffeehouses—busily thrived. A fairground, the whole garden, with one painter's dream view of a domed ducal residence. Every couple of feet a brave young tree, shouting green with, as often as not, bold flags and ribbons caught in its hair. Between the trees and the views, a squeeze of stalls, jugglers, puppets, singers, stingers, and thieves. Between that and the pavilioned Café Chinois with flowers on its roof, the bivouac of the "patriot" soldiers, garlanded by bottles and warriors on the grass. Originally, officially, these men were stationed west and over the river on Mars Meadow, along with the Royal Allemande and the proud Swiss. But they had this problem, the French troops. Their king, persuaded by his foreign Austrian queen, had decided to set up a martial presence in the city. But who said a Frenchman should be willing to open fire on another Frenchman? Well, she said it, Austrian Antoinette, *la reine blonde*. And what did the French troops say then? They said, Well, *Madame la Reine,* good luck. Let's go and sit on the grass in the Palais-Royal.

It was more fun over here. Or over there by the linked-arm arcades where the coffee shops and the wineshops breathed out their welcoming fumes, and vast quantities of eager young lawyers seemed always about, solely in order to buy you a drink. And besides, there were some lovely girls in the Palais-Royal. A number of them only charged a few sous.

The garden, gifted as a pleasance to the People, was owned by the People's favorite aristocrat, the Duc d'Orléans. Sometimes he would appear on a balcony of the domed domicile and wave. There was generally news here, too. Here the first of that day's rain of pamphlets always seemed to fall. Everyone in palpitating Paris who could write (or thought he could) was printing the things. In charming colors, too, powder-pink, pastel gray, or beige. When you'd (if you'd) read them, you could resell or tear them up small and throw them out the brothel windows on the heads of the orators underneath.

Because there was always some orator, orating. Up on a table, making a speech. There were several who were good. They had style and pace. You could take your rhythm from them, which was valuable to a man used to marching. And how many of the absent-without-leave soldiers had come to the roar of a chap under the window bellowing about the rights of man—or, if you timed it *perfectly,* to the cheers of the crowd.

⚜

Where did the trouble start? At least five centuries before, when men of noble birth became gods and men of no birth became their slaves.

More immediately, it started with rotten harvests, an appalling winter, and a rise in the price of bread, so that eating became what the rich did. It started with a new king named Louis, shambling into history, shortsightedly and benignly nodding, too shy to say good morning and too slow to say anything more apposite. It started with Louis being a vacillator, now agreeing to this, now that. His name swiftly became a pun: L'oui—King Yes-Yes. When you have very little and you are offered what appears might be rescue and then there is no rescue, it hurts far worse than if they had left you alone.

In May, King Yes-Yes called together the ancient ideal of a *parlement,* the Three Estates. The First Estate was composed of the nobility, the first vampire of the nation. The Second Estate comprised the clergy, vampire number two. The Third Estate represented the People, the envampirized.

Having nothing, you will tend to hope for something. At the onset it seemed that here it would be. A political voice, justice. All under the aegis of a kind, kingly father who cared. But the new *parlement* was a sham and a shambles, for what can one third of a whole do against two? Then the growling started. Then the anger began. Then the troops moved in a swarm around the city, into the city, marched through the streets banging drums. The kind father had got out the strap.

It now stood, this July day of heat and impending thunder, that two hopes remained in the eyes of the People. First, the Third Estate had grown militant. It had sworn an oath to form a constitution and to fight for the rights of ordinary citizens, indeed for the whole citizenry of France. And so far, the Third Estate had not been disbanded but went on shouting and demanding in the Butterfly Town of Versailles under King L'oui's nose. The second hope was a finance minister named Jacques Necker, out of whom Paris had made an idol. Necker did not believe, apparently, in crippling the masses to pay for France's financial stumblings. It almost seemed he worked magic, for cash figures improved overnight, and no one had been bled to death. A wizard, he was also the People's foot inside the glittering door. He alone could lead them to prosperity. Necker mattered a great deal. And just this morning –

❦

"Hey, Windmill! Windmill!"

Someone thrust through the green-treed crowd and grabbed him. Friends in full cry.

"Where have you been? You look half mad as usual. What's been happening you obviously know and we don't? Come and have a drink."

He stood in the arcade, pushed at by soldiers, early revelers, a carpenter with a chair frame, handsome whores who eyed him askance, for patently he had no money. He opened his mouth.

"It's something important, then?" The three or four acquaintances who now surrounded him laughed at him or cursed him, and one tapped him on the chest the way you did with a faulty clock. As usual, because it mattered, he couldn't get it out: the stammer, which would affect him in excitement or nerves. Damn it, damn it – the sounds coming from him were absurd, like a mechanical chicken, choking. In desperation he turned his back on them and tore his hair.

"Here you are," said Louis-Mer, inserting a glass of cloudy wine between Windmill and this frenzy.

Windmill drank the wine. It might loosen his tongue, more likely his brains. He hadn't eaten anything since seven o'clock last night.

"What time is it?" he asked Louis-Mer quite coherently.

The friends jeeringly applauded. "Two-thirty. Didn't you hear the bell?"

"So late – md-my God. Haven't you heard anything *but* bloody bells?"

"Heard what? You're going to tell us. Slowly now, Camille. Though preferably before the suspense kills us."

"The king," said Windmill, "has dismissed Necker."

They stared at him. All around, the generalized fairground noise of the Palais-Royal went on. Close at hand a group of soldiers was singing, in the embrace of another group of sawdusty joiners and out-of-work artisans. Everyone came here. Even lordlings. Even the lowest and most frantic class might be seen as represented playing cards among the arches, black-nailed, or wandering like lost souls, trying to find someone to read the latest pamphlet to them. A lewd, merry, wandering, or puzzled throng. Still uninformed.

"The one minister the People approve and trust," said Louis-Mer. His face was intense with concentration. He was weighing the information. What would it bring him? "Truly? Out?"

Windmill shrugged, nervous spasm of the shoulders. "Wh-what else? Paris is starving and Paris asks for bread and the aristos put troops into the Champ-de-Mars. The Third Estate talks about rights, and the aristos tell the king, Sack Necker."

Someone said, almost gaily, "They told the Austrian bitch the people had no bread and she said, Let them eat cakes, then."

"No, René, idiot. That was another bitch one hundred and fifty years ago. If you said it to Antoinette she'd say, Let them eat hemlock and die and stop complaining."

Louis-Mer said, "You're sure, Camille?"

"I was at Versailles."

"Still, *sure?*"

"I'm sure, goddamn it, sure. As sure as I am they'll depend on us to bleat about it and do nothing. Oh, God help the cowardice of the whole lot of us!"

Windmill-like, he waved his arms, feeling with a bitter hilarity the frayed seams of his coat give way.

The wine sprang through him now, bringing him not strength or wit but something that was almost terror. Caught in this tense little whirlpool within the vaster whirlpool of the garden, he felt himself suddenly on the brink of some colossal unknown thing. He was afraid he could not seize the swordlike moment which was so abruptly offered him. And, too, he was afraid he *would* seize it.

"Well, we must—" said Louis-Mer Fréron, but already someone was leaning into their circle, a big man with tattooed arms.

"What's up?"

"He says—"

"Let Camille tell it. It's his news."

"Go on, Camille. You've got Paris in the palm of your hand."

"Jesus Christ, so he has. Don't stammer, Camille."

Louis-Mer cuffed the speaker.

There was a scramble up onto chairs. A wine bottle went over. The wine ran out, too thin to mimic blood, along the paving, and not red enough, either.

The table onto which Windmill found himself being shoved, the chair on the table which someone else held steady with one shoulder, appalled him. It was like a mountain. It was so precarious.

And there he stood, a lamp hanging in the arch much nearer than a minute ago. And the sprawling crowd—Oh, look, another speechmaker. What's this one want to say?—turning, swirling about him like a huge multicolored wheel. The whole garden reeling. The tops of the trees. The sky. Well, he had spoken to them before. Sometimes. It was like a Roman forum. You picked a corner, waited your turn, said a few words. They booed or applauded. But if you said what they wanted, and it was fairly blatant what they wanted, they cheered.

But this time the news was black. And the garden would be full of the king's agents, no doubt of that. God knew, someone might take aim and shoot him—but it was two-thirty, it was hot enough to blast the soul—and the fire in him was not the sun, not the wine, but this extraordinary thing compounded of terror and life lust and the yearning for some power over events, always denied.

He stared at the carefree crowd, and it turned its eyes toward the shrill blaze of his.

"Listen!" he screamed into their chatter. "For God's sake, listen! By tomorrow morning every one of you could be dead!"

That did the trick. They listened.

And in those seconds he heard, or sensed, the silence spread away from him, across the garden, as if every clock in Paris, or every heart, had stopped.

And in those seconds, too, the terror almost throttled him. For one moment he was stifled, and then the words came, tumbling out of him, clear and formed, too fast to hold back. "Necker—you remember him, the People's good angel? Necker is dismissed."

The decision was made, the terror lost. Then, even as he shouted, the subsidiary fear brushed him, of the stuttering catching him again, or his voice, never strong, going. But this, too, was dashed away and left behind, for the final argument and stage into which he passed was passion. It came in like a wave, and picked him up, and carried him, so he was lifted higher in the air than a table and a chair could take him. He seemed then to be standing on the roof, on the shoulders of the sky. It made him drunker than the wine had done. His blood was full of electricity, his weak voice somehow carried like thunder. It appeared six thousand people surrounded him; all Paris surrounded him, eyes wide, only on him, ears straining to receive his words.

There had been a roar of dismay and rage. Necker, star of the nation's wishes, flung on the scrap heap along with all cries for food and justice.

"*This* is how they treat you!" he yelled now. "This is how they have always treated you and always will treat you till the sun goes out. You," he said. "*You* and *you,*" but he scarcely saw the individual faces, though he felt the words pass into them like arrows. Their faces were all one face, all tilted up and craning toward him, altering, inflamed, and at his mercy, like—yes, like the face of a woman in the act of love. "And now they've done this, what next? Listen, they'll do anything. You have dared show you have opinions, but your lord king doesn't like them—or, should I say, the polished scum of his court doesn't. You've frightened them badly. The aristos shook in their shoes. So now they'll try to frighten you: Back into the kennel, dogs, and lie down and lick the ground. But if you do lie down under this, God help you all. Do you know the numbers of His Majesty's troops waiting around Paris? Thirty thousand men. But forget those. He has enough Germans and Swiss in Mars Field to send them through the streets tonight *and murder every citizen in his bed.*" Outcry and curses. The response! They gazed up at him, open eyes like an open embrace, pleading, ready: Tell us what to do. "Well," he called to them, "will you wait to be killed like sheep? For God's sake, arm yourselves—*fight,* for the love of God!" Clamoring now. The table shook as someone thumped on it. The cheers of that fellow with the tattooed arms were deafening. They were all shrieking at each other: Arms! Weapons! Guns!

(What have I done? Cold little question. But the raging passion thrust it away. What does it matter what I've done? I've told the truth.) And he found himself dragging the old derelict of a pistol, which he had taken along the Versailles road against possible cutthroats, out of his coat, showing them, saying, "And I'll lay a bet the king's darling police are watching me—let them! Look, gentlemen. What am I doing? Calling Paris to freedom! What is better to die for than truth?"

And someone bellowed, "Don't fret, citizen, we'll protect you. Let them just try to lay a finger on you if I'm by." And other voices joined in, offering him a guard of honor all the days of his life. And he knew himself held fast in their love. In turn, the love in him flowed back to them. His eyes were wet. Theirs too. And now one of the patriot soldiers shouted, "We're with you. Give us our new colors, general!"

There was a girl close by the table with a pure green ribbon in her hair. He looked down at her, at the ribbon the color of July's trees. It seemed she knew. She twisted the ribbon free and held it up to him the length of her warm, smooth arm. Instead of the pistol now he showed the crowd the ribbon.

"Green," he said. "For hope."

At that instant, on that last word, his voice gave out. It didn't matter anymore.

The great wheel which he alone seemed to have set in motion now turned fiercely all by itself. Not just passion but the crowd, carrying him. And snow was falling, green snow. They were tearing the leaves off the chestnut trees, pinning them on hats and coats and in the bosoms of dresses. *Le vert ou la mort* they cawed at each other now, furious and laughing. Whoever lacked a green cockade would be awarded this offer. Whoever would not don the People's color was a traitor to the People.

Windmill, borne through the gardens, no longer on the sky's shoulders, on human ones.

Full:

Lead us! they cried to him. The soldiers shook him, happily, savagely: You're the captain.

"No," he said. He felt boneless and very tired. He wanted it to stop. In a play, a curtain would have come down at this point. But this was life, where curtains came down only at the wrong times. "The People," he said, "can have no leaders. The People is one brain, one heart." They exploded with zeal at his words. And let him go.

For a few seconds the crowd rushed by, and Windmill stood leaning on one of the stripped chestnut trees, a carpet of torn leaves around his feet. He looked at the trees; a gale seemed to have passed through them, or it might have been winter. He looked at the torn leaves and began to feel surprise. Then Louis-Mer and the tattooed man had hold of him, taking the green ribbon from his neurasthenic fingers and pinning it on his coat.

Louis-Mer was also rather green. "You've started something," he said.

❊

Men are not the causers of history. History itself, by a pressure of events, causes men to resort to particular actions. Anyone could have jumped on that table. It is quite irrelevant who did.

❊

In any case, it started before this. Is anything really so simple? Aren't there twenty — a hundred — reasons for everything that is ever done?

The stammer, for example. Where did *that* begin? Not a physical impediment, a nervous one. My father, perhaps. We didn't always understand one another. His universe was ordered, and though he loved me, child of misrule, and I him, this only made it more difficult. My God, he could exasperate me! I recall that great black ledger of his, some treatise he was always writing on the law — clever, never finished. No hurry. A hobby.

And then I remember a funeral of some relative virtually unknown to me, and at the funeral dinner where we had gathered like crows, I said something they all thought was funny and they started to giggle. And because I was young and liked to be amusing (and attention's center) I brought out all my best Parisian jokes, and toward the end a couple I believe were even rather improper. But they were all in hysterics by then. Even the widow was sobbing, and not with grief. While I gather that outside, in the village street, passersby clustered in shock to listen to this sad funeral party howling with mirth till the windows rattled. Of none of which my refined scholarly father approved. So I said, "Solemn lament over someone one doesn't know is ridiculous. Why should I make myself more ridiculous than I am already?" To which he replied, "Your thoughts are your own. What you say—worse, what you write down—becomes the property of others and may be used against you." "Yes," I said. "Hn-n-I know. I'm no success at it, but I'm a lawyer too." (I was home in the country at the time because of unsuccess, having no money to stay in Paris.) "Nn-n-and anyway, I cn-can h-hardly ever get a word-wd out." My mother, who might have reconciled us, was seriously ailing. (She had been so since the birth of my sisters.) She lived with those who could care for her, and my visits to her were diffident and painful. I suppose laughter at funerals was also somewhat tactless, given such circumstances. But I didn't understand, or wouldn't.

Then, only five months after that stammered discussion, I harangued the crowd in the Palais-Royal. Word perfect. A sort of lie. I did not properly know it. I was swept away, for it can go to your head to be nothing, a nonentity, burning with talent and ignored—and then six thousand people stretch toward you, like a woman in the last seconds of love. (Were there really six thousand?)

Years before, in the town where I was born and where my father lived all his life, I'd already jumped on a table and shouted. My aunt thought me very amusing, not for my jokes but for my radical ideas, the Roman republic, the fact that men are equal regardless of birth. A true provincial, she mocked me, and set on a couple of more amenable nephews (blockheads) to "cunning" parody of every phrase I came out with, saying herself always, "You must learn to take a little teasing, Camille." And finally I leapt onto her dinner table, smashing half a dozen of her best dishes and I think three wine goblets, ranting and raving about things none of them could ever grasp since they had no wish to.

King Yes-Yes and Queen Marie-Antoinette were in their beautiful butterfly palace playing milkmaids and shepherdesses, and cabinetmaking (with half the joiners in Paris on the streets with begging bowls), because God had put them there. We of the bourgeois were in our place for the same reason, though we might boast of the odd aristocratic connection. As for the rabble, one could take them soup and a prayer if they were dying, but try to change anything? Blasphemy. (Which is much what I said standing on the porcelain while the nephews catcalled and my aunt clenched her plump ringed talons. I'm sorry I broke her plates. But she would have broken my heart if she could. And at the end, she would have settled for breaking my neck.)

That town. My birthplace. Guise. Its Guisard jibes dogged me. For it was always jibing.

Having got my scholarship as a child, and a school in the capital, I reckoned I was on the stairway to greatness. That would remove the smug smile from those provincial faces. Even the street curved like a smug smile, up to the big gray church. I never felt warm in that church, even when the sun shone in through the pale windows. The confessional—how I would dread it! All my miniature sins, amounting to nothing—*nothing*. I would cringe, nearly vomiting from shame. I was alive; I had feelings. For that I must be punished. Then I learned to lie and waited for God to strike me. He refrained. I went on lying. Then I absented myself. I could, by that time, have brought them exploits to make their eyes pop out. Oh, Paris, City of Indulgent Sin. Beautiful Paris-sur-Seine, *sur-sin.*

I have always claimed to be a patriot, an ardent champion of the rights of my country. But Paris was my mistress. Paris I loved. Always her.

The town priests would have liked my schoolfellow, Derobespierre, far better. He loved with a cool, untainted, unfleshly ardor. Petit Pierre, as he was sometimes called, was short and neat, always scented with toilet water, and well combed. Go away, you stink, said the looks he gave us, if we had been running about climbing walls or scrapping in the schoolyards or eating anything highly spiced. But he was lonely too. And since he admired the same poets and philosophies, we sometimes ended up under the shade trees, talking. And, of course, I would make him laugh. I remember Fréron and myself in a fit of laughter, but when we recovered, little Pierre was curled up in a ball shedding *tears* of anguished mirth. I thought I'd killed him. I'll never forget that. He was like a fastidious little cat, a quality he always kept. But he had genius. There was a time I would have followed him into the mythical hypothetical hell. I did it, too. Then I found I hadn't actually followed him. He wasn't even beside me.

But I'm still trying to explain the lie or the deception in the Palais-Royal— which can best be done, I think, by another detour back in time, to the précis of just one day, that spring before Necker was thrown out of office.

1789: Spring

Windmill: As in tilting at

THERE WERE advantages to the garret room. First of all, he could pay for it. Or at least, he could pay frequently enough they had not yet slung him on the street. Up here, under the gray roof, freezing to death, burning with anger or exultation, or in furious despair or weeping despair (or just flatly despairing), he lurked or paced around, or lay about on the mattress, or half lay across the rickety table with his head on his arms and papers and black hair spilling everywhere. The other advantage to the garret was that its small lidded windows looked across the street and straight in at another, larger window. Looked straight, therefore, into another life. This life was represented by a young girl— she could appear fifteen or less but was actually rather older. She moved in the window there, always infallibly catching the sunlight with her whiteness and her gold.

Odd combination, the poverty and unencouragement of the room and so close, so visible, this Dream, this girl.

There were a lot of pages on the table today: neatly copied petitions for others, who could obtain cases, at a couple of pence each. Also one long paper over which feverish sentences curled like the long hair of the one who had scribbled them. Humanitarian justice. Out in the muddy fields serfs stooped to their labors, their bellies hollow. Their lords bled them of everything they had. Their children died, their wives and sisters were made into whores for the seigneur's pleasure. *In the schools they teach us of the republic of Rome, where each man had as loud a voice as another. Then we are cast out into the world to live under the tyranny of Caesars.*

He dipped his pen deep (there was hardly any ink left; most of what he had seemed to be on his fingers) and wrote briskly:

My dear Father, much as I realize this must irritate you, I have again to *beg* you to send me some *money.*

He scowled at the words, stabbed in the pen again, and wrote:

If this were an ideal world I would not have to ask you. But gaze about: It is not an ideal world, and I do have to ask. I mean to get something else printed. That should improve things. What I'm writing now is so apposite to conditions that sometimes I must get up from the desk in a white-hot rage.

Enthusiasm flagged. Was there any point in saying this?

Windmill sat and thought about the calling together of the Three Estates at Versailles. He himself had tried to get elected to its third portion. Three hundred electors had offered their support. (Eyes glowing in firelight, warmed wine pressed on him. It was, after a summer of hail, a biting winter. Rivers froze, the Seine with them—and eventually Windmill's chances with the voters.) He got as far as Laon and after that disappeared from the running. His father, conversely, who could have won a place, refused to stand. (Windmill sighed and coughed. The stove was smoking again.) Nevertheless, the failure had gone to the Butterfly Town and watched a procession of elected representatives. Nobles in snowdrifts of lace, a poultry yard of feathers, blinding you at every step with the spears of diamonds. Soldiery, the "King's Swiss." Clergy like crows. The glowing dais with the Sacrament. The king, who was cheered. The queen, who was not. The Third Estate straight out of the 1600s, costume coined to show its place. (Mirabeau stalking by. Magnificent, like Jupiter Black-browed, though his usual nickname was That Devil. The count had got himself elected into the Third, pedigree and all. Having peaceably stopped two riots, in Aix and at Marseilles, the crowds lacing his feet with tears and laurels, he received more than the royal share of cheering now. Orléans was also present, smiling on the People. He was always to hand.) A week of festival. Here was the millennium. Now the commons had a voice and would be listened to. The age of miracles was just around the corner, the endless power of the aristocracy about to be curbed. Taken up by a little coterie of deputies, wined and dined, Windmill's head was turned and anything seemed possible. Hearing *le grand* Mirabeau was about to print a gazette covering the proceedings of the magic parliament, hopeful Windmill wrote asking for a place on it. And got no answer.

Presently, the popularity of King Yes-Yes and tolerance of his blond queen declined. It had become apparent nothing was going to happen after all, except an attempt to thrust the Third Estate back into line.

L'oui went on tinkering with his clocks. Antoinette went on bouncing about upstairs with whoever took her fancy.

The People groaned. Windmill gave up on Mirabeau's gazette.

Windmill returned to the letter.

But until something happens, *cher Papa*, I am on my knees. I don't object to living on bread, coffee, and cheap wine. I do rather regret having only two shirts worn to within an inch of their lives. And to sleeping on the floor. There was a couch *insomnie*. I threw it out and, full of lice as it was, it ran away up the street by itself. So, if you won't allow me cash, why not send me a bed?

He visualized the bed, wreathed in flowers, coming up the Womb River like Cleopatra's barge.

Meanwhile, I remain your devoted, malnourished, and miserable son, Lucius Sulpicius Camillus Desmoulins.

(Desmoulins. . . . There had, at the time of the Deluge, been a windmill on their land. What was the latest joke? And how is our stammering little donkey of the mills?)

Across space where buds opened and pigeons flew, there was human movement. Windmill glanced up. There in the opposite window—not the Dream, but the Dream's father. His long pipe extruded from his mouth like the tongue of some fly-questing toad, his bulging little eyes were fixed in return on the writer through two panes of glass and a sandwich filling of air.

Getting up to drag on a disreputable topcoat, Windmill offered the apparition his crooked smile. The apparition did not smile. It turned its shoulder and blotted out the whole window with a fat blank of back.

Windmill flung himself down the narrow stairs like a dog let out of a cage. Gaining the street, his slight figure was overtaken by a surprisingly authoritative walk. It was an almost military stride, with something of a swagger—although God knew he had nothing to swagger about. Wild hair, wild faun's eyes, wicked mouth always tensed, almost smiling, like a bow ready to let fly arrows, and a wicked tongue that half the t-t-time would not get out what it wanted to. As a struggling hopeless lawyer he could look malign and dangerous and partly, when excited, insane. But then the smiling mouth opened and the stuttering began, and those on the verge of running for their lives stayed for a scoffing session.

He had wanted to make his name. He was twenty-nine (in March, Sign of the Fishes, weakness and talent, pulled both ways), twenty-nine and had not made it, despite all the early promise. Here he was, in clothes a charitable institution would refuse, unrecognized. And it began to seem that every stranger who passed him on the street, unrecognizing, was a slap across the cheek, the heart. I'm being wasted. He knew it. Why the patterned fortune of his youth if it was to end in this? Penniless, luckless, silly on a girl he could never have, a lawyer who st-stammered, a writer with one printed pamphlet to his credit (three sales, or was it four?). How they would laugh in his birthplace, that wretched parochial little town. Hadn't they always said he would come to nothing? And here he was, arrived.

He left the begging letter in the *office de poste,* aware it would quite probably be opened and read. With the king's foreign troops being pushed up against the city and drumming like wasps in Martian Meadow, what else could you expect? *Send me a bed,* they would read. Well, let them enjoy it.

A few turnings and crossings over the grid of small streets brought him a view of the Church of Saint-Sulpice. An elegant tower, the top of which seemed to have been hammered back in a playful sculpting blow, let out the four o'clock bell as he turned again, into Harp Street.

Like his room, this slim thoroughfare was also full of smoke, from a tannery and forge half down the way. Up on a second story was a smudged painting of revelry and grapes. Strangest of all, the item which either gave the street its name or borrowed existence from it, a large stone harp hung braced between the walls. It had steel-wire strings, replaced when necessary by the sellers of instruments who had put it there, and through these wires there stirred faint music with the breeze. In winter, the harp could wail like a ghoul, to the consternation of surrounding lodgers. For their part, the pigeons who sunned themselves on the harp kept its pillar freshly whitened.

In the door of his shop, between the dulcet harp and the rank smoke, Momoro the printer stood and glared about.

"What's this?" he said, looking at the sheets of paper Windmill handed him.

"Hn. Whirr," said Windmill, coughed, and said, "Wh-what do you think?"

"No," said Momoro.

"Wh—?"

"No." Momoro handed back the sheets. His waist, inside the conscientious workman's apron, had thickened. His coarse thick hands looked better fitted for murder than printing. Something prophetic, possibly, in that. "It's stuff of the

sort you brought here yesterday? Well, you can take the rest of it back too. Christ. You think I want my press smashed and my skull under it? I know you're bloody mad, but you'd better listen. Print this and I'd have soldiers here in five minutes. How does it go? 'We cry out for liberty and will die for it'? God protect me. And here—'In this just war, what richer spoil was ever offered the victors—forty thousand palaces to spill golden trophies into their hands—this the prize of courage. But we will turn our eyes from such horrors.' I'll say we will. Take this trash and burn it, you raving lunatic. I won't print it. No way."

Momoro threw the writings to the earth. Windmill coursed after them as they blew down the street to the sweet song of the harp.

✻

And that night, with half a crust and three glasses of vinegary wine inside him, scurrying in through the door of a tall old house with piled lintels and imprisoned windows on Iron Jar Street, there came the other element of Windmill's quixotic winter-spring existence. No, not a brothel, though he was familiar with one or two of those. Perhaps, or perhaps not curiously, plenty of the men he met going in and out of Paris' bordellos he also sat down with here.

Despite the candles, the room was always in semidarkness. In the beginning the mystery had appealed limitlessly to Windmill. Now, sometimes, it exacerbated him. Occasionally there were dinners. Warmed by food, he got drunk, and all the initial enthusiasm came rushing back to him. Once or twice he had even made a coherent, rather dashing speech, and been lauded. It was better when friends were here: Fréron, Brissot, or one of the elusive Chéniers, who were less friends than a debating society. Both poets, they fascinated Windmill and made him jealous. There had been conversations after a meeting, long into the night, in some wineshop or even on the summer riverbank. Then a wavering sprint home to begin writing some poetic epic of his own. Once, he wrote something to the Dream. He had dared show a verse of it to André, the elder Chénier, who said, "Hmm. Winter is spring. That's an interesting line." And nothing else. But André was in love with Homer the way the radicals were in love with Rousseau.

Tonight the hall of the lodge gave up from the shadows only the figure of the peculiar Georges d'Anton, whom Windmill knew merely to nod to, *en passant*, in whorehouse doors.

D'Anton filled Windmill with misgiving. Tall, overweight, and strutting, with a voice like a trumpeting bull, a lion's mane still powdered, and blue eyes like the aquamarine lights on a razor's edge, he looked, sounded, and was a bully. Again, though, when he spoke to the lodge gathering, this powdered lion-bull was as radical as any of them, and his private menagerie of animal types imbued him with enormous vigor. On a night of full esoteric activity, when robes and aprons with the embroidery of squares and compasses had been donned, d'Anton had taken his part, roaring out a kind of extempore prose-poetry even the proud Chéniers might have acknowledged. In the robe his elemental power was maximized, he seemed clad in a toga straight from the senate house, and Windmill had been moved to a pitch of wonder and violence, literally possessed. But he shook it off next day. He did not much like the idea of d'Anton.

Mirabeau was another (often absent) of the lodge brethren. Despite the disappointment of the gazette, this devilish gentleman had won Windmill's emotional vote. An aristocrat who dared to be Republican—residing at Versailles; vehemently taking the part of doctors, lawyers, and serfs together in the Third Estate. It was Mirabeau who, when the Assembly had been threatened with eviction from the state of being, had magnificently shouted at the king's envoy, "Get us out with bayonets, otherwise you won't get us out."

One hero at a time. The quasi-occult meeting was now called to attention. The banners came in, scarlet, green, and white. Foremost was the great red and white triangle which showed the legendary pelican, tearing her breast to feed her starving children on her own blood. The message was naked. It kept the strength to wound. Windmill looked at it and shivered. Very well, he would do anything—but without a voice, without a printing press, nature and fate had conspired against him.

Various ceremonials began. He went through them with his mind still wandering. He noticed the Inner Sanctum of the lodge was present in force. These magicians bending over their red light . . . practitioners of alchemy, experimenters in things psychic against which Mother Church spoke coldly. Belonging to the Outer Circle, Windmill was intrigued by the Inner. He was drawn to it, and repelled. Even the carnal d'Anton had shown some curiosity. But confronted by statements on the immortality of the soul, d'Anton had spent an evening in a café proving to the company there was no God. His arguments were so sound they left everyone depressed. At which the fat beast rose from its kill and strolled off into the Palais-Royal, whistling. God, extant or not, knew how his wife put up with him. He was never home and, when he was, could have passed on to her half the diseases of Paris.

Windmill's neighbor at the long table was de Polignac, who now said, "Good evening, Camille. I see your thoughts are elsewhere."

Windmill gazed at him.

"Or did you mean to set your sleeve on fire? If so, I'm sorry for rudely mentioning it."

So Windmill now peered down and saw his worn shirt cuff with its poor gray ruffle was in the way of a candle flame and singeing. He removed it. His stomach growled at Gabriel de Polignac with emptiness and annoyance. Gabriel was not tall, or lightly built, but good-looking and very nicely turned out. An aristocrat born in Africa, what was he doing here with a pearl in his ear, playing social conscience and penning odes? He knew nothing about the plight of the

People and nothing about the bourgeois whose ambitions were so continuously thwarted by the upper class. Gabriel in turn plainly considered Windmill dangerous. He had once said, after one of Windmill's more inspired exclamations, "Really, Desmoulins, you should think before you disembowel. If you knock down all the buildings, where will you shelter when it rains?" "In the sh-shd-shade of your well-fed gut," Windmill had retorted. For some reason Gabriel had not killed him on the spot or demanded a duel. Six or seven years younger than Windmill, Gabriel seemed older. He had, too, a mistress ten years his senior, *très élégante,* with brown curly hair.

"Thank you," said Windmill.

"My pleasure," said Gabriel.

A man in black and masked, like some minister of death, paced down the table, delivering to each of them a folded paper. He reached Windmill and hissed, "Read, and burn!" The words of Momoro the printer hung in the echo: *Take this trash and burn it.* Windmill let fall the paper, unread. Then put his head in his hands, staring at the candle flame through his fingers. While on every side there was the sound of paper being opened, crushed, crackling in fire.

❖

Actually, when he read it, the message was in Latin. Nor was its import novel. It said, as others had said:

> The city is a brew which you must work continually to ferment. Speak softly and sow discord. Speak, when you are able, loudly, sending out a clarion call to the masses. Educated men, it is your right and duty to lead these desolate children by the hand into the paths of victory.

❖

And latest of all then, going back to that wretched garret, to the stove that smoked, the mattress on the floor, the pamphlet no one would print (discouraged by the last image of d'Anton striding off into the black night like some king to his rich wife), fumbling for the candle on the table. Then the candle lit and suddenly, as if it were a mirror, the window over the way also softly blushed into light.

There she was, his Dream. She had a name, of course, a lovely name—Lucile—as well suited to her as the quiet clear candle shine that displayed her now so utterly and perfectly. Whiteness, gold. She was demurely dressed for bed, and over everything a folded wing of lacy shawl—like an angel, all the pale gold hair loose, a halo of curling lights around her face and shoulders. And in that angel's face, eyes as black as his own, feathered with dark lashes and dark brows. So beautiful she took his breath away. And looking at her through the grimy glass of his window, the sparkling-clean glass of hers, he framed her name inadvertently with his lips, and some endearment too, that normally he only spoke to her when he was alone. She apparently read his lips, for she lowered her eyes. Then they flashed up again, two black flames. It seemed to him her color had heightened, but she smiled at him so kindly, lifting one hand in the smallest fluttering wave. Then she turned and with her candle melted like a mist into the dark lake of the house.

❈

> *In the winter of my life*
> *Day is cold and dark as night.*
> *Yet one flower is blooming,*
> *Younger than the morning.*
>
> *L'hiver, l'hiver est printemps,*
> *Il n'est pas neige, du lilas blanc;*
> *L'hiver est printemps.*

❈

It was Fréron who had introduced him to the family Duplessis. The two young men were then still at college in Paris and all their hopes before them, flavored with promise. A well-to-do ménage, this one. The father some important clerk or other, cherishing his own opinions but apparently disposed to be generous. Madame, his wife, was so pretty she seemed to put your eyes out. The two little daughters, children, played about merrily, providing an endearing background, reminding Windmill of his own sisters, who had always made rather a fuss of him.

So the irregular routine was established. Afternoons in the country, for monsieur and madame owned a farm out along the Paris road. Neither of them seemed to mind two student gallants paying madame courtly love. The little girls positively aided and abetted it.

Tell us a story, Camille. . . .

"You're very good with my children, Camille," said madame. "But then. You're such a child yourself." He had flushed with embarrassment and chagrin. But madame touched his hair. "I'm sorry, don't be offended."

"I could never be offended by anything you say," he said, or tried to, starting to stammer. And then she had been truly sorry. Somehow the incident was brushed aside in some game or discussion.

By then Fréron had fallen by the wayside. Why was that? Some years Camille's senior, he had left the college; gone—somewhere. Fréron took life seriously—or, rather, treated it with a kind of serious challenge—to show it, maybe, what he expected in return. Yet even he was capable of sudden wild flights. Once, this considered creature had put on an absurd play for the children, becoming for them a gigantic rabbit that hopped about, nibbled grass, and twitchily sniffed the air. For some time Lucile, the blonder daughter, would say wistfully, "When will we see Lapin again?" Yet Fréron the Rabbit did not return. It was windblown Windmill alone who became the regular, and even he left spaces when he did not see the family, or when the family, busy with its own affairs, excluded him.

How Lucile adored her mother. He had mind pictures of her always, that Dresden figure of a child with skin like milk crystal, so the sun seemed to shine right through it, and the golden fleece of hair. ("There was a hero called Jason, who set out to find the Golden Fleece. . . .") There she lay against her mother's side, singing in a low private voice, as she made a chain of flowers to crown the mother's hair. Proserpina and Demeter.

The father would go off to village junketings and leave the four of them there, lolling about in the burned summer grass seething with purple daisies and the blinding blots of poppies. Beyond their nest, the lines of the land rolled away, honey-green to honey-blue distance. Birds and insects drowsily dipping through the fields. Sky like blue death, a blue to smother in. All those years become one summer afternoon.

He loved her as a child. A pure love, he supposed. She was so beautiful, and sweet, the scent of her that of all natural good wholesome flowerlike things. Such a pretty child. The stirring of lust was for the mother, and that only flirtatious. The idyll was too good to spoil, and appetite could be appeased elsewhere. But then one day, one day—there was another woman sitting there before him under the dapple of the favorite tree. A woman with a white neck, the sun blazing on her, slender and formed, a woman who looked up at him from her book and said seriously, "Will you explain this passage to me? I don't understand it." And abruptly tongue-tied, he had gone over the piece of philosophy with her and then got up and walked off alone, downhill, through the rows of young wheat. Shaking. But she had come after him, taking his hand, saying, "How have I angered you? Is it because you think I'm stupid? I try not to be." God in heaven.

After that, he stayed away. He stayed away a hundred years, all of a month.

The college days were long over. He had reached his era of being the notably unsuccessful lawyer. How did the Duplessises tolerate him, this shabby tattered bright-eyed young scarecrow perched on the rim of their opulent complaisancy? At first, despite life's teaching, he thought himself clever and assumed they reckoned him clever too, thus bound to succeed through talent, and worth cultivating. But he saw the glint of that go out of monsieur's eyes, at least.

The mother, then, must genuinely like him. He could imagine her saying, He never eats, he has no comforts, his own family is miles away. We must be supportive and share with him what we have come by so easily. A very radical argument. And Lucile would concur with all her mother thought fitting. Besides, she liked, Lucile, the stories. Until he stopped being able to tell her stories because it would be so simple, sitting with her innocence and the others out of hearing, to speak of Theseus' love for Ariadne and erupt into some protestation of Camille's love, devouring him alive like a furnace, for Lucile. A dreadful time. He could not keep away. He ached to be with her. He could not talk when he was. He stammered so much in those months Lucile had suddenly laughed and said to him, "I shall call you Monsieur Mm-er-hmm." "Lucile!" cried madame in reproof, afraid for his sensitive hide. But for some reason he too burst out laughing. And the stammer, shocked itself, retreated again.

But the furnace did not go out. There were willing girls free or for sale. Ugly or not, women liked him. He was never rough, and the passion and need of his lovemaking could surprise response even in the reticent. Now all at once, the willing or selling girls could not satisfy. *She* moved between him and them like a cool blade. So then he avoided the brothels and the friendly ladies of the wineshops. He was left in the end with just a mirage in a window.

And what did she feel for him beyond adoptive affection? Not love. Of course not. Chaste as snow. He could woo her with wit when he had it, and with reason and intellect he could excite her so she would clap her hands and say, Yes! You are so wise! With her eyes alight. But what else did he have to offer? Nothing. Neither the princely looks a romantic child-girl would find appealing nor wealth or fame, nor prospects of either. The veiled glances the father cast at him were sufficient to tell him he was currently with them, when he was, on sufferance. And she, hadn't she once said to him, dreamily, his Dream, "I shall never marry. Never fall in love. It is the way I am."

❈

And so, what happened in the Palais-Royal at two-thirty that July afternoon—you note there were reasons for it, beyond the misery of the People, the injustice meted out to them, the indifference of King L'oui and his wicked court, and my anguished need to put all right.

My anguished needs.

In the hovels, children made of bones with an inch of skin stretched over and nightmare eyes, babies dying at a dry breast; and in the prisons men rotting, not even informed by the ungrace of their accusers as to why they had been sent there. And the rich priests taking their tithes, fat as hills, riding on the spine of a skinny peasant. The whole world, my country, writhing and moaning in agony without redress. Yes, I know, I raged against it. My every action tended toward that damnable table and that cry against the assassins who—if they did not slaughter us en masse in a single night—would still rend us to death piece by piece through the ensuing years.

But yet.

I had nothing but ambition and a road for ambition to ride going nowhere. My stage was the mystery of the lodge where we played Knights Templar under the bleeding beak of the pelican and burned our instructions that told us Stir the stew, sound the bell. Otherwise there was the smoky room without a bed, the smoky street where Momoro informed me the one door I thought to open was firmly closed. And there was Proserpina in a field of poppies, which surely made me surly ugly Pluto, trapped in the cellar of the underworld, never to get out.

One other thing. There had by now manifested before me a fine contrary example, a final straw to break this little donkey's back.

At some juncture my Petit Pierre had returned into my life. I had come out on the street one day and found him there, dapperly preening himself in a light green coat, snow-drift linen, with a gentlemanly walking stick, in a cloud of hair powder. And of all things, this little cat had with him an enormous rabbit chaser of a dog. I had laughed with delight at the spectacle, which Maximilien Derobespierre took, plainly, as my sheer pleasure at finding him. Naturally, he was rather ashamed of me in my tatters, but it seemed he wanted someone to talk radicalism and riot with.

Oh, my aching soul. He was like a witch's looking glass, what my image should have been. A successful lawyer, and in his home town at that, he had got himself elected to the Third Estate—which was now calling itself the Only True Voice of the People, the National Assembly. You would have thought he got enough debating over there at the Butterflies. But he could hardly ever get a hearing, my little cat. Now he shoved me into the darkest corner of the Café Procope and began sharpening his claws. Since he could afford to get his speeches printed, he frequently did so. Every speech he made, Maxime the Rose, everyone got a copy. He was no writer. Have a speech. Thank you, Maximilien. But the works bubbled with thought under the surface. "I am a slave to equality," he said. "I would die for it. But the lack of organization. Where are they going, this National Assembly? What have we achieved?" (Mirabeau had said, "Everyone wishes to talk, no one to listen.")

The big dog lay on our feet and snored. Even though it couldn't read his speeches, he liked the dog a lot. Sometimes he even let it gnaw his walking stick, only saying mildly, "Now, Spartan. Now, now." It was d'Anton called him the Rose, first from some semisecret society named for that flower, which Maximilien had belonged to in the provinces. But he always liked flowers. Saint-Just used to bring him roses by the armful, like a young bride.

After we had become impassioned over the Assembly and he'd paid me the compliment of saying I should have been part of it, the two of us could have shaken them up, I presently invited him with me to visit my Duplessis family. Thinking always neatly, two by two, he attached himself instantly to madame's second daughter, Adèle. Thereafter, he too became an occasional regular on the picnics in the country.

Very courteous and stiff and proper. I suppose he must have had his women, sometime or other. There was talk later about the family he roomed with, and about some aristocrat who refused him with the direst consequences to herself. But I remember one of d'Anton's comments: Rose-Peter? *Il baise jamais.* Certainly Maxime was very liberal about the rest of us, particularly d'Anton's sexual exploits, clearing the throat with a slight smile, Yes, yes, of course I realize it's necessary for *you.*

Monsieur Duplessis looked quite beamingly on Derobespierre and his second daughter promenading up and down the herb garden at Bourg-la-Reine. There would be no opposition surely to such a union. For Adèle, I don't know what she thought. She was a silent girl. But I don't think she minded having her own pet escort when Lucile and I went pacing about, deep in Rousseau's humanities. If Adèle's escort talked to her he probably treated her to those long, kindly lectures at which he was proficient, but generally they both kept rather quiet, or he would read her something, or now and then oddly flirt. I can see them now under the tree, Derobespierre saying, "But is this your hat? Or is it a beautiful bird?" And Adèle simpering properly. While Lucile was passionately declaring to me, "The queen—to be the mother of her people and feed her children on cold venom!"

By then the passion in Lucile, always directed at these external figures, had the power to drive me mad. I would do maniac things: climb up trees to get her unripe fruit or, coatless and mindless, turn somersaults.

And just over my shoulder, Derobespierre tripping through the daisies, bright mirror to show me my own failure.

Even he, then, pushed me onto the rickety table in the Palais-Royal as, a few years after, he would push me into hell.

⚜

I make free confession. I do not say mea culpa. Who sins pays for his sin. Finally, the sword is mightier than the pen.

1789: Summer

Le vert ou la mort (Wear the green or die)

THE CROWD, which had begun in the gardens of the Palais-Royal, red with patriotic deserting soldiery and green with chestnut leaves, now boiled through the streets of the city like a flood, catching up into itself anything that might be moved. And anything, indeed, might be.

All through the alleys, from out of cobbled yards behind the high grass of iron railings, from hole-in-the-wall drinking places and simple holes, the discontented and abused ran out. They had seen much traffic through their thoroughfares. The carriages of lords going by like racing chariots and God help who didn't get from the way. The soldiers of the Allemande and the Swiss, flaunting after a drizzle of drums. Now they saw July madness, waving leaves like a forest on the march. An outlet for five centuries of torture.

Eastward, to begin with. The progress of the flood was marked first maybe by an anxious query called from a rooftop or high window – some lookout who had spied the storm far off. Presently the anxious queries merged to form screams, and next the thudding to of doors, slam of shutters, shooting of bolts, and crack of hammers fixing up boards.

Close the theaters! the mob had howled, for what fair-minded man could sit down to a play at such a time? The theaters closed.

The sound of the flood was audible as a dull booming roar. Before it, yipping and squeaking like animals fleeing a forest fire, hurtled would-be playgoers, afternoon strollers, bank clerks, curés – anyone who had been out of doors and now badly wanted to get back in.

Around a curve, then, and on to the tree-plumed avenue of the Temple Boulevard, the flood poured. It had somewhat altered its aspect. It was packed more closely; it had a look of business about it. And true to the exhortation in the garden it was armed: sabers, pistols, even torn-up railings, even pitchforks brought in from the country.

The gate of Curtius' Temple Waxworks, too, had been locked, but the crowd rattled it. They remembered, quite a lot of them, coming here at two sous a head to see The Royal Family at Dinner: *La Vie en Cire.* It was an eye-opener to some, not just the meticulously reproduced finery on these wax dolls of king and queen but the wax banquet spread before them.

Rattle, rattle, roar. The gate quakes as if it will come out of its sockets. The crowd rumbles as if *it* will shake down the whole, salon and house, like Jericho.

Monsieur Curtius advanced into the courtyard to be greeted by estatic noises. Popular, he tacked always to the wind, running swiftly as Mercury from one point to another. He had been used to having aristos as dinner guests. In the climate of this summer he had entertained instead renegade greedy Mirabeau, radical greedy d'Anton, and Derobespierre, who was recently shedding the "de" from his name and ate nothing at all.

"What, my friends, do you want?" Mercury Curtius asked the crowd.

They waved green leaves at him. He accepted some and tucked them in his coat. Someone helped him tie a branch on the gate. But Curtius didn't unlock it. "Necker!" the crowd shouted. They wanted the wax bust of the finance minister. "And good old Orléans!"

A genius with wax, the artist in Curtius now had a stand-up fight with the political wind-tacker. There they were, waving bits of trees and hay forks, and terrible old guns from some museum they had broken into, that would perhaps blow up and take off their fists, black teeth snarling and grinning and insane-asylum eyes. And they asked him to give them wax modeled from the life, every lock of hair placed individually, eyes of real glass.

A carpenter armed with a piece of chair frame said, "We'll take good care of them. We'll bring them back. Not a scratch on 'em, eh, boys?" The boys volleyed an assent. And the gate *shook* again.

Curtius smiled. His face remained composed throughout. "Of course," he said. "The People's wishes are paramount."

He kissed the busts farewell and brought them forth with his own hands. They were passed up by his assistants and over the gate, where the composite monster caught them with a cheer and made off with them up the road.

"Well. I shall never see either of those again," Curtius remarked.

Wrong. Someone brought Necker back days later, its face slashed, eyes out, hair burned. It was in much the same condition as the corpse of the man who had been carrying it when it fell.

⚜

East, the crowd went. But not all. As one portion bore off heads of valued idols, flanked by banners of black and white stripes (black for mourning, white for Bourbon murderers), another vandalized a café or two and forced closed shops to open. Wine barrels were broached in the street, and the bizarre clacking of empties rolling over the cobbles augmented the squall of the crowd as it too rolled up and down.

It was later than it had been, a habit of time. The sun was going west, toward the Champ-de-Mars, and somehow gave the crowd a funny idea it might do the same. There had been no opposition so far. Though it had lost one spokesman, there were still plenty of excitable young men with black curly hair waving their arms. Offered the green, most took it or ran.

The sun stained the walls of the city, yellow for fading primroses, warm gray in a golden lace of light. The river stretched like a blade behind the trees of the Tuileries garden with its mathematical palace set block by block alongside. It was hot. Thunder up there, waiting. But for now the thunder was down on the ground.

Unstopped and unchallenged and full of the rare treat of doing as it wanted, the crowd danced on, kicking up its heels, into the green garden and into the green sprawl known as Heaven's Fields. Where it collided head on with the troops of the king's Royal Allemande.

They had come over the Seine at a gallop. Someone in command, who happened to be a prince, now lined them up across the Champs-Élysées, so the fragrant trees brushed the shoulders of the bright uniforms.

The crowd, seeing this array, was meant to halt, rip itself apart, retreat, or fall on its faces.

The crowd, which had casually been arming itself for hours with stones, broken-up paving, sticks, bottles, and turds, now hurled them. Caught in a hail of missiles and muck, men ducked and horses reared, and *le prince* barked out an order. It was the usual one where an elite obtains, a mob is on the ground, and a trained fighting force sits mounted on horses.

The soldiers charged.

They came down like a red avalanche, hooves and spurs, the flame of swords and bayonets, and struck the crowd full in its mouth. The sound of impact was fearful. As if the foliage took flight, birds spurted from the trees. Horses skidded in an instant slick of blood and kneeled. Men were falling on their faces now, and the cries of the women were the noise of every such encounter, not less terrible for that.

Very soon the crowd was running, back toward the Tuileries or up into the Place Vendôme. Some of the soldiers pursued, and in that moment, when discipline was permitted to absent itself, a couple of shots splintered the leaves in the branches overhead. They were firing high; the actual work was being done with long steel, not bullets. No matter. It did the trick, which was not the trick their lordly commander intended: The sound of guns travels a good way.

Pushed and heaped back into the Tuileries, the crowd had panicked. Returning blows were random. It could not decide whether to escape or make a stand, but it had no order, and the bodies of the horses came between the men on the earth and the men in the saddle, whose elongated arms were bayonets. Here and there a stolen pistol went off. Where were their own patriot soldiers? Lost on the way to wine barrels or trying to fight somewhere in the macabre muddle. A formal open-plan garden is no spot for conflict. Nor the Place Vendôme, like a bull ring.

To be in the crowd now was to feel it close over your head.

In these seconds there came a concerted wail of horror, caught up and magnified—for more troops had been sighted, coming full pelt, swarming across the sheet of green.

They raced into the center of the mêlée and parted it. On foot, but armed to the teeth and yowling with fury. They divided off at once the prince's battalion from the fracas in the garden, walled the latter in, then proceeded to lop down there all the uniformed flowers, flinging them back into the Champs-Élysées, while their horses ran amok up a hoof-carved avenue. The new arrivals were a French regiment which had decided for a fact Frenchmen do not fire upon Frenchmen. They ranged themselves now between the People and the Royal Allemande and called the Germans names that broke their ranks again. An abortive second charge, with no command, started down the vista and floundered into coitus interruptus as *le prince* screamed it off. The new pack of patriot soldiers, who had bristled to resist it, stood easy, jeering.

Skulking, the Germans turned their horses, which were defecating in excitement on the trampled avenue and the trampled wounded lying there.

Ten minutes later the crowd, safe behind a bulwark of loving soldiery, had the delight of witnessing the Royal Allemande trotting back to Mars Meadow, its collective tail between its collective legs.

Those lying crying and writhing did not raise a shout. Though only one of their number was dead, there were a host who would carry for all their days the marks of this evening's adventure.

If it was not quite yet a revolution, the first blood had been shed. The virginity of peace was gone.

⚜

He had, Windmill, been part of it. Most of it. Some of it.

Afterward, he was unsure what had followed his descent from the shoulders of the crowd. First hesitant; then dragged like a zombie; then, again carried, but only by pressure. Louis-Mer had vanished. Everyone he had ever known had vanished. Presently, he too . . . vanished.

The crowd: one brain, one heart. He became, in some sense, merely a figment of it. He forgot who he was, why he had done what he had, or if he had done it at all. And for a fact, the confusion spread to others, for at some point, in a street, a band of men had caught at him: "Citizen, we're looking for the boy who called us out—a bit like you he was." And Windmill remembered, and said, "Mn, it *was* me." But the men had replied, "*No*. He was taller." "I was standing on a chair on a table," said Windmill reproachfully. And he thought, I was standing in the sky. And the men patted him good-naturedly and went on looking for him through the crowd. Windmill thought, with irony, Better be quick. They'll forget me. And then himself forgot it all.

He was exhausted, and while the drinking had not made him drunk, it had unhinged some facet of his mind. (There had been drinking.) Then, too, his whole mechanism was like that of some creature which was awakening from dormancy. The first stage was power but then it collapsed, unused to its own energies; the second stage was this. The third would be power again, but he had not yet reached it.

So the crowd moved, and he moved with it. Afterward he imagined he had been involved in that forward rush which brought the mob of Paris up against the soldiers. But also, he was never sure. I was, or I dreamed I was. Or some part of me, since all of me was one with the crowd, *that* was. Or I had gone home to my room and was asleep over the table.

Certainly there was a memory, an afterimage of the terrifying folding back into the Tuileries and the instants of panic. And then the miracle of the French soldiers who would not fight Frenchmen.

But he had not seen that. They had told him. They had told him in the café where he was drinking and everyone was singing, for some reason, a song about shepherdesses, at the tops of their voices, all because the king's bullies had turned tail, which made the People king.

And on this table he *had* slept. When he woke up, the spirit of the city had changed.

There was an unseen shimmer in the air, and the café was empty as if abandoned. Then, from somewhere far off across the city, came a blast of shouts, crashes, as if a stack of houses had gone toppling. It sounded immediate yet miles away. He went out. The street was dark, no lamps, or else none lit, and the windows blind. He nearly fell over a man lying in the gutter and thought him only a drunk till the man said, "Nothing, yet."

"What?"

"I can't hear any. Yet."

"Any what?"

"Are you a fool or what are you? Cannon."

The man was lying with his ear to the ground listening for the vibration of King Louis's guns turned on the People.

"Montmartre would be the place," said Windmill. He pointed away, vaguely, northward. "Height with almost perfect vantage. They could put them there and raze the city."

"Shut up," said the man. "I want to listen for the cannon."

Windmill walked on. At first, only furtive darkness with all lights out. Then after a while a wider street, and he had come straight into the scene of another museum being plundered for weapons, complete with torches and bawling. He stood and watched and then was given something to carry and thought, I had nothing to do with this. A spectator, still.

When he got up nearer to the islands in the River Womb, he saw fire in the sky at the city's edges. People ran about here, hordes of them, preparing to evacuate their goods and their lives. He was told the king had already shown up and houses were being burned with their inhabitants in them, but also that, no, it was smugglers burning down the customs barriers at the city gates.

From the darkness and chaos of limbo he came to an area where there was nothing but light. It was as if scales fell from his eyes at last. He recognized René Hébert making some speech or other under one lantern and then saw ten magnificent whores dancing in feathers and red petticoats under another, one of whom ran to him and kissed him.

Up in the Hôtel de Ville the windows were yellow. A committee of Paris electors, brooding there for several days, was now calling for a voluntary Paris militia. Brissot told him this, having banged into him in the roadway where a carriage had been overturned and broken up for a barricade, then abandoned.

"And tomorrow," said Brissot breezily, "the mob must be given a target. Don't let their fire go out."

"Or the pot boil over. Versailles?" said Windmill, searching after elusive excitement down the electric night. "Go to Louis before he gets to us?"

"Hang Versailles. They won't do that, or do any good. I say, on the authority of Nine Ladies Lodge, the Bastille."

"Why?" said Windmill. There seemed all the time in the world, nothing important. "Because L'oui once shut you up there for scurrilous pamphleteering?"

Brissot turned his head and spat on the pavement. "This was all discussed weeks ago. But you're drunk, my child, and useless. Go and find a pen. Write it down, whatever it is." He flung one arm over Windmill's shoulders. "Look. Did you ever see Paris like this?"

They looked. Night sky somber, tinged by fire. Gold lights in the river. Air full of thunder. Paris like a black egg about to shatter on a phoenix.

"So we'll creep about, whispering, *Take the Bastille*."

Windmill nodded. A shudder ran over him, dislodging Brissot's arm.

Brissot said, "They can get proper ammunition there, and it's bursting with gunpowder. A hundred and twenty men to guard it—less. Half of those pensioned off." Windmill shuddered again. Brissot said, "D'Anton's jealous, by the way."

"Nw-what? Why?"

"Leaping on tables all night. The new fashion as set by Monsieur Desmoulins. But only Camille could be Shakespearean enough to bring Birnam Wood to Dunsinane."

Then he realized Brissot too had leaves pinned wilting on his coat.

They parted.

He knows what I did. The girl by the Café Flambé knew. And bloody d'Anton's jealous.

He laughed as he walked now. He turned a corner slap into a gang of men, bakers, clerks, green-leaved as Bacchites, who hailed him by name, and toasted him by it, and offered him wine. They *know* me.

Then he got over the river by a bridge with a bonfire blazing on it, where they were roasting pilfered chickens, and ran to the Duplessis house on the rue de Condé. It, too, was dark and close-seamed, like most of its neighbors, but the streetlights over toward the Théâtre were burning. Upstairs opposite he found paper and scribbled on it.

Monsieur, the city is in arms and all is not accomplished yet. Keep your family close at home, I beg you. Your friend, Camille.

That left for them, he stood a moment in the shadow of the door, his forehead pressed there, with something that was almost pain and not quite joy raw as a dagger through his heart, or through his soul's heart.

Dors-tu, mon ange? Ma plus belle, mon amour. . . .

When the Sunday sun rose, it rose on Windmill in the slums of Saint-Antoine. In that grim tangle of streets, the sun made a favorite of him. The sun was shining on Windmill.

Otherwise it dripped down walls that seemed made of paper and filth. Running with damp in winter, stinking in summer. Stinking now. Here the rags ran on the lines like flags. Here the bone-and-skin children scuttled like rats. He went into the drinking shops, one of countless agitators, and muttered the things that were suitable, but someone would come in and say *This* is the one spoke out in the Palais. And then he would stop muttering and address them. They were respectful, though their eyes were like the eyes of devils. It seemed to him he had a passport in their hell country, but without a passport one could not rely on safety. But you said what they wanted to hear—and the devil eyes ignited. His eyes, too, though he did not see them. ("Look at Lucifer," the women said. One took his hand in a doorway. He nearly flinched. A crone out of some fairy tale, the witch with the blood of *La Belle Dormante* on her spinning wheel. "Savior," she said. "You'll show them. You'll make it right." And the tears sprang up like stars in his Lucifer eyes. He was charged with pity and a will to fight for them all.)

❊

On Monday morning the bells were ringing the tocsin from every tower in Paris. The guts churned at the very sound of them. Next to that sound, the racket of the armorers' shops, which belched smoke as high as the towers. Scythes might be welded to poles, pikes could be beaten out, neater than bayonets. But the Bastille is full of gunpowder. Full of men praying for release. A thousand prisoners, immured without trial, chained up in cells by shackles of iron. Fed once a week on the leavings of dogs.

Going out? Don't forget your hat and your chestnut branch. It's dangerous to be seen on the street without leaves.

Over at Les Invalides the crowd, the mob, the entity of Paris (all leafy) was shouting for weapons. Jammed in the crowd, Windmill. This time, identity not lost. ("Tell 'em we want muskets, Camille!" So Camille called the message. Everyone called it: One, two, three, *muskets!*)

Then someone went in to parley and they rushed the gate.

The vaults were stifling, hot, reeking of guns. Out came the rioters again in a riot, with over two thousand muskets—empty—over ten cannon—chargeless. The gunpowder's in the Bastille.

And at the Hôtel de Ville they were handing out bullets like sweets, and outside, broken barrels and boxes of vegetables were being rifled by people who remembered food was useful too—at one point the Place de Grève was full of woolly sheep, turned back on the road from Paris. But if you were a prisoner in the foul eight-towered dungeon, you got the leavings of dogs.

We could use catapults, like the Romans, shoot up over the walls. Or set the place on fire. We could pump oil — or turpentine — through the hoses of fire engines (the ones that didn't put out the customs barriers on Saturday). Fire engines converge on the Bastille. (Dreams of fire. On Sunday there had been plans to burn down the Opéra.)

Meanwhile, a courier who has come from Versailles and was attempting to reach the Bastille is being murdered in an alley. His message was for de Launay, the governor of the prison: *Hold out at all costs.* Or this may be apocryphal. Maybe there is no courier sliding down a wall in his blood. It's a good story. It's like the woman who says, No. To which the lazy lover replies, But *yes.*

❋

If that fellow was still lying on his ear in the street by the wineshop, he would have heard it then: the long ragged *brooum* of the cannon. July 14. *Le Premier Jour.*

❋

The faubourg Saint-Antoine, pointing back at the city like an arrowhead with, on its tip, the Bastille. Mad Charles V had built it, in the thirteen hundreds. Vast walls of yellowish stone darkening with their great age, like tusks; eight towers, a spider. Darkest of all, the stories. Rooms of torture. Rooms whose walls were paneled in prisoners' skull plates. At midnight, the knock on the door, the covered carriage. Whisked away without knowing why and buried alive in the Bastille.

De Launay, governor of the fortress prison, had for days been on tenterhooks. He subscribed to the general notion that violence must spend itself somewhere and that his prison, emblem of all things intolerable, was a God-given choice. Peering by night out at the surrounding district, movements of the trees would set him off, yelping for the cannon embrasures to be widened and the windows blocked up. If there were to be an offensive, the troops across the city might not come to his aid. Massive army absenteeism was now the order of the day. It was no longer, Someone has deserted, but, Who has deserted now and how many? So far, a detachment of thirty Swiss soldiers had been sent to help him, under a captain who obviously held him in contempt. Otherwise he could count on his pensioners, his Invalides, eighty-odd superannuated veterans. Invalid was the word. They had done their fighting and did not expect to take it up again. Besides, de Launay had seen the looks they gave him, seen them glaring down possessively on the slummy streets where they went out drinking. If it came to it, they might refuse to fire on good old Jacques from the Red Cup.

Meanwhile, on the evening of the thirteenth, a Bastille sentry upon a tower had been well and truly fired on—if uselessly—from the thoroughfare below.

De Launay had the Swiss carry a couple of tons of paving stones onto the battlements for purposes of flinging down. Then he got them to lug all the gunpowder into the cellars from the arsenal. He came on them, in the morning of the fourteenth, propped up on walls, worn out.

Soon after that, the crowd started to arrive.

The newly cleaned guns were poking out of the newly widened embrasures like black liquorice sticks, covering with their snouts every dangerous approach route. The drawbridges were firmly up. To look at it, it seemed the Bastille was unshakable and untakable. But the word had been going round and round: the prison was a shell, ill defended, rotten with weak spots. More, that the valor of the People must prevail.

At the commencement, the war was not uncivilized. A delegation arrived to see the governor. Its purpose was to gain means to arms and to protest at the obvious aggressiveness of the cannon. The governor let the delegation in. No, no, arms were not his for the distribution of, but weren't they hungry? They all sat down to breakfast together. Outside, without any breakfast, the crowd waited, calling for weapons itself quite musically, sometimes even in the king's name. Then de Launay, waxing expansive over the chocolate, gave the order to pull the guns back out of the ramparts, to show he had no intention ever of firing them. The people underneath, seeing the guns disappearing, assumed they were being pulled back for loading. They also decided that the delegation, still cramming itself with white rolls and oranges, had been taken hostage.

Presently, when gentlemanly pledges of cordiality began to filter out, the crowd, suspicious, set up the shout: We're here to take the Bastille. Give!

The Invalides up on the walls were skipping about like goats and warningly waving their hats, which the crowd took to be a gesture of threat or encouragement.

Already into the outer court, the entity of the People began to stretch its eager tentacles forward to find some way to grasp and prize the stone box wide. The plan of the fire engines had long since been shelved, but not necessarily the plan of climbing up on one. From here the roofs of the shops that crowded the outer court were accessible. And so on upward, across the rampart wall alongside and over into the inner court the other side of the moat. It was such a simple move, no one had seriously considered it.

Arrived, with axes and mallets, the advance party began work on the chains of the two drawbridges.

If there had been a moment to open fire, this was it. But the fire was held, cups of chocolate chuntering happily about, Invalides looking the wrong way, the Swiss nonplussed or nobly waiting for directions, the chopping noises covered by the uproar of the crowd. Shortly both the drawbridges, tethers shorn, came crashing out and down across the moat, killing or maiming any unable to get from the way. But the crowd, leaping across such sacrificial victims, tore on into the inner courtyard—to find another moat and drawbridge. To the charging mob this was an affront. But to the serious defenders on the walls, *they* were now an invasion.

The mob roiled, feeling its power, thwarted and not to *be* thwarted, an outraged dragon of many heads. It raised its multitudinous arms and howled for the final bridge to be let down. And its muskets, those with bullets and powder, began, as if of their own accord, to go off.

A rain of stinging bees came in over de Launay's precious ramparts. Then the cannon slid smiling back into view, licked their lips, and coughed out the thunder of death.

❊

The streets were full of two-way traffic. In carts, on litters, or hobbling between comrades, powdered with the black dust of shot and painted with blood, the wounded were going back west and south, toward the Hôtel de Ville or the houses of friends who would care for them. Undeterred by these visions of anguish—or inspired by them—the alternative crowd thrust its way on toward the arena of action. While, as they pass:

"Who's winning up there, us or them?"

"It's no joke. Two hundred dead. This blood isn't mine. A woman, standing beside me—"

"All right. We'll kill the bastards. We'll drag 'em on the street and fuck 'em to death with pikes."

And a wild cheer, because blood is spilled and blood is up and the scent of blood is still new, bestial and inciting.

While over the cheer, again the rumble of cannon, and the cobbles vibrate at it. "Oh, Christ Jesus!" the girls cry out, who were craning down from their windows to look at the street a moment before, and now the shutters bang to. And the cannon comes again and the earth throbs.

❊

No one is worse at describing an event than those who were in the thick of it.

Whether any of them knew, those patriots clamoring at the first stone door of tyranny, what was happening four yards away from any one of them, is moot.

To fight was all. Battle madness. The Romans and the Greeks have fine names for it. There comes a point when you know you are invulnerable, and if you are not, you care not. Let the bullets pass through me, the cannon shock explode at my feet—nothing can prevent me. I am only the Revolution now. The

man at my side is my brother, the woman I snatch up in my arms (thinking her
dead, tears streaming down my face, ready to avenge her—who takes me by the
hair, embraces me, and is gone, unhurt or only resurrected), my sister, my wife.
The children—there are many—are my sons. And more. We are one being and
one will.

Coming into it, it seemed a monumental conflagration. Clouds of jet-black
smoke were gushing up, from the cannon and the musket fire but also from
wagons of burning straw brought from a nearby brewery, doused with liquor,
and touched off, first beside the inner drawbridge to afford cover, but now
dragged out again into the thoroughfare. Through the smoke came the tear and
crack of bullets. You got on your knees and crawled to navigate it, coming in
under the storm of shot from the towers and the returning blown kisses of the
People's side, who were in the Bastille kitchens to the right of the gate. Here,
lying across trestles and stuffed in windows, flesh-and-blood men fired to hit the
eyes of the toy men up on the ramparts, using the muskets they had claimed at
Les Invalides. You got few enough of them, those ramparteers, though if one
fell you yelled, or even if one dodged down you yelled, and this was mainly what
they did. Now and then their love tokens flew in over your heads and shattered
things behind you. It sounded like a world of mirrors going. At some stage a
pellet might cut through the sleeve of your coat. You felt the heat of it, but it was
not important. Death had, curiously, never seemed so far off. It was nothing.
Even those who went down, the flame in their eyes growing suddenly fixed and
dull, seemed only mistaken information, or fakes, as if the mighty soul of the
People, which had used them, now left them and came back into those who lived
and were its true expression.

There was a mass of the "People's" soldiery in the yard. These, too, had
brought up cannon and employed them. At least half the booming fanfare that
had shaken the surrounding streets had started from patriot guns. These men
had also, recklessly forging forward, pushed away the wagons of smoldering
straw from the inner drawbridge, on which they aimed to fire. Meanwhile,
behind this length of wooden planks, now the only recognized barrier that stood
between the crowd and its goal, hidden but well-famed, de Launay's eight-
pounders waited in readiness.

❉

I had done my duty by Nine Sisters Lodge. Though I found, where I came to
insinuate I was called on to exclaim; so exclaimed. I had been in Saint-Antoine
and to the pig run of Les Halles. I had even got back into the Palais-Royal and
been ushered up onto a chair again to sing out further pronouncements. There I
hardly needed to say one word. As soon as I opened my lips there was a carnival
of accord. Hardly sleeping, eating as a horse does when presented to a trough, I

slogged from one end of Paris to another, days and nights evaporating around me, and the phoenix in the egg straining at its shell.

I had been standing in a street by an old dye works, in the middle of a crowd some two hundred strong, when we heard the roar of the prison guns. Someone shouted, "They're killing them!" and we sprang forward and ran, the legion of us. Nobody said Who? or Where?

But it was back across the city again, and in a dozen places, where barricades had already gone up or some unfortunate's shop was being looted— the brigands of Paris rarely missed such opportunities—the way was inaccessible and detours must be found.

When I reached, at last, the rue Saint-Antoine, the noise of firing had stopped. There was only a sullen roaring of the huge crowd, but with a lawless note of acquisition mixed in it. Then I did run—I would have laid bets de Launay was on the verge of surrender.

By dint of force, I got myself a vantage, along with dozens of others, on the roof of one of the houses that crowded near the prison. All around, windows were packed by spectators. One looked down and straight into the maelstrom.

It was not quite over. Through that inner court they had taken by sheer impudence, the smoke was fading like a blue spring mist. Now and then a handful of muskets still cracked, but without reply from the heights.

The multitude in the court—it looked like some savage flower bed come alive. It had, this sprawling sea, its islands of dead and wounded too. Some had been propped against the stonework or tumbled carts, faint, no longer caring what happened, which seemed an incredible thing.

It was possible for them now to get in near the foot of the walls, where some attempt had been made to fill the moat with rubbish and furnishings and so cross it. But paving stones had been hurled from the ramparts and neatly brained several of the attackers. From the debris all about, already it looked as if the giant towers were falling apart.

The crowd was like a press. It got hold of its own members and held them. Once in, there was no way out but one—over that drawbridge which was still upright. But despite the shouting, there had begun to be dialogues.

The crowded roof was a debating society. Some of them said that only two of the prison guns had been fired. Others declared five had spoken and a thousand citizens lay dead or close to it. One man said one gun and nearly got himself lynched. He retracted. I was also assured the Swiss had opened fire when the People came in over the first drawbridge. This seemed very likely.

Otherwise, twice there had been a cease-fire, not from the prison but on the People's side, as delegates tried to get some sense from de Launay. Had he given in at that time and handed over the Bastille to the deputies of the Nation, all could have been well. But he was an aristocrat who had grown accustomed to lording it in his aerie. Even as the People paused in order for their delegations to be heard, the Swiss on the walls had redoubled their onslaught, and men standing with weapons obviously reversed, or unarmed, fell dead.

Now, however, with our patriot soldiers here in force and gallant as lions — with not a single aristo master to lesson them how to fight — it seemed de Launay had reconsidered. To the crowd's scornful acclaim, drummers had trotted around the walls beating a retreat and waving white scarves. The firing continued for some time on the People's side, despite this show. They did not trust him, and small surprise.

Nevertheless, there had come to be a curious throbbing lull. We stood and waited, huddled together like cattle before a storm. Some of my fellow spectators presently identified me and said, "Hey, Camille. Speaking as our lawyer, what's your verdict?"

"Well, if he's offering, let them take it." But all over down below they were beginning to scream. It sounded like the tongues of twenty nations. "What are they shouting?" "Just that they want the Bastille, and they won't play truces anymore." And to encourage them, or unable to keep silent, the crowd on the roofs and in the windows began to join in. My comrades were jumping up and down until I thought the leads would give way under us.

It was like dry tinder all around, combusting. If the mob on the roof poured down into the courtyard, I should be taken with it. No choice in the matter.

At the same time, his lordship of the prison had his own business to attend to, in his study. Here he was writing us a billet-doux. It was a scheme for which, if he had managed it, history would not have forgiven him, and of which, since he did not and history forgets, I will remind history.

Having been a king in a castle, he had not liked to let it go. Having fired repeatedly and mercilessly upon the crowd, telling it all the while he would not do so (and afterward saying, I believe, he had not), having used our side's truceful interruptions in firing as a signal to intensify his own, having seen his bridges beaten flat, and the last bridge with our own primed cannon before it, and that we, like the Hydra, grew more ferocious with every pitiless blow he struck (and no help arriving to exterminate us from the rear), de Launay wrote us this:

> *We will surrender. Accept that. Or, by igniting the twenty thousand pounds of gunpowder you know we have here, we shall obliterate the garrison, yourselves, and the whole neighborhood that surrounds us.*

Previously a hole had been smashed in the door, on this man's orders, that his soldiers might fire on us through it more fortuitously. Now the note waved there. Our men improvised a log over the moat — I reckoned they would be shot as they did so, but no — and ran to fetch the paper. The substance of the "request" was passed through the veins of the crowd like venom. It came up to the housetops too, via calls and inquiries. "Jesus, he's going to blow up the whole suburb. Ma, get down the cellar." "I won't," said Ma, braver than I. Every one of us stared in electric fascination at the prison. Nobody ran for cover. Next, someone came up on the roof to tell us the exact words of the message—or as exact as he could get them fifteenth-hand. "He wants a safe conduct; then he'll come quiet." For a fact, some part of the congregation below, getting it garbled, was now convinced the governor threatened gunpowder if the People did not capitulate to *him*. No one disillusioned them. I was cold with rage and fear and wished I had my hands around de Launay's throat. He must be taken an honorable prisoner, this brute who had been discharging guns on the heads of women and boys and men the bulk of whose armament consisted of hay forks. Who said one thing, did another, denied it, did it again. If spared, no doubt in five minutes he would find some ploy for regaining ascendancy. Probably we should be thrown, in a day or less, every one of us, into the dungeons of this place he had so zealously guarded. While if we did not take him on his terms he would blast all of us to hell, and a neighborhood of innocents with us. Gentle gentleman. Here was the aristo's honor. Yes, I realized, he was mad enough to do the thing simply to save his bloody fortress from falling into our hands.

"Let him try," one of the roofites snarled. "But he won't. He'll wet himself with fright and damp the powder before he can set light to it."

And then below us we saw the crowd surge like a tidal wave, rushing *inward,* up past its own guns, the People's soldiers leading it, bellowing: *Down the bridge! No surrender!* You could even hear the words, this time.

I imagined at any second the light and the roar would hit us, blow us out like a thousand candles. A soldier will shout in battle, to alter terror to passion, and I found myself howling too, for the Bastille's black blood, with all the rest below and around me, my hair on end.

I heard he was in the cellar with his tinderbox, de Launay, when some of the old men, the pensioned soldiers who had not wanted to fire on French citizens, intervened.

That huge thud of agony and death, we missed it, though it almost came, the thunderbolt, to send us blind and winged with fire to glory.

When the gate suddenly opened and the final drawbridge fell to offer invasion a road, there was a universal shriek of insanity and mirth in which I have no doubt I collaborated. I don't recall. I have the dimmest memory of that last plunge—theirs—and ours off the roof, downward, forward, and into the broken core of the Bastille, the prison built to outlive us all. Running, grinning and trembling, shouting—but unable, any man, to distinguish his own voice.

Even the Swiss threw down their guns, telling us they never fired. The dead imagined it, then.

⚜

Il pleut, il pleut des bergères,
Des brunettes et des blondes,
Des petites et des grandes,
Il pleut, il pleut des bergères —
Quelle joie pour les moutons!

Attention, bergères,
Mes très jolies femmes,
Très jolies mesdames,
Attention, bergères —
Vos moutons ont des dents!

It's raining shepherdesses,
Dark and fair,
Short and tall,
It's raining shepherdesses —
How delightful for the sheep!

Look out, shepherdesses,
My pretty girls,
My pretty ladies,
Look out, shepherdesses —
Your sheep have teeth!

❊

At the Butterflies they were acting shepherdesses. Acting being anything but what they were. An untroubled life can be so boring.

A collection of dolls who played with dolls.

The impression of them all is whiteness, Bourbon white. The white powdered hair and the white powdered faces, maybe with a pastel rose on the cheeks and the lips; and the white lace, white silk — a winter court. And their palaces bulging with mechanical marvels with which, too, they play. Elephants that exude tinkly tunes, waving their jointed ears and tails and trunks, while all around them flowers open their diamond petals. And golden clocks with dancing figures. And then there is the creative skill, taught them by a pale clever little girl named Marie, of making exquisite models in wax. Wax fruit and flowers, and jewelry fruit and flowers, that never die.

But while they play, the great sea of hungry wolves, dark and sanguine for their whiteness, is pressed panting and hating to the transparent walls of the bubble. Wolves in sheep's clothing . . . but whoever could have mistaken them for sheep?

Ah, the elfin gods and goddesses in their make-believe land of undying flowers, how could they dream it would all end in tears, and in tears of blood at that?

❧

King Yes-Yes, up early, was noting down in a ledger the number of game in the forest, crossing off the animals he had shot yesterday. He had just been told of the fall of the Bastille.

"An uprising?" he had inquired.

"No, sire. A revolution."

"What," asked the king, "is a revolution?"

❧

A revolution is a turn. In some cases, a funny turn.

❧

When we had broken through into the fortress, we found them, the ones we had come to rescue: the multitude of starving, tortured, broken prisoners, who would hold out their shackled hands, weeping with gratitude.

There were seven of them. Unshackled. Well-dressed—better than I was. They gazed at us in terror and astonishment. Had we come to kill them?

One said he was Julius Caesar. It seemed we were his Rubicon. One hid under his bed with a pet canary in a cage.

The cells were nicely ordered, furnished as the inmates wished and could afford, with fireplaces; even apples and bottles of wine standing about. No evidence of fiendish tortures save some antique armor. The bones below were centuries out of date.

On the stair an old man was crying, clutching at us. He seized my wrist. "They don't understand. You're a lettered man. You'll help me?"

I thought he had some request, some long-lost family he was desperate to find. I nodded.

"I don't want to go. Not out there. I've been here years. I've got all my things here, all I want. Let me go back. Please, son, tell them I just want to go back quietly in my room."

I persuaded him it wasn't possible and tried to reassure him, asking where his relatives might be. But either he had none or had forgotten or did not like them much. He held on to my wrist, sobbing, until the victorious soldiers came and pulled him away into the city where he did not want to go.

How the old gods laugh at us.

Given a sworn word of safe-conduct, de Launay and others were set on and killed in the street near the Hôtel de Ville, their heads hacked off with swords and penknives, piked, and borne through Paris. To which deed I added my heartfelt approval. All I could see were men who had refused us arms when our fate hung in the balance, the aristocrats perhaps at any second falling upon us with their thirty thousand troops, the shot already railing red hot against us. And de Launay promising to flatten the whole district with gunpowder because we would not act like gentlemen. But no, more than that. I had drunk the sacrament of the mob and been a part of it, loved by it and in love with it. I had been reckless if not quite fearless, and it went to my head along with the tributes and the cries of triumph, and the promise of things to come.

I should have known, finding those seven sad scared men who did not desire their liberation, that we were in a game now for heaven's titillation. Black farce. I should have known.

How could I know?

I mounted guard all night, along with the soldiers and the embryonic militia. There were barricades everywhere across Paris in case cavalry might be sent against us, and the bells rang until they tired themselves out. But bonfires were burning on the streets; hardly a café attempted to stay shut. Fright and bold hilarity mingled. At every turn someone ran up to sing your praises, to curse the old order, to ask: Have you heard anything? Any news? What will happen now? Later the thunder came and broke open the sky, and we drowned. But Zeus did not strike us with his levin bolts.

It seemed the king had gone to call on the Assembly. And they had been fawning at the door, gasping to receive him. It was le Comte de Mirabeau who recalled them sharply to their places. "Before you lick his hand, wait and see first if he will treat you as dogs, or men." For once, they did listen and sat down soberly. The king took his cue from this and behaved well, if belatedly so. He admitted that now he perceived the needs of the People.

They brought His Majesty into Paris before the sun in the morning, with spluttering torches and trumpets. We all paraded with him, many of us with the drawn rain-wet swords of action yet in our hands. The excitement after the hours of doubt was insurmountable. Benighted Paris shone bright as day.

One of the deputies from Dauphiné was walking beside me. He had given me dinner at Versailles. Now he said, "You were there. You saw the prison fall."

"Yes, I-ul-I was one of the first through the gate."

It seemed to me I had been. I had heard it said, too, I was one of the men who climbed up to the roofs of the shops and had the drawbridge down.

The green cockade was withered and gone. Green, after all that, turned out to be some aristocrat's blazon. A new badge was swiftly devised for Paris' newborn militia, the blue and red of the city in two stripes or two rings. But these did not erase my name or what I had done.

A day or so later, Momoro accosted me at the Café Procope. "Where is it?"

"Where is what?"

He held out his hands to me and I gave him the pamphlet. I had revised it; I was circuitously on my way to him, but he never mentioned he knew. Shortly my words were issuing from his press. Harp Street was blocked by those who came to buy them. Over his door Momoro had written up: FIRST PRINTER OF THE NATIONAL LIBERTY.

That night I was asked to dinner at Curtius' house on the Temple Boulevard, the true Mercury barometer of whether or not you were in fashion. And going in, there sat Mirabeau, who stood up and raised his glass to me, and said in his ringing, beautiful voice, "Gentlemen, salute, if you please, Monsieur Camille Desmoulins, the Author of the Revolution."

TWO

❋ ❋ ❋

1789: Summer

SINCE THE BEAST *is in the trap, someone should put it out of its misery.*

FRANCE SET FREE

For centuries there have been those in France, who love her, who have groaned aloud or in silence, for liberty. The restoration of that liberty to the French people has been reserved for this era — our own. I thank God, therefore, that I was born when I was.

The *restoration* of liberty. The phrase assumes, then, that at the commencement there was freedom. But if once we were free, who gave that freedom to us? God.

Then, if since we have lost that freedom, who took it from us? Men.

Who are these men? Look about.

It is easy enough to see them, dressed as they are in finery and jewels, fat with what they have battened on. Church and nobility — vampires, suckers of the People's blood. It is they who have subjugated France. Observe the color of their faces and the pallor of your own.

For my own part, I would have been willing to die to rid my country of this enslavement. But if the righteousness of the cause is insufficient, one other powerful motive may inspire. In this just war, what richer spoil was ever offered the victors? Forty thousand palaces to spill golden trophies into their hands. This the prize of courage.

But we will avert our eyes from so terrible an image (and may God avert the temptation). Such a holocaust will never take place. The aristocrats will pardon my mentioning it — I do so only that they may be aware of the *possibility* of extinction. Oh, let them listen to our entreaties for justice while the cry is still a gentle one. Why ever should we covet their great riches? We want merely the right to life.

45

Let us have, then, a constitution.

To begin, let us have a fair means by which the voice of the People may make itself heard.

What, overthrow the established laws? Yes. It was the People who first assented to them, and now, the needs of the People having altered, so these laws should alter to accommodate them. The things of the past must cede to us their authority, for we are the present. Or let the dead rise and debate the matter with us.

By which, however, I do not advocate the passing of laws which plainly will not function, such as that Agrarian Law which would parcel up all the land equally, without regard to profit or common sense. Even the Romans, who had half a universe to play with (and could give away a town apiece to their cooks to show enjoyment of a sauce), found such a law unworkable and abandoned it. It is a fact, certain sections of the People, ill-educated and burdened by cares as they are, have gained no knowledge of the practicality of lawmaking and will do better to leave the task to others able to accomplish it. Though more numerous, these sections may receive a lesser share—for he who leans upon the gateway cannot expect the same pay as the architect who built it. Yet still it shall be a fair share. Their legislators will be men who will work tirelessly on their behalf.

Not as the nobles and the priests have worked—solely for themselves.

But surely, the clergy at least is necessary to us? No.

It is the priesthood alone which creates the need for priesthood. Do not make the error of thinking it was God. For if we are to believe the teachings of Christ, he tells us his ministers will be the lowliest and most modest among men. Are the priests, then, lowly and modest? (Do I hear you laughing?)

You may dismiss me from the charge of atheism. Manifestly, there *is* a God, the complexity of Life and all things reveals as much. Yet we are like children bereft of our father. By the consequential rule of nature we know we must have had one, yet he has deserted us. We call to him in vain. It is also useless to search out, in order to please him, which cult of worship will delight him most. He hurls lightning alike against our churches and the mosques of others.

No, it is not God who has need of religion. It is we. We, craving for hope in despair, consolation in wretchedness, a reward for goodness and endurance. Come, then, if this is our need, let us please *ourselves*. Let us take up a religion like those of the Romans and the Greeks, a cult which incorporates music, theater—the best aspects of the true Dionysia, which has long been misunderstood. A religion to bring happiness and courage to its participants. Who can wish to embrace a doctrine that promises only sorrow in the world? I would point out that the pious among us have frequently been our kings, the *most* pious often, too, the cruelest of their kind. Behold them on their knees, worshiping the naked god of poverty, in their robes of cloth-of-gold stretched to bursting after a good dinner.

How is it conceivable one man should live in this way while another lies starving under his window? It is the accident of birth, the tyranny of heredity.

By such arbitrary barriers are men segregated and abused. The son of the aristocrat is an aristocrat; the world is at his feet. The son of the People may advance no further than the dirt beneath him.

What are these nobles, then, that they deserve the best of everything? A parasitic plague on the face of the earth.

For five centuries we have writhed under the heel of these princes. In ancient law, the king is the symbol of his people; the gods judge the people by their king. For this reason, he was to be perfect, without flaw. The monarchs of France have been poisoners, thieves, and lechers, the wicked or, at best, the stupid and the mad. Through this, history has been able to call one of them "well beloved" who has treated his nation like cattle. He who left you to eat the snow and drink water from a ditch, he was not evil. What might he have done with you if he had been? The Romans cast out their corrupt masters. And we — are we not greater than the Romans?

Yet it is not the solitary man but the overwhelming power bestowed upon that solitary agent which cripples and makes a monster of him. God send us and make of us a Republic. We have seen what a monarchy will do. Only by a balanced dispersal of power can France be saved. At which time, having taken from his hands these dangerous toys, we might retain our prince as our figurehead; I have no argument with him. I believe there is virtue in him. Let him show it, by relinquishing those rights we may no longer allow him, and take his place among men — he is not a god. Yes, let him display virtue, that we may offer our love to him, for the man may be loved even while the institution of kings must be hated. Indeed, let all this court renounce their rights, admitting our just quarrel; would not their rights be returned them, freely, by free men?

Above all, then, our hopes rest finally upon that future condition of freedom we have it in our means to bring to pass. It is for us to strive to complete the mighty work only just begun. And strive we must. For beyond the labor I see the dream-come-true. A land the very stones of which are liberty, and liberty the dazzling sky which contains it.

Here, there is no stricture of word or pen, of conscience or deed. Here no child starves. No door is bolted against the cry of pain. In this future country, the riches are for all and all enjoy them. It is defended by strength and guarded by love and is *invulnerable*. See it, this flawless land where the nation may partake of everything and *is* everything, one single blazing flame that burns so brightly for — and of — itself.

Who, in that day, will wish to be any but the Child of France? Who will not fight for that day? Like some warrior of the antique earth, who perishes that his country may live, I know that I too might die gladly for such a cause as this, if to write in my blood at the last:

FRANCE IS SET FREE!

❋

I paraphrase, I elide. I unremember and unsay, and say again, freshly. (And I sense here, too, the whispering of the Lie, like a snake in a green tree, along with the passion, the anger, and the ideal. There are things which now I try to hide, even from myself.)

Those hours in the garret room, smoke and ink, my heart in my mouth. A second in time, and long ago.

Much blood has flowed under the bridge since then.

❊

Two days after the Bastille fell, Necker was recalled to office. Oh, the power of the People. It is unwise to give in to a child which throws a tantrum, or a dog which bites when refused a bone. The lesson is too clear: when refused again, *bite* again.

1789 : Late Summer

Lucile: The alabaster priestess

THE YOUNG man and the young girl had walked across the river, using of course a bridge, and now stood in the enormous nave of Our Lady of Paris, the alchemical cathedral.

The great eyes of the dreaming beast still looked inward; not for too much longer. The mob had also visited the cathedral, and the musket fire of July already shattered jagged little portions out of the windows: a premonition. Nevertheless, untouched, the burning blue petals of the huge roses, threaded with purple and vermilion, remained open wide and dense with profound, supernatural thought.

The alchemical formula, to which every pillar that had gone up and every statue that had been planted was said to offer a key—for those who could read it (even the misplaced crab in the zodiac was intended to emphasize some vital clue)—was lost on Windmill, and probably certainly lost on Lucile, though in her way she seemed to know it all as she stood there, calmly looking about her. What better backdrop for her than this? The submarine lights, the soaring forest roof of stone, and the slender white image of her figure caught between heaven and earth, so fragile, yet the sudden interpretive force of everything. He could see her, here, the acolyte of some high altar, casting white doves into the air in a column of incense. Her hair had turned to silver in the temple. Outside, in the sun, it was golden coins, a fortune of gold *rouleaux*.

"What a strange summer it's been," she said, inconsequently yet truthfully. "And it's almost over."

But time could not run swiftly for her. She was nineteen. And even for him the terrible static dragging of time, alternating with the equally terrible rushes, when life had appeared to be escaping from under his feet, had steadied. He leaned on a pillar, conscious of being rather smartly dressed and in a new coat, dull green, for which he was in debt. There were by now three pamphlets; each sold spectacularly well. But they had not brought him much money—*cher* Momoro had seen to that. Even so, in abrupt revulsion, he had cleared out of the garret and into a suite at the Hôtel de Nivernais. Thereby losing the romantic Duplessis window, but that too had begun to embarrass him. What had they ever seen of him through it save his poverty? Also lost in the extravagant move was a great deal of money; it had eaten up all the slight remuneration his pamphleteering had brought. And still there was, in the well-appointed apartment, no *bed*.

Actually, you could not come back to an attic from Mirabeau's extraordinary domicile at the Butterflies. Two weeks surrounded by gold lions' feet, laughing marble nymphs holding up a ton of finest wax candles, lackeys in pastel satin: Will you have the footstool here, monsieur? And Mirabeau: Have some more burgundy. Keep the inkstand, since you like it. Besides, people on the street still came up to Windmill, asking him if he was himself, shaking his hand, flinging their arms around him (oh, God, mind the new coat!). While at the Palais-Royal he was clamored for, invited, *pressed* to mount tables and give his opinion on everything. No. An attic was out of the question. What, after all, were a few debts? (It would seem Mirabeau himself had debts—one wouldn't know, looking at him: the ruby buttons, the lace.) If only Desmoulins *père* would answer his son's last ninety letters.

He liked himself in the new clothes. He was unaware of the vehemency in him, the sheer drive which could, on occasion, make him so attractive. Unaware of his own peculiar and pagan eyes, holding all the lights of the glass in their blackness. He was simply looking at Lucile, who looked in turn so utterly like a vestal, and so completely unobtainable, he was consumed by violent, nearly agonizing lust.

They had all met in the street close to the Luxembourg. Madame Demeter and her two girls. The meeting seemed oddly prearranged, though of course it had not been so. Although of course again, on balmy days, mothers and daughters did walk gently up and down those green spoons of lawns nailed in by white statuary. Over past weeks, calling at the house in the rue de Condé, Windmill had noticed Monsieur Duplessis's mode of greeting was altered. It had been: Oh. It's Camille. (As if we didn't know.) Now it was: Why, look who it is! It's Camille! *(Parfait!)* And maybe a glass of wine and a biscuit. At some point one was thanked again, sotto voce, for the timely warning of July twelfth. As if anyone wouldn't have been aware of the city's turmoil without notes being left at doors. Windmill sensed that, rather than feeling an increase in friendliness, monsieur was playing safe. The penniless nobody had become a penniless somebody. He was an idol of the Paris crowds, which now might be observed lying down drugged in the heat, waiting for the slow medicine of the come-to-pass-millennium to take effect. Dangerous as hell. So best, too, be careful of this weird Camille. God knew what he might do—or write—next. So far he had surely written what the mob wanted to hear (assuming they understood it). He had given a voice, in black ink, to a tongueless howl, and neatly at that, with classical allusions to burnish and the odd pun thrown in for good measure. Yes, better be careful of this Camille. Which didn't mean you were any more inclined to let him parade about Paris with your daughter.

Demeter had said, "Adèle and I are taking the carriage over to Madame Something-or-other's. But Lucile must fetch something or other from somewhere or other, and I am rather uneasy about the streets in the present state of things. I wonder if you'd be so kind, Camille, my dear, as to escort her?"

So they went somewhere or other and fetched the something or other—where had it been? What? Ribbons, a book?—and then crossed the river, and through the clutter of dwellings shaped to points like wedges of blond cheese, and around the chapter house, and so in a carven door. There was a lectern in the cathedral, blue stone with bronze angels, created by one who bore the name DUPLESSIS. Lucile had told him this when she was a child. She was a child no longer. She was a woman on whom several suitors were now in the habit of calling, some well off. Lust went out like the fierce sun fading from the glass rose, leaving him melancholy after all.

"Mama will be here soon," she said.

She had saluted the altar on entering; he had not. For him, that was all done with. He took a scathing pride in omitting it (out with the fat priests, on with the Dionysia). But she, a priestess, performed the genuflection very charmingly. It might have been a reverence to Apollo—or Diana. (Lifting her hands, doves flying. . . .)

"Yes," he said. Mama would be here soon. What now? He wanted to tell her more about Mirabeau, but he had been boasting enough about all that. He couldn't stop. In fact, he didn't want to say anything to her at this moment. He wanted everything of her but speech.

"With all your great patrons and friends," she said, "you're too proud to talk to me anymore, your silly Lucile. Yes, you are. Look at you, proud Camille in his green coat, like a peacock."

"Oh," he said. "The coat." He touched it, pleased. And remembered the debts and was worried.

"Sometimes I wish I was a child again," she said. "It was so simple then. Nothing changed."

He was surprised, thinking as he had been, too, of her childhood. But he said, "Things change constantly. We don't always see them. But you're still a child."

"No," she said, very sadly. "That's all gone away."

He wanted to hold her in the shadow sheen of the windows, as tightly as it required to possess. The crown of her head would rest against his lips, and the scent of her fleecy hair fill his brain. She was grieving over something; he should make her laugh.

"I'm so sorry they broke the windows—there, look," she said. His fault,
perhaps? *To arms!* he had screamed, and they had run off and stormed the
Bastille and punctured the windows of Notre Dame. "It confuses me," she said.
"I know so little. When you speak about it, I understand. The death of the old
wicked order, and the birth of something new and fine—"

Birth? Nothing was happening. Everything should be. The prison was now
being dismantled, stone by stone, the towers, where the Swiss had shot at them,
crashing on the ground. The bits, you heard, were becoming souvenirs. Somewhere in the dungeon a printing press had been shown off to tourists as an
instrument of torture. Curtius' little niece (or daughter) had fallen down a
Bastille stair into Robespierre's gallant arms. (I've got you safe, mademoiselle.
Shall I let you go? And petite Marie simpered properly.) Paris had been
sectioned into districts. There had also been a quantity of hangings. And
Windmill's second pamphlet, beak dipped in blood, had flown out into the city.
He had put no signature to it; its black humor had disconcerted even him. It
purported to have been written by an iron lantern hook in the Place de Grève,
which spent some time in declaring its value as a much-used popular gallows.
"The wicked fear light; aristos object to the lamppost." But the pamphlet had
sold like hotcakes, had there been any hotcakes, and soon the cry was up: Only
that Desmoulins could have written this.

He was unsure if Lucile had been permitted to read this piece of work. It
was, with all its macabre jest ("Dear People, you have made me Empress of
Lanterns"), not as blazingly dark as the masses subsequently tinted it. Dark
enough, though. ("Plenty of villains escaped my embrace. How is it you let the
Marquis de Lambert go free? How is it you could overlook the Abbé de
Calonne? Evening is close—let me give you some light!") You said, naturally,
what they wanted, and they cheered it. Well, someone must say it. (*Your
thoughts are your own property. What you say—worse, what you write down—
becomes the property of others and may be used—*Yes, Father. Thank you.)

"The birth of something fine?" he now said. "It *will* be fine. But the court
party slings every weight they have on the king's back, against us, and so holds
the Assembly down."

In late July to August there had been some fun and games. A plot was
"discovered," supposedly "Antoinette's," to blow the Assembly off its benches
with gunpowder; summer sky full of dismembered deputies (it's raining—?),
while through all France ran the story of the bitch queen's contrivance to bring
in her brother's Austrian troops to restore absolute monarchy. Austrian troops
were accordingly seen the length and breadth of back-barnyard France. Mean-
time, rumor had it, the Poles had landed on the coast and the Spaniards were
at Bordeaux.

Then, one August Tuesday, the nobles began to stand up, one by one or in
sobbing groups, at the Assembly, renouncing their rights to almost everything.
Either they had been reading Windmill's first pamphlet, *France Set Free,* or they

had caught that interesting virus known as mass hysteria. The orgy went on until Wednesday morning when, in the clear light of day, their sacrifices became to them more apparent and were, one by one or in sobbing groups, rescinded.

The harvest might have been good. But the madhouse of fearful pastoral France, with Austrians in every hayrick, let husbandry slip. The bread shops of Paris now tended to have guards in them.

The king, when seen, still sported his three-color cockade, red, blue, and white for the Bourbon lily. Generally he was away hunting at Versailles, killing animals and diligently crossing them off his forestry lists.

On August 26, there issued from the National Assembly a declaration of the Rights of Man. Which had also been summed up in an anonymous back-street placard seen here and there, so scorching in its simplicity Windmill had half a mind to plagiarize it:

> *Les Droits d'Être*
> *Je suis*
> *Tu es*
> *Il est*
> *Nous sommes*
> *Vous êtes*
> *Ils sont*

"The right to be, dictated solely by the fact of existence," he said to the windows of the cathedral. "But the People still starve. I was talking to Maximilien—"

"Yes," Lucile said. "*De*robespierre." She was cruel as a kitten, silk with claws. "He hasn't been to see us for ages. Do you suppose Adèle will pine away?"

Their eyes met, and the smiling cruelty vanished. She searched his face. "But you were saying?"

"I don't know what I was saying. It's in chaos, this dream of ours, and the damnable king is in the middle and nothing moves. Did we lie on our stomachs in a whirlwind of bullets and cannon shot for this? My God, you can shout till you're black in the face, and write until Paris drowns in the ink, but it seems the only way is through violence and through blood—and if that is the only way, then we must take it. And *all* the windows will be smashed, Lucile. There won't be a single pane of blue glass left standing in its frame." He stopped, panting. Her eyes on his were full of fires, violet and rose and silver. "And I love you," he said. "Y-you know I love you. What do you m-want me t-to do, tear out my heart and throw it on the p-pav-paving at your feet? I-I'll go mad—you—*know*—"

"Don't," she whispered. It seemed to him she was afraid, and he did not believe her fear. "Hush."

"Hn-h-hush? What-wh-what in Christ's nm-name—how cn-I-can I h-hush—af-ter eight years of keep-keeping quiet ab-about it—*Lucile!*"

"No," she said. "Please, please."

"Priestess," he got out. "Stone. Ice and st-stone."

She turned away and he was frantic, for he had never meant to say any of it, and she seemed to be crying. But then she said, very softly and levelly, "It doesn't matter. It's all right. The sun's still shining. And . . . here's Mama."

He looked and saw Demeter and reticent composed Adèle, arm in arm, floating to them through the cathedral's soul.

Lucile was all smiles, welcoming them. Nothing untoward had happened.

Deceiver. White priestess, cold as ice – but it wasn't true. She – warmth and sweetness – and how could he unsay it? Windmill looked imploringly at the mother, who guessed, smiles or not, something was quite wrong. She glanced at both of them, the ripple of concern swiftly banished from that pretty face. They would wait till he was gone to discuss it. Then Adèle would giggle at Maxime, and presently they would all laugh at Camille, going insane, again, under the eyes of the heartless marble saints. But surely they wouldn't laugh at him? Yes, they would laugh till they wept.

He bade them all a very stilted stuttered good-day and strode out of the enormous cathedral, miles and miles of floor that echoed under his footfalls. Leaving the three women standing there getting ready to laugh themselves into stitches.

⚜

When he had walked into Curtius' house in July, and Mirabeau had come to his feet and toasted him on the spot with that unpedantic, devastating toast, the book of Camille Desmoulins's own life seemed abruptly to fly open all about him. He felt a wave of emotion – a self-consciousness like a bolt of light – cover and absorb him. He sat down stunned in the place he had been given, at Mirabeau's side. Mercury Curtius' banquets were seldom average.

For one thing the food – oh, God, the food – was wonderful. Curtius' German, Swiss, or Alsace mistress was also first lady of his kitchen. The aroma of the cooking had formerly had the power to trap Rousseau and Voltaire swooning in the dining room. If anything, she had improved with the years.

There was a scatter of women at the table, one the little sphinx Marie, all eyes. "She is as clever as her father," said Mirabeau, aside, but making no secret of her parentage, "at getting a perfect likeness in wax." Then, more loudly, "and when they've made the doll, they stick pins in it. Witches."

"What?" Curtius inquired down the table.

"I said you are a witch, sir. Who doesn't know the whole waxworks comes to life after the lamps go out."

"All but one," said Curtius.

Ah yes, Monsieur Necker – hairless, eyeless, and shot in the face by the King's troops. You know, mu dear Camille," he added, "in a month or so they'll be clamouring for a similar fate for the original."

Curtius laughed, ears pricked. He looked like a fox, handsome and spruce, up in the wood now, but with several secret holes wherin to go immediately to ground.

"Now, now, Count—"

"Don't tell me, Mercure. Now, now, indeed. Sell me your cook and I'll leave at once and stop causing trouble." Curtius smiled. Mirabeau said, "Our Camille has all Paris up in arms at Necker's dismissal, but I'm afraid the old . . . there are ladies present . . . the old wretch fooled the lot of us. Necker's been fiddling figures since he got his job. None of what he published was accurate. He cleared the deficit by pure imagination. While I can admire audacity, I think it has its limits. If he's wise, he'll cut and run."

Dazed, Windmill said, "I see."

"Of course you do. Go home tonight, and if you still *can* see—Monsieur Curtius' dinners carry no guarantee of that—write it all down. Bear in mind, however, that we may be doing Cher Necker an ultimate injustice. Popularity may galvanize him after all to some feat of genius that will save France from total bankruptcy. In which case it will be out duty to support him. And do you see *now*? The Paris mob will follow you to perdition at present, so be choice where you lead it. I gather it followed you into the Bastille?"

"Nn-not quite."

"Truthful too," said Mirabeau, and sat back to gaze on Windmill as if surveying some priceless work of art. "My God. And young. Look at him." Everyone looked at Windmill. "You have the gift of words," said Mirabeau. "I respect it wherever I find it. Not too often." Then, lightly to Curtius again, "I hear de Sade was in the prison two days before the People liberated it. Somebody caught him shrieking from his window that all the prisoners were being murdered by de Launay. He was hastily moved elsewhere. If he'd kept his mouth shut, he too might have been carried shoulder high out into the city. Ah, the price of free speech. And where, dearest Mercure, did you come by this wine? I am becoming very jealous of your cellar."

Mirabeau. Black hair and blacker eyes, a face life had stamped upon and also indelibly stamped, which had yet the intensity of a gathering tempest or could split into a devastating smile, like lightning. Mirabeau, *diableau*—Devil or Jupiter, god of sky bolt and libido. Depending on values, a clever man warped by appetites, or an intellect which also celebrated the fleshly state. A rioter, whatever else. He soon told the tale of how Curtius periodically would ban him from the house. A notorious tavern over the way, the Blue Staff or, in local parlance, the Sticky Blue Limit, had then received him, mourning for Alsacia's apple-goose.

The flash of sword blades in his eyes when he laughed, or spoke politics peripherally, the eyes far ahead of the words. Duels in his past. Every kind of aristocratic crime. When he turned his head or raised his hand he held the room. It was a power he had cultivated, expected to work, and which did so, tremendously. And his beautiful orator's voice, the beautiful eyes, were perhaps the

greatest and most effective weapons of all, sheathed in his life-blown ugliness.
Certainly his deeds with women were notorious as highly successful. You could watch him charm them now, the starched ladies at the Waxworker's table, making them flutter just a little, crisp clean linen in a strong breeze. He had that knack of presenting you with his own majesty, then demonstrating that very willingly it had come to offer you—exclusively you—its whole attention. It was a flame he could turn on anyone, of either sex, as he chose. He directed the barrage at Windmill and overwhelmed him. With simple honesty that laid the younger man flat, Mirabeau informed him, "I'm taking you up, my boy. You'll be useful to me. And I'd rather have that assassin's knife you dip in poisoned ink on my side. No, it's a cunning style. But don't ever lick your pen. You're coming to Versailles, of course. Next month? I recall you wrote me a letter about that poor gazette of mine which never got to its feet. Things to discuss there. With the plethora of lame limping nonsense that is being printed, have you considered bringing out a paper? All Paris, most of France, would be after it."

With the dessert a dish of strawberries arrived, exquisite scarlet things. Mirabeau tipped the dish onto the table and the strawberries rolled about, staining nothing, but with a curious bonging sound. "See how he tests us, Mercure the Magician. Well, Camille, if we hadn't liked you we'd have let you eat them. Tell him about d'Anton, Curtius."

"You tell it much better than I."

Mirabeau shrugged, accepting the possibility.

"Georges was invited one night—you know d'Anton? Well, you know *of* him. Curtius uses the entire house as his workshop. One evening dear Georges arrived ahead of everyone, bellowing for food, and charged in here—you picture it?—where he found, seated at the table, a luscious young woman. It was love at first sight. (Ladies, forgive me; if you should wish to stop your ears?) I entered with Curtius and there is Georges in an absolute outrage, as he tells us, and the whole street—probably that voice of his was heard as far as Lyons—because he put his hand into the neck of her dress and found only the wire frame."

Windmill was struck by this as by something supremely funny, all the more so since patently it was unbelievable.

When the women had left the room, the jokes grew rougher and the political talk started up with a vengeance. A dish of candied nuts was discovered to be only partly the real thing.

"Virtue in the king, you wrote, I recollect," said Mirabeau, forming up the wax candies on the tablecloth to spell FREE FRANCE, knowing an author's eternal helpless fascination. "But do you think it?"

"I think it might be. He'd be good if they let him."

"Thank God. The cry of reason. But what was all that romance about hating the institution of kings—yes, a spiced rehash of Brutus. But otherwise? Without the figurehead, as you put it, do you know what it will be for France? Seven or eight cold-blooded monsters, who'll squat atop the pile like the gargoyles on the churches and rip at anything they spot moving below. Figureheads are needful. Trappings. Cushioning. Let's keep them. But mold them a little, maybe, as Mercure does his waxes. Now, Curtius, where's that maraschino you promised me? If it matches my own stock, I'll call you out."

"Then it had better not," said Curtius.

Finally, out in the hall, which was lit by subtle painted oil lamps of colored porcelain, Mirabeau announced they would visit the *cabinet de cire*. Curtius somehow restricted the viewing to an alcove upstairs, or downstairs, or perhaps in a cupboard. . . . The other guests had gone or been kidnapped, Windmill was in a state of unaccustomed hilarity. . . . Here they confronted another Mirabeau, standing in a suit of courtly cut and material.

"Good lord, Curtius, you'll have to redress it. The People will never tolerate this."

They stood in the narrow place, the world swinging round with good wine and fine fellowship. The world had never been quite this way before.

"You're next, Desmoulins, next to be immortalized." Mirabeau described the procedure, the face coated with pomade, the plaster applied and left to set, breathing the while through quills and claustrophobia. "But I gather de Launay didn't object?"

"No," said Curtius quietly.

(Somewhere in the shadowy dark gallery, the wax head of the governor of the Bastille hung, listening. That cast had been taken after death, the mob arriving back at the gate with their trophy on its pike, shouting for Curtius, who obliged them. A student of human anatomy, he had handled bits of carcass before.)

They were going out when a woman came gliding across their path. She wore a gown of rosy silk, and her hair was ghostly and worn high. As she went by Windmill, Curtius' candle flickered in her glacial eyes. Windmill saw her breathing in and out, though she was made of wax. He concluded afterward he was drunk, and dreamed it.

All his dreams, waking and sleeping, were bizarre that night, after the sauces and wines and waxes.

Anon, the well-sprung carriage with its Mirabesque coat of arms carried him to the Butterflies.

❖

March-born. The sign of the fishes. Talent and weakness. May be led, and in opposite directions.

It was flattering to be taken up—to be told: Genius, you'll be useful to me—by someone you yourself had placed on a pedestal. Mirabeau's patronage could be invaluable, while the idea of a paper, which Mirabeau seemed in the way of offering a financial start, excited Camille to the point of nervous agony. Then came the house built of honey, the dinner tables collapsing under the weight of the food, beauteous blinding wines. And the other aspect of Versailles, Versailles the shining bubble seen now from *inside*. . . .

My God, he's turning me into an aristocrat, into a royalist—fight it? Oh, yes, flat out on the sofa full of venison and burgundy. Fight it? Forget it.

Out there, the landscape of Versailles, vistas of terraces with marble faunal gods, and fountains, and flower beds like jewelry. Inside, these rooms paneled in brocade, with pictures from Italy two hundred years old, and servants in opalescent liveries of the ancien régime. Chocolate served in bed. The pure decadence of it was wonderful. No surprise they didn't want to let go. You found you didn't want to either. . . .

In the evening there were often supper parties, presided over by the great man's beautiful cold-eyed mistress, Madame Lejay. (Medea Lejay she was privately christened. Stories of her crooked financial dealings abounded. She's ruined Mirabeau scores of times, they told you, but he forgives her in bed.)

In the mornings, there were visits to the artist's studio. Mirabeau's court sat about to amuse him while the busy bee fussed and buzzed with its brushes. At one stage the bee said to Windmill, "You have a very interesting face, Monsieur Desmoulins." "Oh, certainly, popular with mirror makers; it cracks the glass." "Now," said Mirabeau, "no competitions in ugliness. I am here. You'd lose."

In the Assembly, fighting the pettiness and noise of an undisciplined body of men all eager to speak but not to listen, Mirabeau worked wonders. He's missed his true vocation, the actors said, jealously admiring. The Windmill, hurled downstream with the torrent, applauded, leapt to his feet, afterward approached Mirabeau radiantly. "Did you like that, Camille? Good. You make me very happy."

And in Mirabeau's library they worked on the drafts of things, on speeches and on articles. They also debated the germs of ideas, until trees of thought towered through the room and hit the painted ceiling. Once, Mirabeau's eyes, which from time to time troubled him, became inflamed. He sat there in herbal bandages, in a subfusc atmosphere of drawn drapes, losing no power or dignity. "Well, I can't see it for myself. Read it to me." And the towering of ideas did not stop. Actually, always Mirabeau's ideas. His was a swordlike mind, cutting to the core. ("No, Camille. You see it doesn't rest on that but on *this*. Let me try to explain." It rested exactly where he had stipulated.) But the sword strokes came wreathed in a flowering trellis of presentation. Suddenly you found your own mind was the toy, though you could wield a tongue like a needle. So what could you do but follow *his* mind that had this greatness to it, merely humbly providing a whetstone? When they walked, Windmill noticed with interest, it was automatically in step. In conversation, the same. But that was because he marched to the tune of Mirabeau's band.

All the while, it was like being a favorite officer in the service of a king. No denying it. You could relax, because *he* had the final word, and quite justly. You did not tell a clever captain how to guide his ship. God almighty, if Louis had had one half—Dangerous waters, these.

Then there came a moment when you walked in and found him silent, brooding, heavy with some darkness, vulnerable and dismayed. A private shadow, shown you since you were a trusted friend. (At his feet: Oh, sire, how may I aid you?)

"Is something wrong?"

"Yes. And no. An old wrong from my colorful past. I won't burden you with it."

"Burden me. Unless you'd rather—"

"Sit down, then, and comfort me."

And seated there, you listened. He told you, very briefly, with great delicacy, of a woman he had loved long ago: "When I was the age you are now. A lovely gentle tender woman, who lost everything she had, threw it away willingly, only for me. And what was I? A hapless penniless prisoner in the fortress of Vincennes. Sweet Sophie, who even convinced herself she found me handsome . . . you must forgive me. But I—find I must speak of it, after all. My poor father, who always hated me, to the very moment of his death and from the moment of my arrival in the world—but you'll have heard all the choice stories." (One had. All France had done so. The implacable father who pursued his son, even with a *lettre de cachet,* placing him in detention, securing his imprisonment, striving for his deportation, slandering all he did, restraining his genius from expression wherever possible, carping publicly where not. Supporting against him any who were his enemies. Incredible.) "I must have sprung to life owing him some debt. My early years were all and only that never-ending struggle. And in the midst of black misery, this dulcet child, with her high forehead and her beautiful breasts—God in heaven! We've been parted years; it seems to me a century. And yet, only yesterday I said farewell to her. Burned hearts, Camille. Ashes that take fire and blaze again but finally grow cold. She's dead. She killed herself. I heard ten days ago. Oh, Sophie!" And he put his hand over his eyes and, shuddering with pain, he wept in front of you. Impulsively, moved beyond endurance, every anguish finding its echo at once (Oh, Lucile!), Camille took the other hand. Presently Mirabeau collected himself. He pressed the hand of the follower who had witnessed and sustained him. He thanked the follower as if for some perfect service.

Five minutes later, they were working on the draft of a motion to be put forward at the Assembly. Nothing had happened. No burdens. And yet, dealers in emotion are never unmarked by such deep encounters.

Meanwhile the chocolate, the suppers, the powerful chats.

After fourteen days, a reeling Camille Desmoulins found himself enmeshed with his own ideals, not blaming anyone in particular. Floundering, he finally said to Mirabeau, "But if Louis is useless, he must go."

"Ah, you're wantonly missing the mark, Camille. It isn't always necessary to level the forest. Trees can also be pruned. This attitude of the clean sweep—

it's easy to pen, but your readers verge too readily on a sword. Which has been
proved by the message of your blood-red lantern in the Place de Grève."

"Well, I know you frown on the lantern pamphlet."

"String up every aristocrat? Naturally I frown. What am I?"

"An exception which proves a rule."

Mirabeau laughed. "Drink your coffee, and let us forget the awful lantern. Really, my dear, it was a scurrilous piece, for which nevertheless I will forgive you."

The hard school of jeered-at nonentity had not taught Windmill to like criticism, particularly criticism which "forgave." Irked, he frowned but could not bring himself to retort to this god of his. Who in any case had now plucked a rose out of a vase and deposited it on his plate.

"How can Camille, so conscious of things beautiful as he is, dwell so intransigently on matters of destruction? Study this flower. Are you going to blast her with a glance or set her in your inkwell to be poisoned? In the true world there must be some ethic of improvement for all, along with justice and bread. Do you want them to stay wolves or change back into men? The way to heaven-on-earth, Camille, is not through a colonnade of gallows and axes. Meanwhile, if you pull down every standing structure there will only be rubble to work with. I've warned you what will replace a monarchy—a tyranny. Thus, for the king . . . he must stay. If only as our waxwork."

"A puppet?" Camille looked at him. "Who pulls the wires?"

Mirabeau looked back, gracious and unruffled.

"Whom do you suppose?" said Mirabeau, and tore him across the heart with that incredible smile of power, dominance, attention.

He was in love with Mirabeau, in every way but sexually. Here on Olympus with Jupiter, courted and made much of, now the Windmill could feel its sails begin to spin in the tornado of someone else's ambition. He tried to say something that agreed while part of him drew inward and tried to deny. Consciously he balked; nothing came out.

Mirabeau glossed over the stammer with a sudden jovial, utterly unexpected, "And today you must go back to Paris. Off with you. Go and put those other writings on the street, and then we'll mount the paper and grasp the city by its ears." And he got up from the rose-strewn breakfast table where they had been idling, apparently the whole day before them. "Out, out! You've done enough for me; now go and do some work for yourself. My doors are always open to you. Come for a few days whenever you like."

Kicked onto the avenue with such looks of kindness and instantaneous beckonings to return, Windmill picked himself up and covered his own tracks in his mind all the way back to Paris. He was totally confused by it all. The implicit gist—Are you failing me? Then *out*—this he could not countenance. That it was a rap on the knuckles meant to make the boy do better next time vaguely suggested itself, but that too he thrust from sight. The open invitation he did not put to its test, though almost at once the most affectionate of letters from Mirabeau pursued him to the garret.

But he was Mirabeau's friend, of course. Mirabeau, benign god laboring for the People. Little Mother Mirabeau, the whores called him, and the seamstresses.

An intuitive name-dropper, Windmill dropped Mirabeau's name into everything. There even came the day at the Palais-Royal, in an excess of feeling and intimacy, threatened by rumors, Camille had informed the crowd (from the regulation table) that Mirabeau's life was in danger from the court.

But face it. Mirabeau is *working* for the court. He has his voice in the Assembly, and he will use the voice to hold the aristos aloft, safe as linnets in their starry birdcage, where the teeth of the wolves can't get them. Then, balancing the birdcage, he will fly up in the air and the net will come down on anyone left on the ground. There was profit to be made that way.

Wolf or birdcage balancer, Desmoulins? Or don't you know anymore? Or did you ever? Slam-bang go the mind's shutters, shutting out anything the mind doesn't want to deal with.

Did we lie on our bellies in the hail of bullets for this? To get chocolate in bed and a pat on the head and a silk shirt with ruffles on it like the cluster of a hyacinth?

Who powdered his hair when he was eighteen?

Who helped Derobespierre compose a flattering speech to the monarch, years ago at the college, and watched him kneel in the rain to deliver it to Louis's carriage, and didn't everyone clap and cry loudly, *Life to the king?*

Yes. It makes you writhe now, doesn't it?

❋

My dear Father — which tender address I hesitate to use, for I wonder at last if there is any love or understanding between us — what in the name of heaven must I do to convince you that you should rather take my word for what I have done than listen to the carping of your neighbors, the good people of my birthplace?

You are full of reproaches. It seems I am a cause of shame to you — yet once more. You say you fear I have dragged our family name through the gutter, or some words to that effect, by — here let me quote you — my irresponsible and unthinking outspokenness. Have you *read* what I have written? *No.* My best reply, therefore, is to send you forthwith copies of each of my pamphlets, so you may look and decide for yourself, instead of on the hearsay of those who hate me. "A prophet has no honor in his own country, and in his own house." It appears Jesus was nobody's fool.

For FRANCE SET FREE, it speaks for itself. THE LANTERN, I agree, is strong meat, but what else can you expect of a lamp-hook that has been through so much? Conversely, you will note the third leaflet deals with a defense of a marquis—most unjustly treated—to whose aid I came and did some good. I am not, you perceive, "content only to demand blood and the death of aristocrats."

I have been lauded everywhere for these works. Momoro's press practically caught fire, the speed at which it worked, while they clamored in the street to buy. No less a person than Mirabeau praises me; he has had me to stay with him and almost slain me with good food and kind attentions. Derobespierre, too, congratulates me, and countless deputies of our Assembly. (I will enclose, also, a copy of the *Chronique de Paris,* so you may read how others go into print to shower praise on me. Do you think I bought them all? With *what?*) I am called the Author of the Revolution. And revolution was necessary. Perhaps I saved Paris from ruin. Time will tell. Certainly the name I have made myself (with help from *no one*) is neither minor nor despised. Why do you listen to these slanderers rather than to your own son? If their sons had done such deeds, we might all be treated to a different story. Does it occur to you they could be envious?

But why should it? With all your cleverness, you have never fathomed me. I am a prodigal and wastrel, and you blush with shame at me.

In the end, it has actually been easier for me to destroy the Bastille, start a revolution, and overturn all France—than to get from *you* the money to buy a bed! C.D.

❀

Ça ira, ça ira, ça ira—
Les aristocrates à la lanterne.

Just as they had turned the nice little song of Fabre d'Églantine about rain and shepherdesses into a storm warning of savage sheep, so now they had hold of this one. It'll be, it'll be, it'll be—aristocrats on lanterns. "Lord So-and-so?" they said, grunting under the long summer heat, bellies stuck empty to backbones. "We'll *lantern* him."

And Lord So-and-so knew just what it meant. If he was sensible, he took to his heels.

The aristos flooded out, to England, to Austria.

The mob sweated and starved.

The lamppost lawyer, Camille Desmoulins, tried to find ways to pay the rent in the Hôtel de Nivernais.

Summer westered and began to go down.

1789: Autumn

A Burlesque

VERSAILLES, GARDEN OF white lilies.

Enter Antoinette, Austrian queen of the French. She is young enough and comely enough to be looked at awhile. That skin of hers is not jaded but still pure and succulent, and the powdered hair, even if some be false, makes a pretty impression round that apple-blossom face. Her dress is green, the palest, palest green of a pale, pale frozen cucumber under frost. The frost is actually silver lace, with emerald buttons. This is the new "simple" fashion Antoinette has introduced at court. She can play the clavichord, too. In this burlesque she says then, not for the first time, "We should leave."

"Leave?" says King L'oui, crossing off six more stags in the ledger.

"Pack the gold and the ornaments and escape this terrible wicked place." (Remember, this is a burlesque.)

"Oh, we're quite safe, really," says the king.

"How can we be, with that mob in the city only twelve miles away?"

"You don't understand the people," says the king. "They get upset sometimes but they don't really want trouble. I'd like them to be happy. They know I would. Besides, there's a dinner tonight, one of these traditional things. The Flanders Regiment is marching in, and my own King's Bodyguard will feast them in the theater."

"Flanders?" says Antoinette. "You mean they're not French? Then they can be trusted to be loyal."

So they could. So could the Bodyguard, for that matter, well-born to a man. There in the Butterfly theater this 3rd October, the officers of the Flanders Regiment, banqueting with the king's Praetorians, begin to say what an outrage it all is, God's Anointed going in fear and trembling of a pack of filthy stinking rabble.

Dispense with burlesque. This is a fact:

Up leaps a young officer. He has seen the king and queen in a box above the stage where the tables are. He falls in love: the green dress, the apple blossom. "I would die for her," he murmurs. "Gentlemen! The queen!"

They drink the queen's health and, sequentially, the king's.

Encouraged, the monarchs come down among the tables. The court ladies arrive too, snowy white, with lilies in their hair and on their dresses. All the powdered heads nod like lilies, in a gentle breeze. Everything somehow blends into Bourbon white: the green gown, the king's puce, even the uniforms and the gold braid; everything grows whiter and whiter, blanched almonds, icicles. Well, almost everything. For something is clashing nastily. What the devil can it be? The fiery young officers, Flemings and French together, who have already been allowed to kiss the queen's hand and are reeling from perfume, wine, and fine sentiment, stare about, trying to discover this single jarring note.

They do discover it.

"Some insect has alighted on me, some carrier of pestilence," says one. "Shall I brush it off?"

The queen laughs. It is a silver bell.

All along the tables the men laugh too, banging their fists till the plates bounce. "Remove the insect! Off!"

So he unpins it, this beastly contagion-bearing fly.

"And shall I step on it?" he asks.

A roar of pleasure.

"Step on it! Trample the thing!"

With a lordly gesture the man throws down the tricolor cockade he has just unpinned from his jacket and jumps on it with the glee of a child demolishing a sand castle. The theater goes wild. Everywhere you look they are wrenching off the hated cockade, the emblem of the rabble, treading on it, kicking it, cutting it up with knives, and pretending to eat it.

And through the pandemonium the orchestra, which has so far contained itself, begins to play a famous air from the opera *Richard Coeur de Lion,* "O my king, abandoned by the world!"

"Never!" shriek the officers, hurling themselves at Louis's fat feet and at the queen's daintier ones. "Abandon you? We are yours, sire, till death."

They drink the health of the monarchy. They will *not* drink the health of the Nation. They drink to its downfall and chastisement, lilies behind their ears, and the *bleu et rouge et blanc du Peuple* ripped in the wine slops under the tables.

While various journalists sitting in the boxes take rapid notes.

❈

When the news came to hungry Paris of the bread queues, Paris reacted.

At his district assembly, Georges d'Anton was bawling, with wings of sulfur. He suggested the city might care to rise and march on Versailles. He was not alone in giving this advice.

Part of Paris, at least, took its advisers at their word.

❈

They had gone through the Place de Grève, just conceivably saluting the Empress of Lantern Hooks. They had torn through the Hôtel de Ville, ripping up any paper they could find and eyeing the human beings there as if they might be taken for paper too. Women. Fishwives, prostitutes, dye workers, beggars, and a fair turnout of the *bourgeoise militante*. Now, armed with pikes and sticks and toting a cannon, they were making for the Butterfly Town to tell the butterflies they wanted the usual dull old thing: bread and justice. Some distance behind the women marched the People's Militia, the National Guard—it had a *tricoleur* uniform now, blue with facings of white, and red splashes for the collars, and white-tan legs, and it came from sixty districts, one of them d'Anton's. (D'Anton, conscientious lawyer, had gone home to work on a case.)

At Sèvres, being hungry, the women broke into shops. They sat in the street eating pastries—eating, actually, cake. Some got drunk. A lot got drunk. If it was all right for the rich officers of the Royal Bodyguard, it was all right for them.

It had to be said, there were a lot of very funny-looking ladies among the women. Big noses and feet, flat-breasted, some even with a day's growth of beard. In their aprons and ribboned caps, they stood under the trees swilling beer and smoking pipes. Everyone knew they were agitators, but still they had been given friendly female names. "Come on, Suzette," the *women* women said, as the march resumed its tread Versailles-ward. "Come on, Bernadine." And Suzette and Bernadine picked up their scythes and schlomocked after, holding high their skirts above their very hairy legs.

It was raining. Pouring. *Il pleut, il pleut, bergère. . . .* Go home, shepherdess, make a run for it, the woolly white sheep of Paris are on their way with Bernadine and Suzette and four hundred pikes and a cannon.

The National Assembly was sitting at Versailles (as the women were saying, what does it ever do but sit?) when the deluge burst in. Suddenly this hall of politics and debating men was awash with shrilling harpies. They clambered everywhere, effing and blinding, throwing up the wine they had recently thrown down on the august benches, between inappropriate calls for bread. One, not sick and not a man and not ugly, found Mirabeau and embraced him.

Another one, part of a more organized group, had got into the palace, received an audience, and embraced the king. Louis promised bread would be collected and distributed. What else did they want? Mission accomplished.

But Suzette and Bernadine (and Julie with the mustache) had been busy, and it now turned out the crowd in the streets around the palace didn't want bread anymore but the aristocrats, and mostly the queen, served up in a nice hot pie.

The rain streamed. The National Guard arrived, their new blue shape cleaving the water, from the hips down men of mud on mud horses. Their leader was the aristocrat (my, my, the People's Militia led by an aristo) La Fayette. (Bear in mind he was in the thick of the American War of Independence, on the proper side. Bear in mind, too, he didn't want to follow this collection to Versailles but was . . . persuaded.) A fine figure of a man, muddy but honorable. He has halted his battalions, in the downpour, and sworn them with upraised hands – the water running down their sleeves – in loyalty to Assembly and to king. Now, entering the Butterfly Château, La Fayette approaches the chief butterfly, Louis the Hunter. La Fayette puts a suggestion to the chief butterfly that he, the butterfly, and his family, should return to Paris. It is what the People want. Out here, sire, so far off, all they have is rumor to mislead them. Louis is dubious. He will sleep on it. On it, and on a soft bed.

Outside, on wet stones . . . the wingless harpies in the rain. A horse of the Flanders Regiment shot – or brained – by accident during the first exciting hours of confrontation has been skinned, broiled, and eaten. But one slim horse, unlike the loaves and fishes, has not satisfied the multitude, nor the pastries of Sèvres, nor the kisses of Mirabeau. The young girl who was embraced by the king has become an aristo by infectious touch and was nearly "lanterned" before gallants rescued her.

But falling water is something of a leveler, it would seem. *(Après nous, le déluge?)* Flattened by this water, everything was sinking: bonfires, horse cracklings, human heads filled by thoughts. In abeyance. The screams for Antoinette's liver and lights had sunk to a wheezy murmur; the Flanders battalion had been sent back to its barracks. Tomorrow, as it generally is, was another day.

A fire smolders in rain. Maybe it doesn't go out. How *can* such a fire die? The rain only feeds it. Here we crouch in mud and water, nauseated by stolen liquor and emptiness, chilled to the bone. And there *she* lies, a woman like us but all wrapped in her cocoon of silk, well fed, pretty, and clean and comfortable. I could be pretty like her if I had what she has. I could sleep if I had her bed, her money, her lovers. And smell as sweet, and look down my nose, like her. But I reek of the stench of poverty. My head isn't bowed with humility but weariness. I'm wet through, and I've lost a day's wages. I could die tomorrow and be better off. But then, remember, *she's* only human, she can die *too,* just like *me.*

In the theater that 3rd October, falling in love with chivalry, the young men had vowed to die for their queen. Now they were going to do it.

The light was in the sky: first light, the new day. There was a gate leading into a courtyard, and someone had been bribed to leave it unlocked. . . .

The guards who stood against them met scythes and axes, met a tumult of hate. There were now men dressed as men in the crowd, bloody already to their armpits. Red sunrise, red in the east, red between the cobbles. Some of the guards were very young. They died, calling a warning up the stairway, as the crowd went over them like a colossal wheel.

When it reached the queen's apartments, the queen had fled. Damn. No Antoinette for the casserole.

Then the People's own guard came in and shoved the People out again, naughty children, tut-tut, and just look at all this mess you've made, all these heads rolling about. That's right, pick them up neatly, like good children, on your pikes.

Out again, queenless, into the palace courts. And here, in the ecstasy of some state which, since humanity dares not yet coin a name for it, has yet no name, they danced, waving aloft the trophies, the faces of eighteen-year-old men on the tall pikes, along with bayoneted loaves. They had a song, too. It went: *The king to Paris — Yah! The king to Paris — Yaah!*

So, in the end, the king went to Paris.

❊

Birnam Wood was going to Dunsinane again. The crowd had plucked the branches off the trees, their leaves jaundiced for the year's ending, no longer the green of hope.

Flags made from discarded petticoats flapped like great wings, and on the roof of the royal carriage human ravens perched, cawing. Muskets were fired in the air. They were shooting at God now, and why not?

Other carriages toiled through the mud slick, the National Assembly going off to the city too. Presently it would create its own headquarters in the Tuileries Garden, north side, near the middle, in a riding school revamped for the purpose. Thereby earning the Assembly the sometime nickname of the Stable. King Yes-Yes and the uncasseroled queen were also going to the Tuileries, into that well-proportioned palace of the painted ceilings which for some years had been occupied only by mice and beetles.

❊

And presently, in the Place de Grève, the crowd hanged another baker from the hook of the Empress of Lanterns.

❊

The mood of Paris was such, you went to bed to the noise of patriot drums and got out of it in the morning to the strains of some bad National Guard band.

And I now actually had a bed, though I hadn't slept for a week. Or so little it hardly counted. I walked about in a fog, half numb, my heart crashing in my ears and chest. The reasons, other than drums and bands, were various, good and bad.

Some money had been arriving. It came in blatantly and didn't deign to reveal its source, but there was the petal of a rose in the first packet. Just one petal. So easily missed, so subtle, the jest in the screaming bribe. And I accepted the bribe and started the journal, because now I could employ a printer. Danton said to me once, "Let them pay you, if they like. Then show them you can't be bought. Just think how it would have looked, Judas Iscariot pocketing his thirty pieces of silver, then walking into the Garden of Gethsemane and kissing the local butcher." Which was all very well for Danton, who also told me, "If they're

dishonorable enough to offer you a bribe, why deal honorably with them
after you've taken it?" To my mind, Mirabeau was simply helping me out
because he saw potential in me. Not a bribe: a gift from my patron, who
cared for the woes of the People as I did. What he'd said to me at Versailles—
keep the king, I'll be pulling the wires—I'd muddled all that out of my way.
All I wanted to do was write and hold my power on the streets with a pen. How
could I give up the chance? Mirabeau was a complex god. He hadn't meant
anything so obvious.

So I started the paper, my *Brabant Messenger,* and in it I made an immediate
point of knocking all the aristos off their perches with singular regularity.
Mirabeau didn't chide me at first. The only little reproof was this: "My dear,
Brabant? Brabant is in Belgium, and though you and I have passionately
debated their rebellion, the way France now stands would you not prefer
something more *French?*"

To which I replied that No, I would not. The Rights of Man had given
freedom to the press, but I'd dreamed up the title beforehand, a decoy against
suppression (after such titles as *France Freed* and *The Gallow's (Lantern's)
Lesson for the People of Paris* they were watching out for it). Despite so-called
lack of censorship, I was still pleased with it. France had her Revolution on
hand, so what was more natural than a message from a neighbor who was also
engaged in revolt, and—most ironically—against an *Austrian* administration.

I got the paper out as often as possible, sometimes daily, working flat out,
now and then half the night. I had my forum and I was driven to use it. I admit, it
was like my first experience of sex: I couldn't get enough.

Occasionally my dear father even sent me money; officially my financing
was all his.

There was a lot to say. Sometimes the same thing must be said over and
over, but each time another way, to drive the nail home. Sometimes it even
meant praising d'Anton, who was fast becoming king of the Cordeliers district.
In his sledgehammer mode, he was getting things done, or showing things up.
I'd attracted his attention by singing of him and been invited to supper at his
apartment. I went there resolving to be careful but blew that, of course.
D'Anton's ambiance threw me into confusion and a strange premature high
spirits, in my excitement and tiredness. My impression this far had been of
three extraordinary rooms, bright yellow, bright red, and dark purple, and that
I'd drunk too much. Oh, and Gabi, his fat little pigeon of a wife, who sat playing
a clavichord with no mistakes in the fingering and no expression. There were
just the three of us by then, and I'd remembered Lucile playing, quite differently, and started to cry. At which d'Anton had shaken me and thumped me on
the back and nearly choked me, not asking what was the matter, thank God (it
was a sad tune), until the whole thing struck the three of us as amusing and we
almost died of mirth. Gabi, of course, laughed because he did. She adored him.
I could hardly bear it, to see this great bull so worshiped.

Remembering it all afterward, and the fact that the whole party had previously insulted everybody, from the pope in Rome to Robespierre to Antoinette's hairdresser (d'Anton, fluent in several languages, was a master at English puns), I was embarrassed and rather unnerved. The blows on the back from his sympathy—or irritation—were typical. I felt, rather than going to supper with him I had been jumped on from a great height by fifteen stone of mammoth. I thereafter kept out of his way, which was fairly easy. He was into everything. I was working on my paper compulsively. Despite that, I heard the usual reports that he and I were co-conspirators, seen everywhere together, and even one rumor I took women to his house for him, and something else about Gabi too idiotic to think of. People said they had sat at table with us and recounted our comments—always reprehensible. I didn't like any of this, either. It wasn't true.

Meanwhile, cheap bread in the capital was said to be poisoned; it had, apparently, such a bad effect on the insides. Apart from armed guards at the bakers, one began to meet one of Commander La Fayette's patrols at every corner. "This street's closed." Why? "Well, it is." First they sent you one way, then another, and finally it was easier to walk in the gutter (with all *that* meant).

In the midst of everything came October 5 and 6. The mood in Paris was sheer scared fury, and I was hardly immune. My wood seller even showed me a pure white cockade under his ledgers, "For when the Austrians march in." We had trusted those two at Versailles to pull themselves together and admit change was stalking the land. They gave in gracefully, but the minute you looked the other way out came the lilies and the whip. I had gone into print once before and made excuses for Louis. Now I went into print and villified him. There was nothing else I could do. The whole rumpus made me sick—it was de Launay all over again.

The morning the women went out, in the streaming rain, was like a scene from the opera; it lacked only a colossal chorus. Bacchantes on cannon, with pikes; drum-beating matrons; little girls only fourteen or so, all sheeny innocence. The ones who didn't want to go hid themselves: This army of Deborahs acted like an English press gang in the matter of swelling its ranks.

At Versailles came the usual matters: promises, procrastinations, disorder. Finally the whole royal brood was dragged to Paris and locked up in the Tuileries. It seemed some solution to the problem—Versailles being, after all, another planet. The Assembly, following, was an added improvement. Under the direct glare of Paris, away from the courtly influence of Versailles, Louis would have to stop doing things, and the Assembly might have to start. But if Mirabeau wanted to be the puppetmaster, he'd better hurry. I had said something to that effect, too, at d'Anton's party. I wondered just what I *had* said.

The capital was riotous, as usual, for a few days after the event. Everywhere, armies of those men the aristos scathingly termed the Breechless

Wonders — workers who didn't ape the aristo-bourgeois culottes but wore their long untidy trousers to the ankle. Glorying in the slight, the name was now becoming a *title d'honneur.* The breechless ones took to trousers striped red, blue, and white, to make their *sans-culottes* condition more obvious. When I went on the street, prowling in a dream, I would still jump out of my skin when some stripy stranger grabbed me. The well-known are common property. It was more like being arrested than hailed. I was aware, I think now, always of the undercurrent, the tightrope I walked. I had not grown blasé yet, accustomed to "staying popular." And I was always shouting now, in print, for the rights of the People. *How* I could shout! And weep at their sufferings, and go flaming mad at the excesses of fat clergy. Sometimes, the sight of humanity rushing about the thoroughfares was enough to precipitate me also into the tempest. At other times I had no margin for physical involvement; a shouted inquiry and its answer would fling me on the inkwell.

I hadn't seen Lucile, or one of her family, since the drama in Notre Dame.

One morning, I woke from two hours' disjointed sleep feeling a strange happiness — which evaporated, before I had drunk my coffee, to the most leaden pessimism. The dual state was not unknown to me, but it drove me out into the air. I walked circuitously but ended up as if compelled in the gardens of the Luxembourg.

The first leaves were falling, moist and sad, the tears of trees, and a slight mist hung over everything like an impediment of vision. Out of the lawns the formal buildings of the palace rose, their gray tops flat and cold. I remember looking up at the windows.

I went around the basin of water and crossed into some trees. The green was railed by images of whiteness, still stones, or persons wandering as I was. Everyone looked as aimless as I, except a child with a ball. Then, coming along an avenue from the Odéon, I saw Demeter and Lucile.

I stopped, became a statue, understood I was not, greeted them across the distance in an absent, hurried sort of way — and turned aside into cover like a startled rabbit. Hidden, I felt as stupid as it was possible to feel. I had meant to give the impression I was preoccupied and on urgent business. Obviously, that would fool no one. Demeter had, at least, known me very well for some eight years. She had even put up with the poetry I wrote her. What were they doing now, laughing at me? Or concerned, perhaps. There I stood under my shield of verdure, trying to decide if I should go after them.

Having made a resolution that I should, and turning around with the intention of going quite another way, I discovered Lucile poised there under the trees with me. I had not heard her light footfalls. She was alone, not ten feet away.

I stood and stared at her, blinded and deafened by my own heartbeat. There was no color in her face at all. She looked so fragile in the misty half-light, like one of the leaves that fluttered down. I stammered something, I don't know what, I suppose I said good-day and how was she. She ignored this inanity. She only stood as I did and stared back at me, as I stared at her, as if we were both terrified.

Inside the trees, where little light and no other people ventured, there seemed no time, either, no pressure to say anything after all. This sensation stole over me, like some physician's steadying draft. No sooner had I felt it than I think I knew. And my heart's rhythm altered, became like the blows of death but stronger than a lion's.

Then she moved forward, came to me. "Camille . . ." she said. And I had her in my arms.

There was no world at all. It shattered and blew away, tactfully and without a sound. That moment at last. All her exquisite beauty that had the fragility of ice crystal and leaves but was so warm, so real, and which clung to me so frantically, the luminous scent of her and her soft hair like a cloud of flowers, and her mouth given to me and taking me. Lucile. I named her again and again as I held her, kissed her, received her kisses like a rain of fire — Lucile, my Lucile, my most beautiful, my love.

"I couldn't bear it," she said, "to hear you say I was cold, that I had no feeling — when all the while —"

"I know, I know, my love, my beautiful darling love."

"I wrote you a letter. I never sent it. Better you should think I didn't love you — when my heart was breaking with love —"

"Yes, whatever you say, but you're here with me now."

"I love you. I love you. I love you more than anything in the world, more than myself. Camille — I love you — I love you — I couldn't even tell Mama — I couldn't tell anyone. Oh, to say it: *I love you.*"

The trees were swaying with a feverish autumn wind. I heard it blow them miles away, and a storm of foliage come down. She was crying. Her tears were on my lips.

She put her head on my breast and said, "Just this once. To remember." And then she drew herself out of my arms, took her hands away from mine. "I shall never see you again," she said. And I laughed, because this was so absurd and she so serious, like a child saying prayers.

"Never? Until this afternoon. I'll speak to your father. He knows anyway."

"No," she said. "You mustn't." The trees were silent, as if they could never be blown anymore. She looked at me and put me back with her upraised hand, this white priestess in the grove. "My father won't ever agree. I know this. If you go to him you'll make me ashamed. You'll shame us both."

"What?"

"Because I don't want him to *speak* of it to me. He has no — sensitive feelings. He would — make it less than it is."

"Lucile, this is ridiculous. I —"

"No," she said. Her stubbornness awed me. "Forget that I came to you."

"How-how can I? Oh, Lucile, for God's sake—"

"If you love me, *forget*. I won't see you again. If you come to our house, I shall keep to my room. I'll never love anyone else. Only you. I tried not to." She lowered her eyes. Her hands plucked at her skirt, so couthly. "I would sit and tell myself your faults. But I love your silly faults, too, because they're yours. But I won't say it anymore, that I love you or how I love you. Don't hurt me by making vain attempts on my father. Forget me. I shall always remember you, but that doesn't matter." And she turned and walked away, between the columns of the trunks, and vanished.

She was nineteen, but I had overlooked that, or never taken it into account. In one moment she had filled my life with sunlight and in the next flung me down into the pit. Because I valued her, I accepted her reasoning. What she said was true enough. Her father was not prepared to accept me as her suitor. I could foresee how he would mention the matter to her, perhaps he had already done so, and why she would loathe it.

There had been little light under the trees. Now there was total darkness. And the promise of winter.

❊

> *There'd be no winter on the earth*
> *If we were together,*
> *Nothing else but springtime,*
> *Only golden weather.*
> *Winter, winter is spring,*
> *It isn't snow, it's white lilac;*
> *Winter is spring.*

1789: Winter

COMING UP the stairs with an armful of books, I found d'Anton prowling about on the landing.

"I was just going out," I said, as we walked into my rooms.

"So was I."

He glanced around, eyeing the apartment, the best I'd had to date, not really with any interest in things artistic or personal but, for all that, interested.

"I've been going around," he said, "to see what you're all up to. Fabre's in his foxhole, writing a play. Robespierre's making another speech at the Jacobins." President of the Cordeliers district as he now was, d'Anton would preside at his assembly and pointedly eschew the Jacobin Club, where he would only be an invitee. Unless, of course, there was some skeleton he could barge in and haul out of a cupboard.

"And what am I doing?" I began to set out the books on my desk. I'd been pleased with them. One was a beautiful edition of Plato, in leather, only slightly marked. But the room was nearly black; I hadn't struck a light and the sun was gone.

"You? Oh, you're eating your heart out as usual."

I ignored that and went on fumbling in the dark till one of the books fell on the floor. I picked it up. I was going out, apparently, so I'd better go. We went, and down the stairs again.

The streetlamps had been lit, hanging at the center of their wires, just perfectly placed to hit the sheen of muck in the center of the cobbles.

"There's been a terrible tragedy," said d'Anton. His voice was so ominous and large I went cold. It sounded as if he knew the date of doomsday. What, in God's name—? "It's Robespierre's dog," said d'Anton. This was so faultless I fell against the wall laughing. "Come on, now," said d'Anton reprovingly. "Poor bugger. Show some pity."

"What happened to it?"

"A cart went over it."

I was sorry for the dog and said so. Poor bloody great thing, its eyes had been full of trust. It had followed him, I supposed, not looking where it was going.

"The wheel came down on its neck. That quick."

"At least it didn't suffer."

"*He* did. He was kneeling in the street holding it. That flouncy mare of a sister of his was telling all the neighbors how upset he was, such a sensitive compassionate man, even a dog—et cetera."

I felt sorry for Robespierre then, poor little Pierre. The dog was so much larger than he was on its own scale. Maybe he'd got a thrill out of it, being able to call something that big and potentially savage to heel.

We walked, came to the river like a bale of black silk, and onto a bridge.

"It looks like Lethe tonight," said d'Anton. "Still, that'll suit you."

Going out before, in the afternoon, I had met Brissot on the street, who'd hailed me cheerily. But I still had a chip on my shoulder and had given him a cold one. I had had all this time to think about the night just before the Bastille, when he and I met beside the barricade. *You're drunk, child, useless.* I'd forgotten that at first and recalled only the formless silent passion that lay quivering under the city's darkness, which he had somehow made me see more clearly. And I had been warmed and tickled by his crack about d'Anton's jealousy. Later, it occurred to me Brissot had been mocking me. He stood there, with the leaves of liberty I'd coined on his coat, and called me "child." That I'd ignored the slander and missed the "jest" only made me more distempered with him now. His long face was full of goodwill. Back in July, they'd given him the Bastille keys, and sometimes, despite his Quaker attire, he affected a key-shaped "gold" pin through his cravat.

After Brissot, in a bookshop, I came on Louis-Mer Fréron, who told me presently, in an offhand way, that he had called on the Duplessis family the previous night and was, actually, often there. He said nothing about Lucile. He didn't need to. It was obvious from every breath he took, and every angle of his body, why he had gone and why he would go back.

D'Anton had paused on the bridge, viewing the river. Suddenly he heaved a sigh and said, "My God, don't I know what it's like when there's only one woman in the whole of Paris you want to fuck and you can't get at her."

I said nothing. It felt as if someone had tipped scalding water over me. We started to walk again. Was this unconscionable brute reading my mind? In case he was, I said to him mentally, Be careful, Brother Georges, how you proceed with this. If you say something coarse about her, somehow I'll heave your fat arse off this bridge. He could swim though, damn him, everyone knew that. He had even swum the River Womb plenty of times.

Then he said, contemplatively, "Lucile," and my stomach hit me in the throat and I got ready to kill him. "Yes," he said, "like a little white bird. She looks like an angel. And you're like bloody Lucifer, so it's a good match."

The breath I had been holding, ready to leap the required six feet for his bull's throat, came out in a kind of sob.

"I beg your pardon?" said d'Anton solicitously.

I knew if I tried to speak now I'd stutter myself into a fit, so kept quiet, couldn't even look at him.

"You know," said d'Anton, "I've heard it said the two of you are unofficially engaged and ready to run off together, shaking the dust from your shoes over Monsieur Duplessis. Don't do it, Camille. My God, no. She's got a dowry coming. They're nicely off. Just keep up the barrage. Charm Mama. Flatter Dad. Tell the girl you're dying. And wait." We were off the bridge, walking north toward the bright lights. "That's what I did. It worked. You think I don't care about my Gabi, *mia cara* Gabriella, because I screw half the girls in Paris? I can't do without women. Why should I? But she means a lot to me. And the child that's coming. We lost the last."

I did glance at him then, this big bulk strolling along beside me. He'd told me he knew my private life and given me a pinch of his own in exchange.

❋

In the Italian Café at the Palais-Royal, everyone was clustered around the large pod of the stove for warmth. We were drinking a second glass when d'Anton got up and said, "Come on, there's tonight's final quarry."

We went out again, and I discovered we were after the darting figure of Swiss Mara, or Marat, as he now preferred to style himself.

I'd begun not speaking a word for an hour, drinking the wine and listening to d'Anton—like everyone else in the café, since he'd decided to treat us all to an epic recital. First some of Shakespeare's *Hamlet* (freely translated), d'Anton playing every part, including a squeaky Ophélie who reduced the room to jelly, myself not excluded. Then some Dante (what else?) in pure Italian, followed by a Latin couplet or two, translated and un, which I was asked each time to cap and did so, since it was irresistible. The entertainment proved as enticing as the stove, and they had come in in droves because, Look, here were those two clowns of the Revolution, d'Anton and Desmoulins, giving their famous double act. "My God," said d'Anton as we left, "wouldn't you think that bastard" (the proprietor) "would give us a handout for the business we've brought in?"

There was soon some more talk of bribery and corruption.

Mara(t), once an affluent doctor, rather than taking the opportunities of upheaval to improve his situation, had quit it to bathe in the slime. I'd heard his broadsheet, *The People's Friend*, called a rival to mine, or mine a rival to his. D'Anton had been making capital out of Mara's vituperative brand of truth. When the nobility went after Mara, there was d'Anton brandishing his fists, saying, This man speaks for the People; touch him who dares. Which was fine. But never very healthy, and now never clean, to pursue Mara in person seemed an unnecessary penance.

Then I saw where we were hunting him into. It was the house the Palais-Royal sometimes called the Unfading Flower. I hesitated. But d'Anton sailed in, so sure I was following that I did.

Business was good, as ever. The cards were going like fans, and piles of gold louis tottering ceilingward from the tables. A chandelier dropped champagne light on a buffet with china that could have come from Mirabeau's table (and maybe had). The Unfading Flower was there in person, in a gown of amaranthine amethyst. She greeted us like old honored guests; probably d'Anton was. After swooning into her neckline a minute or so he marched off across the room to find Mara reekingly ensconced in an armchair, eating duck.

There were no introductions, no hellos. Mara with a T looked at us and said, "Oh, the hog and the scarecrow. How's the paper, Windmill, found anything worth saying yet? But you can't, can you, unless Daddy Riquetti says yes." He smirked when he used Mirabeau's family name, as if he had done something clever.

D'Anton drew up a chair. I wondered how he could stand to be that close to Marat's entrail-churning smell. Perhaps the perfume of madame had disarmed the poison, like Ulysses' bloom of white moly.

"Now, Marat," said d'Anton. But because I hadn't answered him, Marat said, "Sp-sp-speak up, Windmill. How many more bakers are you going to send to the gibbet?"

"If you read what I wrote," I said, "you'd know I protested against indiscriminate use of lantern hooks."

"Oh, was it a protest? It looked more like applause. But there's Riquetti-Mirabeau, you see. Get the people to kill off the people and leave the dear aristocrats alone."

D'Anton was watching. He looked interested again.

I felt the sting. Though I'd camouflaged it for myself, I'd taken money. But I had a glass of the Flower's champagne inside me. "You're saying what?" I said to Marat.

"Let's see. How does it go? Oh, yes. Robespierre the Incorruptible, Mirabeau the Corrupter, d'Anton the Corrupted, and Desmoulins, who's such a fool he doesn't know when he's been given a bribe."

"Who's been given a bribe?"

"You see?"

"You're a stinking liar," I said.

Marat only looked pleased. He said, "I never lie, which is why I'm hated. I stink because I'm a sick man. What's your excuse for being ugly?"

"I'm a m-mirror."

D'Anton gave a roar, actor turned audience.

"A distorting mirror, then," said Marat, his green greasy snake's eyes gleaming. "A *warped* mirror. A mirror that misleads. No, you're not wicked, just stupid. Despite your clever tongue, which works better when you pin it on your pen, you know as much about politics as a gosling."

"Gn-go back to Switzerland, Marat," I said. "Ln-leave the French to run France."

"And game, set, and match," boomed d'Anton. "Gentlemen. He admires you, really," he said to Marat. "We all admire you." There was deliberately no trace of admiration in his voice.

"You're all scared," said Marat, biting at the dead duck.

I walked away and left them to it.

I stood and watched the *rouleaux* of gold staggering up on the tables at the whim of piquet and rouge-et-noir. Thought about taking Mirabeau's handouts and trying to smash all the harder at the roots of privilege. But had I?

I was utterly disconsolate, like a child in the rain outside lighted windows. Actually I was turning to leave when there was d'Anton again. He said in English, "What a pain in the balls that son of a bitch Marat is. Cheer up. You scored at least two points. *Les mots comme des flèches.* He likes to be beaten. Or so they tell me."

We went through another room, then up a stair. I was thinking, worrying, and scarcely noticed. A girl stood in a doorway, and I saw she was like the beautiful breathing wax doll at Curtius' house, in rose silk, with hair dressed high and powdered white as porcelain.

"Hallo, Rosie," said d'Anton. He was still playing with English. We all walked into the room.

It was a lady's bedchamber out of the Butterflies. Damask walls, flowering carpet, bedposts that seemed to touch heaven. A fire danced in the fireplace, which had girls carved either side. The warm reflection slid on their white breasts and limbs.

There was a bowl of fruit on a table, with grapes and a pineapple, and it was November. When I started to say something, d'Anton snatched up some of the grapes and put them in my mouth, quite gently. "Eat that and be quiet." He pushed me down on a sofa and sat down next to me with the girl in his lap. I ate the grapes and drank the champagne that appeared on the table. I felt removed from it all, removed enough to sit there listening to d'Anton talking to the girl.

Something happened to his voice when he did so. It wasn't the great spoiling bellow anymore. His voice had gone soft, all the power in it held like a volcano under honey – and the girl responded, her arms around his neck, rubbing her pretty face against his with its broken nose and scars and the eyes like little bright blue gems. But I wasn't thinking of that. I was becoming mesmerized by the firelight licking and playing on the carved naked girls either side of the grate. Then the real girl, still lying across d'Anton, was lying in my lap too.

He had already half undressed her. She came to me warm from his hands, bare-breasted out of her lace and aristocratic corsetry, a nymph rising from foam. My own hands went over her, and my mouth was in hers. Blinded, my fingers brushed against his, both of us intent on the same destination, and the girl moaned, but her own fingers were as active as mine. My whole body had clenched with need. It all seemed perfectly reasonable. When I got to my feet I wouldn't let go of her, but he said good-humoredly, "Here, children, *this* way," and we followed him over to the heaven-touching bed.

When I took her he let me have all of her, only keeping one hand under her back, lazily, lying so close I could feel the heat of his body. I felt him watching us, some huge lion stretched out on a rock, waiting, eyes like slits. She was beautiful as any of the lush fruit. The lust I had been saving a century was like torture. I held her and forced myself through her to reach the end of everything, and suddenly she was screaming, arching her spine and writhing, and the muscles inside her rippled and fastened on me like an earthquake. In that moment I felt his hand run down my back and push me against her, as if it were possible to go deeper, as if he brought both of us together in a master stroke. The eruption came at that, groaning and crying out, my mouth tasting her chalky scented hair.

I was lying dead on her when he moved me aside and himself spread out over her and had her. I could see them as sight came back. He growled as he came, not particularly loudly, more a note of enormous satisfaction. But the girl was as violently responsive as she had been with me. It didn't seem to be an act.

When he rolled off her, she lay giggling between us, happy as a child.

"Sweet Rosanne," said d'Anton. "Little maenad. She can keep doing that all night. What marvelous clockwork. A natural gift. You'll see." He leaned over and kissed her a friendly kiss. "But you'll die young," he said. I recall, when he said it, he looked at both of us.

Somewhere in the small hours, I went home before he did. He hadn't finished yet. "No one's going to want money off you," he said. I suppose I seemed uncertain, and he said, "I don't give bribes to my friends, I give my friends presents. Go and write up the virtues of the Palais-Royal. And by the way, don't forget my advice."

"What advice?"

"Kiss the mother, kneel to the father, and tell the girl you'll die. And *wait*."

The early morning struck cold outside, and at first I thought all this would too. But I slept a month in a night, and the paper lay in a heap of unread proofs. Plato had fallen on the floor again. Something in that.

❦

The next evening, literary work accomplished, I went over to the Duplessis house and invited myself in. There was no need to flatter Demeter; I had always been very sensible of her. But I shook Citizen Duplessis firmly by the hand and commended some hideous idea he had, something about poultry.

Lucile did not appear until suppertime, and then her mother went up to get her. She came in looking grave and cold, not glancing at me. I didn't get the chance for two hours; then there arrived a second of privacy. I wasn't going to lie to her. I said only what was true. "How could I keep away?" I took her hand and she said, "I was wrong." "Wrong?" "I can't bear not to see you." "Then you'll see me." "Yes, oh, yes." And then there was a knock and the maid went clattering down and Robespierre of all people came pattering up, with copies of some speech he'd had printed. And he said, "Oh, Camille, if only I'd known, I'd have brought one for you."

❦

The title of the journal had changed. Bulkier and neater in its gray cover, complete with woodcut illustrations at the hands of the printer—there had been arguments over the subject matter of these—it was now *The Revolutionary News (from France and Brabant)*. It promised to lash out, and lash out it did. ("I await the curses of the aristos. I can see them, lolling like cats on their sofas, then leaping up foaming at the mouth to seize the fire tongs—'Obscene writer, if I could get my hands on you!' But we live by the promise of our epigraph: What's new?")

The sales were excellent. *The Revolutionary News* held its own on the streets alongside Marat's snapping and snarling *People's Friend* and René Hébert's nasty little rag *Father Duchesne,* which appeared always with its pipe-smoking eponym on the cover and the charming salutation, "Father Duchesne? I'm the genuine article, fuck it."

Windmill's daggers went another way to work. A frequent laughingstock himself, he had a genius for making an absolute laughingstock of others. No one's safe. Even Necker gets it in the neck. And for Jupiter Mirabeau? "Sometimes a fanfare, sometimes a whipping."

The ideas of the Windmill have, of course, a passionate clarity, black and white, without quarter tones. He seems to remain mostly unaware that the Assembly itself is in the process of breaking Mirabeau's possible ascent to anything. And that the court, for whom he supposedly frequently works, will have nothing to do with him.

But oh, the freedom of the press. Leap, leap into the precipice. Don't stop to think. The faun dances madly in its savage forest of print, its Dionysia of wild words.

❊

Near Christmas, Windmill moved into No. 1, rue de Théâtre Français, and so into the kingdom of King d'Anton (or Danton, as he was now known), the Cordeliers district.

There was some snow coming down, and the furniture movers also made heavy weather of going up the stairs with the desk, the bed, and all the rest, cheered on throughout by a gang of interested citizens who had formed up to escort Camille to his new home. They clustered in the street, applauding him as he tore his hair over the sounds of wood being thumped into doorposts. In the end he gave the crowd money to clear off and drink the health of the Republic.

They went away along the street, saying how wonderful he was. The wind blew cold across the river from the Tuileries. Fatty the King had been wont to throw money to the People. The wind blew cold, but Windmill rushed upstairs to see how many corners had been knocked off his furniture.

THREE

❦ ❦ ❦

1790: Winter—Spring

WHAT IS HAPPENING? Nothing. What should be happening? Everything. The aristocrats renounced their rights. Church property has been taken from the priests and nationalized. Pieces of paper—assignats, revolutionary bonds—have been issued to give everyone a fair share. Of course they're not just pieces of paper.

❦

Baa, baa, mouton noir,
Avez-vous d'la laine?
Oui, monsieur, oui, monsieur,
Trois sacs pleins.
Un pour le maître,
Et un pour la maîtresse,
Et un pour le petit garçon
Qui habite en chemin.

(Ah, vous dirai-je!)

❦

IANUARIUS: *The Revolutionary News*

Sanson, the public executioner of Paris, is after the writer of the *Revolutionary News* (D.F.E.D.B.) with a libel suit, since the aforementioned writer has called him, in print, a torturer.

My God, he's the executioner and I said so. What does the man expect? Torture, let us face facts, has long been one of the arts of his honorable trade.

Other citizens are also bringing lawsuits. Sometimes one must print an apology in preference to paying damages of thousands of livres.

Not having thousands of livres at my disposal, I apologize. Naturally.

Yes, as a lawyer I know I should have proof positive before I accuse anyone of anything. The lawyer says, Turn a blind eye. But the journalist says, Sound the tocsin and make the stones ring. Probably I should go into the wilderness and live on locusts in a cave, wearing the while a blindfold. Dishonesty, after all, is everywhere. Who is safe from it? Our own National Assembly, for example. One imagines even the excellent deputies are from time to time approached by that smiling creature with the outstretched golden hands, so prettily named Bribery. Mademoiselle Bribery is to be found at every corner, it would seem. Even this humble author has been introduced to the lady on more than one occasion: Ah, Citizen Desmoulins, would you care to meet—? Other journalists are bought by the dozen lot. And I? I ask my readers to judge, on the evidence of what I have written and the libel suits that flock behind my paper like gulls after the teeth of the plow, whether or not I am guilty.

⚜

Speaking of livres, Danton was now handing them out like biscuits.

"Stop shying away," he would say to a Windmill gazing at him like an appalled antelope. "I've got the money. Share in my luck. We could all be out in the provinces again next week on our collective ears. No, I'm not bribing you. In any event, they were saying I was bribing you months ago. And the lark was singing my praises for nothing. Whenever I met you on the street, you ran down some alley in terror."

"You're not bribing me. Who's bribing *you?*"

"Take your pick. Orléans. The king. The English."

"Why the English?"

"Why not?"

"Which is it?"

"All of them, obviously. Our dear Duc d'Orléans pays me to stir up the mob. The king pays me to calm the mob down. The English slip me a couple of sous to tell their ambassador when it'll be safe to cross the road. Then Orléans slips me tuppence to tell him why the ambassador *wanted* to cross the road. But *you* know Orléans."

"Do I?"

"You've dined in the Palais."

"With plenty of others."

"What did he say to you?"

"Had I enjoyed the dinner."

"Had you?"

"Yes. They ask me to dinners, now, Orléans, Curtius, d'Anton—"

"And the Sillerys. Had one of the daughters yet?"

"No."

"And Mirabeau."

"I forget when I was last fed by Mirabeau's kitchens."

"Well, they say you are on Mirabeau's payroll and, through Sillery, on the payroll of Orléans."

"Bl-bloody—"

"Who do you think bribed me last Thursday?"

"W-well, who?"

"Do you think I'm the kind to kiss and tell?"

Windmill sighs. "None of it's true."

"Maybe."

"I don't want to hear about it. Leave me out of it."

"Dearest Windmill-Camille, you are in it up to your eyeballs. At least, up to your balls."

"So the fight for liberty and right is a game?"

Danton's eyes flash. His voice becomes a cannon.

"Goddamn it, why must every bloody thing go in a different basket? My country—I love France, the great glorious bitch-hag. If I could I'd fornicate with every inch of her. I'd lay her. My bastards would leap out of her soil like the children of the dragon's teeth. And so it matters—Jesus, it matters to me—to break the chains of her slaves, to set her free, this mistress of mine. Serve France? Yes, to my last breath, the last drop of blood!" He stops shouting. The windows grow quiet in their frames. "But if I'm to serve my country, why shouldn't I get paid for it? Huh? Gabi-Gabriella, play us a tune." The clavichord starts quietly in the other room. "Then there's Little Blondie," says Danton, referring to La Fayette, commander of the National Guard, for no particular reason save that La Fayette also exasperates him. "And then there are our illustrious Jacobins over at Saint-Honoré. Sometimes I go over there and roar at them. Robespierre is about to be elected president."

"How do you know?"

"How do I know I have scars on my face? Did I ever tell you about those scars?"

"Wh-at?"

"When I was a youth I fell in love with a cow."

"Wha-tt?"

"A cow. As God is my judge. I loved this cow with a pure and filial love. And one day when I was lying down under her sucking the wholesome milk from her udder—"

"All right, d'Anton, no one in their right mind—"

"Yes, they do. And as I lay there flat on my back in bliss, the lady's husband, the local prize bull, comes galloping over and calls me out. Jealous wretch. He got me on his horns and ripped my face apart. When I picked myself up, there he is, so I took to my heels—"

"Well, you would, wouldn't you."

"And what happens but the damnable old brute chases me over a wall and slap into a herd of pigs, who panic and mow me down again, and the entire herd crashes across me, clipping me with their pigs' feet. Well, next day, I went back to see that bull—why are you trying not to laugh?—And guess what happened?"

"What happened?"

"The damn thing broke my nose. . . ." Presently: "All right, Camille. Stop laughing, you'll be sick. To get back to Robespierre."

"Who?"

"You know Robespierre, Saint Maxime. Little chap. Glasses. Anyone can see, except perhaps yourself, that he will be next month's president of the Jacobins, whose influence, you acknowledge, is beginning to rival the Assembly's in the Stable. So what's the answer?"

"Join the Jacobins."

"The Jacobins and I are not yet on terms which facilitate joining the Jacobins."

"Blow up the Jacobins."

"A thought. Meanwhile—"

"Train Robespierre to suck cows."

"Oh, Christ," says Danton, and shakes the windows again with laughter.

Later he says, "Fight fire with fire. Maxime has the Jacobins and Blondie has the Feuillants. We of the illustrious Cordeliers district are going to get a Cordeliers club."

❋

On fine days, as the spring reluctantly flowered the trees with green, he would walk in the Luxembourg Gardens. And, turning the angle of a path, would discover Madame Duplessis and her daughter. Such surprise. Fancy meeting you! They would walk about; then Demeter would get tired or remember some errand. There were places in the thickness of the greater trees, where once demons had dwelled. Here he would take Lucile to him and light fires there was no possibility of quenching. Sometimes there was an exchange of gifts to interrupt and augment the agony of kisses. Some of these things she would at once plan to hide; no one must know. But others—this ribbon—I can say Annette gave it to me.

He wanted her in his bed, he wanted her in his life. There were moments when he would weep from lust and impatience. Once, when some royalist had specifically threatened to kill him (it happened occasionally now; he was not used to it, though he could sneer at it in print), he actually found himself in her arms, trembling with fright and nerves and anger and saying to her, "I could die tomorrow. What would you do? My God, you'd forget me in half an hour and marry Fréron." At which she burst into tears, and he cursed himself and spun her a pack of nonsense, some stupid thing about a shop on Iron Jar Street where they sold magic carpets, and he would spirit her away on one, and they would be together in a house built of clouds far above Paris. Then she had laughed. But when they parted that morning, she went very pale, and suddenly she said, "Don't die, Camille, don't ever die and leave me alone here." As if "here" were some alien place where they had both been lost by God. "How can I die if you love me?" he said. "Your love's my sorcerous armor." She said, "But I should give you a talisman."

When he met her again she had brought him a lock of her hair, one long golden curl, so shining, so perfectly coiled it seemed alive, imbued with *her* life and carrying the sweet scent of her. Alone in the darkness of night, or working on the *Revolutionary News* by three drab candles, he would take out the curl of hair, look at it, touch it, breathe in its perfume. The romanticism of the gestures appealed to him. He wrote:

> *Now I'm invulnerable,*
> *Nothing can harm me,*
> *No slings or cruel shocks*
> *Hurt or disarm me;*
> *Through bitter acts and mocks*
> *Your love will charm me,*
> *Your love will warm me,*
> *Your love will calm me.*
> *By your safeguard bound,*
> *Here in my hand,*
> *No ill can find,*
> *No sword can wound.*

❋

Not long after that, one day when he left her (and watched the figures of mother and daughter growing smaller and smaller along the avenue until out of sight), Windmill turned and nearly fell over a large mouse.

It was a friendly mouse, chocolate and cream, with long ears, and it jumped to touch his leg with little muddy paws.

"Broo! Broo! Here, come here!"

Windmill looked up at the call beyond the mouse and saw the president of the Jacobins on the path, taking in the mouse-dog and Windmill and the day, all with utter equanimity and serene good fellowship.

Scooping up the dog, which could have been fitted in a pocket, Windmill bore it back to Robespierre.

"Camille. Well, it's been some weeks." Robespierre accepted the dog in one hand and embraced Windmill. Maximilien's embraces were always rather odd—a rush forward, culminating in a curious aloof rigidity. The dog yapped and nearly punctured Camille's left eardrum. He was then aware of a third figure standing under a tree, just at Maximilien's back, in a graceful attendant attitude, like that of some well-born page. "And let me introduce Louis Antoine Saint-Just."

The figure came forward, slim and gracious, and the light fell like a white blade on his ice-blond hair.

"We're cousins," said Windmill, shaking hands with the blond apparition.

"Yes, so we are, Maxime," said Saint-Just, in a cool, exactly modulated voice. It seemed to amuse him, the relationship to someone so unlike. Saint-Just was indeed a fabulous beast, a unicorn. The cousinship had to be, and was, rather a distant one; Windmill had had nothing much to do with him, had seen him around here and there (a lowly junior at the school in Paris), all some while ago. Actually, written to this March, Camille had inserted notice, in the announcement section of his paper, of a poem by an anonymous author—twenty years of age, twenty cantos—the poem was itself some two years old. On sale, it caused quite a situation, being popularly termed "*hot*." But now Camille felt an instant aversion, as to the touch of ice, which is what the young man most resembled. Chiseled from an ice floe. Was there blood in there anywhere? And Saint-Just himself: you could tell he hadn't liked the familiar embrace between two men who had shared together their years at school. Climbing, then. Today, friend of the leader of the Jacobins, tomorrow the world.

"How is the home province?" said Windmill.

"As ever," said the unicorn.

"I haven't been back for some time."

"No," said Saint-Just. No need, you carry it with you.

Between them, Robespierre stood preening a little, pleased to be fought over. "Well, I'm so glad you're already friends," he said.

Saint-Just and Windmill both smiled. Each smile had the identical edge to it. The dog, sensing undercurrents, growled.

"Now, now, Broo."

"Shall I take him for a walk, Maxime?" said Saint-Just, exquisitely helpful. "If you have something to discuss with Desmoulins—"

"No, no. Let's all stroll together." Robespierre put the dog down. It looked at him and then went scampering off.

So they strolled, and Robespierre talked, candidly, about what he had been saying at the Jacobins and in the Assembly—had Camille heard any of it? Yes? Good, good. "Camille is an excellent critic," said Robespierre. "An honest man."

"So I've heard," said Saint-Just.

"Who did you hear it from," said Windmill, "my friends or an enemy?"

"Now, now," said Robespierre, as he had said to his dog. But he was pleased; they were still fighting.

God almighty, we must look like his bad angel and the good: black hair, scowling, and ugly one side; blond and gorgeous as some girl the other. The hair shivered with iridescence on the shoulders of Saint-Just's smart coat, and in both of his ears rings flamed a silvery gold. The buckles of his shoes blinded you. His cravat blinded you, so white, white as Robespierre's own, but far more complex in its knot. Perhaps Saint-Just's cravat would choke him.

The flower beds lay empty. Robespierre pointed at them with his stick. "Like our Republic, you see. Dormant. But soon, spring. You have said it, Camille, in your *Free France:* This is the time to be alive. We are on the brink of great events."

"But even a republic," said Saint-Just smoothly, "requires wise leadership. To dream is human, to *achieve* is the work of mightier men."

"And to forgive, of course, is divine," said Windmill.

Robespierre's good angel actually whitened under his clear complexion. He was twenty-three and someone had just made him look damn silly. Like Windmill himself, he carried about with him a sort of mental blacklist. The name of the journalist was now added to it.

Robespierre frowned a little. He was losing pleasure in the quarrel because, when matters of moment were debated, bickering should be shelved, even bickering about who was Robespierre's pet. The real pet solved the problem. With an explosion of insane squeaks, it abruptly set off across the gardens, in pursuit of some impossible dream of its own.

"Oh!" said Robespierre.

"I'll get him," said Saint-Just. He nodded to Windmill. The nod said, I trust you'll be gone when I get back. Then he went after the tiny dog.

Rosepeter looked at Camille. They were alone and he became stern. "Be careful of Orléans. And the Sillerys. Those dinner parties. Champagne. Poison."

"You never liked wine."

"It never liked me." He looked dissatisfied and sad. "I find I can eat less and less that will agree with me."

"You used to love pastry." Windmill glanced up and saw a rift of blue in the sky. "You once wrote an ode to a jam tart."

Robespierre laughed. It sounded rusty, and yet there was a note in it, something heartfelt, wanting to be recollected, utilized.

"My God, so I did. Yes. Oh, dear. Well" – he looked sadder – "I can't even eat pastry now." They started to walk, slowly, in the direction the unicorn had taken. "Oh, you know, Camille, my life hasn't been such a happy one. My mother – she died when I was just a child, but I still remember her so very well. I used to think, If I go straight home today I'll find her there again. But she never was. And I remember all you boys tearing about. I never had the energy for that. Do you recall the fat boy, the one who used to call me Old-Before-His-Time?"

"Yes, and do you recall how we put a stop to it?"

Maximilien giggled. "Well, I think what you wrote on the wall about him was grossly unfair. You could see the letters right across the yard. Even I could, with my poor eyes."

"A good prophet always writes on a wall," said Camille. "After all, God is supposed to have done it."

In the distance, Saint-Just tried to secure the dog.

"But you know," said Maximilien, "sometimes this weakness in my body, this constant struggle—it wears me out. I say to myself, Why do I do it? Why do I put myself through so much? I've felt so alone. But then—well, I believe you'll understand me—I sense a presence by me, something that watches over me, that won't let me fall. I want to serve, Camille. I need to do it. This frailty—there must be some purpose for me beyond this inefficient flesh of mine."

Camille turned to him and saw tears fill the round gray eyes, just as he had seen them do twenty years ago in the smoky classrooms of Louis-le-Grand.

"It's all right, Maxime. You're not going to fall. Look at you. Power is coming into your hands, all the power to do what you need."

"I feel—I feel I must have been chosen to do something for France. Why else have I lived? Why else am I tested in this way?"

On an impulse, moved by sympathy, Camille put his arm over the other's shoulders.

"You'll end up a saint, Maxime. Or the next king."

"God forbid. If I could just do some *good*."

"How can you fail? Look at you. Listen to the crowds. The People have more faith in you than you do yourself."

Robespierre's face altered. It was suddenly like a mask, heroic and sculpted.

"I do believe," he said, his voice low and vibrant, "that it would be possible to alter the world, to cleanse it and cure it and make it fine, by work and faith and dedication. I *do* believe it, Camille."

They stood and looked down the avenue at the future, each of them seeing different things. But Saint-Just had caught the dog. The sky clouded over.

1790: Spring–Summer

CLUB. THE word, chosen first by the Bretons, then by the Jacobins, was a kind of pun—since in English that word "club" also meant a blunt heavy stick, by employment of which one's enemies might be brained.

The Convent of the Jacobins over on Saint Honoré Street. Well, you only got in there if you had the appropriate card or an invitation. The wooden benches went up in tiers from the flat tombstones in the floor, and over these sat a resonant ceiling which produced some unhelpful acoustics. You had to be careful what you said and how you said it. Sophisticates at the Jacobins. Choosy. That Danton had made a couple of scenes in there, plagiarizing someone else's speech, bringing all out again in fire and thunder. But what could you expect of that Danton, who had nearly started a civil war over on the left bank, calling out the militia of the Cordeliers district to protect Swiss Marat, when La Fayette's troops were bearing down on him by order of the mayor of Paris (Marat had been slandering the mayor again in his paper)? There they were, cordons of People's soldiery in concentric rings, glaring at each other, when someone thought to ask, Where's Marat? It transpired he had walked out of the battle zone half an hour before. Presently, of course, that Desmoulins fellow was going to get someone's army detail charging down on *him* for slanders in the *Revolutionary News*. Then Danton would be at it again.

No, Danton and his gang did not really suit the style of the Jacobins.

The new club, on the other hand, started by Danton and his gang under a set of false identities (the mayor was still touchy), began life inappropriately in a ballroom, then moved across into its own church, the Cordeliers.

The Cordeliers Club was a madhouse. What else?

Anyone could get in, and did. Anyone could speak, and did. The only requirement for speaking was a red Phrygian cap jammed on the head—the *chapeau obligatoire* of the Revolution. Then again, there was so much bellowing and trumpeting and crowing going on in there, who heard you anyway? If the Assembly was the Stable, this was surely the Barnyard.

The chapel had been bare before the influx of chairs and slogans, all ornamentation gone. The east window, a stone rose lacking glass, was set instead with panes of weather and brisk east winds. Now and then someone would climb up there and appear, deus ex machina, amid even louder catcalls and jeering from below. You could always get a drink at the Cordeliers, too. There were wine barrels in the annex, sometimes with good-looking citizenesses managing taps and glasses.

Danton had coined a motto for the club, or cribbed it from the Latin. It was written up on a tricolor banner nailed onto the wall: LIBERTY, EQUALITY, BROTHERHOOD (and PANDEMONIUM, the wits might add).

Peculiar, though, the madhouse barnyard radiated a power and influence all its own. It was lively, patently. It was non-aristo, pro-populo, and not even (overtly) bourgeois. All types of persons, able to invade it, upheld its virtues. Then suddenly it was taking up issues, sending delegations to the National Assembly at the Riding School. Getting a hearing. And who was it spoke? Guess who.

That voice. It was going to break the windows.

The deputies looked at each other, and back at the towering elemental addressing them below the speakers' platform. What is this monster up to? Where does he think he is? Danton knew quite well where he was. In high oratorical form (what vocality the opera had lost in him!) he sang his busy cannonade, assassinating the characters of the king's ministers. When he stopped, the hall went on vibrating. Though the complaints of the Cordeliers district did not get the winning vote, there were going to be a lot of ministerial resignations in a minute. As for the leader of the Cordeliers Club, he had left his mark in the place of the Assembly, that draperied chamber near the middle of the Tuileries Garden, north side. Left it as if his personality, his gargantuan roar, had cut into the very walls like shot.

⚜

A summons had arrived from Mirabeau. I was to go to his new house in Paris. As I walked along the handsome boulevard I tried to be interested in the trees. Ah, yes, returning summer. Then I got to his door and rang its bell and forgot the season.

When the door opened, there you were in Versailles again. A servant with powdered hair and a pastel silk coat, the vista of a shining floor, the smell of beeswax and pomanders. I stood around on the floor, reflective as a pond—it made me giddy—and gnawed my nails. I'd arrived dressed in my best, and my hands were icy. My patron's request of a visit had come in the wake of several letters, which had had a certain tone, and an accidental (in the sense of accidentally stubbing one's toe) meeting near the Tuileries when, having just torn him in pieces in print, I'd almost walked slap into him. He was utterly charming, took my arm, said I had misunderstood his motives in supporting the king, invited me to call on him.

But I had realized this was a public act. He was furious, and I was here to be upbraided. Like a pupil at the college, called out to be dressed down, I was defiant, had been arguing with him all the way here, had already lost my temper and was already stammering in my very thoughts.

Sure enough, when they let me in to him, he allowed me to sit and then said, "Camille, this won't do."

"Wn-won't do what?"

He looked me over and said, with an unpleasing accuracy, "I see. I have an impertinent schoolboy to deal with."

"B-boy be-be damned. You want a t-talking parrot."

"Ah, so he knows."

"Hn-he-h-he knows. It was your king's st-strings you were going to gan-organize, I thought-t, no-n-not mine. It was a payment then? Hn-hmnb-barter?"

"An agreement," he said. "I understood we were of like mind."

"It seems—it seems—it seems—"

"Not? What I wished from you was little enough. If my policy made sense to you, you would offer it, in your own inimitable style, to the People. But instead I have been made the butt for your most puerile literary antics. I have enemies enough. Must I add you?"

"Wn-when you were ng-wrong, I s-s-said so."

"No. When you *decided* I was wrong. You are so utterly infallible then? You know everything? All these classical allusions you are so fond of using, all this reverence for Tacitus and Plato, and yet you've learnt no subtlety, no *awareness*. Without consulting me, you reckon you can divine my every gambit? What training have you had to enable you to be so wise? A few school debates, a couple of idiotic court cases in the Styx, which you *lost*. A seat in the gallery at the Assembly, where you are far more concerned with how to frame your insults than in attending to what is *said*."

I could have burst with the words I couldn't get out. They came from him in seamless skinning concertos.

"Iv-if you w-work as a court lackey, s-sir, I'll tre-treat you as one."

"All this is a child's nonsense. You have no respect for me. Very well. But *think* before you attack my policies. I am trying to save France from a blood-bath. And you, vaunting your love of country, are thrusting her into the abyss."

"Well," I got out. "Now Mirabeau confuses hm-himself with al-all France."

He flung up his arm like an actor acting a passion, then turned his eyes full on me, blazing with genuine rage. But I too was shaking with rage, and the ice in my hands seemed to have spread into my heart.

"You dreamer of Roman ideals," he said to me, "you worshiper of republics, heroes, gods—let me enlighten you. You are a bourgeois plebian to your soul."

In absolute turmoil, stupidly I said, "Soul? What soul?" Because I knew he was an unbeliever.

"What soul indeed. Well, I expected better."

"Your heart bl-bleeding at having noticed me in-nn the gutter."

"Yes! Bleeding, you fool. I saw fires I thought might have been trained to light the whole of France. But you're only, I'm afraid, a torch-bearing arsonist. Yes. Bleeding. I thought you could be persuaded to grow up, if we were gentle with you. But no, there you still are, a little attorney with a toy lamppost, who thinks he is Jesus Christ, son of God."

"Thn-then God will no doubt disown me. When d-do you plan to do it?"

"You have become tiresome," he said.

"Yes. I can't be bought."

"Can't you? What are you doing at this Rights-of-Man Cordeliers Society, in the left ear of Georges d'Anton, if you are unbuyable?"

My throat closed entirely, something that hadn't happened to me since I was nineteen. While I sat there silently strangling, he said, turning away, "Get out."

I found I could breathe though I couldn't speak. I was cold, but also hot with the horrible anger, and my eyes congested by water, or even tears, I suppose. I stood up and snatched out the last array of his payments I had brought with me — I hadn't used a sou — and flung the bundle on the elegant Savonnerie carpet.

He turned back and looked at it.

"Fine gestures now," he said. "What about the rest, you black dog? No. Pick it up. Keep it. Buy yourself a bone. It may improve your bark."

There was a story that once, involved in a lawsuit to do with his wife, this man had been maligned by one of the lady's lawyers and eventually returned such a broadside the fellow fainted headlong and was borne from the courtroom insensible. I thought of it then and believed it.

I stood there another moment staring at him. I remember how he looked against the light of the window. His dark clothing, as if for a funeral; I had scarcely noted it till now. His springing hair lay flat across his large skull. There was a muddy pallor behind his skin, nothing to do with its natural sallowness, and a new sharp line between his eyes I took for fury, but it may have been from physical pain.

Aristocrat that he was, he merely allowed me to stand at last, with a dreadful impervious slightly smiling courtesy. Finally I turned and walked out. There was nothing else to do. I left the money lying on the carpet. Maybe he would call a servant to tidy it up, throw it in the fire.

He had his own journal on the streets by now, Mirabeau (one of my soundest omens was that he had not asked me to write for it). I waited. Sure enough, I received another answer, in print.

'A specter is stalking the streets of Paris, filling the hearts of the innocent with terror. The name of this demon? An epic by the misleading title of *The Revolutionary News*. Its editor, an impudent journalist who will try any trick to gain sales. M. Camille Desmoulins, lashing out left and right like a child in a tantrum, strikes the guilty and the blameless together, randomly. Clearly, he believes none of us is brave enough to defy his wrath and denounce him to the Nation. We would suggest he should not rely too blindly on the slowness of the law.'

'The good *Count* Mirabeau may be aware of the biblical story in which the Angel of Death, detouring by the innocent lambs' blood, passed over the homes of the oppressed and struck only at the houses of the slave masters. Perhaps, in this case, the marks of innocence on aristocrat lintels are not convincing enough.'

I noticed that, promptly after this exchange, an invitation by the urbane Sillerys to dine in their Apollo Chamber, with the divine daughters in attendance, was apologetically canceled. I met Sillery a day or so after, and he spoke

to me so kindly, attentively, and flatteringly, under his powder and wig, I knew I
was—for the moment at least—persona non grata.

For Mirabeau, with his rallying cry that I escaped justice, had shown the way. A host of lawsuits and threats followed in the wake of his essay, enough to jolt me at every knock on the door.

I had got accustomed by now, in the Palais-Royal, to the slap of somebody's glove across my cheek. It was a favorite game among the royalists, to call us out or try to. I had a stock answer: "Monsieur, if I liked, I could spend my whole life fighting duels. I have better things to do. Besides, I can hardly accommodate you and let down the three who challenged me yesterday; they'd be jealous. Cheer up. The way things are going, someone's sure to kill me very soon." Having delivered this, and my audacity being applauded by supporters at nearby tables, the aristo in question would go up the wall. On one occasion, a plot was loudly laid to take me into a private garden and hang me. This ruined for me the meal I was trying to eat; while a group of Cordelierites who were hanging around, led by d'Anton's butcher, Legendre, who was at least seven feet tall, came up and awarded me a guard of honor. Another time, in the Swiss Restaurant at the Luxembourg, some maniac actor actually drew on me (Why is one always attacked when eating or drinking or in bed? Hérault de Séchelles was to say). I was so appalled I couldn't even stutter, and in desperation I wrote the actor a note on someone's handy napkin, as follows:

You forget, I am only a man of the People, untrained in the use of sword or pistol. Pay for me to have three years of lessons to get me to your standard, and I'll meet you in the Bois.

The restaurantful, now crowding around sufficiently to protect me, went crazy with delight. The napkin was borne away to be immortalized. The royalist put up his sword, spat at my feet, and said, "Cut off your hands, Desmoulins, and you'd be dumb."

To which d'Anton, who had just come in, shouted, "Cut out your anus and so would you be."

His son, brand-new and healthy, and bawling in his father's tradition, had been born in mid-May. Since then d'Anton had been into every pie—at the Cordeliers, at the Jacobins by invitation, and pressing for votes for every job of esteem that was on the market. Sometimes he would drag me off to the theater or some wine fountain. Usually he was hedged in by two hundred and fifty possible voters. When gloves hit me in the face, he was seldom about.

None of the threats stopped me writing. The more they sharpened their daggers, the more I nicked them with mine. Yet there were days I was afraid to leave my rooms. I had stopped meeting Lucile save at her house, or that of some mutual friend, for fear something would start when she was with me. I began to suffer a series of dreams, incoherently connected to the legions of ancient

Rome, battles and being mortally stabbed in the back. Why then was I unable to control the killing pen? My hysterical belief, even so early, I was invulnerable — for the crowd liked me and was everywhere? Who reckons he can die? At the same time, I was paying off my debt, showing the world no one had ever bought me like his whore.

I had, even after the personal aggression in his journal, a couple of curious letters from my erstwhile god. They were . . . placatory. Full of goodwill. He even began one: *My wretched eyes are playing me false again today. Bad enough, the jest is I may lose one. Nevertheless, my concern to write to you brings me to pen and paper.*

I could not make him out. What did he think he could have from me now? I noticed, too, he put the blame for our falling out (never really specified) on me. As if we had had a lovers' tiff and now I must come around. As if I had invented for myself the scene in his study at Paris. It is a fact, reading these letters (*despite all the fireworks of your brain, my Camille, you deserve to be valued*), I was tempted to go back to him. The genius of Mirabeau — everywhere demonstrated — one could not put it aside lightly. His affectionate words hurt me more than the insults that went before. Was I, after all, betraying him? For God's sake, must I put him before my country and all I believed in? Even the play for sympathy: his eyes. I remembered how he shed tears for a woman once dear to him in front of me. I had been moved, disturbed. Touched by his trust. But then he might have been able to gauge me susceptible to such a performance: first dazzle, then elicit sympathy. Cunning stratagem. Women do it. Well, I would think his grief had been genuine, but maybe carefully permitted to overmaster him when I was at hand. And she was safely dead when he allowed himself to cry for her.

I answered his letters blankly and coldly, assuring him I would support him, as always, when and only when I could do so in conscience. And, thereafter, there were times when I did speak out for him. Impartial, I. But I wondered if he were laughing at me.

By late June, I foresaw real trouble dropping on my shoulders. I had been saying loudly that those royalists who backed the Revolution had done it solely to get a better deal for themselves, as reigning aristocrats. Now I was warned some royalist Third Estate deputy, a provocateur, Malouet, was out for my blood, not on a sword's end this time but through the courts. I had tapped his knuckles twice or thrice, but that was the excuse. He was to be spokesman for the whole tribe, and I the scapegoat for the Revolution — a put-up job constructed by the nobles. Well, they had to get rid of me somehow.

Then, nothing happened. All the biting dogs seemed lying down. July dawned and plans for a celebration of the Bastille's fall. Abruptly I was being grabbed and embraced on the street again. Here and there you saw the green cockade being worn with the red cap and the tricolor. No one would attack me now.

Seen from the air, it looks like a mole's paradise. Thousands of moles in it too, working away, chucking up the earth in mounds. Over there, the silver ribbon of the Seine, over *there* the courtyards of the military school. And between, this place with moles in it making molehills.

Fly down, little bird, fly down and see on this summer evening, what goes on in Mars Field. Moles with *wheelbarrows?*

The idea had been to create an amphitheater for the festival, something like the Roman circuses of old, an oval center, turf seats going up all around. But the army of workmen was found not to be enough. The work wouldn't be finished in time for July 14. And suddenly a beautiful silly enthusiasm flooded Paris. They had come forth to level the Bastille with shouts of hate. Now, lapped in the lovely summer weather, they streamed out smiling to complete the task the workmen couldn't handle.

Actually, they came from everywhere. From the hovels and the bars, off the college benches, out of the pulpits, and from under the latest client. They jumped down from the heights of cosy apartments, and out of the gabled galleries of rich houses, and ran off to become laborers in a bowl of powdery soil.

Look at them, trundling their barrows, banging into each other, laughing uproariously, sharing wine and fruit and the symbolic loaf.

There is a minor aristocrat down on his knees murdering his silk stockings, helping two wood merchants and a soldier fix a broken barrow shaft. And there, three market women, a bourgeoise lady, and a lady no better than she should be, sunstruck, dancing around a makeshift Tree of Liberty—a pole they have unearthed and hung with garters. And here some excitement because someone thinks he has dug up a Roman coin. And here a group of children from every walk of life, playing a complex game, covered in dirt. But they are all behaving like children. Caught in this colossal daft exercise—and what is it? Heaving earth out of a crater so they can all sit around it and toast the unhealth of the Bastille tomorrow—they've gone mad as midges. It's so serious. Got to be done. And shoulder to shoulder the Three Estates of Paris toil, singing and cursing and howling with mirth, to get it done.

My God, my God, if they can work like this to make a circus for a festival, what can't they do, together, arm in arm, shoulder to shoulder, bold and loud and singing, to unify France?

Look at them, look at them. Full of fun, happy to be one. Not caring about the mess or somebody's rough accent. Lending a hand each to another. Oh, people, children of eternity and light, born to love and joy, dampening your flames with the rubbish of untrue creeds and false premises, what are you feeling *now?* Who's starving, who thirsts, who hurts, who complains, who abuses? None of you. You're all in love with each other. You'd give each other anything you asked and give it gladly. *Look at you.* My heart will break. This you could do for a festival. But for the sake of your lives and your souls and the world, you could not do it.

And when the sun goes, the torches burst up in flowering bushes. You can see them winding away along the streets, fine streets and foul, and down the alleys, everywhere. And hear that song, the *Ça ira:*

> *Oh, it'll be, it'll be, it'll be,*
> *That day of the people, unparalleled day—*
> *It'll be, wait and see, it'll be,*
> *Come against us what may—we'll be free!*

But the torches go out, the song dies down, the soft winds blow over Martian Meadow where the soldiers put up their tents. And by that sign of darkness and that sign of silence, the gods who watch in the air can tell just exactly *how* it'll be, it'll be, *it'll be.*

⚜

The weather was perfection. Then, the day of the festival, it rained. Water, like a wave, came down ("Christ, you wouldn't think there could be that much up there, would you?"). *Il pleut, il pleut . . . de l'eau.* Smack. It blasted the gray hats of the towers, and the red "freed-slave" hats of the populace, and the bearskins of the marching People's soldiers, and it washed clean the powdered faces of ladies—with a puritanical spirit rather lacking in charity.

Well, all right, it's raining. It's still *14 Juillet.* What's a drop of rain? Have a drop of sausage. Have another drop of wine. We had the cannon and red-hot bullets raining on us then. Water? It's only wet.

A procession.

Beginning at the sight of the Bastille (all torn down now; so much for five centuries) going street by street westward, the way the sound of the cannons traveled, crossing the Womb by a bridge of rocking boats.

The soldiers had come in from everywhere and been welcomed with open houses, open arms (and, quite frequently, open legs). Now they marched swaggering behind the drums and bands, through the rain of water and flowers and apples and wine-bottles-let-down-on-strings. Soldiers of the Federation, National Guard, frontiersmen—no one was going to say, Shoot your brother. No one would dare.

The priests wore the white surplices of the angels, slashed with the tricolor. They were the People's priests. When they reached the oval basin of the amphitheater Paris had carved with her own willing hands and ornamented with Greco-Roman fancies of platforms and thunderously flaming and smoking cressets, the priests herded in. They blessed every banner that came to them:

those of the state, of the People, the gorgeous panoply of every one of the eighty-three Paris sections. It was like some fantastic Roman triumph or medieval joust. Even the king's oriflamme arrived and was blessed, one of the crowd.

The king looked on, under a canopy, complacent. What with the rain and his rotten eyesight it was just a pretty blur. Easy enough to look complacent at a blur. But he could hardly not have been here.

Still raining.

In the amphitheater, the Vanquishers of the Bastille were being recognized with medallions specially struck for the occasion. (Just a blur.) Some were old enough to have known better and some too young to know anything. Some had imagined it, that they were there at all, and convinced others. But they all got their war medals. Just think, when we're ancient, grasshoppers crouched by the hearth, we'll show these disks of honor—Vanquishers of Tyranny, that's us, eh?

Still raining.

The mass was said, before the altar built to the Nation. The crowd responded, hymned, wept, cheered. Like the backs of tortoises the umbrellas quivered with emotions. (Just a blur.)

Still raining.

Then there was a huge marriage ceremony at the altar. France married, one by one, her Parisian Assembly, her priests, all her soldiers. Love, honor, obey the constitution, till death. And finally the king, whom someone (the devil, Mirabeau?) had told it might be a notion, stood up before his flower-decked throne and swore the marriage oath too. The crowd swayed, opening now its heart. The queen rose, raising her fair-haired child in her arms (Think, madame, who can resist a madonna?) She too married France—the Austrian woman.

As would sometimes happen when, at a dark Easter, the Host was elevated, signifying the release of Christ from agony on the cross, a miracle occurred. The rain stopped. The sun melted out of the cloud and bathed the Champ-de-Mars and all Paris in a glaze of jeweler's gold.

"Life to the queen! Long life to the king!"

What a time to be alive. What a day it'll be.

Anything's possible now.

❦

Lights everywhere; Paris might have been on fire that night.

Half the hotels had arranged some banquet or ball, but they were dining and dancing in the streets too. First in the long sunlit evening, then in a deep lavender twilight that went on and on, till the stars were lighted and gave the signal to the lamps and torches. Over at the site of the prison, also, they had made a dance floor. There, where the stories had grown, and the fight had been fought, and we had burst in and rescued our seven men, an orchestra was playing and the heels of young women hitting the ground in quick little slaps. In the gardens by the river they picnicked. On the river the boats wore necklaces of lamps. Someone had let loose a flotilla of swans, new-minted gold in the lamp shine, swimming so gracefully I think nobody potted any of them.

In the Heavenly Fields, the dusk came close as velvet, a sky of purple coffee. What a night, so much scent in it, crushed out by rain and marching feet and eager lips; flowers bruised to fragrance by the bosoms of girls. Colored lights were touched to life under the mass of the trees. It looked like a dream, some fairy-tale thing. And then the sky itself broke into flames, fireworks crossing each other with their silver traceries and peacock's tails.

Everybody was laughing and in love. In love with the night, with Paris, with hope, with whatever humanity was adjacent.

Keyed up still with shouting, the oaths, and the passion in the Champ-de-Mars, we knew it was a night to climb trees, or the greased fairground poles in the park, or, better yet, the tall stems of Our Lady, and hang a tricolor there big as the soul of France.

What didn't seem possible? You could see everywhere, on every face, this same optimism and avid pleasure in being alive. It was all coming right after all. And Fréron and I, and Maxime, were jabbering at each other about how it was all going to be, now the court was bending to the whim of the city. One last shove to get all in order—reforms, programs—Christ, we had all France reeducated, reclothed, fed till it had colic, turned into the Chosen People, and installed on the moon. From where the Nation began, naturally, to give directions to the earth.

Even Maxime had blossomed. He skipped merrily along with us, shadowed by the tiny dog like a sprite, Adèle on his arm, and he was showering the dog and Adèle with attentions, buying them gingerbread, and her a knot of ribbons and armfuls of flowers. At which Fréron and I, who were sharing (so he imagined) Lucile for the evening, entered the lists and began to shower Lucile and Demeter with ribbons and flowers and sugar almonds. The three women laughed, their faces tonight much resembling each other, uptilted, fluttered now by a green lamp in acid-green leaves, or a pink lamp that turned the leaves to candy. Through it all the debate went on. "And schools," Robespierre was saying. "An education that will help them, place them in the scheme of things, and away from parents who, through ignorance, may hold them back." Saint-Just was in Paris again and somewhere about. Now and then he would come slipping through the Elysian avenues, like a white greyhound, say something to Robespierre. Once he handed Adèle a flower (the prince's lady) and went gravely off again.

Here and there, recognition. At a certain point a surge of people, one of the multitude of sporting groups, came and clustered around me and around Maxime, knowing us by sight or description and delighted to have trapped two birds in one snare. They wanted a speech, so Robespierre climbed up on a box

and told them for twenty minutes the day of the People was almost at hand.
When they called for me, I backed out of it. They let me off with proposing a toast to Paris and her Revolution two thousand years ahead of its time. I heard the phrase repeated twice, during the rest of the evening, and meant to use it in the paper. But eventually I forgot.

There were still unofficial processions tearing around the streets. Tomorrow night there would be a dinner over at the Cordeliers, but I hadn't seen d'Anton later than five o'clock this afternoon. He too had had a crowd round him. He was buying them all drinks. Always canvassing, d'Anton.

"Education is the font," said Maxime. "The bench of learning is where a good citizen starts."

"Give me a child until he's seven," quoted Fréron.

"Just so."

I remembered Maxime at school, working so hard to get everything right.

I leaned to Lucile's ear (any excuse, my God) and whispered, "Well, we're boring you."

"No. I like to listen."

"What are we saying?"

"You're talking about saving your country, as usual. But all those cold classrooms with the poor children being taught what sort of people to grow up into—"

"No, Maxime isn't saying that."

"Yes, he is. You see, Camille, you don't hear him as well as I do."

"Such exquisite ears. How could they help hearing everything better than anyone else's?"

"Lucile," said Fréron, not to be left out (some chance), "would you like one of those triangles of silk? Over there, that woman's selling them."

"No, Rabbit, thank you." (She still called him that sometimes.)

"But I'd enjoy buying it for you, seeing you wear it."

"Buy her a shackle, Fréron. You'd enjoy seeing her wear that even more."

"Shut up, you corn grinder. Wait a minute." And he went off to buy the thing.

I said, "If you wear it, I'll rip it in two pieces."

"Only two?"

"Two pieces of twenty-two pieces each."

Brissot passed, escorted by a clamor of friends and supporters. On the tricolor sash at his waist was a huge key, presumably one of those he had been presented with last year. He grinned and waved his hat at me. I lifted my hand to him. It wasn't a night to keep count of old scores. I could even put up with Fréron. Probably.

When the business with the silk fichu had been seen to and Lucile ceremoniously draped in it, we found a long table under the trees and lamps, and the party sat down. It was a warm night, but Lucile said to her mother, "Oh, dear, are you cold, Mama?" And insisted on lending her the scarf.

Of the eating and drinking that went on, all of it came to us free. I'd made the provision of bringing paper and pencil and scribbling some stuff for the *News,* there in the midst of everything. As I wrote, and the gratis bottles and pastries and slices of fowls came over, and my name, with Robespierre's, was yelled across Arcadia in tones of high if sozzled approbation, I looked to see how Monsieur Duplessis was taking it all. He was very jolly tonight and hardly immune to Federation fever. He'd slapped me on the back a couple of times and slapped Maxime on the back and nearly crippled him. Now the Toad looked pleased and sly. Yes, dear sir, I thought, think about it. Think about how much has changed, and who changed it. Forget that scrawler you saw through the grimy window. I speak at the Cordeliers now, and they listen. I have a journal on the streets that sells as far as Marseilles.

Some maniac of a juggler came around the plank tables with a torch, gulping the fire. Robespierre looked at him in awed disapproval.

"Well, even Camille can't do that," said Fréron.

"No, Camille doesn't swallow fire. When he speaks, whole institutions burn."

I looked up from my notes and Lucile's hand I had been playing with under the table. There stood de Polignac, immaculate as starch. Not with his *très élégante* lady friend, Clodie; probably he'd be going there later.

"Good evening," he said. "How did you like the king's performance today?"

"The oath? It would have looked better if he'd hopped off his perch to make it. That throne they gave him should have been properly vacated, left empty. He sat down again there too firmly for my liking."

"Well, he's maybe used to it."

"He'll have to get unused then."

The tableful, our party and others, watched me. I flapped my feathers for them.

"Well, where are we going? Back to Louis Quinze the fifteenth and lying on our faces in the mud?"

"Impatient Camille," said Gabriel. "Is that what the *News* will be saying?"

"Buy it and find out."

"Um," said Gabriel.

His eyes went by me and fixed on Demeter and Adèle, and he bowed. Then Lucile. He bowed again, but with his eyes never leaving her. Then he walked off. Five minutes later (when we were heatedly discussing King Capet's popularity), Gabriel came back and placed before Lucile, wrapped around three roses, a paper.

"It's not a night," said Gabriel, "when one omits to pay homage to goddesses."

Lucile blushed, de Polignac bowed again, was gone again, did not return.

I unwrapped the paper and laid it out for her. It was a poem.

"Let's go after him, he can't have got far," said Fréron, who was by now fairly viciously drunk.

Lucile and I read the poem silently.
"Like music on the summer air," it said.

Like music on the summer air,
Some orchestra in heaven playing,
Falling to earth, these notes formed her,
A symphony that stars make, praying.

What are the wars of men, the words of kings wrung dry?
Shattering blasts of noise and pain.
When all the riots end, the triumphs die,
Beauty and love alone remain;
Flowers after rain.

"Aristo," said Fréron scornfully.

"Poet," I said. "And he wrote it in five minutes. I w-wish I could have written it in-in five hours."

I was saddened then, sad with an elation that she had brought that from him, despite his manners, the pearl in his ear, that he had put into words something I felt for her and had never known. That somehow he had seen beyond it all, out into space and distance, and it had perhaps surprised him, too. Sad for the sense of the joy that passes, the triumphs that die. But we drank up, and more fireworks wheeled across heaven. No night for this, no night for that. It was no night for being sad.

When we got back to the Duplessis château in the early morning, the whole neighborhood was still up and about, windows blazing, and the orgies of Nero and Antony taking place by every door. Not to be outdone, our entire party, now larger and frankly formidable, was asked in and settled or unsettled in the drawing room.

There was some singing and some improvisation. Even Maxime warbled out a verse to Adèle and himself flushed with pleasure, while she sat, demure and smiling. Saint-Just was nowhere to be seen, so absent, unless he had slithered in and coiled himself behind a sofa.

Mercier staidly suggested giving the little dog some brandy in milk, and with Robespierre mildly protesting this was done. But the dog put its nose to the mixture, sneezed, and walked away disgusted. Too much milk perhaps? "No," said Mercier. "Like master, like hound. Your beast's no d'Anton, Maxime."

"I won't hear a word against d'Anton," said Robespierre, who actually had been drinking quite dedicatedly, for him. "Whatever his shortcomings, the man is a staunch patriot."

"The Cordeliers thank the Jacobins. Bravo!"

Presently the wine ran out. No one thought they had had enough. Duplessis set off down the stair for his cellar, with an enormous key the rival of Brissot's from the Bastille. I staggered after him.

"There go the bells again." He chortled, as three o'clock sounded from a clock in the passage. "This is a noisy town, Queen's Market—like the grave," he added, reaching the cellar door and trying to see to get the key in it. "Here, you try." Somehow we got the key in. Upstairs, they sounded like mad people. "I'm bound to regret this in the morning," said Lucile's father.

"It's morning now."

He thought this was funny. So did I.

"You're a good boy, Camille," he said, as we floundered into his cellar among cheeses and bottles and spiders.

"Success hasn't gone to my head."

"Success? Yes, you are. Well, why not? You know"—he fell over a basket and I caught him—"You know, I started out as nothing—nothing."

And ended up as nothing. No, he was all right, Papa Duplessis. Yes, he was. Flatter him. He'd decided to like me. "Now you're an important man."

"Yes. But then? Nobody cared a damn. Till I got my position in the finance office. I came up in the world. Got some land—through madame, you understand. And now they bow to me on the street. They say, Duplessis, old man, can you give us a hand with this—?"

"Look out," I said. I intercepted the wine bottle as it fell.

"Well caught! Good boy. Let's see—Oh, yes, this ought to do nicely. 'Nother couple of these. Wonder what the king's drinking tonight?"

"Pride, with a little water."

"Oh—oh, that's good. Oh, yes, oh, ha-ha-ha. But you shouldn't—ha-ha—you shouldn't speak about him like—ha-ha. God's Anointed—"

"I didn't know God had done it personally."

"Oh—ha-ha—oh, my—ha—here, hold this other bottle. Ha-ha, yes, you're dead right. Like me. Man of the people. You know, I put myself in mind of that fellow in the Bible. Judge of Israel. Despised, pushed out, and then he gets somewhere and they all want to know him."

I hazarded a guess. "Jephthah?"

"Jefthap. 'S right. You know, we'd better see what this wine is like. Can't offer the guests rubbish." He took off the seal and uncorked the bottle. He drank and said, "Am I pissed, or is it you?"

"I, O Jephthah, judge of Israel."

"I like that. Yes, Jepfaff, judge of Israel."

He passed me the bottle. I accepted it.

"Jephthah had a daughter," I said.

"Right, so he did."

I looked at his fat hard body wedged between the narrow walls, and his fat little eyes bulging with good humor.

I said, "Jephthah, give me your daughter."

"Oh, ha-ha-ha," he said. "Ha-ha-ha. Camille, you're a good fellow."

"Splendid. So, will you?"

"Will I? Oh, ha-ha."

"Lucile," I said.

"That's right," he said. "Lucile and Adèle."

"Just Lucile."

"Ha-ha-ha."

Upstairs they were all laughing too. The whole confounded house was going into fits because I'd asked to marry his daughter.

"Listen," I said. "I'm serious."

"Yes, yes, Camille, my lad. I know you are." His jollity was shrinking.

"Well, what do you say?"

He grunted. He didn't want to be having this talk down here in the cellar. "You must see it my way."

"Oh, y-yes. Now we get to it."

"She's very young. A child. And pretty."

"S-sh-she's beautiful."

"And you'll have noticed the way we have young men calling at our house. I've had offers for her. There's one of them with an income of a hundred thousand francs a year. And another one – twenty-five thousand livres."

"You propose to sell her, then. What did she s-say to these su-suitors?"

"She turned them down, but then –"

"But th-then she m-might want somebody else."

"All right." He sounded sober now. That boded ill. I leaned on the wall glaring at him, the wine I'd drunk curdling in my guts. How had we got into this? "Now listen, Desmoulins. I know she's young and impressionable –"

"Oh G-God *almighty!*"

"And she perhaps thinks she feels something for you. But she's nineteen. She knows nothing. And you. Look at you."

"Ln-l-look at me. W-well?"

"You believe you're climbing up on top of the heap, but anything could happen. What are you? Some bloody libeling writer. There are more prisons than the Bastille. The way you carry on you could get carted off to the Châtelet tomorrow and locked up for thirty years. Where'd she be then?"

I spluttered.

He said, "Or worse, if the court party gets the upper hand again, you could find yourself hanged, and not off any blasted lamp-iron either. And if she's your wife, she'll go with you. Yes, she will. You know what happens to families if it's treason. They'd have you, and then they'd have her. You like the idea of that, do you? Lucile executed because you can't stop your idiotic scratching with a pen? I've got nothing against you –"

"You've got everything st-ag-ainst me."

Then he shouted. "Then I've got everything against you! Satisfied?"

Upstairs, they were singing. They didn't know what was happening down here.

I had got between him and the door. Suddenly he looked scared. I tried to tell him what I thought of him but I couldn't get it out, only gibberish, and in the end, desperate with fury, I flung the two bottles of wine at his feet. They smashed with a terrible noise. Somehow this sound penetrated above. Almost at once there was a concerned rumbling, and voices calling down to know what had happened. Ignoring all that, I rushed up the stairs and out of the house.

In the streets the lights were dying. Smoke and a stink of lamp oil and the sewers. I was beside myself, with a roaring like death in my ears. I had done the one thing she'd begged me not to. It had seemed so easy and so sure. But the old bastard, even with the ecstasy of the federation in him, wouldn't budge.

Somewhere in the Cordeliers district I paused in an alley to throw up. I wasn't alone in this act. The returning dark was shot with spewings and groanings on all sides. A brotherhood of sufferers, if not the liberated, we hung on house corners to rid ourselves of wine, July 14, the memory of the Bastille, all dreams of justice and love.

⚜

The king in reverse, at the Cordeliers dinner d'Anton would drink none of the toasts save that to the Nation. I didn't drink very much that night. "He's turning into Robespierre," said d'Anton. Momoro, once my printer, now a Cordelierite, tried to force some wine down my throat. I called him some name and he pulled out a dagger. I forget what happened next. Obviously, nothing.

⚜

I wrote to her, told her what I had done, asked her to forgive me, got no reply. I thought Duplessis had prevented her receiving the note. Or prevented her answering. I went to the Luxembourg, hoping to see her with Demeter in the gardens. Women and girls went up and down the walks, some even smiled at me, but they were the wrong ones.

Falling behind on the paper. Fréron began working on it with me. I relied on him for a third of the copy and news from the Duplessis house, which he was cagey with. Everything was normal, he said. Why didn't I call and see for myself?

⚜

The Revolutionary News

Certain persons are suggesting that the voting franchise be limited. How? In this way: that only the man who pays the tax equivalent of one silver mark is entitled to have a say in how his country is run.

To demonstrate the absurdity of this, I only need to point out that such a decree would push Rousseau himself from the electorate, while Jesus Christ would be outlawed as a "member of the Rabble." Suitable voters, I suggest, are those who have taken a Bastille. They are those who labor, at the bench, in the field. Such do-nothings as churchmen and courtiers are only the parasitic weeds which, at tilling time, are flung on a bonfire.

What if, on learning of this distinction of a silver mark, the ten million Frenchmen it disenfranchises—or their Paris representatives of Saint-Antoine—had fallen on Malouet and Co., crying, "Yes, you are stronger than we in the Assembly, but we outnumber you on the streets. If you deprive us of a vote—our civic life—we will have your *physical* life from *you.*" Is that not justice? Where, without hope of redress, a minority enslaves a majority, there is only one law: *Retaliate!*

⚜

Then the business with that dearest of royalist deputies, Malouet, started up again. He'd written to the Châtelet. . . . An Israelite curse, maybe, on behalf of Jephthah Duplessis.

⚜

"Gentlemen, I thank you for this opportunity to speak before the Assembly. For a year, I have withstood the slings and arrows of an outrageous fortune whom his father saw fit to award the name of Camille Desmoulins."

Some laughter. Malouet, who has played for it, accepts it graciously. Tall and dark, he has a presence, and no one is about to deny it. He looks around. On all sides the tiers of seats go up, but the acoustics here, at the Riding School, are very good. You should merely pitch a little, to overcome the swallowing power of so much draped cloth. But he's used to the Assembly, being the deputy from Riom. How else did he get to speak today?

"Please don't think," he continues, "that I am here to avenge a personal injury—though it would be true to say that personally injured I have been."

Someone calls, "Tell us what you wrote to the Châtelet."

Assent general.

Malouet clears his throat. This fad for heckling and interruption is getting worse lately. Copying the influential Jacobin Club no doubt. Never mind.

"If the Assembly thinks it will serve, I'm prepared to say what was written to the prison of the Châtelet by myself."

They tell him they would like that, though most of them know (apart from a brace of members who have nodded off after their lunch). So he reminds them.

"In a nutshell, citizens, I recommended that Monsieur Desmoulins be examined by the prison doctors, who would then certainly commit him to a lunatic asylum as certifiably insane."

A lot of laughter now. Particularly, of course, from the royalist element. But even Desmoulins's own political confrères, some of them, look amused. "Windmill," they call him. Everyone knows he's crazy. Clever and crazy. And writes and is *read*.

"What else can I suppose of a man," says Malouet blandly, "who has—for no more reason than that I am a lover of France, who would not see her traduced of all nations—enraged the masses against me for the last twelve months? It is a fact. A country which disowns and dishonors its king is a country defiled. Monsieur Desmoulins, with his constantly brandished classical leanings, should be aware of how the gods frown upon such a land and blast it with pestilence and sorrow. Yes, I would see France brought into the sunlight of liberation, but not by way of a dung heap."

Applause. Well and good.

"So I will simply mention the fact that I have been insulted, spat on, actually attacked, at Versailles, at my home, even here at the Assembly's door. That I am forced to carry a pistol at all times to protect myself, and that my feminine relatives dare not stir out of the house for fear of abuse—and all this due to a madman's persecution, the lies he has told about me in this scurrilous, felonious *thing* he terms a journal.

"No, gentlemen. I would only draw your attention to the insanity of his 'journalism' and the insane violence of it—which discredits any who take his part.

"You will have attended and perhaps read descriptions of the Festival of the Federation, that day of harmony and goodwill which did so much both for the heart of France and for the opinion that is held concerning her abroad. Did you then not see this lunatic rabble-rouser's paragraphs on the subject, put forth with the sole purpose of causing a riot in Paris? The king, who swore to honor the constitution before us all—what does this Desmoulins say of him? He recalls the triumph of some Roman—Paulus Emilius—which was 'Transformed into a festival because a king was dragged behind the general's chariot *in chains.*' "

Silence. Attentive silence. The royalist element is watching and waiting. The others are digesting. Someone has woken up a bevy of the sleepers, who all seem agitated.

"What," says Malouet, "is this—this *windmill* trying to do, turn Paris into an Armageddon? Plainly, his god is not after all Dionysos, patron of theater and wine, but anarchy. Or else it is the devil. Doubtless, gentlemen, even the most complacent among you would be unnerved if you were to learn that there is a movement afoot which has as its aim the arrest of the king, the incarceration of his family, the placing of the principal leaders of law and order in irons, and the death of as many as six thousand persons."

A great murmuring now. He lets it reach a crescendo. He hears two phrases: "It's a lie!" and "Name names!"

Malouet lets the crescendo die. He says, "I have been persecuted for saying I love the king as much as the People, equal love, and cannot change my heart. I am not such a fool as to name names, even if I knew them all."

Yes. I've done well.

"I'm known among you, I hope, as a good constitutionalist. Let my life and actions speak for me. I don't believe either Camille Desmoulins or his works can say very much for him."

Sitting down, amid royalist exultation, he takes a pinch of snuff from the new box with the tricolor blazoned on it and the chip of Bastille stone set in.

❊

"So what are you going to do about it? You've got to do something."

"They didn't read the paper publicly—the offending passages Ml-Malouet was mo-moaning over. Therefore how can the Assembly judge them? I've wr-written a defense to that effect. Sm-som-someone will read it."

"Who?"

"Who-whoever reads d-defenses."

"Not you."

"Nn-no. But I'll be there, to make sure it gets a hn-h-hearing."

"If you're there, they'll come down on you like vultures. You'll be called out to speak."

"Then I'll sp—I'll speak."

"Yes, just so, you'll sper-sper-speak." Louis-Mer frowned. He said, "Bloody Garney makes more setting errors in my articles than in yours." Windmill, worried to death and trying not to show it, shrugged. "Camille, you do know you're in serious trouble? They could arrest you."

"Yes, yes. But they w-w-w—"

"Why not?"

"The People. They matter. They wouldn't let—"

"Come down from the clouds. The mob's fickle."

Camille tore spitefully at his nails, crumpled up a sheaf of galleys, and threw it across the room.

"You say that because it's never loved you."

"Oh, *dear*," said Lapin Fréron. "Don't let's romanticize the rabble. Forget your Rousseau a minute. Men are animals, and animals bite. While the mob— that's a beast with no memory and no mind."

Windmill was at the door. "All right. Hn-nth-the—they'll kill me. I'll r-rot in a dun-dungeon. It's all I *think* about. Be happy."

"And Lucile," said Fréron, "won't visit you in jail."

"Yes, oh—yes, yes. No, she wo-n't." Windmill propped the doorpost.

"You should," said Fréron, "be more adroit in what you write."

"Mn-stm-st-stop talking like m-my—I can only say the truth. The *truth*. They've pushed Fatty back on his pedestal and everyone's crying Hurrah for the king! And the rats are gnawing the foundations away. Someone has to—and you—you write like a machine."

"Thank you."

"A butcher's cleaver for cutting throats. They'll have you up there next, roped and tied in the Stable."

"I'm more careful than you where I make the incision."

"Bloody machine. I'm off. G-going out."

"This is your room."

"And y-you're in it."

❧

So they'd ask me to speak. I'd spoken at the Cordeliers, to some effect. Sometimes, I'd even stammered, but the ideas had got across. (And sometimes I'd waived my turn, if I'm honest: My throat's sore, I'm hoarse, excuse me.)

I'd spoken in the Palais-Royal, too, and it had snowed green leaves. Bastille stones.

I couldn't sleep. I went to the hall of judgment and sat among the tiers of seats, right in the middle of it all, in the beautiful ruffled shirt that had been one of the first bonuses from Mirabeau the Magician, cheat and liar. I sat it all out, till they crawled around to my business. It was a good defense. I was lawyer enough to get that much right. They listened: also good.

My hands were slick with sweat; there was a raw feeling in my stomach that had been there off and on since that morning of July 15, three weeks of days and nights. I'd looked around to find any helpful faces, but I could only make out Robespierre, who was jotting notes quietly and gave me the idea he was completing a laundry list, not attending.

I didn't see Mirabeau that night. I think he wasn't there. Of the one or two who'd caught my arm and praised my arrival in the entrance, none seemed to remain.

Early August darkness. Outside the open windows, Paris breathed softly. She sounded far away as another country.

I shouldn't be here. My God, if they decided to arrest me, there I sat, like an Easter goose. I should have done Marat's trick, stayed home, with some mistress posted as lookout, all ready to leap down into the sewers and be lost.

And then Malouet got up and wanted to speak again.

He looks very tall. I think I'm seeing him taller than he is. Nobody is that tall. D'Anton, maybe.

"Very well." Malouet, also looking all around. Oh, marvelous, this one's an actor. Looks at me. Involuntarily I flinch, and he's tickled by that. "A very neat defense by the lawyer of the lamp-iron. But what does it prove? We haven't read the whole paper out." Staring at me. Damn him. Try to swallow. Yes, I'm going to have to speak. "We *can* always read it. All I say is this: If Camille Desmoulins is innocent of my charges, let him explain himself." Yes, this is what it felt like, my very first legal case. Botched it, failure. Twenty-five, then. Tongue-tied; perfect English description. Older now. Tongue-tied. T-tongue-t-t-tied. Aristos. Born in a golden bed, born to a golden world. Love the king, boot the People in the backside. Always you, tripping us, in our way, *you* taking the food from our mouths, putting the cord around our necks. Now he's shouting at me: "Let him justify himself. If he dares."

I came to my feet, burning, terrified of what they would do to me but in a spasm of anger that gave me speech.

"Yes, I dare. I *dare.*"

And the dull twisting in my belly seemed to rip apart as if a knife had gone into me. I caught my breath at it. The pain—was execrable. Sweat broke out all over me now, icy as well water. Stunned on the echo of the pain, I tried physically to turn from it as it came at me again.

The great room was swelling, walled in by those bloodless soulless faces, the somber draperies sinking into black. I stared at Malouet. Who was he? I started to speak in the grip of the pain, confused; it came out like the mouthings of an imbecile. God alone knows what I said. Unless someone wrote it down.

The tall man stood and postured mockingly at me, and soon they all began to howl and jeer like things in a jungle. I must have sat down then. I didn't care.

Robespierre. He had given up making out the laundry list and was speaking in my place. What was the deputy from Arras, Robespierre, saying? His voice sounded moistureless, a well-tuned dusty instrument.

The pain is going to stop. It can't last.

A spear of fire ran into my groin, another upward into my ribs.

Robespierre's . . . saying: I was not at fault. My zeal tended to prove greater than my tact. *No, Maxime.* A sound patriot, I must be forgiven these flights. I did not always think. *No, Maxime, don't betray what I've tried to do by making it into some kid's witless prank.* But I couldn't protest. I was grateful.

I sat there with the pain tearing away inside me. I'd seen someone die of this, or had I only been told? A blade in one side of the pelvis. Nothing to be done. Opium, and still screaming in agony, dead in two days.

I got out and into the street. I don't recall how. It was late. Mirabeau's thirsty drunken brother would be grateful when they rang the bell to end the session. Bells out here. The river. Streets. Theater-of-France Street. Up the stairs. Crash down on the bed. I'm dying. I'm thirty, and I'm dying of an incurable poisoning in the right side of the intestines. Thirty and dying and I haven't done anything, haven't done what I meant to; my mother will cry when she gets the news. She's so ill, and I haven't seen her for months, and Lucile—

The thought of her made it worse.

The pain was my only companion. It came and went in long thunderings. I was soaked in sweat as hot as spilled blood, drowning in the fine shirt, trying to throw the base of my spine and the soles of my feet up through my guts.

Sometimes I was still answering Malouet, whoever Malouet was.

I dare. I dare because, while I am not, truth is fearless. Imprison me then, shut me up and gag me. They burned *France Set Free* in Toulon. But the ashes of that pyre blew up and came down and every speck of ash marked some wall or heart with a wonderful smudge which read WE WILL NO LONGER BE SLAVES. If I persecute, then, I do it for a cause. For yourself, I did not order the populace to attack you, I am not some great captain or king, sir, to do as much. It seems they saw some fault in you that I had pointed out—but I am the light that showed it, not its maker. And where I struck at you with a pen, they took up sticks and stones. Well, if you feel the edge of the sword, disarm the swordsman—correct yourself. Leave your visions of a golden monarchy and put France in its stead.

And then again I thought the pain was the pain of hunger, I was starving to death in some heat-blasted landscape, I the persecuted one, who died.

Near morning I was cold, so cold I shook and the bed rattled, or my bones, or my chattering teeth. Then the vast ocean of the pain began to grow dry and small, till in the end it ebbed away and I slept.

They woke me an hour or so later, crying under the windows: Malouet and the aristos routed! Desmoulins wins the day!

I lay there shuddering, afraid the pain would come back. But there was only the stink of illness blending with the sticky sweetness of summer city dawn. I closed my eyes and slept again.

Nobody came to arrest me, not even death. My apologist, Maximilien Robespierre, had saved my skin. (Have a speech. Thank you, Maximilien.)

⚜

But the lie, the lie. In everything it threads its way, the snake in the tree.

The printed word becomes a weapon better than swords. Hound, then, the despots and the reactionaries with these word swords. But when does the workman's use of the sword become the *love* of the use of the sword?

It is not the solitary man, but the overwhelming power bestowed upon that solitary agent, which cripples and makes a monster of him. It was I who said it.

If I say I believed in what I wrote, that does not excuse me. If I say I enjoyed my vocation, that to write was an exhilaration, I shall probably be condemned. If I say that when I lay in the delirium of horrible illness, thinking I was dying of perityphilitis, I believed my death would matter to France—it is not so much the admission of ego as of my own pitiableness.

Was there ever a man born who did not reckon he had some vital place in the world? Who could bear to live, otherwise.

The People's Friend

My dear Camille, for all your wit, you know as much about politics as a cuckoo. Though your song is always interesting, it never says anything sensible.

Have a kick in the teeth. Thank you, Marat.

A Queen: Diamonds or hearts?

Marie-Antoinette was visiting the poor, appearing like an apple-blossom mirage in the hospitals. "How are you today?" "Oh, very well, Your Majesty," said the terminal cases, astonished. But King Yes-Yes was ruling now by right of law, and not by Divine Right. King and queen of the French. Poor things, making do there in the Tuileries with the flaking painted ceilings, the mice eating the candles (my, *these* taste good—best wax), the army of servants at pains with scent and ceremony among the disturbed dust and beetles.

One would say she knew, Antoinette, almost from the very first, that a great staircase lay before her and the only way was down.

Married to a fool in a kingdom of foreigners who hated her, had always hated her, because she liked to dance and dress up and—nervously afraid of ennui—would dash from the card table to the ballroom, always in a new dress. But she was born to it. She was as conditioned as anyone. From the moment her eyes opened on the world, her only proper education had been that she was a goddess and would always be a goddess. The first sights were silk and satin, servants who worshiped, peasants who knelt and threw flowers. Everything came to her on a golden plate and in a silver spoon that was inserted, so very gently, lovingly, into her rosy mouth.

But now, after all these years of being one thing, the wolves came howling and she must become something else. You're like us, they shouted, grimacing their filthy ugly masks at her. No, no, her heart cried out. She could not help her heart.

But she tried. Give her her due. In October, at the Butterflies, when they had screamed for her blood in the courtyard, she had come out onto the balcony and faced them, even as she heard the cocking of maybe twenty muskets, each with a ball of obliteration aimed at her breast, her forehead. And here now, having lost so much of the luxurious pleasure that to her was only a normal everyday thing, she tried to adapt. She verified the oath of July 14, she went to the reeking hovels and hospitals and gazed like a marble saint on creatures so alien to her in all things they were like beings from another planet.

She knew the staircase only went down. First the threats, then the reality. She didn't like it, didn't see why she should have to put up with it. What else had she had but her dresses and her dancing? She had Louis, so good at venery and joinery, who had taken several years of trial and error to relieve her of her virgin state.

She plotted. She wrote letters to Austria: Dear Homeland, help me. Of course she did. Who, deprived of their security and all hope of joy, for no reason they can properly understand, would not attempt to correct matters? If she had been an intellectual, then her conduct would be unforgivable. An intellectual, presumably, could have worked it out that one man (or woman) should not live by the anguish of another. But Antoinette was only a little clever, and that in all the wrong ways.

Sad, feckless queen. She saw the steps go down and down. Did she also see the shiny edge that lay across the staircase bottom?

1790: Autumn – Winter

IN SEPTEMBER, Necker resigned. Once the idol, he was now the totem of all things bad. And when you think it was all because —

Meanwhile, the great religious quarrel, which had started the year before, churned on and on, and villages still resounded to the slamming of doors as sons who told their fathers priests were only men were thrown onto the street.

In fact there were now two sorts of priest. The People's priests had sworn their loyalty to France, given away bits of church furniture, and toyed with the idea of getting married. The others held on tooth and claw to their altar candlesticks, their celibacy, and the supreme authority of the pope. The pope himself (that "Bishop of Rome") had been applied to, that the schism should be mitigated. As yet, no reply. But what kind of reply did they reckon they'd get?

In the northeast of France, matters military had got seriously out of hand with mutinies over arrears in pay. The mutinies had been — crushed.

In Paris, the assignats still boldly flapped, paper money. . . . Were they worth a bit less than they had been?

And don't forget there are a lot of émigrés in England, in Austria, and in the towery town of Koblenz, stirring up trouble. Some quiet nights along the borders of France, you heard the rattle of sabers in the distance. Who says it's only cowbells?

⚜

Rather than calling Windmill into his studio, which was a messy attic located somewhere in the Cordeliers district, the artist was working on his sketch in the apartment on Theater-of-France Street. More comfortable, if somewhat untidy. These *nouveaux messieurs*—all the same, if they didn't keep servants and a wife and a couple of mistresses to clear up after them. Books everywhere, paper everywhere, and dead quill pens (this one broke a lot; the kind of stuff he wrote, a wonder they didn't naturally combust like phosphorus matches) lying all over the desk as if someone had been plucking a goose.

The artist was preparing the drawing for a stippled etching which would be executed over at the shop in the rue Saint-Honoré. No problem selling. He must be careful the Honoréites didn't swindle him over the fee.

An interesting face, this Camille. Skin rather livid, as if he'd been ill, but they said he always looked like that, sallow; Derobespierre—whoops, *Rob*sepierre—was the same. But there any resemblance ended. The features were easy to capture, if you were careful. Arrogant apple of jaw, nose that could have been classical if someone hadn't once lightly stepped on it, flattening it near the apex and lengthening it. Wicked mouth. Always that nervous tension which held the lips upward, like a sarcastic, pitiless smile. Fine eyes, wet-black, power there—but noticeably wide-set, so the ignoramus who didn't know Desmoulins by sight would say, This can't be right. But it was. Very odd. What did it mean? All facial characteristics did mean something: like hands, now. This one's hands were neurasthenic. Long thin fingers, with no tapering at the ends, covered in ink. Callus on the second finger of the right hand where the pen always dug. Bitten nails. But what were the eyes all about, spaced there under the intelligent forehead, which was well-shaped if somewhat aggressive? Staring out into glory now, of course; he'd taken his pose and held it rigidly, sometimes twitching with nerves, so the artist could catch it all just *so* for posterity. But the artist hadn't himself been caught that way. He'd retained the look of the eyes gazing straight at him, with something uneasy and veiled in them under the brilliant black, something that almost seemed to be asking, W-well?

"I'll put leaves into the hat," said the artist.

"Wh—?" muttered Windmill, far off in the pose.

"Chestnut leaves. Every hero has his symbol."

"Ohh."

Funny. He didn't react to the word "hero." Most of them did. A student of men, the artist from the messy attic.

It was going to be a good likeness, without flattery. They said this one was ugly, but he wasn't. Every age has its vogue. This age liked people of either sex who resembled porcelain dollies, and *that* Monsieur Windmill decidedly did not. Some other era, they'd have said Attractive, crankily handsome. Yes, they would. Some era where they found irregularity appealing and truthful and, so, valid.

"Thank you, monsieur," said the artist.

"Wh—?"

"I've done."

Windmill wriggled out of the pose like a statue coming alive, not sure if it liked the new conditions. He put up one hand and removed the hat and set it down carefully, but stayed wrapped up in the cloak as if he were cold despite the fire. (The cloak had been a good idea, a heavy hint of the Roman drapery there. And the shoulders were very straight for a man who spent half his time bowed over a desk. Yes, it was not bad, this sketch.) The artist squinted to see if Camille was coming across to inspect. But he didn't. He eyed the drawing warily upside down from a distance. No high opinion of his looks, obviously. But a vanity nevertheless. The dramatic flinging around himself of the cloak: I am Brutus! The pose. The very greeting at the door—Oh, yes, I'm ready. Which meant Come in and make me immortal.

The artist finished up the wine his sitter had been generous enough to supply, and agreed to the final arrangements standing over the fire, the standard of which his own did not often approach.

When they had shaken hands, and everything been tented up in its covers (it was raining outside), the artist sought the apartment door, opened it, and paused spontaneously in admiration. A lady bloomed in the doorway, in her early forties and proving the adage that the ripened fruit is always the best.

There was a stifled, surprised exclamation behind the artist, in the room: Brutus coming back to Paris with a bump. The lady raised her brows and smiled upon everyone.

If this were the attachment who came to clear up the quill pens, no wonder the bastard had been biting his nails.

"Well, good-day, madame," said the artist, "Just off." Unfortunately. He went down the stairs and heard Windmill vocalize after a long silence, "Yn-you'll be compromised." But then the door shut. Oh, well, out into *la pluie*. Rain me a nice plump shepherdess, why don't you?

"Not at all," said Demeter in the apartment. "Don't you ever listen to gossip, Camille? They've said you and I were lovers for years; then you got tired of me and went to work on my daughter."

Windmill looked uncomfortable. Her mission was not to distress him, so she added, "We seem not to have seen you for some time."

"Hn-nn. No."

"Lucile," said Demeter, "is not the kind of girl who cries into her pillow every night. But now she cries into her pillow every night. Very softly, so as to disturb no one, which Adèle finds very disturbing. Adèle, you see, isn't able to cry into *her* pillow when she is separated from your friend Maxime, and she's grown very envious of such *grande passion*. This is not good for a young girl. Otherwise, there have been breakages in the cellar. It seems a whole shelf of bottles came down on my poor husband on the night of July fourteenth."

Windmill didn't speak. He stood and fiddled with papers on the desk, peculiarly graceful in his utter gracelessness.

"We anticipated a full assault by the mob at any moment. The infants of the streets don't like their new lords upset." Playful, but finding the play got no response, she left it. "Then, Lapin tells us you've been ill."

"Frér-eron. Wh-what does he know?"

"We've had described to us a feeble Camille who crawls to the door to open it, falls into a chair, writes like a fiend for five minutes, then collapses asleep over the copy with his hair in the ink."

"Hn-wn-once, last mn-m-m—"

"And all this while, one very foolish note to Lucile."

"Dd-did *he*—"

"Lucile's father, I believe, has had a discussion with her, regarding her intentions toward a certain rather bizarre personage who sometimes calls at our house and throws things. Oh, dear. My dear Camille. What can I say?"

Windmill stared at her smiling calm. She looked at him tolerantly. She was well aware, Demeter, of the hot water this wild male child could have got her into those few years ago, with all the courtly poems and the intense eyes. She had put up immediately between them a barrier of genuine affection. Never once did she let the barrier slip. If she had ever permitted there to be anything else, it could have ushered in disaster. The twenty-two-year-old child could not have coped with the repercussions. For herself, she was too sensible to trust herself to that brink where amusement might give way to feeling. When he began to love her daughter, she knew almost at the selfsame instant he did. There had been just a moment's jealousy, then, very light, only a little regretful. Actually she was relieved. It took the knife edge away from her fingers, and she didn't like to be cut.

"You've begun the chase, sir," she now said, "and are supposed to continue your pursuit gallantly. Throw a bottle at my husband's head by all means. I'm sure it was very good for him. But then pray don't fly into the forest and hide. You're required to come back and consolidate the victory."

"V-vh-*victory?*"

"Well," she said, "you do also have two advocates earnestly pleading your case at all times. Not to mention our maid, who calls you that 'truly good citizen, Monsieur C.' "

"I wrote to Lucile and got no an-answer."

"Oh, come now. Her father's got her under his eye. Besides, what should she answer? She's told you she loves you over and over. My heavens, she even brought herself to tell *me* she loves you. Whatever you do she assents, gives in. She can't oppose you. What does she care about some ridiculous promise she exacted? She won't be your conscience, Camille. You'll have to be your own. All my daughter can give you is blind love and absolute loyalty. Be careful. I warn you. If you're wrong, she won't ever believe it. She'll only say, My Camille has decided, and it's as clear as day: That's that."

Windmill put both hands over his face. Eventually he said, "What am I supposed to do?"

"Come to the house. Give my poor husband some wine."

"And he—?"

"We're wearing him down."

"D-Dem-Demeter—"

"Now, now. I am to be Madame your mother-in-law."

He came at her in a pantherish rush, and took her hand as if it were glass, and kissed it as if to bury himself alive in it. Demeter sighed. She patted his head bowed over her hand, the beautiful black waves of hair, so unlike the balding cranium of her big fat unenterprising spouse.

❀

The talisman was around his neck in a small cloth bag—Lucile's lock of hair, still bright and alive. He entered the door and looked at the maid who thought he was a truly good citizen. Then he looked at Papa Duplessis, who had just been the recipient of a gift of wine. For a moment they circled each other warily. Then, "Well, look who it is," said Lucile's father.

There were some other people there. Who? No one. Supper was a stiff-backed affair. What did they eat? Nothing.

Lucile, like a golden-white lamp in the middle of the room. Laughing and alight. Because I'm here.

Everything has to change. I don't want any of it, only her. Peace. Peace with her. It's all I want. The rest of it: swimming against the might of an ocean, upstream.

By the door, ten o'clock or midnight.

"Why did you stay away?"

"I thought—"

"He understood you were in earnest. You properly frightened him. He rushed up and said, That idiot Desmoulins has just gone mad and thrown half my cellar at me—and the best wine, too. Next day he said to me, Now, Lucie, you've got to start thinking like a woman. You're quite old enough to marry. How do you consider this writer fellow? And I said sweetly, You mean Rabbit, Father? And he was quite furious with me. But you didn't come back."

"I thought—"

"You always *think*. You never *think*. Stop thinking, Camille. Why were you ill, and you never sent word to Mama or to me?"

"There's an illness that kills, and I thought—"

"Thought, thought—"

"I thought I'd die and never see you again."

She looked up at me, inside my arms, her beautiful face with its mirroring eyes. "But you believe in God, Camille."

"Yes. Sometimes. The kind father who abandons his children."

"*No.* How can you say that if we're together?"

"Share your faith with me," I said. "Share it with me, Lucile."
"Don't be afraid," she said. "Dear love."

❀

And two months later I was saying to the curé of Saint-Sulpice, "Well, if you'll only marry me to her if I'm a Catholic, then I'm a Catholic for God's sake."

"Now, monsieur," said the curé, folding his hands and his disparaging face, "this won't do. We all know about your *liberal* opinions. When did you last attend confession?"

"I forget. Twenty-three—"

"And you are now thirty years of age?"

"If it's 1790."

"Please don't try to jest with me. This is no joking matter."

"Well, wha-what do you want me to do? Walk b-barefoot to Rheims?"

"I am not attempting to salvage your immortal soul at this juncture. But I really can't unite you to a daughter of the Church, and under the canon of holy law, if you persistently demonstrate yourself to be an unbeliever."

"What do I have to demonstrate myself as believing in?"

"You're quite well aware."

"Then I believe it, all of it."

"There is also the point that if you wish to marry at this unusual season, directly upon Christmas, you'll require a special dispensation."

"Yes."

"Which will most certainly be refused. Several of our clergy contend that various properties of theirs have been burned to the ground as a result of comments in your paper."

"I'm not responsible f-for-or *everything*."

"Compose yourself. We will try the catechism."

We tried the catechism. Who was God? Who was God's son? I told him what Rome decrees they are. I must have passed the test. I was a boy again, back in the cold-eyed church. Presently:

"You will also, of course, make a confession."

"Of course."

"After which—"

"Yes?"

"You'll take some thought about the next issues of your journal, perhaps. If Mother Church consents to marry you, it would be rather churlish of you to go on as you have, castigating the priesthood and attempting to bring Christianity into contempt."

We considered one another. Oh, Lady Bribery. But I hadn't gone there to say no. I could always pocket my silver and give Pilate the butcher, after all. . . .

Demeter took us both to make our confession, Lucile and myself. I tailored my sins to the occasion and spoke up bravely. I heard all Lucile's as I stood in the church by the booth, and my heart beat crazily because she said she had paid more attention to worldly things than to God, and I knew by "worldly things" she spoke of me.

I'd been astute enough to go to one of the priests of Louis-le-Grand, my old college (or did Maxime suggest it?), and I'd asked this priest if he would marry us. And with his help, the dispensation was arrived at.

My father had also delayed everything. First of all withholding consent and then—my fault—not getting sufficient information of my betrothed's names and similar paraphernalia to award it, though he had agreed. To be fair, they had never, my parents, set eyes on Lucile, this apparition I had so constantly conjured for them in word pictures. I suspect my father had some notion she was from the theater or the Palais-Royal and further monumental disgrace was about to tumble on him, courtesy of his son. Then, at last, all was resolved; I got parental blessing on us both.

My father. Having cursed him and raged against him all that month, I was suddenly disarmed by a final communication. (This letter, which I always kept, the very night I looked for it—all of thirty-nine months after, when he wrote to tell me of my mother's death—I could not find. I remember fumbling after it, turning out bureau drawers, in a shadow darker than that of the low-burning candles. But all this was to come.) That winter he spoke to me of how he had fallen in love with my mother, my entire life ago, a love not like Camille's shouted passion but quiet and mannerly. Still, love. She was so ill and frail now he seldom saw her, I less often than he. She was with the nuns. To see her in this way was painful, a strain, the chains of duty, aching helpless hopeless compassion. Nothing to be done. We did not frequently speak of her. But in the climate of that warm December, his gentle confession brought him close to me as he had never been close, till then. Since we were both mortal, both men, both lovers, despite all other differences.

❋

And despite the altering world, the fever dreams which rocked France like great earth movements, planetary shifts, two human beings were married that Wednesday the twenty-ninth of December, 1790.

A portion of the city had come to the hem of smoky Saint-Sulpice, with its summits of creamy architectural icing. The carriages, not being the chariots of nobles, had some trouble getting through the crowd to the doors. No one was mown down or whipped from the way. It was: Pardon me. Excuse me. Thank you. And the crowd was not at all tame. It reared and squealed. It patted Brissot of the key on the back, and embraced Robespierre and fat cute Pétion. And when d'Anton Danton arrived (late), it barked at him as if for bones.

When the bridegroom turned up in all the splendor of new clothes, he was cheered and stroked and kissed all the way along the live cordon to the church and only let go, laughing with excitement, egomania, and embarrassment, at the last possible second.

When the bride appeared, the crowd fell almost silent with glee. For the bride was gorgeous, her face like a flower through her lacy veil, there in the winter day.

Her wedding dress was the pink of a shell from the dawn sea, with the sheen of the waves still on it. So warm and sweet she was, and so young. So young, Lucile, lovely Lucile, going up the aisle on the arm of her father, who, outnumbered (and terrorized?), had ultimately given in with scarcely a squeak.

A dowry of one hundred thousand francs (and a house in the country): worth having. No fool, that Camille. No fool anyway to win over a girl like this one. Well, it always helps to be famous. And if he couldn't get a word out, he could always write her very witty letters.

The solstice light that fell into the Geneviève Chapel was of a platinum color until it touched the candles; then it mellowed to clear amber.

The old priest from the college, who was fond of Camille and had always looked for success for him (and who had been slightly scandalized, actually), still maintained an overall belief in the basic goodness of most persons, providing they could be brought to heel. But love was a great leveler. The priest's eyes, watering a little but seeming only luminous in the wintry candle-smoothed crepuscule, had a wonderful aesthetic holiness. He gazed, with these miraculously profound eyes, at the couple before him, seeing children.

"The sacrament of marriage," said Father Bérardier, "as commonly, in religious things . . ."

The outward form is not the All.

From the first man and the first woman who drew together in the loneliness of being, even to the last man and the last woman who will walk the earth—in these conjunctions, forever and always, the symbol of the definitive Love is made manifest.

As the man and the woman turn to each other, just so does the benighted soul reach out to God. There on the hillside, bereft of companions and having only the starry sky for company, the dreamer yearns to find his complement in the moon. But how much greater than that wandering changeable lamp the vast and unquenchable ray that steals from the Creator to envelop him.

Each searches for the mirror of himself, like and unlike. And whoever finds it, in his own miniature universe of self, demonstrates the love of the Heart of all universes, which encompasses mankind.

Then love one another, that through such earthly love you may learn the lesson of a far mightier love. For the greatest of all virtues is love. Nothing can flourish unless there is love to nurture it. Nothing can find rest unless there is love to cradle and defend it.

Love one another; it is the command of Christ himself, and through your love behold the power of love, which casts down mountains, triumphs over deserts, divides and raises the waters of great seas.

And in your love, remember: There is One whose love is eternal, the Father of all things, that were, and are, and have yet to be. Nor shall His love leave you till the world's end and beyond.

It was the morning of the Romantic age. One did not scruple to be moved. Emotion was not something to be shut in a cupboard. And if you shed tears easily, so, you shed them.

And to Camille, who could not hold back his tears, moved unbearably by happiness and strain and the creed of universal love, Maximilien Robespierre whispered unnecessarily, "Cry if you want to cry."

I remember it. Maxime, along with Sébastien Mercier, Brissot, and Pétion, balancing the bridal canopy over us, and that voice, very quiet, tactful, and kind: *Cry if you want.* Giving me — what was it? — encouragement or permission?

❄

(Long after, the sight of the marriage document from the wedding of Camille Desmoulins and Lucile Duplessis, with its list of signatures, curlicued, scrawled, imprisoned by insecure underlinings, would have the ability to startle. It reads like a celebrity billing of Who's Who in the Revolution.)

❄

The wedding breakfast was spirited and merry. And like every event of its kind, it lasted too long.

❄

They had all gone away. The rooms were empty but for the wreck of the feast, which in the morning the domestic, Jeanette, would efficiently clear. Empty — but not empty. Through the wall there was a movement like that of a small bird, spreading its wings, ruffling them a little. Probably I imagined it. She wasn't there, beyond the door to the bedroom.

Her mother had been the last to leave, coming out of the bedroom, closing that door on its mystery, stealing by me with only one long glance, closing the outer door as if it were made of eggshell.

Finally, silence in the inner room. Was the girl in there going to call to me? No. Was she there at all? I opened the door.

She was sitting on the bed, demure and self-possessed as a child for whom the world is timeless and safe. She wore a sweeping white nightdress, so totally modest, with gathered little ribbons. Her hair shone, every soft rivulet, with a faint lemony light from the few candles. I was almost afraid of her, I don't know why. As if she were another girl, not the one I had been after so long and so urgently, because that girl was never to be won or to be had, but here this beautiful image was, like one of Curtius' waxes—

"Your Jeanette," said Lucile, "makes horrible coffee. I'll have to speak to her. Or better still, I'll always see to it myself." And that was so much Lucile that the macabre idea of false images was chased out of the room shrieking. "Oh, what a very glamorous waistcoat you were wearing," said Lucile, leaving the bed and moving toward me with lights shimmering all over her, hair and gown and skin. "So many flowers embroidered—"

"I married you," I said. "Did I?"

"Oh, yes. And I married you."

"And we're here."

"Here in our own apartment, with hundreds of books and thousands of broken quill pens—how do you *break* so many, Camille?—and wood for the fire and awful Jeanette to make awful coffee, and we'll be happy."

She raised her arms to put them around my neck, and I lifted her off her feet and held her to me.

I meant to be very gentle with her, but all too soon carried away, I couldn't be gentle. Ultimately, unable to change a thing, I was afraid I might have hurt her, until I heard her laugh at me, a sweet wild breathless devilish little laugh in my ear, as the world divided at its center and ended.

She was the only one in all my life whose laughter could never sting or anger me. That's because, I believe, for all those to whom I stupidly betrayed myself, she was the only one I ever trusted.

"My love," I said, at two in the morning, "go to sleep."

"No. Let me lie here and look at you. Let me watch over you like the sphinx."

The candles were finished, but through the window came a faint light still; it might have been the winter moon. The pillows stared palely at it, and the marriage ring on her finger glimmered like her eyes. She seemed a supernatural creature. "Indefinable being," I said. "Priestess from Apollo's grove. Sphinx. Angel. Go to sleep."

But it was I who slept. And maybe she did watch over me. It seemed to me I felt her eyes glowing on me through that boat journey of slumber. Though in the early morning when I woke she was up, investigating the rooms like a squirrel. I brought her back to bed and, in the end, Jeanette made the coffee.

Janvier-miel 1791: *Winter is spring*

Much of the honey month was spent at Bourg-la-Reine. The smart little house at the end of Madame Duplessis's estate, with its rectangular shutters and porthole-windowed attic, was occupied by two tenants running up and down its stairs, anxiously overseeing the advent of a small piano, busts of Rousseau, and various noble Romans; otherwise appearing at windows or disappearing utterly as if into the heart of a cave. Sometimes, a volcano of unexpected sun erupted over the landscape. Then the tenants emerged from their pagan privacy to wander the linden walk hand in hand. They would appear to belong to no particular time or country, regardless of costume. They had an air of complete ignorance – or rather innocence, primitive as two animals who live only to live. Their conversations, overheard by a scatter of birds in the trees, were hardly representative of what you would expect of an incendiary Revolutionary and his wife. Were they discussing the state of the economy, the monarchy, or the duties of the bourgeois position? Well, the girl looks stern. Some pronouncement is going to be made. "My name is Lucile. Lu, indeed! Are you addressing a wolf?" "An exquisite blond wolf, Lu-loup-Lulotte." "Then you're twice wolf." What a sensible and philosophic dialogue. So much so, it's repeated, several times.

The family house, a grand two-to-three-story farm, whitewashed and with tall gate pillars of mellowed stone surmounted by haughty globes, lay just off the Paris road. There was a well with a walnut tree that occasionally dropped nuts. There was the large garden with its trees and shrubs, abutting the long roll of fields and copses, and the toy village that rambled on down the street, providing the availability of wonderful cream, dark cheeses, and herds of cows who left the public thoroughfare not as they had found it. The Duplessises, too, had their share of provincial animal life. The pond in their yard bustled with ducks; rabbits made constant forays into the herb garden. A tribe of cats seemed permanently just delivered of their pretty and lawless children, so no one need ever be without a kitten or six. When Lucile's court began to arrive on weekends out of Paris, worn to a frazzle and grumbling about everything from the sewers to the Assembly, from wheels coming off coaches to toothache, they were let into the smart small house, installed in armchairs on the lake of polished floor, handed a couple of kittens and some very good coffee. Presently they fell asleep in a rapture of relaxation. "Look at them. They only come here to sleep," said Windmill, slightly surprised that they were even able to stay alive in conditions so unlike his own.

Letters also arrived. Maximilien's was one of the first, but it came to chide:

> A promise is a promise, Camille, and I scan your paper in vain to find this speech of mine you assured me you would include. The issue is a vital one. You mustn't allow yourself to be distracted from your task as a patriot by the loveliness and the adoring eyes of the new Madame Desmoulins.

(Rosepeter? He fucketh never, as d'Anton said.) A letter from Danton too, now a card-holding member of the Jacobins and so able to invite others. *Come and give us a talk on wedded bliss, you bloody libertine.*

Also other letters, the usual outpourings of strangers, that great army of unknowns who wrote to Camille and had written since the first pamphlet blazed out onto the streets. Save us, they'd said; or, You're the only one who cares about us; or, You and Marat, the rest are liars—we know you'll speak for us. (They had touched him deeply. A cloud of responsibility had floated around his head like a shadowy halo. But it was difficult to go on being Jesus twenty-four hours of every day. In the end he'd read the letters, sigh, feel exasperated and pressured. Get up at half past three in the black morning to write about some injustice perpetrated at Toulon or Lyons. Sometimes he let the letters pile up for days, not reading them at all.) And now the letters said, *Where are you?*

It was true. The paper was mostly in Fréron's hands, and they missed the particular style they'd come to recognize as Camille's. "The royalists are having a field day," Fréron had said, turning up in grave-quiet Queen's Market in January, like a shipwrecked mariner reaching an island. Louis-Mer had renounced his claims to Lucile, or he had never had any; it had been another variation of a Robespierrean courtship. But no, not quite that. Still the visitor stared at her, eating her up with his rather cold eyes. Fréron was altered altogether. It was not that he was less himself—but *more* himself that he had been wont to be. There was a sort of hectic passivity about him. He was tired out, but even so, still waiting—for what? The old quarrels were extinguished, just as the quarrel with Brissot (actually all one-sided; Camille had never informed Monsieur la Clé that they'd fallen out) had been swept away. Brissot had been part of the wedding, sat at the wedding breakfast, and made a silly speech, just like everyone else.

But Fréron, shipwrecked in his chair, said to Lucile, "Play the piano. No more talking, no more words." Which state of mind lasted perhaps three quarters of an hour.

They all flirted with her. Pétion ("Watch him, he means to be important." "As what?" "Oh, mayor or something. He's got paid coteries going around the slums to tell everyone he's wonderful." "I thought that was Kiddy-Blond's act." "La Fayette? He does it in person on a big shiny horse.") Jérôme Pétion pretended to die of unrequited love every time he met Lucile. As did Mercier, who, being a great deal older, did it with a great deal more finesse. She laughed at them, took them for walks, and fed them winter salad from the garden as if they were yet more examples of her country pets: the rabbits, the kittens. And Camille himself, removed from her by two rooms' distance, was liable to go into helpless vocal ecstasies over her beauty and her grace, as if he hadn't even had her yet, which, it was quite plain to anyone who stayed in the house, he had done and did very regularly. The "cottage" resounded with sexuality and high spirits, and now and then with intellect.

In the unseasonably fine weather, there would be strolls along lanes, Adèle, Lucile, and Demeter in becomingly rustic straw hats, the male party growing wildly Rousseauesque over the countryside, the sheep, or whatever happened to be on view, the fabulous gloss of reawakening on trees and hedges. There was also some lolling about on the lawn in chairs; the discovery of a print of the tragic muse who so resembled Madame Duplessis that she was again "rechristened" – Melpomene; a supper in the farmhouse with several jolly retainers at, and a hen or two under, the table. There were card games, impromptu dances, a mock tribunal set up to try Robespierre for the terrible wickedness of refusing a ham pancake. Then the inevitable disgruntled return to the capital of the guests on Monday morning.

"When are you coming back to Paris, Camille, eh? Back to the drudgery of work?"

"Never. I'm giving up the literary life."

"Oh, yes? *Oh,* yes!"

"I'll resume my former profession. Lawyer."

"A practice established no doubt in the Place de Grève under the lantern hook."

"I'm serious."

"Hang them, *then* defend them, eh, Camille?"

"Ha-ha. Look at the pack of you. Collapsing at your posts. There are too many sword fights. Someone else can do it."

"Hey, the razor's saying it wants to be blunt. That only happens with constant use."

But the razor said, "Have some more lemonade before you go."

They went. They sent back letters. There was even a strange epistle from Windmill's birthplace, some fellow wanting to "serve the People" by working with Citizen Camille. Shattered to find someone from the wretched town who admired him, Windmill almost answered it.

The last letter of that era, however, came by night, flung over the wall and wrapped about a stone. Not intended to cause damage, save to the conscience, it landed in thick grass, was nevertheless found and brought to Windmill, who was laboriously working on a poem. He opened the paper and read: *You sleep, Camille, while Paris is enslaved.*

"What does it say?"

"Some nonsense. A play on the Latin. . . ."

But something stirred in him. All those years of unrecognition; then the leap to power by means of the table and the green leaf; now this simple sheer flattery. Because you of all men, *you* abandon us, we are enslaved.

Think about it.

He thought.

❦

Frère Camille, frère Camille,
Dormez-vous? Dormez-vous?
Sonnez la toquassen, sonnez la toquassen:
Din-din-dong!

FOUR

1791: Spring

Mirabeau: The fallen warrior

THE WHEEL OF *Progress has begun to turn and cannot now be stopped till it has run over someone.*

Mirabeau was dying. All Paris knew. And much of Paris was around the house wall, on Antin Drive, waiting for the wings of the dark angel to pass over me-and-thee but not him.

Inside the house, all the friends had gathered. They were clustered around the bed, and wedged between them there were vases on pedestals full of April flowers: narcissi, early lilac, transparent lilies. The air was soaked with perfumes and the scent of fresh young blooms. Just as he had commanded it to be. No stink of death. "The raven's coming," he had said. "No need to signpost. He knows where the carrion is."

It might have been Alexander's tent. The god-warrior stretched out, elegant in the finest nightshirt, shaved, anointed, and powdered over the ghastly mask of pain. The grieving admirers. The incense burned in little silver dishes. Drapes drawn back, the day itself providing just the perfect golden shade: classical.

And all the while he was dictating things, coining phrases. Bons mots littered the room and piled up in the antechamber, to be collected or misremembered later. He'd used every minute of his life. Why stop now? It would be a long silence, oblivion. When one of the many who loved him rested the dying heavy kingly head on his young man's arm, Mirabeau said, "Yes, support this skull carefully, my dear. It's housed a cunning mind."

"Oh, God, you'll live," the young disciple said, crying bitter tears.

"Oh, God, I won't, and God has nothing to do with the matter. Have I taught you all nothing? If you must worship a symbol, worship the sun. Look at it, streaming through the window. What a splendid god the sun makes. I'll tell you this. If I'd lived and had the power I wanted, I would have made slaves of every one of you. You're too genuine, too spontaneous, unconsidered—dangerous. Only a skeptic like Mirabeau could have controlled you. Now you must do without me. You'll see. This thing called a Revolution is going to run away downhill. Get out of its path before it crushes you to pulp. The first to perish will be the king. Look at me, I haven't the strength anymore to raise my arm, but as I fall I shall pull the monarchy of France after me into the bottomless pit."

※

Sitting in the Café Procope, working on copy, I glanced up along with others when Mercier's secretary came in and said to the table generally, "Guess who's dying today? The king."

"Louis?" There were startled exclamations all around.

The messenger looked smug. "No, my friends. The *real* king. Riquetti-Mirabeau."

My hand moved on its own and knocked my glass over. I'd hardly touched the wine, so it spilled red all across the copy. Wine spilled too often.

"Camille's gone white. Or should I say green? Stop it, Windmill, you clash with the marble."

"Shall I get some ammoniac salts? I forgot you were in love with him."

"Shut up. Go on. Who told you?"

"All the city knows, except you hibernating hedgehogs in here. He went to the Assembly to make a speech to save the mining interests of some crook, some banker friend—"

"Lamarck."

"—swung the vote in favor, then had to be assisted to his house. Five doctors were called. Or fifteen. *Father Duchesne* says Mirabeau caught his death off a brothel-ful of duchesses."

"Bloody Hébert."

"Anyway, all this wasn't after the debate. He was at the theater, taken ill in his box—"

"Oh, so you know something too, Jean? *You* tell it, then."

"Well, I heard he was better."

Mercier's secretary resumed his eminence. "There are crowds packing the roads all up to the house. They've been going crazy at the Hôtel de Ville. The royalist lot are up in the trees screaming hurrah and wetting themselves with fear."

"Fat Louis was paying Riquetti for two years to get the monarchy off the hook, only Fat Louis can never make up his mind to follow any advice—except Bitch Austrienne's."

"Mirabeau could've been minister-in-chief months ago."

I said, "In which case the Revolution would be snugly dead."

"Watch out, Camille. Don't repeat that on the street, they'll tear you in bits. The women are already crying like a Greek tragedy, saying he was the People's only hope for peace."

"Once you're dead it's safe to make you a hero." I got up.

The whole café was piled around the table asking for the gospel over again. I went outside and stood there in the light April sunshine. I don't think I even believed it. He was clever enough it could be some kind of trick, a ploy to catch the sympathy of the mob, then rise from the sickbed and be borne in majesty anywhere he felt like going. (But I had seen him a couple of days ago at the Assembly. There had been occasions I'd watched him, sick enough, yet mounting the Tribune and giving his silver roar at us, the illness falling off him in shards. No longer. This time, illness had wrecked him. I hadn't acknowledged it as the mark of death.)

I walked about awhile. Everywhere I met people who cried, "Mirabeau's on his last legs." Somebody informed me the Revolutionaries had poisoned him. Someone else: the queen had seen to it. Up by Ninth Bridge, a crowd of women and young girls were moving in a weird procession toward the cathedral. They looked and sounded unearthly, with their tapers burning half invisible and the smoke hovering like ghosts, voices wailing like creatures from mythology. Notre Dame, since the pope had answered no in March to a constitutional clergy, was a shell of sinister discard, walls already scrawled with slogans and glass like sugar in the aisles. Nevertheless, they were going there to pray for Mirabeau, the atheist. I said aloud, "He won't thank you for that." But in the throng idling about to watch, someone heard me and glared at me, a sullen unshaven giant. I'd better save my comments for the *News*. (Besides, he might have thanked them. Love always found a response in him, perhaps only a shallow one but enough to feed the fire. I had found that.)

Finally I discovered myself close to the Chaussée d'Antin. Under the trees, huge clots of people, looking dismal, even afraid. Fools. What had he ever done for them? One lordly gesture for the Third Estate. A few magnificent speeches that hid his heart. His eyes and his voice shot lightning, and we were on our knees. Working in the pay of the Capet king. Saving the old regime. Have some more burgundy, Camille. Keep the inkstand, Camille. You're a bourgeois plebian to your soul. D'Anton's bought you. A child in a tantrum.

I pushed through the crowd and got to the wall and then up to his door. There were long shadows there already.

Finally, someone came to answer the bell. It took awhile, but it was the usual pristine lackey in satin. His face was very pale and still, and that was the moment I realized for sure it was true.

He let me in, rather uncertainly. I stood there, twisting my hat in my hands, scowling, feeling light-headed, stupid.

"Who shall I say, monsieur?"

I told him who he should say. He went off, and I turned my hat some more. Even the sheen on the floor was dull. There was an overpowering aroma of flowers and sweet things, as if he were dead already and being embalmed in Egyptian honey. I thought, What the hell am I doing here? Apparently he thought that too, for presently the servant came back and said to me, "I'm sorry, monsieur. The count is very sick. Only friends—"

"I *am* his friend," I said. "Was his—h-his friend. Gn-go back an-nd—" I stopped, humiliated, at a loss.

The servant looked at me with a polite, dehumanized compassion. It's a doll, one of Curtius' moving breathing waxworks, dressed in a court coat and set to guard the house. Of course he means to see me, and this automaton won't tell him, or else won't let me by.

It was the case; the servant was immovable. He would only show me to a book on a side table left there to be signed by visitors. With my hand shaking, I signed it and went away.

I got through the crowd again, who all clamored and pulled at my coat, asking me how he was, and it seemed I was going to strike some of them, but thank God I managed not to; it would have started a riot. I mumbled, "The same, the same," and somehow escaped. My eyes were wet, but I scarcely knew even then what I felt.

When I got back home, Lucile and Jeanette were down on the lower floor in the kitchen there, at work on some dish; I could hear swirls of circling laughter from them both. Our rooms were still at odds with our return, boxes about and an unpacked chest from Bourg-la-Reine. A pair of Lucile's "country" gloves were lying on the sofa. I picked them up and held them to my face.

Soon she came up, swathed in her apron, very proud to be mistress of the establishment, but she lost her brightness at the door. She carried a bunch of yellow daffodils. I said, "Were you putting those in the soup?" She said, "What is it?"

"Mirabeau's dying."

"Have you been there?"

"Y-yes, but they did-didn't tell him I-I'd come as a friend—or he w-w-would-wouldn't see me."

She put the flowers on the table. Drops of moisture fell from each lacy corner and starred the mahogany like a still life by the Flemish school. I watched the daffodils weep for Mirabeau. Lucile put her arms around me and laid my head against her.

I said, "He was a liar, a cheat. Hn-h-he'd have pushed the Revolution in-into the gutter, b-buried it al-alive. And I was to have helped. But I was too m-much of a fool to nd-understand what I was sup-posed to do."

Outside there didn't seem to be, as yet, any lamentation in the Cordeliers district. Carts crackled across the stones, someone was singing, a dog yowling, and Saint-Sulpice ringing a gentle two-tongued four o'clock over the roofs.

Beyond the windows, pigeons were investigating the flower pots inside the twisted-iron balcony cages, including those Lucile had placed there yesterday inside ours.

"I kn-know how it will be," I said. "Eulogies. They—they'll all turn on like fountains and sh-shower his name with gd-gold. Jupiter, slinger of div-divine thun-under. S-sa-vior of the People."

The carts jumped along the cobbles. The dog began to bark. The pigeons flew up in the air.

I said, "I love you. I'm all right. Let go of me and mop the table."

It had been daffodils I'd smelled in the perfumery reek of his house. The embalming honey had yet to come from all those votive offerings of the journals. Even René Hébert would alter his tune.

That evening d'Anton came over with Gabi and the huge Herculean baby named Antoine d'Anton. As Gabi sat down with Lucile and the child, d'Anton said to me, "He won't get through the night."

"So I heard."

"No tears? Everywhere I've been, they're in mourning."

"Naturally."

"You've decided to play the woman spurned, have you? Listen, Camille, take my word for it. This once toe the line."

"Which line? Yours?"

"There'll be a funeral like the burial of Achilles. Recall, he had the Presidency of the Assembly two months ago and impressed the hell out of everybody. You included. They'll be throwing effusions on the coffin lid like bouquets."

"I'll stay at home."

"That's what Pétion says. He won't. But you'll stay home to write a nice funerary notice."

"To write, certainly."

"He was a great man, Mirabeau. If he'd been called Capet and had the throne of France, none of this crap would be going on now."

"Which would have left *you* out in the bloody c-cold."

D'Anton shrugged. "All right. But don't say I didn't warn you."

"His eyes are as blue as his father's!" exclaimed Gabi joyously. D'Anton looked at his wife fondly and then at mine, with open uncomplex lust. Last, he looked back at me and shook his lion's head, the mane tonight unpowdered. "You were too long taking it easy in that rural retreat of yours. I know. I go off to the home province now and then, even if the house is falling apart. . . ." (He'd bought some land recently. This was his way of saying, You see, I really *had* to—not acquisition, only maintenance.) "But you come back, and the real world strikes you in the belly. It's a damnable nuisance, this Mirabeau affair. They're sure to close the theaters, and there's an actress I've got my eye out for." He rambled on. All the time, his gaze was sharp and burning on me. It was a gambit of his: say one thing, think another. Studying me. Trying to make me out or see how to alter my intention.

When they were leaving, with a fellow to escort them two streets' distance with a torch and cudgel (all show—d'Anton could see in the dark and kill with a kick), he thrust me back in at the door and said in my ear, "Well, give her one for me." "Go to hell." "And you, go to the funeral. Then pen something to make us all cry over him."

I woke up in the night to Lucile saying, "You were shouting out loud."

I said, after I lit the candles, "Mirabeau's dead. I loved him; which makes no difference."

But I suppose I did go to the funeral.

❀

The passing of a god is marked by fire in heaven, and fire there was. A crimson sky, with a core of throbbing molten light far broader than the wound of the sun's death. It lay over all Paris, from the southern tops of Montparnasse to the sable heights of Montmartre in the north. The west was drowned in it. Only eastward did the color mitigate, first to claret, next to the red of dying carnations, eventually into mourning darkness. ("Look at the sky." Just as Mirabeau would have wished it.)

As the coffin came from Saint-Eustache, men reached up and dipped their brands in the flaming air. The sunset fell in the streets of the city, burning there on the heads of the torches.

Dead-as-the-dead slow, the marching procession.

The brass instruments of a mighty band, shearing off scalding gleams of afterglow, released the pent groans and clashes of a dead march.

The draped box, on its litter, was carried by relays of soldiers. A constantly igniting flash of drawn swords: tall La Fayette, leading his National Guard along in slow motion. Every funeral should have a handsome La Fayette. But the procession was three miles long; they were all out tonight. The Assembly, the collective judiciary of City Hall, Jacobins, Feuillants, Cordeliers, nonaffiliates. And every man in black. Under the red tumult of sky, moving between the darkening houses, in whose crowded apertures the lamps had been put out, forward into the mouth of night.

When the relays replaced each other to take up the heavy cadaver, there would be a pause.

Those at the wayside craned from doorways, windows, roofs. *Look, look.* This was the last time they'd see Mirabeau. Mirabeau who had cared about them and fought for them. Oh, the tears rained down. *Pleuvoir et pleurer.* The men who walked behind the coffin were weeping. The women wept from their balconies. The children wept, because the adults did. One day they would be able to say, I cried at Mirabeau's funeral. Providing, of course, they themselves lived to grow up.

They were taking him to the Geneviève, which was to be his Panthéon. The People would come there to lay flowers on the sepulcher. And more—a fire should burn there, never let go out, tended by young girls, pretty, with long fine hair. He would like that.

The banker Lamarck was in the procession, the one he'd saved almost with his last breath. Lamarck leaned on a friend, sobbing. Sometimes he would turn to those who shed their tears along the route. "Yes, lament. We don't know yet what we've lost. It's finished, gone with him." And such a dismal howl of grief would go up, even the dead march failed to contain it.

And there, too, was Danton, walking with his shaggy head bowed, black-clad like the rest. The day after Mirabeau's death, the entire Jacobin Club had stood, to demonstrate its respect. Then one by one, a bevy of the deceased's most savage detractors had stepped forward to speak of his virtues. Danton joined the praise-singing. (Also using the opportunity of his platform to throw a few more cats among a few more pigeons.)

Those who now beheld the enormous walking tower of Danton felt a flicker of interest amid their mass depression. That one so big could be so grave. Capable of making such a lot of noise, stirring up so much dust; to see this robe of quiet and massive dignity upon him was awe-inspiring. There had used to be a saying: *Le roi est mort. Vive le roi.*

Behind the domed temple that was to enshrine Mirabeau, the night was now completely formed and very black.

Where is the light? Only the torches now, to keep faith, and the torches have grown pale and venomous and twisting, like snakes' tongues. The faces of men, seen by this flare, look desperate or sickened: plague faces marked for terminus, as all faces are. Fire has many forms and images. It does not always summon the illusion of splendor, festival, or the domestic memory of hearthside—leaping flames suggest, too, subterranean places, tortures, the pillage of a metropolis, hell.

The band offers its last crescendo. Midnight strikes in the sky and slams a door into silence. Rather awkwardly, the coffin is taken up and maneuvered into the hollow stone temple of the night-pierced windows.

Men stand at attention. Almost static, but there is a wind blowing, frisking hair and clothes. And the fire wings ripple on the torches, and the lines of fire on the cheeks of men, which are the tracks of tears. And eyes move too, even sharp attentive dry ones, like those of Georges-Jacques Danton.

They had spoken aloud to his glory, even the opponents of Mirabeau. Now Paris wrote him odes. Poems to Mirabeau the father, the leader, were printed and sold at nearly every corner. Even the Chéniers joined in. The journals went to press with tears mixed in the ink. Rage throughout the royalist issues—he had been worn to death by the sniping of the Revolutionaries. The revolutionary papers meanwhile accused the royalists of misleading and muddying his endeavors, exhausting him by their petty spites. Everyone suggested statues might be put up to him. Several recommended his bust be placed in the Assembly and at the Jacobins, an invocation of a guiding spirit. Mirabeau the genius, a true lover of France.

Yes, the honey flowed. It flowed from almost every pen and press in the city. Except one.

There on the flower heap, a single searing flung clod of dung.

It was *The Revolutionary News,* which said:

Go then, you fools who can judge nothing, you nation bought by cheap words and bribed by golden ones: Fling yourselves on your faces before the tomb of this man of honor. He was your god. Yes. Mercury, the patron of orators, whores, liars, and thieves!

(And actually, Monsieur Desmoulins, also of writers.)

❋

You see, I was getting used to it. The guardsmen who promised to cut me in half with their sabers, the plotters who brought lengths of rope into the Palais-Royal and laid them out at nearby tables. The ominous lack of noise on entering some bookshop or café. With it all, there I was, unharmed. I'd been threatened, lawsuited, spat at, drawn on, and received a quantity of abusive letters which Jeanette found excellent for starting the fire. But to myself? Nothing, after all, had happened. I learned thereby an invaluable lesson. Camille could get away with anything. And once you have learned that? Those whom the gods wish to punish, they first deceive into supposing themselves invulnerable.

Indeed, as days went by, various ruffians would approach me and say, "Ah, *you* saw through the bastard, Camille. You and Marat, they can't pull the wool over *your* eyes." In fact, Marat—who the People loved to insanity—was hounded more vigorously than I. In the matter of Mirabeau, too, he had been violent but late. Marat's literary motto was (and we all knew it), Give me a name and I'll finish the beggar. This applied to rich and poor, aristo and bourgeois, army, civilian—he hated us all in equal measure. I think he hated himself, the world, everything, but had come to it tardily, this exciting hater's passion. When you showed the feeling was mutual, he reveled in it, like a lover. The mob, which he let make free of his verminous domestic styes, knew he would work thoroughly on its behalf. But the People's Friend—he and his paper were now synonymous—would only aid one side in order to have the leverage whereby to leap for the throat of the other. D'Anton, who courted him in public, called him, for his underground adventures, and since the *T* had been added to his Swiss name, "The Sewer RaT."

Nevertheless, he was pure gold on the street, and to have my name consistently marshaled with his meant something. Particularly here, where I had, for once, sprung sooner than he.

Well, well. Desmoulins: The one honest writer in Paris.

I'd been determined not to join the crowd fawning on Mirabeau's corpse. I'd castigated him as abrasively after death as before it. He had hated my censure, I suppose quite rightly, if he reckoned he'd bought my connivance. Once he had sent his servant with some out-of-season fruit. The message said I would be doing him a great service if I withheld such and such a comment he knew I was about to make. But I withheld none of it, and the fruit, which would have choked me by then, went rotten in its basket. Now he couldn't ask and couldn't answer. But somebody must speak. Death doesn't wipe out all blame or alter a man's character like the turning of a page. Men who had called him traitor two months earlier, who had loathed the very syllables of his name, had stood up before France and said fine and gracious things of Mirabeau. I'd loved him, and I hurled the mud.

I wonder how much of my truth-telling and my defiance was only that love, gone rotten as the fruit he had once sent me. I wonder – how can I help it? – if he had seen me that day when he was dying, let me go in to him and kneel by him like all the rest of them who were his friends. . . . *For all your fireworks,* he wrote to me, *you deserve to be loved.* But he turned me away like a jackal that had come scratching at his deathbed's door. And like a jackal I ran out into the desert and set up a raw loud mocking sound. . . . Maybe I judge myself too harshly. But why not? How else did I judge others from the unassailable height of my brave bold verity, wielding that paper sword the *Revolutionary News?*

Well, Mirabeau. You were a great man, with all the merits that I lacked, including an unfaltering and magnificent voice, including the ability to act a powerful rage and hold a powerful rage in check. If you'd gone on, you could have won your war, made slaves of us all, halted the rolling bloody wheel of Revolution. A dictator in the end, perhaps; at least a sane one. But we lost you. Yes, Olympian Jupiter, you outstripped us all, outshone us all. Nothing glorious they said of you, those enemies over your body, none of it was false. They didn't praise you enough. I add my voice, when no one can any longer hear me. It doesn't matter what I say – drape purple; let the trumpets cry – I'll praise you now with all my heart. I give you back your rose. Take it. The dew on it will be my blood.

At least, you died with an actor's style, there in that ocean of scent and flowers and lamenting love. You said your last words clearly, all the scores of them, and saw faithful scribes record them for history. And when you drank the opiate, and slept, and woke to revile pain like an enemy, bravely, and died with dignity, your final vision of yourself was something to be proud of. But there are other ways. We don't all have your damnable flair for the perfect exit, my Mirabeau, uncrowned king and atheistic god.

✤

It's a terrible thing, being religious. Take Capet now; he can't accept Communion from one of the People's priests, not since old pope-face decided only the priest who keeps loyalty to Rome is worth anything. So L'oui got this popery priest in, and they all ate God in the Tuileries. Then what happens? You might well ask. Yes-Yes and Austrianette and the royal sister-in-law and the kids all decide they'll go off to Saint-Cloud to have a pious Easter. And, of course, who's to swear they'll stop at Saint-Cloud? They'll be off and over the border and into Austria's arms before you can say *Resurgat*.

Now you've got to understand, I've got nothing against the monarchy. It's very pretty. But Austrian sabers are something else.

Anyhow. April 18, there are the royal carriages all ready to set off, and there La Fayette is, waving his sword about, and all these battalions of National Guard ready to escort Their Majesties. Only La Fayette screwed up. He's called in, as part of the deal, the battalion from the Cordeliers district. Oh, boy. Well, I ask you. All I say is, La Fayette must've been brighter when he was in America.

So there's Danton roaring away, Nuts to Saint-Cloud, nobody's going anywhere except straight back in the Tuileries. And there's La Fayette going white in the face for Danton's red, and Antoinette turning blue with funk and fury, so the three of them make up the tricolor really nicely. The Dauphin's bawling (well, he would), and the crowd is throwing flowers at the guard and invective at the royal carriages, and in the end the whole expedition gives over and does what Danton said. As the queen flounces up the steps, she remarks to us, "Well, nobody can say we've got any freedom now."

Which, thinking it over as I chew my crust (and she gets through her *poule* and pastry), I reckon may be true.

Then again, with La Fayette supposed to be guarding the Tuileries, Watch out! is what *I* say.

✤

The pope's cold return had split France, but the split was mostly obvious out in the wilds, where, between listening for the tramp of invading armies and trying to till the soil occasionally, certain villages still sheltered their orthodox popish priests. In Paris the sophisticate, for the most part the priests who clung to Rome were not popular.

The theaters were showing religious plays. The subjects were twofold. One, bawdy: the naughty nun, the well-endowed bishop with an itch. Two, historical: the Inquisition. This is what the priesthood does, you see. It uses the cover of the cloth to fornicate itself silly, or it tortures you to death in the name of the one true God. Ouch.

Slogans scrawled on church walls. THE POPE IS A — The pope burning on two hundred bonfires.

Into the Papal Nuncio's carriage someone tosses a head. (Whose?) Oh, it was a pig's head, and they'd put a wig on it. No, it was the head of a priest, died in the hospital. Or wasn't it a wax head, one of Curtius' rivals made it — very lifelike. Anyway, it gave the Papal Nuncio a nasty turn.

At a few churches, persons broke in and insisted the organ play the *Ça Ira* very loudly.

Meanwhile, Louis Capet was in a religious dilemma. (I would point out that the pious among us have frequently been our kings. Kings have something to be pious about.) But Louis? He protested at the Assembly about being prevented from visiting Saint-Cloud. And they told him Hard luck, there's a Revolution going on.

What did they say to each other, the king and his wife?

"We must leave. I told you before."

"Yes, well. . . ."

Not only the mice and beetles creeping and whispering at the Tuileries now. Spies everywhere. Plots everywhere.

There's this tall handsome Swede, for instance, been *her* fancy-man for years, rolling in money and just bought a very large carriage.

They're going tonight. No, it's tomorrow morning. I tell you, it's tonight. Actually, it's next Wednesday. Or Saturday. Or June 20.

June: Le deuxième burlesque

Coming out of the Jacobin Club about ten-thirty, the last blue drifts of last dark light still webbed high in the sky: the streets were so quiescent that when the patrol of National Guardsmen went by, the whole city seemed to echo at their tread.

"It's quiet this evening."

"Yes, Camille. All the virtuous citizens are in bed ensuring the future generations of Paris." D'Anton looked up at heaven. For him, nobody at all was up there. He drew in a deep breath, as if to drag the sky into his lungs.

"I meant, that's the only patrol which seems to be about."

They stood and looked around them.

"Come and have something to drink," said d'Anton. "The night's so sweetly corruptibly young."

They had been involved for hours in endless public vituperative discussion concerning the legislative reelection of the National Assembly next autumn. The problem being a restriction on voters to those who paid the tax equivalent to one silver mark. The Jacobin debate was, as the Jacobin debates were so often, a continuation and extension of the Assembly's own debate. The Theater-of-France section, ably represented by d'Anton in vocal gunpowder and Camille in incendiary ink, was up in arms against that tax restriction. Today, a petition had been presented at the Stable. "And they'll take as much notice of it as of some gnat. Swat the thing out the window," Fréron averred. He had not written the petition.

They walked on. Presently, Windmill said, "Three more patrols should have passed us by now. What's the matter with Kiddy-Blond?" He looked over his shoulder at the invisible Tuileries. "I suppose it isn't tonight Fatty's going to give us all the slip?"

"Who'd have thought," said d'Anton, "they'd have named that church for your little editor."

"Wh-at?"

"He means Saint-Roch," said Fréron moodily.

They stared at d'Anton, who showed evidence of wanting to step aside into a courtyard, where the somber yellow glow of an establishment beckoned.

"D'Anton," said Windmill. "Wait a minute."

"As the actress said desperately to her incompetent lover."

"*D'Anton.*"

"Yes?"

"You know," said Louis-Mer. "Because I showed it you—that letter I had, warning me about a possible attempt at escape tonight."

"Escape?" D'Anton was mystified. "Who is a prisoner that he should wish to escape?"

"So you want to ignore it?"

"Dear Fréron, we've all had so many letters recently saying old Fatty's about to take off. On a winged horse. In a balloon. By tunneling under the walls. Or the Roman bishop is sending God over to lift him up through the roof." Regretfully, he walked beyond the enticing lamps. "No. Let's stop speculating and get home to bed." He was ahead of them now.

"What's he playing at?" said Louis-Mer.

"Well, it's true. We've all had these letters."

"This feels different. And *he's* up to something."

Windmill shrugged. After the irritant of the debate, Fréron was also irritating him.

"How do I know? I'm not h-his confessor."

"That's not what I heard."

"So what do you hear?"

"You're in each other's pockets. In more ways than one."

D'Anton strolled, a great lion under the lights, casting a gigantic shadow onto housefronts. Fréron and Windmill faced each other.

"Which means?"

"God knows. Gabi and Lucile sit at home and embroider, and you two are out at all the theaters . . . said the actress. Well, I'm sure the pair of you take care to please."

"Jn-jackass."

"Added to which, the common talk is you go back and call Lucile to strip naked for him and you watch while they—"

Camille's open hand caught him across the face. Fréron made a spluttering, growling noise, then struck out in return. D'Anton had turned at the ring of the first slap. He beheld the two men struggling untidily and violently and came over, pulling them off each other with casual brute force.

Fréron fell back against a wall, breathing noisily, head down, like a big cat lashing its tail. Camille hurled five or six incoherent words at him and d'Anton pushed him in turn out of Fréron's reach.

Aside from the obscenities, nothing more was said. The two quarrelers breathed and glared. D'Anton watched them, noncommittal. Presently Louis-Mer straightened up, straightened his coat, turned, and walked off toward the markets. Equally silent, D'Anton and Windmill turned toward the Pont Neuf.

Under the bridge the river rocked like ink, enough ink to feed the inkwells of every pamphleteer in Paris. D'Anton tended to pause on bridges. He paused now, and Camille waited for some query or comment. Nothing.

They walked, two dumb people, off the bridge onto the left bank, footsteps loud. Sometimes a vague noise came from some house or hotel; otherwise the city was like a tomb. Windmill bit his nails. They got to d'Anton's corner.

"Well. And good night."

Camille mumbled good night. D'Anton walked off, his lazy powerful stride taking him miles away in three seconds. Suddenly Windmill shook himself. He ran after d'Anton and caught up.

"Wait!"

"All right. I'm waiting."

"What *are* you up to?"

"Me? Nothing."

"But what are you going to do?"

"Go in. Wake Gabi and kiss her a bit. Then we'll see how tired I am."

"D'Anton, for God's sake—"

"Calm down. Fréron's a tiger that's sat in the fire. And you talk too much about your wife. You say to them all, Look at her; she's so beautiful; her skin's so white. You take her to bed and wake the whole bloody street up. It gives them ideas. What do you expect? To hell with the lot of 'em. What does it matter? Have a good time."

Camille reeled away from him. "Th-that's not-not—"

"The king's plans to get out of Paris? Wait and see."

"W-wait and see *what?*"

"I wonder."

D'Anton left Windmill standing, physically and mentally, and went ambling on along the street, the monstrous swimming steps devouring yards at a time.

❧

Roch-Marcandier, for whom Saint-Roch by the Saint-Honoré road had most definitely not been named, had appeared at the printers one May morning, fresh off a coach, with a box and a bag and a wild unslept look. Guillaume Brune, who was in the middle of printing a relay of the *News,* and Camille, who was idling about with the galleys, half deciding to rewrite something and call for a resetting (in other words, an argument), had looked up.

"Citizen Desmoulins," declared Roch-Marcandier, "I'm here to serve you."

"It's a waiter," said Windmill.

"Coffee," said Fréron, who had also been in the shop, not to be outdone. "Make sure it's hot."

Roch-Marcandier, small, slight, with very black hair and a preying falcon's beak, went scarlet. A fellow Guisard, he had Camille's own flailing ability to lose his temper.

"I didn't come here to be laughed at."

"Shall we all go somewhere else and do it?"

"I wrote to you—I've spoken to your father—I wrote to you in January."

"Aah," said Camille.

"You didn't answer."

"Oh, dear."

"But I came to Paris. I don't think you'll turn me away. I have a testimonial here—"

"What do you think I'm running? Some sort of army?"

"Exactly," said Marcandier.

Windmill blinked. He looked across at Brune. "Gui, I want this first page reset."

"Why, what's wrong with it?"

"There's something needs to go in."

"No, Camille. Not again. You can't pay for it, or you don't, and I've got a further two commissions here. It'll take me all night as it is."

Roch-Marcandier came across the floor like a little red and black fighting cock. He seized Brune's large arm and shook it. "This man is one of the foremost writers in France!" he shouted, pointing at Camille as if to skewer him with a finger's end. "Don't you know? He's done more for his country with a pen than the pack of them with their debates and marches and so-called laws. If he says reset—*reset* it!"

Brune retrieved his arm. He laughed uneasily, looking down on the fanatic bantam as if it might flap up and take a peck at his eyes.

"Someone's on your side, Windmill."

"Windmill!" wailed Marcandier. "How can you joke about this man? His family name is an honorable one! Very well, he insults me; I'll put up with it. But the rest of you—you'd better do what he says."

Fréron had gazed blankly. Brune looked at Camille.

Camille got up and walked to the door. Marcandier's black furious eyes irresistibly followed him. As if whistling a dog, experimentally, Camille said, "All right. Leave your luggage there. Since you didn't bring the coffee we'll go and get some." And as Marcandier rushed immediately after him, Camille swung into the street, saying, "And how's my father these days?"

Hero-worshiping Marcandier. (It would seem I'm his Mirabeau.) He did what Camille told him. Sometimes he flew off the handle and became the resident clown (which makes a nice change from its being myself). But he had sharp eyes for printers' errors and neat spiky small handwriting with which to answer the more pressing letters piled up to the ceiling on desk corners. He was efficient even when ruffled. He'd come a long way on the off-chance. Camille took him up teasingly and loaded work on him: My editor.

The editor was now running up the stone stair of No. 1 rue de Théâtre Français, his revolutionary bootheels making a clatter. It was half past seven in the morning on June 21. Jeanette, the Desmoulins's domestic treasure, opened the door in a cowlike morning mood. Marcandier burst past her, screaming for Camille. Jeanette squealed. Neighbors from other floors came cursing and quavering onto the landings.

Camille, who had been shaving, walked into his study with the razor still in his hand as if for a purpose. His chin was bleeding because he had just begun work on it when Marcandier hit the front door.

"What the hell's the matter?"

"*He's gone!*"

"Oh, Christ," said Windmill, knowing just who Marcandier meant.

He wasn't aware a similar scene was taking place over at d'Anton's rooms, where Fabre d'Églantine and a couple of others had gone rushing, not to read aloud a piece of verse but to announce Louis XVI had fled, complete with all the family and some spectacular family heirlooms.

❈

"They used the Swede's carriage. Disguised themselves. Got through with fake passports the Swede had made for them. They're halfway to Austria by now."

"And where was bloody La Fayette while all this was happening?"

Wherever he had been, bloody La Fayette was now much in evidence. Clad in full uniform, he had braved the savage crowds, gone to consult the mayor, and sent out National Guard in all directions to intercept the royal party, who had plainly been abducted by enemies of the Revolution.

Eh?

He says somebody took them. They didn't want to leave, you see, they like it here so much; and they like the Revolution so much, they wanted to stay and enjoy it. But someone's kidnapped 'em.

Who?

Better ask La Fayette. He wrote it, not me.

All over Paris, the tocsin was clanging from every bell tower.

At nine in the morning, the Assembly met in chaos.

At the Cordeliers, Danton stood up and said, "Well, we trusted them, and you see what's happened. Doesn't this prove it? A hereditary monarchy is a hereditary stone around our necks. Let's get rid of the thing. Out with the king, in with the Republic." Zoolike noises of agreement. The vote is passed. By midnight the streets will be placarded, all the walls changing color (again), a poster asking for the People's sanction on this drastic, inevitable move— because it's what the People wants that counts, isn't it?

"And La Fayette's beautifully in the shit," said Danton to Windmill, over by the Hôtel de Ville.

"So that's what you were up to," said Windmill.

"Don't look so scared. What do you think is going to happen but the great reshuffle we've been panting for?"

"If Capet gets to—"

"What makes you think they'll get anywhere?" said Danton. The crowd pressed close, patting him, wringing his hand: *You tell 'em, Danton.* "Oh, I will, brother. I will." *Life to Danton!* "Thank you. Too kind."

"You were saying, What made me think they'd get anywhere."

"The point is, you and I have both been prophesying the king would run off if he could. Now he has. It's the finish for him and the finish for the supporters' club that's been holding him up. The court party is now—" Danton made a sign indicating what the court party now was.

"And you're so sure."

"One hears a few things in the circles I frequent: the king's law benches, certain back rooms. . . . What a charming flower, you pretty girl, thank you. And can I have a kiss to go with it?"

⚜

Robespierre looked ghastly. He'd been ill again, with all the fuss that entailed, his sister muscling in, shriek-voiced Charlotte. Now he was up and about in time to find Paris standing once more firmly on its ear.

He and d'Anton shook hands gravely in the Jacobin refectory. I couldn't hear what they were saying. Someone was speaking to me and congratulating me on my clear predictions. I could see Saint-Just, a pale shadow balanced behind Robespierre's right shoulder. Attentively waiting to catch him if he tottered, or just to give Maxime's shining shoes another lick. Truant from Picardy again.

I'd disliked Saint-Just from the moment I'd formally met him. To say the hideous Camille resented this one's sugary looks is foolish, though I've heard it said, along with a few other choice comments. Why then was I ever a friend to Hérault, who they claimed was so handsome women fought to get a piece of his hair? It's all rubbish. No jealousy, either, though the bastard may have been jealous of *me;* I'd known his Maxime since childhood. Or thought I had.

I got the impression now d'Anton and Robespierre were discussing something they had discussed earlier and not very long ago. But with the dry tinderbox feel of the city as it had been all day, and the ringing bells driving you mad, my own nervous excitement made me a poor judge of almost everything. D'Anton was hardly reassuring. I'd followed him, arch plotter in the cabbage patch, about like a dog, reading more into each thing he said, storing up his advice anxiously, and drinking the way I hadn't been drinking for five months, not noticing.

Into the middle of it all had come Fréron, declaring that after he left us the previous night (one way of putting it) he had seen La Fayette go toward the palace in a torch-lit carriage—complicity on complicity. When the shouting had died down he came roughly up to me and said, "Will you accept an apology or shouldn't I bother to give one?" "Don't bother to give one." He looked at the wine in my hand disdainfully. "Did you repeat it all to her?" "Her? You mean my wife? Why tell her, when she's already Georges's whore?" Someone came to drag him off and retell the La Fayette story—if it was true. Fréron tended to capitalize. He went, bending to the last a fishy stare on me. I still needed him to get the paper out, and he knew it. It would have to be smoothed over somehow. Poor devil, he was gnawed in half by wanting. If I loaned my wife to my friends, he too could cool his ardor—I drank the wine in a gulp to stop myself from going after to strangle him.

Now at the Jacobins, the meeting was called to order and its minutes got through somehow in a furor of impatience. Tonight it was going to be nearly as noisy and lacking in protocol as anything we Cordeliers could put on.

D'Anton had shoved me into a seat and sat down next to me as if to keep me there. It was a fact; I had a sensation Paris might be burning outside and in here we wouldn't find out until the flames filled the windows. "Are you going to speak?" I said to him several times. "Maybe." They were all yodeling away, calling Fat Louis the more elegant bad names. Any minute we'd have an Austrian invasion—alarum! Treachery! Get the Republic on the road! D'Anton only looked complacent, as if he had thought some of it up, which meant he must have a connection to the court I'd never known about—though of course, he'd told me, had he not? Everyone pays *me.*

"Well, *are* you going to speak?"

"Yes, yes, Camille, there, there. Hush-a-bye."

It was all so formless I was getting very angry with it, nerving my legs and my vocal cords to take the floor myself and speak. Then Robespierre walked out and asked for a hearing, and he got it.

I had heard him speak before, of course, here and at the Assembly. I hadn't paid a great deal of attention. Well, I had looked at him but not seen him, I suppose. For all the motions he put forward, I don't think one had ever been passed. There was an odd quality he seemed to have, standing there, Petit Pierre, not apologetic exactly, but—what? Somehow essentially *small*. You thought, Behold the exact example of one who has no authority. It's just some little crib who theorizes a lot, getting up and saying the death penalty should be abolished (he was very concerned it should be) or that somebody had gone too far or not far enough. Or the windows ought to be opened. (He had actually proposed that once, at the Stable, and brought the house down laughing. It was a hot day. Now I come to think of it, they didn't take any notice of that, either, until women started fainting in the public gallery.)

So now there he stood, strutting a bit, which he inclined to do, from one neat dancing-master's foot to the other, in the bright shoes Louis Saint-Just had licked for him.

Oh, it's only Maximilien going to give us a lecture. They'll put up with him. Former president, et cetera—I can rest my eyes a moment. (The candle flames are jumping even when they stay still.)

Then he started to speak. He never had a big voice, Rosepeter, but he must have had the measure of the refectory acoustics by then. All right, I'll listen. He'll want it reported in the *News* tomorrow. He gets so damned upset if you don't report what he says. And he saved my skin once, to be honest. When Malouet had me on his line.

"Why are you so afraid?" Robespierre said. "You talk as if this is a tragedy. But the flight of the Nation's chief *servant* is hardly, I would say, a disaster. Invasion is *not* imminent. Europe is a disunited body which, if it comes precariously together to attack France, will just as precariously discover itself defeated."

I opened my eyes. No invasion. . . . He's in on it, then, whatever it is. Is he?

I stared at Robespierre. The wine had got at my eyes, and it was this, I presume, which made the summer darkness hang around the edges of the hall like curtains, but slice off from the candles in a white blur where the speaker poised, his feet on the tombstones. His voice was strong tonight. He was speaking well. The illness must have done him good.

His pallor appeared incandescent, and as usual the spectacles he wore were pushed idiotically up on his forehead, giving him two sets of eyes, one set transparent, one opaque.

"Actually, the citizen Capet has done us all a great service. I think you understand what it is, though no one yet has had the temerity to mention it aloud. I will mention it. My life is at the service of France and otherwise meaningless. My life is the only sword I can offer her."

He turned and looked at all of us. Half blind as he was, he couldn't see anyone. And yet the flaming blank gaze seemed to go around the hall like a knife. By not seeing our faces, he somehow seemed to look into our thoughts.

When he looked at me, the hair rose on my neck. What had got into him? He was taller. When he lifted his hand, I felt the room rise up with it, as if he drew the air. The last one I saw could do that was . . . was *Mirabeau*. What's got into him?

"The National Assembly," said Robespierre, and suddenly that shallow voice of his was deep with passion, so again the hair stirred on my body, "our Nation's representatives — of whose number I make one — is rotten to its core. Yes, rotten. This is what Capet has shown us by running away. For how else could he have contrived it? There are traitors everywhere, in absolute collusion with the monarchy. No, not merely these bought men, of whom we hear so much. Our Judases we have, and to spare. But also, the Nation is betrayed by a tribe of Simon Peters thirty times over before each cockcrow. Those men who let us down through fear, ignorance, envy, wounded pride. There are even those who sell France by their blind optimism, which refuses to acknowledge the pit at our feet."

There was a sound through the hall. You hear it sometimes — a murmur stirred and unable to keep quiet, but somehow never wanting to get loud enough to drown the orator. He had them, mastered them. Little Robespierre. Not because he was in some game of d'Anton's. This power of Maxime's was unique.

"Yes, then. I'm accusing almost the whole of the National Assembly. I *will* stand here and I *will* say it. And yes, I can detect the rasp of daggers being sharpened. Very well. Let me be the sacrifice. I know what fate lies in store for those of us who speak the truth."

Across the room he gazed at me again. He couldn't see me — but he did see me. How could he not, when he was saying what I had said?

There was all the strength in the world in his face. I remembered how he had looked in the gardens of the Luxembourg, poor wretched Maxime telling me how he couldn't eat anything and how exhausted he was, let down by his own physical weakness. And that sudden steely light which rose behind his face and changed it. It was there now. He seemed possessed. No, not by any sort of demon or god, but by some inner blazing thing which was *himself*. All at once you saw what Robespierre was. And the studious gray child, the tremblingly pedantic little man with the lace ruffles and the hair powder — he had gone. *This* was Robespierre. A formless shining fire, shaped to the confines of a man and breaking him in fragments to get free.

He spread his hands. It was a very simple gesture, of calm resignation. He said softly, but the vaulted roof took the words and passed them down to us like feathers, as if he spoke to each man privately, "I may die tonight. That means nothing. To die for liberty. I ask no more."

I was on my feet before I knew it, and shouting to him, "You're not alone! I'm with you!" Or something of that nature.

The whole hall-ful, on my lead, was springing up and shouting, swearing to stand by him. He stood there and smiled at us with a sort of still joy.

This man looks like a saint.

There was a perfect clarity to him, a cleanness; you could see right through him—not a smudge or stain—to the utter purity of mind and heart. And he smiled at me.

Something broke the spell. D'Anton grunting.

"Bravo, Camille. And I never even prompted you." And then he was past me, plunging down to the floor, embracing Robespierre, lifting him off his feet. "If they threaten you," he bellowed, and the roof cracked under the cannonade, "you've got eight hundred men here ready to die in your defense."

The benches roared. D'Anton showed Robespierre off to them, turning him around like a doll or something he, d'Anton, had just invented. He took all the credit for Robespierre.

I sat down stunned and dizzy, put my hand over my face, and found I was trying not to laugh.

Having got the floor, d'Anton was now in full operatic cadenza. He had, of course, automatically retained all Maxime's speech and was redelivering most of it with gilded knobs on. (He had another phrase for it.)

I leaned back on the bench. I was grinning stupidly, nor was I alone.

"These traitors!" d'Anton thundered.

"Names!" someone demanded. Everyone, inappropriately, catcalled and guffawed.

"Names? You want names, do you? No, you want the flesh. You want heads. I swear, if one of those devils shows his face here tonight, I'll give him *names*."

"One of them *is* here, Georges d'Anton!" somebody else yelled out. "Look behind you."

We all looked. Theater. There in the door stood La Fayette.

This is going to be interesting. What is the dolt *doing* here? The obvious answer was, someone had invited him. He had been dashing around Paris all day on foot so the mob could see that he, in his unsmirched honor and innocence, wasn't afraid. Perhaps this appearance was a similar venturesome ploy. The Jacobins were influential and dangerous. On the other hand, the somebody who invited La Fayette must also have promised La Fayette that, if he looked in, a friend would speak up for him.

D'Anton moved slowly and heavily. He regarded La Fayette as if he had found the man in his soup. D'Anton said, cat's-paw tone, the huge voice furred by velvet, "As God's my judge, I'm very glad to see Monsieur La Fayette. There are a couple of things I'd like to say to him."

The commander of the National Guard stared at d'Anton in a sort of frozen horror. This, patently, hadn't been what he expected. Had d'Anton been bought and decided to renege? Or had d'Anton himself paid to have La Fayette misled into arriving here? Whatever it was, d'Anton began a recital of every suspect antipopular thing La Fayette had ever attempted, tearing the aristo limb from bleeding limb. When he had scattered portions of him all over the club, lawyerly, d'Anton summed up.

"You swore the king was safe in the Tuileries and couldn't get by you. You went surety for him. So one of two things is a fact. Either you're a liar who betrayed us all, or else you're an incompetent blithering twit. Well, speak up, sir, which is it?"

La Fayette could find nothing to say to this delectable choice of personas.

The Feuillant deputy who'd come in with him shouted after d'Anton, who was now coming back to the benches, "I myself have criticized La Fayette harshly, no one can deny it. But I'll say this: I maintain utter faith in his patriotism. I'll take an oath he'd rather die than allow counterrevolution. Even Georges d'Anton knows I've said this."

D'Anton halfway back to his seat by me, reversed and looked at the Feuillant, de Lameth, one long amused look. Gentle as thick syrup, and with a most specific menace, d'Anton said, "It's perfectly true Monsieur de Lameth has so expressed himself, on several occasions." Which shut de Lameth up like a gag.

D'Anton thudded into place beside me, and the whole bench shook.

La Fayette had found something to declare after all. He said, "I came here because I know freedom of speech is respected here, and no good citizen need be afraid under your eyes. You remember my record. I believe any people will be free when they wish to be so. Presently they seem unstoppable."

"Watch him go down," said d'Anton to me.

I needed some more wine, and to get rid of the last lot.

❦

A day after, when the capital was still waiting for news of L'oui, the Austrians, and so on, Orléans turned up at the Jacobins to be admired, in case we might be considering a regency. Thereupon, d'Anton gave a phenomenal display of having been bribed by everyone to do everything, and more or less doing it. One had the impression with him that he loved the game as much as the pay. And then again, so many of them told me he was bought, and so many of them told me I'd been bought, I'd taken to carrying around a large mental salt cellar. Aside from anything else, as I'd said, d'Anton got things done, woke things up. A walking powder keg. You could no longer envisage the Revolution without him.

Robespierre surprised me again too. In the middle of the old republic debate he suddenly inquired, "Precisely, what *is* a republic?" Either a very clever or a very sportive question. It was hard to believe this fiddling little figure was the one we'd all vowed to die defending the previous evening. Then, I'd said, at home, "Tonight the god came and spoke through Robespierre. I've never seen anything like it. The way the Greek actor would invoke Dionysos when he took up his mask for the play—like that." "Oh, surely not?" said Lucile, teasingly incredulous, taking off my coat because by then I was so tired I no longer recalled how. "His face altered," I said. "Like the mask, too. I couldn't take my eyes off him. None of us could." "Maxime? You're certain it was our Maxime?" "No. I'm not certain. He said, once, something about being 'chosen.' I almost believed it, tonight."

When I read over what he'd said, written down it looked fairly flat. Just some different angle, to get publicity perhaps, with a martyr's tail tied on the end.

Maxime didn't appear to take bribes. But he could nevertheless have agreed on a certain line with d'Anton. D'Anton was always agreeing on lines with this or that member of this or that club. Once he said to me, "I never need to work anything out with you, you always do what I want before I tell you." I instantly objected to the word *tell* and pointed out ten occasions when I had favored another path to his. As a general rule, though, it had to be admitted, we were sufficiently like-minded. He also once commented, "If ever they cut out my tongue or somebody steals your inkwell, we'll be in serious trouble."

He still gave me money. I still took it. I was not alone in being his beneficiary. Fabre, to name only one, had financed his latest play on d'Anton's handouts. And there were all the other bribes, too: Orléans's habit, for example, if you dined at the Palais-Égalité (once Royal) of saying two and a quarter words to you but insisting you keep the silver fruit knife. One evening he left a gift on the table for everybody's wife. Lucile, with his jewelry around her neck, said, "Dare I?" To which I replied yes, but I didn't like the idea, and she knew as much and never wore the necklace after. And then there were the country flowers that sometimes got left, dew fresh, at the door, or the man who'd arrive with a brace of rabbits or a bottle of wine, or the girl who fell against you coming around an unlit corner and put her hands where no woman puts them unless she means business.

"Perks of power," would say d'Anton, who for all I knew was constantly guzzling rabbit and free wine, up to his ears in flowers, fruit knives, and labor in unlit doorways.

Maxime went home alone or sat in a respectable café, drinking watered wine and outlining utopian dreams to Saint-Unicorn.

I went home to Lucile and next week's edition of my paper.

It seems to me now there was a lot going on on every side of me I never saw at all. Or if I did, with defective vision.

⚜

So let's eat intrigue over at the Jacobins. The People prefer more obvious fare.

The mob's in the Tuileries. Making a mess. Fingering the riches that, in the normal course of events, they would never have come within fifty paces of. Selling and chomping fruit and making sure the stones and pips go on the rugs. Holding stair parties. Dressed up in bed curtains. They've hung a sign on the gate: HOUSE VACANT. Who'll come and live in the Tuileries? Well, Granny could have the boudoir, and you and I could have *her* room with the nice big bed with cherry pits all over it.

The original tenants won't be back. They've gone camping in Austria. Better have a good time while we can.

⚜

They should have reached it too, that Austrian border. Loaded down with jewels and gold-mounted dressing cases as they were, with baskets of bread and fowl and wine for the king's snacks — even so, it should have been possible for that glorious painted equipage to get them east through the little towns and villages, where surely not many knew them by sight, east and east, picking up at Châlons a prearranged escort of royal loyal bodyguard. But something happened to the bodyguard. Peculiar, that. Somehow the local peasants distrusted smart soldiers on horses loitering, and the smart soldiers smartly went off to alleviate suspicion and . . . got lost.

North, then, toward Varennes-en-Argonne, pleasant quiet little place.

Why is that fool running out in front of the carriage shouting for it to stop? Why is the local militia all across the street? Aristos can always drive over one man, but not over this many. The falling bodies would pile up and impede the progress of the horses. Besides, the men in the street have muskets.

The carriage halts.

A man with a culinary name (Sauce) says, "Are we making a mistake?" But another one, who's clever, says, "I've seen the king and queen on a number of occasions, and I recognize them. Get them out and hold them, or you'll be in trouble."

Sauce doesn't want to be in trouble. Handy for his name, he keeps a grocer's, and now he opens up and pushes the flour and coffee out of the way.

In this manner, the royal family end up in a grocer's shop, and that's that.

Strangest of all (though a burlesque is always permitted a certain number of coincidences and fortuitous discoveries to help it along), a great many people seem to have been able to overhear things, guess things, pace and find and pin down the truants. Supposedly, if you know someone is up to something and you think it will be a fine idea, for various reasons, to give them enough rope to hang themselves, you also have ways of stopping them in their tracks at the perfect moment.

⚜

Twelve hours, going back to Paris. Carriage crammed by royalty and staunch revolutionary deputies of the Assembly. One's fallen in love with Antoinette already. Another is cute vain stupid Pétion, who has ants in his pants for Élisabeth, the king's virginal sister, and reckons her in the same condition on account of himself.

"The English are an interesting people," says Yes-Yes.

Everyone looks at him as if he's gone mad.

In Varennes, the crowd had seemed ready for murder. In Paris it's going to be a cold reception at the end of this hot, dusty, bladder-bursting ride.

❧

The Revolutionary News, JUNE

The Capet family, returning to Paris after their spur-of-the-moment holiday, did not receive a very tender welcome. A placard carried on a stick informed the crowd at large: Whoever insults the king will be hanged; whoever cheers him will be bludgeoned. It was very quiet in the city today. . . .

Madame got out of her carriage with a depressed look, but next stalked up the stairs as arrogantly as ever. The stately male Capet, as usual a model of grace and decorum, announced, "What a bloody awful journey. Well, I realize I've been a bit unwise, but why can't I be a fool now and then like everyone else? Come on, bring me my dinner." After this majestic utterance he fell to and put the kitchens to some difficulties.

We confess, we are puzzled. What is this blockhead, this crowned turnip, doing, ensconced in his palace again, stuffing himself with food? Is this how the People reward their betrayers? And Madame Messalina, his evil genius (no one surely supposes he had the brains himself to think of leaving?), she would be better off in some nunnery, where hauteur is generally the subject for chastisement by rods.

Humanity, like many other species, has always tended to allocate some person the role of king animal. But since this position has now, unfortunately, been fixed in the political structure of the country, it seems needful whoever holds it should also be answerable to the laws.

What do these laws say?

They say that any man who takes up arms against the Nation is punishable by death.

By the natural law, also, if a man tries to stab me through the heart, do I have no right to kill him?

This king of ours has called the Nation out, in the aristocratic fashion: begun a duel with us. The first shot, which he took before we had even learned we were in the Bois fighting for our lives—that first shot missed. The bullet went over our heads and lodged in some tree. No matter. By the rule of the duelist's code, the second shot is *ours*.

PREPARE TO FIRE!

Father Duchesne, **June**

Out with them, these stinking Capets! Out with Louis, the drunken wimp, Bitch Austrienne, and her *belle-soeur* Big Arse. Kick the fuckers to perdition!

The People's Friend, **June–July**

What is needed is a military tribune. However, the military may not be trusted, as we perceive. M. La Fayette, for example, loves the People as he would some disease, and given an opportunity will doubtless, so rumor has it, wish to dose it from the body of France by a draft of shot. (A possible alternative remedy would be to have M. La Fayette assassinated.) Meanwhile, why should the People not elect their own dictator? And who rises to mind for this illustrious post but that very one the multitude so vociferously acclaims as its father, Citizen Danton?

("Confound the bugger," was Danton's reaction. "The villain's done it on purpose to drop me in it and get me lynched. Why not have me crowned *king,* you bloody Swiss sewer rat?")

1791: Summer–Autumn

July. The celebration of the glorious fourteenth had been moved three days on, to the seventeenth, a Sunday. It was thought a public holiday on a Thursday would cause too much disruption, aside from the loss of wages. Nevertheless, there were some gatherings in the parks on Thursday, and some marching about by the Breechless Wonders, and the city was pretty with posters, the gist of all which was that Fatty really ought to go.

What was Marat saying, and Desmoulins? The flight to Varennes should be taken as an abdication.

What was the king, anyway? The Capet line descended from a common advocate, of all things, as the *Revolutionary News* had pointed out.

King Midas, who fell out with a god, had been somewhat changed about the ears, as his barber discovered when he saw Midas minus his crown. Unable to keep the secret, the barber dug a hole in the riverbank and spoke the truth into it. Presently the reeds which grew there, blowing in the wind, called out, "King Midas has asses' ears!" I find myself in the position of the king's barber. Having seen through his crown, I am forced to seek the riverbank—

> *And since I dare not ever write it down,*
> *I'll dig a hole and whisper to the ground,*
> *So all the reeds can have a lot of fun*
> *Shouting, "Royal King Capet is a lawyer's son!"*

On July 16, at the Cordeliers, Danton read a petition for the king's removal from power. The zoo rendered its applause. Desmoulins, poet of the Revolution, crossed over the river, not noticeably pausing to dig any holes, and asked if the Jacobins would care to join in. But the Jacobins declined. The Assembly had just got through a motion declaring the king's person inviolate. (Remember those deputies in a carriage, falling in love with Austrian apple blossom, virginal Frenchness?)

However, crowds burst into the Assembly and complained, and crowds burst into the Jacobins and howled. Robespierre's protocolic club decided it would join in after all. . . .

Danton, of course, is in favor of a regency, because Orléans is paying Danton to be aware of how good a regent Orléans would be. And Desmoulins gives his stuttering yap whenever Danton tells him. Brissot of the Bastille key draws up an even better petition, and everyone is going to be by the Altar of the Nation in Martian Meadow tomorrow to hear the Cordeliers Club read it. The new petition is obdurately for the king's ousting (and possibly even for his trial), and the citizens of Paris will be called on to sign it.

During the afternoon of the sixteenth, the Breechless Wonders are out in force, roaming the thoroughfares.

By the night of the sixteenth, La Fayette has troops out instead, en masse: around the Stable, around the palace, along the river, and beside the bridges. Horses go by in tides, and even the ubiquitous cannon are heard rolling across the cobbles.

Late walkers find themselves arrested. Not all. A few get over to Danton's apartment.

⚜

When the dawn started to come, we opened the windows again. The red study was full of smoke and stale, overused air. Soft summer stench hung on the city, and a strong smell of horses. No wonder. A whole troop of La Fayette's regulars had positioned itself below us in the street for half an hour the previous night. Fabre was petrified. "They've come to arrest us." This brought a general discomfort, but d'Anton laughed it off. "Rubbish, they're hoping for a free drink." And he went at once and saw to it. After a time, the troop departed, with a few comradely whoops. Fabre had by then chewed his nails down to the wrist, modeling himself flatteringly on me.

(Gabi, whenever she came into the room to bring us coffee, gave me a look as if she hated me, something I wasn't used to from a woman, which made me very nervous and depressed.)

The desk and floor were covered in papers. The one lying nearest my foot I could still just read. Ill-scrawled and fascinatingly spelled, it said, *Julit 17 is a badd dae, Camille, to sho yourself on Marts Meadoe.*

The warnings had come thick and fast. We'd all had them, every man in the room. Even the seven-foot butchering Legendre had come crashing up the stairs with frightened eyes. Friends had told him to get out of Paris.

Marat had, apparently, already disappeared down the sewers again. Brissot also was absent. I'd recently had another disagreement with him, telling him I'd knock his teeth into this throat, over a couple of terms he had applied to me in his skim-milk-and-brimstone paper. He always knew better than anyone how everything must be done. But this time, maybe not.

"Well. Something's going to happen," said d'Anton, looking over the rooftops of the Cordeliers district.

"You think we'll be in jail tonight?" said Santerre, who was drinking wine from the bottle, lying on a sofa with his waistcoat under his head.

"Let's wait and see," said enigmatic d'Anton. You wanted to kick him in the ear. But I'd given up trying to get an opinion out of him.

"What about the club members who'll be reading the petition?" said Fréron, still stirring, as he had been for hours.

"Oh, they'll be safe enough."

"No, d'Anton," I said, furious with him. "They'll be as safe as we'd be if we were there. And none of us is going to be there, is he?"

"O brave Camille, always notable for his daring," said Santerre.

I picked one of the journals off the floor and threw it at him. It caught him on the cheek, and he jumped up with wine spilled down his neck on the wrong side.

"Stop it," said d'Anton. "Bloody maniacs. Do you know what that brocade cost, to have vinegary claret all over it? The spokesmen at Mars Field will be safe since they are not *us*. We would not be, as we *are*."

There was some crooked applause.

"Robespierre told me," said Fréron, "he would present himself at the Altar of the Nation."

"He opposed the petition!"

"He opposed it on legal grounds. Now the Jacobins are converted. Like all converts, they're extra ferocious. L'oui the Lout, out, out!"

"All right. But what are we supposed to do?"

"Wait," said d'Anton inexorably.

He went through into the purple room and I followed him. Morning light fell on Gabi's clavichord. It was delicately dusty. She hadn't played it for some days.

"You know," d'Anton said to me, "things aren't going quite as I foresaw." He smiled, in his shirtsleeves as most of us were, his eyes dead still as pieces of blue glass dropped in cement.

"It was supposed to be easy? Topple the monarchy and the military backup—"

"You've been fighting with print. This isn't an essay."

"—and put *who* into power, d'Anton?"

"That would be telling."

"Yes. So tell me."

"Where's Lucile?" he said.

"Where do you think?"

"She should, perhaps, visit her mother out at Queen's Market. . . . Sunday in the country. Nice."

"Christ," I said. I had gone cold in the heat.

"Don't," he said to me, "go to the same place."

"*What?*"

"A bit farther. Confuse the trail."

"You're explaining you've started something that's about to come down on our heads. The court par-party is st-stronger than you—"

"Bargained for. You could say that. We've gone too far too soon. Don't you want my advice?"

"W-was it your v-advice to sign the per—the petition?"

"Not quite. And I don't write your paper. You do."

"Fine. Ver-everyone s-says you dictate it. Oh, my God. Lucile—"

"Get off now and tell her to pack."

I ran back into the study and grabbed my coat. Santerre said, "What haste. Rushing to Mars Field? Or the privy."

"To get aw-way from your brewery stink."

"Coward."

"C-clod."

I pelted down the stair and rushed out on the street, running almost slap into a bread cart and then Roch-Marcandier the other side of it.

"Camille!"

"For God's sake, what is it?"

"Are you going to the Champ-de-Mars?"

"Yes," I said, lying angrily because I wanted to get rid of him.

He stared at me. He said, "They say it's dangerous, but you've never been afraid where truth was concerned. I'll do my part." And leaving me shamed and infuriated, he hurried off. Idiot.

I ran for home.

Lucile was before the mirror, exquisitely cool in a pale dress, combing her
hair into its long curls. Unbelievable mirage. I told her in a flood that she must
go at once, there was about to be some military upheaval. She came to me and
took my hands. "Yes, Camille." So serene and matter-of-fact, it calmed me.
"But you?"

I improvised. "With d'Anton—the country."

Then her eyes flickered; she put her head on my breast. I held her for a
moment, and then she left me and went away, serenely, matter-of-factly seeing
to everything, as if flight were a daily domestic occurrence. Which, of course, it
could well become.

❧

The firing started a little before midday.

❧

The petition, when it was read by various of the Cordeliers' second-in-
command, had changed somewhat in tune. Orléans's conspirators had been at
it. The Jacobins, in new mood *féroce,* had been at it. A night full of troop
movements had had its effect. And despite the candy sellers, and the musicians
strolling through the crowds with their old-woman-wheels churning out popular songs, despite the sale of sugary drinks, the children with hoops, and the
girls in their best clothes all out in the sun on Mars Field, the general temper was
aggrieved, not to say militant. After all, they *were* going up to the Altar of the
Nation and signing—or at least making a mark on—a paper which called for the
abolition of the rule of kings fourteen centuries old.

There had also been an Incident, earlier: two drunks found under the Altar.
The Breechless Wonders had got hold of them, considered them spies, considered their wine barrel was gunpowder, and separated (in what was fast becoming the *mode révolutionnaire*) skull from torso.

So the day had begun in blood, anyway. The gods seldom ignore such a cue.

When they saw the troops coming, the People grew unsure. But they said to
themselves, The National Guard is made *up* from the People: friends and
relations. They won't fire on us. They saw the mayor up front, hair powdered,
coat brushed, and lace at his throat, and they thought, Well, we elected him; the
Paris sections put him where he is. They won't fire on us. Then they saw La
Fayette and they said, *Will* they? Then they saw the blood-red flag, symbol of
war and threat. Then somebody took a potshot at La Fayette. At which—

One moment the grass is green, the sky is blue, the sweetmeat sticky in the
hand and all life before us—and then the pistol speaks its smoky message.
Death, the sudden-winged. It was always so. Just so. Since the beginning: the
shard, the spear, the arrow, the bullet. The dead fall down like broken birds in

the green grass turning red, among the scattered gingerbread and the hurdy-gurdy cries of pain and terror.

⚜

Who's responsible this time? Who'll take the blame for the young artisan lying on his back in a vest of blood? Or the woman with a piece of lead in her thigh, shrieking, and only taking breath to shriek again? Come on, own up; who'll carry the can for this day's work? Who'll be the scapegoat now to be driven out into the desert with the sins of Paris on his back?

It wasn't us, the guardsmen say, they who have been shooting their brothers stone red dead on the green grass. The general gave the order. Or the mayor. A man in the crowd fired at them, and that started everything. It was Marat invited someone to assassinate La Fayette, so it's Marat's fault. Hunt Marat. Otherwise, who began the whole thing but those rabble-rousing Cordeliers with their petitions, overexciting the sans-culottes, enticing the mob to come out and cause an affray and get itself blown to bits by these guns that went off in our hands when we never meant to hurt a fly.

The guard is running wild now in all directions. If you see a crowd of bluecoats faced with white, slashed at the neck with scarlet, shut and bolt the doors and shutters.

The bolted doors of the Jacobin Church are hammered on, and bottles thrown. It's your fault too, you bloody Jacobins. (The besieged cower.) We'll have you, and we'll have those Cordeliers. You can't miss Danton, it'll need about ten of us to bring him down, the filthy pig. Look! There's one of the swine now—long black hair and ugly as Lucifer; it's that shit Desmoulins—let's get him! And in one public garden and two back streets, three young men mistaken for Camille are beaten to within a quarter inch of their lives or rescued by screaming neighbors—"Leave him alone, it's my Gaspard!" On Ninth Bridge, Louis-Mer Fréron (who for some while has preferred, like so many men christened for the king, to be addressed by another name: Stanislas) is correctly recognized as co-writer of the *Revolutionary News* (D.F.E.D.B.). Backed up against the parapet, he hears, "Throw him over"; "Tickle him first." And feels the first blow land. But Stanislas (L-M) Fréron is saved by the advent of guardsmen from his own section. If anyone is going to kill him, the right should be theirs. Having learned a thing or two from Danton, Stanislas (L-M) uses the interlude to commiserate with the men and offer them a drink. Their blood lust stems from horrible guilt, and by negotiating it he saves his life. Later that night, Stanislas Louis-Mer Lapin Fréron gets out of the city and makes for Versailles, with a speed any rabbit would be proud of.

See how they run!

Whatever game you were playing this time, Georges-Jacques Danton, if you were, it's a mess.

Maximilien Robespierre, leaving the Jacobin Club, pauses under the Tree of Liberty (a poplar) in the courtyard. The meeting has finished early, in case the guardsmen get drunk enough to want to come back and kick the doors down properly.

It's fact, supposed to be, the Incorruptible One was there, on the Champ-de-Mars, chancing the bullets, trying to bring some decorum and sense to the occasion.

"You've risked your life enough for one day, Maxime," says the joiner Duplay, in the somewhat self-conscious, admiring tone his voice always gets when he employs Maximilien's familiar name. Duplay is a big man, strong-armed from his trade, which prospers. To him, Robespierre represents something rather specialized, rare. A pale exhausted prince, Robespierre leans by the tree and passes his hand over his eyes.

"Madame and I," says Duplay, boldly, nervously, "would be delighted to offer you a bed for the night. It'd save you going back across half Paris and coming up against the lawless element." He thinks Robespierre will like that phrase.

Robespierre seems to. He gives Duplay a smile, very tired, oddly sweet. The times are refining Robespierre, never very coarse-grained. He is indeed becoming specialized and rare, startling those who have known him, binding those who come to it fresh. In order to be so purified, one must bow to the pressures of a choosing fate. He is bowing. The slave of Equality imparts to Duplay the sensation that great saints are always capable of imparting: You are good to me? For this you will be blessed. "You're most considerate," says Robespierre, gently, almost inaudibly.

"Oh, not at all—Maxime—a pleasure. Really."

The Duplay domicile existed just along the road, like the club situated in Saint-Honoré Street.

Coming from between the house walls into the court, Maurice Duplay became busy guiding the immaculate Maxime among the seasoning boards, deals, and battens stacked up in the yard. Having climbed through a window frame and over some tall pots of glue (Maxime is by now coughing a little, wearily, at the strong aromas and wood dust), the door flies open. As in all the fables, there in yellow lamplight the welcoming wife, the three daughters, who, if not exceptionally comely, are certainly beaming.

Maybe Maximilien was aware this might be a put-up job, an excuse to entertain the star Jacobin. But ever conscious of his physical reliance on some support or other, and of the loneliness of a creature of destiny, Robespierre always responded with a definite and genuine gratitude to kindness. Gravely he stepped over the threshold into the embrace of the lamplight. How good these people were, to shelter him! Almost curtseying, the women conducted him into the house which was about to become home for the rest of his life.

Meanwhile, Brune the printer, having had a narrow squeak out in the alleys, was still crazy enough to open up the printing shop and slip inside. Here Brune found Roch-Marcandier curled up asleep by the press, guard-dog style, who promptly bounded to his feet and assaulted him.

"Take that pistol out of my eye," said Brune, as they untangled themselves. "Is it loaded?"

Marcandier had not yet been driven to the sort of humor which would comment that Gui Brune should himself know if his own eye is loaded or not.

"Yes! What else?"

"Have you seen Camille?"

"No," said Marcandier. He looked stricken. "He may be dead."

"What of? Gabi's servants' cooking?"

"He was at Mars Field."

"I have news for you."

"Liar! With his own lips he told me."

"Then with his own lips he—er, misinformed you."

Marcandier, disconcerted, disgruntled, lapsed back on the floor. He was beginning to rehearse the old saw about idols with clay feet and that perhaps, in some instances, the idol might be solely composed of clay *but* for the feet.

Somewhere during the muggy night, when the press was clattering and heaving away, a surreptitious knock announced Windmill.

"So there you are. Where have you been?"

"All the way out at Gabi's father's house. D'Anton dragged us off there for a meal. I walked back and one of my damned feet is bleeding."

This seemed rather to support the Marcandier philosophy. Brune augmented it by saying, "Ah, you see, Roch. He *is* wounded."

Windmill glanced at Marcandier, peremptorily and uneasily, then shoved some paper into Brune's hands. "Print it."

"*What?* I've got—"

"Fuck what you've g-got. Print *this.*"

"There isn't much. You'll be adding to it? What is it?"

"Look at the dedication."

Brune looked. "To M. La Fayette, the unputdownable Vizier of Paris. Oh, *I* see. You *want* to go live in the prison."

"Don-n't start. D'Anton was in the oddest mood I've ever seen him."

"D'Anton's blown it."

"So I ga-gather. He's talking about England."

In the shadows, Marcandier spat.

"If Georges is talking about England, why are *you* here?"

"I'm not. Now w-will you—?"

Brune gazed critically at the press.

❧

July 18. The National Assembly, motivated by the mayor and the general feeling of the judiciary at the Hôtel de Ville (since blame must and will go somewhere), passes a decree. Individuals guilty of persuading the citizens to unlawful disobedience, whether by means of bills, or the making of speeches, or through the publishing of inflammatory writing, are to be arrested downright and—wait for this—condemned to the chain gangs. A warrant for the apprehension of such culprits (for example, Danton, Fréron, Desmoulins) is being drawn up. (Visualize, if you will, Camille in a chain gang.)

But they're gone. Of course. The four winds have them. Or do they?

That evening at the Jacobins—rather an edgy meeting, with several notable absentees—in walks Windmill, unshaven, uncombed, in disgraceful linen and a dusty coat. Also slightly drunk.

From the middle of the floor he gives a short shouted speech, playing heck with the acoustics but lacking all stammer.

"I'm flying for my life—you know it. Will Marseilles be far enough? Perhaps I should try Austria; it seems there's more justice there than here. Paris is in the charge of two arch-devils and an overweight moron. I refer, of course, to Messrs. Lord La Fayette, beast-mayor Bailly, and King Capet the clot. Paris under the bootheel, then. You're welcome to it. A city where two men can commit red-handed murder, mow down hundreds of innocent people simply for stating a widely held view. Traitors and killers—and still they're strutting about, passing laws against the rest of us. So. I give you Paris, citizens. Take her. A capital dishonored and betrayed."

He stalked out with a furling cloak of black rage blowing around him. Seldom had they been more impressed with him. While not catching everything he said, that he had spoken tonight seemed an act of extreme bravery. Or silliness. Either way they saw, for the time being, he was apparently unbought and passionately sincere.

There were soon, too, a few copies of the *Revolutionary News* flapping along the streets. The last line read, "It breaks my heart to lay down my pen."

Written like a noble suicide.

But writers always break their hearts on every last line.

✤

The police who reached the offices of the *Revolutionary News* forced their way in, and a mad dog leaped for their throats.

Roch-Marcandier, firing off his pistol, was chucked on his face and battered into a black-and-blue coma. He lay therefore oblivious as the printing press was attended to, the "coffin" dislocated, and the wooden frame crippled. Marcandier also missed the happy bonfire party which followed. He roused in jail to the inhumane irritated faces of Brune, and the once-so-careful Momoro, and a handful of other Cordeliers.

"If you want the dashing Camille," said Brune noncommittally. "You'd better send to Marseilles."

This time, Roch-Marcandier spat blood.

❧

THE SONG OF THE BULLET
(IN THE ARTISAN'S HEART)

There in the dark of the gun,
Sleeping and harmless and numb,
Woken by fireblast, and flung
Up in an arc to the sun.
Bright is the flight—quickly done—
Winning, the race is not won—
Brought to a standstill in some
Substance that cries and grows dumb,
Beaten to death like a drum.
Now in this thing I have stung,
Still as the stone in the plum,
Trapped in the dark, to become
Sleeping and harmless and numb,
As at the first, in the gun.

Innocent, I, of the sum.
Powder and murder are one.

(To which the powder retorted, Not guilty; the gun did it. But the gun, being called, said very firmly it was all the soldier's fault. The soldier then stood up and said his commander had ordered him to fire. The commander said he had been driven to it by the riotous people. The people said it was the political writers and other madmen who had egged them on. Which is the reason why I am in this stifling damn coach, jolting north, scribbling doggerel.)

❧

Saint-Quentin was the outpost leading to the villages of the Picard landscape of my birth. Marseilles—a ruse. I'd thought of it, and also of the shelter Fréron offered me in Versailles. But Marat, who had told him of it, had not used it. I did not, at that point, trust either of them. I didn't trust anyone. D'Anton had let me down. I felt lost.

First of all going off to Fontenay, where d'Anton's in-laws received us. That was almost a joke. The dinner had been scrappy and the company unnerved. We all made jesting references to Bailly, Kiddy-Blond, Fat Louis. It was the Drink-up, tomorrow-they-throw-us-to-the-lions type of wit. When the country-scented dark began to arrive, d'Anton terrified me by waxing first poetic and then bursting into tears. I say terrified, and I mean it. It seemed to me the floor had given way and now we were falling into the abyss.

Supposedly there had been a plot to discredit the power hierarchy of Paris, and supposedly we'd all been party to it, and myself too, through allegiance. I was taken by surprise. Things had grown so monstrous and so out-of-control I didn't believe them.

I still wasn't believing them when d'Anton cast his great lion's head down on the table and wept. At once Gabi jumped up and threw her arms around him. Then he cried on her breast.

We all sat and stared, between embarrassment and alarm. I'd never seen him moved to panic or lament. His mirth and his anger, which were colossal, had long since ceased to intimidate or offend me. I admired the man. Now he was crying, and Gabi was shooting us looks of venom over his shaken mane, as if we were all responsible and he our hapless victim. *D'Anton!*

I was worn out, at my wit's end; I flung back my chair and said, "All right. I'm off to the city. I'm going to give La Fayette what he deserves, a pot of blackwash over his confounded head."

But I was just a minor character. Mesmerized by the lion-bull's Trojan grief, no one took much notice. I walked out, feeling as if I'd been knifed. It wasn't till I was well on the road I experienced any compassion for him, felt any of my loyalty to him stir and rise to abash me. I was the proverbial son whose father abandons him. (Yes, the abandoning father—I see now; I equate d'Anton with God.) Never mind. I'd trusted him—no, not to be unbreakable, not that, but to be *consistent,* yes. Whatever mistakes he had made, chaos he had engen-dered, he could have put it right if he had stuck to his guns. This I was assured of. But I thought of how I'd left him there, that enormous baby sobbing, and Gabi hating me, and of Lucile at Bourg-la-Reine—and I walked for nearly three hours back to Paris, wretched as a whipped dog, all the while writing lines on bits of crumpled paper by starlight and the passing flare of inns.

And I still didn't truly believe in any of it. To come into Paris, get out that last portion of my paper, storm the Jacobins and shout—it did not require courage. I felt that any moment everything would change. I would have laid bets; besides, the mob would protect me, the People. I was so incensed on behalf of the People, it must work both ways. I think my greatest rage had to do with the compulsion others put on me to act the fugitive when all the while it was *unnecessary.* I know that when I went back into the dusk and found the stagecoach for the provinces, I made no attempt to pretend I was anyone but myself. I said, not one of them would stay to fight this through, so I have no choice. I, too, fly prison, darkness, this frightening demon that pursues, scares the hell out of me, and in which I don't believe. But it's all a dream. Maybe d'Anton never even cried those tears on the table. Maybe he's over at City Hall right now, wringing Bailly's lacy neck, and I should be there with him.

But the coach plowed on through the low-slung black of night.

By the time I reached the elm-locked lanes which divide the landscape beyond Saint-Quentin, I was confused enough to be bitterly merry. I sang as I strode, and plucked branches off bushes, and when the dawn began I even asked a girl with some goats for a drink of the milk and got it. She probably thought me some bandit and was too timid to refuse. When I came to the door of my Uncle Godart, the farmhand who opened it literally stepped backward, as if I were Satan himself.

❄

Green land, around that place. Green land, and sun clustered in the trees with the birds. And golden straw in the barn. I hadn't been so stupid as to run directly to Guise and my father's house. Or perhaps, prophet without honor as I was there, I hadn't wanted to show myself a refugee to the smug faces, winding streets, gray church, and attendant château.

It was safer here. Not inevitably friendlier.

So you're in trouble with the law? Well, we always knew you would be in the end. We don't turn family away. For your mother's sake, we will put up with you. You can help us out on the farm. This time of year, it could be useful.

The groom's quarters over the barn were very well appointed. Plainly, the groom had been more valuable than I was.

Tossing hay. Years since I'd done that. I'd been a boy then. Memory, just on the edge of vision. Always the sunlight, except once an explosion of hail. Geese with long necks hissing like snakes. All the time, the little coiled worm of anger and desolate tension nestled in my side.

I got letters, now and then, meandering through a couple of addresses before they reached me. D'Anton was indeed over the sea in England. It was a business concern. He'd only gone to help out his father-in-law, Georges speaking as he did such fluent *anglais*. Goddamn it. I wondered if I would see him again. I wondered if he'd wept again on the boat, as the shores of France drew away like a misty sigh. He had said, "My country, my darling country, if I desert her, what do I have left? If I could, I'd carry her earth in my shoes the way the antique wizard did, to keep me vital. Like the Greek giant, I need to touch the ground, the flesh of my mother, to be strong. An exile—then nothing, I'm nothing."

And for Lucile . . . I had told her she must on no account write to me. She obeyed the injunction. And how I longed for the sight of the beautiful childlike seriousness of her careful hand. And how I longed for her. There were nights then, up in the comfortable loft apartment, silent country nights, not a sound, no breath of wind, not even the sailing of an owl, when my own exile was poison. Less than a month, and the city seemed a year and many continents away. I could send for Lucile and she would join me. We too could take ship for England, and with my poor English (I could read it well enough to know how well I should be able to speak it), we would flounder through that mud-brown metropolis, London of the cold summers and the closed hearts. Outlawry from France for me, as for d'Anton, was an unbearable nightmare. Sprawled on the solid empty bed in the silent night, I felt I was ready to die before I was ready to leave. France was my flesh, my blood, my very mind and soul. If they killed me, my bones could rest in no other soil. And they would have to kill me to quiet me. I was still feverishly writing.

"Well, you're a miraculous help," said Uncle Godart. "If we've got two days work out of you I doubt."

"I'll pay you."

"I'm the innkeeper and you're my generous guest?"

"I mean, to recompense you. But I *must* finish this."

"Why? So you can get yourself hanged? They want to lock you up and lose the key down a sewer because of what you've written already."

It was early September, and the news from Paris was not good. The writ for my arrest had been altered to a summons—as with all of us. One of my sources told me now was the time to go back and plead my cause. Another source warned me to stay put. I knew my press was gone, but even so I'd managed to enlist the services of a couple of reckless jobbing printers, who'd been perpetrating for me various placards to jollify the bricks of the city. I was not alone in this enterprise. According to my optimist source, the bombardment was having an effect. The Stable grew agitated. Every time its members walked out on the streets, it found a new green or pink fungus over the walls proclaiming: *There is no evidence against me! How can there be such corruption rife amid the elected representatives of the Nation, that a man may stand accused without any accusation?* "Their fingernails are full of paper from tearing these posters down. I've heard it said that, on days there are no bills to be read, it's because the mayor hires gangs of urchins to rip them away overnight." My optimist source also told me d'Anton had been spotted in Paris. The pessimist source presently confirmed the report, adding that if d'Anton showed himself on the right bank he would be imprisoned immediately.

Now I spent days tossing the Godart hay and nights merely tossing and turning, sleepless, getting up to read and reread the books I had brought with me. It began, despite the warnings, to seem imperative I too get back to Paris. There was also another problem with the Godart house. She had been away with relatives when I first turned up, but someone must have told her I was there and soon she appeared, my little cousin named for the goddess of flowers.

It was some years since I had seen her and she, then thirteen years of age, had extracted a promise of marriage from a young idiot of twenty-two, in the orchard. The young idiot was myself, and I think I had meant it at the time. To wait three years would just have given me the margin to achieve brilliant success. The family furor which came on the heels of our "announcement" had not been very polite. I recall even the frowning uncle, who now sheltered me, had pushed me into a corner and demanded to know if I had ravished his child.

At this date, the Flower Goddess, twenty-two herself, unwed, and very charming, began to visit me in the seclusion of the barn. Sometimes she brought apples, sometimes she came to look at the "scholar's" books. She bent over me, her fair hair brushing my cheek and the page and her hand on my shoulder. I was seduced in five minutes and, I will add, never satisfied the whole two months I was there. She had been demure at thirteen, and I very honorable. I still would not have harmed her or thrown her in the way of risk, but since she presented me with the opportunity, I felt more could have been done with it than was. To the Flower Goddess anything was permissible, provided it stopped at the waist. Whenever I put my hands anywhere else, I was reprimanded. As for herself, she was a teaser who liked to pay me out for marrying elsewhere, I believe. I told her she would kill me, and she laughed and left me, perishing of lust. There was always the chance, too, Daddy would come in. My God. The thought of Paris grew more appealing every day.

One late morning, having combed the straw out of my hair and restored some measure of calm, I was lying on my bed upstairs, reading Catullus, when Uncle Godart came thundering up the ladder and into the room. She's told him something even though there's nothing to tell—accused without any accusation!—and I got ready for a fight, not very cheerfully; he was a big man. But he flung a letter at me.

"One of your very clever big-noise friends who are saving France. Sends his own courier with instructions—*instructions*—to place this in the hands of Monsieur Desmoulins. Well, there you are, *monsieur.*"

I retrieved the letter from the floor. I could already see it was d'Anton's handwriting.

"Do you want to dismiss me, or will you read it in my presence?"

I ignored this. My fingers were trembling. I opened the letter. It said:

> Paris lacks a windmill, no wonder there's no bread. Someone who reckoned he would see me in jail ended up in jail himself. Here I am and here I stay. By the 10th, or 12th at the latest, there will be an amnesty. You have my word. Gaius Marius, Tribune of the Plebs.

Marius—that was a nickname I'd given him. I noted he hadn't signed his actual name.

It was September 8. I'd been perfectly calm a second or so before; now I was suddenly shaking with a violent reaction. I started to laugh, too. D'Anton the Charioteer had the reins again.

"Good news, I take it," said my uncle, dislikingly.

"Paris is burning," I said. I came off the bed and embraced him, thanking him for his hospitality and his kindness over and over until in the end he relented and took me down into the house for some ale. Even my flowerlike cousin looked benignly on me and wished me joy of my return home—though later she chased me back into the barn and, having kissed me tumultuously farewell, bit my ear so savagely I had to tell her father I'd cut myself shaving.

❧

Oh, September.

As the leaves get ready to fall, so does almost everything else.

The National Assembly ends its term and—due to the protestations of that extraordinary being from Arras, Citizen Robespierre—its members vote not to be reelected. A whole new Assembly will sit down in October. Nevertheless, that amnesty stands. Danton and all his tribe are back—though, it's noticeable, more reticent. Danton doesn't get elected to the Assembly. Camille hasn't got a paper. Quiet around here, isn't it?

Then again, La Fayette resigns, and the mayor, too, is in the process of an exit.

On the other hand, the Capets are walking at liberty, and torchlit, on Heaven's Fields, visiting the theaters and the cathedral (cleaned up after the latest graffiti and smashery), and fond cheers greet them. They've recognized the Constitution. They're going to be good. Let's all be friends. Let's stop the wheel. Let's settle down.

We only want peace. Peace to raise children, peace to grow and to be and to die in bed. Ah, friends. Don't you know you're part of history? And history itself, by a pressure of events, causes men to resort to particular actions.

Peace? You ruffians, do you want to live forever?

❧

Notre bon roi
(Our good king)
A tout fait;
(Did everything)
Et notre bonne reine
(And our good queen)
Qu'elle eut de peine!
(She's had her share of pain)
Enfin les v'là
(Well, now here they sit)
Hors d'embarras!
(Out of the—)

❦

"Were we parted?" said Lucile. "It was a bad dream. I used to wake up crying."

That's the only true peace. To be with her, still holding her after the frenzy of lust and love, just the love remaining, and her tears warm, and her arms around me. Beautiful Lucile, *aimante, amante, âme de moi.* When there was trouble, she never wept. She only wept with gladness when I came back to her, staggering coach-drunk up the stairs to our apartment, which was already welcoming in the evening light, candles lit, autumn flowers burning on the table, and she standing in the middle of the room blinding me with my own tears.

The windows were filled by the strange, softly draining, smudged gold of a city sunset, caught up on all the lights that grew more flagrant as the sky more modest. There was the scent of polished wood, the earthy scent of flowers, the dust and smoke of Paris, the fresh bread on its platter, and the sweet fruit. The pastel rain-fresh scent of her skin and hair.

The sheets were crisp. No straw. No lies.

"I shall never let you go anywhere near Guise again, to this cousin who bites," she said, at her most playful. She didn't care. She knew me through, my priestess.

Among those warm dark forests, amber-leaved with candles (the last nights of September), she conceived our child.

FIVE

⚜ ⚜ ⚜

1792: Winter

Dearest Father, are you pleased to get so many letters from me? I am afraid the surfeit is partly due to having nothing else to write. For writing, I find, once one is afflicted, proves an incurable disease. Yes, I should be content. I know it. My marriage has brought me such utter happiness. . . . I lost all faith in the existence of God because of it. I thought paradise was a state reserved for the afterlife. To achieve paradise while still living seems to preclude all hope of a spiritual heaven. Lucile fills my every hour with brightness. I'm reminded of that biblical line in Psalms: for thou wilt light my candle – illumine my darkness. She shows hardly any sign. Except, if it were possible, she may be even more beautiful. No. Of course not possible at all. Perfection is not improvable.

I am, as you know, honestly lawyering once more. I can get work quite easily (ah, reputation!) and cut a splendid figure, strutting about the courts. I've only to use those words "non-republican" to throw the prosecution into an acute dither. On the other hand, the king is now most popular. (To be a popular king, it turns out, one need only lie to and cheat the populace, repeatedly betray it, attempt flight to and embracement of an enemy, setting all off at last by throwing a few sous on the wet ground outside the cathedral for the penniless to trample each other groveling after. He should write a book of guidance for the other monarchs of Europe!) Besides this, I never heard that word "republic" aired so often by those who have no notion of its meaning and no actual inclination toward it if they do. My Robespierre was wise – I find he often is – when he asked us all that evening: What *is* a republic?

Meanwhile, I go mad. Chide me if you will. My days are full, and at night my sleep is peaceful. But my hand itches and aches to wield a pen. My paper – that I left in the coffin of a broken press – was a *power*. Again and again I say I should never have let go of it. But what choice did I have?

D'Anton is now back for sure. At first he seemed set on wintering in the country on his grand estate. The house is considerably beautified – we've stayed there a couple of times. Gabrielle confides Antoine can expect "a sister" later in the year. I think I've been forgiven my transgressions, whatever they were. Gabi's condition, it may have been, which clouded her views of us. Now all is sweetness. She and Lucile sit and converse intently, like two birds on a bough. For Georges – well, he's in top form. Greedy for action, as I still am, he was stamping around the Sur-Aube woodland in the snow, where I was treated to a constant rehash of the idiocy of voters. The house was full of relatives and guests. You took two steps and stumbled over some beatific antique aunt or nurse of his with her tatting. Outside, oxen and horses have been poured into the empty fields. *Seigneur* Danton? No. Whatever he does, he'll never be that. I have grown to have an absolute trust in this man. Discount whatever tales you may hear. He is so honest with those close to him, one rocks in one's shoes. But like any great man, he has a squadron of foes capable of dreaming up and spreading slander.

His comments on England are mostly derogatory, but the word games grow more numerous.

You'll have heard Jérôme Pétion is mayor of Paris. The people love him and go about wearing pictures of his handsome face. Our fretting d'Anton, however, at the start of December, braved another election and found himself at the end of it First Deputy Public Prosecutor, with well over one thousand votes. It transpires, not all voters are "idiots" after all. Now his Paris apartment is being done up like some sultan's pavilion, with the odd treasure spilled over into the tents of the two Desmoulins in Theater-of-France Street. He made a brilliant speech on assuming his office at the Hôtel de Ville. All the whispered calumnies were brought out and given a trouncing. After that he spoke of his allegiance to France, his vital dedication to the Constitution of Rights. He spoke so much solid sense, with such glowing passion, we were stunned. He vowed, as Brutus did, to put truth and justice before any personal tie and moved the whole place – royalists included – to a roaring ovation. I believe at that point he could have led us all into the mouth of hell. If I ever doubted him, I would never do so again. The fire in d'Anton! He is the very torch of France. And when he came and talked to me presently, I confess I missed half of what he said. I was thinking, with awe, This man is my friend!

Yes, I predict there will be war. There has to be. I don't say it lightly, but certain persons have kept up their liaison with Austria, and the coalition of monarchies mutters the vilest of threats. The stories coming out of Koblenz can turn you gray overnight! Feeling grows high. With such spirits, can you doubt France would be the victrix? The paid (or *un*paid) slaves of Prussia, Austria, and England: what do they have fighting on their side but discontent? France has her glorious dream, the flame of Liberty, which only a fool would think is dormant, despite the curious, nonrepresentative Assembly we now have sitting in the Manège and the blindness (temporary) which has kept the Bourbon lily from being uprooted.

Our fresh-minted constitution, that monument to hope, still stands. It was Maximilien who said to me that a belief in the power of truth was as vital as that truth's enactment. We may be delayed on our path, we may sometimes wander from it, but in the end the monstrous Minotaur will be slain and the ball of twine will lead us out of the labyrinth into the sunlight.

Well. I see I'm writing you a paper, not a letter.

As for your proposal, that I should consider buying the house at Guise . . . it seems unlikely I'll have cash enough. Remember, I've never been rich, and now I have no journalistic employment, we are already making economies here.

D'Anton meanwhile is generous and won't let us starve. We're dining there tonight. The Key will also be present. I have some bones to pick with Monsieur Brissot that have nothing to do with cooked fowls.

With my loving affection and kind thoughts, your son,
C.D.

꘍

"For Christ's sake, be quiet!" Danton roared, rising from his chair like a boar from a thicket, lightning in his jewelry eyes.

Jacques Brissot and Camille Desmoulins, who had been spitting vitriol at each other across the table, obeyed involuntarily.

"My wife," said Danton, "does not need to put up with all this bloody nonsense." (Gabi lowered her velvet gaze. You could see she loved it, to be so protected.) "One more – only one – crack out of either of you and I'll put you down in the street through the window. If you want to fight, do it out there."

Camille rose. "*Do* you want to?"

Brissot laughed affectedly. "Oh, my, when will he grow up?"

Danton made a noise at them, pawing the ground.

Windmill looked across at Gabrielle. "I'm sorry, Gabi. I thought he would discuss it rationally."

"He can't," said Danton. "*You* can't."

Camille reddened. He said, "He-hn-he's been calling me name-nm-names in his damned paper for six months. Not that anybody *reads* Brissot's paper – except Brissot, who, it's well known, buys ev-every copy–"

"And who bought your rag? People wanting to make fires who couldn't afford wood."

"Wn-when they found your journal was so bloody wet it wou-wouldn't even burn."

Lucile had gone over to Gabi and, putting her arm around her, drawn the elder woman away into a corner by the hearth. Lucile had made no move to reproach anyone. Her eyes were lowered and a touch too innocent.

Now Brissot got up. Everyone was on their feet save Brissot's little wife and the one bachelor of the evening.

War had been declared with the entrée and continued until the petits fours were about to come in. Brissot's wife looked frightened. She thought Windmill was mad, and Danton appalled her for she found him attractive and considered herself virtuous.

"If," said Brissot. "You want me to leave—"

"I want you to sit down, shut up, drink up, and finish your dinner. There are things that need to be discussed," said Danton, "that have nothing to do with Camille's activities as a lawyer, or the running battle between the now-defunct *Revolutionary News* and that still-operative journal *The Committed Frenchman*."

"Oh, God," said Windmill. "Thank you." He threw his napkin on the table and walked across the room to the window.

"It's a nice view," said Danton. "We like it." To Brissot he added, "Maybe the ladies would prefer to get out of this bull ring into the other room. Then we can begin the boring business of reviewing politics." He was all urbanity now. He smiled down at Brissot's wife, who blushed.

Brissot shrugged. He said, "Don't credit all you read in the papers. The ministry isn't about to be replaced."

"No?" said Danton.

At the window, Camille looked over his shoulder through a curtain of black hair and said sharply, "The Roland bitch is backing her husband and his hangers-on for the next government of France."

"Why must little boys be so rude?" said Brissot. "Manon Roland is a charming, intelligent—"

"Bitch," repeated Camille.

Danton laughed. He pushed past Brissot and drew all the women to him and so through into the adjacent room. Brissot's wife went unwillingly. She had just begun to think Camille Desmoulins was on the side of the angels after all. Danton returned, shutting the intervening door.

"Gironde." Camille was sneering. "A party named for deputies from an estuary, now dominated by sl-self-s-seekers from every rut of Paris. A name as out of date as the Machiavellian intrigues of its m-members."

"A party that wants to keep France afloat," said Brissot, furious, "not submerge her and dance on the wreckage, which is *your* trick."

"You're a bloody liar. Who do you think l-l-listens to you?"

"You don't grasp the meaning? And we thought you such a sparkling scholar. I'll quote Danton then. What he said to La Fayette that day can equally well be applied to you. What are you, a villain or a blind blithering twit?"

"Now!" Danton bawled at them. Silence. Danton nodded to everyone, ironically. "We are *all* aware, the party of the Gironde, name outmoded or not, bursts with sincerity and talent. You, Monsieur Vergniaud, Monsieur Brissot: leading lights. *I* am aware, also, that your Gironde will soon have the king's current ministers justly disgraced. It will then insert new ministers into the void. All this is very interesting. It appeals to me. As for the wife of Monsieur Roland, I'm entranced every time I meet her. Brunettes—I have a distinct weakness for them."

"Then I'll take Lucile home," said Camille. He went toward the doorway, pausing by Brissot. "As for you—"

Brissot appealed to heaven.

"No speeches, now," said Danton.

Camille flinched, but he failed to stop. "As for you, Brissot, if I choose to defend a man accused of the ridiculous *crime* of running a gambling establishment—"

"And lose the case," interpolated Brissot smugly.

"Hn-vn-very well. I *lost* the c-case. Because the court was full of mb-imbeciles like you who pretend to be horrified by na-any infringement of so-called mr-moral law."

"Oh, really, Desmoulins. You'll give me indigestion."

"I'll give you more th-than that."

"Threats, little child?"

"You, in your guh-gutless sheet, the *Committed Chastity Belt,* dare to revile me for defending a gambler, when you—"

"Yes?"

"Think back. A b-bell may ring."

Brissot abruptly looked uneasy. "*Those* lies? Even you—you're not going to—"

"Well, why worry, Brissot? Nn-nobody reads what I write."

"Camille—"

Observe him now, the Windmill, poised in the doorway. Yes, he looks like Lucifer, all right. The black eyes like fiery gems of ink and the smiling bow-and-arrow mouth. Demonic and dangerous. He doesn't like to be faulted (who does, much?) or to be laughed at; his skin is thinner than any paper. Too late, Brissot wonders what he's unleashed.

"Camille, you—"

"I tried to talk to you but you think that's funny. Do you r-rem-ember the night before the Bastille? You stood outside City Hall with leaves on your coat and you said-d I was a drunken child. Yes? It-it c-comes to you? Well. We'll see."

"You ass. Come back."

"I'll see you in hell," said Camille.

No one who heard it was quite immune to the effect it had. There was something fearsome about the beast in the doorway. Slight, dark, elegantly dressed, eyes blazing, white as only the sallow of complexion can fantastically whiten, the hand already shaped around an imagined quill, as if around a slender dagger.

They had been arguing all evening, and nobody had believed it would end up in an attempt at murder. Even Camille, as he left the house, was torn along in the wake of his own fury. He already had the pamphlet's title: BRISSOT UNMASKED!

More irremedial than insulting his former friend, Brissot had given him the opening to write again.

⚜

On the home stair, Camille stopped. He looked back, as if someone had called his name. Then up at Lucile, tragically. Her smile was so beautiful it could have lighted every candle in Paris, woken every flower under the frost. Ah, lovely Lucile.

"I'm sorry," he said.

"I'm not Gabi," said Lucile. "Besides, we were all pressed to the door after Marius closed it, poor sensitive Gabi foremost, avidly listening. Then you fumbled the handle wonderfully to give us all warning to step away and be demure by the time the door opened."

"My hand was shaking."

"Dear love." She took his hand in hers. "Not now. And do you know, your unborn child listens to you too? I can feel his attention; he lies so still."

Camille walked up two stairs and caught her to him. "Divine wolfess. It may be a girl."

"Never. A boy. I know."

"My God, if he's like me. . . . Does he hurt you?"

"No. Sometimes he dreams of writing, and then he turns over. Sometimes he laughs. He has your laugh. It makes me laugh too, for no reason anybody can see, and everyone thinks I'm mad. But Georges's children never laugh inside Gabi. Now and then she winces. I imagine the baby starts to give a speech and probably bellows and strikes her with his fist."

"*Her* fist."

"Gabi is wrong. That's another boy too."

"How do you know so much?"

"I don't know anything. *You* know things. I only feel them."

They reached the apartment and went in.

The moment he sees the desk, the lightness of the staircase is gone. He turns toward it, changed, that large somber crouching thing resting slantwise from the wall. The first new candle blooms there, a pale eye. He stands and looks down at the virgin surface, black-browed, unblinking.

"He's been hounding me," said Camille. "Brissot the breakable, a man of glass, throwing stones." But he was at my wedding. What does that matter? My wedding, his funeral.

Lucile moved quietly, settling the room to light and warmth about him. She said nothing of Brissot, who, on her wedding day, had kissed her with tears in his eyes, placed flowers in her hand, held the canopy, wished her lifelong joy. She had seen her husband's frustrated nail-gnawing rages at Brissot's condescending diatribes. A known enemy of Camille's could be no friend of Lucile's. Though, if Camille forgave the man, she too would forgive him. ("I warn you. If you're wrong, she won't ever believe it. She'll only say, He has decided. That's that.") The High Altar, which the priest will always serve. The alabaster priestess had found hers in a wayward, talented, impassioned, clever imp of the perverse who only a Brissot, at this moment, would dare call childish.

The long-term row had come to a head tonight through the gambling-house trial and its owners' stern sentence — six months' imprisonment. Allied to losing the case, Windmill had inevitably had to read an article in the *Committed Frenchman* which told him:

> Camille Desmoulins brings the Nation into disrepute by the laxness of his attitude to gaming. This pursuit is not the slight recreation as which he sees it, but a vice and a sin which fritters away the money of the poor even as it feeds the avarice of the villainous dens which shelter it. This man, whose faults we have often excused in the past on the grounds of his intellectual immaturity, is nothing but a flag-waver, while that banner he flaunts so often, his "love of his country and its people," is nothing but a *performance*. Desmoulins, we fear, calls himself a patriot only in order to devalue patriotism.

It was true Camille had intended to talk to Brissot. He had greeted him stiffly with the words, "We know you can't write, so who wrote your paper this time? Did you know he's an ill-informed halfwit? What do you think I should do to him?"

Brissot had shrugged this off. Windmill had then left matters until everyone was seated at the table enjoying a roast. By the time the next course arrived, Camille at least had been too angrily distrait to retain any appetite, and Brissot was paying more attention to goblet than giblet. Danton had sat in his theater seat, offering no support, finally intervening when he got bored. That Danton had *not* supported him was perhaps now a part of Camille's overall aggression. For some while, prey to his heroic allegiances, he had felt himself capable of laying his life in the dust for the lion-bull. But the lion-bull did not necessarily return such frantic loyalty in absolute kind. If Camille had not consciously examined such an aspect, his annoyance was nonetheless increased, and his general sensation of misuse. The desire to write (even more than the desire to follow his exquisite wife into their bed) now had him by the throat. One by one, the candles burned down and the quills snapped.

❧

They joked about it. Brune said to me, "Well, you've killed him."

I smiled. Glad as a child (yes, yes, a child) who has managed to make the school bully a figure of fun.

Brissot . . .

He'd swiped and niggled at me. He'd called me "boy" and silly brat, in print and out of it, enough. Who did he think I was now, some kid, some impoverished adolescent clinging importunately to the hem of Nine Sisters Lodge, some ne'er-do-never-will-do-well, an unknown hack? He'd overlooked what I'd achieved in three years. I would not let him. To refuse to see me as I now was: established, famous, a writer who—not only far superior to Brissot in ability but in *sales*—had already made an indelible mark in the history book of France we were writing. At the Cordeliers I had an official position, was recognized and attended to. At the right-bank Jacobins, much the same. But Brissot, peering through the steam of his stupidity, refused to see me. He was like one more sorcerous mirror, showing back at me only my former image, scruffy little Windmill the buffoon—goddamn it, to make me *nothing* all over again. (And I remember Maxime's room at the Duplays, full of portraits and small statuettes, all of himself. As if he needed a constant reminder of who he was.)

Brissot de Warville, Jean-Jacques-Pierre. You starch-spined creep. Kill him? I'd plaster him with dirt and let him suffocate in it.

I was the fool and the infant and the discreditor?

He had been all those things, and foremost the fool, when he made an enemy of me.

It was his pamphlet *The Devil's Holy Chalice* which put him in the Bastille. But he had also been had up for fraud. Having promised a literary work and pocketed all the subscriptions for it, this wise, mature, honest patriot Brissot failed to deliver the goods. It became a practice thereafter to name such double-dealings "brisso-ing." He told one it was only a calumny, not true. But I did not need to prove it; we were not in court. I simply told Paris that her Monsieur la Clé had once become a proverb and recalled to their minds exactly how.

I made him look a fool, an infant, a brat, a cheat, the intellectual precursor to the roach. *Touché,* Monsieur de Warville, son of the innkeeper, husband of a lady's maid, chaser after the skirts of la Rolande, which fashion plate thought him even less interesting than she thought her elderly spouse. But then, wise and wonderful Brissot would not be the next minister for the interior, as le Roland was about to be. I could just picture Brissot slimily crawling about the Roland salon, fawning, a footstool.

I remember being twenty-five, and conversations I had with him far into the night. I remember being dizzy and sick with hunger and he bought me something to eat in some smoky café, nameless—where was it? I remember his upright too-rigid declarations at the lodge meetings. That damned key he was so amused by. The way he laughed at my wedding and kissed Lucile and pulled my hair as if we both were boys. My God. If there are debts to pay, how can I pay them now?

You've killed him, said Brune. But actually I'd only made him the satire of Paris. I had not killed him. That was a present I had yet to give.

❧

And after the farce, the melodrama. Paris, long afraid of invasion, turning to Fear's counteractivity, aggression (soaked in propaganda and fin-de-siècle madness, to aid things along), begins to bay for war. And the Assembly, motivated by the Estuary Party, otherwise termed the Girondins, are able to dislodge the extant ministry—since it did not so bay—and replace it with baying Girondins, headed by bitch-pecked Monsieur Roland.

Thus, while the whole scenario boils into red rolling clouds conveying at least two of the Horsemen of the Apocalypse, Camille is doing what? Baying.

Having smashed Brissot, to coin a phrase (he will coin it), Desmoulins prepares to deluge the city with a new paper (*Patriotic Tribune*), all four issues of it.

But who said Danton pays Desmoulins? Who said Robespierre can influence him? It's well known Citizen D'A (who'll stand you dinner if you meet him in the Palais-Égalité-used-to-be-Royal-and-often-still-is) or Citizen R (who won't stand you dinner but enjoys a nice cool drink of water with his friends); neither of these two luminaries wants a war at all. Both dead set against it.

It's Deputy Brissot and the Gironde who want war, who say: England sympathizes, Prussia's involved elsewhere, Spain faints at the idea—let's get Austria, who is out there all alone. So there's Brissot and the Gironde calling for war. And Camille calling for it. Camille who just said, *J'ai brissé Brissot.*

This gets clearer by the minute.

❧

The fake marble of the Café Procope was darkening as the lights darkened into shadows the color of the coffee.

They'd made a great fuss of d'Anton tonight. A second (third) son had been born in February. For some while you only saw the mighty First Deputy Public Prosecutor if you went across to his apartment. There he was, cooing over the cradle. The baby was enormous, like the first. Drop it, you foresaw it bouncing. But d'Anton, with that always surprising, often very moving finesse and delicacy of touch he would employ with women, children—d'Anton held the child like a precious crystal. Then mother and sons went off for a country convalescence, and he was on the loose again. Everywhere they toasted him and his "good wife" and his "heirs." They had something to be heir to, as well. He'd gathered a lot of money. He made very little secret of it. Cunning clever d'Anton, taking the silver, handing Pilate the butcher. . . . Presumably he was bought over and over, but he had never sold out. I had got used to it. Whatever he did, the blinding fire was there in him. You trusted it; it warmed you. He had even made me relax a little at Brissot. "Well, so you've made a laughingstock of him. He was due for it. But you want to keep half a handshake going with the Gironde. They're powerful. Look, Camille, at the nice ladder made of people."

Tonight he said, idly, "Of course there'll be war. And they'll make a bloody awful mess of it. Prussia *won't* keep out. England will certainly feel inclined to do something. And as Rose-Robed-Peter says, Where's the ammunition, where's the transport, and where's the food to feed our new-birthed army? So. Whoever cries for a fight now will be remembered as crying for it when the muck begins to fly."

"Mars Field again? Let's keep quiet? Unlucky for me."

"Oh, you. You're only battling in print again. Have we drunk all this wine already?"

"You have."

"Hell. Never mind, here's the next bottle. *Ah, grazie. Ahi me, il terzo fiasco sempre me apporta la sete.* (Are we getting tired of those actresses at the Théâtre? Well, you never do anything with them.) As I was saying, you know nothing about war, Camille, which makes it forgivable if you tell us all you want it. You know you'll never have to fight."

"I would," I said hotly.

"Don't be a fool. Chance getting that witty brain blown out of your skull? Aside from anything else useful you might lose."

"I've brothers who'll fight."

"Yes, so you do. Better think about them, then, and stay your fiery flights. This won't be a scrap in the yard. This'll be a mess. It doesn't bear thinking about. But it's inevitable, yes. Maximilien talks about holy war, preaching to the world's masses, who will then rise as one and overthrow their oppressors: in other words, their kings and governments. Which is very stirring and very doubtful. I sometimes ponder what Robespierre's glasses are made of, he seems to see things so differently. But then he lives in a block of ice on top of Mount Sinai."

"Too warm."

"What?"

"Sinai's too warm for ice. Leave Maxime alone."

"I won't leave him alone. Come on. He thinks the chicken on his plate died because it wanted to, with an ecstatic squawk of consent. He thinks children should be made by wishing on the moon. If it was left to him, that's how it would be."

"You don't understand Maxime."

"Agreed. You do?"

"He's struggling for something he believes in and can visualize. It's a dream, but it's a good dream. No, I don't understand him."

"Then stop quoting him in the *Tribune*."

"Fréron supplies the *Tribune* too."

"Made up again?"

"Truce again."

This was a fact. As it was a fact I had quoted Robespierre now and then. And as I had told the Nation, Strike now for freedom while the swords of the enemy are slow. It *would* come. There was no way around. To me, it seemed better to attack than to fall back and defend. The vibrations of the court party, the feel of the very earth under my feet, were threatening. And there was, too, such a mood of instability, such a chance of turning tail and running from all that had so far been achieved, you felt you must push them the opposite way. I was only doing what I had done when I first shouted the call to arms: to make them move in the right direction, since the other led into the pit. Strike outward, I had been crying, *outward,* or the blow will cleave the heart of France.

(Or did I only suppose we were too glorious to go down, like those murderous clods who state God is on *their* side and see half their side killed to prove it? Winged with blue and white and red, and the golden promise of Right on our foreheads. Those indomitable Roman legions of brass and drums that for some reason were in my blood. . . . I ask this now. Then, I thought I spoke and wrote the obvious. I had even been prepared to clamor alongside Brissot's Gironde for it, Brissot's posturing nonsense. You do not have to love a man to support his cause, nor hate him to hate everything he stands for.)

"Roland, of course, is an old fool," said d'Anton, as we finally set out for the bridge. "But his wife's clever. She'll run the ministry quite well."

I didn't care for Manon. Now he glanced at me and said, "I know what she says about me, when I'm not in earshot. All the bribes I take and the plots I lay. And how repulsive she finds me, how can Gabi stand to have me in the bed? La Rolande has made a cult of beauty. All her lovers are Adonis and Narcissus. She knows if she got with me she'd like it a whole lot better. Why do you think she says all that? She wants me to hear and come over and have it out with her, ending with her on her back." I saw the logic of this and grinned. "But that's too much trouble. I never had to take that much trouble to have a woman. You should hear what she said about you." "I can imagine." " 'Such eyes!' she said. And compared them to a couple of poetic visions—night seas and so on. And then added, 'Pity about the rest of it.' " We found this funny and went over the bridge laughing.

We were nearly at the place of parting when he said, "I'll tell you this. We've thrown the whole caboodle sideways. I'll tell you another thing. At the end of every century, there's a silly season. What's the year?"

"Ninety-two."

"One thousand seven hundred and ninety-two. In eight years, the dawn of a new era: one thousand eight hundred. Superstition, since the first century ended, says the world may end with every ending century."

"I'll be forty," I said. I thought about that. It went through my mind, almost inconsequently, how it would be: Lucile a rapturous thirty, the number of our children and of the books I had yet to write.

"Yes, you'll be forty," he said. His voice, held low as it now was, had a quality of the night's own darkness that set the air tingling. He could be such an actor, d'Anton. "And I'll be forty-one and look like Gabi's aged father if I go on at this rate. Or the world may end. Or," he said, standing between me and the last scatter of lamps, the stars, "It may end for some."

"Cassandra d'Anton."

"We can always die," he said. There was nothing special in his voice anymore. "Don't you think so?"

"Why should we?"

"The knife's edge. You're not aware you're on it?"

"I'm aware of being alive. Breathing—seeing—the city, the sky. I'm aware my wife will have a child in June."

"July. The first ones are always late. All right. We're alive. Do you know how little a thing can alter that?"

I suddenly recalled two–three years before. The threatened duels, the Bastille gunpowder, the pain in my guts I'd thought would kill me. Or had I truly thought that? The night was dark, this huge genius of a creature blotting out the stars to which I was entitled.

"My God, you're depressing."

"Cheer up," he said. "I hear you've got Marat writing for your paper."

"Hardly. Fréron wanted him. Not my idea."

"And Marat jumped at it."

"Marat girded up his sores and carbuncles and replied, 'The eagle flies alone, it's you donkeys who like crowds.' "

D'Anton roared with laughter till the house walls shook. In twenty bedrooms they would be waking up and saying, Oh, it's those damn Cordeliers going home again.

"What's death?" I said. "What *is* it?"

"Nothing. Nothing to worry about."

"I'm not content with that. This moment; then—*nothing?*"

"Live enough, then it won't bother you."

"Always."

"If you believe in the lying whore Immortality—yes, lying whore; you pay her all you've got and she takes you to her room and ushers you through the floorboards into the cellar—if you believe in her, why do you pretend to care so much for the rotten lives of the People? Or for getting your own life sorted out?

If there's something else, what does any of this matter? It takes an atheist," he said to me, "to *care*. This *is* all there is, so let's make it worthwhile. Now Robespierre, for example. He, like you, my friend, thinks there is a God and there is an afterlife. Robespierre's motto is Liberty, Equality, *Eternity.* Yes. And once you know that, you know he doesn't care a mouse's fart for anything that happens to anyone here, himself perhaps included."

"Oh, for Christ's sake—"

"Don't bring Christ into it. Christ was a revolutionary entrepreneur who panicked and got himself crucified. Christ didn't care either. All he ever said was, Suffer, I'll make it up to you sometime, later."

"Rubbish, d'Anton—" Now he had me defending Christianity. I checked.

"Robespierre dreams of a land of scrubbed shining people, none of whom eats, drinks, sneezes, pisses, craps, fucks, or tells jokes. That's what heaven is like. Didn't you know?"

I pictured all the ears listening in the bedrooms and garrets overhead. I was laughing. At the same time my heart raced. I wanted to go on arguing with him till we had had it through, and I had convinced him of some nebulous hope I cherished which I did not even comprehend. But he grabbed me, kissed my forehead like some saintly grandfather, pushed me off, and went away into the streets.

I turned for home. The scent of spring was on the night air; even the sewers had it.

Lucile was asleep but woke up softly and moved toward me, her silken hands on my neck; the warmth of her pressed the length of my body, with only the curve of the child now between us. I drew out of her that night one of her shivering little cries, scarcely audible, very rare. As if she too had caught the mania of the affirmation of life, in face of the utter emptiness beyond it.

1792: Spring–Early Summer

ON APRIL 20, the king declared war on Austria. He did not wish to, but there you go. Brought from the Tuileries on his invisible (visible, risible) leash, he was paraded before the people and the Assembly and said what he had to say. No doubt, his domestic conditions were not, at this time, ideal.

❊

> *Come, children of the Fatherland,*
> *The day of glory is at hand.*
> *Against tyranny we raise the standard of blood.*
> *Hear, in the heartlands,*

The roar of these beasts — called soldiers —
Who rush headlong to cut the throats of your sons,
*   your lovers.*
To arms, citizens!
Form your legions.
March, march,
That the alien blood
Shall quench the thirst of the furrows of France!

⚜

And they did march, even before they heard the song.

Across the landscape, then, just turning to its fulvous early summer colors, going northward or northeast, through the sometimes misty mornings and the high clouds of noon dust, under the wide French sky. Soldiers. The men of the militias and the volunteering men, in their blue jackets, their boots that don't stand the mileage, cracked and gaping, or the wooden shoes of provincials, and some barefoot. Whole battalions of musketmen and pikemen, sappers with axes, cannoneers with half-moon hats or red handkerchiefs, which were cheaper. And the great guns grumbling by through the villages, so the children and dogs pelted out to see. ("Where are they going, Ma?" "To tear the damned Austries to bits and bring us back some fine heads. Now keep quiet and mind the geese, or those bastards'll have 'em away.") Which was true enough. Rations were low even at the start. Although the promised pay was good. Fifteen sous a day; what work (if you could *get* work) would bring you that? Leave the joinery and the day laboring. Yes, sir, we'll go and kill Austrians for the Fatherland. The baggage trains go by last of all, the donkeys pulling the enormous tonnage of ammunition (though it's not enough, it's hard on a donkey), the cannon, the equipment for camping and killing that attend on war. Bags of flour, tents and posts, gunpowder and cooking pots. Rattle, bump, twang. A gypsy caravan of the battle-god Mars, singing the *Ça Ira* sometimes, for they haven't yet heard the hymn of Marseilles.

But the paths are rough and long. The shoes drop off your feet; the dust gets in your eyes, down your throat. Flour bags burst. Donkeys go lame, and men end up pulling the cannon. At dusk you make your camp, and the aristos ride up and down on their horses, with the People's tricolor on their hats. They give you a look, as if you're scum — *je suis, tu es* all you like — and if you don't salute properly they can order you a parcel of lashes.

As the artisan soldiers and the laborer soldiers sit over the fires by night, drinking coffee with sugar in — and that's a luxury, but they say it won't last — you hear the Prussians have joined up with Austria, alliance fashion, and they're coming down the road toward you, three days, two days away, over the border already.

What'll it be like when we meet them? How does a battle go? It goes in blood, my boy. You stick him first before he gets his mitts on you. But a cannon can do things to you from half a mile off. I remember my dad telling me – he was in the Seven Years do – he's talking to this feller and there's this kind of roar, and he looks and the feller is shorter by two legs, there on the grass on his stumps, not realizing yet properly he's lost anything.

And the Prussians are devils. Why else are they fighting – they didn't have to, some old treaty – except for pleasure? What did Mirabeau say? War is Prussia's main export.

A few fires off, the regular troops, hardened to most things, cock-campaign-sure, stare over at the raw troops and spit. They'll do for us, this bunch. Where did they dig them up? Pimps in blue jackets. Are you calling me a pimp? Maybe I am. And under the hedge there, they'll be fighting, the regular with the volunteer, gouging each other's faces, bashing each other's ribs, trying to make eunuchs of each other, as if there wasn't enough enemy to go round five times over.

But in the morning it's turn out and march, march for the Fatherland, and it'll be, it'll be – it'll be a bloodbath, won't it? These aristo generals in charge of us, they don't know what they're doing. Did you hear 'em last night? Drinking each other under the camp tables in the tent, toasting the Nation, but if you cough in the ranks they punch you in the stomach. They don't give *that* for us. So when it comes to it, they'll shout some order, and it'll be the wrong order. This Prusso-Austrian wedding: our aristos'll send us, a handful, up against thousands of *them* and their guns. Do you know we haven't got enough gunpowder? Well, I heard some bastard sold it, some contractor, like the meat they said we'd get and didn't. They're selling it to the Prussians, our gunpowder and our meat, so they can eat themselves sick before they blow us to shreds. And when it comes to the crunch, these aristos are going to run. They'll run and leave us – why else are they riding horses? Jesus, we shouldn't have got into this. We need more men. We need help from Paris. We shouldn't have come.

And the aristo generals and captains say, Look at them, this rabble. No discipline. No idea. My God, they won't fight. They'll run. The charming Assembly has sent us here to be massacred. Then they recall all the deserting officers who refused to swear the new oath to the Nation and the constitution because allegiance to the king was excluded. Off somewhere, noble and safe.

And the Prussians are on the road, holding hands with the Austrians.

Look! That's them! See the smoke? They must be burning the villages. And on the plain, through the standing of the young wheat, the glint of metal, many thousand bayonets. Don't wait to hear the muskets' prattle or the cannons' call.

Back. Fall back.

The French army falls back. On every frontier, falls back. Murdering the occasional commander on its way.

"The Prussians could be here in two weeks. In Paris."

"And the king's own guard'll be there to open the gates for them."

But the king's Household Guard has been disbanded by order of the Assembly. Around twenty thousand men from the provincial militias have been summoned to form a defensive ring around the capital.

The news comes and goes, passing on wings of Fear. The streets of the city are not restful. Crowds, everywhere crowds. A man who shouted *The Austrians are coming!* in a marketplace was strung up among the fish.

The Breechless Wonders are out en masse on their candy-striped legs, carrying pikes, even those not permitted to bear arms. They have their own secret societies by now, own dire watchwords to be whispered at corners. You don't, if you're wise, go anywhere save in a group, preferably with a couple of your own section militia to escort you. Your wife or domestic does her shopping on the doorstep, and the tradesman glances over his shoulder all the time.

Up at the Stable, the Gironde is less popular than it has been. Did it call for war at L'oui's urging, to invite the invader in? But the Jacobins are in a panic too. They *didn't* call for war, so someone must have paid them. You can't win. It's Robespierre's fault, of course. Though no longer president, he does exert a peculiar influence—even lives in the same street, now, as the club. And he was right, which makes it worse. In the midst of the tumult, the migratory presidency of the Jacobin Club is resigned and promptly offered to Danton, who had been merely sitting there sunning himself in the heat like a dozing lion. Now he springs and snaps up the tidbit in his jaws. That done, he shoves the rest back in their seats.

"One more slander of Maximilien Robespierre, and there will be trouble. That man only told you the truth."

What is Robespierre thinking, blinking at Danton across the tombstones in the floor? Tied up on the rock for the monster, Maxime beholds his heroic deliverer swoop down.

"To the bravery of this man, his own career bears ample witness. Too good for you, perhaps? Leave the lies to his enemies. We are his friends and will speak well of him. Whoever doubts the courage, integrity, and dedication of Monsieur Robespierre is no ally of the Revolution."

Obviously, you may be useful to him, Maxime. He, too, the sleepy lion, has seen the god come upon you, the white power latent in your short little frame. Danton is not about to discard what may become a sturdy cloak come wintertime. Danton, too, cherishes the mighty dream of Liberty. He views it otherwise, but still, he views it. We can all be comrades while our opponents are mutual. No fool, Georges Danton. Never that. Only, sometimes, a touch too clever. For genius brings its own calamities. Besides which, he can speak with a candid passion in his defense of Robespierre. For at such moments, like any marvelous actor, Danton also convinces himself.

Robespierre blinks. His eyes have tears in them. The kindness of others, their loyalty, always moves him to a genuine gratitude.

The genius of Robespierre (yes, he too has genius) operates quite differently; this is plain. For Robespierre is motivated by those very driving terrible Furies Danton has just described: Courage, Integrity, Dedication. Robespierre is truthful. He does not have to fool himself or try to fool others. He knows what is right, will serve only that. Would give his life for it. For when Robespierre offers his life for the cause it is not the fiery theater of Danton, essentially doubtful even of itself, nor the self-swept almost-sincerity of Camille, who is in love with the runaway carriage of thought. No, when Robespierre gives himself for a sacrifice, he means it. He is also prepared to trust. He trusts those who befriend him. Trusts them to notice, probably, the mark of God on his forehead—for yes, too, he has come, only partly unconsciously, to the conclusion that something has singled him out. It would be hard for such a man, placed in this historical gateway, to think anything else. So, he trusts. And so that inevitable paranoia, the companion of trust, will come to him. If all who help are friends, when they grow cool, or simply busy elsewhere, then they are unfriends. It is Maxime's fate to see himself as constantly betrayed. Those terrible nights of burning ice are before him, only a dog to comfort him, when all alone he must suffer his Gethsemane over and over again and sign, in the blood of his heart, the words of death for so many traitorous disciples.

Meanwhile, back in the war zone, the Royal Allemande and the Saxony Hussars are trotting quietly through the dawn mist, making very little sound above the muted clink of sword hilts and spurs and the cluck of hoofs on dewy ground. They are advancing toward the Prusso-Austrian lines. What can this be? Some act of incredible valor? The storming of the camp of the foe?

Well, actually—

The leaders present arms and white flags. Able to converse fluently in the tongue of the opposing forces, they soon make everything clear. The German regiment and the Saxony Hussars are going over to fight for Austria.

❧

What is going *on* out there? Have you heard the latest, about de Biron's troops? He formed them up, raised his sword, yelled *"Charge!"* And they took a vote on it, and the majority decision was they wouldn't.

❧

The king says he is not having twenty thousand men of the militia stationed around Paris, ostensibly to defend it. They will cause upheaval and be potentially more dangerous than the enemy. What he means is they might just keep

Austrian rescue out, now things are going so well. L'oui applies his veto (which the Assembly left him as a toy). Doubtless *she* made him do it.

The ministry, so fresh and new, begins to go down. One by one, ministers resign or, tearing L'oui off a strip, are thrown out. A Feuillant ministry commences to rise from the ashes.

Danton suggests Antoinette should be returned to Austria, with such attentions as may be awarded a used article. Paris, in the throes of upsurge, gives a hysterical laugh.

La Fayette, having retreated with his troops just like everybody else, sends word that this "Rule of Clubs" is ruining France. Marat recommends *all* troops should murder their officers. Danton recommends La Fayette should come and repeat what he has just said before the Assembly. The Assembly says, privately, it agrees with La Fayette. Not a day passes without petitions: from the Cordeliers, to do this; the Jacobins, to do that; the Feuillants, not to dare do either; the numerous sections, roused by insane linguistic gymnastics, to do everything at once and altogether! But the elected deputies are not about to go hunting such People's pets as Marat, Danton, Robespierre, the way things are right now. . . . And isn't the crowd getting bigger down there?

⚜

June sunlight was coming in at the windows, sometimes winking as a bird flew by. An afternoon quiet had descended, though there had been some running to and fro, earlier, and a fight involving a fruit cart. Even the bourgeois areas now caught their share of the turbulent currents. The weather was thundery. Storms still came on cue, hanging over Paris to mimic the thunder in the blood. Did these storms inaugurate or heighten the biological tension below, or were they themselves summoned, like wasps to jam, by the mood of the metropolis?

Camille had been writing (though not for the *Tribune;* tussles with Fréron had killed it) in his usual quick nearly mesmerized way. Now he paused. He looked through the doorway. Lucile was in the next room, arranging some flowers in a vase. She had been arranging them a long, long while. It appeared she had fallen into a graceful dreaming state, but every line of her stance denied this. Heavy with pregnancy now, she moved slowly. Even her hands, when she raised them, seemed made of lead. Her head wilted on her beautiful neck, a flower parched by the heat. How pale she was! He had been seeing all this for some time, but when he anxiously spoke to her she would tell him she was very well, only a little tired. This was how it went with women—at least, with women of the towns; one saw how the peasant girls, where nourished, sailed to term like laughing galleons. The last months were taxing, and the child was due in some two weeks. The pallor, laxness—nothing uncommon.

He got up and walked into the room and put his arm around her. She leaned
on him, her weight and the child's. He felt with a kind of alarm how solid the
bulk of the child was against him.

"Here you are," he said. "Always doing things like a busy little hen."

"A few flowers." She sighed. She left the flowers and let him lead her to the
sofa. She sat there, resting on the cushions. She closed her eyes. "Push back the
shutters. I like to see the trees in the gardens. Don't worry for me. I don't mind. I
love him already, your handsome son."

"You'll make me jealous."

He got open one of the shutters and wrestled with the other, which tended to
stick. Outside the carnations were fading in their pots, curling away from the
sun that turned their leaves to paper. Down on the street Fabre d'Églantine was
standing looking up at the window, a slender dark being, with suitably poetic
hands, one of which he raised.

"Can I come up?"

"Or we can play Romeo and Juliet," said Windmill. "Mind the squashed
fruit by the stairs, a cart went over earlier."

He kissed Lucile – already she was asleep – and went out to greet Fabre by
the apartment door.

"D'Anton asked me to come here. He wants to see you."

"And has lost the use of his legs."

"Oh? No. He's being inconspicuous. There's trouble brewing again."

"You're telling me something? I haven't made any speeches. I haven't signed
any petitions. I'm not running off to the backlands now."

"Don't go on to me about it. This is just another interruption to me. I was
writing a play."

"You're always writing a play."

"Don't you wish you could do it."

"Yes. One day."

They went down into the street.

"Wrong turning."

"No," said Fabre. "He's in my room."

When they had got all the way up the badly tiled staircase, they found
d'Anton seated at Fabre's table playing Pyramid as though there were no other
purpose in life.

"There you are," he said. "Things are once more going too far too fast."

Fabre moved sheets of manuscript away from d'Anton as if mere proximity
might prove injurious. Windmill glowered. "It's too hot for all this again. Why
aren't you at home?"

"Doing the rounds. You know the way I have. Seeing what you're all up to.
Informing you of what you're likely to be up to."

"Too kind. *Well?*"

"*That's* a challenge. My word. Come and sit down."

"Say what's happening."

"Sit first."

Camille pulled a face, came over, and sat.

"What about La Rolande then? Those two, which means her, made a mess of things," said d'Anton, ordering the cards industriously. "I thought Manon was sharper than that. But no. She gets the old man to write a letter to L'oui saying he gets first prize as prat of the year. Naturally L'oui throws Roland out with the night soil. But then, that's just as well. Now we can all blame the aristocratic Feuillants in the ministry for the wreck our war's turning out. Pull a few stones from a wall and it'll start to give way."

"Down with the wall," said Camille. "I thought we liked walls to come down."

"Not until there's someone suitable standing under them. A waste, and a dangerous waste. Nothing's stronger than a rebuilt wall. Santerre, lord of the back streets, has been hearing a whole lot of things. Some of the Cordelier fools are agitating, getting the mob at it."

"The mob is already at it. And with a Prussian army supposedly halfway down all the north and east roads—"

"Ssh, now. (Fabre, stop fidgeting.) There is a scheme to plant a tree of liberty in the Tuileries Garden. This scheme is going to blow up into a full-scale riot. The problem being that there is not yet enough support for such a riot, either in low or high places. It's poorly planned if planned at all. It'll end up like the Champ-de-Mars fiasco. So it's got to be stamped on."

D'Anton was no longer employing the cards. Absently Camille moved one of them into line with another. D'Anton struck at his hand. "Are you following me?"

"From what you were saying the other night—"

"Certainly I was saying we'd put the fear of Christ into the court. And certainly there is going to be an explosion. But the timing has to be precise. Nobody's riled enough yet. When the fuse burns through to the powder this time, everything will go. Or else nothing. It's the last fuse we've got."

"Look," said Camille. "Your game's come out."

"Not yet it hasn't. Idiot, leave the cards alone. Fiddling about like some old fortune-teller."

Fabre, perched by the table, gazed mournfully at his manuscript, that second, safer home.

D'Anton glared at these accomplices, exasperated.

"It's too hot," said Camille.

"Damn it, it's hot in hell. What's the matter with you? You're scared? I tell you, if this thing goes wrong you'll have a right to be."

"Plots, schemes."

"Everybody's doing it. La Fayette, for example, is planning a coup d'état. Give him an inch of ground and he'll be in. What then?"

"Well, th-there's always England," said Camille, surprising himself. He looked at d'Anton to see how the remark had struck its recipient, but d'Anton only shrugged. He pushed the cards away and stood. He looked down on them.

"Now listen," said d'Anton. "We speak at the Jacobins and the Cordeliers and tell the pack of them, including the manic Swiss Rat, that there is to be *no* public madhouse. We mingle with the crowds and we murmur in their ears, as in the old Lodge days. If we can write, we go into print and express our disapproval of any attempt to disrupt law and order at this point."

"W-wh-*why?*" shouted Camille, slamming the table with his fist.

"I've been telling you. The proper date is not yet marked on the calendar. When it is, we want it to go with a swing."

"Who does?"

D'Anton met Camille's eyes. D'Anton was amused and irritated, but the colossal power came streaming from him like a fierce light and he turned it on this sometime friend of his as if only to experiment, to tease, blasting a hole through him and out the brickwork at his back, so for three miles you could hear the houses fall down smoking before the blue ray.

"Very well. *I* do. *I,* Georges Danton, son of a scoundrel from the provinces, scar-faced lawyer up from the country. Danton, Tribune of the fucking Plebs. *I do.* And whoever is paying me is irrelevant. *I'm* the one decides. *I'm* the one I'm doing it for. *Me.*"

Fabre looked petrified. Camille swallowed noisily.

D'Anton relaxed. He smiled at Fabre.

"How's the play? Going to read us any?"

⚜

The crowd, the mob. It was an entity now, and maybe always it was. One does not any longer need to speak of individuals—except, of course, when they step forward to represent the being's sight, hearing, or vocal cords. For there are no positive individuals in a mob. An independent act—that is only an impulse of the great singular brain which drives the multiform machine, the thousands of arms, legs, eyes, voices, minds. (As if there were a dream in all men that once they had, every one of them, been a part of each other, or that one day they *would* be—the loss of ego then, or to be, not fearful but marvelous.) The mob is a telepathic creature. One thought, and they all know it. One emotion, and they all share it. In face of uncertainty, hunger, terror, what cosier or more comforting place than the union of a mob?

It swarms, the amoeboid beast, up from the eastern faubourgs through the streets, crashes against the doors of the Manège, and gets in. It marches through the august hall, waving the hearts and innards of animals on those pandemic pikes, variously labeled OFFAL OF AN ARISTO and TREMBLE, THE HEARTS OF TYRANTS. It waves also banners and placards: THE RIGHTS OF MAN—OR DEATH!

KILL THE VETO! BEHOLD! THE WONDERFUL BREECHLESS ONES. There is even a young tree, festooned with blue, white, and red, paper slogans, and driblets of calf's blood. They had said they meant to plant a tree.

All sections of the Assembly sit very still, this late June day. They watch, Feuillant with Jacobin with Girondin.

When the mob finally marches out of the riding school, you hear with trepidation the way the roar of it subsides by only a little distance and then holds steady. They're at the palace now. And it's happened again: some bribe and a side door left open. In any case, they use a cannon as a battering ram, and now the beast is on the stairs. It bursts into a room—and finds before it Louis XVI.

The king looks at the beast of many eyes, arms, legs. He says tiredly, "Yes. I'm here."

The mob fills up the room, leaving just the little pocket for Louis to stand in. When it can't see him with all its eyes, it tells him to get up on a table, just like one of its own orators. So there he is, on the table, looking down at the beast. He doesn't seem to be afraid. When the beast yowls, the king answers it, slowly, frankly. "You know I support the Nation. I have sworn it. And to abide by the Constitution." The beast shrieks that he must revoke all these vetoes—damn nonconstitutional priests, let in the defending troops. The king looks at it. "My friends," he says, "I will consider anything you say to me. But to change my mind under duress? No."

Startled, the beast reviews the words in its enormous composite mind, and the telepathic tentacles that stretch into each of its animate atoms convey a weird little frisson. Well, he's talking like a king at last.

Then a very tall man, muscular, red-faced, used to hacking (already) things to bits, steps forward with the latest petition and becomes the mouthpiece of the beast. Framed by the wilting yet-unplanted tree of liberty, Legendre (d'Anton's butcher, whom Santerre has not been able to dissuade from this headlong course) reads every demand in a stentorian howl, orchestrated by the cries of the crowd. The demands are mainly a reiteration of what has just been "discussed." When Legendre has finished, the king stands and gazes at him. Nothing else. "*Well?*" The king looks at the butcher. "I am the Nation's friend," says the king. But that's all. Legendre bridles his rump-steak features. He yells, "Sir, you're a bloody traitor to the People!" "Never," says Louis mildly. And finds a pike thrust in his face. On the end of the pike not a bloody heart but a blood-red cap, the obligatory headgear of the Revolution, copied from the Phrygian cap worn by freed slaves in the antique world—a symbol and a half. The king looks at the cap sadly, self-consciously. He takes it off the pike and attempts to put it on himself. It's too small for such a large bulbous head. Centuries of plebian malnourishment have gone to make the bald, narrow skull that wore it with ease. The mob snatches the cap back, laughing. They sense the joke. They stretch the cap and hand it up again, a shapeless gigantic sock, and the king puts it on. He looks now like some poor provincial dunce, some ninny made to stand on a table at school for wrongdoing or stupidity. The scatter of guards who have managed to get to him, circling the table, writhe with embarrassment. When the mob offers Louis a bottle – to "drink the People's health" – a guard catches at him. "Sire! It may be poisoned." Louis's eyes, as he raises the bottle to his lips, say dully, *So?*

They had poisoned him already. He's already dying of the Nation's venom.

Calmed by his acquiescence and his obstinacy, the beast lies down, growling softly. Eventually, it slinks away.

Louis sits in a chair, forgetting the red dunce's cap still on his powdered head.

He isn't a bad man. He's always prayed earnestly and been notably devout. He has done nothing that countless kings have not done. Less than most. He has even offered orisons for the souls of the masses. For Louis, it should all have been rather like a medieval Book of Hours: the court in splendor overflown by admiring angels, the plump jolly peasants happily tending the fields or romping with the lambs, everyone comfortable in their place. He's done his best. That day in 1775, when a slight bespectacled youth knelt by his carriage door, soaked in the pouring rain, delivering in Latin a speech of homage and a prediction of future joy (Robespierre, with a little help from his friends), the king had not realized the flattery was anything but the truth. (Or, at least what he understood of it. Louis's secular Latin, actually, was nowhere near as fine as Maximilien's.) What have I done to deserve this? Louis's heart of hearts was now asking. And if the Austro-Prussians broke through, what then? Would Louis turn tyrant to assuage his wrongs? Mow down all Paris, scythe it to stubble and rubble to avenge the wearing of a scarlet cap?

He remembers it now, the misshapen sock, and throws it on the ground, blushing at the memory of how he will have looked wearing it.

❧

I was keeping out of d'Anton's way. Since the twentieth he'd been in a sulky rage: at himself, at France. All right, I said to him, after we'd been arguing half the night, I've done my best. "That's what our glorious king says," said d'Anton. He picked up the pamphlet I'd put out, which was selling well. "Too late," he said. When I was partway down the street, he stood in the café door shouting after me to come back and have another drink. But I ignored him. I was as prickly as he was. He let me go. I hadn't wanted particularly to take his orders, but I'd done it and apparently failed him.

Even so, the riot of the twentieth had been contained. It had also restored some sort of temporary calm to Paris. The pus would form again and need letting again, naturally; there was still thunder in the air. But La Fayette had not brought his troops into the city, and the Prussians, despite rumors, were not over the border. Yet. My pamphlet, which assured the populace it had been the wrong hour for revolt, also patted everyone on the head for keeping matters within bounds. (Almost everyone.) I'd also squawked myself hoarse at the Jacobins prior to the event, despite heckling from all sides, stammering out a written address, with sweat pouring down my back, wishing the lot of them in hell – though it would need to be invented for the purpose. "Reduce Paris to a beast pit – what better service can we do Prussia and Koblenz?"

"Desmoulins the royalist champion!" Somebody yelled repeatedly. It could have been a trained parrot. Or it could have been that maniac Roch-Marcandier, who, rather than work for me, had now become the classic thorn in my heel. I gathered he had gone to jail for my sake, though his term in the arms of justice had not been long. Needless to say, I was blamed. Unable to get anything individually printed (I had had a word with one or two acquaintances), he had taken to sticking handwritten bills on the workshop door extolling my unvirtues. He also sent me letters, asking when I would "gulp some more courage out of a bottle." I doubted my fellow Jacobins would actually let him past the sacred portals, but he spent a lot of time at the Cordeliers, where he reviled not only myself, his special fallen idol, but everyone else in the bargain. I had put up with him in the beginning because he was useful. I think I sometimes enjoyed, too, if I'm honest, having this abject slave who practically lay down in the street for me to walk on, in order to save my shoes from the mud. But mostly he exasperated me. He got in the way. He made me look a fool by his fool's ideas of making much of me. Then, when he decided I was not a hero fit for his worship, he gathered up all the muck he could find to throw. Stories had begun to go around. I could not be sure he was the source. One or two concerned Lucile. Probably others of my legion of enemies inspired them. But what he did not start I have no doubt he spread. Wretched little bastard. Once he turned up at the apartment again, when I was out. Jeanette slapped his face. He was lucky. I would have pushed him down the stairs.

On the streets they told you the king (still *the king*) was brave. Mirabeau once said to me, "If Louis died, it would be necessary to have him stuffed." Figureheads. However rough, angry, or afraid, the People seemed determined to clutch the old symbols to itself, a man hugging the serpent in his bosom.

My concentration for any work was virtually gone. My concern about Lucile had grown. Her paleness, which had been like crystal, was now like chalk. She slept fitfully all day. At night she could not sleep and sat by the light of a candle, reading, embroidering or pretending to read, embroider. I would sometimes sit up with her and fall asleep, and wake with a cricked neck, feeling wretched and guilty. I half began to dislike the child, which was doing these things to her. He had no personality for me. Yet I sensed a sort of communion between my wife and my son, intense and silent. It seemed to console her. Taking the doctor aside, I had put a lot of questions. He was cheery. Everything was well. My insistence puzzled him. Women at such a stage were bound to be in discomfort. It was the natural law. We nearly came to blows when he added

some rubbish to the effect that even the Bible told us so, since Eve bore her
children in pain. After I had shouted for some moments, I think he reckoned I
would denounce him as a supporter of refractory priests and hurried off,
assuring me he had been joking, but even religion sometimes spoke fact, by
accident as it were.

But I had begun to be frightened for her. Her own mother had, delicately
and euphemistically, assured me Lucile was quite strong enough, and at the
perfect age, to produce children. But there seemed a shadow on the apartment. I
knew it was my own. Superstitiously troubled lest I should infect her with it, I
would go out and leave her to the attentive, watchful Jeanette.

Some days I sat up in the gallery at the Assembly and listened to them bark.
I recollected Mirabeau telling me I never attended to what was said, I was too
busy planning how to warp it with my insults. It was certain; not reporting on
the sessions took much of the savor from them. The Stable needed new blood,
besides. It was gasping for Robespierre's flat logic or sudden unearthly possessions, or the cannonades of d'Anton. But Georges had never yet been an elected
member, and Maxime, by getting through his proposal that none of the former
deputies be reelected, had also excluded himself.

Now and then I met Robespierre in the rue Saint-Honoré, walking with
his cane and new dog. (Sister Charlotte had kidnapped the last one; or
else, somebody told me, Robespierre had given it away to a sick child who
loved it and cried when it was taken away. Another version had it the dog ate a
present of fruit intended for Maxime and died in a fit, leaving the obvious
conclusion. I never mentioned any of these tales, though I was curious.) The
new dog was, like the first, large. The Duplays persisted in thinking he named it
Brown, for its color. But the dog was not called Brun but Brount ("t" pro-
nounced), after some obscure but worthy Englishman Robespierre had read of
and wished to commemorate.

At this period I found Maxime calmed me down.

He would wean me, for the afternoon, off wine onto coffee, and I was even
permitted to choose for myself an orange from the dish in the Duplays' drawing
room—kept solely for God. For he was God to the Duplays. It was funny, and
touching, the fuss they made of him and how he needed, enjoyed, responded to
it all. As a workable theory, perhaps we become what others think us to be, like
a chameleon, changing color to match our surroundings. So grave and gentle
and nearly playful was Robespierre in this house. The three daughters were his
priestesses. I'd swear he never laid a finger on any of them save in the most
brotherly manner.

Upstairs, his room had contrived to be a tricolor. Blue bed curtains around
the austere monk's bed, white walls, a vase of singing red roses kept always full,
by the virgin vestals, from a briar that grew in the yard. The window looked out
on Duplay's joinery sheds and the stacks of wood. The scent of sawdust mingled
with the scent of roses and made the dog sneeze.

"Here is your book back," said Maxime, when we were down in his study.

I looked to be sure which of them it was talked, for he was everywhere. Paintings of Robespierre on two walls, engravings on other walls, busts and statuettes all around. A crowd of little Maximes. I myself had come in, the last year or two, for my fair share of portrayal. We did not display any examples at home. One of me was surely enough.

I took the book, which contained some of the writings of Pietro Aretino. "There was a passage I marked. I thought you might find it interesting. They didn't call him the 'scourge of princes' for nothing."

"Yes, I was interested. But really, Camille, to leave the book with Betsi" — this was one of the vestals — "with such engravings."

"Oh. Did she look at them?" His reprimand made me smile. "Have I led her astray?"

"Not at all. She has a pure mind and an innocent soul."

"Unlike myself. Never mind. When she marries, it may give her an idea or two."

"Oh, Camille. I despair of you." But he, too, smiled. Fallible mortals such as I — well, he could be lenient. It was only saints who must not stray.

I'd wondered how much d'Anton had discussed with Maxime. Certainly Maxime had stood out against the uprising on the twentieth.

Since May, he had been putting out a newspaper (financed by Duplay, probably). He never asked me to read the copy, only, unspokenly, to praise the results. Generally the *Defender* contained a reprint of the latest Robespierrean speeches. It saved the rest of us from having to quote them.

That afternoon he began to talk about the danger of a dictator arising out of the mess. I thought at first he meant La Fayette, whom, along with the rest of us, he cordially disliked. Then, by some shift, he seemed to be indicating Pétion. "Oh, him," I said. "No. You're wrong."

Maxime looked at me and said, "To whom do you think I'm referring?" I saw I was still wrong and hazarded, Brissot? "Brissot is a danger, yes. But no. I don't mean Brissot." I saw then, and said, "The heat's making me extra slow. So tell me. Who *do* you mean?"

Robespierre contemplated his manicured fingernails. "Marat, the wretch, has already postulated it."

"Oh, has he?"

"I see you have loyalties, Camille. Other than our own old ties of friendship."

D'Anton was who he meant. Maxime might have been there in Fabre's room that day d'Anton glared at us and shouted, *I'm the one I'm doing it for.* I hadn't made my mind up yet as to what I thought of that. There had been too many other worries.

"No, no, Camille," Robespierre said. "I don't mean to make you uneasy. But I trust you. We've known each other many long years. You must believe, I'd always speak openly to you. And now I say I think you should perhaps consider the possibility that even the very strong, when very much tempted, can fall prey to baseness. Temptations surround him. And you're associated with this man. Be careful."

I didn't like this. I lost my temper. "Th-that's a threat?"

He looked concerned, stood up, and came and put his hand on my shoulder. "No—oh, never that. Please, believe me. I know you for an honest and committed patriot. But sometimes, your very clarity of vision may hide from you what others—"

"You're saying I'm a fool?" He simply regarded me, very quiet, until I relaxed. "All right. I'm sorry, Maxime."

"You are a genius," said Maxime. He had never said anything like that to me. I sat and gaped. "A clean, honed blade that can cut the way for us to freedom. I don't say this to flatter you. You can no more take credit for your gift than for the coat you have put on. God awarded you your talent. How you employ it is another thing. If I repeat now that you should be careful, will you heed me?"

I was suddenly overcome by a sense of utter despondency—no, more: tragedy. Not truly knowing what it was, I put my head in my hands.

"There," he said. "We shouldn't be having such a conversation when you're so worried about your wife, so precious to you, dear Lucile."

Then I began a terrible dry sobbing, choking out to him that she seemed a mile off from me, beyond my grasp, that I thought she would die, that if I lost her there was nothing else left for me, either, but death. He heard it all through. When I subsided, he took my hand and spoke very comfortingly, with great understanding and tenderness, calming me again. Finally he said, "Any man who cares about his wife might feel as you do. But you'll see. Soon there will be a new life to give joy to both of you. A child, the sum of both parents. What happiness he'll bring you, a happiness I shall never know. But perhaps you'll let me share him a little?"

His eyes, without the spectacles, were full of kindness, full of knowledge. He knew she would live. He promised her life to me. As one day he would promise to take her life away.

⚜

June smoldered on into July. I began to haunt the apartment now, finding excuses to be on hand. The doctor told me he imagined there might be some further delay, the tenth, perhaps, or the twelfth.

The usual round of crazy things was going on. A band of Cordeliers had burnt La Fayette (in effigy) at the Palais-Royal-Égalité. D'Anton was speech-making everywhere. Mercier walked in one morning and told me, "You ought to be over at the Assembly, my Windmill. The king's about to send some vital letter in."

"He's always sending in letters."

"True. But word has it this could be an abdication."

"Never."

"I agree. Then it's something to do with the war, and there'll be a reaction. Anyway, Melpomene bribed me with some wonderful chocolate to get you out of the house."

Lucile's mother had been coming over every day. She was due to arrive in half an hour. I let Mercier persuade me, as the confines of our rooms had by now been well and truly paced out, my pen was dry, tides were rushing, and I was missing all of them.

I went in to Lucile, who was still in bed, white on whiteness.

"I was thinking about the queen," she said, when I asked her how she was. "So cold, that wicked creature. If I had committed so many wrongs . . . I'd sacrifice myself." She stared through me dreamily. "They should build me a pyre, like Dido's, and an altar where I should pray for atonement to God—all this in the sight of the people I'd so abused."

This scared me very much. "What on earth are you saying?" I took her hands, which felt like ice. But she smiled. "Did I hear you say to Mercier you'd go with him?"

"Well—"

"Do go. Mama will be here in a few minutes."

"Shall I send in Jeanette?"

"Oh, no."

I bent and kissed her. Her mouth was fresh and sweet, tasting of an apple she had been eating but discarded. Wanting to escape and not wanting to leave her, I took the apple and finished it as Mercier and I crossed the river.

We hung about in the boiling hot Stable all day, all evening, but the king's message never came. Everyone was in the know and waiting for it. News was up that the number of Prussian troops on the border was now estimated at sixty thousand, which caused paroxysms. You discredited the number on reflection. It's usual in these cases to knock off at least a third.

At nine, when we were about to give up, Arthur Dillon came in and approached Mercier to inquire for news. Officer and royalist, impeccably French—but an Irishman to his nails' extremities—he listened to Mercier's comments, which were restrained enough, then looked at me. "I suppose Monsieur Desmoulins is awaiting an abdication." "I've been awaiting that since they crowned him." Dillon smiled. "Oh, now," he said engagingly. "You spoke quite well of the poor king once upon a time." "I hoped he'd change his ways." "Has he not?" said Dillon. "Yes," I said. "He's much worse." At that, with his inappropriate charm, he tactfully converted the subject. "And may I ask, monsieur, are you a father yet?" Which caught me off guard. I told him shortly I was not. Dillon gave me a blue-eyed Irish nod. "The best of all wishes to your wife," he said, bowed to Mercier, and passed on as if at some ball. I could have kicked him.

I returned to our street about ten o'clock, light still netted in the sky, and suddenly started to run. When I reached the door, Jeanette came out and held me back. "There now, monsieur. It's started."

I must have treated her to some choice phrases, but Jeanette's mind was broad; she only smiled. "All's as it should be. I've made up the bed for monsieur in the other room."

Monsieur, needless to say, did not use the made-up bed. He lurked in the other room and went mad.

The midwife had already arrived and now and then appeared, looking at me with boundless genial contempt. Demeter came out of the bedroom, and said something absently, and vanished again. The place was full of women, to whom I was only a shadow and who, when they saw I was not peaceably going to bed with a book, began to try to coax me into departure once more. God knows what happened to the night. It went somewhere. Every minute lasted a year, but whole hours disappeared like smoke. The silence was dreadful. I was waiting for it to be broken by cries.

Eventually the open windows started to lighten. I did go out then and walked up and down the streets, pestered by a succession of late-roaming prostitutes, milk sellers, a knife grinder, and an ill drunk. The churches were shut, bolted and barred against nocturnal civil displeasure or else already turned over to civic uses. I think if Saint-Sulpice had been accessible I would have gone in there and prayed to something, to a God stripped of lies.

Virtually since the day she gave it to me, I had worn that coil of Lucile's hair about my neck. Soon after we were married, she had awarded me a locket in which the talisman might be placed. (She said, I recall, she would check the locket's contents when I slept, to make sure the hair had not changed color, become black or red: another's.) Now I found myself afraid to take out and open the locket, in case the curl had turned to dust. One of the reasons I so hated superstition—I was never able to cure myself of it.

I went home. It was half past six. I sat down at the desk and woke up to Demeter saying gently but firmly, "I bring you an invitation from my daughter to go in and meet your newborn son."

When I went into the room, everything had been set to rights. Lucile was lying on the high pillows, her hair combed off her forehead, her eyes bruised, paler than marble, but utterly *present*. She had come back, out of the vast distances, come back with the second life safe in a white bundle in her arms.

"Look," she said. "No, not at me, silly one. At *him*."

So I stopped looking at her, and I looked at him.

He lay there, this extraordinary little miracle of a thing, every small feature perfect and in situ, fur already on his head, wide dark eyes swimming on me.

"C-can he see me?"

"Yes, of course he can see you. He's been wanting to see you for so long. Pick him up. Hold him. Tell him who you are."

I remembered d'Anton holding his child, so respectfully and with such care. I took up my child, out of his mother's arms, and I held him. Even now, I can feel the texture of his wrappings and the astonishing smoothness of that new-cast skin to which life had not yet laid a single scourge but one, the act of birth. My son. I told him who I was. He watched me attentively, this living, astounding element we had formed between us, she and I.

I gave him back to her because I was weeping, and a baptism of tears for this child was not what I intended.

SIX

THE DRAMATIC CLIMAXES are all in the wrong places in this affair called History. If a writer had made it up, he'd do it very differently, more neatly, and with ten times more impact. But real life's a bloody mess." I once said that to Mercier, who had written a great deal of drama years before. I forget if he agreed.

1792: Summer

WHEN THE king's letter was finally delivered to the Assembly (on July 6) it was nothing much. It concurred that France was in danger from the Prussian advance and announced that the monarchy expected every man to do his duty: resist. In other words Yes-Yes was saying, Yes, yes, I'm on your side. Just look, I'm telling you to drive off these nasty foreigners. Somehow, coming at the time it did, the mood of alarm and disorder straining on a leash, the letter threw a lever for action. By July 11 the Assembly had declared a State of Emergency. All over Paris the patriotic platforms went up, roped with tricolors, fringed by tubbed trees of liberty, noisy with bugles and gallant men in blue or red coats and the bright white faces of excitement. Over here, brothers. Our beautiful mother, France, implores you to rally to her aid.

On Ninth Bridge the bands played all day, and they fired cannon across the river. The enrolled flung up their arms for cheers, kisses, and wine gratis from the bystanders. The military processions went marching over: horses, gun carriages, and men, the banners on their wreathed poles like the trophies and eagles of the legions. *Come, children of the Fatherland, the day of glory is at hand.* And by the fourteenth they were beginning to sing it too, that wonderful, oddly modulating rhythmic aria of the Republic. The federal soldiers had stridden back into the city for the annual festival of Bastille Day and brought the battle hymn with them. You heard it everywhere. In the alleys, parks, and gardens, in private houses, in the theaters where, at some rousing phrase in the play, the audience might spontaneously combust, rise, and sing, the orchestra (not slow, the music ready on their stands), joining in at once. Raise the standard of blood! the pale-limbed actresses fluted in high wild maenads' voices. *Aux armes, citoyens! Marchons! Marchons! Q'un sang impur abreuve nos sillons!* Till the rafters rang, and the great chandeliers quivered like the sweat and tears on the faces below.

But on the day of the festival, the patriot king, requested to fire a tree of feudalism hung with badges of the aristocracy, had refused. *No, no,* said Yes-Yes, backing away.

The fête of the fourteenth was altogether not as it had been. If there were lights under the trees of Heaven's Fields this year, they were dull and cast a bloody glow. Those walking there *en famille* spoke in harsh voices and had already donated their sons to France. Mostly they stayed home and started to dig up their cellar floors for nitre to keep the cannons going.

Danton: Scholar of greeds

The dinner party at Orléans's place in the country had gone very couthly: the fish with the cream and the lamb basted in some sort of toffee, with fruit, and the fowl drowned in wine, poor little devils, and the pastry dishes, and the interesting trifles that summed everything up, the confectionery and liqueurs and cigars and aristocratic snuff—which led to a discussion of an aphrodisiac snuff that apparently now came out of Spain.

Little Robespierre, powdered head down, busy peeling and stoning cherries before deigning to put them in his mouth, not listening. "Have some more vinegar, Maxime." And Maximilien smiling a touch, and putting his pale hand over his goblet so the exquisite wine must stay in the exquisite decanter or go all over the exquisite tablecloth. But he had looked as if everything he ate and drank *was* vinegar, or sawdust. Eating to be polite. Here to be polite, and politic, in the nest of the wicked republican aristo who now had himself titled Citizen Égalité—Philippe-Equality—certainly, no longer Louis, Duc d'Orléans.

Danton, meanwhile, the greedy pig, had obviously enjoyed everything: every mouthful, every dish, every glass, every word of lewd or artistic conversation, every opportunity to speak—the tableware, the paintings, the estate, the earth. Everything, everyone. Over there, the gold-faced clock with the marble cherubs ticks because the clockwork is nicely oiled and wound. But what makes Danton tick? Greed and lust for life. Don't make any mistake with him. When he straddles a woman, he is piercing the universe. When he eats that candied apricot, that's France he's swallowing. Nothing is of small significance here. Genius embraces all, and all is symbols. He's so clever, this one, his name should be scrawled across the sky in fireworks, and maybe it will be, one day. In a way his very appetites are intellectual, because every one of them has an intrinsic depth. There's more to him than even he himself will ever find out. To see him as some enormous cunning hog, shouldering through the forest, gobbling up the flowers on the way, is to miss the essence of Danton. While he shoulders and tramples and chews, he notices every petal, every vein of every leaf. He could dissect a spider's web and reassemble it. Because he seldom bothers, don't suppose he can't. Remember how he holds his children, and remember how well capable he is of offering the preliminaries of love, and that appalling voice, softer than honey, and those little porcine eyes bluer than bright stars.

Camille the Windmill — who isn't here, but if he had been would also have behaved like a greedy pig — tends to be forgiven because he is thin and looks frail, as if he starved to death recently and has come back to haunt the supper tables and get his rights. Camille's physical appetites are only accessories, anyway. And Robespierre has none, apparently.

But now there is something else on the table, nothing to do with dinner. Even so, Danton regards it just as hungrily as he did the cuisine. And like the cuisine, actually, without having been apprised of the exact menu, he seems to have had some idea, too, that this dish would be served.

The dish was a document, drawn up by a section of the king's current aristo ministry, and with notes made by no lesser person than Queen Austrianette. A sort of list of who was going to be doing what, once France was back in royalist hands. For example, certain members of the Girondins would be rowing galleys about, for life. A few others, including Robespierre and Pétion, would be in less energetic employment, nourishing small areas of soil, in Robespierre's case only five feet three inches of it. Hardly anyone at the table was not threatened with something, and quantities of absent friends and hangers-on with them. (It was the type of brochure that makes for energetic after-dinner conversation and is repeated everywhere for days to come.)

Oddly enough, Danton was not mentioned, not even in the banished-forever category. But of course, the court had been paying Danton, so there was no need to exile, imprison, enslave, or hang him. As yet. Maybe the idea of the *as yet* had occurred to him, for he seemed as incensed as the rest of them, if not, perhaps, as scared.

"What do we do?"

"*Do?* We get the Marseilles soldiery together, strike up their battle chant, and march on the palace. Get them, the bloodsucking, plotting bastards."

"Or we could get out—"

"*Out?*" bellowed Danton. He told them where they could put such a notion. "Listen. They are sitting there on their padded arses at the Tuileries, playing piquet for our heads. Maxime, what did you say the other day about the palace guard?"

Maximilien, looking startled but composed (the combination, with Robes-pierre, was possible), replied, "Reportedly the palace is guarded chiefly by the King's favorite Swiss battalions, each man armed with fifteen cartridges, every man looking the other way. The king is almost certainly about to attempt another escape."

"Straight into the arms of the Prussians, which will make this death list immediately operational."

"The National Guard—"

"The present commander of the National Guard," said Danton, "is a royalist and a traitor to the People. Pétion wants him forced out, and I want him shot. I think that's plain." They were quiet now, staring at him. Danton was used to this. He lowered his voice considerably and shouted, "Good God, it's them or us. It always was, but the game's getting dirty. Do you think the Austrian cat will hesitate to scratch? She lies in bed dreaming about it. And have you heard what's coming out of Prussia? They say when they get here they'll raze Paris, make a modern Troy of her. No city—they'll blast it out of the ground. No river—it'll be dammed by corpses. And they *will* get to Paris the way things are. An untrained army, sold out at home by the bloody Assembly quacking away like a lot of old virgins over their knitting. *Christ!* We wake up and we do it now. What do you say?" They sat and stared on. Philippe-Equality raised his hands and let them fall. Danton shot a look at Robespierre. Danton said to him, as if appealing to the one sane, reliable man in France, "For God's sake, say something. Help me out."

Robespierre awarded Danton a (half-conscious) little bow. He said to the disconcerted table, where he had patiently lapped vinegar and avoided the discussion of aphrodisiacs, "Gentlemen, we're at the summit of the constitutional drama. The Revolution must move faster or be overwhelmed. This king—who is he?—a shadow. A terrible disease may require a terrible remedy. Use the knife, or our poor patient, the dream of French freedom, will die in front of us."

"Thank God," said Danton. "Thank God for you!" And leaning across, he embraced him. Maximilien allowed it, gentle, stern, giving Danton credit for recognizing him. While the table broke into uproar again.

※

28 July 1792

DECLARATION

Of his Serene Highness the Duke of Brunswick and of Lunebourg, Commander of the Combined Armies of their Majesties the Austrian Emperor and the King of Prussia

To the Inhabitants of France

Their Majesties the Austrian Emperor and the King of Prussia having entrusted to me the command of the Combined Armies, which they have caused to gather on the frontiers of France, I wished to set before the inhabitants of this Kingdom the steps to be taken by the two sovereigns, and the policy which guides them. . . .

Their Majesties Imperial and Royal have set their hearts on this: to cause to cease the reign of anarchy within France, to end the attacks carried out against Throne and Altar, to reestablish law and order, and to give back to the King of France the security and freedom of which he has been deprived, returning him to that rightful eminence wherefrom he may exercise the authority which is his due.

In the name of the King of France, we outlaw the "Revolution" and the "Revolutionaries". . . .

The armies of our coalition will protect French cities, towns, and villages, their people and possessions, providing all submit to their King.

We enjoin the "National Guard" to make provision for the keeping of the peace in city and countryside until our arrival; for this we shall hold them personally responsible. On the contrary, those "National Guard" who have contested with the troops of the allied advance, and who are taken in arms, will be regarded as traitors and duly punished for their treason. . . .

The commanders, officers, noncommissioned officers, and common soldiery of the French troops are to return to their ordained allegiance and kneel to their King. The members of the departments, districts, and municipalities are likewise deemed responsible; their heads and their goods will be at stake for all crimes, arson, murder, looting, which they condone or which they have not made sufficient effort to prevent in their respective areas.

The inhabitants of cities, towns, and villages who attempt to defend themselves against the troops of their Majesties the Austrian Emperor and the King of the Prussians, who shoot at them either in open country or from windows, doors, or other openings of their dwellings, will be punished on the spot, according to the rules of war, their houses being pulled down or burned.

The City of Paris and all her citizens, without distinction, will be required to demonstrate submission, immediately, to their King, to award this Prince his full and unmitigated freedom, and to ensure for him, and all royal persons of his household, the inviolability and honor due to God's Anointed by considerations both natural and civilized.

Their warlike Majesties, whose Commander I am, declare that these events rest on your heads. They will hold responsible the members of the "National Assembly," those of the local assemblies of districts and departments, the municipality, the justiciary body, and the "National Guard" of Paris. All these will subsequently be judged by a military court, without hope of mercy.

Their Majesties have further declared, on their word as Austrian Emperor and King of Prussia, that if the least violence, the smallest insult was offered to their French Majesties, the King, the Queen, the Royal Family, if their security and liberty are not restored, and protected in that restoration—at once—there would be exercised a vengeance never to be forgotten, that shall serve the peoples of the future as a warning: To deliver the entire population of Paris to military restraint, exacting of fines and other strictures, and her stones to total destruction; while the treasonable perpetrators of the outrage will face tortures and all capital penalties they have merited.

Conversely, if you lie in the mud like good little slaves, we'll march in, your friendly local invaders, and shower you with smiles.

❧

That, coming out of Koblenz, turned the pallor in French cheeks to a stamping red. Who was this—this Prussian earwig, to tell them what they could and could not do? (Or, some sources had it, it was the Swedish earwig, *her* lover, he of the big carriage that got all the way to a grocer's at Varennes. He'd run off and left her, but now he was composing threats.) Whoever did it, said it, wrote it, it reacted on them like a dare. They gathered around the river, the Parisian "Inhabitants of France," stared off at the Tuileries, joking: Oh, *much* too scared now to go up there and say anything to L'oui. And they sharpened their pikes on the air, the "National Guard," the backbone of which was becoming almost pure Sans-Culotterie. (And some other sources had it Danton had bribed Brunswick to write it, to cause an opposite effect, bribed him the way he would bribe him in another matter. But that was later.)

Otherwise, Danton had been demanding equal suffrage for every male citizen. Votes for all, power for all. Any man could carry a pike and enlist to save his country. Now and then Danton gave an incredible speech on some corner or over at the old fairground, the Palais-Égalité. The Breechless Wonders liked Danton. And the federal soldiers liked him. They'd decided not to disperse in the usual way, after the fourteenth. The provinces could take care of themselves for a while. It was better to be here in the capital, just turning the corner into August, copies of the famous Brunswick Manifesto appearing all over the place with pretty drawings on them of the Brunswick duke doing various things to himself with his quill. And even chamber pots going on sale with his picture . . . inside. . . . Anyway, the pressures on the borders were intense, and where would the allied enemy forces come but straight here? On the way plunging through Arras (Robespierre's home town), the Aube department (Danton's), possibly crashing about a bit in Picardy (Desmoulins's). (Not surprising the ones with wives they liked had them all stored around Paris and the babies off somewhere else again.)

As for general entertainment? Well, it must be said the girls in the Palais had put up the prices, and they wouldn't accept assignats. But there *was* an endless selection of spirit-elevating processions and cavalcades taking place, arranged by the municipality. And free dinners by the score.

It was Robespierre, over at the Jacobins, who warned the federal soldiers to watch out for the blandishments of serpentine aristocrats: "Avoid the false embraces, the banquets, and the cups of gold which hold the waters of Lethe — deadly forgetfulness of duty and honor." Frankly, the soldiery did let the royalist faction treat them to the odd banquet, but they bore in mind all the while Robespierre's warning, holding it before their mental noses like Ulysses' magic flower, so the sorcerous feast should not corrupt them.

Robespierre had in fact begun to extol a republic. It seemed he had found out what it was, having asked everybody. He spoke out boldly. Once the king was overthrown, the Assembly, unreliable as rotten floorboards, must be removed. It would be replaced by a National Convention, elected on universal suffrage — no more distinctions between taxpayer and poor man; all had the right to vote. (Just what Danton said. Or had Danton said just what Robespierre said?)

Mayor Pétion was in a panic, meanwhile. The Gironde party was entirely in a panic. The death list could be a forgery, but if the king went down, God knew what would happen. They dashed about, diving in on L'oui like frantic herons, but L'oui didn't trust them and shooed them out again. "These traitors," said Robespierre, with a sad and terrible distaste. "And when the storm breaks," cawed Marat, pointing at Robespierre across the tombstones, "where will the little Pierre be? We all know he swoons at the rattle of a sword." It was Desmoulins who stood up at that point and yelled across the room at Marat: "Then can we take it you're offering to lend him the cellar *you* always hide in?"

Laughter. Marat sneered, sitting on his bench off which everyone else had moved to avoid his smell, his loathsome illness, and his tongue. He had referred to certain persons as the Three Ds, having reawarded Maximilien the *De* prefix. "When one barks," had said Marat, "the other two wag their tails." Now he did not bother to be witty.

Camille was getting too noisy these days, he stammered less and shouted more, and generally successful stupidity was going to his head.

Marat lifted his mask of running sores and called, "I only say this. I shall respect the lot of you far more when I see something done. Yes, Robespierre. Away with the king. Then what?"

"Then the program as I have outlined it."

"Milk and water!" shouted Marat. "You drink it, you talk it. The only way to save this Revolution is through blood."

And then Desmoulins yelled, "Did you think we were speaking of going over to the palace to *dance?*"

Robespierre broke in. He fixed Marat with his blind strange gaze and said, "The People's Friend is speaking of a scaffold." And the room turned noiseless for a moment. Then Robespierre went on. "Death, as a solution, is the last resort. I abhor it. You, Marat, with these constant cries for an ultimate violence, destroy your credit with the People."

Marat sprang up: repulsive, as his sickness had made him, that infection contracted underground in those very cellars of hiding Camille Desmoulins had just jibed at and which caused him an endless torment, a ceaseless misery of itching, burning, writhing, suppurating agony. His own body disintegrating about him, Marat bound his fearsome soul with iron. "I can never lose my credit with France!" he screamed now. "My credit is my utter sincerity. When I say kill, I mean *kill.* The rest of you"—he raked them with his slimy, pain-seared eyes—"you speak of fighting and you mean crawling; you say *death* and you mean compromise. But one day the tables will turn. You'll start speaking of comradeship—then watch out, it'll be murder. And poor France, on her cross, waiting to be remembered, while you pack of fools hack about. Future generations will spit on your names."

Draw a heart on a wall: Marat hates everybody; everybody hates Marat.

Except the People. Who love Marat. For whom Marat, if he doesn't love, for Marat surely loves no one, has yet conceived a flaming passion. His springboard, whereby to leap for the throats of all the rest. Rabid little Marat, lurking foaming and snarling, to bite. Marat, who for years never took a bath, forced now to lie in an herbal bath half the day, to ease the earthly hell his body has become. And the faithful laundress mistress, tirelessly tending him (and presumably his laundry), this hate-filled stenchful little fiend. Whyever does she do it?

※

The great cavalcade, having swept around into Carousel Place, poised like a glittering alligator under the red light of a westering sun. Surrounded by the legions of the National Guard, the black-wheeled gun carriages, on a horse that now glowed like copper, the man shouted to the soldiers and the crowd, managing briefly to be magnificent, a figure of authority and power. "That's Camille," they said. They leaned out of windows, elbows on sills still hot from the August day, framed by crisp dry flowers. In the doorways they watched him, and when the soldiers roared their assent, those in the doorways—roused by the idea of response, not really having heard—also roared.

He looked exalted. Caught by the sun, gilded under the wings of black hair, the old Roman mirage somewhere in his brain, eyes like black lights, this rabble-rouser worked away at them, filled with that former magical sense of moving the world. Inspired, inspiring. He only told them they were in danger, which they knew; that the day was coming when a blow must be struck to release them, which they had heard about and were not necessarily convinced of. Proud as a commander, invested with a bizarre authority, up on the chestnut (what else?) horse, he looked patrician, even beautiful. And he took their shouts of acclaim and affirmation into himself like drafts of wine. It had all happened before: the crowd, the soldiers, the chariots, the blood-red sinking of the sun. I led them to victory, and the earth shifted on her axis. Long ago, far off. I can almost remember.

❋

"And I went around to Danton's and banged on the door, and the maid comes out and says, Oh, he's gone away."

"You're joking."

"No. All this in the air, and Orléans's mob involved up to its earrings, and Santerre saying the slums are going crazy and he can't hold them. And Danton's in the country visiting his mother."

"He's gone there to make his will."

They looked at Fréron. "Who says?"

"He says. Or ask Camille. Danton said, This is kill or cure. And he went off to say good-bye to his aged parent and arrange his affairs with the notary. He'll be back on the eighth." Fréron looks away into the smoke of the crowded café. Lucile, too, will be returning to the capital on the eighth. She has been staying with her mother at the holiday house in Queen's Market. But the child has gone off to be nursed in another direction, to the same nurse who cares for Danton's latest. God. One on each tit, the future princes of France. Fréron, miserable and glorying in it, calls to mind how Lucile fed him thyme in the garden. He thinks about her brightness. He thinks about the riot that is due in Paris, and how any one of them may get himself killed in it. Fréron, his head in his hands, thinks about Lucile Desmoulins in a black dress and looking very pale, and how kind he would be, providing she isn't wearing the black, remorsefully, for him.

❋

August 9. *Sonnez la Toquassen.* The bells start in the late afternoon, then stop. A bell practice, perhaps. Everyone's poised. Everyone's ready for a showdown. Paris packed by People's soldiery, raring to go, and the Sans-Culottid National Guard. Even the speechmaking has tailed off. That's always a sure sign, the moment of silence that attends the indrawn breath before the great scream begins.

At the Stable, snowed in by petitions, the Assembly has been debating the suspension of the king. The debate took about five minutes and was adjourned. Interesting. They have all been saying: Make a decision on the king, or at midnight tonight the tocsin will sound and the People will rise in answer. And no decision. So presumably at midnight—

The will maker's returned. He's been strolling around the Theater-of-France division, patting men on the shoulder and kissing babies.

⚜

"You didn't want me to come back?" Lucile said. She stood before the mirror in the dark gold light, taking from her hair the flowers she had worn during dinner. She spoke playfully, but her eyes did not meet her husband's in the glass.

"Not want you? I hate the place when you're not here."

"But I shall be in the way. Danton's scheme."

"No. But things will be unsettled."

"Dangerous. How could I stay in Bourg-la-Reine when you—"

"Nothing will happen to me."

He looked away. She knew he was afraid, excited and afraid, wildly elated and grimly disturbed by turns. He had written to tell her how he had stood in the stirrups of his horse, calling on the People. She had visualized it and wept, for a hundred reasons, mostly without names.

There had been soldiers to dinner tonight. (Persons of importance wined and dined the Patriot Army.) Marseillais, the men had inevitably sung the "Marseillaise," until the china trembled and, outside, some passersby enthusiastically joined in. Everybody was otherwise most respectful. The soldiers lowered their eyelids modestly at Lucile, and one of them blushed when passed the salt. He was the very one who then made a dramatic pass at Jeanette, downstairs. Whether rebuffed or welcomed, there had been a squeal and a sort of thud, and the fellow in charge went out on the landing and squawked something into the stairwell. Returning, Lucile's pardon was begged. Lucile was demure. Jeanette was also demure, coming up with the dessert and the soldier in tow innocently carrying a cheese. When the soldiers left, Lucile burst out laughing. The two of them, the crowd agitator and his wife, stood in their apartment and giggled. The tears of reuniting had already been celebrated the day before. Then had come the questions. His were all about the child (whose mighty Roman name, Horatius, had already been commuted to the title of Little Lizard). Her questions concerned the plans Camille had intimated and not explained. Their complexity did not concern her. She was concerned only with his part in them.

She was in a strange mood. Her body, which had been the traveling house of a child born only a month ago, was still dazed, curiously empty. The last months

of pregnancy had made her more ill than she would have admitted or allowed
herself properly to understand. Delivered, she contained, instead of life, a kind
of fear now. She had felt a dream of it once before, when she cried, "Don't die
and leave me here." When she said to him, Didn't you want me to come back?
she was saying, Are you going to leave me after all?

(But it's guesswork. I can't swear to what she thought. I was frightened and
excited and the blaze of light on her was like an omen of all things splendid but
perilous. I wanted to make love to her, and it wasn't possible at this time, and it
drove me mad. I suggested we go around to Danton's. I saw only her love that
was like a form of immortality, and that I desired her. Only the light shining on
everything, like the future, which was to be won.)

❋

The Key to Camille is Danton.

❋

I was twenty-three when, across the slaty November sky, a great gleaming
planet had sailed. The windows and the yards of Louis-le-Grand were packed,
every face turned upward. I recall seeing some of our priestly tutors cross
themselves, for surely such a thing went against the laws of God. But I, nearly
falling out of the tree I had climbed, craned after the golden dream, in love
with it. It was de Rozier's wonderful balloon. With it, he had conquered the
air, become a bird, giving to man the promise of the power of flight. The
gorgeous globe had all the figures of the zodiac around it, and lions' heads,
and sunbursts—you couldn't see them, only the flash and flame of the gold. Out
in the countryside, the peasantry fled under their henhouses, thinking France
was being invaded, not by Austrians or Prussians, then, but by beings from
the stars.

The vision of the supernal balloon came to me again that August night when
I was thirty-two, how men could aspire to and achieve the impossible. (Robespierre missed seeing the balloon. I forget why. He missed August ninth and
tenth, too.)

❋

The Marseillais soldiers had been very cheerful. We (and the rest of those
who "spread the word") had done a fair piece of work in Paris. The hours of the
monarchy were numbered. And we, too, were pretty blind drunk with believing
our own propaganda. My God, who was I then, striding down the street with
Lucile on my arm, already hearing trumpets and firecrackers? Again and again
I see it and I say, I? Did I do this, say this, reckon *this?* I know I did. And like a

dim distant noise, the agonized exhilaration and the crawling doubt of that evening come back to me.

Lucile caught my hysteria. By the time we reached Danton's residence we were both silly as two children (I the more so; my son, Horace, one month old, could have put me to shame with his sensible demeanor). We chased a flock of pigeons by the street door; having enhanced *their* evening, we then sprang up the stairs and attacked the Dantons' bell. When the maid answered it I said to her, "Tell him it's La Fayette and I have five thousand men with me." Even the maid tittered, rather nervously, and we all rushed into the purple room to find Gabi in tears in the arms of her Italian mother. Danton came out of the red study, relieved at rescue, though I'd arrived too early.

Danton embraced Lucile, in the usual way lifting her up in the air. Gabi glared at me. Here we go again.

"How can you laugh?" demanded Gabi. She sank once more on her mother. Danton put down Lucile and came over.

"How are the streets?"

"People rushing about, but farther up, near the bridge. A lot of horses have been through, with the usual result to one's footwear."

"Mmm. So you're in a frivolous condition. Keep going. Either the monarchy's finished off tonight or I am."

Just then, as if on cue, a vague roaring sounded from over toward the Cordeliers Club. You could make out the words, *Life to the Nation!* One huge blurred tipsy voice. Then it died off suddenly.

"How drunk are they going to get?" said Danton.

"When they fall in the horseshit, it'll sober them up."

Italian madame raised her eyebrows at me and looked away displeased. Danton generally reined his language in her presence, but she wasn't *my* mother-in-law.

"Is it true," said Lucile abruptly (she had gone to sit with Danton's elder son, Antoine, who looked unnerved, and she was playing pat-hands to stop him thinking about Gabi's distress), "is it true Maxime was threatened?"

"There's some story. Somebody ran out at him with a dagger. Or Madame Duplay has it his sister—you know how jealous Charlotte is of the Duplays— sent him some poisoned jam." Lucile and I both collapsed, laughing insanely, and Antoine laughed insanely too, because it was better than copying the other adult, who cried.

"Well," said Italian madame, lifting Gabi off herself and onto Lucile. "I'm going home while it's quiet."

"Yes. You'll be safe enough," said Danton. He went to her and kissed her hand. He said something in her ear as he kissed her cheek. They flirted a moment; then she said to Gabi, "Come. Walk with me to the corner, like a dutiful daughter should. The air will be good for you."

"No!" cried Gabi.

But Lucile caught the drift. She handed Antoine over to the domestic, who had come to take him to bed, and also stood up. "Yes, Gabi. It's a lovely sunny evening. Let's walk a little way. Really, it's perfectly safe. Camille and I just came along—"

"That shouting!" exclaimed Gabi.

"It was several streets off, in the other direction," said Danton. "Go on, *mia cara.*"

She rose, then, and flashed a look at him which said, I know you are sending me out to be rid of me. I will go, dutifully. I will never forget it, either. She swept to the door ahead of her mother and Lucile. And I realized Gabi was pregnant again.

"I suppose the streets *are* safe?" I said to Danton.

"Safer than in here if you don't stop pestering me about them."

As Lucile went by me, nevertheless, I muttered something to her about being careful. "Oh, everything will be quite all right," she said. "Everything. I *know.*" Her confidence was sparkling. She was playing my tune better than I was, now. Last through the doorway, she paused, turning to Danton and raising an imaginary glass. "To freedom, Marius!" Captivated, he grinned and nodded. But when she was gone, he shook his head and murmured again, "Freedom, or death."

Now we had the main room to ourselves. Danton plonked some wine on the table and we started to drink it. We said very little. This space was valuable mostly because it was the quiet before the storm. The eve of battle. The windows filled slowly with a beautiful translucent dusk, the melancholy of day's ending. I didn't think, Will I see another evening? You don't, until you're very sure. The wine kept me calm, as it did him. And then I grew confident, detached. Presently he did start to talk. He said, "You remember that afternoon at Fabre's bolt-hole? I told you, Wait for the day marked on the calendar. Well, it's here. Everything's right, now. As right as it can be. We've been slaving for it. If it works—" And he left the sentence to all its possibilities. The last light drew a thin blue line along his broken profile. His eyes were glowing; not a muscle moved. He looked implacable and awesome; I'd have backed him against the world. It would have been the most alien thing to me to have left him in those moments. I recalled Maximilien's telling me to watch out, Danton was hungry to rule, and I couldn't any longer, after the discussions and plans of the past month, deny it. I thought, I'll follow you. I wanted it, to ride after him into the night and the battle, knee deep in blood if I had to. Detached and out of time, I was already doing it. I have to say, at this point, the blood was only colored water.

Then they started to come up the stairs, the rest of the captains of Danton's army. We lit the lamps. There were guns everywhere, stacked in corners, on the sofa. "Don't scratch the damn table," said Danton. Fréron and one of the leaders from the Luxembourg section were quarreling over some unimportant matter.

Every one of us had had our "orders." To me, Danton had constantly said, "Stay by me. I'll tell you what and when." He meant, Shout when I shout. The peculiar high-strung whistling note of tension was in the room and in my bones. I looked out the window at the peaceful darkness of the street. The doorbell kept ringing, training for the tocsin. Robert's wife had appeared and was demanding of Danton where her husband had been sent. When he brushed her off, she came to me. "He's over at the Luxembourg section." "I know that." "Well then, you know as much as I do." "Do any of you know what you're up to?" she hissed at me. But she seemed so concerned I kissed her. "Yes. *He* knows." She glared at Danton furiously and went away across the room as if setting off for another country.

We were arming ourselves when Lucile and Gabi came back. Gabi declared the streets nearer the river were in ferment. She was terrified and had obviously done an excellent job on Lucile, who stood in the shadows, very small and still. All her optimism—gone?

Fréron swaggered over to her, toting a musket. Striking a pose he declared hoarsely, "Well, I'll probably die tonight. Why not? What's so wonderful in my life I should want to go on living?" But she turned from him as if she despised him and walked quickly into the other room. As I passed him, he said, "Well, we all want your wife." "I know you do," I said, and pushed him out of my way. She was standing in Danton's salon, sobbing, her hands over her face. In that moment I wished she had stayed in Bourg-la-Reine. I couldn't bear her pain, even if it was for me. I went to her and put my arms around her, consoling her with whispered random endearments, her heart dashing against mine, as if they were in a race.

"You're crying for Fréron," I said at last.

"For you. Why are you involved in this? How can it have happened?"

"I was always involved."

"But such danger—please don't go with them."

"Oh, Lucile—"

"For my sake, for the child. It isn't necessary."

"You're frightened of the guns. It looks worse than it is. We'll just walk over the river and call on the Hôtel de Ville. The soldiers will be doing the fighting. There may not even—we could do it without a shot being fired." As I said it I didn't believe it, nor did she. "And Danton," I said. "Our friend, this great Roman leader of ours—I couldn't let him down. Besides, he's invulnerable. He's magic. I'll be next to him the whole time. His gods will have to look out for me too."

"He doesn't have any gods," she said.

"He thinks he doesn't."

She drew away and said, the tears still running down her cheeks, "I'm sorry. I shouldn't have said what I did. You have to do what you think is right. And you'll be safe. God won't let anything happen to you."

I was kissing her when Danton called through the doorway, "Come on, the celebration comes *after* the victory."

She was so brave and gentle when I left her, I could have cried myself. She didn't, after all, want to send me out with her forebodings on my neck. But I felt as invulnerable as I supposed Danton to be. I went down into the streets with the sense that I already owned and had responsibilities for them.

The Assembly was still sitting, over by the Tuileries. The municipality at City Hall was also sitting, quaking in its seats, waiting for Danton to come in and throw it out. Which he duly did. An Insurrectionary Commune was set up in place, with full support from all the Paris sections. Pétion had vanished. The present commander of the National Guard, Mandat, was called in and arrived, like the priceless dolt he was. He had been declaring he was going to give the order to fire on the crowds over by the Tuileries from the rear – clearly a keen student of La Fayette. Danton met him among the maze of rooms the Judiciary kept for itself, and inside ten minutes the commander, relieved of command, was under arrest. In the early morning he was shot on the way to prison. Very few wept over that.

A new commander of the National Guard was next elected, Santerre. This neatly removed that most awkward aristo-pleb split, which till then had crippled the Guard in any civil action. No one had any doubt now that, called to combat, these forces would fight solely for the People. However much of a blundering loudmouth, Santerre was no aristocrat.

Getting to the Hôtel de Ville, in the first place, had been fairly fascinating. No sooner were we up by the Cordeliers Club than we ran into a mass of men, women, children, all out and seething with the wish to do something but not entirely certain yet as to what. Danton was recognized, I was recognized, everyone was. Danton gave one brief impromptu speech he had had ready about him, and which he rendered quite a few more times during the night. I hardly recollect any of it. Everybody shouted in the most incendiary language. The pack on the streets applauded everyone who *did* shout. Over the other side of the river, the business with the replacing Commune was seen to with the minimum of fuss. (And exactly according to plan.) Initially thereafter, events seemed likely to move on their own, needing only the first shove to set them rolling. But, despite the takeover of the municipality and the arrest of Mandat, the great explosion didn't happen. An atmosphere of strained excitement persisted. The Hôtel was full of rushing figures, alarmists, volunteers, voluntary alarmists, messengers. Outside, the mob of people, seemingly covering every surface, was stuck to the sides of the building like molasses. Periodically Danton disappeared, even going home to bed at one juncture – but, unable to sleep for the "loud crying of women," came back again. Always he arrived in time to do the crucial thing: arrest Mandat, or sign some paper, or detail some squad of stripy Wonders into some useful or at least nondisastrous manuever. At one juncture, Westermann, an Alsace NCO now become a general in Santerre's

National Guard, rolled in with a batch of Marseillais and Federals from Finistère, the Land's End of the west. Backslapping and congratulation all around with nothing to have caused it. I remember thinking abruptly how volatile we had all become, and that still the spark failed to be struck—but then forgot that. It was all *tomorrow* now. They're too bloody drunk to manage it tonight, said Danton, handing me the next bottle. ("The third one always makes me so thirsty.") Later, he told me, "We can screw this bitch all night and not get a result." I had been going about to encourage whoever I was supposed to ("There's so-and-so, go and give him a kiss for me"). And now I'd sat down on his desk in the Judiciary, eaten up with nervous energy and nerves. He came in, scowled, and then sent me back to his apartment. "Go on, go and tell them we're all thriving. Nothing's going to start till the morning, now." "It *is* morning." "Daylight, then, you pedant." I remonstrated. Despite the *tomorrows,* the tocsin had begun from the left bank, at the Cordeliers, promptly on the stroke of midnight, and all the other bells in Paris had taken it up. The constant ringing, now and then jaggedly lessening as new relays of bellringers took over in one or other of the inumerable bell towers, drove me crazy. But ignoring the protest and the bells, he kicked me out and I went, because he had the battle command; I'd geared myself to obey him.

There were massive crowds still, as far as, and thrust out onto, the bridges. I was crossing when a solid wedge of cavalry came clattering, forcing a path through. To my surprise, though God knows why I *was* surprised, I saw they were Swiss, king's men. The crowd pressed away from them, but one of these redcoats, staring at me, checked his mount and snarled my name. It seemed he knew me, or of me. He yanked out his sword and raised it. So desensitized was I with my lust for victory, and surrounded by a mass of human supporters who growled at him in turn, I made no move, felt no harm could come to me, and my face must have shown as much. He cursed me in his Swiss French and abruptly lowered the sword, plunging on after his fellows. I continued toward the Cordeliers district, laughing to myself, like the madman I was that night (do I hear you say, Always?). He could have cut me in two pieces and had maybe meant to. What actually stopped him? Perhaps he only feared to be lynched. As indeed he doubtless was, the following day.

When I reached Danton's home I discovered the three women had taken off like scared pigeons for Theater-of-France Street. Here I duly found my wife in our home, with Danton's wife and Robert's wife, and for a minute wished myself somewhere else. Gabi, ghastly pale as if painted to look ill, greeted me with "Have you come to tell me he's dead?" I assured her I hadn't. La Roberte would not speak to me at all. Lucile and I went into our bedroom. I began telling her the news and fell asleep lying against her in the middle of my recital.

We woke up at seven o'clock because Jeanette was leaning from the lower window shrieking at some ruffians in the street. It turned out they had been cursing me and had the intention of writing something on the door. Jeanette's

offer of boiling coffee over their heads decided them against the enterprise. (It
was true, her coffee was fairly dreadful.)

Jeanette went on bleating as she brought us the beverage instead.

"Why is everything Monsieur Camille's fault?" she demanded of me ferociously. She looked as if she would like to strike me for being unjustly accused.

"I have to go back," I said to Lucile. I was afraid she would start to cry again, but she nodded and made a great pretense of drinking the awful coffee. Poor Lucile. This morning, things seemed rather annoyingly funny to me. But obviously she no longer saw anything of humor, or the reckless glamour of events. She'd had, besides, a night of Gabi and Louise Robert fainting and exclaiming. Louise had threatened to stab Danton if her husband was harmed. Lucile was terrified this death warrant would swell to include me. "Please," I said. "Stay indoors. No, there isn't any great danger. But there are always troublemakers at times like these."

"We haven't any bread!" she cried wildly.

"Then send Jeanette. Get the concierge's boy to go with her."

Outside, the day was already like the interior of a stewpan. Three pale faces and one bleating pink one window-watched me down the street. No sign of my unfriends the sloganists. The local thoroughfares were empty, as if a stopper had been pulled and all the fluid run off somewhere else. The concert of bells had died down during the night or early morning; a few still sounded, but isolated and tinny with distance. From the river came a vague dull rumble.

When I drew level with the Cordeliers Club, I found a crowd of members marshaled there in the courtyard, making a flower garden of revolutionary cockades. Immediately I had a guard of honor to escort me over the bridge – one of the tall recruiting platforms had caught alight, or been fired, during the night, and was still smoldering. The crowd let us through. Many were shoveling themselves along on the same route.

It was starting, for sure. You could smell it: the scent of human sweat sharp with the acids of fear and fury and intention, and a stormy overtone in the air, gunpowder, and the smoke of burned ribbons.

Where the crowd was thickest, my guard beat a good-natured, determined way through for me. At the City Hall, somehow, someone had got a tricolor banner up on the clock. It hung there, obscuring the time, which was symbol enough for anyone.

I was hardly in the door before I met Pétion being marched down a corridor under his own escort, less friendly than mine.

"For God's sake, Camille"—he grasped me and brought us all to a halt—"this has to be prevented." He was green and sweating. I laughed aloud. "Rubbish. It's everything we wanted." "Oh, you fool," he said. "It'll go wrong." "It won't. Let go of me. Where are you taking him?" "Just back into his nice room, Danton says, and lock him up quietly. Can't have little dogs around our feet on a day like this." They all went off. So much for popular Mayor Pétion.

Perhaps he was scared for his princess. Well, we'd give him Élisabeth on a plate, presently.

I walked into Danton's room whistling. Not the "Marseillaise." A crowd of men was in there, Fréron blocking the door till I elbowed him aside. Danton's eyes were bloodshot, and where I had slept in my clothes, he looked as if he had been through a third-rate laundry in his.

"Rested well, I trust?" he said to me.

"Not bad. You?"

"Yes. Some dreams, though. Mandat got shot in one of them."

I was going to say something to cap that when there was a long hollow thud that tipped the floor against my shoes and shook the windowpanes. Utter silence came down on the building, on the crowd in the street. In the silence Danton said, "That's it." It was the first cannon.

Outside, the crowd began to scream and to rush in all directions.

For some reason—it had not properly occurred before—I *did* feel then the true enormity of the undertaking. My stomach jolted over and I could taste the gunpowder in my mouth. But Danton's fist thudded down on the desktop. Sunburst by his disheveled mane, he shouted, "The first cannon! The first day of hope! What are you looking like that for, like a pack of rabbits? That's history out there. Waiting for us. Don't disappoint her, gentlemen. You are standing in the gate of freedom." I could have gone on my knees to him at that moment. He lifted us, one thing, and hurled us back to the summit. "Forget the past. There have been no years till now. Here, we start. Year One," Danton announced. "Which we have fought toward all this while, and which we are on the point of beginning. The dawn of liberty."

⚜

An aristocratic public attorney and department president had arrived in the Tuileries. Before the cannons spoke, he had informed the king that, No, it was useless to try and inspire the guard in a coat the royal color of the viola flower. One would do better to go over to the Assembly and ask for sanctuary.

They had been stormed before. You could say they had become accustomed to the People of France bursting in on them without knocking.

But this was not like the other times. They must not be taken now. The deputies could protect them, because the deputies were the People's elected representatives and therefore holy.

"We are betrayed," said the queen. She said it very softly, with the usual dignity. But oh, the descending staircase! How near the last treads of it must have seemed to her, even if she could not yet make them out quite clearly.

The king, standing close to the aristocratic attorney, remarked, "Ah, so Danton doesn't want my life today?" Even a fool can sometimes be astute.

The segment of the National Guard which, with the Swiss, had been left at the Tuileries to protect (or enjail) their constitutional Majesties, watched the royal family retreat along the terrace through the crowds and sneered. A vast number of palace servants were running after the procession, imploring the benefit of sanctuary too. But the small detail of men conducting L'oui and the Austrian woman pushed these poor gadflies off. The National Guard jeered. Once the viola coat and the pale muslin dress had vanished up the path to the Stable, the National Guard stepped off their positions like toy soldiers come to life. They marched over into the arms of the enthusiastic crowd, and as they went they turned a couple of the Tuileries cannons around so they faced the palace.

In the Stable, the royal family had been ushered into the writers' box. Here it was that the scribbled accounts of speeches and proceedings, made at the round table below, were brought to be transcribed and occasionally got wrong. The railing which separated the box from the main hall was uprooted. It must be possible for the king and queen to jump straight into the arms of their protectors, in case of invasion.

"I've told the Swiss not to fire on the people," said L'oui, hauling up railings with a will. The moment of astuteness had passed.

Out there they stood, then, on the Tuileries steps, the Swiss battalions, who must not leave their posts, who must not fire. Of course they would fire.

The bellicose Marseilles soldiery was pressing in on them now, coming at a kind of slow run, a battle trot, singing its operatic anthem, mingled here and there with the other song, the "It'll Be," decked with its most savage words. But the advancing soldiery made some sense, even when it sang. The mob that came in behind and around the Marseillais—that was primal chaos. And as it flowed forward, chaos and order joined, becoming all chaos.

The sun detonated from the upraised sabers and pikes: It was the sluggish unstoppable stampede of a herd of hellish beasts with metal horns.

"You want to die?" the stampede mooed, in gusts of its multi-throated voice (Did they? Who does?), while others of the throats cried, "To the lantern!" Cried, "Quake tyrants at your crimes—your schemes against the People are tottering! To arms! We are legions! March, march!"

They waited, the Swiss, in their bright uniforms, in the glory of the sunlight, to defend the house of a king who had gone away, to defend it without firing on the metal-horned herds of chaos which sang.

The metal horns lowered and slashed forward, and the Swiss muskets cracked out a rain of lead. Back at them, at once, the reply of the Marseillais. Smoke like puffs of powder, blood glittering like jewelry in the sunshine. Is that what the gods see, that, which make it all so beautiful, so attractive to them, they long for more?

The cannons, clichéd, boomed. The first, second, third, fourth. But now the Federals have the cannons. They kill to get them. The fire winds rip both ways. There is a momentarily continuous earth-shocking growl, and the ground trembles. The statues on their pedestals *thrum* like harps. Flesh falls. Garlands of smoke, black, putting out the sun. The sun is going out in smoke, out in a hundred eyes.

"You bloody *traitor,*" the man says, as he rams his pike through the breast of the Swiss soldier. The soldier, sinking, looks at him. Their eyes meet; it happens. In some mountain valley where he was born, a Swiss child, he had never, the one young man, looked for this. Nor had the other, born in some hovel of Saint-Antoine, looked for this. It's no good talking of mobs and battalions. It's human beings here, as it always is, pushing through each other's hearts with steel, cutting through each other's minds with bullets, their eyes meeting, their feet treading in each other's faces.

But the king's order has been reiterated and supplemented. It says, Lay down your arms and return to barracks.

The federal soldiers are on the steps, running, drumming, singing. But even as their flood tide crashes in, under the spray of smoke and lead, to engulf everything, the Swiss—begin to turn, like clockwork, to obey this fresh order.

The cannons are now all pointing at the Tuileries. Fire-*flash!* Coal-black roses of smoke. The world *rocks*.

The Swiss are running.

The mob chases them, almost playfully.

It chases them away across the square, into the gardens, away toward the Hôtel de Ville. And upward, too, into the vistas of the old palace. The mob will tell you, it knows its way around the palace now, it's been here before.

Death to the traitors!

Who are the traitors? Why, anyone who helped them, the bloodsucking king, the vampire queen. Not just soldiers, oh, no. Kill them, then, all of them. Kill the startled white-faced porter by the staircase, kill the page fifteen years old, trying to hide behind a drape. Kill her, that bitch of a maid in her flouncy gown. They've cosseted monsters, fed them on the People's blood, dressed them in the People's rent skin, taught them they were special, opened doors for them so they could walk through and leave us behind. Kill them! *Kill them all.*

It's raining . . . it's raining death. From the high windows, where once the dainty faces peeped, the flowers nestled, the little birds tweeted in their cages of gold. Don't look. Look away. No, look, *look* at it. Look at what is in the soul of all men just as, in all men's souls, there is the seed of perfect good.

The broken bodies falling on the walks below. And in the gardens, among the fragrant topiary, the women plummeting on corpses like carrion crows and with their ready knives slicing off trophies.

There goes one, see? Running. Let's get him.

The frantic man climbs up a statue, clings to its marble with his legs and arms. But darkness gathers around the pedestal. The searing pain of pikes jabs at him. *Come down.* Don't hurt me, I'm only a cook–not even that. I scrubbed pots in the scullery. *Yes, and got fat on it, didn't you?* He clings there till the pikes and the marble's slipperiness exhaust him. When he slithers into their arms they wrench back his head. "That's a fine specimen. His eyes are still open." "They don't close when you do it right. Too quick. Haven't you noticed?" One man clucks in disapproval. He wipes the jugular blood, which has splashed, off the pure limbs of the statue. For the statue belongs to the People and will be preserved.

But everything trickles with blood. Carpets of blood, hangings, wall paintings, chandeliers–of blood. The Tuileries run red. Get used to it. This is just the beginning.

⚜

The first image, in one of the avenues of trees west of the Tuileries, was of a lovely woman, with curling hair under a plumed hat, firing a pistol at a man; then, as he went down, seizing a blade to stab him and to hack off his head. I recollected her once at the Cordeliers, proposing a temple to Reason to be put up on the site of the felled Bastille. I knew the man rather better; we had been at school together. He had royalist sympathies which he paraded in pamphlet form. Days ago I'd warned him to be careful. Now, caught in Heaven's Fields stealing about on apparent aristo business, he took his death blows from a beautiful executioner in plumes. But no amazement in that. As I went on to the Tuileries where the rushing human river plunged, I met the maenads of the mad god, those women, their sans-culottid skirts striped blue, white, and red, their white arms striped only with red blood.

It's possible, when death is so broadcast, so multiform, to gloss over it. I had myself run on corpses to reach the Bastille. I saw *this* spread everywhere in front of me, and only cant filled my mind: That it was a pity the citizens were so indiscriminate, that where the hell was Santerre, this wretched beer merchant we had made commander, to control it? That bloodshed was inevitable, owed them, and the way to sanity and peace lay over the back of . . . this. That one did not flinch at what one had helped to cause but stood by the action. The slaughter of the man I had known, by a woman I recognized, shocked me, but in the way only a personal matter can. I regretted it. It angered me, for though there had been times I felt I could have killed him myself (we fought in our papers, when I possessed one), he had not seemed to merit death. Nor, of course, had these others strewn all over the lawns and under the hedges. But I didn't know them, having not yet learned every human thing is known to every other–even while I had, for God's sake, *preached* as much. As to the horror of the spectacle, I'd steeled myself. I didn't look closely. Though somehow I saw. I saw . . . the girl, abused and abandoned, her skirts pushed up to her dead eyes, the secondary wounds on her skin where the little bracelets had been pulled off and the earrings torn out of her ears. I saw the headless dead, the mutilated. Even now, the victors were at that. But mostly they were in the king's house, hunting and mutilating *there,* or smashing, or soiling, or carrying off the loot. I heard it remarked the integrity of the People was so pure that, though they would destroy or deface, they would never steal from their slave masters. Which is a bloody lie. Joyful ant colonies swarming away with bric-a-brac, clothes, jewelry—even chairs and writing desks—passed me on the walks. They went by with piked heads, too. These didn't look at all real, only like badly painted, unlifelike masks up in the air, open-eyed, open-mouthed. Not even Curtius' waxworks, some inferior rival's. Once or twice I was recognized. Fellows with sabers, brown with old blood, scarlet with fresh, clasped my hand (and those of the two escorting guards I'd brought with me). Such greetings happened more than once. I was not so brainless as to turn away. By a miracle no blood got on my clothes. (The stink of it, in the heat, was unspeakable.) Presently I washed my hands in a fountain's basin. Yes. Just like Pilate.

Westermann was in one of the lower rooms, with a group of his command around him, ransacking cabinets, shouting, the floor littered with trodden papers. He shrugged when he saw me.

"They've killed all the Swiss in the palace," he said. "Tell Danton it's a damn good thing old Fat Arse was off the premises. He'd have got it, for sure." (Westermann was usually more mannered. But formal manners were hardly appropriate at this stage.)

I said, "And now they're killing the Swiss in the streets."

"Some of them ran for City Hall. The crowd'll be after them there, too. Santerre says, and I concur, we've got what *we* want. Now let the People do what *they* want."

"Oh, and could you stop them?"

One of the busy soldiers left his work to turn on me. "Why should we? We *are* the People. Stopping them's for the stinking aristos, and haven't they been doing it for years?"

There was an awful screaming somewhere up among the carved stairways and the painted ceilings. My heart shuddered. The guardsmen in the room laughed or swore. "Someone's objecting to something." A couple went out to see, join in. Then the screaming ended.

Westermann had a reputation for bravery. He had been brave today, thrusting across the cannons and the muskets with just the wild Federals and a wilder rabble behind him. He glanced at me with contempt. I hadn't done any fighting, merely come as Danton's envoy, to assess, to tell the warriors where they should be next. Danton had said nothing about not permitting wholesale butchery. He had got the king out because he reckoned on that butchery. Whatever would become of the monarchy must be effected legally. He had stressed as much. A rioting city that tore its former masters personally in shreds was a psychological induction to the kind of anarchy no one who dreamed of better days could allow. But the rest – it was only a necessary bloodletting. (Danton the doctor, applying the leeches.) Let the People have their day of vengeance, their cup of blood. They'd been centuries gasping for it.

When I'd settled a few details with Westermann, I went back out again and walked prosaically over dead Swiss soldiers lying in the flower beds.

The maenads of the mad god, Dionysos' dark side, seemed to have drawn off. Perhaps to twine more ivy around their thyrsus pikes, tipped by severed heads, not pinecones. The men had dispersed too. Just a patrol of guards drinking, a shrubbery or two away, the bodies, my escort and I. Over toward the Stables there was some smoke but no attention paid to it. For the moment, activity had collected beneath the palace windows, from which satins and mirrors now seemed to be cascading.

As I turned east, I saw a young woman standing under a lilac tree. Ah, another maenad. A new version, cold and cruel, not burning crazy like the others. Come to scavenge for further trinkets, no doubt, though the corpses had been thoroughly stripped of them. I was about to go by her without pause when I recognized the white little face. "Mariette," I said. It was the diminutive her uncle-father sometimes gave her; I'd heard him use it on several occasions. Marie, Curtius' niece.

She looked up at me then. Her face, which never showed much except small polite smiles or the odd small careful frown – concentration, disapproval – tilted up at me. She stared. For a second I saw in her eyes absolute horror. Then she looked down again.

I waved my guard back and went close to her.

"For God's sake, you shouldn't be here, Marie. He didn't send you?" I knew he took waxes from cadavers; one of his shows was all hanged murderers. But it seemed unlikely. She shook her head. "Then why – ?" But she wasn't going to answer. She had had to do with the Capets, a voluntary slave companion to Élisabeth. "The king and his family," I said, "are safe with the Assembly." If it reassured her I don't know. I was a monster to her, and for an instant saw myself as she saw me (with all my young man's puzzlement and affront) and was unpleasantly startled. Though she was in her thirties, yet she was like an adolescent and also peculiarly old, this one, a prim chilly clever old lady of thirteen. ("Witches," Mirabeau had titled the entire household.) She'd always rather unnerved me, if I thought of her at all. Never more than now. "Do you want me to take you home?" I said, halfwit that I was. And she recoiled, shrank from me. Camille Desmoulins, *cauchemar,* black beast with whom to frighten babies just a little older than my own son – Do as you're told, or Camille will come and *get you!* I shivered and sweated and said to her harshly, "For Christ's sake, go home, you silly little fool." And she turned and ran away. I never found out who she was looking for. Maybe, incredibly, she had a lover among the palace staff, or the Swiss.

I went back to the Hôtel de Ville and sat down to listen to Danton, addressing his Insurrectionary Committee and making beautiful majestic good sense of everything. There was even some laughter, in which I joined.

Yes, you had to let the children have their treat out there. Let them play hard till bedtime; then they'd be easy to lead gently, wherever was necessary.

❀

Riot unraveled from the Tuileries and was soon all over the city. I was vaguely but persistently gnawed by worries for Lucile. I couldn't be sure she had stayed put as I told her. (It turned out she hadn't. She, like all the rest of us, seemed compelled to hurry, mostly pointlessly, from place to place in a sort of dull frenzy. It was the pervading mood of Paris, other than the inclinations to kill or flee. Only Danton, presiding over events, was consistent. It was simply his brain which raced.)

In the tail end of the boiling morning, lacking an escort now, I dashed back across the river to the Théâtre Français section and met Fréron as I did so. Unguarded, companions in arms, we grudgingly fell in together and walked fast and unspeaking. At corners and intersections there were crowds. All the shops were shut. (There had been corpses on the bridge.) We were stopped and asked for news. We gave it.

At the entry to Theater-of-France Street, there was a mass of people arguing, one of whom came straight at me, a big devil in a leather apron, demanding was I Camille, the bugger who'd started a massacre, he'd skin me alive. I was stupefied. Before I could try to gather my wits, Fréron pushed the man away from me and snapped at him, "Don't be a bloody fool. Desmoulins is at the Luxembourg if you want him." Very curiously, right on top of my own apartment, all these were strangers to me. Which was probably why nobody debated with Fréron but seemed to accept what he said. We walked on, I with my mouth hanging wide. As we got on to the street, Fréron took my arm and hauled me past my building. "Not *yet,* you idiot." So we proceeded beyond and turned into a side court, where we stood under some appallingly normal washing. "So, why did you?" "Because he wanted your guts on the road, and I thought I'd save you the business of denying *yourself* and every bloody chicken in a three-mile radius crowing." He looked white, as if he were ill; he had looked like that when I met him. "Why not let them get me," I said. "Cheer them on." "Don't give me good ideas, Camille."

Suddenly I felt deathly; my excitement and sense of purpose were no more. And I was ashamed of so petty a thing as not pompously thanking him, I who had, not long ago, walked out of a corpse garden. So I did thank him. He said, "I take it you were at the Tuileries too. You look the way you did when they told you

Mirabeau was dying." "That's hardly—" I said, then had to break off and go across into a corner to vomit. He left me to it. Over my own retching and groans I could hear him kicking his heels and cursing softly. Then I was leaning on the wall, choking back to life from the racking sickness, saying things to the bricks, asking them what had happened, what had we done. I didn't know what I was saying, or what it meant, or even why I had vomited.

"The crowd's gone," he said, coming up to me. "Pull yourself together. You've helped make this happen, don't get squeamish. It's dangerous, stop it, you damned chump. Pull yourself together," he said again. "You can't go up to her like that. She's scared enough as it is."

I had forgotten where I was, too, and that I'd come to see if Lucile was safe. Now, like a lunatic, I burst out—to him, of all people—that I couldn't go up into the house, Gabi would be there, and Gabi would say, You've come to tell me Georges is dead, and dear Georges was sitting in the Hôtel de Ville, one of the few people who *wasn't* dead, with those who were, half of Paris, piled around the doorstep.

"I won't tell him you said that," said Fréron.

"Tell him. He knows. Tell him."

We finally went out and got into the house and to the apartment. They were there; they'd been eating breakfast. The room looked far off and everyone very small, as if revealed through the wrong end of a spyglass. The questions came, and I answered them calmly and not illogically. Gabi started to cry again. She looked worse than any of us. Lucile scarcely said a word to me. For my part I didn't want to touch her and could barely say her name; I was afraid to, as if it might break me. All the time I stood in the room, I felt myself on the edge of utter insanity. The world had become an alien place.

Not until we went out again and walked back into hell, did I steady. Someone offered me wine on that horror of a bridge, and I took it from their hands, the way La Fayette had once done, and Louis, not caring anymore if it were poisoned, or not understanding the efficacy of poison, since poison was everywhere—natural.

⚜

Later I thought, when the darkness began, and the torches streamed along the streets and seemed to set fire to the river, and Danton's name had become a new sort of "Marseillaise" sung down the arteries of the city, and the old order lay in rubble, and the dream stirred once more, the phoenix, rising in gold, unstained by anyone's blood, and I heard him speaking to them, and forgot him sitting at his desk—later, then, I thought, I've been acting like a moron. What was wrong with me? Blood washes clean. Every worthwhile god demands his sacrifice.

❉

Bullets had cracked the windows of the Assembly Hall. Terrified, speakers got up and said things and sat down. The mob had already visited them once, but went away.

In the unrailed box, the king has watched the proceedings through an opera glass and presently eaten an early dinner, then a late dinner. The queen has been posed on the comfortless chairs, listening to the distant music of the riot, for hours. Surely not recalling how once she reclined on a silken sofa catching, like butterflies in her brain, the measured rhythms of Haydn.

The afternoon hovered, faltered, dropped dead on Paris. In the hot black dark, the perfume of decaying things begins to rise, like odors of a night-blooming flower.

The royal family will be going to sleep in a handy convent tonight. But where tomorrow?

> For who forgets a murdered queen?
> The names of leaders, when they die,
> Are written in the books of men.
> My blood ran by the fountain's stem,
> Where flowers grow. I was nineteen
> And quite immortal, till that day
> I lost my life which leaves no name.
>
> Ah, vous! Ils ne vous oublient pas,
> Mais moi, je n'ai pas d'la mémoire.

In a few more days, the last trailing ends of the insurrection were picked up and tied neatly, in ribboned bows.

Danton, lying low eventually in the long grass of prostrated sleep, had left enough of his gigantic paw marks on the authorities of Paris to swing them as intended. It needed only a deputation from City Hall, backed by howling on the streets outside, for the Assembly to vote the king into official suspension and protective custody, *en famille,* in the Temple. Also for the Assembly to vote itself into proposed dissolution in the near future.

It took, too, only arch-enemy Desmoulins to visit Brissot's Girondins, pushing his way among them armed solely with the aura of that day of Danton's work, to crowd the Gironde over into promising Danton its conciliative support. Windmill's agitator activities were by that time enormously forceful, with all the drive and glitter of the last hours of total exhaustion—analyzed, were unreasonable, even idiotic. But who did analyze? Everywhere he jammed his foot in the door, the door was flung wide for him with screeches of welcome. You said *Danton* and the world jumped. And though others of Danton's gang completed their tasks more skillfully, it was the chosen acolytes, such as

Camille, Fabre, Robert, who were most effective. The imparted genius of their lord and master clothed them with tongues of fire.

Without L'oui, Antoinette, and their troublesome toy veto, the ministry was soon disbanded and put together again.

The Legislative Assembly elected, as minister of justice and keeper of seals, Georges-Jacques Danton. All right, a minister, fancy titles, what's in a name? This. The king was out. With the support of all still-standing authorities in Paris, and of the military and civilian wolf packs on the streets, the Assembly decreed that whichever minister of the reshuffled, refurbished government achieved the majority of votes would thereby assume the foremost authority in the executive. Thus, in Paris. So, in France. And Danton had the majority of the votes.

There may well have been some expressions of surprise and displeasure elsewhere, but in the fiery cauldron of the capital there came only the noise of applause.

Even aristocrats, such was the stature of this colossus, the ambiance of his power, had voted him to the peak. Even those who had spoken ill of the sacred name suddenly came down with a cry that turmoil would only bend to such extraordinary strengths, such single-mindedness of spirit and intellect. In time of chaos, only the pillar of a Danton was worth clinging to. They had watched him overthrow the giant, the dragon, which reared in his path. It was fear and an astounded respect which threw them at his feet. He was commended so vigorously by his detractors, he was heard to remark, "With such enemies, who needs friends?"

But in the sunrise of this day, the blue-eyed lion up on his high rock surveyed the landscape spread before him with appetite and consideration. France: a lush game park, a woman on her back, an esoteric opened book. He saw the smudges of war at the edges, the fissures that traced the interior, each slicing deep down to hell. And he saw the floods of milk and honey. He waited a space, enjoying the view, before he sprang. Few men, not born on high rocks, ever *climb* so high or see so far.

❖

1792: *Late Summer*

AND SO the prince and princess stepped aboard their magic carpet, and it whisked them away to a beautiful castle of fine carved furniture and brocade walls, in the Place Vendôme. . . .

Well, Father, although you only ever prophesied for me disgrace and ruin, here I am living like a lord, in a palace. Danton is minister of justice and has made me his secretary. We got to our glorious situation by the grace of those black deities, the cannons. As Georges said in the Assembly, "If I'd lost, I would be a felon." But our cause, Liberty, has triumphed. We're safe, and seated far up the grand stairway. (Don't mention how well I've done to your neighbors. The beautiful townsfolk of Guise will have a fit. What? That wretched Camille? Not possible. Or, Well, the undeserving are often *lucky* — because in *my* case, ability and talent could have nothing to do with it.)

For myself, I'm less vain than I was. Success has calmed me. Yet — disillusioned, too. Well, I'm older, I see through the masks, the smiling faces, the loud cries of love of country, goodwill, the rest of it. Sometimes I'm sickened by what I find under the lifted stone. But set aside that for now. My rise to prosperity will also be felt by you, believe it, and soon. As for France (poor France on her cross, as Marat said), now we have the means to press toward our goals unhindered, finally. Though it is a fact, sometimes I'm beset by despair: misgiving, hopeless melancholy. You know how I am. Even as a child, one instant exalted, then in the blackest of sorrows. But I confess I can't understand how it can be put right, this sea of miseries all about me. The most simple happenings. . . . The People were offended by the statue of Louis XIV in the square below our windows. But in pulling the thing down, it fell and crushed a woman beneath itself. Lucile is haunted by the memory, as well she might be. Thank God she saw none of the sights vouchsafed to me on August tenth and eleventh.

What is to be done with it, then, this random vast torture chamber we call Human Life?

The able talented lucky author, who had been working on memoranda and public circulars for the minister all morning, now walked across and into the ministerial office. The door stood open, surprisingly — the heat, perhaps. Sunlight burned on the patterned walls, the impressive desk: tidy because, unlike the author's desk over the way, not much paperwork had yet been done on it.

"Come in, worthy secretary," said Danton. "You know my secretary, do you, Monsieur Robespierre? May I present him? Desmoulins, Robespierre. Robespierre, Desmoulins."

Robespierre, by the window, nodded to Camille. He looked jumpily affronted, a cat whose tail has been stepped on — ridiculous. Camille stretched, his shoulder joints cracking. He put papers on Danton's spectacular desk.

"God almighty, don't make a mess of that. Maximilien," said Danton to Camille, "has just been offered a beneficial and important job on my staff, which he's turned down. What am I to think?"

"I have explained," said Robespierre. "I have no intention of burdening the People with the expense. I need nothing beyond what I have and can work very well, for those things I believe in, from where I am."

"But not with me," said Danton.

"If we're fighting for the same cause," said Robespierre, "of course, with you. I don't need to be in the same building."

"Suppose that I would *like* you in the same building."

"I'm very sorry, Georges. You mean for the best, I'm sure. But my life is very simple—"

"Don't squirm out of the issue, damn it," said Danton loudly. Camille, on an instinct, turned and kicked the door shut. Both men glanced at him. "How subtle," said Danton. He walked past Camille and opened the door wide. He bellowed out into the golden rooms and lofty corridors. "For Christ's sake, Maxime, I need you! Please help me out! Join this great enterprise! Aid me in the saving of France!"

"Oh, my God," said Camille.

Danton grinned amiably at them. At Maximilien. "And now everyone knows what you'll be saying no *to,* say no again."

Robespierre cleared his throat. He looked at Camille. "Do please tell Lucile how much I'm looking forward to calling on you tomorrow and seeing the child."

"All right," said Camille. "If I saw you I was requested to ask what you wanted to eat."

"It's all one to me. You know my poor appetite."

"Yes," said Danton. "We're beginning to. Just beginning." He leaned forward, putting his hand on Camille's shoulder as if to steady himself. "I'm hurt, Maxime, by your refusal. Wounded."

Robespierre looked at Danton, leaning—towering—over Camille. Robespierre said, "It's my fate, Georges, to struggle alone." He nodded again to both of them and walked neatly out, his polished, heeled shoes clicking like a tiny horse across the sun-blazed floor.

Presently Danton himself kicked the fine-paneled door shut. The building shook a little. "Fucking jumped-up bastard," said Danton. "He's as good as told me he won't have anything to do with this corrupt nest of vipers." He pawed the papers on the desk. "What the hell's this? I haven't got time for it; I'm going over to the Assembly."

"It's what you asked for. A new batch of corrupt plots and lies with which to mislead the people of France."

"Splendid. Get Fabre to deal with it. What do I have him paid for, Christ blast it?"

"Temper," said Camille. He went to the window and watched, until in a minute Robespierre appeared below, walking off between the pale yellow masonry in the deep yellow sunlight. "Twelve thousand livres," said Camille. "What did you offer *him?*"

"What he was worth. Are you ready to leave?"

"I once asked Mirabeau, Are you bought? Trying to be clever."

"You're always trying that. Sometimes it works. Not now."

"Now, I ask myself, Well, Camille, are *you* bought?"

"You're bought," said Danton. "We all are. Get a move on."

Camille went on looking out of the window. He and Danton, sparring along the borderline between joke and earnest. The publicity memoranda of Swiss and Austrian plots at the Tuileries—they had been real, or could have been. It had not particularly offended him to make a lawyer's case of it. But Robespierre the Incorruptible One, pitter-patting off over the cobbles, *virtu intacta.* Oh, confound him!

When Camille went back to his own office—the luxury of it—someone came in and courteously informed him a Citizen Fouquier was outside. The Windmill rotated its arms airily. "All right." This one I'll see. This one I won't. Danton, brilliant in the Assembly. Lucile clinging to me, weeping, dreaming about death out in the oval square—no longer Place Vendôme, they called it the Place of the Pikes. And the child—the child staring at me with his night-black eyes—my God, what I've looked on since I held you last. Can a man infect his son with horror by a glance? But it passed. You could tickle the child and make it laugh and kick and squeal. Sometimes he held the child and a wave of estatic happiness made him bury his face in its wrappings and warm body. Happiness or pain. Or some emotion unnamable. Is this mine? This life truly a part of me? He'll grow up. He'll be a living man. A man named Horatius, young and strong. Don't let us fall out the way I've done so often with my own father. I can learn by those mistakes. Get it right. I can be the best father on earth to this son of mine, I know what *not* to do. (Remember Mirabeau. His bloody damnable father I'd have liked to crucify, when he told me the little he did. But Mirabeau's dead. Why am I thinking about Mirabeau?)

A shadow slipped around the door.

This one, another relation. (Saint-Just, the beautiful cousin; Fouquier-Tinville, the ugly cousin.) It had written him a letter, this creature in the doorway.

Stop. Stop looking at him with hindsight. Go back. Unremember. That day he was only a funny little crawler from the home province.

Fouquier's letter had said:

> *My dear kinsman, you alone can help me, through your particular illustrious contacts and acquaintances. You know I am committed to the freedom and prosperity of France. I count upon old ties, your well-known and esteemed sense of duty—*

Splutter, puke. Hello, Antoine-Quentin.

From time to time he had been wealthy, had married it. Then lost it in the brothels and over crates of brandy. Black-clad, with little bulging sperm-colored eyes.

"Good-day, Fouquier."

(Danton was going to coin an English name for Fouquier-Tinville too. *Fork-Tongue*. Danton had already spotted him, in fact. He wants a job? Tell him yes. What? Stall him. He's a lawyer, like the rest of us. Something on the legal side. You can see, he'll do what he's told.)

"Well, Camille," said Fouquier Fork-Tongue, looking all around: his eyes slithering everywhere; his hands slithering, picking up a paperweight, a dish of blotting powder; his body slithering in the chair in a sort of seated dance. "It's very kind of you to see me."

"True," said Windmill, putting his feet, in their elegantly buckled shoes, up on the desktop. Fouquier studied, admiring, the shoes. He smiled, promptingly. "You're searching for employment?" idly queried Windmill.

"In a manner of speaking."

"And you want me to help you?"

"Danton – has shown me some marks of favor."

"My, my."

"And to you, of course, he listens."

There was a black-clad Fouquier-type fly droning and crawling somewhere up amid the curlicues of the ceiling. Camille tilted back his head to look at it and strained his neck.

Oh, Christ, the symbolism of gesture. I can't unremember. Not with this one. He sat and hung on my every breath. And I made him wait. Not knowing he was the angel of the angel of the Angel of Death.

⚜

"Don't cry. My darling love, what's the *matter?*" Frantic, thinking I'd hurt her, harmed her. She clung to me and I held her. She told me she loved me over and over again. I assured her it was mutual. My heart was still thudding in the aftermath of pleasure which seemed to have made avowals superfluous. "But I'm afraid," she whispered at last. "Of what are you afraid, my Lucile, my love?" "The child, he's so adorable, such a miracle, I'm so glad for him, I love him so, but – you see, Gabi – child after child – it was like" – I could hardly hear her; she murmured so very low, ashamed to speak of it to me, as if *that* was important – "a long illness. I couldn't think. I couldn't help *you*. Everything was like a horrible dream – not again, I can't stand – oh, my God, my God!" And she wept violently now, loudly, harshly, coughing and gasping for breath, her tears burning through my skin, the searing grip of her nails in my flesh. I lay and held her, murmuring to her, kissing her gently, recounting for her every kind of nonsense, every old wives' tale, every reassurance, every pledge of faith. Until she rested trembling and shuddering against me, sweet lovely Lucile, who had just told me, if she even realized it, I could never possess her again.

I'd seen the lesson of it in my mother. I couldn't, with such an example, kill my wife that way. If I needed any proof, I had beheld it all those last three months she carried the child, terrified I'd lose her. She had said nothing then. That was like her. And this—was not.

In the end she fell asleep, curled against me, her beautiful hair brushing my lips, her breasts molded to my body, and I must learn some means of being with her like this and not desiring her, holding her like this, as if she were my sister.

There under the ceiling of the Lamoignon Palace, which had on it gods frolicking, and girls with swans, and rosy amorous clouds, all of it coming clear as daylight entered the long windows, lying with what she had told me, what must not be, heavy in my heart. Bereft of any answer, with a hundred glib solutions learned in brothels, all useless against her basic innocence, my need. Sometimes entertaining her change of heart, that she would grow less afraid— she wouldn't. She was wise. Saying to myself I loved her and this didn't matter— it did. Every unquiet nerve of my body sang out to me that it did.

⚜

Longwy, girdled with iron, its fortress a pinnacle above the valley of the Chiers—a town suddenly famous. Because the Prussians have taken Longwy.

Look at a map. Germany and Belgium poured over into France. That's all you need say—*the Prussians . . . Longwy*—for rooms to explode. The roads to Paris lie open now to the invader. To those who have vowed to mur- der all Revolutionaries without mercy, to raze Paris and dam the River Womb with corpses.

The patriotic troops have got to stop them. Quick, send them a message. Send them more arms, and more saltpeter, and do we need all these bells? We could melt some down for the cannons. And meanwhile, the city must be shown no traitor will be tolerated. An army only flourishes when there are no plots behind its back, at home. There have been upsets from the start. Contractors selling bad meat to our legions, supplies that never reached them. And there have been wicked tongues spreading dissent and despair. One sown doubt is worth pure gold to the enemy. For that reason alone, you can be sure two-thirds of the pessimists in Paris have been *bought*. So the traitors will be gathered together and brought to justice. Danton has set up an arena of judgment, a Tribunal of August.

In the war zone La Fayette, the golden-haired boy, the blond kid, veteran of the American War of Independence, had just learned the August Tribunal was eager to see him. The eagerness was not mutual. Well, he'd been this way before. Ingratitude and danger. "I must drink this bitter cup to its dregs. Again." Brooding over it all in the dark of dawn, remembering being nineteen in America. In 1789, La Fayette had sent one of the keys of the felled Bastille to George Washington: the tribute of Liberty's disciple to Liberty's Founding

Father. And now? Well, the horse was nicely trained and did as it was bid. Slipping through the cornfields and through the woods (he'd be damned if he'd see any of Danton's justice), and over a stream and over the border, and into the arms of the Austrians—who were not as innocently rejoiced as La Fayette had hoped—and so, instead of Danton's, he will see instead several years of *Austrian* justice: the inside of an Austrian dungeon.

But maybe that was just as well, the August Tribunal in Paris turning out so harsh Robespierre apparently refused to sit as judge on it. Well, it's the old abstemiousness, Maximilien's aversion to capital punishment. For, naturally enough, the Tribunal has to mete out the occasional death sentence. Though fashions change, even in death.

Quid novi?

❀

There is a new goddess in Paris. She is, in her way, impressive, tall and slender, her silhouette against the sky. When the coverings are on her, she is a high-shouldered woman, curiously missing a head. When the cloak comes off, her naked frame holds air, and in her belly is a round navel of emptiness. You must climb upward to reach her, and then you must lie down, as it's always well to do with any deity, on your face. She puts her wooden hands about your throat. And then: the cold steel kiss.

She was first brought in by night, muffled like a rare courtesan for a king. Did anyone see that bizarre procession, at the margin before dawn? Hear, down in the street, a faint rumble of wheels? What passes? Ah, it is only She.

Since she is a fledgling goddess, brought in quietly under the shield of darkness and newborn to the world, she is not yet a celebrity, though given many playful names.

Sometimes she is called the Piano, since a piano maker is said to have created her. Does she resemble a piano, maybe, to the analogous eye? If so, the keyboard is metaphysical, a block of space over which death can run his fingers. Yes, the Piano, she'll play today, but only one note.

They will call her Mignonette, and Louisette too, as if she were a young girl, a virgin. (Frankly, she has had one man before, but only one.) She has not attained, as yet, her mature status. She will have to grow to that through practice and experience.

Through cold steel kisses.

How cold or hot is the blade today, the blade of Louisette the cat goddess, who has only one tooth, though her bite is fatal?

Far off, looking out of windows across the Place du Carrousel, you can watch the two small figures, those criminals, go up the ladder to the platform where the goddess stands. Or, at the back of the crowd, craning—hold the children up or they'll miss it.

One man is lying on the plank now, face down. The collar of wood goes around his neck. There's a flash in the sky, between the wooden uprights, a flash—and the crowd makes a noise. What? Is that it? Is it over? I didn't see— well, alas, it can't be done again with the same man, but there is the other one. Watch now, concentrate and fix the gaze. Don't blink, it happens in the wink of an eye. And a second flash, and a spurt of red, just like before. The crowd shouts, and some of them laugh. But it's a fact; it happens too quickly. The crowd tries to cheer itself up. Don't those fellows look silly with their heads bitten off? It's good to be rid of traitors. But: a pity it's so fast.

Probably the only way around the problem is to have more of them done at a time, quantity if not quality.

The black goddess, now adorned with ruby ribbons, makes no sign of being aware she has disappointed anybody. She hangs in the air, still and waiting. Perhaps she knows something we don't.

And they will call her, too, for the glorious revolutionary month of July, *La Juilletine.*

Actually, her shape, in forward silhouette, is less like that of a musical instrument than, strangely, of a printing press. And like a press, of course, part of her comes *down* to do the work.

Go to sleep now, black goddess, though the round eye in your belly never closes. Go to sleep now, for a little while.

SEVEN

1792: Septembre (Sanglant)

Fraternité ou la mort (Be my brother or I'll kill you)

THE CONVOY OF coaches, which trundled toward the Abbey Prison, appropriately contained a group of priests. They were not People's priests, these, naturally, but recalcitrants who would not take the oath to the Nation. Arrested, as so many hundreds of various persons had been arrested over the past few days, their mood was grimly miserable and apprehensive. Their escort of federal soldiers now and then insulted them, and this might bring a flash of fear. But what they expected was dank walls, prison straw, a vile detention. Some were already quietly praying for release.

Release arrived.

It arrived out of the September Sunday afternoon, between two streets, shouting in one long, incredibly sinister howl, with nothing human in it, except that only human things are capable of such noises.

They saw, the prisoners in the coaches, a wall of men built in a moment around them.

The windows were open—it was such a hot, close day. Now, through the apertures, white light came slicing in. And slicing out again, the white was red.

"Hey, you," the Federals said.

"Yes. Us. Are you going to try and stop us, or join in? Are you for the People or against the People, eh, Citizen Heyyou?"

A few streets on, those who had heard the shouting and the cries stood back, as the first of the teams of carriage horses presently moved into sight. The passage of the convoy was now almost silent. The tumult of three or four streets off had died away. The horses hauled, their heads down, sweat steaming. Above the roll and judder of the wheels came the faintest strangest noise, a ceaseless whining and whimpering. . . . From under the doors of every carriage, blood had run—and was running still, in scarlet streams, spangling the cobbles, making bright rivulets, left behind as the trembling horses toiled on toward the prison of l'Abbaye.

⚜

Every one of the prisons was full of traitor priests and conniving aristocrats. Who didn't know it? And they had money, of course, the papist clergy and the lords and ladies. They lived in the prisons in luxury, and when they got tired of being there they paid to be sprung. (Everything's a game to the rich and noble. You'd seen them on the streets earlier, in ribbons and waistcoats of a color they called *rouge séparé*—for the severed heads of the Bastille's governor and certain persons taken off lantern hooks.) Escapes were a commonplace from all prisons. Patently the nobility stayed incarcerated only just as long as it took to hatch plots. Places of chastisement were a hotbed of treacheries. How many evil cutthroats dumped in the dungeons of the Châtelet, la Force, the Conciergerie had not been taken up to the elegantly appointed cells of aristos, offered and given gold, assured of freedom on some particular day. Once Paris was duly stripped of her young men, who left in droves every hour for the war front, paid assassins would fall upon the remaining citizens—the weak, the sick, the aged, the women, even the children—and murder them. Paris, who did not forget her heritage, knew such wholesale massacres were possible. She had, for example, seen the Huguenots butchered, just over a thousand of them, on the Feast of St. Bartholomew, late in an August only some two hundred years ago.

It was this way. Brunswick's Prussians had taken Verdun. Apparently nothing could (or would) stand against them. They might now reach Paris inside two days. Think about it: *two days*—Brunswick of the Manifesto, rivers dammed with corpses. Meanwhile, there was this horde of enemies within the walls. You saw it. You dreamed of it. A night sky red with things on fire, the gates of Paris broken, the crimson thunderclouds of the cannons. And as the army of death thrust forward, the second death rose snarling at your back with a dagger, rose upward at your side, your dead child in its teeth.

There had been an interim of panic. Pure panic. Nothing alloyed about it. The ministry met foaming and tweeting for a mass evacuation of the city. Let's get out. Out, away. Run for your lives and save himself who can!

It was the minister of justice, Danton, who marched to the speaker's rostrum at the Stable, dressed in the colors of fire and blood, gaudy as hell, and red in the face for the quaking pallor of the rest.

"*Run?* Over my body. Does Paris mean nothing to you, then, this empress of cities, that you'll abandon her? I would rather put her to the torch myself, kill her myself in the Roman way, than let her be the raped plaything of some alien conqueror." And the shivering hall begins to sparkle and to fizz. Oh, when the god comes to Danton, it isn't like any other man's god. Mars is the patron today, maybe, from the meadow over the Seine, Mars lifting his burning war plumes. "Listen to me. We will have defenses. We will reorganize our troops. We will *fight,* both the enemy without and the enemy within. It is with joy, gentlemen, that we shall today inform the masses of Paris that France will be saved and that France will be the victrix. The line between terror and valor is thinner than a thread. We have only to inspire them to make warriors of them all. And those who fail France, we will give them only what the enemy offers—death!" Loud applause. He has them. Terror, valor. The thread breaks and they stand on the benches, brave as eagles, lions. "When the bells ring out on this occasion, it will be no mere alarm signal. It will be the sounding of a charge against our enemies. For in order to throw down a foe, what is needed? Superior arms? No. Moral ascendancy? No. The hand of God? No, no, and no! What is needed is *audacity,* and more audacity yet."

And standing on the benches they roar and cheer. Outside, the crowds catch the words and go wild. Terror and valor. ("But it also needs," Danton remarks privately, "a blooding.")

❀

When the blood-spilling carriages reached the Abbey Prison, there was a mob waiting to meet them at the gates.

Those priests who had so far kept their lives were pulled onto the roadway and cut in pieces.

A short little carpenter went around, quieting the horses, which were now neighing and stamping at the stench of blood and offal. "There, there, my beauty, my love." And to reach their heads more easily, he climbed up on the back of a dying priest.

❀

I'd said to him, "Well, will they get here?"

"Who get where?" he asked me lazily.

"Come on, Danton. The Prussians."

"No. They won't get here."

"You're with *me* now, alone. Not out there rallying the world."

"And don't you need rallying, dear Camille? Aren't you shitting yourself with funk like everyone else?"

"Barring you."

"Barring me. They won't get here. We'll portion them in chops. Longwy and Verdun: the defenses were lousy, and the army's still a rabble. But it'll get better. I've given our bold captains a talking to. The only recent general to desert us is La Fayette, which is like losing a rotten tooth. Now? I'd put my cash on the Marne department, if I were you, for some kind of decisive victory."

"Oh? Why?"

"Near enough to Paris to make our wretches wake up and work. Far enough off to make a German withdrawal feasible. Besides."

"Besides."

"I gather there are a lot of windmills in the Marne department."

⚜

Since August, there had been thousands of arrests. The prisons were bursting at the seams.

Bursting with plotters, traitors.

In league with the émigrés, whose army of Koblenz–whose pact with Prussia–whose agents were already–

And they rise up with daggers at your back and dead children in their teeth.

And those who fail France–we'll give them only what the enemy offers–death.

Danton, awarded plenary powers, had authorized the searching of houses for secret caches of arms, hoards of illegal money. All able citizens should be mobilized and given weapons. Those who refused to aid the city would be shot.

The roads out of Paris are closed.

The Assembly is electing a war committee.

"*What's happening?*"

"They're killing them–like flies. Oh, God, we'll be next."

"But *why?*"

The prisoners crowd to their narrow windows, some of which are so low down they must lie on the floor to do it, beholding in the court beneath the great bath of blood, with some men splashing merrily in it and others drowned.

Some of the prisoners leave the windows and attempt to hide. They find crannies in the walls and burrow there, they climb the chimneys. Bullets and lighted straw bring them out and down.

Into the cells men come bounding. They look cheerful, hearty, and their eyes shine. They carry bottles with them, as if they have rushed here to offer the prisoners a drink. But they only offer steel: the last face you see, grinning, with nothing human in its shining burning eyes. But slaughter is not always so precipitate.

At the Châtelet they take you, on legs nerveless with fear, along the corridors to a wondrous dreamlike tribunal set up in the jailors' rest room.

"In here." (Don't ask *why?* anymore. Step over the dead body in the doorway.) "Stand there."

Stand, then, or kneel if your legs give way.

Torchlight and pipe smoke. They're smoking and drinking brandy. A couple snore, tired out by exhausting labor. One of the jailor's dogs crouches,

chained and quivering, in a corner, lusting for the blood it smells, frightened
almost to dementia by the other smell: hatred, horror.

"Name."

My name? Give it. An ordinary name. I'm only a common thief. Just stole
to keep alive.

"But you've been seen speaking to aristos."

In the yard, once. Did I? No, he said to me —

"Don't lie. We can tell. We can read your mind. If you lie to us you're lost."

But you're probably lost anyway, whatever you did or didn't do or say.

"This court finds you guilty. Take him out and see to him."

You are taken out and seen to.

❋

Rivers fount and begin to flood. Rivers redder than wine. From the
churches that have sheltered or incarcerated criminal priests, from the prisons,
those hives of perfidy.

The gutters blush, as if a million butchers' shops —

It's only water. Turgid red water.

Though in Egypt, once, water turned to blood.

The tocsin sounding from the towers and steeples. Thunder in the air.
Rivers of sound, and water into blood.

How can I go on with this?

Because I must. Because, naïve blaspheming fool that I was, I always said
and believed I would tell the truth, and even while I believed, knew I did not,
and did not.

❋

People came and went in Danton's office. You heard them arriving, like the
whirlwind; leaving, spent. They came to ask if he knew there was a massacre
going on. He told them it was simply summary justice. No, it wouldn't go as far
as all that. A look at me.

"There are provisional prison courts being set up. The local authorities
have been, in each case, approached, and where they can vouch for a man's
innocence they'll protect him."

"Camille's right. Oh, it may get a little out of bounds. But it's better they
work off their high spirits on the criminal element than on those citizens, like
you or me, monsieur, who are working for their salvation."

On the other hand, there had been maneuvers to get certain prisoners away
from, or keep them out of, Paris. "He's too useful to risk in this. Oh, these.
Yes, they're owed a favor." Then there had been the usual hosts of petitioners,
some of the women arriving very décolleté for our benefit. There had also

been: "The scum of the earth is in jail this year. Good for nothing but to start a compost heap."

He knew, of course, as I did, what was going on. It wasn't planned exactly, nor was it prevented. When the howling in the streets became audible, I remembered Fréron's *The People? Forget your Rousseau. They're animals, and they bite.*

So fling them something to blunt their teeth.

Some of the assassins were paid, and others joined in from sheer bonhomie. Malhomie.

Danton's Committee for Security—the names give a clue. Hébert. Marat. Billaud-Varenne, who took off at one point to go around the prisons congratulating the sabered patriots on their hard work. Rossignole, our nightingale, who had shot that awkward cuss Mandat so obligingly on the steps of City Hall. A Chénier was presiding on it, too, counterweight of poetry. And Fabre, the playwright. And Robespierre, the saint of our order.

For Danton himself: what did he say, and how did he seem? Recollection gives me three panels of a triptych. In the first, smug, mocking, contemptuous, and—hungry. Yes, greedy. The taste of power—or of blood. In the second, uneasy. Damn it, it's going further than it should. No longer in control. Blandness rolled across the surface of unease like printer's ink. Third panel—which he actually came to act out for me, for all of us, for himself—indignant baffled rage. *I? No.* A cry which alternated with: All right then, *yes.* It was *me. Septembriseur.* To save the world.

I must add, I didn't, at the time, analyze or therefore see it that way at all.

I didn't even question him then. The streets were awash with blood. Walking forests of heads and hearts traipsed past. I didn't look, and I didn't argue.

And when the visitors pelted in, I said, "The innocent will be protected."

In a funny way, I think I even meant it. Some blind fate, or God, was delivering the blameless. It had to. There *was* a lot of intrigue in the prisons, there *were* buyings and sellings and engineered escapes. And there was the fear madness of the People, which must be turned, as always, in the right direction.

But there was also, within me, a dull weight of uninterviewed things, petitioners on the mind's stairs, and their décolletée revealed a skeleton.

(At such moments as this, the load of guilt makes me weary. Makes me wish only to turn aside, to say, Very well, I was a damnable idiot, which is no excuse. Condemn me. Get it over with. But no. Too easy.)

While Danton glowed in the triptych, I hid my poisoned feelings: from him, from our visitors, from myself. I was even cheerful and once or twice joked. I had, in any case, long since written to the populace at large, in my paper, that there were times when the People must take judgment into their own hands. They were right. Of course they were right. God and nature guided every sweep of every knife, every jab of every pike. Only the guilty would be struck down.

Later, the committee over at City Hall was discussing National Defense with sober attention to detail: trenches, cannons, provisioning.

Sophisticated Paris came out of the theaters which had had the temerity to stay open. Thirsty Paris sought the wineshops that did not have the temerity to close.

One always avoided the reeking sewers. Nothing exceptional in that. The ignorant asked what that screaming and shouting was over by the Carmelite Prison.

When it grew dark, the sky was bestially lit in a score of places by the flare of bonfires. To come back from the country to the city and see all this would have been to think Paris already taken, invaded.

By night, the blood in the gutters ran black.

Oh, September.

⚜

In the undark dark of torches and bonfires, it's a festival. And at festival time, we drink and dance.

The carts went by, loaded with strange contorted shapes, like tangled washing. Meaningless rag-doll hands hung down and trailed. Look, there's one still got a ring. *I'll* have that—a memento. No, *I'll* have it. The men laugh as they part their fighting women.

Up on a cart, a young girl with a red rose pinned to her bodice embraces a naked dead priest—"Oh, kiss me, Father, for I have sinned!" Shrieks of mirth on all sides.

"You won't do any sinning with that one. I did him myself, with my own knife." The girl laughs too, and springs from the cart. She links hands with her sisters of the night and they dance, their wild hair flying. It is not, after all, a rose pinned on her breast, it's a—

> *Vive le son, vive le son*
> *(Dansons la carmagnole),*
> *Vive le son du canon!*

Was there ever such a night (anything's possible now) and days to follow it, days of the People's judgment? Who fears Prussians now? Let them all come, let them all come and we'll do *this* to them, and maybe *this*. Ah, Danton, our father Danton, you knew us well and taught us well. You have made us *brave*.

And in the wineshops they're roasting human hearts and eating them. (They say.) And, seated on dead bodies (pull up a corpse, Jacques, and sit down), eating bread dipped in human blood. (They say.)

And on the counter of a tavern, a beautiful face with fair hair, wide-eyed. "Drink to the unhealth of a princess!"—an aristo woman's severed head. (They say? Very well. All right. It's true.)

Here's health to the sound, health to the sound
(As we dance the Carmagnole),
Here's health to the sound of the cannon's pound!

Antoinette used to play that tune on her harpsichord—the Carmagnole. But now she's locked up in the Temple, and they've shown her one of her aristocratic girlfriend's heads on a pike. Antoinette doesn't play the harpsichord anymore.

❈

Un, deux, trois, quatre, cinq, six . . .
Six days, inclusive.
Well, this massacre has a better total even than St. Bartholomew. Nearly one and a half thousand dead.

❈

They paid the men twenty-four livres each, by means of agents; I mean the men who went around the prisons, on the advice of the Commune at City Hall. They were encouraged with the words, "You're executing your enemies, as it is your duty to do."

We knew, if we didn't get them first, they would get us. We thought we'd be murdered in our beds.

Naturally, when justice was placed in our hands, we accepted our responsibility and carried it out. And we rejoiced and had a party afterward, because we were so relieved.

And because now we knew we could shed blood, better than any Prussian bastard.

❈

The Commune of Paris hereby informs its brothers of France that ferocious conspirators, apprehended in our prisons, have been purged by the populace, to safeguard itself from their treason. We believe the entire Nation will wish to adopt such measures, in order to safeguard public security, and that all France will cry out, with us, "We march against our foe, but leaving no monsters behind us to cut the throats of our wives and children."

❈

Don't be squeamish, Fréron said. You helped start it. But Fréron is away in the Moselle region on Danton's orders, a commissioner, looking into matters—there, not here.

Don't be squeamish. And don't tell them they were wrong. They bite.
"I can't sleep. That's why I'm writing. Go back to bed."

"But you can't see. Only one candle."

"I can see, Lucile." Too well. Or not enough.

I hadn't meant to be sharp with her. But she, knowing my sharpness was irrelevant (Oh, God, how did I deserve such a wife? Some mistake, no doubt, in the itinerary of rewards and punishments), took no notice. She lit a lamp and brought it to me.

"I'm telling them," I said, "how wonderful they are. The People are God and can do no wrong. It would be most unwise to say anything else. Luckily, they don't properly realize yet what an insult you pay them, if you tell them they're God. And then, I'm trying to get myself elected to the convention when it starts, am I not? And so have to remain popular, faithful to the mob."

She touched, caressed my hair. Don't, Lucile, if you don't want to drive me mad. She heard my thoughts. She kissed me gently and turned away. I caught her hand and held her there.

"You're married to a fool," I said. "A fool and a coward. I don't know what to do. What are the answers to all this? Are there any answers?"

"Yes. You'll find them."

"How?"

"Through waiting and working. By listening to your own good heart."

"*Good?* Fool, coward, corrupt, incendiary—yes. 'Good' isn't a name I've earned."

"But you will," she said. "When they pay attention."

"They have. Look where it's gone."

"Ah, don't blame only yourself."

"That's fair. Yes, I accept that. Why should I? The king is to blame," I said, "for all this." I let go her hand and stood up and went to the window, open, airless, night as hot as a flame. Outside, the streets were very quiet. A few nights earlier, we had kept the windows closed, despite the heat. "A strange circular process of reasoning," I said. "You don't want to query it? Why is the innocuous ignoramus ostrich of a king to blame? Just because he is all that. If he hadn't got in the way simply by existing, if he hadn't laid his plots, tried his escapes and botched them, fiddled and fumbled and fucked around, if he hadn't *been* there, we wouldn't have come to this. If someone had axed the stupid ox the day after the Bastille went down, there'd be no Prussians at the gates, no heaps of dead harmless women from a mad-house piled up all along the road because obviously they were planning to kill us all. It's Ll-*Louis*. It's cen-centuries of bloody devouring v-vicious soulless *monarchy* that have brought us where we are. That mob, those poor bloody stupid vampires with their pikes: *he* m-made them. Not Danton. Not me. *The holy kings of France.*" I stopped, breathless, trembling. I added, "And I hear all the windows are smashed in Notre Dame. Do you remember that day I prophesied it would happen? The day I so gracelessly told you you were loved by me?"

She came to me swiftly, silent but for the whisper of her nightrobe, and took hold of me so strongly. She murmured to me, "Forget all the silly things I said, I was being fanciful. Come with me now."

But I only held her in turn, in the window, lit up for any to see who looked out of the black maw of the city.

"No," I said. "I only need you beside me, here. I'm insane tonight. Is he asleep?" I meant the child, which of course she knew. "Yes. Fast asleep. He looks so peaceful and so happy." "He's a baby. We were all happy and peaceful then." I felt her tears, falling against my burning skin through the open cravatless collar for which Danton had started a thankful summer fashion. (Danton, always Danton.) "I didn't mean to make you cry. When our son is my age, the world will have been set to rights." And I thought, And what will he say to me then, my son? What will there *be* to say to me?

❅

The bodies were slung down into quarries. Insects, feasting, died in the quicklime which was then thrown on.

So many limbs, torsos, skeins of hair. Tenantless, festering, obliterated, anonymous, under the burning toxic snow.

❅

Oh, you! They do not forget *you.*
But I, I have no fame.

Oh, mother, when you bore your child,
Oh, mother, when you watched it thrive,
You knew that life's an unsure thing.
Oh, August, when the flowers brim,
September, when the knives bloom wild.
Yes, all must reach, in turn, the grave.
No need to drag, to thrust us in.

Ah, vous! Ils ne vous oublient pas,
Mais moi, je n'ai pas d'la mémoire.
Ma chère, ma petite vie, sans gloire.
(My unglorious, dear, precious little life.)

❅

Camille presented his resignation to Danton with a slightly shaking hand and a slightly stammering voice. His face, however, looked frozen, as if he had had a brush with the Gorgon Medusa on the way upstairs.

"Because you're concentrating on election to the brand new National Convention?" said Danton.

"And writing."

"Not your own paper anymore."

"Whatever, I'm better at that than clerking here, even if all your secretaries are princes."

"Everyone's dying to get into this Convention. I'm thinking about it myself."

"Then you know."

"Mm. What about the nice salary I've been seeing you paid? And the lovesome furniture, and all the books you've bought?" (Some of Mirabeau's famous library, or is that hearsay? What a thrill. The very volumes that sat on shelves and watched Jupiter tick you off, now subsequently in your own bookcases.) "But you'll be leaving all that. Leaving me. Taking the vision of the exquisite Lucile away from my glazed eyes. How can you do that to me?"

"Ha-ha."

"And after I sent fretful Fréron off so he couldn't stab you in an alley. And what about that new coat? And all the wine that's been clanking up to your apartment? And the new dinner service Lucile—?"

"Danton. I'm going. This isn't for me. I'm no good at it."

"Correction, you're very good at it. Which is just what all the little actresses have been telling me too, but how are you going to afford them—and that little redhead? You have to think of these things." Playful. Playful as a big cat with a gazelle in its paws. "Do you want to take this back?"

"I want you to roll it up and stuff it right—"

"Now, that's better. You're getting wild. Lose your temper for me, darling, then I can handle you."

"Fabre can work on your propaganda and draft the motions for your speeches. You never stick to a word of them anyway."

"Oh, true. But I'll miss you. I'll miss your flattering phrases, your sycophantic attentions. The musical sound of your singing, which cracks all the inkwells. Your anchoring calm in moments of stress. Besides which, Robespierre is lurking somewhere outside, waiting to take a snap at you. The camps are splitting. Stay with me."

"I *am* w-with you. But this bloody great palace—I want election to the Convention, and I want to wr—to work for the things I've said are important."

"Still think they are?"

"You *know* I do! Christ, you can be—"

"Then will you take my word for it that I, too, believe in the same ideals as formerly?"

Camille turned away. "Yes? Do you?"

Danton thundered. The words came out like cannon fire. The old words. I love France. I'd die for France. My life's blood. . . . But there are ways to achieve results, not all of them straight or narrow. . . . Camille, absorbing the onslaught, or resisting it, appeared to grow smaller, bowing over, withering. Danton suddenly seemed to become aware he was blasting, not uplifting. In a terrible rage he roared, "Well, I thought I could count on you! I thought you knew me. I thought I could turn my back and not get a stiletto between my shoulders from *your* hand. You're as bad as Gabi. *I'm* the one went out and stood at La Force and called the mob over. I'm the one waded bollocks-high in the blood and shouted, Sharpen your knives, lads! It was Danton, wasn't it? Danton was September. Tell history. Make it stick. Give the girls something to scare their kids with. Write it on the piss-house walls."

"We both—" Camille said. He said, "All of us."

"It was inevitable and unstoppable, and it's irretrievable now. Come out of the sky. It did what it was meant to. If I could have got their courage up any other way—but I only had an ax. Instead of pretending it was a rosebush, I used it like an ax." Danton relapsed. He mopped his face. "Why are you doing this to me? What the hell are we arguing about?"

"We're not arguing. We're both saying the same thing. I'm getting out because this scares me. I wonder, will you?"

"Oh, you wonder that, do you?" Danton's angry eyes cut at him. "Don't you think I value the power I've got right now? But my mistake. Power corrupts, doesn't it?"

Camille went to the door and looked out. Nobody appeared to have been there, listening. Not much need. Five streets distant they would have heard that enormous voice: *Danton—September.*

"By the way," said Danton. Camille looked back at him apprehensively. "Do you mind if I try that redhead of yours?"

Camille shrugged. "She isn't mine. I'm sure she'll be delighted."

"I can, in turn, recommend the blonde at the other establishment. She asks after you pointedly."

"I'll remember."

❦

The artist whose *Andromache* and *Oath of the Horatians* I had viewed with astonished enthusiasm at twenty-five was now busy painting me *en famille.* David, dwarfish and fiendishly ugly enough to make me look tall and chiseled, prowled around us half the day at the Lamoignon; one fell over him behind bookcases or cross-legged in corners. Even alone, he would rest his head in one hand, concealing what he considered to be the fouler side of his face. The attitude had caused persons to inquire of him if he had a toothache. Working, he forgot. In our rooms he prepared random sketches. Conversely, captives in his studio, Lucile and I posed, ricking our necks, trying to conduct civilized conversation while craned around at each other at a dramatic angle. He had

Roman intentions for us: I, seated; Lucile standing behind my chair. When I
saw the result later, I particularly liked the smallness and delicacy of her hand,
resting on mine. Her hair had darkened since the birth of our son. (Nevertheless, he didn't quite catch the shade of it, which disappointed me.) But she wore
it, for David, loose and girlishly. There is an unlikely curious indescribable
resemblance between us, in that picture. Then, of all things, the artist placed the
child, balanced on the chair back, on my shoulder like a pet owl. Extraordinary.
(Danton was to call the piece "Madonna and Child, with Satan (seated).")

All was not done by the time we vacated the palace and moved back over
into the Cordeliers district. David followed us across the river. He had to
make a prompt alteration, or said he did. No longer possessed of a desk, as
he discovered, I found it also taken from me in the canvas, replaced by the
table where now I worked. He was a stickler for realism. His plasters from
antiquity, lined up along the banks of the Womb, were to gain it the names of
Nile and *Tiber.*

He was fascinated by Horace, never playing with him, but staring at him.
Horace stared back. They would stare at each other for hours.

"Jajot, stop mesmerizing my son!" Lucile would cry.

"It's your son who is mesmerizing me. Do you think he'll be a famous
man?"

"Therefore overworked and at his wits' end. Let's wish him obscurity." I
said it glumly, with all the self-importance of such gloom. (When had I ever
courted obscurity? It had been my plague. My son, naturally, would be a hero.) I
was tensed to responsibilities; like our painter, I had been elected a deputy for
the Paris section, securing my seat in the Convention by a sound majority of
votes. (Brissot apparently remarked, my electors were now buying large quantities of land with the bribes I'd given them.) But I'd wanted the job (redemp-
tion?). I was falling over myself telling everyone the importance of the mission.
"What greater laurel, what greater hope of glory? Such tasks in our hands: the
punishment of oppression, the building of justice. To astound the nations of
Europe by showing them the door. To create men anew, and give to them the gift
of Liberty's fire."

Now David, fiercely nursing his face, said softly, "Obscurity? Well, Pétion's been blessed, then." (Pétion had lost out to Robespierre, installed by three
hundred and thirty-eight votes out of just over five hundred.)

"Oh, Pétion. Brissot and the Rolands have made a donkey of *that* one."

I took the child up and held him. I realize he must have cried now and then,
but I scarcely ever recall him doing so. Even David captured his look of benign
amusement. (Lucile would gaze at us, when I cradled him, and assume her
"indefinable" resonance, a moon priestess. He would be fair, as she was.)

"I wonder," said David, "if I'll finish the canvas before Brunswick arrives."

"He isn't arriving, didn't they tell you?"

"They were too busy digging trenches."

A city besieged by German armies, with Lucile and my son trapped inside it. The child looked up at me. Am I risking you?

David said, "I was talking to Maxime. . . . We've picked up an odd story at the Jacobins. You're never there, you miss things."

"I'm there. I come disguised."

"The story is, Danton has bought Brunswick."

"No, Jajot. You've got it wrong. The story is Brunswick bought Brissot and the Gironde."

"Excuse me. *This* is the story of the crown jewels."

A hoard of loot had been stolen from the Archives on Louis XV Square. The journals were full of speculation. Obviously, anything that happened involved Danton. I said, "Another Necklace scandal. Where did we hear this before? If someone robbed you, it's Danton. If someone pushed you out of the window—Danton."

"Alternatively, how else do you stop Brunswick?"

"Rely on his own cocksure incompetence. If that commander is as poor a judge of his men as he is of the citizens of Paris, they'll probably lynch him before much longer."

"And what do you think of our own generals?" asked David craftily, in that way he had, talking you out, as if he were not an artist but somebody's spy.

"We have a few worth the name. Westermann . . . well. Dumouriez seems sound enough. And Dillon."

"Oh, Dillon. Your friend."

"Is he?"

"You dine together."

"I've been known to share a table with him, and other foreigners, in company."

Lucile said mischievously, "A gentleman with perfect manners." At which David and I congratulated each other on being mannerless and not gentlemen. "And speaking of dining," I added, "this oaf has been here three hours. I suppose that means we've invited him to eat with us." (We were, in fact, never quite comfortable with David.)

But no, I didn't anymore believe in the fact of invasion. Everything had been wildly exaggerated; while "two days away," the Prussians had failed to materialize inside two weeks. Something—and maybe it was only, ultimately, the sureness of Danton—had pushed the idea out of my head. Cynically, I'd reviewed the fiasco of the Champ-de-Mars; if our leader stayed put now, there was no reason to do otherwise. I thought of him, back over the river, in his goldenly appointed office. We had celebrated the elections at the cafés and theaters. He too had won a seat, was full of glee at the prospect as if he had nothing else. We ended in a place of women, and he vanished at last with a tall whore dark as a negress, her neck ringed with gold. You waited for some sort of lead from him. Even there, with blood full of champagne, and white arms, purple petticoats, blown flowers smothering the breath from the lungs, some niche of the mind, waiting—But no. Off he went with his dark lady, leaving me to the celebrated blonde.

And besides. I was now committed to a different course. While he—behind the bombast, oratory, jokes, desk—seemed committed to nothing. His greeds had reached their pitch and been fed. He was digesting it: the red of September.

Something had changed within me. I felt it, never named it. I sought about for a broom to rid the yard of blood-red fallen leaves. They were the debris of centuries. And the broom? A pen, as usual.

Writing for a *Revolutionary News* no longer my own, whose motto ran, "The gods like best a willing sacrifice. A king goes consenting for his people."

And with these thoughts around the edges of my mind, tigers in a thicket, I, deputy for the Paris section, played with the child on my knees, who trusted me not to let him fall.

Some evenings, the deputy would be discovered galloping through his apartment with his son on one shoulder (David had got his pose from the habitual), the child unafraid, up in the air, his hands clutching my collar and nearly pulling my hair out, squeaking and chortling, and I informing him we were a horse and rider in the Arabian desert. "If you give him a colic, you'll be contrite," said Lucile. There had been a nurse to wait on him at the palace. Now Lucile had resumed full rights. "Your mother says I shall give you a colic. Do you agree with this?" *Plm-slp,* averred my son jovially. "Lucile, he spoke—he said something!" "Yes. He said *plm-slp*. What do you expect the poor thing to say at two months old, with all the breath jolted out of him?"

I would lift him up in both hands and watch him laughing back at me under his bonnet. It seemed we took great pleasure in each other. He knew me. When I came into a room where he was, he would wave his arms and drum his heels, all attention on me.

And I scripted the future somewhat. I began to see him growing, before he had done so very much. I wondered what he would ask me, what he would want to know. Everything. What had I wanted as a little child? God knew. I didn't remember. What all children wanted, I supposed. Freedom—if you translate it. Not only children, then. The whole adult world. Is it really so simple?

Little Lizard, basking in the sun, crawling earnest inch by inch, those incredible minute exquisitely formed hands that one day would be as large and dextrous as my own, grasping my fingers, the buttons of my coat, and on my face very gentle, careful, as if, even so young, you didn't want to hurt or startle me. Oh, my son, my son, my son. I never knew you. Only the bud, never the flowering. They took that from me too. I wonder if you will ever forgive me, or understand why I left you?

❧

The plain stretched out an apron of checkering sunlight; it was an autumn-weather day. Only one thing dominated the flat terrain, like a dark quixotic chess piece: a windmill. The sails were nailed to the sky this morning. The village was deserted; all one and a half souls who lived there had abruptly moved away. Either side of the chessboard, however, there was a temporary increase in population, a thousand of whom were due never to leave.

When the great guns first barked, the waters broke inside twenty women. Crouching in ditches under the trees of Valmy, these camp followers labored to bring forth replacement life. Others had different business. They swarmed through the battalions offering their reviving flasks of liquor, their eyes full of promises. Later, some would stoop over their fallen men in the dusk, howling like bitch wolves. Or they would lie in the ditches silently.

When the great guns first barked, the waters also broke in heaven.

Westermann, who had now been out with the army some while, ignored the rain. He was impressed by the new genius which possessed the troops. They were aggressive, full of fire. They knew the king had lost his crown. Some peculiar barrier had gone with it. After that they heard of the treason in the prisons, and the vast wave that had swept over and dealt with it. News filtered through to them in a blazing fog of truth, lies, imaginative conjecture. Prudence, which had made fear possible, gave way to recklessness. Now they had it, the vaunted audacity. Not daring, or boldness, or even courage—this was an insolent thing. It made crude gestures at death. (Up yours, Prussia, as far as it will go.) *That* was the brand of valor now. You burn your boats, and then, since there's no way back across the river, you *fight*. So, damn the rain. Let it fall on the enemy.

The great guns.

Beautiful and black as polished wet jet, lean and powdered with an aspiration to rust: long phallic guns, stubby antique cranky guns that in their dreams dream of exploding on the spot. Guns with curlicues, and guns without curlicues. Cantankerous guns formerly retired. Young guns knowing nothing.

Marroomb!

The plain rocks gently. Partly lost now in cloud, the sails of the deserted windmill stir a fraction. Half a seed of grain, left behind, may be ground by reverberation alone. Or half a seed of phantom grain haunting the mill may think it has been.

Here's to the sound of the cannons' *murrmb.*

The revolutionary commanders stride from emplacement to emplacement. Their troops cheer. Red handkerchiefs and rain-sweating faces. The stink of gunpowder, and damp smut settling like flies. (In the field hospitals, already some work being done. Rain drips through tent roofs. Not much. Cannon can do things to you—I remember my dad telling me—shorter by two legs.) It's a busy morning. Busy raining, busy giving birth, busy dying, busy firing.

Across the plain, the guns of Prussia roar back from the overcast. They have
a heavy German accent.

Vrrarumb!

On the leaded rain clouds, fresher clouds of frothing white, as in an etching.

Sraanbrr.

(Don't hit the windmill.)

Up in the air, the wet birds look down at it. Wingless flesh blasting itself to bits again. Tonight there may be an avian banquet.

The Prussians go on firing because the French go on firing. This dawn, the Germans have been telling each other what they would do to the French when they got near enough. It had been thought, in fact, the French would scatter long before midday, retreating fast and messily, like a flock of panicky tricolor sheep. Previously, this was what had always happened. But today, nobody's run yet.

Frankly, while new recruits, fresh spirit, have been poured ceaselessly into the French battalions, the Prussian army is the same old crowd that marched away from home months ago. The popular proverb has it Prussians will set aside anything, leaving kith and kin and every comfort, to go slogging off into foreign lands with the military purpose of killing, when once ordered to do so. Mirabeau made a comment on this phenomenon: the human machine, the massed automata of Germany. Give it a shove and it starts marching. Then again, though, what's it all for? It's for Austria, isn't it? It's alliance warfare. It's Go and do that because that's what you're going to go and do.

Which is all right, if *they* turn and run. All right, all this long way, if they scream and fall down every time they see us. And if their generals come creeping over into our lines at night and kiss our boots. And we get to sack Paris at the end of it. But—

The cannons of the sheep continue to shear off fleeces of smoke.

Baaannbb!

And now it would appear they are getting ready to charge. *Ah! Diese Schafen haben die Zahnen.*

We're tired and cooled of heart. Our guts ache from the traditional dysentery we've been saddled with. The guns are swamped with water, stuck in the mud. And we're stuck there too. You wound us up and we started marching, your toy soldiers. But that lot over there, they're alive; they're fighting drunk for every single thing that's dear to them: body, country, hearth. Children of the Fatherland, they shriek at each other, the day of glory's here! March! They wail, That the alien blood shall drown the furrows! They're not just men, they're *remade* men, and the gods have given them the fire of Liberty. Remember the old legends, the berserkers who could cut their way through bone and stone, who could fight on with an ax bedded in spine or skull, not deigning to admit they were dead?

Find an explanation for it. Say the Prussian commanders were bought. Or say they felt, the men of Prussia, all across that level plain, the unquenchable sea change of fire in the souls of the French. Felt it—and shrank away from scorching.

Consternation.

Brunswick, sitting there in person, like a gray statue on his rainy horse, has glanced at the French lines, back across his own: sullen, sodden, and shifting, clockwork running down.

And his verdict? Not today, thank you.

❋

"They're in retreat! The effing Prussians ran like rabbits!"
"No, the rabbits couldn't keep up with 'em."

❋

The gods could scarcely have sent a better omen. The news from Valmy descended on Paris in a golden rain the very evening of the Convention's inauguration. They had been applauding Danton all day, in the Convention and out of it. Once the victory was common knowledge, he got a standing ovation on every side. I could picture him basking in it, like a great seal in an ocean of warm light.

For myself, I managed to miss the opening sessions.

Now and then, infrequently and usually faint as a ghost, the stomach pain of two years ago came back to haunt me. Fasting seemed to cure it, along with Lucile's cosseting and reassurances. This time, not so. It laid me up. A doctor entered the scene, with all the wretched paraphernalia this entailed. Although the fever was slight and the pain never so bad as that first time, when I had fought it alone, these attentions, and being quite unable to work, put me again into utter despair. I was dying. Would die. Everyone was left unprovided for. What would become of Lucile and the child? And France? Thank God for my wife, who began softly laughing in the midst of it all and, putting her cool hand on my forehead, told me, "I never heard such nonsense. You are *not* dying. I have it from the doctor directly. Lie still, stop fretting, and get well." I obeyed her, and in two days was back on my feet. The Little Lizard, who had appeared to miss his father's mobility, rendered me his own baby form of *un*standing ovation, crowing and waving furiously every time I walked across a room. (I recall sitting writing some notes for a sort of history of events I'd begun compiling, and Lucile's sweet voice saying to him at my back, "See, there is Papa, working and blinding himself with only one candle," and his dear little hand alighting on my head as if in blessing, before they both stole away again.)

I'd meanwhile been appointed overseer for the Guise and Laon area, a mission I indefinitely deferred—while savoring its irony. (*Dear Father, the village idiot of Guise has been put in charge of your affairs. Tell them to watch out. They'd better start singing my praises there, or put up a statue to me, or something.*) Ignoring all alternatives, determination to take my seat in the Convention drove me over the river, in good time to find internal war had already broken out.

❋

The road to hell is paved with good conventions.

❋

The Convention had taken a geographical turn. The higher benches of those draperied tiers had gained the name the Mountain. Up there, in the rarefied airs of Olympus, the Mountaineers sat looking down in disapproving contempt. The Mountain was also the left, and militantly Jacobin. On the crag, such as Danton; Robespierre (and his handsome drunkard brother, both recently escaped from the clutches of Charlotte); Billaud-Varenne, the saber patter; itchy-bitchy Marat, the friend of Spilled Blood; crippled Couthon (paralyzed at thirty-seven, stuck in a chair and presently ready to kill anyone with two usable legs); David, sketchbook in one hand, toothache-cupping his warty cheek; beautiful newly elected deputy Saint-Just, providing, with Robespierre, the Mountain's snow caps of purest cravat muslin; Desmoulins, just strolled in, yellow as a primrose, Lucifer-eyed, with notebook and *porte-crayon* to complement David's sketching apparatus.

Opposite, and lower down, the Gironde Estuary: Long-faced Brissot of the Key (enemy to Windmills); Vergniaud, balding but elegant; Louvet, bald and inelegant, writer; Marseillois "Antinoüs" Barbaroux, fat and gorgeous as a peacock chock-fed for the pot; gray Sillery, still powdered—Roland's protégés, or *Manon* Roland's.

Centrally, the Marsh, full of croaking Toads, prepared to burble yes to anything, no to everything: the unexciting, irritating, undercommitted majority.

A pretty landscape, though hardly by Fragonard. Mucky, muddled, and noisy.

The glory of world-making had already taken place. On September 21 and 22, the monarchy was abolished. Fourteen centuries of granite feudalism had melted like mist and might never have been. It was now the first year of Liberty, *l'an un*. The very nature of the phrase: consider its implications. Quicker and more efficient, for once, than God, the Convention had destroyed and re-modeled the earth in only two days.

It meant so much. And it's all in a name. Wherever, whenever else, did anyone dare to do it? To shake the universe, to cry out: Nothing, till now. And now: Everything.

Year One.

For a split second the heartbeat of eternity faltered, then began to race.

For a split second every man who had shared in the dream was at one. And to augment it, the crown of Valmy.

But only for a split second.

"I denounce the scum of the top tiers. Who doesn't know they intend to subdue France by a dictatorship? And the chosen master? I'll tell you: Maximilien *De* Robespierre."

That from Louvet of the Gironde, with sugar on it.

Robespierre, on the rostrum, looks about him. Practice has taught Maximilien a great deal. The little fellow who used always to be shouted down, says, "Citizen, I admire your courage. I have demanded always the right of a man to speak freely. If you use your freedom to defame me, I can only commend you for demonstrating the liberal tolerance of this institution. I fought for it, and I thank you." And when he tells them, as he so often has told them, how persecuted he is by all factions, and the jeering starts ("File it, Robespierre!" "Précis, Robespierre!"), he waits implacably for a tailing off and says calmly, "No, you're going to listen to me." And they do. He moves into the attack and takes the Gironde to the laundry. The god comes, and Robespierre stands flaming with a clear pale flame, summoning like a sorcerer the vision of the Republic that has already been declared.

When he sits down, trembling in a sort of ecstasy, his lieutenant says quietly, "Brilliantly said, Maxime. Oh, yes."

"No, no, Antoine. Oh, God, I sometimes despair of them. God give me strength. To end this formless bickering and come at the soul of what we need. I had some hopes Danton might do it." Robespierre sighs. He says, "Nothing changes." And where David is hiding his cheek, Robespierre hides his trembling eyes.

Louis Antoine Saint-Just, his own icy gaze gleaming, a white wolf guarding a man on a mountain-top, says softly now, "Corrupted Danton. But they listen to you. One day they'll know what they hear."

"Yes, perhaps. Thank you, my dear comrade."

In the evening, walking in rain over on the left bank, Saint-Just escorts his lord and leader to the doorway of the Duplessis home and declines to go in. The disdainful shiver of the ice-blond head declares, I've no friends here. Have *you?*

The white angel goes away into the rain, to which he appears nearly impervious. The door opens and Robespierre potters up the stairs to where the dark fallen angel greets him. "Well done. You trounced them. But now you know what a lot of rubbish gets talked about dictatorship."

"Do I, Camille? Well."

The supper is excellent, Demeter presiding, her husband, the good Citizen Duplessis, off on patriotic business for the Commune. The soft gray light dies in the windows. Nights and leaves are falling early for the season. The fire is lighted. There is a card game. Lucile and her mother are prevailed on to produce a duet, something of that talented German's, Mozart. Should they sing it at all? But it's so tuneful. In the orange firelight, Robespierre plays gravely and awkwardly with the child named Horatius, an unchristened, non-Catholic son of the Republic, to whom Maximilien stands, nonetheless, in place of a godfather. It's a sentimental evening, pleasant, to be remembered. The rain striking the windows lightly, but here all warm and well and safe.

"How I envy you your son."

"You wouldn't, when he starts exercising his lungs in the middle of the night. No, he's usually very quiet."

Demeter calls for more coffee, but Maximilien must be leaving. He resumes an abstracted manner. He looks out at the street as if afraid of it.

Lucile is dancing gently with the baby, a minuet in strict 3/4 time as accords to Demeter's playing on the piano. "How well you dance, monsieur! So much better than your father."

"And he never treads on your toes," comments Camille. "Come on, Maxime, if you're leaving, I'll walk you back."

"Now, you've been ill. You must take care of yourself."

"If I stay here, I'll end up in a duel with Horace."

On the stair, Robespierre hesitates. He says, "I sometimes have the foolish idea there are assassins waiting in each shadow. Not, perhaps, so foolish. I've often been promised death. I'd give my life — but there's so much still to do."

"You're allowing that bag of wind Brissot to frighten you. The Gironde is all talk."

"Dangerous talk. Paris isn't done with its plots. Corruption everywhere. We tread on rotten boards. The whole edifice needs to be pulled down and rebuilt."

Camille opens the street door to reveal, on the dark threshold, Saint-Just, pale wolf-unicorn and angel.

Robespierre starts. Collects himself. "Good heavens!"

"He's been faithfully waiting for you," says Camille. "Have you? You should have rung the bell."

"And intrude? No."

"No? How sensitive. And in the rain, too."

They walk. Robespierre says philosophical things about the night's darkness and the hope of daybreak. Camille says he heard Saint-Just has become engaged to one of the Duplay daughters. Saint-Just haughtily corrects him. Saint-Just suggests the Gironde should be smashed. He makes a reference that postulates Danton and Camille have some sort of arrangement with the Gironde. Camille asks Saint-Just if he's written any more poems lately. "And what was that last one: 'The Orgy'? 'The Catamite'? Oh, dear, it slips my mind."

On the bridge Camille, who has been drinking if no one else has, pushes Saint-Just hard enough that he nearly falls. Saint-Just retaliates with a blow that Camille manages to sidestep, mostly. Saint-Just, who was once in prison and picked up something of the vocabulary, forgets himself and becomes more than usually entertaining. All this stops when Camille and Saint-Just both realize simultaneously that Robespierre is trotting briskly away from them, head bowed as if in sadness, exhaustion, embarrassment.

"Go on, run after him, you fucking bootlicker," sneers the awful Camille, leaning on a handy railing. "Buy some roses for him on the way."

Saint-Just shudders. His cold face has not altered, even when letting out the anatomical words. He stares at Camille, memorizing him.

Camille says, enjoying himself, "I heard how you met him. Wrote to him, went up, and accosted him: 'You are not the deputy for Arras, but the deputy who represents the whole world. Oh, let me shake your hand. No, let me kneel. Let me shake your *foot* —"

Saint-Just walks away after his master.

Camille stands on the bridge, aware, oddly, that he has not, after all, been clever. But it's too late now.

He swore to kill me. That was later. But probably he also swore it then.

Striding back toward the *maison* Duplessis, the night was dry and sour. Year One, and nothing special. Some more black scandal, as usual, hurled at Danton: jewel robberies, fornication with the wives of close colleagues, particularly one. Lucile no longer paid any visits to Gabi. Nothing had been said, but Gabi, pregnant, was in her unreasonable stage, believing anything bad. She knew her spouse rode with half Paris, but straddling her friends was another matter. Camille, who could never keep his mouth shut, always boasting of Lucile's beauty and of her constant stream of courtiers, had by now been awarded the idiotic untrue name of the deceived or complacent husband. Perhaps Lucile had also now and then unhelped matters. How often, as I heard her once, in reply to someone's remark that I kept two mistresses in the Palais-Égalité, had she frivolously answered, "Oh, that's nothing. I number two bankers, three poets, and a dragoon among *my* itinerary."

(And the girl with red hair, for whom he had a fondness because she was kind and vivacious, because she woke and appeased hunger. And the red leaves, falling.)

Oh, September . . .

Miserable now, wretched. It should be a time of triumph.

❊

Politics is one of the poorer schools of life. It teaches mostly the states of false camaraderie, false failure, and false victory.

❊

Danton's latest idea had been to start a periodical, edited by Camille, which would push opinion where it needed to be pushed. In the restaurant where the contrivance was discussed, it had shone bright as the lamps. Which soon enough went out. Danton lost interest. He had already proposed his resignation from the ministry. The great power had proved boring, too taxing, or finally ineffectual, beside the wilder rogue power of a deputy. You couldn't pin him down to an explanation. Slothful and beneficent, he played games with every question. You looked for the razor edge in his eyes, but they were cloudy with good living. At the Stable he hardly ever left the rostrum. Christ, hasn't it taken me long enough to get here? He spoke on everything from munitions to morals. Out and at large (appropriate description) in the cafés, he recited torrents from theatrical productions to which he had dragged you two hours before. He had a phase of singing, shattering thunder. At the Café Procope, as in former days, he chatted for hours to the proprietor in Italian. *Dantonations,* Camille baptized them, these verbal uproars which went nowhere. Though he had timidly predicted it all (*I'm getting out; I wonder, will you?*), it was no consolation to Camille to be a wise prophet, even with honor thrown in. (Yes, you were right. Desk jobs, not for me. Too much sitting. I need a pulpit. Scared? Scared of ennui. The fulcrum whereby to move the world is *here.* Gabi'll miss the palatial furnishings. I'll have the apartment done up again. Must do something to please her. The pregnancy's wearing her out this time.) Danton had put on a great deal of flesh. His face had sunk backward into its own environs. His hair, of course, was never powdered now. The eyes smoldered languidly on the women he went after, the dinners he devoured. His wit sprang like a leopard from a tree—but it was the wit of the banquet table and the brothel.

In the beginning, one followed him blindly, not needing to see, since he saw everything. Then one backed out, as gracefully as possible, stepping free of the swamp and mire of false values. But leaderless? No, not possible. The elected Tribune does not go to a party at the burning gates of Carthage. If he goes to a party, then one has somehow made some sort of mistake about the nature of flames.

Following still, the Key and the Clue. If Danton takes his ease, up to a point so must I or it's a denial; it's a denial of the leader, the following, every single thing undertaken in his name. And memory, thick with running red, comes boiling through the mind's alleys—see, see, this you did with him, and if his shadow is less, it gives more light to see *by.*

So. The restaurants, theaters, dinners, cards, chandeliers, orchestras, wine bottles, glass-eyed women with smiling thighs.

Only the odd symptom. Pain. Depression. Excessive laughter. Extravagance in peripheral things.

Turned theater critic, the Windmill crucifies half the productions, full as they are of revolutionary zeal, witless activity, even gunpowder. The description "An explosion in four acts" has brought two playwrights to the Stable demanding the expulsion of one C. Desmoulins.

"Nearly out on your ass that time." "It'll take more than that. What's next?" "Another bottle. Have you heard what the Chéniers are up to?"

The Chéniers had fallen out, brother with brother, almost to the point of pistols in the Bois. André, the poet, is running with royalists — or moderates — Joseph, the playwright, whose bedroom tastes stretch to maenads, standing firm for patriotism, the rights of the People. Robespierre persuades the two gentlemen apart. There are biblical allusions enough in the scenario without including Cain and Abel.

"And have you heard what Robespierre's up to?"

As the nights draw in and the French army harries Brunswick's retreat into Belgium, or storms into Nice and holds it, Robespierre, declaiming coldly at the Jacobins, succeeds in expelling from the club every member of the Gironde.

And Danton is officially out of the ministry.

What's next?

Another bottle. Another set of massive Dantonian clothes, a new massive Dantonian baby due in February, a high-class tart and an actress, another speech about the war. . . .

And you say Robespierre has outlawed the Gironde from the Jacobins? (Which included the moderate André Chénier. One way to stop a fight.)

Interesting. He's become very influential, our Maximilien. The namesake almost of the club. Too modest to admit it. Too high-minded. People kissing his hands in the streets. Robespierre the sans-culotte, who *is* still powdering his hair, wearing lace at his throat. But it's the thought that counts.

Brissot's gang, the Girondin Estuary, in revolt against the Jacobin Mountain, are not above starting physical fights around the Tribune. The intellectual boxing matches incorporate a recurring theme: accusations that Danton was appropriating public funds while in the ministry. (Fabre in a sweat, nearly fainting; he's done his fair share. Is he about to be dropped right in it? As for Camille, there were those dinner services and crates of wine. But the Lion-Bull roars and paws the earth and stamps, and they get away with it.)

Next . . . the Gironde goes after Maximilien. A letter had been read out, accusing a number of persons (particularly a Citizen M. B. I. Robespierre), of wishing to renew the excitements of September (you know, the ones with battered-in prison doors and pikes). The net result is that there are universal cries the Incorruptible One is about to be martyred, as he has always foretold. A bodyguard armed with bludgeons begins to trail him everywhere. He affects not to notice. "Maxime, *who* are those fellows?" Where? "*There.* The ones about ten feet away with sticks, beaming at you and glaring at everyone else." Don't be ridiculous. Workmen on their way somewhere. "They were walking behind you along Saint-Honoré Street last Tuesday, Friday, and Saturday. On Wednesday and Thursday it was three others. The same expressions, however, and similar cudgels." Robespierre is self-conscious. He admits he has asked these good men to leave him only to the protection of God. If people want to speak to him (kiss his hands, shake his feet), how can they get close? (Suffer little children to come unto—)

And next?

This upheaval, this alternative explosion in four acts, is a backdrop to another drama, a drama about to be played out to a final steel curtain falling with a rasping thud.

DAUPHIN: Papa, what did *you* do during the Revolution?

KING: Well, son, I got myself guillotined.

1792–93: Winter

IT WAS the old quarrel: his support of the monarchy. I threw him a look as full of contemptuous indignation as I could muster. But he only smiled. The smile said, Come now. Between *us?* If there's some problem, walk over and have it out with me. So I was borne after him, almost will-less, not yet decided whether to dress him down in public or fall back. But he'd seen me advancing, turned and waited for me. When I arrived, he took my hand, then my arm. We walked, somewhere. I said, "I'm surprised you're abroad. I expected, if I saw you anywhere, to find you hanging from a lamp-iron. How large a bribe did you get off the king this time? I hope it was worth all the trouble you took for him."

"Ah," Mirabeau said, in that voice of his that was like no other voice, unforgettable – the voice which, singing, had seduced women from the battlements of his prison. "You know that if I wanted to, I could make you an explanation which would convince you, totally."

"The only explanations I get from you come in the form of charming dinners."

"I could suborn you, Camille. Don't pretend I couldn't because I never did."

We had arrived on a high tower. A river passed below in a great shining sweep. It was sunset. The stones were gilded by it, and on the stones lay peaches in a brown dish, clear as anything seen awake. There was dust in the air, the smell of leather and horses, and somewhere behind me, no need to turn and see it, the blinding flash of the legion's eagle on its painted wreathed pole. And he said to me, in Latin, but the oddest Latin I ever heard, "Are you betting on the race?"

What race? And betting, or running . . . ?

Up there, a man was running already, along the sky which had become the slope of a mountain. But the maenads, too, ran fast up the mountain, crying in those high piercing voices such writers as Euripides describe. Like birds falling on a carcass – but the man still lives. At a distance, I could watch them settle, bees to a screaming tree:

Then from his high perch, dragged down,
The king falls, with one unbroken scream—
His pitiable head,
Fastened on a thyrsus point,
Carried over pastures
Among the maenads dancing.

My father was looking at me from his black ledger, his ever-unfinished treatise. "Don't do it, don't vote for his death. All you have to say is that you are a staunch Republican; your every activity proves it. When the king was still fêted, Camille Desmoulins denounced him as a tyrant. For that very reason, Camille Desmoulins now withholds his vote."

"My God, how can I get you to understand anything? *For that very reason.* For that very reason, Father, if *I* don't face up to the vote, and give it, how many others can use that as an excuse? There goes that Windmill, hiding under a table. No, we won't vote on it either."

"And you insist, then, you must vote for his execution?"

"Yes. In God's name, *yes.* Yes!"

"Your writing indicates you have some special grudge. You speak and write of him as if he were a personal enemy."

"He is. To every free man. You should have heard Saint-Just. Cold as frozen milk. His first speech at the Convention. This man, he said, can be neither imprisoned nor exiled. He is the enemy of the People. For that crime there is only one penalty."

"Do you know what you're saying?"

"I know what's been said. I know what's been done. So let's clear the board and start the game afresh."

"Not chesspieces; men. Flesh and blood."

The maenads shrieked on the upland above Guise, where the old battlemented tower stood. I'd played around it as a child; I was a child now, to my father. I refused to shrink and grow ten years of age for him again.

"Don't talk to me," I said. "Anything you advise at this stage I would reject. If you'd wanted me to let the bastard off, you should have told me to parcel him in slices."

"What you say," he said. "What you write down—can be used against you."

"So far, not very successfully."

My mother was standing in the frail sunlight. Her brown hair was graying. She held out her tired hand to me. I went to greet her. I dreaded these visits to her sickness, cursing the necessity of duty, putting it off, weeping when I left her.

But she was gone. A woman stood laughing at me, blood clotted in her hair, between her *teeth.* She rattled the head of Louis Capet at me, and the red spillage of it dewed my face—

"No, no," someone said. "Now, *no.* These dreams of yours. What are we going to do with you?"

"Lucile," I said.

But it wasn't Lucile who bent over me. The soft lamp haloed her hair like blood, but the red was merely its own fiery color.

"Christ." I put my arm up over my face.

"Ah, there," she said. "You're back now. Just in time, too. You gave the bed a worse shaking than the other thing."

"Was I talking?"

"Yes."

"What? For Christ's sake, what?"

"I know better than to listen."

"I didn't mean to fall asleep."

"But you're so tired. Poor tired boy."

"Yes. Tired."

I'd dreamed of Mirabeau too. The latest scandal would have triggered that. An iron safe had been found concealed in the wall of the Tuileries. It contained correspondence between the king and certain others, one being Mirabeau. Now all France knew he had betrayed her. He had been working for the Capets. They threw down the bust that all this time had presided over the Assembly, the plaster Mirabeau. Plaster that shattered in a hundred shards. They made plans to haul his body from the Panthéon, to cast the bones into some unmarked hole, a dog's grave. It would have been a second death to him. Perhaps he was aware of it, perhaps he raged and lamented in Elysium or hell or some limbo for lost souls who believe in nothing. Or did he only mock at our misunderstanding? "I was no traitor. I tried to hold the balance. To save the king from all of you, that I might then save all of you from yourselves."

"*Sur la chatte, sur la chatte,*" softly sang the girl. "Oh, let me see your beautiful eyes. Why are you hiding from me? Are you thinking of someone else, making me jealous—cruel nasty unkind—"

I took my arm from my face and looked at her, lying there beside me now, rimmed by lamp gold, her young skin, in its playful daisy field of opened lace, her rust-red hair with the smell of smoky grass. I wanted to go at once, but I only lay there on my back, looking up at the painting, crude in all senses, that elaborated the ceiling.

I wanted to be at home, but the dream was becoming confused and leaving me. Any sudden return to reality seemed likely to bring it back.

The girl lay watching me. She put one pretty plump little hand on my chest and walked it up and down. Her fingers felt like feathers, and then like hard cool pearls, and every touching "step" began to send a silken line down under my skin.

She sang her quaint little song as she did it:

"Sur la chatte, le chat,
Et sur la reine, le roi,
Et aussi toi sur moi."

"Why are you always singing about kings? Are you a damn royalist?"

"Oh, of course I am. And cats, I like cats, ever so much. And the other thing, I like that. You know how I like that. Put your hand here. Aah, that's better, isn't it? Oh, that's so lovely. Lovely Camille – oh –"

The dream went farther and farther off, the nearer I reached to the core of her. My body was heavy and my muscles ached but the point of flame forced me on and on, until it met itself inside her, twisting and soaring, senseless agonized pleasure, over in so few seconds. But by then the dream was gone.

❈

But I digress. This didn't happen until 1793, until the river began looking like blood, or perhaps a short while before that – the dream. To excuse myself with the dream *beforehand* is also too easy. It was after, months after. Or not at all. Maybe I never dreamed it, only some trivial nightmare in that bed of the Palais-Égalité.

Damn Louis. Damn the centuries of feudal France. Why seek to excuse myself for that murder in the midst of so many?

The fat simpleton, the turnip dunce. The enemy. Kill him. Get rid of him. I vote for death.

❈

And Danton? Danton was going to inspect Belgium.

"The army's in a mess. I told you before, don't believe everything you write. Yes. Belgium's a triumph, as far as it's gone. But there's no organization. The contractors are only supplying enough to keep the fleas bright. Supplying the fleas too, I gather. And the desertions –"

"The king will be brought to trial any day now."

"Hmm."

"You want to avoid it."

"That's right."

"Too boring for you."

"It's tricky. There's an old saying in the Aube region. When you think the roof's going to fall in, leave the house. I've had twenty letters promising to kill me if I try to put Louis to death. And a couple of hundred promising to kill me –"

"If you don't. We'd better compare letters sometime."

"You get threats too? The Gironde agents, the rampant royalists. And some
offers of money either way. The best thing is to find something patriotic and
useful to do somewhere else. Want to come too?"

"No."

"I could swing it."

"No."

"Then don't sulk. Stay and paddle in the blood. I said, don't sulk. I had
Gabi on at me all night. Crying and sobbing. The baby will come and you'll be
in Belgium! She's surrounded by friends, family, servants: even the blonde
thirteen-year-old nymph from upstairs wafts round her all day. (The father
sends her down. Suck up to the Dantons, he got me a job.) God above. It isn't
due till February. I'll be here by then. Does she want me to hang about now and
be assassinated?"

But in the end, he came back from the mud of Belgium to bawl out the
Convention on absenteeism and dithering. He stayed to vote, with the rest of us.
And, like the rest of us, for death.

❆

The Convention had stated that the king could not be tried. His offense sprang
from his very existence, his hereditary entitlement to, and assumption of, the role
of tyrant. On the other hand, he must *have* a trial. One could not appeal for a
verdict from the People. One had seen the People's justice was somewhat
headlong (and, worse, the People's opinions conflicted). Besides, the National
Convention represented the People. Why else had deputies been elected?

The Convention next declared that the non-trial would be conducted, not in
the Hôtel de Ville, before the Justiciary, but at the Stable. Court and judge—
both would be formed by the Convention itself. And the vote must be absolute.

In accordance with this wonder, a dock was built below the draperied
benches, for the accused to stand in.

The accused.

Confined in the Temple, alternately baked or iced as summer fell to winter,
the fat pious king had carried on the rags of living as best he could. Eating,
always eating (there had already been terrible complaints about his food bills,
his hoarding of coffee and flour and sweet things). Sleeping, rocking the Temple
towers with great snores. Tutoring his young son diligently. Reading a dozen
books in a week. Praying: I will lift up mine eyes unto . . . the lamppost?

Every day, a constitutional. The Family Capet would step cautiously into
the walled garden.

Four or five jailers accompanied them, and a captain of the National Guard,
or somebody passing for a captain.

But there was surely no point to caution. No sooner were they out on the
lawn than soldiers, artisans who worked in the building, any sightseers who had

bribed their way in, pressed closely around. Some only wanted to touch. (I got her, I did. On the boob. You don't believe me? Well, you'd like the chance. What did she do? Just pretended nothing had happened.) Some, however, wished to pass on to the Capet family items of news, or the current hit songs. Everything was obscene, of execution or dirt. Through a stinking breathing fog of it, they pressed their quiet way.

Over the walls, from surrounding houses, faces looked down, pale feature-less shapes, ever changing, ever the same. (Five sous to watch the Capet family take the air. And you get a glass of lemonade free!)

Inside the walls, the brickwork was papered by sketches and scrawled with *tricoleur* slogans. A gallows: Madame Veto's Dance. A pig with a crown and a crowned she-wolf with long dugs. And there, an upright skeletal drawing of the city's new machine. Some called it the Juilletine, for glorious July fourteenth. In turn, others seemed to have corrupted the name to Guillotine, after the fidgety little doctor deputy who had recommended its use. It was very humane. Very quick. One kiss and then good night! (That was written on the wall too.)

"Did you know, Citizen Capet, at the front they're running out of ammuni-tion? It's a fact. But the gunners said, Never mind, they'd soon have a nice big head with a little crown on it to use as a cannonball."

Indoors again, at dinner, every single roll of bread had always been torn into bits, in case some weapon or message were ever smuggled inside in them. The fish lay mashed. The macaroni dish—was no longer macaroni. Cut oranges stained the table linen.

"The oranges are bleeding, Papa!"

"Oranges don't bleed, little boy," said one of the guards to the Dauphin. "It's people do that."

The sightseers had even once witnessed Austrianette sweeping the floor. She wasn't so pretty now. Now she'd had a taste of the hardship that had always been the People's lot, she had lost her looks. Thin and wan, her hair graying without powder, she wielded the broom, sweeping away bread crumbs from torn rolls, the husks of leaves.

When the Republic was declared, monarchy abolished, and Year One dawned upon the earth of France, Louis Capet was separated from his family. Soldiers trundled him into the Temple's largest tower. Here he was to be strictly guarded. It was, at last, a proper prison.

I will lift up mine eyes.

He was a fool, but not so much of a fool as all that. He knew. There had been, too, a rather clever drawing on the wall in October. It showed the wall itself, with a single door in it, apparently standing open. When you looked carefully (he had been encouraged to do so) you saw the door was actually Dr. Guillotin's recommended instrument, marked (in red letters, which ran) EXIT. On the eleventh of December, the current mayor of Paris arrived with a couple of Jacobin Mountaineers. Louis was wanted over at the Convention, for trial.

It was raining. The carriage drove quite fast through the beating water (why, at these crisis moments, does it always *rain? Il pleut, il−*), but fists also struck the windows, and thrown clods. "Let's see his blood!" they screamed. Louis, formerly King Yes-Yes of France, stared ahead of him, not looking at the excited wet faces.

As they went up the path to the Stable, some attempt was made to shelter Louis from the rain.

They said he entered, and stood in his cage, at the prisoner's bar, and acted like a blushing, bumbling moron.

They said he entered, and stood in his cage, at the prisoner's bar, and acted with enormous dignity and self-control.

It depends, of course, on who recounts the story: pro-royalist, Revolutionary.

To leave him alive, Maximilien Robespierre had said (fresh from a sickbed, blazing with the sheen of his god upon him), is to renounce and disown every deed of our Revolution. If he is not to die, then he is blameless, and all else that has been done is the crime. We must go to him and beg his pardon, lying on the ground. I, who abhor the death sentence and have fought against it for so long, in this instance demand its use.

What did Louis demand? He had a right, he said, to legal counsel. It was not refused. They read the indictment out to him, the list of his felonies, his tyrannies, and he listened with a vague, almost bewildered look, then mastered it and seemed only to attend to some recital of music that required his politeness (its composers were present) but which failed to interest him.

It would be hard for him to equate all these things with himself.

The trial, once begun, drags on. December wanes and fades to an uncelebrated Christmas. They have him brought before them and they bombard him. Then he is sent away and they discuss, shrieking and bellowing, what has been said.

The legal aid annoys them. A man who has served the king before, now bravely and boastfully coming to his help, refers to Capet as "Your Majesty" and "Sire." "Who is this person, Citizen Sire?" demands someone from the Mountain, producing howls of laughter.

"I shall never convince them to spare my life," Louis says to the three advocates of his defense who visit him in prison. "And to throw myself on their pity is not my intention."

I pray with all my heart that Merciful God will bend His gaze upon my wife, my little ones, my dear sister. They have shared, so great a while, my misery. When I am taken, I pray that He, from Whom alone I hope for justice, will support them for as long as they may live. (Although I am much afraid for my wife's safety, that she may be implicated in these fabricated plots and, pulled down by my fall, fall after me.) To the guardianship of my wife, so uplifted and made fine by all that we have suffered, I give our son and daughter. Should they ever attain to any height of the world, I entreat her to assure them that all worldly glory is a transient, deceptive thing.

December. January. Gray days, cold nights of rain, and misty mornings.

Louis's youngest counsel spoke fiercely now before the Convention. He ignored the murmurings and growlings from the benches. When he was done, Louis himself lifted his bulbous head and spoke.

"I think this is the last thing I shall say to you. But I have done my best. I have answered every question. I have never lied."

"Yes, you *lied!*" someone yells.

Louis pays no heed. He says, "My conscience is clear. I have never shunned the passage of light upon my actions. I deny, in particular, any statement which sets on me the desire to shed the blood of my subjects."

"Subjects! What subjects? For Christ's sake, does he think he's still a king?"

"Be quiet, Camille."

"The accusation alone, that I may have wished to shed their blood, causes me pain."

"Camille, stop writhing about, for God's sake. If you punch me on the arm again I'll knock your teeth out."

"They let him say that—they let him say he never wanted any blood to be spilled." Struggling to stand up, to shout, but pulled down. "Whn-nr-whrr—"

"Camille, shut up."

"Wh-hn—wh-what about Mars Field? Wha-at about that? Wurra-nesh never shed any blood—what about de Launay? What bt-about the guard riding with bn-bar-bayonets on thra-the Third Estate at Ver-Versailles?"

The disturbance on the top tiers was limited. The voice trying to shout, impeded by its own unstrength and the fits of stammering, made a very minor stir. Protocol denies that there be an altercation at this point. The Convention wants dignity. A dignified doomed king, a dignified, implacably honest judgment. No squeals for naked truth from the upper benches. (Shut *up,* Camille.) Probably not even recorded, this outburst. Only the words of Louis, to stand for history in their own curious glare. I never wanted to spill your blood. The very idea hurts me.

"Damn him. I don't believe this. Does anyone accept one word of what he says?"

Oh, yes, Camille. Many people will accept it. First and foremost, Louis himself.

In the midst of January, that dark month, in the winter season which so mimics the last black hours before sunrise, the voting, then, began.

The Gironde had made noises. "We are not royalists!" Manon Roland's latest courtly lover had shouted in fury. "But this goes over the edge into the abyss." "Rubbish," said Danton, interval-ing from Belgium. "We have all monarchic Europe at our throats—the Gironde's favorite war, I believe, or didn't I hear those gentlemen baying for it last year like a pack of dogs after a bone?

Well, now, what better battle gage can we throw down before them than the head of a king?"

But in the aftermath of the uproar, even the Gironde fell back. Barbaroux had risen and said, "I, for one, will vote for death." And Vergniaud, who had sworn to abstain, was due to walk white-faced into the Convention and break his oath with the words *la mort.*

Dark month. Dark days. And that large hall of the Stable dimly lit, as if for a meeting of murderers. What else?

And like the untrial trial, the voting goes on and on.

One by one, they came to the tribune, mounted it, gave their vote, said whatever else they felt was needful. It began to have a hideous kind of music, a song with differing verses. but its refrain always the same: I this, I that, we must, we shall, *la mort, la mort, la mort.*

Why was it so dark? The way that great room would look before the eyes blackened in a faint, swimming and shadowy, with disconcerting specks of light, restless, almost nauseating, on candles, spectacles, shoe buckles, rings.

Up on the public gallery things were cheerier. A horde of people had come crowding in, sitting, watching eagerly, applauding uncommon favorites, cheering specifically violent speeches, and—if the expected refrain of the song (*la mort, la mort*) failed to come—booing and catcalling as if at an actor who had forgotten his lines. Between while they ate fruit, ices, drank, and played cards. If one went out, ten others rushed forward to get his place.

On and on. On the gallery, and out in the cafés of the city, they were laying bets as to which way the vote would go. Those who gambled on a reprieve were taking a big chance with their money, and they knew it. But it was also possible to vote on particular deputies. Someone had made some cash on Vergniaud's retraction, pure luck. Danton, Robespierre—they were not worth a sou. Everyone knew they wanted blood and wouldn't change their minds.

On and on. On the benches, starving deputies tried, like vultures, to figure out if they had time to snatch a meal before they were interrupted. Others, in the late hours, sagged asleep and had to be kicked awake to go and sing their song. Some had been waiting for days. The sessions started early, went on till midnight; presently went on all night long. Voting. Votes piling up.

Walking through the hellish dismal light. Mounting the tribune. Their eyes glittering, and their teeth, when they open their lips.

One hundred and thirty: Robespierre—Death. (Loud cheers.)

One hundred and thirty-one: Danton—Death. (Louder, wilder cheers.)

One hundred and thirty-two: Collot d'Herbois—Death. (Much approval.)

Not due to be counted, for: Manuel—Detention in—(Drowned by a raucous squall. Someone throws an orange. Manuel finishes for the recorder's benefit, pale and trembling, and walks quickly away.)

One hundred and thirty-three: Billaud-Varenne—Death inside twenty-four hours. (The crowd throws a fit of joy; the painted well-dressed women on the lower seats, the ones who look like aristos; they seem the most delighted of all. But shush, now. Look who's next.)

One hundred and thirty-four: Camille Desmoulins. (As pale as Manuel, and quivering like him, but with a sort of feverish anger, he stares around, draws in a breath, and pitches his voice to carry. The voice shakes, but there's a malicious power in it. His eyes blaze like a fanatic's. Only *like?*) "Manuel forgets himself. He already said, two months ago, in print: A dead king is not one man the less." (The gallery resounds. Camille waits for quiet, gets it—he's had a couple of years now, to study Danton's tricks—his voice is faltering, but still pitched, thin as a wire.) "So, not one man the less. Perhaps too late for the honor of this Convention, I vote for death."

And they scream for him; he grimly grins at them, like a wolf, and turns and marches, with his warrior's stride, off the tribune and back across the hall, the pressure of his blood almost bursting his skull, his trembling hands clenched at his sides. (Still doing what the crowd wants. Still a darling of the mob.) (The recorder has made a blot above the reproduction of Camille's *la mort*. He clicks his tongue and wipes the pen.)

And on.

And the count reaches one hundred and fifty: L.-P. Égalité (formerly Orléans, cousin to the king.) He takes a stand, his eyes flash frantically, and the gallery whispers. *Death!* shouts Égalité, and his scented ladies in gowns of red rise to drink his health on the gallery in their cherry liqueurs. Well, cousins are not always faithful.

And on, until—

It's done.

In a rushing torrent of false camaraderie, false victory, they have sung their song to its ringing conclusion. Despite dissenters, sleepers, rumbling bellies, arguments. Despite the sick light. Despite the skewered-moth fluttering of the Gironde Estuary, trying to get a delay in the sentence. Despite threats of retaliation, and a couple of murders of convention members who voted in a way displeasing to the murderers. Despite. Almost four hundred deputies have voted for *la mort*. Enough to do the job. To send one overweight, silly, mortal man to the scaffold.

Louis, called Capet, though, as he had mentioned, Capet hadn't been the family name for centuries, was up early, noting down in a book his son's progress at his lessons, when he was told—by the speechless collapse of his oldest advocate—that he was due to die the next day.

"Don't be grieved," said the king. "This is my release you bring me."

"Oh, sire. There is God's curse on this Revolution."

"What," asked the king, quietly, stubbornly, "is a revolution?"

❊

Monday, January 21, 1793. The day is somber under its umber sky. Wet river mist clings to the city. The frost has made patterns on the windows.

There is a great new terror of conspiracy. Plots were apparently laid to rescue the king against this advent. There is even a rumor Swedish Fersen of the Varennes carriage is in Paris with a band of armed desperadoes. They will ambush the conveyance taking Louis to the scaffold. But the guard is thick around the vehicle, and the number of armed men who line the route is estimated at eighty thousand. The crowds who shrilled for blood are softer, now, and more sparse. Every shop is shut.

The loudest noise, above the tramp and clop and clatter of the escorted conveyance, is the voice of Louis himself, reading psalms.

She has been moved, the goddess Juilletine-Guillotine. She stands now in Louis XV Square, which has become Revolution Square, casting down the old gods who occupied the place before her, the statues of kings. Some of the jewel thieves who robbed the Archives were kissed by her, and this had been thought an ideal spot for the embrace, the very scene of the robbery, the square against which the Archives stand. There are other advantages. The Tuileries Garden runs toward it from the east; south, one reaches the open river. Northwestward spreads the woodland of Heaven's Fields, and southwest those huddled slums and tenements jokingly retitled the Cours République. The two gray-yellow facades, of the Archives and the Hôtel Crillon, check the northeast surge of the city at the end of Nation's Road (once the rue Royale). A wide vista here; it gives space to be filled by spectators, who have duly filled it. Also, the relatively open spot recommends itself for the letting loose of high spirits.

Although there is little evidence of any of those at the moment.

Unrescued, mouth full of psalms, the king alighted from his carriage. He lifted his head. He saw, across a little distance, the tall gateway, black on the miasmic sky. The mist was drifting, lifting reluctantly. The trees of the Tuileries hung like wet colorless plumes; the Champs-Élysées was lost in the haze.

He was placid and resolute until they tried to bind his hands. Then he fought them. The crowd rustled expectantly. Was Old Fatty going to lose his nerve? But the accompanying priest said something that appeared to calm him. (A wretch of a Roman priest, at that.)

Finally, he did allow his hands to be tied. He had already stripped himself of his collar. They cut his hair. He went up among the executioners.

Sanson, the master executioner, stood waiting, and beside him a young assistant, who held a scarlet flower, a rose, by its stem between his teeth. At this odd sight, the king's leaden uninterest lapses.

"Against the stench," one of the men tells Louis, reading his look. "He doesn't like the odor of blood and the rest of it. Don't worry, Citizen Capet, you'll stink just like all the others." But Louis has already averted his eyes. He moves forward on the platform and sees the crowd in the mist between the dripping trees, the shadowy scattered buildings, the low sky. Drums are thudding, but Louis shouts for silence and, as if amazed, the drummers' hands are stilled.

"I die in perfect innocence of the crimes I am accused of," Louis calls—to whom? Who listens or believes or cares? Does one heart beat for him, out there, in that theater full of puppets and mist? "I beg God that the blood you are shedding will not bring anathema on France—"

"Bloody hell on earth." Santerre, lord of the guard, steps forward and gives an order: "Shut the bastard up!"

The drums burst back to life and drown the voice on the platform. Suddenly the crowd begins shouting for the sentence to be carried out.

The executioners take hold of Louis. Bound and shorn and helpless, having been prevented from speaking, he is pushed forward on the plank. The big head appears on the underpiece of the round window, which now closes upon him, the loving clasp of Louisette, Louis's little girl.

The blade comes down abruptly. The sound is horribly mundane, as if someone had chopped a large cabbage in half. But a ghastly cry is shot out in the midst of it, and the crowd makes a weird pleased frightened squeaking.

"Jesus! Get it right, you infernal butcher." Appalled despite himself, Santerre grits his teeth. But Sanson only orders the blade up again, and again it falls, and the croupy groaning finishes. This time, the too-thick neck of the victim has been severed.

Very humane. We'll have to watch that, with the fat ones.

At a nod from Sanson, the young man with the rose in his teeth steps forward. (It's winter; the rose is silk at this time of the year, drenched in perfume from a shop at the Palais. The young man might be Sanson's son. Even executioners may become fathers.) The youth picks up the fruit of the guillotine. He holds it by the hair and raises it high for the crowd to see. The eyes are wide, and the mouth remains fixed in its first astonished protest.

The crowd stays very silent, now. Then somebody shouts. And another. *Life to the Nation!* And then the whole morning is shouting it.

They have killed their king. They've done the inconceivable. Dance, then. Dance, and run forward to dip handkerchiefs and clothing in the gouts of blood: souvenirs. One man leans down and licks the blood spilled on the steps under the scaffold. "It's disgustingly salty," he says, and laughs. "Salty, like the sea."

⚜

The body was buried, having the usual ceremonies, in the churchyard of the Madeleine. With the devotional chants were mingled the noises of carouse and festivity. Most of the houses along the route, or near it, kept their shutters and their gates closed.

The Duplays' house in Saint-Honoré Street was one of these.

The girl, Betsi, knocking timidly on the door of Robespierre's room, stole in when he quietly told her to. "Mama says, shall she bring you anything?"

"No, child. Thank you."

"You don't look well," says Betsi soulfully. The whole room seems thick with sadness, its white walls gray, bed-curtains in mourning, the vase empty of flowers—for even Saint-Just (like other executioners' assistants) can't find roses in the dead of winter.

"Something terrible happened today," says Robespierre. "Something it was better not to see. In order to save ourselves, a limb was amputated. A useless, poisoned limb. But it was a terrible thing, for all that."

His dog lies grievously at his feet, its eyes empathically tear-wet, in the way of the eyes of dogs.

Robespierre's tragedy is grave but quite real.

There is a man to be careful of, Mirabeau had once commented. He believes every word he says.

❦

At the news of Louis's death, the English close their theaters. When the English close their theaters, they're getting ready to open the gates of war.

❦

Gray January. Sallow February. Black March. The dark hours before the April dawn of spring—for those who get through the night.

❦

"Well, there was this dear little dog on the stairs wagging its tail, so naturally I scratched it kindly behind the ears—and got my fingernails full of dried glue—wax and clockwork."

"There's a sequel to that. When Marat was hiding here—oh, go on, Curtius, you know he *lived* in your cellar at one time—one evening the Rat surfaced, drawn up by a scent of cooking, and stalked into the drawing room. And there is this same waxwork dog plonked in the best armchair. So Marat seizes hold of it to chuck it on the floor, and—"

Three or four voices, my own included, said in weary chorus, "It bit him."

"Not the waxwork, then?"

"Absolutely not."

Lucile was laughing, beautifully.

"Naturally the dog died," went on Fréron. "Poor little devil. One nip at Marat. It'd kill any of us."

"Rat poison," I added.

That set everyone off again. The company was diverse but excluded Marat. Maximilien, who had been invited, had not arrived. A pity, since anyone not present tended to be the butt of our hilarity. The jokes were hare-brained but fairly clean; we had a roomful of women with us, including Marie-glacée. (I'd looked askance at her on my last visit, which had come after the episodes of August. But she'd given no sign of anything, except she didn't like me much, which I had always known, and because of which my pillow had never been wet with tears.) Danton was spending February back in Brussels. We had even had a moderate go at him tonight, in an amiable way. Most of the men round Curtius' table this evening were part of what the city loosely termed Danton's Gang. Fréron was still in the capital and had got himself onto the guest list through my own auspices. The ill feeling between us was under the mat. He had come up to me, calling, and flung his arms around me, in the middle of that infernal vote. My nerves standing on end, I'd been glad enough to see him. For some reason we sat talking about school, pausing only to jibe at or concur with other voters who took our fancy. No worse than the bloody gallery, where they were already playing *paille-maille* with the head. Since then, we'd had him to dinner with us, and he had behaved impeccably. Gossip about Lucile had at one time got so bad (if they couldn't hit us directly, they would always start on our wives), I had been up the wall and around the ceiling over it. Louis-Mer had decided on tact. His eyes yearned now and then, but the rest of it was not inflicted on us. He had a new mistress he was being mysterious about. She'd taken off his edge, it would seem.

      The dinner was all Curtius' dinners ever were—several lush foretastes of paradise. He, the cunning fox, laughed and smiled and chivied us on from course to course, jest to jest, indiscretion to indiscretion.

      "He's been passing some story around that Maxime is bribable," had said Fréron in my ear.

      "So that's why the Slave of Liberty isn't here. I thought he was sick again."

      "In a paddy, more likely. Mercure had better watch out."

      "What, for Maxime?"

      "Yes, for Maxime. Don't you see the way he's going? All right, smile if you like. Maxime is this: If you slight him, he bears a grudge. If he slights *you*—then he'll never forgive you."

      "Listen, it's too far into the wine for me to work that out."

      "I'm saying anything that makes him uncomfortable has to be blamed on someone else. Every mistake he makes, since he's infallible, is therefore someone else's mistake."

      "Oh, he's all right with me."

      "He thinks you're an innocent, that's why."

      "Well, if he thinks *that*—"

      "But show him you know what you're doing, and *then* do something he doesn't like. Damn it, Camille. Look at the Gironde. Out of the Jacobins."

      "Splendid."

"Yes, but how did he do it?"

"Pressure of opinion was behind him."

"No, little Windmill. He was behind *it.*"

"Bloody rubbish."

"Fine. And don't tell him I said any of this. I don't want to be on his blacklist, or that earringed thief's he keeps as a henchman. You know Saint-Just's new nickname?"

"I've heard a few."

"You've coined a few. This one is the Angel of Death. That speech he made against Capet in that flat cold bloodless voice. And his arm going up and down, like the blade itself."

Something touched my mind. It had to do with gray January, vomitous bad lighting, a slice of steel that hadn't, they said, worked as it should.

"Camille?" said the lovely vision beside me, looking into my face, questioning and sweet, against a background of candied apricots and wax apples.

"My God, who's this beautiful girl they've sat me by? If I ask her, will she run off with me?"

"She might," said Lucile sternly. "But I hear you have a wife and child, monsieur."

"That's true. And strangely enough, I heard my wife at least was dining somewhere in the vicinity."

"I discard my mask. Your wife is revealed, oh, traitor."

"Heaven help me. Discovered!"

"Heaven help you indeed. And my poor mother looking after the baby at home, thinking we're out behaving like two adults."

I offered her a wax apple. Lucile threw it over my head to Fréron, who tossed it across the table to Marie. She, with a surprised cry, caught it. At a loss, she was persuaded into throwing the apple on, but only to Curtius, to accompanying shouts of cowardice.

Mirabeau would have liked all that, I thought. Genteel wildness in women, their raised arms, and breasts dancing in the candlelight. Where was he; did he see, or look to see? I drank off my glass before he came between me and the present. I had first met him at this table. It was a world away. I had had nothing, then, but wings of light from green July and the roar of the Bastille's surrender. Now all Paris knew me. And he — they would cast him into an unmarked grave, that god of the Third Estate.

After dessert, the women went away and the black brandies appeared.

Curtius came over, urbane as always. We had a little talk about the National Guard, in which he remained a captain. (His men were generally termed the Wax Cohort.) Presently, by circuitous routes, he was asking me if I had heard a story of something he was supposed to have said about Maxime.

"Oh, Maxime's used to slander. We all are."

"But I, you understand, Camille, am not the slanderer."

"I didn't say you were. He won't think so."

"I hope not. I have great respect for Robespierre. I trust he knows that." (And you want me to remind him. What is all this fuss about Maxime?) "There are those who like to set friends at each other's throats."

"For example," said Fréron, appearing out of the brandy murk, "Roch-Marcandier."

Curtius raised his brows. "But I heard he was a protégé of Camille's."

"You heard wrong. He's a pest. He should be exterminated." I was uncomfortable, as mention of Marcandier tended to make me currently. Some more handwritten bills of his had been circulating. He had choice things to say of the September business which had caused me to fling the items on my fire (an act I had heard my own journals frequently brought forth in others) and nearly set light to the chimney. "Meanwhile," I said, "talking of bad company. If Curtius wishes Robespierre to love him, he shouldn't invite Brissot to dinner."

"It would be difficult not to. Wherever one's commitment lies, the other factions—in my business, I try to cold-shoulder nobody. It wouldn't do."

"Don't," I said, "let your niece send messages to the Temple."

"I wouldn't dream of it. Nor would Maria, I assure you." He rarely used the real version of her name, the Germanic one. It seemed deliberate now. As if he said, We are after all aliens. We're too sharp to do *anything* stupid. Bear that in mind. Chilled cleverness, all of them, however warm the greeting. Ready to ally with any party that was on the staircase top: Capets, Gironde, Mountain.

"But you have a new exhibit," said Fréron.

"Ah, yes." Curtius lowered his eyes.

"Be careful," said Fréron. "*That* could cause trouble too."

I said stupidly, "What the hell is it? The king's head?"

"Precisely," said Fréron.

"What?"

"Gentlemen," said Mercury Curtius, "people pay to stare at such items. Though my heart belongs to Liberty and the cause of the Revolution, how else am I to afford my cook? It's business." He looked at us carefully to see if we would accept this line of reasoning. Then he offered to let us see the unfinished cast of the head. We went off with him, Fréron and I, into that other part of the house. So we found, in the light of a curdled lamp, the unfinished wax Louis lying eyeless on a table.

"Christ. How did you get it?"

"My niece took the impression."

"You sent Marie—"

"You know how it is: in times of excitement, women are frequently safer. Just before the funeral, a small side chapel. . . . And she carried a bribe, I'm afraid. The bribe, I fear, is where this other untrue story began. While the poor and base can be bought, we all know better than to tempt fleshly appetites in the Incorruptible."

I laughed and turned away from the wax head. I'd never been so near the original. And cool little prudish Marie, scared out of her wits under the lilac tree in August, her cold January hands patting the plaster over this clammy flesh. A wave of dull nausea swept through me. I fought it off, turned back, and picked up the valuable head and shook it at them. (Eyeless, unbleeding.) Curtius composed his face. He didn't like his precious toys manhandled, but he wasn't going to say anything about it to me. I was one of the Leaders of the Revolution, not to be got on the wrong side of at any cost.

No, I wasn't about to let a tyrant's severed head intimidate me. For that very reason I improvised a black farce on the spot. Fréron abetted me instantly. We had Louis's head speaking to Curtius, telling him off for his discourtesies. ("Where are my eyes? Don't you know royalty is unused to being kept waiting?" "But, *sire,*" said Fréron, his own eyes glittering, "we didn't. We had your head off just as soon as we could." "What's this nonsense?" I said for Louis. "My head is firmly attached to my body. Now where's my handkerchief? Now where's my coat? Now where's my *hand?*") The jokes got broader. Where is my—my God, Antoinette, I've some bad news. Curtius reacted with polite mirth throughout. It was in poor taste, and only Fréron and I received any benefit. Finally I returned the head to the table. Curtius cast a quick glance over it, but it was unharmed. Laughing like madmen, each for our own unalike reasons, we went back to the main party. I was tired to death.

※

Lucile and I went home in the hired carriage. I held her in my arms and was at peace again.

"Where would I be without you?"

"Still upstairs with Curtius?"

I told her about the latest waxwork. Despite my personal antics, I said, "Magicians, or ghouls, the tribe of Curtius. Every famous death will see one of them popping up with carpetbag and plaster."

"The queen," said Lucile, strangely. "I wonder if she loved him."

"Louis? Which queen? There *is* no queen. No. She's a strumpet and a bitch, and he was a dolt, ugly *and* stupid. One can't be both and be loved. Or, yes one can. Look how you love me."

"You are clever, and I always tell you, to me you are handsome. But if she did love him, she must want very much to die. She's a wicked woman, heartless—but still I pity her. I think how I love you; how must it be for her? So much hatred, and alone. If I lost you, I couldn't bear it, even if I had all the world to love me in your place. I wouldn't want their love. Only yours. I wouldn't want to live here without you."

"Ssh. Where's this going? Sad solemn talk of death. Don't love me so much if it hurts you in this way. Little Lucile. Silly beautiful Loulou. You're with me."

"What, when I caught you in the very act of running off with that hussy at dinner?"

"True. She was lovely, though."

"Now are you about to confess there's someone else who has your heart?"

"You've got that. It isn't even in my body anymore. Doesn't it ever confuse you, Lucile, the sound of my heart beating inside your own?"

"Ah, but that's the way it was when I carried your son. *His* heart and mine."

The carriage jolted and threw us together, a gift from heaven. There were nights we had learned to play the old pagan games of love. Never enough, but better than no love at all. She found me sufficiently ready for that, even in the carriage. It had a marvelous sinfulness to bring her pleasure in this way, jolting over the hacking roads. We emerged, flushed and stupefied, at our destination. She said to me on the stairs, "Marius should be home with Gabi." "Write and reprimand him." "She's very ill. The little Gély girl told me." Lucile fell silent. The gossip had turned Gabi against both of us. Her eyes had said it all. At our door, my wife slipped her arms around my neck in the old way. "Don't ever leave me. Don't go off to Belgium, or Guise. Don't you dare."

"Damn Belgium and double-damn Guise. There's only Lucile."

In the apartment were warm light, scents of lavender and wood, utter order and serenity. The child asleep in his cradle, pretending to be a cherub. Demeter saying to Lucile, "Whoever are those enamored lovers I heard at your door, just before you came in?"

※

We were hardly out of bed the next morning when, opening the outer door to entreaties, I found the Gély girl on our threshold. Danton's "blonde nymph" was about sixteen or so, though one gathered the family tended to pass her off as anything up to two years younger—to enhance her forwardness, presumably. It was true Danton had got Gély a job at the ministry. The daughter had no special beauty, but some quality one became aware of, like a sharp fragrance among flowerless reeds. Her fair hair was usually little-girlish and pretty, but now tousled. Her eyes were all dilated stare. She practically fell into my arms.

We put her on a sofa and asked her what was wrong. She kept whispering to herself, *Poor Danton, poor Danton,* with no prefix, not even "citizen" appended to the name. I felt I was meant to hear her distress. She had leaned rather heavily on me, not out of deliberate design, exactly; more as if to give me a message that was my due.

The coffee had arrived, but Sophie-Louise Gély would not touch it. She told us Gabi's pains had come on during the evening, and she had given birth in the early hours. The child was ailing and not expected to survive the week. Gabi was already dead.

I remembered, after Martian Meadow, how he had cried in Gabrielle's arms. Now he cried in Lucile's. He talked, on and on, reasoning with himself, accusing himself, reassuring himself out of the accusations, then accusing himself into them again.

"She didn't want me to go, she knew something was wrong this time. I was in bed with some girl in Brussels. They thumped on the door. I shouted at them, thought it was funny. Three days to get back. Bloody roads. Thick with deserters whining excuses, rabble. What was it for? This glorious rebirth, this shining Revolution, this great miracle of human shit, what am I doing in it? Why wasn't I here? The times I promised her. I'll leave it, I said. Retire. We'll go to the country house, plant trees, breed horses. I promised her. God, it's too late."

Sometimes he would get up and walk out. You heard him in the other room, taking her clothes from the closets, holding the clothes and weeping, in terrible loud chokings of furious anguish. He kept everything under seal. He would, he said, never be rid of anything that had been hers. "It hurts me to see her things," he shouted at me. "It drives me crazy. I want that. I deserve it. The way I treated her."

Seeing him as he was racked me. I was helpless in front of this thundering grief. His heart's blood spilled everywhere. He wouldn't stop crying. In the end I verbally set on him, in a panic, trying to make him sober for one minute, by means of rage if nothing else would work. But the colossus slumped there in front of me, letting me beat him over the ears, until I couldn't stand it and went away. Alone, I found myself in tears for him. But it was desperation too.

The threnody continued for days, with no sign of abatement. When not weeping into Gabrielle's clothing, he was pawing and splashing through the letters of condolence. There was one from Maximilien he particularly liked, if such could be said to be the word. Oh, Maxime, he said, *he* understands. (Months later, I saw that same letter held up to the most fantastic ridicule and scorn by Danton.)

At the burial, he went mad at the graveside. I hardly remember what happened. It was, I gather, an insane blur of holding him from the coffin, the pit in the earth. Stunned by his cries.

The servants told you they thought he would take his life. I lost patience with that.

The Gironde was organizing trouble over the prison killings of September, implicating Danton and all his associates. Fabre was terrified and had been around to the apartment four times in three days, each occasion with a different country in his mouth. Something had to be done. Collot d'Herbois took a crack at it by announcing in the Convention that lies spread by the Girondins had shocked Gabrielle to death.

"That's good," said Danton. "I must thank the stupid bastard." Then put his head in his arms and sobbed on the desk.

I couldn't help him and I couldn't cure him, and he wouldn't listen to anything.

The truth is, I was afraid for him. Afraid *of* him. Danton's weakness had every time appalled me, where, if I recall it, Mirabeau in moments of weakness had touched my heart. It was a fact; I'd pinned the ribbons of my hopes on Danton. In some sort I'd followed him, sworn to his service, from the first days of the Cordeliers. Even when I resigned from his ministry, I had only been going on ahead of him, as if I knew for sure he too would leave any palace for the possibilities of a convention. But Carthage is burning, Danton. The fire may die down, but it never goes out, and the archers on the burning walls never sleep. These tears, these endless cries of guilt, won't put out a single spark, deflect a single arrow. Danton, *Danton*.

"I hear you," he said, when I'd returned, a week later. He was sorting through books and financial papers in a leaden, heavy-handed way. "Don't bully me, Camille. I have to go back to Belgium tomorrow."

"Oh, God," I said loudly.

"We'll lose a couple of good generals if I don't."

"And darling Brissot's Gironde?"

"It's nothing. It'll blow over."

"Wl-will it?"

"I'll smooth it over, then, presently. A little tender stroking, till the fur lies down. Don't split France; that's today's motto. We need the Gironde, we need to work with them."

"If you say so. And you always say so. In which case, when are you going to, for Christ's sake, *do* something about it?"

"You remind me," he said, "of my sons. I can't cry in front of them, they get so bloody confused and frightened."

That finished me. I went to him and embraced him, and both of us wept. Presently the Gélys, mother and nymph, came timidly scratching at the door to ask after his health. Even with my reddened eyes, I could see the way Sophie-Louise gazed at him and an almost comic shiftiness about him in her presence. Foolish of me to forget. When it came to women, it was, with Danton, only a matter of time.

❊

Time . . . women . . . girls, hags, goddesses. . . .

She begins to cast her shadow now, long, slender, and black, over the pages. At first, a distant thing, some tower or tree seen on a far-off hill. But as we move nearer to her, she grows and grows, like a monstrous genie released from a bottle. She grows and grows, and her black shadow with her, until she stains and fills the world, and all the world is darkness.

EIGHT

❧ ❧ ❧

1793: *March*

ARTIAL MONTH OF the War God Mars: Martius, March, *Marchons*. Black
March. And the black flag of direst emergency flying from the Hôtel de
Ville: France Endangered.

The war month. And France duly at war. At war with Austria. At war with
Prussia. With Holland, England, and Spain. At war, in effect, with every
monarchist power. At war with the world.

It had to come. The dream of Liberty and the wild boast: We will set the
peoples of the earth free. And that thrown-down gauntlet, the head of a king.
And the victory at Valmy, the splendid pressing home of the advantage into
Belgium, toward Holland. But mud and rain make a cold barrier against
success; the roads are thick with deserters. Danton's carriage, teeming north-
eastwards, has passed through hundreds miserably trudging southwest.

Now and again, he stopped the carriage. Lacroix, his emissary companion,
grabbed his arm. "For God's sake, Georges."

"Leave me alone. It's a pain in the butt anyway, sitting for ten hours at a
stretch." The door's thrust open, and Danton plunges out into the turgid dusk,
staring at the tide of men, which gradually halts. "You don't know me, huh?"
The great voice peals away over the flat wet countryside. "Well, I know you.
Every one of you. And your names? All the same name. Do you want it? *Judas*."
They stare back, the men with the gray rain running from their hats. Someone
says, *That's Danton*. "Yes, God blast the lot of you, it's Danton. Me. Well, have a
good look. Who's going to take a potshot at me?" (In the carriage, Lacroix
covers his face with his hands: *Oh, Jesus*.) "Yes, I'm not usually so reckless. But
something's made me sick. Fine, raise your musket, sonny. Except you'd do
better firing on the bloody enemy, wouldn't you? Yes, France is back that way.
Go on. Go and fall down at her feet and tell her why you won't fight for her.
Because you hate her, this mother of yours, you hate the guts of France. No? It's

283

the act of a son and lover then, to run? You want to live—excellent. You'll live to see the Prussians crawling all over her carcass like flies." He stands and roars at them, there in the desolation of retreat, as the light goes and the carriage lamps remain unlit. No, he's not usually so reckless. Danton the lion-bull, cramped and clawed at by grief and guilt and a host of minor ailments (laughable, if you never had them), rats gnawing at the base of a colossus, the blood of Talos, the giant of bronze, running from his heel—Danton in the rain bawling out the French deserters, till they cowered and came to him with their grievances and fears, like children to their father. "All right, we'll see to that. Trust me, I'll get something done." Some of them he even turned, by his rhetoric and pledges, back toward the front. But, his carriage by then tumbling on through the darkness, he did not pause again to see if they arrived.

Lacroix sighed. "Danton, you're not France."

"Am I not?" said Danton tiredly. "Then tell me who is?"

"Let those pathetic deserting bastards get on with it. The Convention will approve the idea of a levy. You'll get your three hundred thousand men to fight. And Dumouriez will listen to you."

"Perhaps. He's a clever general and he's losing all his battles recently. While all the Convention does is send him the message *Win or die*. What do you really expect? He wants fresh men and fresh promises and some cash and a pat on the head. He's not going to settle for listening to me. Oh, yes, I'll try. I'll try the way I did with those poor bastards on the road. But he'll be over the border, kissing the Austrians, before Robespierre can say *martyrdom* one more time."

"You're worn out," says Lacroix, who is exhausted.

Danton does not at first reply. Then he says, "Audacity, always audacity." Then in English: "Be bold, be bold, and everywhere be bold."

"What?"

"Spenser. An English poet of the sixteenth century. He writes my speeches for me." And after that, in English once more: "*And all for love, and nothing for reward. . . .*"

He slouches uncomfortably, brooding, his flesh pocked and gray as the mud of Belgium in the rainy dark.

But he'll snap out of this. He'll have to.

※

The sun goes, the sun returns. The same blackness, and eventually the same dawn that broke over disgruntled unvictorious French encampments breaks too across Paris. And with the dawn the streets begin to move. What's that noise? It's a matter of course to ask the question and a matter of habit to answer, *Them—shut the door quick.* But who is "them" this time? To an accompaniment of slamming portals, the ragged crowd comes down the street, yipping and yelping, and, forming up outside a baker's, begins to bark and howl.

"That's it, boys. Keep it going."

Woof woof yowl, goes the crowd.

Above, a window shutter moves, a frightened face looks out and is hastily withdrawn.

"Hey, don't be shy! Hey! We saw you. Open up now! *Woof woof yowl!*"

But nobody opens up. So the crowd beats on the door and presently breaks it in.

As they are rifling his shop, the baker comes down. He stands on the stair and faces them in tears of terrified rage.

"You see, you maniacs, I haven't any bread to sell."

"So you say. But you'll be hoarding like the rest of them."

"Come and look then," quavers the baker in hysterical bravado. "You're welcome. Give my children a giggle while you're at it. They can do with that, they're starving."

"All right, all right, Dad. Leave it, boys, he's one of us, he's telling the truth."

"You're the one called Roux," accuses the baker.

"Yes. That's me, Cordelier Jacques Roux, leader of the Mad Dogs." Howling and growling breaks out to emphasize the words. Roux, once a priest, now a man of the People, shouts a piece of coarse religious Latin at his mob, and it guffaws. "Well, why not join us, Dad?"

"And do what? March on the Convention like you, and get thrown out in the street like you?" The baker is becoming more and more valiant. "Robespierre's got your number. Rabid fools, in the pay of the aristos, that's what he called your lot, trying to destroy the People's trust in their Revolution."

"Oh, yes?" says Roux. "Well, I'll tell you. As you say, we all went to this glorious Convention we elected, we went and scratched on its doors, we Mad Dogs. We said to Robespierre, The People have no bread. And Marie-Antoinette Robespierre answered, Let them eat Liberty." There is silence. Roux says, "We had one king, sat on his bum at Versailles, and we were in difficulties, all right. But are we out of the fix now we've got seven hundred and fifty kings sitting on their butts at the Stable? Eat Liberty!" Roux shouts. "Because Robespierre's got no fucking appetite, nobody's got to have an appetite. Well we're hungry. And we're angry. And you'd better watch out, Daddy baker. You'd all better watch out."

The Enragés, the Mad Dogs, stream away along the street barking. The baker sits on his stairs shaking, in the cold March sun.

⚜

"There's going to be trouble, real trouble, in a minute. All the news is bad. The army can't win a game of piquet. There's no food in the capital—"

"And there was another free-for-all yesterday. Roux's Mad Dog pack running amok."

"Well, it's these royalist antirevolutionary hoarders. They buy everything up and hide it. I've heard it said the queen—"

"Eh? What queen?"

"Beg your pardon. The Austrian cow. She's supposed to have been sent sacks of sugar, got it stashed away in the Temple—"

"Sugar's a luxury. It's bread that's the problem. The People can't find a crumb, pecking about like poor starving birds in the snow. Naturally they're getting frantic."

"I said to Marie—"

"What, you still calling your old woman by that lousy aristo name? What's she called *for,* the nonexistent Catholic Virgin or the Austrian whore?"

"Well, I call her Julie, but I forget sometimes. I said to Mar—Julie, anyway, Go to the country. Go and stay with your sister."

"Not very patriotic. Every citizen should stay to support and defend the capital."

"Wherever you go there's trouble. What about Lyons? The rioting's completely out of hand."

"There are aristo plots. That's what's doing it. You know what Robespierre says. You need eyes in the back of your head, they're everywhere: spies, counterrevolutionaries. Everything's going wrong. I get into bed every night and wonder if I'll wake up in the morning with my throat cut."

"Hmm. Speaking about waking up the dead. You heard the latest about Danton?"

"Well?"

"He had that wife of his dug up out of her grave. Embalmed. Or else a waxwork. Some very murky stuff."

"You're suggesting—"

"Not me. Common chat. That gang of Danton's. They're capable of anything. What's a bit of necrophily?"

"Here, that's dirty talk. Shut your trap. Leave Danton alone. He's been fighting the royalist filth tooth and nail."

"Yes, and they all wear good coats, don't they, that crew? And feed like hogs. Camille Desmoulins goes regularly to dine with German bankers. Even a Prussian. Who told me? Everyone knows. Don't you push me, I'll knock your eyes through your head."

"Robespierre's the only one we can trust."

"Robespierre, with his powdered hair and lace cuffs."

Standing watching the ensuing fight, somebody says, "Danton's back anyway. Laying the law down at the Convention."

It keeps the mob happy. The mob always likes Danton.

"It's only that the mob can always *hear* Danton."

Although this evening he had started quietly, standing there on the rostrum in his dark clothes of mourning for Gabrielle. He appeared raddled and threadbare of skin, if not of coat, as if to show them all that he, who had made a great deal out of the Revolution, had given it in turn a great deal back, and maybe too much. Thirty-four years of age, he looked sixty-four.

"Citizen Robespierre," said Danton, "is hardly noted for his partiality toward our generals." (Some amusement; Robespierre has for weeks been blaming every reverse in the war on the generals.) "Yet Citizen Robespierre has nevertheless told us he has confidence in Dumouriez. Myself, I'll go a little further. I have seen a defeated army, gentlemen, standing wounded and wretched in the rain, acclaiming Dumouriez and offering its life for his next assault on the enemy. This is the kind of military genius not to be set aside lightly. All he requires are troops, all he requires is our support – and he can win the battles for us."

Someone shouted, "What about the atrocities this precious army has committed – rape and pillage. Do you deny that, Georges Danton?"

Danton did not look. The voice came from the Estuary Party of the Gironde, as might have been expected.

"A certain amount," Danton said, "has been breezed abroad on this matter. One hears plenty of rumors. But we're not here to gossip. We're here to find remedies against losing a war. If I see a house on fire, what do you advise me to do, leave it to burn while I chase looters up the road? I tell you now," he said, the big voice growing bigger, "if you want to save the Republic you have to act immediately. Don't let's bawl out all our generals, citizens. Let's put the blame squarely where it belongs – here in this hall. Dumouriez only needs men! And France has men by the million. Why are we delaying? Secure Belgium, take Holland, and pull the rug out from under the English. Isn't that the goal?"

There was a racket, of course. Danton attended to it a moment, picked out the relevant word, and shook it at them, drowning the whole vast roomful suddenly with his thunder.

"Money? Yes, let's take it, then. The rich have got plenty, they can pay our debt. The People can only give blood, but they donate it generously. Be as generous with your gold. Yes, make all the row you want. I can shout you down. *Listen!* This endless bickering over every issue, this sniping, one side of this house against the other: *Stop this factiousness.* There should be no passion in this place but a passion for the public good. You dare to waste time with personal recriminations when half the world is baying at our gates for the blood of France? For heaven's sake, gentlemen, stop quarreling and save your country."

The Mountain erupts into applause.

The Estuary makes gestures of mockery and amazement. The president shuffles (a Girondin sympathizer), wanting to adjourn; the ground is dangerous and the hour late. Certain members are already, under cover of the disturbance, creeping toward the exits.

Abruptly, Danton, black-March-mourning figure, comes completely alive, and the years fall off him with a clank. No longer sixty-four, he straightens and hurls that unbelievable voice of his to every wall, through every interstice and crack. "This debate is not finished. That being so, no true citizen is about to desert his post."

And they come to heel. Affronted, nervous, and abashed, the president lapses; the escapees slink again to their seats.

"Yes," comments Danton ironically, towering there in the midst of them all. "And now, I'll pass on to the other business on our collective patriotic mind. You've heard, doubtless, of the situation in the cities. Anarchy is just around the corner. Paris rocks with riots. Who went by a baker's today without armed guards standing outside? We acknowledge, the Republic has enemies both without and within, always busy, stirring up the sections. Such a contingency asks a strong hand. While we secure our frontiers, we must also shore up the interior, before the world gives way on every side. Since plainly Paris is heading for a bloodbath, I suggest—"

"Wrong month!" the voice yelled again from the right-hand benches. "Wrong month for your bloodbath, Danton. It isn't *September!*"

Danton's head jerked up as if yanked by the slack of a tether. His face turned gray, then muddy, then scarlet in a rush of boiling congestion. He opened his mouth. No words came.

Danton-September. Tell history. Make it stick.

Seeing him speechless, the arena went mad. On the Mountain benches, men were jumping to their feet, yelling. Desmoulins, for one, was screaming across at the Gironde—inaudible in the uproar—while apparently trying to push his way through in order to kill someone. The Girondin who had called, Lanjuinais, looked first smug, then alarmed. He fell back into the ranks of his own party, gesticulating.

I can smooth them down. Roland's out of the ministry. Roland's Gironde. We can and must work with them.

But they don't like your power, Danton, your force that can stop the session in its tracks. The Olympian Mountain makes dictators. No, the Gironde isn't about to be smoothed.

Danton's color is cooling off. He stands and waits, almost idly now, on the rostrum, watching the upheaval. His mouth describes a leonine snarl of contempt. Very few of them are close enough to see the rapidity of his breathing, or that his hands, clenched at his sides, tremble. But he waits, and the fast breathing, the trembling, like the frightful strangled color, die down. Fifteen minutes of pandemonium give him the space to collect himself.

When there is order, he picks up the verbal knife cast at him and shows it off, almost casually.

"Since someone here has had the surpassing good taste to remind us of the blood-stained days of September, I will say this. Had we possessed, at that time, a strong lawful body fully empowered to order and to mete out justice on behalf of the citizenry, things would never have got to the pass they did. I therefore propose, as I was about to propose twenty minutes ago, a new Revolutionary Tribunal, which will assume the fullest authority in the weeding out and punishment of crimes against the Nation. Thereby ensuring that never again will the outraged People take the law into its own hands."

More cries exploded: the Gironde, feeling its oats (it had rendered him voiceless, had it not?). Brissot's shrill glassy tones came cutting through the rest.

"For my part, gentlemen, I think I prefer popular anarchy to a Dantonesque version of the Spanish Inquisition. Presumably that's what Citizen Danton is suggesting?"

"It seems Citizen Brissot confuses justice with coercion, a fact some of us have been painfully aware of for some time," was the loud Mountain comment.

Brissot cried, "I fear and foresee a degeneration into ruthlessness—"

"Ruthlessness!" Danton shot back from the floor. "Do you think our enemies will be gentle with *us?* Better the ruthlessness of a legal tribunal than the ruthlessness of pikes on the streets."

The Gironde sneeringly cheered. Another of its members shouted, "And please note, Georges Danton chooses his words just like a king."

"And please note," Danton bellowed, "that gentleman there chooses his words before he knows what he's talking about."

En masse, the Mountain applauds. The strained pale faces, feverish with excitement, boys on the school wall—I am *not!* You are *too!*—Fabre, Billaud, d'Herbois, Camille, all still on their feet, even Marat writhing and twitching with cruel consent. Robespierre gravely nods, making a few notes, while the slim white wolf (Saint-Just) stares over his shoulder at everything.

"But I see I've lost my reputation," says Danton, with unexpected sublime lightness. "Well, let it go. Tarnish my name in blood. What do I care for that, if France is free?" He comes off the rostrum in a storm of plaudits and insults, walks through it all, seemingly untouched.

⚜

"Well. We seem to be at war with the Gironde."

"I told you so. They're scum."

"So are we, by their lights."

"Sons of innkeepers and petty grocers. They're in this to get as much as they can, line their stinking nests."

"And what do you suppose they suppose we're in it for?"

"Oh, the old argument. Danton, we're in it because we believe there can be something better."

"And look at the mess we're making."

"No. I won't look at it. I'm looking at the shining future, the sunrise just over the hill. I believe in *that*."

"You're drunk, Camille."

"Truth speaks in wine."

"That'd make Brissot laugh."

"*Et nam risu inepto res ineptior nulla est.*"

"Thank you, Catullus Desmoulins. It's a fact, though," said Lacroix. "Brissot *does* have a damn silly laugh, like a rusty screw working loose."

"It also remains a fact," said Hérault, "Brissot's clique has now reached the stage of opposing, seemingly on principle, and regardless, any idea coming down from the Mountain. We do know, don't we, Brissot's paper was singing Dumouriez's praises only a day or so ago?"

"*The Committed Frenchman* also accused Robespierre of calling the streets to anarchy."

"The other theory is," said Danton, "Dumouriez is going to La Fayette all over us and is planning a coup d'état."

They looked at Danton, waiting for some more. Finally Hérault de Séchelles uncorked another bottle. Aristocratic not merely in name, he had remained firmly tidy throughout the volatile political session and the drinking bout which followed. Handsome as a doll, his thick fair hair gracefully tied back with a ribbon, frivolous cravat still crisp, he gazed into the ruby of the wine and said, "So we'll be obliged to lose him to the Austrians."

"Probably," said Danton. "Which makes me a blasted idiot for shouting on his behalf tonight."

"More problems, then."

"Many more problems."

Hérault stayed unperturbed. He had not actively aligned himself with any particular party, even the toad-laden plain. He attended the Convention as a man went to his office or, more correctly, rode around his estate, immaculately fulfilling his duty. He had been known to say, "Which side am I with? Oh, with the best dressed, naturally."

"If I had any sense," said Danton, "I'd try to arrange another meeting with Brissot. Or with Vergniaud. Pretty fast."

Camille Desmoulins made a derogatory noise.

"It would," said Hérault, "seem a little late for that."

"My timing's off," said Danton. "No. It isn't that. I'm tired."

"Then wake yourself up," acidly said Camille.

"Or go to sleep," appended Hérault quizzically.

Later, Danton invited himself up to the Desmoulins apartment. "Is the hour too advanced?" he courteously inquired of Lucile, not lifting her up but leaning over three-quarters of a foot to kiss her cheeks and lips. She led him in and sat him down like a large child. "There, Marius. How are you?"

"He's tired," said Camille. "And no surprise. He chased Monsieur Brissot around the Convention three times with a bull whip."

"Take no notice," said Danton. He began to ask Lucile quiet domestic questions. With the shortages, were they able to get sugar? Good. Because if not, he knew someone, more reliable than their dealer, who could get it for them. And the child was at Queen's Market? Yes, that was a fine idea. Lucile sat and abetted the conversation. She had even been known to get out the household accounts and discuss them with him. She was letting him play Gabi-is-alive. Gabi is alive and asking my advice on mundane affairs. Tonight he said, "I don't like to go home. So I inflict myself on you."

"But what about your boys?" Lucile asked, all concern.

"Oh, like yours. They're with their Italian granny in the country. Paris is no place for children with all this going on. Or, if they're in the apartment, little Louise comes down and sees to them."

"Oh, yes, Louise," said Camille.

Lucile did not say to Danton, as she had said to Camille, "That one hennas her hair, I would swear to it—some days it's pinker than her ribbons." Lucile said, "She's a kind girl, Sophie-Louise."

"Very good with the boys," said Danton. "They're crazy about her. Well, poor little devils, what else have they got?" Don't get maudlin, Camille said silently, bristling with defenses.

"You," said Lucile. "*You*, Marius, they've got their father."

"Me. God help them." And Camille walked out of the room (as Lucile sat with Danton's hand held in her own, and Danton began to talk about Gabi), only coming back ten minutes later brightly to interrupt with a brand new edition of Petronius.

⚜

The Convention decrees:

> *That there shall forthwith be established in Paris a Criminal Tribunal Extraordinary, which shall deal with all counterrevolutionary activities and plots, all essays upon the liberty, equal status, unity, and indivisibility of the Republic, the internal and external security of the Nation, and any conspiracies attempting to reinstate royalty or other authority injurious to the freedom of the Sovereign People.*

This Tribunal will be known as the Committee for General Defense.

⚜

He got that to work then. The Tribunal. Law and order—no more rampages and the streets running with blood.

I'll tell you what, though.

What?

Madame Guillotine's going to be busy.

Madame la Chatte, elle a la dent unique, mais elle mord à mort.

Having galloped up the stair, Camille Desmoulins stood irritatedly brushing off his coat the sawdust from Duplay's joiner's yard, waiting for the door of Maximilien's bedroom to open. It did not; instead he was invited to open it himself. Camille walked in, to find Maximilien seated at his desk but in his dressing gown, looking deathly ill, as expected. The brown dog lay patiently, under the window, alleviating its boredom with sleep. The white dog stood in an actorish attitude with an armful of journals. (Camille gives these a funny glance. He's trying to see if there's a pinkish broadsheet in their midst.)

"Ah," said Robespierre, smiling exhaustedly. "Thank you for coming over."

Saint-Just put down the papers neatly. (No broadsheet.) He gave Camille a long flat look, which Camille returned with a curl of the lip.

"Excuse me," said Saint-Just. He began walking out.

"Oh, Antoine," said Maximilien despairingly. "Couldn't you—"

"You'll find it easier to talk, Maxime, if I'm not here. I'll return in an hour."

He passed Camille like a cold draft and slipped through the doorway like a dagger.

The dog made a weird little whining sound in its sleep.

"Exactly," said Camille.

Maximilien put his hand to his brow. "Sit down, won't you."

"Why not? Though I wish you'd get some more comfortable chairs." Camille sat. "How are you?"

"Better."

"What is it?"

"The usual. The fever doesn't last long. And they're very good to me here."

"Of course they are. Élie has made up her mind to marry you. Or are you going to marry that rich widow from Marseilles who writes you love letters every week?"

"Don't be capricious, Camille, please. I really can't stand it this afternoon."

"Oh, dear. You're in *that* condition: *There's nothing wrong with me, I'm dying.*"

Robespierre looked (and was) hurt. He brought his glasses down over lowered eyes and took up one of the newspapers Saint-Just had been holding. He read for a while in silence.

Camille counted cracks in the ceiling. He was in a singularly bad mood, inactivity and nervousness preying on him, along with successions of underslept, overdrunk nights. His rather consistent lack of sympathy with others in their physical or spiritual distresses sprang partly from a fear of illness engendered in him early by the failing of his mother. Yet also, in fact, from his latent respect for—awe of, inadequacy before—nearly everyone else. They seemed stronger to him than he could ever be, far more sure, less confused, less plagued by those terrible malaises of the heart which disfigured his emotions and often made him, incidentally, talented and intelligent though he was, such a very rotten judge of character. Frankly, even where he felt contempt for another, this bizarre awe and respect would run alongside it. Intellectually superior to many, he must still, on some level, acknowledge they seemed to organize their journeys through life more logically. (He was almost envious of their clodhopping progress.) Without being a poet, save half accidentally now and then in his prose, Camille had several affinities with a poet's anguished soul; plus the temperament of a warrior, whose need to be able to *see* the enemy was just now hurtfully if unconsciously predominant.

Presently Robespierre pushed up his spectacles again and, four-eyed, gazed at him.

"Brissot's paper."

"So I noticed. What does he say today? What he said last week, I surmise. We're all villains."

"Something on those lines." Robespierre hesitated. "There is a story, not precisely reported here, that Dumouriez bought Danton in order to—"

"There's always some fucking story some cunt has bought Danton, for Christ's sake. Don't tell *me,* if it worries you. Tell Danton. He's in bloody Belgium. Try shouting."

Robespierre removed his spectacles. He stared at Camille.

Camille sat panting. He said, "Have you seen the pink broadsheet—the one with the fascinating name "Men of Prey: Crimes of the Defense Committee"? No? Look out for it. Printed by a drunk in gray water instead of ink. The spelling is artistic."

Robespierre said, "Whose paper is this?"

"A promising Guisard called Roch-Marcandier. A bloody insane lying little turd—"

"Camille," said Robespierre. "What have *I* done?"

Camille looked sullenly at his feet. "Nothing. I'm sorry. I've been slandered. He calls me—well, you say you haven't read it. It's not a paper, it's a rag. No one will pay any attention to it. He shoots his mouth off all the time. My well-wishers at the Cordeliers always tell me what he's said about me. I made sure he couldn't print any of it with any reputable journal—a word here and there—but now he's found some broken-down alley press. He says I'm an 'everyday murderer and robber.' He says I egged them on in September, shouting for blood. Oh, God, Maxime!"

Robespierre cleared his throat and Camille fell silent. "As you remark," said Robespierre, "no reputable printer will accommodate him. You see, his sheet isn't here. To return where we were: I count on you, Camille, *because* I value your honesty. And because I regard you, to some extent, as an intermediary between myself and Danton, a man I can in some measure admire, but for whom, as you know, I have certain fears—"

"I know about your fears for Danton. You've told me."

"I've trusted you enough to tell you. In this matter of Brissot and the Gironde, the unity of the Jacobin left is essential."

"Brissot isn't popular with the crowd anymore. They've seen through him. He can't do anything."

"Yes, he can. Forgive me, Camille. Don't suppose that I undervalue you when I say that you are not always aware of every base motive and means employed in the Convention. For myself, I too look beyond those closed doors. I look outward, toward France, whenever I speak there, and whatever I try to achieve. I wish the Manège were larger, so that the galleries might be filled by thousands, able to listen and to oversee what goes on. I wish the walls of this Convention of ours were made of glass. Nothing hidden. The will of the Nation safeguarded at all times."

"And damnably cold in winter."

Robespierre blinked. He said, ignoring the quip so pointedly it fell dead to the floor, "There are members of the Gironde on the Committee for Defense. There are still sympathizers of the Gironde in the ministry. That Circe, Manon Roland, continues at work in her salon, corrupting the minds and hearts of the susceptible. For the Convention itself, you see how the Gironde can sway the lower benches. Why do you suppose so many of our party have been periodically dispatched out of the way to inspect the army? Saint-Just, Fréron—even Danton himself is sent hither and thither like an errand boy. There's so much to do," Robespierre said. "Danton spoke very wisely when he upbraided the hallful for its factiousness. I listened, and I was moved. Our only passion should be for the rights of the People. But all this bickering is constantly in the way."

"Yes," said Camille. "They need shutting up."

"Yes," Robespierre said. He arranged the meticulous order on his desk an iota more meticulously, then said softly, "And are you writing anything at present?"

"I'm always writing something. I've told you, I'm trying to put a volume together on the course of the Revolution. No doubt very biased and unaware and blinded."

"I didn't mean to offend you."

"I know. The trouble is, we think . . . Lucile may be going to have another child."

Maximilien's sick face lit up. "But that's wonderful!"

"No, it isn't. It nearly killed her the last time."

"You exaggerate a little, Camille. I understand you're quite properly concerned for her—"

"You understand nothing about it, Maxime. Christ, how can you? You've never had—you've never—bloody hell, you're above and beyond all that. You don't know the first thing about any of it."

"I see," said Robespierre.

"No, you don't see. Your self-righteous attitude to sex: Stop unwanted children! But no, an unwanted child is far better than the grievous sin of contraception. God almighty!"

"If you believe there is a God, Camille, as I know you do—"

"Not God, Maxime. Nn-not now."

Camille had stood up five sentences before and started flying in a limited way round the room. The dog woke and barked at him. Robespierre shushed it. Camille collided with the doorway and halted. "You'd better tell me what you want me to say to Georges for you. Then I'll go—and stop making you feel worse than you do already."

"There's nothing I want you to say to Danton I'm not perfectly capable of saying to him myself," said Robespierre. "It was you yourself I wanted to speak to. I had a suggestion. But we'd better wait until you're in a cooler temper."

"Then let it wait," snapped Camille. He flung wide the door. "I w—I wish you well," he said. "Take care of yourself. Demeter's sending you some butter and eggs from Bourg-la-Reine."

"No," said Robespierre, with utter gentleness. "It's very good of her, but she mustn't."

"What do you mean, 'mustn't'?"

"I have all I need. And if there are shortages in the city, well, I don't mind sharing the People's own lot. For example, we haven't used sugar here for several weeks."

Camille stared at Maximilien.

"You mean you can't get hold of any?"

"I mean I refuse to get hold of any, by underhand means, when the majority of Paris is without."

"So I suppose when I put sugar in my coffee tonight, *by underhand m-mn-means,* you'll expect me to choke on it?"

Robespierre gripped his fingers to his forehead. He looked near to tears of debility and frustration.

"You're willfully misinterpreting what I say. What you do is a matter for your own conscience. Or your own needs. I have no appetite, you know that. It's no sacrifice for me to—"

"Stop making excuses for being a bloody saint, Maxime. None of us can keep up with you. All right, when the butter arrives, and the eggs, send them back or distribute them in the markets to deserving poor. Or shove them somewhere. The venal rest of us will get on as brr-bs-best we can."

The door slammed, and Camille heard the dog bark again behind it as he skirmished down the stairs. At the bottom he paused, went a short distance, paused again. He cursed, and was half turning to go back when he saw Saint-Just looking in at him from the wintry yard. So he walked out instead.

As he passed Saint-Just, who stood with an ethereal silver halo on his white hair, Camille said, "Don't bother to say good-bye. Your mask might crack."

Saint-Just indeed said nothing, only returned across the yard toward Robespierre.

In Saint-Honoré Street, a crowd was milling about near the Jacobins. Camille avoided it with the dexterity of practice. The Tricolor hung from the portico of Saint-Roch, now a sometime section assembly hall. (Saint-Roch-Marcandier. If I meet him, I'll break his neck.) The symbols of religion on the church had been in various ways largely defaced, as on most churches in Paris and throughout France, with, doubtless, the notable exception of the Vendée. There in the west, the Revolution had been surprised by a revolution against itself. La Vendée objected to the military levy. ("A million men in France," said Danton. But the Vendée replied, Count us out.) La Vendée, instead, had organized its own military levy and risen. Kneeling before statues of the Holy Mother, it offered its muskets for her blessing. So now the dream of Liberty was fighting on all France's borders, but also in her heart. And with an empty gut. Camille Desmoulins, walking on, went by several alleys and courts where other small crowds waited hopelessly, or furiously, or both hopelessly and furiously, against chandlers or grocers' shops, kept at bay by National Guardsmen.

What do you do? Is a spoonful less sugar going to put food in these bellies? Can you starve for the sins of the world? *No, Maxime.* You're fighting like a slave.

But then, everyday murderer and thief that I am, casting the innocent in jail and getting them piked so I can seize their goods, a little sugar's a minor affair. Is all Paris reading it? No. No one's read it but me. How can I kill him? Some crater should swallow him whole.

The warmthless bitterness of the day hung low and pressed on Camille. The colors of Paris had altered. They had become uniformly leaden. Even the *tricoleurs* pouring off so many cornices, ledges, seemed drained of their dyes.

If spring and shining sunrise were just over the horizon, you would never know it.

1793: Spring

GENERAL DUMOURIEZ had sent a letter to Paris, full of threats. He had also sent a letter apparently to the Temple, to the Austrian woman or her friends, announcing that he found it impossible to remain, any longer, a passive witness to so many stupidities and crimes. *I will smash this illegal government,* the missive declared, *restore the monarchy, make the Queen regent, and proclaim the Dauphin the next king of France.* And there he went, prancing along the French frontier, wearing in his hat a white Bourbon cockade, with fifty thousand men eagerly bucketing along after, squawking, *Vive la Reine, Vive le Dauphin, la Révolution est fini,* et cetera. In fact, Dumouriez's troops, whatever his madly reported plans had exactly been, refused to assist him. April weather saw him floundering through the crocuses into the arms of Austria.

※

It ceases to be clever to be in company with half the military command in Paris. Boxes at the opera are vacated, restaurants walked out of, because some poor guy with time off from the front—but who once shared a map conference with Dumouriez—has wandered naively in to say hello.

Arturius Dillon, who distinguished himself (beside Dumouriez) at Valmy, receives the oblique looks with a desperado's composure. Though he seldom calls a spade a spade, he has never stopped calling a queen a Queen. A little older and a little taller than most of the men in the room, he gives Camille Desmoulins only the politest of greetings, which signals: No need to recognize me; I'm an awkward commodity. Who knows but I might skedaddle up the Temple walls and rescue the Lily Lady one night. Above his uniform of the Nation, General Dillon's hair is powdered and curled. The eyes are clear with ancestral Irish rain, and all the gypsy boldness of Ireland in them. But he is a Frenchman too, if with a crush on the ancien régime, and moving with the times. Which doesn't mean to say he *likes* the times, though he would never be rude to them unless much provoked. Perhaps he is surprised when Camille walks up to him and exchanges rather more than the greeting of the hour.

Camille certainly looks flustered and uncomfortable. He despises Dillon as a royalist, admires his military skills, has found him in conversation (once they had both of them wriggled out from under Camille's political rhetoric) absorbing, and additionally dismisses him intellectually, as a foreigner, from all understanding of the needs of France. As a rule, Camille avoids Dillon. Now, obviously, Camille is making a show of not toeing anyone's line. Presently Dillon chides him for the risk. Camille glares at him, stands firm, and promptly broaches a new subject, which they duly discuss.

Dillon is highly amused, but also sentimentally rather touched. "When they come to arrest me," he begins lightly. Camille snaps, "Arrest you for what? Winning your battles?" Dillon makes a mild gesture, intransigently aristocratic. "I don't long for prison," says the general. "But who does?" "Don't talk yourself into chains," Camille replies. After this the exchange peters out, and Dillon absents himself from the gathering. Camille is exasperated not to be able to go on proving a point.

※

Lasource, that day's spokesman for the Estuary, shook back his revolutionary hair and said to the Convention, "As we now know, Dumouriez's plan was to put the monarchy once more in power. But to do it, he needed an army. Who provided him one—who, indeed, begged that it be strengthened? Danton, I think. While Desmoulins has backed him up, yapping that Dumouriez's sidekick, Irish Dillon, have supreme command of the northern squadrons. To help the scenario along, it was reckoned useful to sow dissent and misgiving here in the Convention. And who came here and attempted such an act, upbraiding us all with laziness, pettiness—expressing fears of a popular uprising—Danton? Oh, surely *not*."

The cries from the Gironde benches now resemble those of dogs after a quarry.

The Mountain rumbles. The whole room is on the edge of its seat.

"Lacroix, naturally, has been an invaluable aid to Danton in all this. As I am sure are all his friends, who like so much to spend time discussing tactics with such fellows as this Dillon. Then we have the poetic playwright, d'Églantine, Danton's sometime right hand, who has currently been telling the Committee for General Defense that the best thing in the world for us all would be another king."

"*Liar!*" rockets across from the Mountain, a voice large enough, momentarily, to be Danton's own, but he is sitting nearly stock still and silent, a rock with quivering fists and snarling mouth, his eyes riveted on the Gironde benches.

"We are aware large sums of money have gone to Danton and Lacroix on their forays into Belgium. These men—who have conveniently had nothing but garlands for Dumouriez, omitting to mention his little peccadillo of traitorousness."

"All right," said Danton. He stood up. "That's it." As he moved forward, the Mountain clamored, and up in the public gallery, not packed with Robespierre's quota of thousands but still packed, the citizens of Paris wailed and stamped: *Danton! Danton!*

Levasseur remarks to Camille Desmoulins, "Now watch out for spontaneous combustion."

Lasource is shouting at the president, "Yes, let him speak, let him explain himself!"

Danton reaches the rostrum and looks back at the upper tiers he has just left. He breaks into a great avalanche of coherent wrath, such as only he is capable of.

"You told me," he thunders at the Mountain. "You warned me, my friends. Don't have any truck with the perfidious Right. I see good manners have led me astray. But no longer. These very creatures, who—out of ignorance or villainy—have been conspiring for months to save the monarchy and reinflict it on France, now dare to accuse me of *their* crime. They say I held my tongue in the matter of Dumouriez's defection. Did I? Who was it, then, who presented a warning to this Convention that just such an event was likely? Anyone present here today who knows me to be speaking the truth, I call on him to verify that statement." And from many parts of the hall, the yell goes up: *Yes, Danton. Yes! It's true.*

Danton continues, carefully taking to bits what Lasource has been saying, chewing the bits over, ejecting them. "You, talking now of my bribery by Dumouriez, this traitor you yourselves upheld as a great and noble officer. Only three days ago, the Gironde newspapers informed Paris he would never sully his laurels with the *mourning cypress of September.* You say I sow dissent in the Convention. *I* do? You who do nothing but make nonsense of its proceedings. While I value its dignity, even to the point of showing courtesy to sworn enemies."

"Stop waffling!" comes from the Right. "Answer!"

"He *is* answering you!" from the Left. "Shut up and listen!"

Danton shrugs massively. He says to the gallery now, "The best answer of all is in their newspapers. Out of their own mouths—"

The Estuary, having come rather unglued, is jeering for all it's worth.

Conversely, the Mountain opens up to disgorge Marat, who, standing up on a bench (tearing at himself in itching hatred and frothing at the lips), screeches through the din, "And there have been Gironde supper parties, paid for by the royalist faction! Lasource was at them all! Do you hear Marat? Marat will strip the pack of you naked and show you in your dirt."

The gallery bays: *Marat! Marat!*

"I defy any man of the Gironde," comes Danton's gargantuan voice, "to produce a single proof against me. Whereas for yourselves—"

The central benches, Marsh toads, excited, begin to demand names. The Estuary tumultuously joins in. "Go on, then, say who you're defaming."

"You want me to name those members of the Gironde who have behaved treasonably?" Danton roars. "Then I name every one of them!"

Marat leaps and bounds on his bench like a frisky mountain goat. He is a perfect picture in his filthy old coat and flea-ridden collar, in hate almost to a pornographic degree.

Danton rides the chaos and the noise, waits, then launches out again at the Right.

"No more truce with you. It's finished. Your stale trumpery charges, your idiocy, deserve just one response, which only the honor of this pulpit prevents my offering. I say now, to my colleagues," says Danton, "we will close shields against our enemies. My goal is the Republic. Who aspires against the victory of that Republic is at war with *me.* My unassailable fortress is reason, and from its walls I turn the guns of truth against them. Come on, then, and be blown to powder."

"Who needs an army?" somebody cries out from the Left. "Danton—we have you!" And brings the house down.

So there's already quite a lot of powder in the air, or smoke. When it metaphorically clears, Danton has left the rostrum and Robespierre is standing there in his place.

Which is like a mystic metamorphosis. The scarlet giant disarrayed in black, the stentorian rooster off the barnyard fence, altered to a compact and white-faced midget, nattily clad in a green-striped coat, a blue-striped waistcoat, and a red-striped cravat.

Silence falls in aesthetic surprise.

"Conspiracy," said Robespierre. "Such a word, of course, should not be uttered in the same breath with such names as Vergniaud, Brissot. . . . A man, for example, of Brissot's spotless character, a man who corresponds daily with the patriotic general Dumouriez—this sort of man is hardly to be suspected of anything." Robespierre seldom made jokes. As such, it was appreciated. Like a schoolmaster, having enticed the classroom to laugh so he can rap its knuckles, Robespierre became very cold. "It's time this farce was ended," he said. "The Convention must take revolutionary measures—but I doubt if our vaunted Committee for General Defense will be any use."

Drawn again, the Gironde retaliated. Powdered Sillery informed powdered Robespierre he was criticizing a legal arm of the Convention.

"Exactly," said Robespierre. "And as a member of that legal arm, I hereby offer it my resignation. It has ceased to represent justice, the sole purpose for its creation. Where is justice, I say, when persons are able, continually, to slander the Left—the party of freedom—and these persons themselves have supported a traitor. I am astonished."

Brissot said loudly, "Let me astonish you again! I demand a hearing when this citizen has finished. *If* he ever does."

Robespierre turned a fraction and looked at Brissot.

Uncorrupted and incorruptible, Robespierre had come at last to the perfect advantage of virtue. Here in this whirlpool governed by strong emotion, by an oratory that could push and propel, intoxicate and madden—yet never totally conceal the small insidious doubts—here, Saint Maximilien, pale and pure, purged by fever, devoid of sugar, stainless, blameless, fixed the foes of Liberty with his eyes, staring as a cat stares, lidless, nearly alien. His voice that had neither beauty nor power; his phrases that were often too long, occasionally rambling or stilted, and lacking, normally, evocation or cleverness; his rhetoric built on repetition like drops of icy rain wearing away, but only by perpetual abrasion, the hardest stone; his poise, which in that moment seemed terrifying. No showman. This is all sincerity. He believes what he says, he knows he has done no wrong, and God, the Supreme Will of the universe, stands at his shoulder. Everything of this is visible in Robespierre at this instant. Danton can inflame, but Robespierre can freeze—and petrify. And now he does so.

"Since Citizen Brissot demands to speak, in order to blast me with his lightning bolt, I will return the compliment. I will recall, once more, the praises

showered on Dumouriez by Brissot's own journal, *The Committed Frenchman.*
And I will declare, here and now, that the first measure needful in the interests of
general defense and public safety is the investigation of all those who may be
connected in complicity with Dumouriez. In particular, Jacques-Pierre Brissot."

Rather than retaliation, the Gironde sits abruptly silent. Even farther than
Danton's, this attack has swept home and found them out. They stare back at
Robespierre, a panther in spectacles no longer remotely funny.

"Lest this seem precipitate," he continues, "I will remind this assembly of
the ventures of the Gironde. When the dawn of freedom was at hand, it was they
who opposed the removal of the king. Thereafter, they have seemed determined
to replace him with his son, the so-called dauphin. They have plunged the
country into war and sequentially attempted to wreck France by supporting, one
after another, the arch-traitors La Fayette and now Dumouriez. They have
intrigued constantly to interrupt the necessary business of this Convention with
factious squabbles. They have even gone so far as to recommend removal of half
the governing body outside Paris to the provinces, at the first hint of criticism."

Brissot is white and shows no sign of wanting, after all, to say a word. It is
Vergniaud who gets up and says, "No one's infallible. We remember Monsieur
Robespierre sought personal refuge in a cellar in times of danger. I'm rather
amazed he wants to remind us of how he proposed to run off to Marseilles.
Where were you on August tenth, Robespierre, Liberty's dawn? Did you see the
sunrise through the grill of your hiding place? And coming out, all you can call
for is blood. We—what have we done but try to restrain such calls, the famous
Jacobin blood lust? If that's what Revolution is—murder and robbery with
violence—then I'm no Revolutionary."

The personal spears are blunted and fall short. The world knows, and God
knows, Robespierre is not a coward. He stood on Martian Meadow in a hail of
bullets. He walks the streets whose shadows are full of assassins. He has told
them many times, *Kill me then. I will die for Liberty.* And he has asked again and
again, meanwhile, that the death penalty be revoked.

He steps off the rostrum, moving without haste and with enormous dignity.
The currents of the room move with him. It's difficult to take your eyes off him.
But Pétion has gone tearing to secure the rostrum for the Gironde. "All
slanderers," he cries, pointing at Robespierre's back, "must be eradicated. To
the scaffold with them!"

Robespierre turns again. He says, "Now it comes out. *Jacobin* blood lust,
robbery, murder? *We* are the ones who are to be robbed and murdered."

While David the artist, straight out of one of his own canvases, pulls open
his shirt for a hypothetical knife and cries, "Then kill me as well—I too plead
guilty to honesty and virtue."

Bringing everything stylishly back to the accustomed balance of manic uproar.

⚜

The Gironde is fighting for its political life. Since it has now taken the device of moderatism, its next target is likely to be Marat.

He's revolting, but the Mountain can't afford to lose him—his popularity on the street, his convictions, his paper.

However, the Convention has disbanded the Committee for General Defense. It reforms, with no Girondin members. Included in its ranks are, or will be, Danton, Lacroix, David, Saint-Just, Hérault de Séchelles, Robespierre. . . .

And it has a new name.

The Committee of Public Safety.

❧

There had been endless plots, obviously, to get her away, the witch-bitch at the Temple. Even Fersen the Swede had had a hand in them, from a safe distance. (The question was, if he got her out, would he want her now, this hag with baggy eyes and scrawny throat, limping about in her faded pinkish gown, her hair stuffed under a dingy cap. She'd nearly died of grief, they said, after Louis got it in the neck, and that hadn't helped her looks a bit. Neither did the prison diet, the endless insults, the sword of Damocles, commonly called execution, permanently hanging over her skull.)

The latest plan had been that she and Élisabeth should disguise themselves as men and trot out the gate with some bought clerks. The Capet kids, pretending to be children of some lamplighter and odd-job man, would trot out too. But in the end that's not going to work, is it, because Dumouriez has earned a price on his head, and Paris is oh-so-sensitive.

An inspection party from the Commune arrived one night at the Temple. The leader of this group happened to be none other than one René Hébert, renowned perpetrator of *Father Duchesne*. Once he had, at least in mixed company, been fussy and particular in his speech, but the fame of his literary gem has brought him out. A genuine republican calls a spade a spade. And a queen?

"In bed, are they? Well, tell the so-and-sos to get up again."

Antoinette and Élisabeth got up and dressed. They stood together in the bedroom while every inch of it was ransacked. Drawers were pulled from chests, bedclothes and mattresses were heaved onto the floor, and the men trudged over them in their mucky boots, so diligent was the search.

"We understand, Capette, you've got stuff hidden all over the effing place," says—guess who?—Citizen Hébert.

"As you perceive, this isn't so."

"Oh? I don't *perceive* anything of the sort. I just *perceive* we haven't found it yet. Up your skirt, maybe?"

Marie-Antoinette, *reine-jadis de France,* who has played at being a shepherdess on a well-cut meadow dotted with well-brushed sheep; who has danced till dawn, a cage of silver, with diamond and turquoise birds, built into her coiffeur—Marie-Antoinette looks far away and does not see and does not hear.

Hébert glances at the diligent searchers. "Well? What have you got?"

The men reveal they have found a red notebook, a case of pens (damaged: they've dropped it), some blotting powder, some sealing wax, and a picture of a saint praying for France (which can maybe do with it?).

"Look under the bleeding bed."

The bed doesn't bleed, but they comprehend, and under it they look and find something.

"What the hell's this?"

"It's a hat."

The men gather around the hat and regard it with suspicion. It's very large. Plainly it belonged to old Yes-Yes.

"Your late hubby's."

Antoinette pauses, nods. Her hubby. Louis XVI.

"Won't need it now, will he? No head to put it on."

The hat is taken away, along with pens, notebook, sealing wax.

The boy, the eight-year-old child, once a dauphin, isn't well, and his mother and aunt hurry him back into a remade bed. He wakes incessantly at first, saying, "Have they gone, Mama? But *have* they, Mama?" Even so young, he knows, he senses, that in some nonphysical fashion Hébert and his men are still in the room and all the vitriolic thoughts of Paris with them.

Later on, the most frightful shrieks ring through the apartment from somewhere nearby. The boy starts in his sleep but does not wake again. He's grown used to these gothic impromptus. The gatekeeper's wife, eaten alive with guilt at guarding and reviling a queen, is going round the bend. Periodically, she accosts Antoinette in the passages or on the roof, where now exercise is taken, falling on her face, pawing the tattered prisoner's gown, and screaming for mercy. "But I, madame," says Antoinette, "am at yours."

By day there is also the sound of bricklaying as an extra high wall goes up around the Temple garden.

Unable to sleep, Marie-Antoinette sits at her son's bedside and mends clothes by the light of a candle. She has entered, at thirty-nine, somewhat prematurely, the outposts of the *crise féminine*. Sometimes she hemorrhages violently. It weakens her, and frightens her a little, the sight of so much blood.

A former cobbler, Simon, who is the prison overseer and chief jailer, often comes in the early hours to serenade the Capet family from the court below. This morning he arrives and sings loudly and long, banging his bootheels on the cobbles and hitting something—possibly a hammer—on the wall.

(The woman glances at her son from time to time, but he continues to sleep, despite the noise.)

At dawn, danceless, no silver in her hair, only fallible gray, Antoinette kneels at her orisons, as always. She is very meek, very humble before God, who is testing her so sorely—she makes allowances for Him, just as she does now for her human torturers.

She knows, instinctually, she has almost reached the bottom of the staircase.

⚜

Across the river, twenty-two years old and very beautiful in her pink dress, Lucile Desmoulins rocks the cradle of her son. This child is wide awake, watching his mother attentively. Sunlight has got into the room and falls across them, making of them an idyllic representation: the Republican Ideal of Mother and Child.

Yet Lucile is not teaching Horace the Rights of Man. She sings to him very softly.

> *"But Love sees the rose*
> *Her petals unclose,*
> *Though blindfolded he.*
> *And at this fresh flower*
> *He shoots his bright power,*
> *Divine as can be.*
>
> *"The rose bursts in flame!*
> *Her jewellike frame*
> *Is lost in the smoke.*
> *What time shall be spent*
> *In ceaseless lament,*
> *To mark that day's work?"*

Horace coos and Lucile laughs.

"And aren't you properly appreciative of your mother's skills as a poetess? Unkind!"

A worry has been removed from her heart. She feels the goodness of God. From the red notebook in which she wrote them, her songs spring to her voice.

She lifts her baby out of his cradle, and they go together to the window. The streets of the city are very quiet this morning. They might be back at Queen's Market.

> *"Beware then of him,*
> *The fanciful whim*
> *Of the blindfolded sprite.*
> *And bring no fresh rose*
> *Entirely too close*
> *To Love's blazing light."*

At the window, limned by sun, rose-clad and singing of roses, Lucile does not see the staircase bottom. Or, if she ever has seen it (like some vague shadow cast far ahead, from an obstacle she cannot quite make out—a tower, a tree—and which in any case may not exist), she has drawn a thick veil over the eyes of her mind to shut it out.

Lucile, Lucile, why did you love me so much?

❧

On April 13, Jean-Paul Marat was arraigned before the Revolutionary Tribunal and a body of magistrate jurors.

He arrived in his usual mode, disheveled and odious, scarf around his forehead, reeking of vinegar, herbs, disease, and malevolence. He was fifty years of age but looked more like a loathesome child, or perhaps a gnome, as he stood there, or sat there, listening to all the charges the Girondins had succeeded in bringing against him.

But the place throbbed with the crowd, with the mob, the amoeba-beast-being of the city. It walled in Marat and poured out to him its energies. All along the route to the Tribunal it had bawled its encouragement. And now, to all he said or promised, threatened, admitted, or fantasized, the mob gave its loud approval. One was put in mind of one head of a hydra having been sent for trial by all the other heads.

To be popular, you said what they wanted—and they wanted blood. Of course they wanted it. It was the only thing anybody let them have, when you came down to it: the right to tear aristos and clergy, and finally anybody who argued, limb from limb. There was no food at affordable prices, or just no food. There was a war on, to which sons and lovers were regularly dispatched in droves, and from which sons and lovers infrequently returned. There were paper assignats, the Revolution's bonds, now worth, in popular parlance, a cicada turd. So what had they got and what could they sensibly hope to get? Only blood. And then the Gironde said, Blood's off. And Marat was the scapegoat.

Most of Paris turned out to support Marat, and when the Tribunal exonerated him—indeed, vociferously honored him—Paris went crazy.

He was carried through the Tuileries Garden, crowned by oak leaves, borne high on the shoulders of tall men. The populace had garlanded itself and carried bushes torn up along the way. The delicate flowers of spring perished in matted hair. There were banners and singing.

At the Convention there was another break-in. A man with an ax said, "Here is Marat, the People's Friend. Kill him, and you kill us all. Raise a hand against him, and we'll die defending him."

Sabers flashed. Men scrambled over benches.

They put the People's Friend on the rostrum, the honor of which pulpit had prevented Danton, a short while ago, from making a street porter's gesture at the Estuary party.

Marat spoke at some length, burning-eyed. He skinned alive any who had accused him of treason; they were the traitors. He himself—he had nothing to fear from justice, as today had demonstrated.

At the Jacobin Club, presently, it was much the same. With the massive crowds all around, forcing their way into the yard, climbing the poplar there and breaking off its branches, the Jacobins felt obliged to render an ovation, then sit quiet and allow Marat to play god for the night. They had got up a petition protesting his arraignment, though not everyone had signed it. Camille Desmoulins *had* vehemently signed. Almost simultaneously it was Camille who had named Marat the Haphazard Christ-maker—"due to his facility for causing whomsoever he approaches to exclaim, *Noli me tangere*—for Christ's sake *don't touch me!*"

It was, or would have been, full dark when the adoring mob carried Marat back over the river. But torches lit up the faces of the buildings, flared in the water, threatened everything with a penetration of light and the potential of arson.

People leaned from windows, rushed from doorways. They cried out to Marat, up on his throne of shoulders, dappled as a leopard with scabs and petals and the sparks of flambeaux.

Somewhere over there, near the Cordeliers, he addressed them. Perhaps, though, it was only his personality, his aura, which, shooting out telepathic rays, seemed to pass words into their heads.

"I'm yours. I'm part of you. Since this began I've never left your side. When the rest of them climb up on your spines to get to the soft seats and the fine coats and the good dinners, I'm still here in hell with you, starved and dirty, verminous and sick and suffering, just like you. See? I'm the living proof I've never broken faith. The sniffer-out of plots, the exterminator of the faithless. The People's Friend. Marat *is* the People."

And in their flaming eyes, by token of their upraised hands, flung garlands, they call to him, if they even know it: "Save us! Don't desert us. Don't betray us like the others. The Bastille fell, the king fell, but nothing's changed for us. We hurt and want, we always did and always shall. We'll die like rats."

"Then nip like rats, nip and gnaw like Rat Marat. Taste blood. Leave a scar on France she'll never forget. And maybe in a million years your children's children, sheltered by that cicatrice, will be able to live like men."

Is it only hate which fuels the lamp of Marat? Or is the hate, after all, the perversion, the black residue left behind by that other passion—love.

❧

And I never loved them: it—that mass of lives, that *thing* of which I was a part, which moved me to tears or scorn, enraged me with pity or contempt, lifted me in pride, cast me down in dread; which ultimately had no claim on me; to which I had never belonged.

Long, long ago, in the slums of Saint-Antoine, I'd burned for them as Marat burned. I'd sworn to die to set them free. But I saw them through a spyglass, the lens of which was myself. They *were* myself. And when I had freed myself, then, hadn't I freed them too? No? Then if I had not, I must admit, at last, it was an impossible task. I stood on shore and watched the ocean carry them away. Ashamed, I could do nothing. I'd hoped for so much, but who can dam up the sea?

It was too great, too vast. No stopping it. A boy's dream, a *good* dream, but—I'd failed, must always fail. And I didn't love them enough to carry my failure to the cross for them, to die for our sins, both theirs and mine.

And if I knew all this, which I believe I did, yet I knew none of it.

Look, I'm still fighting. Backing up Danton. Challenging the Gironde, the diehards, the enemies of Liberty. Sword in hand on the shore and the sea drawing away, softly crying, into darkness and lost night.

❋

There were three men in my path, three of the Breechless Wonders who now made up a sans-culotte army patrolling most of the city. They wore the usual short Italian jackets of their order, the candy-stripe trousers and revolutionary sash, saber untidily slung on one side of the pelvis, whatever extra armory they could land stuffed in on the other. The three-color cockades were of wool; ribbon was "aristocratic." Two of the men carried pikes. The middle man, who also had a plume in his hat, came up and handed me a letter.

I was alone, and it was late. I too was wearing the *serpent tricoleur* at my waist—it was the Cordelier fashion, which had spread to Convention and Committee. I saw the men knew me, and I said, "What's this?"

"You're Camille? For you."

"All right." I opened the letter under a streetlight. The scratchy writing was at once recognizable as Maxime's. Puzzling. You were often gifted billets-doux on the street, but from strangers. He'd been ill again and now wanted to see me. *Come at once, if you will.* But why then had the letter not been sent to our apartment in the Cordeliers, or even brought to me at the Jacobins, from which hallowed spot I had just emerged?

The men were still hanging around.

"Well," I said, "good night."

They considered me, and the messenger said, "We'll walk along with you. To the Duplays?"

"I'm not—"

"Some of Roux's Dogs are on the loose again. They're furious you Cordeliers disowned them, and anyway, they tend to be a nuisance, like, to any deputy. We'll be glad to give you an escort, citizen."

"But I'm not," I said again, "going to rouse the Duplays at this hour."

"He's expecting you."

Something in all this unnerved me. I was full of political agitation from the Jacobin Club, and tired out. I hadn't seen Maximilien since our sugar debate. This was like a summons. I'd heard the Girondin crack leveled at Robespierre once or twice: "His Revolutionary Majesty."

I tried to make my exhausted face laugh. "You've got a *lettre de cachet,* I trust? I don't have a choice, I can see. I'm dead on my feet, but if I say no, you'll carry me there physically."

So we all "laughed." The flickering lamp slid on the pikes, the watchful eyes.

I let them escort me back up Saint-Honoré and to the gate of the Duplay yard. Here they handed me over to Philippe Lebas, the betrothed of Duplay's youngest daughter, Betsi. In fact, she stood out by the sheds, shawled and a lamp in her hand, waiting on him like his torchbearer—all her demeanor showing her anxiety to have him swiftly returned. Which he ignored. Had Saint-Just been waiting with the torch, doubtless Lebas would have taken more notice; he was the Saintly Paragon's best friend and showed me up Robespierre's stair haughtily.

I could see a light under the bedroom door. I knocked and pushed the door open at one and the same time, then slammed it shut. He was sitting up in bed, looking like a corpse, with a tray of writing materials across his knees.

"This time don't thank me for coming here," I said. "Your admirers gave me very little option."

"I suspected you'd be angry. Again, you misunderstand me."

"Why didn't you come to the apartment?"

"Like this? I can hardly stand, I'm burning with fever. I'd be at the Convention otherwise."

"Fine. You never play truant like the rest of us."

"Besides . . . I'm watched, Camille. We all of us are watched. And listened to."

"Royalist spies in every shadow."

"They *are* in every shadow. But this house, I think, is safe. And the friends of the Republic are out in force tonight. Some of them will be waiting to see you to your home. You're too careless of yourself, Camille."

"Oh, I lead a charmed life. My friends have great power over the People."

"You talk as if you have none." He said, "You talk as if you were jealous of the slight influence I have. *You,* Camille, jealous of *me?* You, who have everything I haven't, and can never have."

"I'm not jealous."

"Sit down," he said.

I sat because I was tired. "What do you want, Maxime?"

"Oh, Camille," he said. "Camille."

"Oh, Camille, Camille, what?"

"Is this all friendship is to you, then? So tenuous a substance a few harsh words can destroy it?"

He made me very uncomfortable. I muttered something about that being nonsense, got up again, and stood at the window. It was so quiet outside that soon I heard a rat scuttling in the yard. Robespierre's dog heard this, too. As if sleepwalking, it padded to the door, glancing back at him for permission. He waved a listless hand, and the dog, disappointed, lay down again.

"And yet," said Robespierre to me, "you're mourning too, your heart's crying out for this thing we began that we see now dying in our arms."

"We can *fight*," I said violently to the window. "We can fight till the sword's cut from our hands."

The dog growled. It wanted to go after rats so badly. I crossed to the door impatiently and let it out.

He seemed not to notice. He was sitting forward. "*Good,*" he said, in the vibrant voice that he sometimes found at the Convention, or the Jacobins. "Thank God. I thought we'd lost you."

I looked back at him and saw he had come alive now. The dead white face glowed, and the eyes were black. I thought, He'll really kill himself at this rate. And looked away again.

"Listen to me, Camille. You're hearing me now, at last. There are great dangers all around us. But the greatest danger is the Gironde."

"They're rubbish."

"Don't underestimate them. They've failed. But how many times does a viper strike? How many times do you ignore its venom because the stroke has missed?"

"Then let's throw them out," I said. "It shouldn't be so hard."

"Turn your mind to it," he said. "It needn't be."

Then I did look at him.

After a moment he shifted and drew out a packet from among the pillows behind his shoulders. "You'll need to read these papers. Will you do it here?"

"What are they?"

"Evidence it's taken some while to gather. Items which, put to the right use, will totally discredit Brissot and his party."

"The right use?"

"You know me," he said. "You've known me since we were boys. You know we're fighting for the same thing. Don't doubt me."

I took the papers out of his hand and put them on the desk. I lit candles there, sat down, and read fairly perfunctorily. My head was reeling inside five minutes.

"It's as bad as this?"

He didn't answer me; I didn't wait for an answer but read on. All Paris knew Orléans's son had run with Dumouriez. There were already tales he had done so mostly out of horror at Jacobin plans for a dictatorship, and because of a proud recital Danton had made him, when drunk, of the revels of September '92. These other matters seemed to attend in logical progression. Many of us had been forewarning of conspiracies. No surprise. The information ran in circles. This one had seen this, and that one learned that. Monsieur A had been apprehended in the reception of cash and confessed, which corroborated what Monsieur B had previously babbled en route to La Force. There was nothing colossal and nothing wholesome. It was like wading in a sewer.

If only one quarter was a fact—

I pushed the papers away in disgust.

"The worst of it is," he murmured, "these men have been our comrades, our friends. But corruption—you see how they go to work. The People starve, but when an attempt is made by the Left to control the price of corn, the Gironde has the motion taken from the agenda. Then they have had themselves formed into a commission—twelve of their members—to sit in judgment on every Jacobin. You guess what they'll do? They've failed with Marat. The next target is Hébert."

"A good thing," I said. My head continued to spin. I needed to employ the vitality unleashed in me. Anger would do.

"Oh, yes," he said faintly. "Hébert is a wretch, his paper an obscenity. But, like Marat, he belongs to the Mountain. At this time, a threat to any one of us is a threat to all, and to everything we've striven for. You've heard Vergniaud's threats—that if the Gironde is insulted further, they'll call their pet provinces to Paris and overthrow the Convention entire?"

"Ludicrous!"

"Are you so sure, now you've read those papers? Oh, Camille. You were more perceptive than any of us. You saw through Brissot when the rest of us were blinded. And you were right, there can be no loyalties before our loyalty to mankind." He sighed. "Then again, despite these proofs of their activities, it's difficult to make it stand. We can't afford a black comedy for the Mountain such as the Gironde brought on itself in the tussle with Marat."

"Well," I said.

"You," he said. "Make a lawyer's case of it."

"They need to be hanged, everyone of them," I said, in a sudden stifling-hot anger that drove me up from his desk and almost knocked all the candles flying.

"You'll do it," he said.

"I've written anything that I felt needed to be put into circulation. You nn-know that."

"But this."

"I'll do—I'll do what I can."

"I have vast confidence in your abilities," he said. "I told you this once before."

"Don't flatter me."

"The truth, only the truth. Your writing has made a record for history of everything we've achieved, or tried to achieve, and of every wickedness sent against us. You speak out, and the innocent are rescued. The guilty tremble. Louis Orléans—"

"I've written as I was asked to, and as it seemed vital t-to do."

"You were always our voice, Camille, a voice speaking through ink that will outlive all the speeches. The Revolution's word, seared in tablets of stone by your pen."

I'd loved praise all my life, most of my life having been starved of it. And now it frightened me. (But not enough.)

"It's this," I said frantically, "all th-this in the way: Brissot—traitors—sl-sold out at every step—yes, I'll make a case of it."

Unaware of how near I'd been magnetized toward him, I started in my skin when he caught my wrist. "You must *never*," he said to me, "lose heart in what we believe. Never lose sight of the Ideal. It's all too easy: the weakness of the body, the frailty of hope. But we must fight, as you said, to the last drop of blood, till the sword is cut from our hands."

Dying gladly for such a cause as this, if to write in our blood at the last: *France is set free.*

The dog scratched on the door, and I let it in to present a dead rat to Robespierre, who turned away in nausea.

I took my leave of him hurriedly and chased the animal with its prize back into the yard.

Walking home, my allotted sans-culotte escort tailed me respectfully.

The streets, the bridge, the streets. The indigo sky with no moon. In battle, to fight the unseen is unthinkable. The invisible must be revealed; the enemy must have a face and a name.

❦

Danton, coming across Camille in the black back of the café, sat himself down and said, "I gather you saw Well-dressed Peter. Are you going to do it?"

"Do what?"

"Oh, come on," said Danton.

"Let me hazard," said Camille. "An English spy followed me. You, being in the pay of England, are also in on the act."

"No. I had it from Maxime. It's been discussed in several quarters. He said to me, Do you think he'll do it? Meaning you."

"Did you say he would?"

"I told him you were breaking your heart to watch Brissot and Company whipped through Paris sewn in donkey hides."

"I take it you've seen the evidence against them?"

"Oh, hush. Walls have ears, look how I shake. What evidence? That trumped-up muddle? It'll do. Good enough to usher them out of the Convention."

"You're telling me it isn't—"

"*Quid est veritas?*"

"They're in the counterrevolution up to their ears. Haven't you heard? They have half Normandy in arms."

"Ah. I'm so glad. Not *il gran rifiuto?* You had me worried." Sitting there, Danton began to sing some old, faintly familiar song:

> *"If the King gave to me*
> *Paris, his great citee,*
> *But it was needful for me*
> *To leave my sweet lovelee,*
> *I'd say to King Henree,*
> *Go stuff Paree!"*

He sang quite well, not so well as he had.

"You're in a jolly mood."

"I can't go on being Black-browed Anguish forever. I'll leave that to you."

"Louise waiting up for you?"

Danton balked a touch. "She's keeping an eye on the boys."

"Have you had her yet?" said Camille. "Or should I say, Has she had you?"

But Danton had decided to be unruffled. "Not yet, alas. She's very young. I think she'll want marrying, first. No, it isn't just that. My sons need a mother. And I need a woman in the house. I need a *home* to go back to at night. Don't grudge me a little comfort. How's Lucile?"

"We were wrong."

"You're always panicking she's pregnant. This is the fourth time this year. What about the wonderful invention from England, the English Overcoat? Or is it a fact the bloody things always break?"

Although he sings and jests, Danton doesn't seem so well. Heavy and inert, his mane falling over his face, which has added to its injurious scars others of pain and trouble. He looks old again. But they are all older than they were four years ago. Even Camille, the Dionysian faun who never grows up, the terrible infant of the Revolution, has thickened a little, if almost imperceptibly, at the waist, while under the brilliant eyes the skin hollows, pressed in like wax against the bones. When writing now, he mostly puts on wire-rimmed spectacles. He is just thirty-three, half a year younger than Danton, two years the junior of Maximilien Robespierre. Brissot is five years older than Camille but has somewhat less of a future.

NINE

❧ ❧ ❧

1793: Early Summer

THE HISTORY OF THE BRISSOT FACTION

A fragment of the Secret Annals of the Revolution: Concerning the Orléans
Game and the Committee for Anglo-Prussian Cooperation

Is it that vermin are an Undying Species?

What a beginning we had! How jealous the world must have been of us.

That climax of sixty-five despotisms — Louis XVI — brought to justice as the
Nation's prisoner; the ruins of avarice and monarchy everywhere, ready to provide
the material for our constitution; ninety thousand Prussians and Austrians halted by
seventeen thousand Frenchmen; God, even, on our side, smiting the enemy with
sickness until the proud Prussian king was harried by our troops to a standstill;
Belgium, Holland, England, Ireland (and half of Germany) leaning toward our
cause and openly wishing us success: So things stood at the beginning. Our task: a
French Republic, to lift Paris from the mud, to quell Europe, and — why not? —
perhaps to free it in turn from its tyrants. While to the French people, sold as slaves
before their birth, were to be awarded those rights that are the due of every human
thing. This was the Divine Call which fired us. Who could hear it with a cold and
miserly heart? Several, it would seem.

Who were they, then? Who, these enemies of our Republic, the men who
would bring us down?

High time they were exposed to our vengeance.

It falls to me to draft their indictment.

A few days ago, at the Convention, Jérôme Pétion was grieving, as follows:
"What's the use of refuting slander? One answers from the tribune, but the day after,
the lies are back on the streets. When is someone going to have the courage to write
out a coherent list of complaints, so we can reply to them?"

315

Well, Pétion, I am going to make you very happy, and all your dear friends with you. Here is the list you asked for. Let's see you answer it.

As long ago as 1791, I myself made a speech at the Assembly in which I pointed out one sinister and alarming aspect of our condition, which was this: To some extent our Revolution had been organized by interested elements in England in collusion with certain of the French nobility. Its object was but too apparent: to bring down the figurehead and replace it with another, to the mutual benefit of the conspirators at home and abroad. I can still recall the starts of guilty horror from such members as Sillery. I did not then press the matter. The Revolution was in its infancy—it was not the hour. But I was determined to show such gentlemen that those of us who truly cared for French freedom were aware of those of us who did not. Invite us to their homes and parade before us as they might their musical wives and dancing daughters, we still kept some attention for their politics.

For heaven's sake, no one could convince me that, standing on that table, when I called the city to arms, it was *my* eloquence that half an hour later dredged up from hell, along with the waxwork of Necker, that of Orléans.

Orléans, Brissot—Brissot, at one time secretary to Sillery's wife. It was Brissot who devised the infamous charter which drove the People onto the Champ-de-Mars that July of '91, and so into the bullet storm of La Fayette's soldiers. It was Brissot who wrote at La Fayette's direction. Those who say Danton is to blame are grossly mistaken; he had no part in the affair. So Orléans, Brissot, La Fayette—all in the game together, surprising as such a polygamous marriage may seem.

And meanwhile we have Pétion returning from a mysterious trip to London, in the sleeping carriage of Madame Sillery and her daughters—the Three Graces indeed—who perhaps tickled, en route, his incorruptible and virtuous . . . knee. And no sooner was Pétion back in Paris than he was made mayor

Can Pétion, with his wish for a list, really suppose I have forgotten those dinners I was invited to at Sillery's house three years back, when I was thought "safe"? So many Republicans sat down there, but strangely they never asked Robespierre, who even then the streets had titled Incorruptible.

But I see I make myself suspect, admitting the company I kept at that time. Frankly, in those days, Republicans were so sparse on the ground, one felt obliged to frequent any gathering that seemed to cherish the common aim. At the same moment, one kept alert and so discovered things. For example, for a long while I even thought Orléans opposed to La Fayette. (I had not then discovered Brissot was their go-between, whom they used, as the lovers Pyramus and Thisbe used the hole in the wall, to whisper through.) I woke up when I learned of a proposed marriage between La Fayette's son and Sillery's granddaughter. There was, too, one choice evening, when Sillery, despite his stiffened joints, had himself chalked the dancing floor. Madame Sillery regaled us, to the accompaniment of that harp of hers, with a song praising the "roving eye." Then came a dance by the daughters, who might have given lessons to Salome—though in this instance if only one severed head would be required for the platter is moot. I had made up my mind to be ice and suffer the same ecstasy of temptation as Saint Antonius. But at the height of the experience (when the Sorceress had, I confess, turned some of the ice to boiling water), the door flew open on our mystery. Who should walk in upon the very private scene, nodding and winking at me and very much at home, but a close associate of La Fayette?

The marvel is that, like the Silver Virgin of Saint-Sulpice, our statue of Liberty has been made from chamber pots. We began with a Tyranny; that we threw down. We progressed through a corrupted Ministry and Assembly in the grip of all the Neckers, Mirabeaus, Rolands. Thereafter we have weathered the plotting of the Pétions, Buzots, and the Brissites—that tribe of Brissot, who is their genius. The fierce determination of the People Militant is freeing us, at last, for a more dedicated regime in the charge of a Danton and a Robespierre.

Now suspect and no longer invited to dinner, I have watched mine host Sillery at the Jacobins (where we have had proposals from that side for the Duke of York as our king!) or over in the war zone with Dumouriez, at meetings with officers of the Prussians.

The Royalist Theater Company meanwhile kept busy making and breaking reputations. In this way Roland has been billed as the modern Cicero—Roland, such an excellent writer that his ministerial correspondence had, on every occasion, to be rewritten by secretaries. Brissot was stagily cursed by an English government now our enemy. As someone said three thousand years ago, No one can help you better than a friend posing as a foe, no one destroy you more quickly than the enemy who comes disguised as your friend.

For four years I have seen fine reputations slung in the gutter and others lifted from the muck and made to shine. And all the while the Anglo-Prussian Gentleman's Club yowls for the heads of Danton, Marat, and Robespierre.

From this volcanic upheaval, the Mountain has been formed. And it is at the Mountain, which has continuously asked the death penalty for any putting forward a king, that these charges of royalism have been cast.

Brissot and his aristocrat friends have been hounding us from the start, to punish us for pulling down the monarchy. And with their London visits and their sleeping carriages, they have wriggled onto every manner of committee, into every key position, and so set at the head of our armies such as Dumouriez, Biron, and La Touche (who has still a command—which, as I informed him, astounds me).

There has altogether been so much double-faced lying that it has become a grim sort of game. Philippe-Égalité himself would come and honor me by sitting at my side on the Mountain benches, thanking me before my colleagues for my "help" in ticking him off from the tribune. Sometimes we could not resist reviling Sillery to Philippe, to see how far this chameleon would go in blackguarding his friend, and to our fascination he would go farther than we. So it is a wonder Sillery's burning ears did not set fire to his hair powder. Though Philippe voted so often with the radicals I baptized him "Robespierre Forever," he was basically neutral, easily led. Sillery led him into the clouds in a royalist balloon, but Philippe would keep getting airsick and wanting to come down.

I should say here that royalists and Orléanists infest not only the right-hand benches but also the "noncommitted" Center.

We should, it seems, have planned the structure of our Convention better, but who could think such frigid Austrian souls would wash in on the crest of Revolution? We were full of hope—and it seems it is after all hope, not love, which is blind.

But the scales fall from one's eyes and one sees—and hears—the Brissites, who six months before demanded total war to "liberate" Europe, shouting, Who gives a fig for the Dutch masses? Their cheese-selling bondage is no concern of ours. I can remember Brissot, too, who screamed for the war of liberation, saying that our defeat and retreat in Belgium was "fine"; it would lead to "peace."

Does it not seem slightly incredible that the army which had smashed and routed the Prussians could not then cut off their retreat? Half the enemy's troops were down with dysentery—it was carrying half its men on litters! While the French battalions had swelled from seventeen to a hundred thousand men. But any soldiers from the French vanguard will tell you what happened. "When the Prussians pulled up, we were pulled up. When they went right we got sent left. When they went over the bridge, we went through the effing river." Rather than pursuing the king of Prussia, Dumouriez was seeing him home. And there was no soldier in our armies who did not know there had been an agreement between the enemy and powerful elements of the Convention.

Of course, one of Brissot's confrères has announced that he noted Dumouriez at the opera with Danton. At that time Dumouriez made a point of being seen with Danton. One does not, however, plot during the performance; that comes afterward. Quite a number of persons saw that it was Brissot's carriage Dumouriez subsequently got into, all the while whistling the most catchy aria.

(Brissot, in his latest literary work—which he had distributed at the Convention—denies all relationship with generals and calls Dumouriez a "despicable intriguer." But is it sensible to trust Brissot? In the same issue he tells us no one could name six people who had acquired positions through his favor. But the following letter was found at Roland's. It said, *My dear Roland, I enclose a list of those you should help. Give a position to no one who is not on this list. J.-P. Brissot.* But the favorite sport for the Brissites at this time is digging up the corpses of September 1792, laying exaggerations and tragedy at our door and so getting all France a bad name. Yet it was Brissot who was so anxious that some personal enemy of his had been overlooked in the prison massacres that he was heard to remark, much peeved, "Hell! Those pikers have forgotten old so-and-so.")

But Pétion, I must remember, wants facts.

Is it not a fact that the treasurer of the Prussian king has the following entry in his account books: *6 million écus for bribes to the French?*

Isn't it a fact that various Brissites have a lot of money—even if, like Roland, they dress like scarecrows?

Fact, that Pétion, when mayor, had thirty thousand francs a month coming in?

Fact, that royalists have always clustered around Pétion like wasps around something they find to their taste?

Fact, that the Gironde knew the white cockade was vaunted in the west but gave no warning until the Vendée went up in flames?

Royalism has been a curse upon Paris, and that *is* a fact.

The men of the Right stand at the tribune and declare, How I hate these maniacs who would soil Paris with blood! Then go home to dinner and talk of pulling Paris apart stone by stone in order to be rid of the Left. They squeal that the Left will impose a dictator on us all. But who was it but Danton who demanded the supreme penalty for anyone suggesting a dictator, or even a triumvirate?

But let's get back to the facts.

For a fact, in the first days of the Convention, the Republican party was paralyzed and could do nothing to help the People. When we could not be kept from the tribune by presidents sympathetic to the Right, they would form up three lines deep and *fight* us off with fists, sticks, even swords. I, for one (examine my newspapers and tell me, please, if you find anything counterrevolutionary in any of them), tried to get a hearing and was pushed away.

While this went on, forty-eight of the Paris sections asked for the expulsion of such men as Lasource. These cries were smothered. If, though, you made anti-Jacobin noises and toasted Austria, next Thursday you would be president.

Finally, I arrive at Roland, who, when I told him I did not trust him, replied, "*That* for your trust." When his papers (which unfortunately Madame Roland had had a chance to "tidy") were investigated, we did find among his financial accounts many "secret expenses." So secret, actually, that though one could see the money had gone, one could not tell on what.

But then it was Roland who, after August tenth, plastered our walls with warnings and wrote us letters as "An Englishman" telling us we were now under the rule of Jacobin tyrants. While he accumulated his millions for those "secret expenses" of his, he placed pet deputies where they would do the most good (harm). One charming tactic of this branch of the Brissites was, if unable to silence Robespierre in the Convention legitimately, to make extraordinary faces at him to throw him out of stride. Robespierre is not so easily put off. But it shows what a strange creature a Brissite is. (One should not exterminate such reptiles. One day, when all Brissites have vanished from the earth, people should be able to see what the thing looked like. Therefore, we must stuff it and put it in the Museum of Natural History.)

Brissot told us poor Roland was so penniless he lived on loans. But it has occurred to me that the virtuous Patriarch (as his wife's gentleman friends like to call him) was the very being who had the diamonds burgled from the National Archives. Although the apparent thieves were taken in the act, no jewels were recovered. Plainly there had been a previous foray, and these wretched devils were the scapegoats. If the diamonds went to Roland, I am sure he Brissoted them about very ably, buying up whole sections of the army and all the monarchists for miles around.

I have left out a lot of *facts*. Never mind, I have filled the canvas.

These are the men who called us "royalists" while they plotted with the aristocracy. Called us "agitators" while they agitated to bring back the king and sell

France to Prussia. Called us "murderers" while they plunged the country in wars both foreign and civil. And "bandits" as they burgled the Archives.

I will pause here to mention, too, that on the eve of the king's trial, Barbaroux (an Antinous for sure!) tried to persuade the Marseilles regiment to attack the Convention, killing, if able, all the deputies of the Mountain.

Will you wonder if I exclaim that, in the matter of the Brissot tribe, the Committee of Public Safety is too lenient?

And yet, despite all this, *still* I foresee a day when courage will bring us to a free Republic.

The Convention has been purged and purged again. At the next purge, conceivably Liberty may triumph (particularly since there are no more diamonds to steal!).

The Convention devotes too much time to speeches, not enough to ability. It needs fewer sessions. And no deputy can be penalized for silence; we are working also when we think. But whatever blunders have been made, we have tried to achieve a sublime ideal — which, even if we go down, will remain as our glorious monument. For the seed of this colossal growth, this thing both bloom and cancer, was the desire to set free the human race. There is poison in our veins now, but eject the Brissot faction and the body of the Convention, though rent, will be sound once more.

There is so much to do.

With proper primary education, had we been permitted to introduce it, the priests — to whom tuition of the young has been left — could not have gone on filling their brains with a murk of superstition incredible in the light of the eighteenth century. Enlightened, the Vendée would hardly now be fighting as it is.

Let us bring the sea to Paris — and with that sea, every land of the world, so we may show them that, far from ruin a city, a Republic will cause her to flower and to flourish as did those republican cities of the ancient earth: Athens, Tyre, Carthage, Rhodes.

There is the dream, still. Why must something beautiful and good be deemed impossible? As Plato said, if a painter set before you a portrait of a girl so lovely you felt she could not exist, would you throw out the painting on these grounds?

Paris, who took her name from that fabled perfection of a city, the peerless Ys, and who dared to call herself the Match of Ys, Parys — why should not Paris be the New Rome, the New Athens, of tomorrow?

Let us forget the diehards who carp and groan that Paris was not fitted to be a Republic. Let us remember Plato's beautiful lady who is not to be found — and *seek* her.

For it is this dream of the Republic, I believe, which will bring to France what all her kings have promised her and never managed: That summer day of the future when there shall be honey and roses for everyone.

May 19, 1793

2nd Year of the Republic

One and Indivisible

❉

I paraphrase, I elide. . . . My memory is full of it. I recall I laughed as I wrote some of those sentences. It was not until it filled the streets my heart turned cold, and then I warmed myself at the last lines of it and assured myself I had spoken well.

❉

It sold. Because of the expertise of the language or in spite of it. First editions were bought second-hand and tenth-hand. Précis were made of it and also bought under the counter. Copies flooded the capital from the spark-flying white-hot pestle-and-mortar presses. Bales of the baleful work were circulated through suburbs and hinterlands and sown deep in the groaning furrows of France's armies of freedom.

Everyone knew about the pamphlet all of seventy-eight pages long. Those who had not read it had read bits of it, or had all or bits read to them. Those who had not read it still learned the content, and some others learned chunks of it by heart. A section or so was set to music: *Silleryette, with her harp made blush / Patriots upon the plush / Of her very lewd settee.*

Aside from the pranks and convolutions of the text, the strength of the idea lay in its utter simplicity. Its appeal to the human dilemma was fiendish. What has gone wrong? *This.* And none of it is your fault. Conversely, since someone is to blame, look over *there.*

❉

"I must say I found it a fairly unbeautiful performance, yes."

"Hérault," said Danton, "we love you, but stop acting like an aristo."

"Oh? Is that what I'm doing? I thought I was suffering from a revulsion of Liberty."

"Whose?"

"Everybody's, actually, as signalized in the Convention."

"Oh, dear. A metaphysical point."

Hérault shrugged. Despite the episode to which he had been referring he remained, as ever, lustrously unruffled. Only the slight frown, the fastidious refusal, so far, to play cards or contemplate the parades of gorgeous women passing up and down the long painted room, gave evidence of his displeasure.

"He means the sanctity of the Convention," said Lacroix. "If it can happen once, it can happen any time. We could all end up—"

"But we won't," said Danton.

At the beginning of May, sick and tired of the limited facilities of the Manège and additionally aggravated by the constant invasions of the mob—the Mob Militant demanding nonexistent food, the Mob Victorious with Marat on its shoulders, or merely the Mob Noisy, fed up with waiting—the Convention had voted itself over to the Tuileries Theater and so relinquished the noble name of Stable.

The theater was reckoned less accessible. Certainly, it was gracious. Its round-topped arches and oblong alcoves, divided vertically by carved persons with upraised arms, horizontally by slender architectural bands, had overseen a different sort of drama in the past but proved adaptable. Reconstructions now rested the upper gallery, rather in the manner of the Philistine temple, on one solitary beam. Who would play Samson and bring it crashing down upon the worshipers of false gods?

Neither biblical allusion nor placement, however, did keep the mob out of it in the end.

It had been ready, of course, the anguished populace, but something touched off the powder. Something it claimed was called "l'Histoire des Brissotins—or, the Second Unveiling of Brissot."

"You know what the devils are doing? They're selling us out to the English."

That makes sense. The English *are* sailing up on all the western ports, and Toulon's in a real fix. And there's the Vendée and these revolts in Normandy. Then the royalists are taking over in Lyons—they've threatened to hang anything Republican. Spain's getting ready to come over the mountains and dine in France, and Prussia is having a hilarious time herding our generals along the borders again. And we're hungry.

"He says it's been going on since the Bastille came down. The Revolution's start was its *finish*. Because every step we've taken, they've had a wire around our ankles, pulling us this way, then that. Never letting us get too far."

It stands to reason. All we've done and been through—the result should be better. So something's been stopping us. *Them.*

Which was, Camille, the cleverest argument. We've suffered so much, why aren't we there? *They* held us back.

The Gironde. Let's get the bastards.

It started on Friday but lacked support. (You lost wages if you didn't work on a weekday, and everything cost enough as it was, if you could even get it.) Sunday was mostly still idle, even if it wasn't godly. So on Sunday the great mob beast of Paris went storming through the gardens, across to the Tuileries Theater, and pulled up there behind an enormous squadron of supportive People's National Guard, plus fifty operative cannon.

"It's a Jacobin plot," said the Gironde.

"Come out!" screamed the mob.

"If those cannon go off we'll all be in a mess," said various deputies on every side of the house.

Presently the regulation mob delegation entered the hall and demanded Justice.

"You have, sitting on these benches, criminals. Give them to us."

The Estuary burst its banks.

Lanjuinais pounds to the rostrum. "This is a disgrace! We are the elected representatives of the People."

"Not anymore!" comes from the public gallery, with a hail of crumpled papers, among which are no inclusions from *The History of the Brissot Faction*. Precious stuff that, selling twelfth-hand, not to be thrown.

And "Get off! Come down!" the Mountaineers sociably yell.

"Is free speech dead in this hall, then?" cries Lanjuinais. Apparently so.

He is dragged from the rostrum by Mountain enthusiasts.

There is voiced a suggestion that, things standing as they do, the Girondins should resign their office.

Barbaroux (Manon's "Antinous"), opens his handsome mouth and shouts, "People write to me every day and thank me for the service I do France. Resign? I'll die at my post rather than leave my country to a Jacobin dictatorship!"

Uproar, pandemonium, imbroglio.

A party of deputies from the nonaffiliate Marsh get up and march out. Five minutes later they return. They have been set on, smacked, punched, their clothes torn, and chased back in, vociferous with fright and fury.

Hérault de Séchelles happens to be president of the Convention on this historic day. He regards the mayhem rather languidly, but his tone is decided. "No, this won't do," he says. He manages to silence his colleagues. "Gentlemen, this body is not subject to the rule of intimidation. We are the People's servant, but not its slave. We will leave en masse."

Outside, in Carousel Place, it seems the whole city is ranged against them. Not a few Jacobins turn pale. You strike a match for a nice warm fire and the whole room goes up in flames.

Hérault behaves gallantly. More, he makes a beautiful spectacle of it (David, get your sketchbook, quick). Hérault goes over to the phalanx of horsemen heading the National Guard. Gesturing with an elegant arm, the other elegantly relaxed at his side, Hérault says, "What do you want?"

"To get something seen to."

"This isn't the way, my friend."

"Don't 'friend' me. You're no friend to us, citizen, if you don't hand over the traitors to us here and now."

"Which traitors are these?"

The gentleman on the horse spits on the ground.

Hérault regards the lucky patch of ground. He adjusts his laundered cuffs. No, Hérault. Wrong.

"It seems to me the only traitors involved here are those trying to harm the authority of the Convention, which, you'll recollect, is a legal body maintained by the wish of the People."

"Bullshit."

"Can it be you are a rebel against the wish of the People?" Hérault looks at the rest of the phalanx. "Don't you arrest rebels?"

But no one moves, and the leader says, "Do you happen to notice, monsieur, we've got a couple of cannon along?" He turns in the saddle toward the battalion of National Guardsmen and booms at the top of considerable lungs, "*Get ready to fire!*"

Hérault appears distracted, with distaste rather than alarm. But since the rest of the Convention is now scuttering back into the theater as fast as its legs can carry it, Hérault can only stroll in after.

A few of the more violent Jacobins pause outside, to shake hands with the people and applaud their vigor. And Marat, recognized, stays to be fêted again.

❀

"Nasty," says Danton to Hérault now, in the Salle Doré. "Hébert's tribe were behind most of it, obviously. He and that excremental paper of his have a lot of influence in the slums. Of course we know what happened thereafter, there being so slight a choice."

"An order passed for the arrest of over twenty Girondins, the names of whom Marat insisted on reading out in that tiresomely squeaky voice."

"Camille'll be thrilled," says Lacroix, though his eyes have wandered; he's getting rather thrilled himself by a girl with blue plumes in her hair and nearly bare-breasted, who has now oozed past his divan seven times. "Camille's . . . languishing to watch Brissot in chains in some public spot and the crowd chucking rotten fruit at him."

"Where can they buy fruit, rotten or otherwise?" inquires Hérault.

Lacroix rises, in one or two contexts. (The young woman seems to have lost something down her neckline; maybe he should offer to find it.) Exit.

"So the Brissot clan is out of the Convention," recaps Danton, "but the arrests are in abeyance."

"The popular term is, They're being surveyed."

"Surveillance, then. Good. Soon we'll reach the stage of pardon, followed by shuffling them off to obscurity."

"You forget. Not just Hébert; Robespierre also wants the Gironde out of the way."

Danton drank down his glass like medicine. "Did you buy those shares, as I advised you?"

"I nearly always do," said Hérault.

"Well, it works, doesn't it? Thank God. Money. A comforting thought."

"Even so, you're not participating tonight?"

"As you may have heard, I've got my eye on something fresher."

"The Gély madonna. Yes. You've made poor Camille very jealous. He thought you were going to marry him."

"Oh, Camille. He's a child."

"Who has learned his letters and now papers the world with pamphlets."

"A clever precocious child. No, Camille's all right."

"I will say, he uses the language exquisitely. In quieter times, France may find a notable dramatist there. I become so entranced by the wordplay, of course, I overlook what he's saying. (I wonder if Camille ever does that himself?) Then again, the theatrical emphasis is nearly always excellent. But perhaps he hasn't quite the sense of structure to make another Molière."

"Molière? Camille?" Danton laughs with enjoyment at the notion; Hérault shrugs again. "I'll tell him you said so. He'll collapse at your feet. Don't in turn tell him I called him a child. He hates that, as any child would. And speaking of children, I must go home. Look at those little harlots. Yes, those. How enlivening. But no. No weakness. Good night. And remember, don't mention to Camille—"

But I heard you, Danton, I heard it in your voice. Your exasperation, your affection, both had it. A clever child, who could precociously form words, drunk on the contents of an inkwell, striking flints to make a spark, playing with the pretty white-hot fire. But to burn is not to answer.

❧

Let us turn our eyes from such horrors. . . .

Let's rest our eyes on something pleasing.

Sophie-Louise Gély.

Sweet sixteen and never been kissed. Lily skin, silky hair. Knowing eyes. But knowing what? One thinks of those girls that their mothers wind up continuously, from a certain age, like clocks, to keep a certain time and strike a certain way at a certain hour. And the hour that this one chimed was *Georges Danton.*

There was a dinner party at the Gélys, one floor up from Danton's rooms. They had quarrelsome domestics, but the food wasn't bad. The set piece was Louise.

She played an Italian guitar with the serious attention of a child who has got her lesson perfectly and expects candy as a reward. She will of course then say, Oh, but I *never* expected candy, Papa! She looked very pretty, playing, transposing, singing in a light thin trill, candle shine on her ringlets and in her eyes, which she only occasionally raised to meet Danton's, for a glimmering instant, at the end of each recital. *Oh, but I never expected. . . .* His applause was hearty. So she rendered an encore.

> *Mon vainqueur encore*
> *Aujourd'hui ignore*
> *De mon coeur le Funest esclavage.*

Stretching a point, and rather risqué, but from an opera. It worked where it was meant to.

Fabre, who had not been allowed to bring his mistress, was also enchanted. He told Sophie-Louise he would create a sonnet for her to set to music (she improvised and composed too, naturally). She flirted demurely with Fabre, with me, with almost every man in the room, including her father. She did not flirt with Danton. She took Danton seriously.

And he, when he sat by her, became a boy. He looked ten years younger consistently, and often twenty years younger, which made him fourteen years old and so two years her junior.

"But did you truly see the coronation?" she had murmured. She had pretensions, even in our day and age of glorious republican *sans rois,* to the aristocratic nuance.

"I truly did. I ran off from school for a few days to do it."

"But weren't you beaten? How brave."

"I used to be brave in those days."

Le père Gély laughed. "Listen to him. Oh, monsieur. 'Used to be'!"

Louise didn't say to Danton, You are of course the bravest and most daring man in France. Her eyes said, You know what I'm not saying to you. She pressed him for details of Capet's crowning (and he gave them), there in this roomful of men who had voted for Capet's decapitation. Innocent infant. What could she possibly know of the guillotine, the war, bloody September?

When he told her white doves had been let free from their cages in the cathedral, she said, "How lovely."

"You'd have been sorry for them," he said. "Their freedom turned out something of a fraud, trapped between four walls and a sky of stone, no air, no food, not even the moss to make a nest."

Fabre, who was also determined to be a charming child tonight, said, "Oh, I expect they made nests from the priests' tonsure clippings, and lived off the Host, and sipped the holy wine and blessed water. And when they perished, being so sanctified, each dear little dove soul went straight to heaven."

"But birds don't have souls," said Sophie-Louise primly. She was yet a Catholic. With almost every church in Paris defaced, the Gély family still found somewhere to kneel and pray and made no great secret of it to us.

"By a process of ordinary logic," I said, "if one type of living thing possesses a soul, why not every type of living thing?"

"Oh, but—" said Louise. She looked at her father.

He said to me, on her behalf, "But the beast is the inferior of man and was put here to serve his needs."

"Or conceivably it was the other way about, but we have accidentally got the upper hand."

Danton laughed. The Gélys were flustered. Madame Gély said, not looking at me, "But it's a pleasure to hear Monsieur Desmoulins admit to the truth of the soul."

Danton said, "You can always rely on Camille to admit to that. Just as you can generally rely on a contra-suggestive argument from him at a certain juncture in the evening."

Fabre said, "If anything has a soul, a bird has one. Besides, they have wings and could fly straight into heaven regardless. Picture old Peter in his nightgown, fumbling about, hopping mad and yelling, No birds allowed! And the birds streaming in over the top of the gates."

Now it was Lucile who exclaimed, "How lovely!"

The Gélys had passed from fluster to disapproval.

"Something that will amuse you," Danton said to me later. "I'm to go to confession."

"I'm amused. You're setting aside a month for it, or do you intend to keep a few things back?"

"It's in the bill of sale," he said.

"I realized that."

"Gély's scared of me, but he wants his rights. He can't marry off his girl to a godless lout."

"He'll be doing that whether or not you perform an act of contrition."

"Thank you, my dear friend."

"Any time. Where will you find a priest? You're taking a trip to Rome?"

"It transpires they can dig one out of the woodwork for me."

"They're not afraid, then, you'll betray everybody to our Tribunal for counterrevolutionary activities?"

"That's not so funny. Try to forget I told you any of this."

"I think you're mad. I'll be glad to forget you are doing it."

"That's typical. A dedicated pagan is always less tolerant than an honest nonbeliever. But you're right, in fact. This is the old thing again, isn't it: kowtow to the father, ogle the mother—get the girl."

I had been thinking that too. Thinking back with the oddest sense of a scene revisited, to that bridge over the river when he had given me his advice as regards Lucile. I'd been afraid of him in those days. Afraid *for* him now, though not precisely at this moment. Yet it was curious. For him to advise me in such matters, skeptically and with such adroitness; one took that to be in the scheme of things. But for him to play the same moves himself, like a lovelorn swain of twenty—it seemed a part of everything else out of kilter. I made some bad joke about whether or not he was in fit shape for a wedding. He countered with some crack or other, and it got back to God.

"There are times I wished I did believe in something. When I was a boy, the ritual, the music—all that made me want to believe. But I can't be as nearsighted as all that. She does, of course. Believes in God."

"Does she?" I bet she flirts with Him too.

"Well, look at her. So young and untouched."

The effect of a virginity, physical and spiritual, upon the libertine—I had had experience of the power of that myself. Yet, while there are some women who remain eternally, in some unfathomable fashion, daughters of Diana-Artemis, others are born in the seething lap of Venus for the whorehouse of the mind. Lucile belonged in the former category. Where Mademoiselle Gély belonged, I refrain from saying.

Don't grudge me comfort, he had said to me. He had come to look so damnably sad. Why shouldn't he have her, if he wanted, four months over Gabi's dead body? Was any other item going as it should?

The Committee of Public Safety, still something of Danton's brainchild, had seemed to be under his direction for one whole week. One or two of his "gang" had had high hopes of this. He'll put France in his pocket this time, for sure, and then we'll see things done. I excluded myself from among these optimists. Danton toyed halfheartedly for a while with the game he'd blown once before when he was minister of justice. (I hadn't seen it that way at the time, but hindsight had ripped the gauze off my eyes with a knife.) At the moment he had a scenario for the placation of Europe. Negotiations were about to be opened, or had been opened, with Switzerland, with Prussia, even with the spider empress of the Russians. This, the man who had cried, *Before the crowned heads of the earth we throw down one more crowned head, cut from the body of a king—our battle gage.* But he had been against the war from the start, saying publically one thing, going a different way in private, as we all did now in so many areas, or supposed that we did. (Though spontaneity may have masqueraded as precision, and lies disguised themselves as passion. God knows.)

Otherwise, Paris was turning into an army factory. Encouraging orders went out continually. Dig up your cellars for saltpeter! And in the parks, the makeshift armorers accomplishing our knights with busy hammers, furnaces blazing away, and black smoke towering into the new skies of summer, choking the birds, so they surely needed their souls.

But something was working against Danton. Rivals, enemies, a dwindling popularity—was such a thing possible?—his own apathy. His deals fell through, both diplomatic and mercantile. It seemed he could manage his country estates but not, after all, the small change of the French war. His plots, which at first excited me, presently lost me. And presently too were altogether lost. It's a real fight, Danton, not chess. "All right, then we'll try this." But it was still chess. He frankly said to me, this very night we talked about the marriage, "The committee is getting ready to vote me out. Don't tell Fabre. He thinks I'm going to be king." What will you do about that? "Leave graciously. Let Maxime get a seat on it and try his hand. The confounded fools won't let me make any headway. It wears me out, fighting the current twenty-eight hours every day." And he turned and smiled at Sophie-Louise in her little-girl bodice with her eyes straight off the walls of Pompeii.

"He's hiding from it all," I said to Lucile, when we were home. "He hides by guzzling the best food and wine, calling in the plasterers, ordering carpets and books. By sprawling along to the opera and the theater. And with women. Even with those tirades of his at the Convention. Now he's trying to hide up her skirts. Literally."

"Poor Marius," said Lucile. "He's so tired. Louise may steady him."

"She's sixteen," I said under my breath. "She'll either freeze him to death or burn him out."

Lucile, who had heard me, smiled secretively and did not answer.

"Are you trying to imply, madame," I said, "she's confided in you she loves him?"

"Why shouldn't she love him?" Lucile challenged me blithely, standing there with one of our son's bonnets in her hand. "Isn't he lovable — infinitely so? You love him. And I. And all his friends. And Gabi loved him to distraction."

"If this one said she loved him, she's lying. She's a decorative vine, which climbs. If Danton hadn't been hooked, any of us would do. Maxime preferably, but he'd run for his life. Me, then, if I didn't have you."

"You could always divorce me. There's a law now."

"Can you see me with her? What could I say to her she'd understand? 'Give me another quaint tune on your guitar'?"

"But Georges doesn't require from a woman —"

"I know what he requires. He'd have you, if I were — absent."

Lucile tucked the ribbons of Horace's bonnet through her sash. She came to me and looked up into my face. "Now what is this?" she asked.

"A discussion."

"No, dear love." She put her hand to my cheek. "I'm here."

"I know."

"And could never be anywhere else."

I stared at her, wondering then what I had said. I was confused. But the insecurity sprang not from any doubt of her. It was a sort of rage. It had been with me so long, I had mislaid its proper name. Rage, and an awareness of broken things. Or things which had been abandoned, torn away. But she had never been a part of those. In all the wreckage in the wake of this mighty ship of Revolution, her fidelity and her light were not included.

In the bed I made love to her and she refused to let me take any care. Since I had first dreamed of her, I had wanted only her. All the others, and there were many, for all their sometime savor, I cannot remember. Who were they, those kind, delightful girls? Were they not Lucile? Lucile red-haired; Lucile who had just sung Eurydice, her arms still chalked with powder; Lucile a little taller or plumper. But Lucile, always Lucile. I never deserved her or her flawless heart, but the gods who gave her to me kept my punishment in hand. Nothing is for nothing.

Yet even making love to her had become a sort of penance, for in the aftermath of every wrenching ecstasy there fell my fear for her, or simply a second nameless fear, which had become mixed with the first. Black despair. I lay in her arms, spent, and felt death in the room. I never told her so. But she knew. She held me and soothed me, stroking my hair, gentle; and she knew.

But Danton went to confess like a lamb, and made various settlements and payments, and on June 12 he married that Gély girl.

There were, for good measure, two weddings. Just as he had made his confession in some attic room to some escaped Roman priest, Danton the atheist now wedded his kitten wife in the webby cave of a neglected village church about five miles out of Paris. ("One expected any minute a patriot patrol to see the lights and burst in, demanding what we were at. At which I'd throw Louisetta down, straddle her, and declare, Why, defiling the blasted altar, what do you think?")

The second wedding was civic. The city came out to stare. The crowd wished them well. Most of it.

The celebration which followed is a vision of lights on endless glass, ornaments, and eyes, or passing through bottles into drifts of softer stuff: veiling, curtains, hair.

He looked happy and stupid that day, that evening, a sly rural impresario with no brain or genius at all to burden him, and he was charged with marvelous energy. It infected all of us. We all became happy and stupid and energized, unknown people with no worries, in a land without time or crime. Nothing was down to us. It didn't matter what we did. We need only be. Even she, with a bride's flush in her face and her grandmother's pearl ear drops, and a jewel or four he had given her, glittered and sparkled like the champagne, which in turn poured over, a Versailles fountain of love, or of eternal youth.

Last seen on the stair, Louise in a cloud of women, flowers and kisses and butterfly hands, the whole thing looking classical, very attractive, so one was pleased with it, as with a painting one liked.

"She is wearing," Lucile confided to me, "a garter embroidered with roses. Which says, *May our hearts be one.*"

"You wore one which said, *Unite us for life.*"

"You remember."

"Why do you cast spells on us when you marry us?"

"Is that a spell? To be sure of you, I would think. Are we witches, then?"

"Women."

"Ah," said Lucile. "Sphinxes, maenads, indefinable beings. Do you trust me at all?"

"Of course not."

"I shall mix glue into your ink."

"That might be no bad thing."

"Don't think of it now," she said.

The bridegroom came over to me before we parted. He embraced me and told me he was reborn and the world was new and we would live forever.

Why shouldn't he be happy? (Why shouldn't I? What had I done but denounce a pack of traitors? No need constantly to justify myself, in speech, on paper. No, I'd done nothing more than must be done.) Let us alone. Let me have quiet and let him laugh. Perhaps his Louise would strew his path with violets, refurbish his strength, not vampirize it all away.

But had he ever been aware of loneliness? I don't mean the sort that comes from lack of company. I mean the somber stranger the horseman finds mounted behind him, the uninvited guest who sits at the left hand. The one who says, Though you are loved and loving, though your friends are in every house, and in the streets they cry your name, and here at your side *she* is, yet you are isolate upon a tiny rock in the midst of a tidal sea by night. And there you stand, dashed by the waves and the wind, crying aloud to emptiness, in a voice unheard, nor is there any to listen. No one will help you. None, none. You are alone.

❈

On Clichy Road there had also been a sort of festivity. A group of Gironde deputies under surveillance had held a Roman feast, before the lictors of Nero Jacobinus came to conduct them to the lions.

"Eat and drink. Tomorrow, truly, we shall be dead."

"This wine is the blood of the Republic."

"And this bread, the body of Liberty."

"Spilled, broken."

Tomorrow (truly) some will be taken to the prisons. Some, left unsuperintended out of jail, will run for Normandy, already roused to anti-Jacobin ire. Others will sit it out in Paris. But the shadow is on them all, the shadow of the open page.

Edamus et bibamus, cras enim moriemur.

Let me admit to my ego, my conceit, now. Let me say I make too much of my influence and am not guilty. Can the pen kill? Even the pen of Camille? No, the sword does that.

Egomania, then.

One takes it too much to heart. Not guilty. Oh, God, if I could believe that — no, I do believe that. *If* only then I could *feel* it to be so.

There at my own wedding, four men held the canopy above our heads: Pétion, Mercier, Brissot, Robespierre. This, the tableau of memory, unshakable. But now that canopy, like some banner held high in battle, some oriflamme of friendship, seems to receive the glancing blow of a shot. And it trembles; one corner gives way suddenly.

Fat cute Pétion, no longer so fat or so cute, blunders through the Normandy countryside with his Girondin companion. Because supervision had been, to begin with, lax, it wasn't too difficult to get out of Paris and away. At first there were welcoming committees everywhere, those who wanted to help, to listen, and to react. If the provinces would only rise as one, they could squash the manic rule now taking seed in the capital. The valiant Vendée provided a lesson. For God's sake, how could a few square miles of city dare dictate a regime to the whole of Free France? (And the one or two evil men behind that dictating.)

At first it went well; there seemed a good chance.

But there were spies everywhere, creatures of dear Maxime's proposed police-state utopia.

The warning had come in the middle of the night.

Pétion and Buzot made a second run for it. Now here they were in open countryside that seemed all alike in the dawn dusk.

"We're lost," Buzot perhaps said. "You're aware of that?"

Pétion would want to be cheered up, not depressed.

"Keep your voice down. Any one of these trees could be working for Maximilien."

They must tramp and trip on. Maybe the morning was cold for June, cold with doubt and empty stomachs. A morning without promise.

Pétion, ignoring his caution, would probably whistle or hum a snatch of tune. (Musical fellow, Pétion. He had been fond of playing the violin—or was it just that the shape of it recalled for him his Princess Élisabeth?) Now, whistling away, he would be saying to nature, I am a city boy, be kind to me. Also, it would be an appeal to God to note his valor, so take pity. Though he had sometimes said otherwise, Pétion was not an atheist. More, he credited a personal destiny, despite reverses. He'd been rescued before, would be rescued again.

Was he still vaunting?

"It's at moments like this I think of Élisabeth."

Buzot, unshaven and looking demented, would snarl, "Who's she?"

"Capet's sister."

"That one. You never had her."

"Don't you take a bet on it. I'll never forget that carriage ride back from the Butterfly Town. She looked to me for protection, and then she got hot for me. She was swooning with lust."

If this was said, Buzot was less likely to crow in turn that he himself had had the muse of their order, ruby-lipped soot-haired Manon. . . .

Then again, there may have been no confessions or arguments or melodics. Just the inept flight, with ears keyed for a pursuit, until one of them said to the other, "Something is behind us."

Either it came swiftly then, leaping upon them, or it did not, and hearing nothing specific, or sounds incoherent that might have been only cattle going to drink across the fallows, they went on along the edge of the wood. Or they may have been dragged there, later.

Everything is conjecture.

It is admissible some band of lawless itinerants came across them and killed them, took their valuables, and left their bodies in the trees. Or it may have been farther on and days later that they dropped down out of exhaustion and hunger, cursed God and the Republic, took up pistols, fired into aching head or heart, and, so, silence. Those things which savaged their corpses could have killed them too. Not wolves, surely, for it was summer and a fair amount of game in the woods. While any child will tell you that if you meet a wolf or two on your journey and shout loudly enough, the animals will flee. Wild dogs are less wary, though. Or perhaps it was the werewolves or two-headed demons of the backlands which set on them. Whatever, in the second half of June, some gnawed human remains were found, a hideous sight, to which were allocated the names of handsome Pétion, once mayor of Paris, and handsome Buzot, once Manon Roland's lover.

"Am I the first to give you the news, Camille? Your old friend Pétion—devoured alive by wolves. Plenty of meat for them there."

Or there's another story. The bodies being so disfigured, it might not have been Pétion and Buzot at all. Anyone could steal clothes, papers, get caught by animals.

But I think not, actually. I think the arrow was fired true and hit to the heart.

And the canopy tilts toward the dust.

❊

There had been a lot of: We never see you at the Convention anymore, Camille; as a deputy, shouldn't you put your head around the door from time to time? At the Jacobins there was sometimes a huge joke, five or six of them exclaiming, Good Lord! Whoever's this? Do you know him? Well, I've never seen him before—wait, though, a dim recollection—no, no, I'm confusing him with Robespierre's dog.

This evening there was another disturbance. Roch-Marcandier.

The traditional screaming match had started in the Jacobin chapel over price controls. Saint-Just had the president's chair, which meant I hadn't bothered to speak. Whenever my exquisite cousin presided, it became strangely difficult to get a hearing, unless you were Maxime or somebody Maxime put up. At one point he offered to do this for me, coming over to me and saying, "You seem anxious, Camille. Do you want to speak?" A genuine offer, but what with one matter and another, I'd been avoiding Robespierre. "If something's on your mind," he pressed me, "give us the benefit of hearing it."

"Tell that blond thing over there, then, not to shuffle papers or ask his friends to have a coughing fit every time I open my mouth."

Robespierre suggested I exaggerated. I suggested a means of hushing Saint-Just and was promptly left alone. I sat on for half an hour and writhed, feverish and irritable. Even I could tell by now that with or without the pristine Antoine in charge, Robespierre seemed to exercise some sway. As others sought the theater, he always spent his evenings at the Jacobins. He occupied his place (which never varied now) and wrote in a notebook or listened with his chin in his palm. When the debates grew heated, he took on the look of a teacher whose class is scrapping in the yard. Initially the Jacobins had had a reputation for decorum and formality. This idea still obtained in various quarters but had ceased to have much foundation. Nevertheless Robespierre, if he felt things were seriously out of hand, removed or donned his glasses, rose to his feet, or merely made some slight gesture, as if at an auction, and somehow everybody rolled to a halt. It was interesting to observe; very unlike Danton's method of bellowing a room to silence. Then again, on occasion, the passions of the club were allowed to soar. He, Robespierre, only looked on, then. Measuring? He was deferred to, here and elsewhere. On the streets even the Mad Dogs, who had gone through a phase of denouncing him, were now at heel. When he took the floor at the Jacobins he was carefully listened to and seldom anything but applauded. I saw better, with gaps between the viewings, what had happened to him. He shone less often and less brilliantly with those curious unearthly visitations of glamour. But there was a different kind of power, which stayed with him. If it was his own, or something he drew from the submission of those about him, I was unsure. For my side, he wore me out with his unassailable virtue. I can no longer be certain if my grudging respect had already altered to a sort of fear.

Tonight was one of those when he said nothing and made no move to stop the rows that were breaking forth in all quarters.

My own reason for being there was a dull perplexed sensation I must keep abreast of events. Having decided to add my own sou's worth of rhetoric I had become excited and nervous, as normally happened. Changing my mind, the wine went flat. I smarted and scowled and finally walked out.

In the doorway, a couple of fellows who had just come over were listening with interest to the shrieks of David, Barère, and seven or eight others engaged in constructive debate. We were dawdling there — I was saying what I'd meant to get up and say inside — when out of the night walked the Guisard falcon with his crest erected in spikes and his eyes on me. He must have come looking for me. Until now, sensibly, he'd kept out of my way. I had seen more of those messy ill-printed broadsheets; I tried not to read them. He attacked everyone — the Gironde, René Hébert, Danton — but was reckoned a joke, which I failed to understand.

Now he stood and glared at me with total familiarity. My mouth filled with acid and my eyes with heat.

"Oh, look," I said. "It's the Pride of Picardy."

Marcandier raised a stubby wing in its impoverished coat and flapped it at me. The flight feathers of the wing were paper.

"An admirer," said one of my companions. "He's got the latest."

"Secret History, Brissot Unmasked Again," said Marcandier loudly. "How about someone unmasking Camille Desmoulins?"

"Dear, dear, are you wearing a mask, Camille?" My doorway friends patted my face, trying to find the mask edge. "Couldn't you have got a prettier one?"

I pushed the hands away and said to Marcandier. "So far as I know, you don't have a pass into this club."

"Who'll stop me? Those drunken court lackeys around the yard?"

There were a handful more men by the door now, potential evacuees from the pitched battle going on in the refectory. A general mocking cheer went up.

"Get out, Roch," I said. "Before someone makes you."

"You'll do it? Save your hands to write your lies. Where's Jérôme Pétion's liver and lights now, Camille? In some dog's guts. Not that he didn't deserve it. But if that's his fate, what's reserved for you?" He plucked about in the papers (all torn and pleated as if he'd been biting at them, and maybe he had). "Listen to this brave statement printed here by Monsieur Desmoulins, author of *France Set Free*. 'It was Brissot who devised the infamous charter which drove the People onto the Champ-de-Mars and into the bullet storm. Brissot who wrote at La Fayette's direction.—Those who say Danton is to blame are grossly mistaken; he had no part in the affair.' Do I quote you aptly, Camille? *Danton had no part?* Not much. The foul swarm of you were there in his rooms, plotting it all, to get what you could out of it. And when it didn't work you ran—I remember how you ran! Brune was in prison, and I was in prison—but you were off in the country sticking yourself into somebody's kitchen maid. And all this crap about bribes and seductions. Who doesn't know you'll adore the arse of anyone who'll give you a handout? And if they like, you'll hire your curly wife out for the night—"

He saw me start for him and he bolted. Somebody shouted after me to let him alone; he was crazy. I don't remember very much except we went around that damned poplar a couple of circuits, and then I got hold of him. He hit me in the face and in the ribs, but I battered him into the wall. Some of the Nationals and the idiots from the doorway were standing around to watch. When he was down I kicked him, and like the mad cur that he was he kicked me back. I knelt on him and held him by the hair, trying to pull it out of his skull, and informed him he must never mention Lucile again.

"Oh, let him alone, you'll kill him."

"Leave it, Camille."

They dragged me off, while someone poured water over Marcandier. Both of us were bleeding, our eyes no doubt redder than the blood. Someone else, it may have been "Père" Vilate, shook my shoulder and said so reasonably I could have throttled him too, "That one makes a set at everybody. Why waste time on him? Nobody takes any notice of what he says." I shook him off and yelled at Marcandier what he could expect if he approached me again. The filthy little wretch went, limping and injured and obscenely agonized. I hated everything about him, even the pain I'd inflicted which was now his.

It seemed the external fracas had been more vehement than the internal verbal one. Jacobins had gathered in legions in the doorway of the building, with Robespierre at their head, gazing at me nonplussed.

He was so short and so astonished, I laughed. There was a response of sorts. One didn't laugh at Robespierre in public now, apparently.

"You had better," he said to me, neatly trotting across, "come back with me and put yourself to rights. You can't go home like that."

"Can't I? How do you know how I can or can't go home?"

And home, as I was, eventually, I went.

❄

For I went elsewhere, first.

I hadn't meant to do it. I was looking for a drink, and a respite from politics. And then it came to me that farther down the side street into which I had turned, between the lamps and the doorways, he was ahead of me, Marcandier, still limping along, like a devil in the dark. And I thought, for I was rage-drunk already, *I could kill you here.*

The broadsheet should have killed him. Why hadn't it? Nobody cared enough, they thought him a nonentity; the "Guisard Hiccup" was a name Danton kept for Roch. Danton didn't give a fuck. Both Marcandier *and I* had been sorry he caused so slight a stir. It was the look of the broadsheet which was to blame. He needed a decent printer — or at least access to a workable press — and then he needed publicity, to make sure the thing was read by everyone he selected for his criticism: the Billauds, the Barères, the Couthons.

He had no friends at court. No one would defend him. He would sting them all. And then, too, did he speak quite strongly enough? He could anger me, but perhaps needed some advice on the weaknesses of others. Why, Roch, didn't you know, Couthon has long been guilty of — Simple, to tip him off. There were letters, copies of letters; the offices at the Convention were knee-deep in paper.

He'd lied about me. He'd cast slurs on Lucile. Oh, Roch, the times are perilous and you are nuts and I hate your soul.

I caught him up and flung my arm over his shoulders.

"Fellow Picardian," I said, "come with me. I'll buy you a drink to ease your broken nose."

He slung me off. But he looked frightened, now.

"Do as you're told," I said.

"I won't drink with you, you traitor."

"A stain on your pure reputation? Don't worry. This is a dark hole." And I got his arm and dragged him into the place I had in mind. He sat huddled in a corner, glowering; the bad wine arrived and we gulped it.

"I admire you, Roch," I said. He sizzled and swore. "No, I do. You're mad and a blathering fool, you put words together the way a crook botches up a brick wall, and your wit is wall-eyed, Roch, and you spell like a child of three. But there it is. You know what you think is right—and all the rest of us are villains—and you say it. Drink up."

"Yes, you're villains. You're shit."

"There's a brave Roch."

"You're sold. You should do penance on a burning spit for twenty thousand years to wipe out the crimes."

"And you're still a *Catholic,* dear Roch?"

"Fuck Catholics. But there should be a hell: for you, and your Danton, and the bitch's men, Brissot, that snake—"

He went on and on. He had an epithet for most of us. I drank the filthy wine and trembled with hate, and he did the same. It bonded us, and in the end, though he cursed me ceaselessly, he lapped what I said. I told him if he thought he was the only honest man in France he'd better prove it. Go on, Roch, shout louder. And you know Citizen X has some knowledge on *that* business, and as for *that,* there's a file so thick; Citizen Y might drop a hint. But that sheet you put out—no one *reads* it.

"*You* saw to that," he said—he was very drunk by now, and tomorrow he would probably be spewing, and good luck to him—"You sto-pped me. They wool-wouldn't let me—"

"Brune," I said.

"What?"

"See Brune."

"Ah!" he said. He crowed, and his lunatic's eyes flared up in the bruises I'd given them. "You think if you help me I'll spare you. Wrong, Camille, you bloody rat. I'll lash you with the rest."

"Lash on, Roch," I said. I got up. "Fire and gunpowder, Roch," I said. "Let's see you skewer the world."

"I will!" he screamed after me. "You'll see! I'll make you writhe, all the corrupt pack of you."

His nausea boiled in my stomach. If I walked over to Brune's, he'd very likely be there, or I could leave a note for him. Generally, he'd do favors for me. Access to a press, perhaps an assistant to check the galleys—if he misspells their names, *that* you can leave in.

I did it, though by now I was beginning to feel ill. The ghostly conversation with Brune, as he set up type, stays back in the shadows, with the smell of metal and ink and the aftertaste of that abysmal wine. "Yes, there's a printer I can send him to." Tell him to keep his name off it. "Yes. He's not one to push himself.

Roch can have the key, and there'll be somebody about to tidy. If you must fight don't bleed on my press—a lot of trouble for a little maniac. You want to see someone hang him?" Twice over, preferably. I want him *stopped.*

The chemistry is bizarre. The gift I gave to Roch-Marcandier, the sinecure I too—but this again is hindsight. I recall the pathetic figure he made, crawling out of the Jacobin yard, bristling in the wineshop. I had good cause to hate him.

Ironically, he had always been associated with me, even after he left off worship and began to hurl the muck. The other Guisard. They called him, at the clubs, "Camille Little-Paws." Fellow Picardian. Print cleanly and I will see to it they all pay attention. I'll see it's handed around at the Tuileries, the beautiful object, your journal. Christ, David, do you see what he says about *you?* (Even once, I would direct the sculptured nose of Saint-Just toward its surface, "Roch has a delightful name for you.") I trained them to read it.

In antique Rome, that night, in the alleys, I'd have run him through with my sword. This was another method, and I could always say I had done nothing, only let him commit suicide. The blade's not mine, I merely put it in his hand and told him how to hit the heart.

I could kill you here.

I owe you then, do I, you damnable little cur, for sending you to the punishment which was also to be mine?

You were myself, I see it now, myself in little, as they said. The part of me which hated me and all I had not done, and all I had become. My devil, my conscience. I cheated, then, also, myself. And, hidden in the dark, passed sentence.

I owe you. I acknowledge the debt.

❧

By the time I reached my shore of the river, my handkerchief was still scarlet under the lamps, I was sweating, and there was the threat of that old familiar ache in my right side. This seemed the final imposition, infuriating me even as it exacted the usual alarm. For a long while I walked about the streets avoiding patrols and scavengers alike, fighting the malady off, telling myself I imagined it—until I could barely stand; at which I hobbled home.

Everyone had gone to bed. I sat in my study, in the armchair. Sometimes I dozed. The pain was not bad. I trusted it would leave me soon. Once or twice it sharpened and woke me. There were also dreams—for example, that I was in the sky outside the gate of heaven, but heaven was the Bastille and Brissot kept the keys. Wolves gently gnawed my vitals. No, I didn't dream that, only pictured it somewhere between sleep and shuddering wakefulness.

In the morning, the sinister pain had abated, as it always did, and always with its promise of return, maybe next time bringing with it an atrocious death. Or maybe not. There was a fuss over me, which falling asleep in the chair in a fever, and the blood from the Jacobins, augmented. Sickness provides refuge. You need no longer think or decide when gripped by it. Who was always a well man has stinted himself.

But now, the magic balm of illness failed me. It seemed to me that never had so much been pressing on me, a chaos of things in disorder. I did not comprehend them, yet they hunted me down, roughshod.

Danton was at Sèvres enjoying his month of honey.

I must do something. What was it? Had it truly fallen to me, as once before? Hadn't I done enough? Write something, then, explain it all over again. Whatever it was.

Paris seemed very quiet under the windows. That meant nothing.

There were still marches, demonstrations, break-ins, and impromptu battles all over the city. The Tribunal was working hard across the river. A world full of traitors, and traitors found out. Miles off. Another country.

(It was about this time that my son spoke to me. How, in the midst of this, can I pause to note such an event? Well, there it is. So we are, bound by our personal limits as if by chains and blindfolds.

(He had begun adventurous forays across the floor, or any surface permitted him. Today he had in tow two particular toys he liked, a sheep on wheels and a patriot rabbit (Fréron had sent it), a white beast with tall ears and a jester's red and blue collar. The sheep, being on wheels, had an advantage of pure volition Horace was still in quest of. Leaving the sanctuary of Lucile for the twentieth time, Horace, the sheep, and the rabbit essayed the score of inches between us and collapsed all three at my feet.

("Oh, Camille, now there are tiny wheel marks on your shoe," said Lucile disapprovingly.

(Horace looked up at me and said, "Cam-eee."

(I waited. He regarded me.

("Again," I said. But Horace only beamed. I lifted him onto my knees; the rabbit came too. "Ridiculous boy, you said my name."

(He was nearly a year old, and had begun to mutter things, under his breath as it were, like a fractious mage. We were constantly saying to him, What?

(Now I sat and embraced him, and perforce the rabbit. He did not say again to me, "Camille." He had never named me for his father. We recognized each other solely as the right hand does the left hand in darkness.

(So, in the coldest ocean, such islands.)

But the sea is audible, and often visible, from every side. Audible, too, on a still day in the Cordeliers district, they would tell you, was the sound of that other thing, snapping its teeth together in Revolution Square.

There were already men, taken in the arms of that, who had had sons, no doubt.

⚜

What do you expect? We said the guillotine would be busy, and it's a fact.

France's generals, fumbling this war so badly, have been sent the traditional message: Victory or death. Those who are not victorious are brought back to Paris by decree of the Committee of Public Safety and ushered over to the Tribunal.

The Tribunal sits at the Palais de Justice daily, hourly. It's like a big, loudly ticking clock that never stops. And the pendulum in the clock is the Public Prosecutor.

An interesting man. Thick-set, pallid of face, with a protruding jaw and a long nose that seem to have fallen in love and to be desirous of one day meeting each other for a kiss. Protruding eyes, pale, like the face. A pale mouth turned down at the corners. Not much of a family resemblance to the "dear kinsman" who helped him to this illustrious, lucrative post: Camille Desmoulins's *unexquisite* cousin, A.-Q. Fouquier-Tinville.

He'll do what he's told, we'll give him a job, Danton had remarked. And so unleashed the creature on France.

Fouquier the Fork-Tongue lives with his work, just upstairs, in a slatecapped paper-yellow tower of the justice building.

When he descends from his legal papers and his brandy, he appears in the jet black of a raven, and a jet-black hat with black plumes, as do the three Judges of the Tribunal. Ah-ha, you think, a funeral cortège. Someone's going to die.

To one side, the magistrate jurors sit, generally fourteen in number. They are patriots to a man, and they get paid for doing this.

The accused (unpaid) sit or stand on the platform or the benches facing the judges and the jury post. Central to the action.

There is a public area, nearly always full. Justice must be seen to be done. And obviously, justice *is* done. Harsh, sometimes, but thorough. Much the same could be said for Fouquier.

Last perceived last year over in the office of Camille at the Place Vendôme, Fouquier's demeanor is altered and might surprise.

He is in a position of power here. He is neither shifty nor shifting, but generally moves only a little, and always with a macabre black dignity. Something to note, however. At certain times, when putting forward some point or raising some specific question, he may fleetingly assume a fawning smile, an almost whining tone of voice—as if he wishes to be careful, even to flatter the one who stands there in the dock: It is then that Fork-Tongue is at his most dangerous. And the answer to this behavioral riddle? Quite easy. A.-Q. F.-T. comes of that stable of thoroughbred sado-masochists who gain pleasure both from crawling and from being crawled before. Now and then, in the coolness of the moment, as one might say, the two delights may be confused. There is also the fact that, if circumstances were only a jot altered, Fouquier would have had to watch his step with some of these people now on trial. So he shows them how it *could* have been, before he rams the dagger home.

"Well, general. And do you think it fair to say that you permitted the enemy to win?"

"I?" blusters the captive, there in his tarnished uniform, almost straight from the front. "What grounds do you have for such—"

And Fouquier steps in, his voice all ingratiation.

"I have a list here, general. The numbers of those who fell in your retreat—it was a retreat? Am I mistaken?"

"No. We retreated."

"You have been heard to say that a kingless army is leaderless."

"A lie!"

"A lie, oh, a lie. So many people seem to have heard you say it."

Someone's going to die.

But not always. Some of them are only sent back to rot in prison until more evidence (against them) arrives (adjournment). Some get off. Really. And then there are displays of emotion in every direction. Fouquier folds his papers. Someone brings him a glass of something. He looks sternly gratified to have been escaped.

The show being over, the prisoner—depending on the verdict—leaves in one of three ways. Normally downstairs. There are those who must dedicate their heads to the Republic.

And the clock of justice ticks on, with its black Fouquier pendulum and all its machinery working to order. Part of this mechanism seems to be a number of rickety open carts that are beginning to run continuously up and down the arteries of Paris.

Tumbril. The word has its origin in the verb *tomber:* to fall. Dung carts, or carts to carry wood, or guns. Now taking condemned criminals to the Place de la Révolution. Two blind wheels without spokes, that ram and bang into the cobbles. From the walls and the windows along the route, you could watch the villains slowly bouncing past. The roads of Paris, which made for such up-and-down riding in a carriage, jarred every vertebra and nerve in the spine through the board benches of these juddering, studdering tomber-tomberils.

How many've gone by this morning?

Two or three. Full, as usual. Oh, it makes you sick, so much wickedness.

The passage was viewed with dismay, sometimes with satisfaction. With so many criminals, spies, plotters, genocides about, thank God the Safety Committee worked as hard as it did. Although . . . although the old woman there, in that cart, see? Isn't she the old biddy sold lemonade on Heaven's Fields? What can *she* have done? She's half silly. No, you must be mistaken. That old hag's been pushing monarchist tracts. She got drunk and had the nerve to yell *God Keep Louis XVI* at some Breechlesses, and obviously they took her over to the Palais d'Justice.

Tumbrils, tumbrils, all fall down.

How many today?

Five or six. Full as usual.

Just missed the tumbril? Never mind, there'll be another one along in a minute.

Girls without husbands. Fathers of sons who will be fatherless.

Don't make a joke of it. Don't, don't.

But—

Maman, maman, you hear it sung,

> *Qu'est que c'est qu'ça?*
> *Est-elle la confiture du cassis?*
> *Alors, mon petit, c'est ton pauvre papa!*
> *Madame, elle a de trop des maris.*

Nearer to the square, itself crowded, they keep their windows *closed.* It isn't against the songs. There's a smell of butchery in the air. Darkness, or even rain, fails to lay it. There have been complaints to the Convention, and there will be a lot more. Who wants to breathe, night and day, the perfume of an open abattoir?

It's quick though, if not clean, this novel method of al fresco slaughter. Sanson, the master craftsman, has spoken highly of its efficiency.

But there are other versions.

You hear the executioners' assistants, pissed out of their minds in some wineshop, telling each other how the wicker wears out in the baskets—gets torn to pieces—those severed heads tumbling about on each other like a panier full of crabs, and the teeth in those severed heads chomping and champing in the ultimate of hideous frustrations, and taking great bites out of the basket sides.

You hear the tale of the times the executioner must lean over the pile and say, "You are dead, monsieur. Be quiet and go to sleep." And it's become a precaution to lift the heads by their hair and show them to the crowd like a tidbit about to be thrown to wolves—during the action of which lifting, the head is also shown its own lost body lying there, strapped to the plank. That, if all else fails (they tell you), does it. That puts them out.

But every device . . . acquires its own legends. Who's going to listen to that, take *that* seriously, when it's a matter of justice?

No, better to concentrate on supplying the bitch. Giving her a food she enjoys.

Come on, now, generals to feed La Guillotine! Can't you see she's got a hole in her belly?

⚜

"Don't do it," said Lacroix.

"He's written to me."

"So let's allow him to write. You never liked him."

"I've sat drinking with him, and so have you."

"Well, I've sat drinking with a lot."

"Let go of my arm."

"That isn't me, Camille, it's Pierre on your other side."

Camille stood up, pushing off restraint like a dog springing from water. He was pale and shaking and enraged. In the past few months you seemed to see him most often publicly in this state, more prone than ever to mercurial outbursts, to arguments in the streets and a series of fistfights at the Cordeliers and even at the Jacobins. (Plenty of these, one gathered, had to do with the virtues and virtue of Lucile.) In the inflammatory atmosphere of the Convention, normally he stayed on the benches. If he was there at all. Now he strode down the tiers and managed to secure the tribune. As he was, he was capable of speaking coherently, even dramatically, if not always with much logic. "Oh-oh, notes," said Lacroix, however. And some of the Mountain groaned. Desmoulins was the clown. He could spell victory on paper and disaster in the flesh. He was capable of anything and apparently conferred with no one these days. Danton, who could have shut him up, was of course off with his child bride, doing what came naturally.

Camille spread his notes on the pulpit's rim and the Convention grumbled, catcalled, and whistled. Suddenly, his face convulsed with fury, Camille flung up his arm. It was the wild savage gesture of long ago, of 1789, the chair and table in the Palais-Royal, the green ribbon and the chestnut leaves. Some blurred recognition, partly unconscious, attended on it and gained him a few seconds' quiet, into which he shouted in that hoarse unreliable voice, strung now with anger, "I demand a hearing. I accuse the Committee of Public Safety of blind stupidity. Of a sentence based on fables told by halfwits."

"Oh, nice," said Lacroix. He glanced along the benches and took in icy Saint-Just and legless Couthon glaring in his wheeled chair, both new members on the aforementioned Committee. Lacroix grinned and put his hand over his mouth.

Camille was apostrophizing (Greeks, Romans, the principles of legality), turning now this way and now that, his hair flying. The voice was annoying. Funny, that, since when he spoke in the ordinary way it was not unpleasant, even musical sometimes, coming out with a line of poetry or offering endearments to his son or wife or some nymph at the theater. . . . But this!

"It's about Dillon, I take it," said "Père" Vilate.

"Right," muttered Lacroix, still smiling around his hand. "One more suspect general lugged off to prison. He sent a letter to Camille. Camille's up in arms. Dillon's all right, despite a certain story he's Camille's wife's fancy man. The problem is, he writes love songs to Antoinette."

"At Valmy," Camille cried, "who held the Prussians pinned, who gave Dumouriez his victory? It was Dillon. Dillon who never for one moment considered politics, but only the fate of his country."

Somebody bawled, "He's Irish!"

And there was laughter.

Camille appeared to ride it out. He gathered himself and went on. His color was up, the way Danton's color would rise, if not so hectic. The whiteness had passed into the clenched hands. He informed the assembly that the charge which had placed Dillon in jail was a pretext to shift blame.

"He's missing his lawyering," said Lacroix. "He wants someone to defend." He was right, in fact, if for the most flippantly wrong reason.

Someone to defend, someone defensible. While in the quiet you heard mechanical Madame snapping her teeth, dribbling bloodily for more fodder, you felt a need to act. Truth, reason, justice, common *sense.*

The way to heaven-on-earth, Camille, is not through a colonnade of gallows and axes. (Ah, Mirabeau!)

The Windmill's display was fiery, and the arms waved a lot. But not bad at all, and with no stammering. Till one of the newer Jacobin converts rose from the lower steppes of the Mountain and hailed Camille in mid-sentence with, "Well, you should know everything about Dillon. You have dinner often enough with *all* the aristos."

"Here we go," said Lacroix.

Camille was in the process of exploding.

The Nouveau Jacobin (he had run with the Gironde six months back) asked the indulgence of the Convention for Citizen Desmoulins. "We have to be lenient with someone so ignorant of the Convention's proceedings. After all, for several weeks he hasn't shown his face here. It's these late suppers with aristocratic generals. That sort of thing gives you a thick head in the morning."

The man standing at the tribune was ranting now, unheard, hopeless. Lacroix had stopped grinning. It's a charge you could level at most of us. You wined and dined where the cooks and the cellars were best. Besides which, could you help it if the restaurant seated you alongside de so-and-so, who sent you over the occasional bottle to drink the Republic's health? There were additionally "well-born" men who were the soul of the Revolution. Feeling his own temper rise, Lacroix took refuge in cynicism. He looked over all their heads at the fine ceiling and told it, "Give it up, Camille. Give it up, Camille. Give it *up.*"

But Camille had not given up. It was Mountaineer and Saberist Billaud-Varenne who got to his feet and shouted, "I call for an end to this!" Billaud's record was unsmirched. When certain people had been thumping about on tables, he had been publishing a three-volume work on ministerial corruption in France. And on August 10, 1792, Billaud had raced amid the legions, commending their efforts, till his coat was ruined by the blood. "Camille Desmoulins," said Billaud, "can't be permitted to go on making a fool of himself. He is requested to leave the tribune."

Camille stood humiliated and saw the sweep of terraces that snarled and jeered. It had a terrible rightness, a summation, and a symbol that had never before been made so plain. He left his ineffectual station at once. He thrust through the group standing ready all around the rostrum, mockingly applauding his departure. He said, as he went by them, "All right, if you won't listen, you'll read it tomorrow."

"Fine. Wonderful."

"It's an interesting business, why he'll speak up for that royalist bastard," someone said. "When the Irish shit's been screwing his wife behind his back all these weeks."

Camille turned, like something cornered, trying to make out who had spoken.

"Married to that one, can you blame her?"

But there was just a wall of faces and a wall of words, unclever but cutting, things said a hundred times in familiar ways by unfamiliar voices.

He did not ask himself, even then, What am I doing in the midst of this? It was an alien land, but he had grown accustomed to it, as the lost traveler grows accustomed to the desert. Water is greeted there with disproportionate joy, the weather is feared but accepted, the mirages still entertain and, sometimes, still mislead. One tries to keep a few stones handy against jackals. But the terrain is dangerous; it may kill.

Somebody, the cruelest god of all (who is named Chance, or Fortune), flung this child down into a nest of vipers, and there he played. He saw their attraction, and their agility fascinated him. He didn't understand the bite was fatal.

Even poisoned ink's no match for pure venom.

❧

Robespierre took me aside. He told me I had caused an upheaval at the Jacobins by my defense of a known royalist. Billaud-Sabers, in particular, had called for my appearance at the club, with my excuses. A proposal seconded by Legendre, the one-time Cordelier butcher. "He should stay with the chicken guts. The Jacobins is the Tribunal now?" I said. "I beg its pardon. I thought one was still allowed to be honest."

Robespierre told me to calm myself, he had personally defended my name. "It's foolishness to think you, of all people, would do anything against the Republic. But you leave yourself open to grave misunderstandings, Camille." Do I? "In these fraught times, try to consider where emphasis needs to be placed." I thanked him ungraciously for his help and the lecture. He went away. And there was Saint-Just down in the street to escort him.

Do they still have their cozy family evenings over at the Duplays? Singing and reciting poetry: Elie, who had her agate eye on Maxime; little Betsi, who had gained Philippe Lebas, of the well-padded chin, for her husband; and Lebas's sister, to whom, one heard, Saint-Just had engaged himself; how long before he could wriggle out of it, and what excuse? (Did Betsi practice with Lebas the naughty games I showed her in my book of Aretino? It seemed millennia ago, that act of folly.)

I watched Saint-Just ushering Robespierre along, moving like a sacerdote in a holy procession.

Robespierre is the truth and the way.

But why joke about it? He's the only one of us who seems to know anymore where he's going, and why, and *how.*

⚜

Now what is this? she had said to me. And now she said, "What is it?"

"Only that I need to choose my words. I mean to say something here that needs to be said, in print."

"Concerning me."

"Yes. Concerning you. Will you forgive me if I publicize your name in this way?"

She looked at me gravely. "Does it matter so much, if you know"—?"

"Yes! Yes, yes! It matters. Christ almighty, all I hear is this bloody lie. You with Dillon. Or with Danton. Or with someone. If Maxime weren't a monk, it would be you with Maxime too, and your sister minding the hats, no doubt."

She lowered her eyes and I could have bitten out my tongue. To bring this putrid rubbish home and spread it before her.

"Lucile, I'm sorry. But I swim through this filth and I drown in it. You remember, don't you, how Gabi began to hate us, all through disgusting rumors like this one? She believed it because she heard it so often."

Lucile raised her eyes again to mine. She said firmly and with a coldness I had forgotten her capable of, "But you don't believe what is said?"

"In God's name you know I don't. For this very reason, because *print* is my only voice, I have to use it to tell them that I don't."

"Then can you say this pamphlet is to champion an innocent man or to champion *us?*"

"Both. Unequivocally. Dillon. And your name."

"My name is yours, and safe with you."

"Then let me defend it."

She came to my chair. I caught her to me and buried my face in the sweetness and scent of her. The impassioned speeches of love came out, and she listened to them, softly, sometimes kissing my hair. Then came a silence. And then she said, "What a terrible time. How have we arrived at this?"

"I don't know."

"Do you recall, in the beginning, how very awful it seemed—those snatched silly meetings in the Luxembourg, Mama with her errands—and I used to cry because I thought I'd lose you and have to marry someone else?"

"Oh, my love."

"It seems only yesterday. But it seems so long ago, too. Have we changed so much? We were children."

"Don't," I said. "Don't. I can't bear it. Don't."

"There," she said. "There."

"It was so very clear, so sparkling," I said. "Everything that had to be, and how it must be done. We've failed. We've broken France on the back of it, this bloody useless dream that can't be made to work."

"Oh, there," she said. "No," she said.

I thought of Danton in the glades of Sèvres, driving himself deep into the forgetfulness of Louise. I thought, Let us go back and unravel the carpet on the loom. Let's start again and make it right. But the swamp dragged at my feet. Time moves inexorably forward, and we with it. I, too, clung to lovely forgetfulness, as if it could help me.

⚜

Reply to General Dillon
(And so to the City of Paris)

And since attack is the surest means of defense, I found myself duly attacked, upon defending you, from all directions, by stalwarts of empty-headedness from every faction. These broadsides do not necessarily draw my fire, but I will pause to answer them. For example, to the newborn Jacobin who announced I had been absent six weeks from the Convention, I must explain that during a month of this time, had he bothered to inquire for me, he would have been told I was ill. But I fear this gentleman is at the traditional game, trying to make us forget his former allegiance to the Gironde by calling me an aristocrat.

Aside from this, it is no use to accuse me of schemes to push any general to a superior command in the army. Dillon has been recommended for such promotion by the many of illustrious reputation I have noted here. While the very one who arrested the escaping Capets at our borders (and who could be more Republican than he?) has said of Dillon, I know *him; he* has saved France.

But doubtless everyone is by now agog that I should take up arms on behalf of the man who has been, all this while, making as much a dupe of me as of the rest of the country. What? You haven't heard the delicious tale? Then let me recount a conversation that took place five minutes after I had left the tribune.

A dear friend approached me. (Are not all my brother deputies dear friends, having, as I do, a wish only for the prosperity and health of France?) He planted himself in my path and said:

DEAR FRIEND: How well do you really know Dillon?

CAMILLE: Well enough to have spoken up for him, it seems.

DEAR FRIEND: So I see. Did your wife plead with you to do it?

CAMILLE: What do you mean by that?

DEAR FRIEND: (*Very concerned*) I don't want to upset you.

CAMILLE: Don't let that trouble you.

DEAR FRIEND: How often does your wife meet Dillon?

CAMILLE: I don't think she's met him more than four times in her entire life.

DEAR FRIEND: A husband can be mistaken in these matters.

(As I did not promptly throw a fit on the ground at his feet, my kind and considerate friend went on.)

KIND AND CONSIDERATE FRIEND: Well, since you're being so stoical about it, I can reveal the rest. Your precious Dillon betrays you in the same way he betrays the Republic. You're not exactly a pretty boy.

CAMILLE: True.

KIND AND CONSIDERATE FRIEND: Your wife, though, is stunning. And Dillon's still a handsome fellow. With you out of the house such a lot, and women being the flirts they are— Well. I'm grieved for you.

To which, seeing he had now finished, Camille responded: "Dear and considerate and grieving friend, I see you know nothing about my wife at all. And if Dillon cuckolds the Republic as he does me, never did the Republic have a more loyal and blameless comrade."

So much set down, I ask you, general, to resign yourself merely to patience. The prison which holds you will soon give you up again. France is not in the grip of an Inquisition, though I admit one sometimes looks askance at several of Liberty's representatives. (Our own Bilious-Varenne, who, despite his energies on August 10, leaps in terror to stop the mouth of anyone speaking up for a friend at the Convention. Or mighty Legendre, who is sure never to say anything unpatriotic—or sensible—but reckons himself above us all because he hits the door lintel with his eyebrows on entering. While after him there minces along Saint-Just, who carries his so-beautiful head as carefully as a priest bearing the Eucharist, for fear its porcelain profile may be chipped. With such cornerstones of Revolution, we might well tremble.) But take heart. I swear to you, by the honor of Paris—for she, your ultimate judge, will deal fairly—you shall be freed.

⚜

I put the pamphlet on the streets with instructions that it be publicized as *Treason Uncovered! Correspondence between Desmoulins and Dillon!*

It was bought and credited, and he was quickly uncaged. Which went to my head again and cheered me up.

It seems now unimportant, a flash of palest fire over distant water. The tempest was to come.

1793: Summer

My very dear Father, forgive my delay in answering your last letters. It is not that I've been idle. Far from it. (I dream at night of clamorous lawsuits brought by all the poor geese whose denuded feathers supply my writing materials.) I enclose for your perusal the pamphlet you may have heard of, my open letter and notes concerning Dillon. I enjoy the success of it (I have immodestly come to expect large sales, but my popularity still surprises me—a strange contradiction; can you fathom it?) But having enjoyed the success, I then feel guilty. The royalist faction, who grasp any straw, are very pleased with me because of this work. I brush off their most unwanted laurels and ask myself anxiously if I'm still a Republican, or have I mysteriously been transformed into a counterrevolutionary as I slept! The other pamphlet, concerning the Orléans conspiracy, has also done much of what was intended, since Brissot's villainous crew are expelled from the Convention where they did so much harm. Orléans himself has been sent to Marseilles under strictest supervision. God help those who attempt to scale our Mountain with rotten ropes. Otherwise, I'm sorry Mercier was caught up in this. But he should have shown more care. In this matter I have nothing to reproach myself with and a good deal to take pride in, seeing how diligently what I write is attended to.

I wish I could find a means of visiting you. But my duties here make the idea a near-impossibility at the moment. Besides, between ourselves, Lucile has formed an unfavorable opinion of most Guisards—particularly one of my female cousins. . . . In fear of dreadful censure, I write this to you from the offices at the Convention, where my wife can't look over my shoulder.

Your description of our troops' passage through Guise, on the way north, is dire enough. Their officers, you may be sure, are the ones to blame for the rowdiness and lack of discipline. It is not the men who should be chastised so much as these petty aristos who set them such a poor example.

My God, I just received your latest letter. Your news of my brother's death in the fighting appalled me. That you hadn't heard from him for so long seemed ominous. But don't, I beg you, give up hope. There is enormous confusion in the war zone. It may well be he has been captured, rather than lost his life, and will be returned to you. Looking at my own son, I understand hourly how the blow must break your heart. The loss of a child—the very love one bears them seems to *make* them vulnerable and thus invite calamities.

Life is surely a precarious balance of good and ill. For some years, evil has appeared to swirl about the little ship of my domestic happiness. It seems my turn must come, to be swept under. To be unknown and to be nothing, that is the only safety. But I have had success. Where can I hide, what deep vault could shelter me and those I love—my wife, my child—and with me those things of the mind I need, my books, a pen? It becomes very hard not to dwell, night and day, on the multitudes who die here. On the notion that such men too have children, wives, fathers. Minute by minute, heads fall. Yet these executions—the responsibility is not mine. I have tried to stand out against all wanton slaughter, as against the latter stupidities of these wars, which move beyond anything ever envisaged.

It seems that visit I jokingly began by putting off will never take place. Well, we'll meet, if I come through this Revolution alive (many are now saying *that*). Then again, I think to myself, why not throw off all this, go to enlist, soldier in the Vendée, find peace among the bayonets. So much I see here fills me with despair. And yet. We freed ourselves from one despotism. The reins are in our hands. We have the *chance* for something better—bricks from the ruins. We are no longer slaves, and only the damned have no hope at all.

❖

No, you're not above rhetoric, Camille.
Even in letters.

❖

> *Mother, Mother, come and see!*
> *This looks like currant jam.*
> *Hush, darling, 'tis your poor papa,*
> *Done over by Madame.*

The Wedding Canopy Begins To Slip: Second Tableau

A very simple picture. Mercier imprisoned.

It was less than that. A detention, at the Luxembourg. Not imprisonment, for this place had been a palace surrounded by gardens not so long ago . . . It was still surrounded by gardens, of course—Supervision only, then, and quite a lot of comfort. They even let you go on writing.

Don't strain your eyes, trying to work in the miserable light of those few candles. You have a lot to say? If you'd said less, you wouldn't be here now.

I met you on the street and you wouldn't talk to me. You slapped your gloves against your hand as if to slap my face. I told others I met you on the street and I averted my head from *you*. In the same manner I also said, What the Guillotine is at is nothing to do with me. And, I was against the war from the very beginning but popular opinion pushed me into calling for it, though I never called for *this*. As if war were an apple of which one could accept a couple of bites, casting it aside when one had had enough.

And I said, I hate Fame, because I chased her and caught her and had her, and now she has pushed me on the street naked in my shirt, and they recognise me and throw stones at me, or they may.

And I said, Let me hide somewhere because I only meant to do good but look what has been done, and the blind wheel runs away down the hill and we can't stop it.

What are you writing, Mercier? My indictment? Beware. I have twisted things even I have said and made them something else.

But no matter. Two corners of the canopy of friendship and love are down in the dust and dead leaves. But two corners are still upright. One, it's true, tilts a little—Brissot of the Gironde. But the other is held firm by Maximilien Robespierre, my good friend.

❧

The day after Horace's first birthday, Marat leaped up in the Convention, squealing about Danton's continual absences and the "Committee of Public Muck-up." But Marat always had a well-honed stiletto ready for each of us.

❧

Marat: Scholar of Daggers. (I will speak—and write—daggers . . . but use none?)

Marianne, Marianne, nobody's wife,
Went to a shop and bought a knife.

The air of the young woman who alighted from the carriage was strangely arresting. It struck, too, the men in Marat's office. She seemed curiously important, so they looked up from the paper and paid attention.

"Good-day," said the young woman. She appeared about twenty-seven, with an oval serious face, unbeautiful but quite fine. She was dressed in a pale brown costume with black braid and a black hat, slightly plumed. "I have an appointment with Citizen Marat."

One man went off to see. The other went on folding up the paper. The young woman stood posed, very still, in the midst of the untidy room. She did not glance about and seemed uninterested in everything, her gaze fixed inward.

The first man came back.

"I'm sorry, citizeness, he says not. He's busy, not seeing anyone." Which was partly true; Marat was writing while lying in his medical bath of herbs. (The stink of his poisoned skin, going up with the steam, was awful.)

"But he must see me," said the young woman. She said it without insistence, but with absolute authority. As if it were an irrefutable fact and they too slow to understand, but in her nobility she would be patient with them. She turned her eyes on them. Fine eyes, too, but decidedly out of this world. "You see, citizens, I've come all the way from the Calvados department, and already I've written to Citizen Marat and called here several times in the hope of seeing him. We're all aware, I think, of the danger of the Girondin faction. I have something I must give to Marat. It's essential, if France is to be saved."

One grew used to this brand of emotive talk. It was in the atmosphere morning, noon, and night, particularly around here at Marat's place. But this girl seemed imbued by such force, they believed her at once.

"All right. Wait here. I'll go and tell him what you said. And your name?"

"Marianne," she said, "Corday."

"You again," says Marat, sitting in the vile steam, writing daggers. He is comfortable in the bath, or more comfortable than at all other times. Although the fearsome *dis*comfort of his flesh, to a certain extent, has become usual to him, therefore forgettable. He listens while his assistant explains. Marat's face, smoothed a little, the steam beading his eyelashes, looks almost innocent. But he says, No, no, he won't see her. She sounds like some fool, a celebrity seeker. He hasn't the time—and just then Marianne walks through the door.

The Revolution, with its nature gods, has liberated Paris from many rituals of etiquette. But there is yet a certain taboo on unrelated females entering upon a man wearing nothing but towels and water in a copper bath.

"Now, now!" exclaims Marat's assistant, shocked.

But, "Citizen Marat," says the arrival steadily, "in the name of Freedom, I demand an audience with you."

And Marat grins. He too is struck by some element about her; also, her lack of "propriety" pleases him. Perhaps he recognizes something lawless and violent, which reminds him of himself. He says, "Very well, since you're in." And motions the man to go away and shut the door. (He obeys and, downstairs, says to the other fellow, "You let her come up." "Well, I thought he'd see her; she just walked by me.")

Once they are alone, Marat has said to his visitor, "You say you know of a Girondin plot in Normandy? Is that it? That's not such news."

"I have names."

"Spit them out, then. I expect I have them already. In which case you can relax; they're on La Guillotine's waiting list."

She comes closer, into the obnoxious steam, apparently not aware of it. She leans near to Marat and whispers, like a lover. He writes. Then a pause. She remains leaning over him. The tube of the bath contains him, but not utterly. "What are you looking for, citizeness from Calvados?" he asks malignly. "I'm eaten away, as you see, but otherwise made just like other men. If you stare at it that way, it may answer."

Marianne Charlotte Corday moves aside from the bath and its leering occupant. "Citizen," she succinctly says, "I'm leaving." She turns toward the door, which in this instance causes her to pass behind him. It's conceivable she has even changed her mind. But then—ah, resolution—she turns back again and from behind his right shoulder, leaning down as if to kiss his lips, she plunges the knife into Marat's chest. The blade—meant to cut meat, but not the human sort—pierces him under the collarbone, slants to sever the great artery leading from the heart, and penetrates finally to the left lung.

Devilish Marat, with a look of sheer bewilderment, falls back and cries out like a frightened child to his mistress, "Oh, come quickly, darling!"

Rushing in, the lady passes his assassin walking out of the door.

Marat's laundress holds him to her, while the bathwater changes color and his eyes glaze.

She fails to look up at the sounds of a scuffle: the murderess is being accosted in the doorway by one of the men who has run up from the office below.

"You bloody bitch, what have you done?"

"Too late," says Marianne Charlotte. "The beast is dead."

❈

Marianne, qui n'a pas de mari,
A acheté un couteau, et comme cela—
Paris n'a plus de Marat.

❈

She carried a fan, and the dagger was hidden in the fan. When they opened out the fan it was painted with viola flowers, and if you held it up against a lighted candle, you saw, behind and beneath each purple bloom, had been painted the face of the guillotined king.

Oh, yes?

❈

"This way, citizeness."

The stair is narrow, overused, unmended, dark, and dangerous. The first young woman with the kingly face went up it with a swift fierce tread. This one, a few years older and a great deal shorter, exercises more caution, while, instead of a fan and a knife, she carries a carpetbag. The National Guardsman — they are also all around the house and on every landing — opens the door for her to go in. The men in the room, standing in a kind of sullen awe, look at her suspiciously. Another *woman*. Has she come to stab him again?

"Citeness Curtius," says the escort, getting her family name wrong, or biologically right, possibly. And the second Marie of the afternoon passes into the presence of Marat's bath.

Outside, there are crowds everywhere, surging but mostly quiet. In some quarters panic threatened to break out — the death of Marat, managed by royalist spies, would be the cue for a wholesale massacre! But the Commune turned out the guard, who kept, and keep, control of things. It took the carriage a long time to make it here, for it was stopped almost at every turning. "What's your business in the Cordeliers section?"

"This citeness is a worker in wax, the assistant of Doctor Curtius on the Temple Boulevard. The Convention's sent her to make a likeness of someone who was murdered this afternoon."

David the artist had stood up in the Convention and asked for Marie to do just that. You assume David knows Marie is used to taking death masks by now. And for some reason David himself, opportunist though he is, doesn't fancy sitting there sketching the corpse. Let little Marie do it. He'll consult her afterward.

Marie gets on with her task, painstakingly. The men watch, faintly appalled, some of them, or interested. When requested to — the day is fading and already overcast — they set up lighted candles. The candles are of the worst sort, naturally, what else would *Marat* buy? They gutter and smoke and hiss. There is hardly any other noise. Sometimes, heavy boots on the stair. Once an outburst of passionate desolate weeping. Can it be the laundress is crying for her loss? Or some woman becoming hysterical in the street.

Marie works meticulously, sometimes with a small theatrical flick of the wrist. The dead do not require straws through which to breathe while the plaster forms hard on the face; this is an advantage. Nor do they grow restless and nervous as the plaster sets, turning to a hot and poreless captivity against the skin, the features, the eyes — intimations of burial, perhaps, a white plaster grave. It is necessary, too, with the men (and sometimes with the ladies) first to shave the face, or when the finished mask comes off what shrieks there would be! But again, in the case of Marat . . .

While the mold hardens, Marie keeps busy. She takes measurements: shoulders, neck, arms, chest. (Here she invites one of the sentries to aid her by lifting the dead man a fraction away from the side of the tub. The sentry obliges but is squeamish and almost gags. Marie herself at no point shows any sign of

distaste. She would appear to have a general distaste, actually. She seems to
perceive in the world others like herself who, for reasons unknown, do not
behave as she would do.)

When the mask has set, it is lifted away and carefully wrapped and packed
in the carpetbag. Marie tidies up. As she walks to the door, one of the
guardsmen bursts into tears. "Show him as he was, citizeness. He was the only
true friend the People had."

Marie nods, severely. They open the door and she goes cautiously back
down the unclean unsafe stair into the darkening street.

She has another call to make, in fact. More sketches, perhaps measurements.

Over at the Conciergerie, Charlotte, called formerly Marianne, Corday, is
royally awaiting her execution. Once decapitated, she'll make a good show in
the waxworks. *La mort en cire.*

❉

So much insurance of immortality.

But immortality is inevitably ensured for such as Marat. At the instant of
his death he became a martyr and the saint of the Revolution.

He will be buried in the Panthéon. All but his heart, which the Cordeliers
Club is determined to suspend from their ceiling in a porphyry urn. Maybe a
type of sword of Maracles: if a traitor to the Republic dares to stand beneath,
down will come the *coeur de Marat* with a nasty thud and brain the wretch.

The Jacobins intend to have made and placed in the Convention a bust,
Marat complete with his bandeau – nicely hygenic now, in marble.

They say that in the schools of the provinces, when the name of Saint Marat
is mentioned, the children are taught to cross themselves. Before the haphazard
altars of Liberty, they light candles in which the name of Saint Marat has been
scored with crimson, so the name is eaten slowly away by fire: Mara-arat-rat-

(Is Maximilien Robespierre, still unmartyredly alive, by any chance jealous?)

The day of the funeral, everyone turns out, as the heartless ashes of Marat
are borne to the Panthéon in their box.

Young men walk by the coffin, which is heaped with flowers, carrying
branches of cypress. And girls in blinding white, the tricolor at their waists or
across their shoulders, sing a melancholy dirge. It's all very Greek, or Roman.

Every section of Paris is represented, and many of the departments of
France. Jacques Roux's Mad Dogs follow in modest howllessness, with banners
of paper or cloth painted with That Face in its scarf and labeled FRIEND TO THE
PEOPLE or THE HEART OF FRANCE, THE HEART OF MARAT.

The Convention, the Commune, the dilapidated tatters of the disorganized
ministry (who?): everybody plods along the funeral route.

Remember Mirabeau? Could this get to be a habit, this dying and burying
in state? But there's no fire in heaven now. And no Girondins on the ground.

Robespierre presides.

At the tribune of the Convention, Robespierre has been known to refer to Marat: "This man is not my friend, yet I believe him to be a true patriot, eager for the salvation of France." There have been, allegedly, secret meetings (as haven't there, allegedly, been between every revolutionary deputy and some enemy of his or other). Marat, they said, announced to Robespierre, "The only way to save this Revolution is through blood." "I won't listen," Robespierre said, "to this talk of scaffolds." Soon enough, Robespierre will walk northeastward, to the Temple Boulevard, and going into the waxworks, having insisted on giving the entrance fee like everyone else ("No, no, Curtius, thank you, but I will pay; you'll embarrass me"), he'll stare at the tableau—Marat in wax, the bath, the towels—and then go out on the street almost fainting. He's been ill, of course, and the waxwork (which good old David is about to rip off on canvas for all he's worth) is extremely lifelike.

"That man," falteringly will say Robespierre, to the concerned passersby who pause to help him. "No, not a friend—his violence always distressed me—yet his heart was sound. It took the knife of a traitress to stop its powerful beating. Yes, go in, go in and look at him. He must be avenged. His foes are ours—and have we only been too blind to see them clearly? If we are stabbed, violated, shot at—what recourse but to retaliate?" You said, my friend, you were a pacifist. "I am. Oh, God, give me peace. But the only way to health is through a letting of blood." What? *Blood?* And is the day coming, Robespierre, when you will say, Better ten thousand innocents should perish than that one guilty man should escape?

But not quite yet. Your perfect utopian dream has not yet driven you to this. At the funeral, you stand above the fallen and are wise.

"My God, look at him," remarks one of the attendant Mountaineers. "Marat's coffin my eye. You'd think Maxime was taking something noxious to the garbage dump."

"Well, isn't he?"

But one doesn't laugh at funerals. It gets one a bad name.

Very different, though, on the road to the scaffold.

⚜

It's raining. But not on any shepherdess.

How brave she is. During the trial, she's never broken down. Now, driven in the cart through a gaping craning multitude, she looks—damn it, she looks like a confounded queen. Doesn't she? Head up, hands (unbound) lightly on the rail, huge eyes blank and far away.

They've dressed her, for the big occasion, in the scarlet shift that marks her as a parricide, an assassin of her country. The rain molds the fabric to her statuesque body, so she seems already dipped in wettest blood.

And there is a kind of jovial quality to it all, a *rightness*. She, her task accomplished, goes consenting and almost smug to meet her death, providing thereby an epic drama to placate the mob, which laments its hero Marat so tirelessly. The crowd which follows her, admiring her in their hatred, sings the "Carmagnole," and there are girls dancing behind the cart. What on earth can it all mean? Is it, then, a game, a scene from some play staged in the streets of war-forlorn Paris? They don't intend to slaughter her? They do? Then this partly joyful celebration means mostly this: She did it, but she'll pay for doing it. Which sets another precedent: All who offend the People will pay. Besides, in a way they're glad. If he had to die, better at the claws of this magnificent lioness than the slither of some spineless worm. (Remember, bear it in mind for later, my friends, my enemies, a courageous death is always popular with the crowd.)

"It's a bumpy ride, miss," Sanson comments to his charge.

"Is it?" The murderess favors him with a calm smile.

"And in a press like this, it takes awhile."

"But we will get there."

Sanson is either slightly abashed or slightly disgruntled; it's difficult to be sure with Sanson.

Now and then, someone has asked this man, chief executioner of Paris, with pleading in their hollow eyes, "It's quick, yes, the new machine? Tell me it is, you monster. You'd *know*." Or others, afraid he'll botch it for them if they're not polite (they say Old Fatty stepped on Sanson's foot, and look what happened to Old Fatty—*two* strokes before it did for him), others fawn. "You'll be kind, won't you, a craftsman like yourself?" Sometimes they swoon or vomit, sitting in the cart. And other things. It scarcely matters anyway how controlled you are. When the noose jerks, the ax slaps home, the blade slices—the reflexes of the body win as every sphincter relaxes. It isn't just blood, *mes chers amis,* makes the killing ground stink so.

Sanson. Does he wonder if he might mention to this woman that she will feel no pain? The mechanism of the instrument is perfect by this time and through the white column of her neck will pass like a silver sigh. You feel the breeze of its passage, but not the fatal kiss.

But oh, God, what comes after?

Does she even think of it?

Hell, angels, oblivion—

No. She's not afraid, not of that, whatever it may be. And not of this.

They could burn her alive, this one, and she probably wouldn't feel it. Jeanne d'Arc in a tumbril, in a scarlet gown.

Along the last stretch of the rue Saint-Honoré, sharp left and down Nation's Road. And the square opens up, with the sun also bleeding to death all over it, through the fire-shot rain.

Sanson helps Charlotte Corday to the ground.

When she walks up the steps to the platform, it is with the same firm fierce tread employed on Marat's stair. They bind her hands; she permits it.

Thunder rolls vaguely over the Tuileries, too disorganized to be melodramatic.

She lies down on the plank. Madame clasps her neck with the famous slender wooden talons.

Away in Normandy, intellectually roused by Girondin refugees, making her simple plans, didn't she guess the end of the road lay here on its face under the blade? Yes, surely she did. Twenty-five years of age, all thrown away on the butcher's block.

A flash of mirror. It's over.

One of the executioner's assistants goes forward and lifts the twenty-five-year-old head up by its shorn hair. Since the action of the machine is so fast, one learns to prolong it in other ways. Because she has killed Marat, the Heart of France, the assistant improvises brilliantly and slaps the head across its face for its impudence.

The blow bruises the last blood up under her cheek, and the crowd, startled, will insist for years they saw the dead woman's severed head flush with rage. Her wide eyes, though, stare far away, tranced and inhuman, looking just as unalive as when she was alive.

❈

Terra incognita, the land beyond Marat's murder.

The murderess had spoken of the Girondins as "Makers of songs which will call again the People of France to wholeness."

The Gironde spoke also of Charlotte. "She's destroyed us."

And the Mountain? The fissures widen. It begins to split.

1793: *Late Summer—Autumn*

DANTON CAME and went and, through the golden burning of that summer of 1793, seemed never in Paris for more than ten days at a stretch. "Even Romans," he remarked, "used to clear out of Rome in the heat. The Tiber was brown with garbage, and there was always some quaint little plague or other tidying up the slums." For most of those who no longer saw Paris as the New Rome, or the countryside of the Seine-et-Oise department as the column-strewn Arcadia, hazed with offering smoke, of the Greco-Roman dream, still slinky Louise furnished Danton excuse enough. (Cascades of hair, bare feet and shoulders.) When he came back to the city he appeared refreshed. He would blow into the Convention like a hurricane, shake everything about a bit. It seemed to watchers that, rather than spend himself, he would abruptly forget why he was

there. Rushing in, seizing the tribune in teeth and paws, then ambling out—
gone. And presently away again, carriage, children, child bride, into the gilded dust of distance.

What was there to stay for, now, anyway? Save a slight canny probing around from time to time, or the odd firework display, to keep the compost healthy. The Committee of Public Safety, to which he had not, for long, seemed to pay much attention, had had a reshuffle and kicked him out. (One less irksome duty to perform.) Otherwise, Danton's protégés seemed not to fare well. Westermann, for example, was making a glorious mess in the Vendée.

"I never thought I could get bored with the political arena," said Danton. "But it's just like a certain sort of woman. One likes to play around with her, but how can you stay faithful? Besides which, I'm tired."

"You've been overdoing it," said Camille, "staying faithful to Louise."

Danton laughed. "What do you think of my Louisa?"

"Three new songs in one evening. Impressive."

"It's better than sitting on your backside at the Tuileries, hearing that bloody madman Hébert, son of Duchesne, screeching for someone's head. Look at these vines. This is a beautiful-looking grape. Louise and I were . . . out here the other night. And afterward I poured a libation of processed wine to your Dionysos, but he seems to have taken it in good part. Do you think I should buy this house?"

"You've got a house. Two. Or is it three?"

"But this is pretty, and Louise likes it. I still hanker for the home province, that rambling old place—all those horses, I wonder how they're getting along? But I need to keep an eye on Paris. And we're not far off here, even with the consolation of the vines."

Danton and those vines. Having proposed the levy, a number of his current speeches concerned the importance of getting the harvest in before sending the farmers off to war. In this spot it was hard to imagine shortage and starvation anywhere in France. While Paris, close enough to keep an eye on, seemed a thousand miles away.

Camille looked about him. Beyond the vine stocks that bordered the dusty little path, the dry lawn went up to the white house with its homely faded shutters. Louise and Lucile were playing there with Danton's children, the figures, pale and bright, flashing in and out of the last bars of evening sunshine. Doves were making dove noises as they settled on the roofs, hopelessly bucolic. There was, too, the restful sound of water from a little stream. Under the clear sky, the trees pressed close, woods dotted with trapped spangles of light yet built into arches of shadow. It could, after all, have been Arcadia. And far off, as the dusk began to come, the syrinx of Pan, eerie and sweet, would pierce the glades, some French shepherd boy who could not read and did not care, kissing music from a pipe.

"You see?" said Danton. "You know what I mean. We've done enough, you and I. We were in the thick of it. Get out now and leave it to the hotheads."

He would say such things, *en pastoral,* perhaps meaning them at the time. But passion would always drive him back to that political she-creature to whom he was "faithless." Or to France, his mistress. He had leapt to the heights, grown dizzy, seen himself encompassed, retreated. He had lazed in the shade and turned to stare again at the dangerous veldt of public life. He did not review now the bitterness or anger of his retreats, dismissals, the resignations which bouts of inadequacy, or seeming inadequacy, had given him to. Let me retire, he said, because the blood thundered in his skull, his heart stamped in his side, because minor pains dogged him and major fears he had never accurately named. But the genius in Danton, pitiless engine that genius always is, tore him back again to the threshing ground, its claws in his soul. How could he leave her, his France, the multitude of living things that composed her, to the Héberts, the Davids, the Robespierres: he, Danton, her lover, her strength? Unlike Camille Desmoulins, Danton—though he would use the label in jest—had no proper conception of the "rabble." Even when he utilized the term as an insult, he insulted *individuals,* not a composite entity. Danton saw people, he saw *lives*— every petal, every filament, every speck and atom.

But pulled two ways now, he will fret at ease, and in the forum of action lose his stride, yearning for quietness. And so learn to bluster in the one, and in the other to speak of cabbages. He has things to forget, as well. He is, like most men, afraid of himself, what he has done, might do. Even now, and here (not listening), he detects the footfalls of events he has set in motion, as does the man beside him. So they examine the vines, and Paris is a thousand miles away.

And the doves sigh, the sky deepens. All the stars come out. The yellow lamps burn on the scrubbed table and change each glass of wine into a scarlet lamp. The big dogs approach and ask for scraps and Danton is outraged, then relents and feeds them, ruffling their heads. Antoine Danton recites a rhyme his second mama has taught him and is as much applauded as *oncle* Fabre. Louise sings to her guitar, skittish tonight, a girl with a wild lyre on an Arcadian hill, waiting for Zeus-Jupiter to dash to her arms in a thunderbolt. (Which, plainly, he has every intention of doing.)

The house creaks through all its boards and beams as the day's fire sinks out of it, up into the moon-set night.

"She does love him. I always told you."

"Yes, she does, I suppose. But what on earth is this?"

"Flowers. I put them on the pillow. Such a fresh cool scent."

"The bed's full of the damn things."

"That's because you won't stay still."

"Come here and quiet me, then."

". . . But this does not seem to quiet you . . . ?"

Summer in the bed, the flesh, summer in the room, and the sky low on the earth, spreading out poppies and wheat and flying birds, and lovely women on their backs. Summer in arcadian France, with gods under every thicket, laughing.

wife; Georges Danton, my friend; this summer is the last.

❄

Things flying up in the air. Royalist Lyons besieged by patriot troops, hit by bombardment, her arsenal exploding, towers in the sky. Paris, celebrating the prior August of Liberation, lets go birds with the label on their necks or legs:

> *We*
> *Are free*
> *Be*
> *As we*

Some of these unfortunately shot at and brought down for the pot, food being scarce. Perhaps allegorical (we are free to be shot at, our skies full of exploding powder towers like parallel-world Bastilles).

And could balloon surveillance not be serviceable above the field of battle? Nothing invented, but it has some other use for war.

On the ground, processions of mules in bishops' miters, chalices holding brandy or melted for the mint. For every substance thrown in the air, plainly heaven is to be reckoned empty of God.

❄

Scenes from Parisian Life:
Unnumbered Issue

All churches are to be officially closed. In a few days' time there will be no longer any Church in Paris, merely buildings given over to civic use. Catholicism is declared dead. Reason is god, and goddess too.

In Notre Dame, Our Lady of Paris, the Goddess of Reason (represented by a noble young whore from the theater), was borne along the aisle in splendor. Her clothing seemed somewhat familiar, a white dress with a blue drapery—had one not beheld such garments on a certain totem called the Virgin? Never, though, the blood-red Liberty cap adorning the flowing hair. Her palanquin, wound with ivy, was deposited under a canopy. Here she presided over the bacchanal—I beg its pardon, the ceremony—which followed.

A Dionysian scene, redolent with the divine madness. National Soldiery having installed revolutionary icons, notably that of Saint Marat, the drinking and dancing began. The "Carmagnole" was performed with vigor.

But just as all men are equal, so there can be no queen of temples; every one must be honored alike.

For each religious edifice, a Goddess of Reason has therefore been found, deity for a day. At Saint-Sulpice in the Cordeliers, the wife of Momoro (first printer of freedom, Jacobin, and good citizen) ladys it. While over at Saint-Germain-in-the-Fields, Cecile was juggled to the high altar, high no more, with roses in her rosy cap; and at Saint-Thomas, Rosalie carried a crozier bound with three-color ribbons; and at Saint-Auguste, Annette, with Marat's picture at her throat, sang the "Marseillaise" to an accompaniment of drums and bugles.

Presently the men will loosen their trousers and the women throw off their scarves. In the maelstrom of the dance one will see portrayed the whirlwind, that destroyer of crops and property, precursor of the tempest.

When the storm drops, seeking the obscure places of their fane, the dancers will conclude their orgy with those acts that have attended every Dionysia since the First Days.

All most reasonable.

(This from the pen of Sébastien Mercier, persistently writing his paper in detention.)

⚜

But you should hear what that Marcandier says about that Mercier in that paper, *Men of Prey.* . . .

⚜

The British have occupied Toulon.

The good harvest, gathered randomly, has not done much for the bread queues. (You should hear what Marcandier says about *that.*)

And the mob prances back and forth between Festival and Fatality— throwing up its hats at the blood-curdling roars in the Convention, throwing up wine (cheap and nasty) around the cathedral, where the great statues of Solomon and Sheba have been smashed, mistaken it seems for Fat Louis and Antoinette. While over in Revolution Square it goes on and on, the only High Mass left in town. (Who's getting a close shave today? Oh, *him.* Well, serves the bugger right.)

There's a new law due. Something about acting on *suspicion* of anti-national feeling. That'll weed the traitors out and no mistake. The Committee thought it up.

Who's on that, now?

Well, Danton's not, though he's still hanging on at the Convention, shouting the roof off at René Hébert, who will keep on accusing him of appropriating funds. Hébert's lot is on the Committee, and Robespierre has a lot of the seats. But Robespierre's a moderate, of course.

And outside, the mob sits howling, or runs howling, or stands howling. The mob, the mighty machine worked by so very few levers. Tell the mob who to cry for, it'll do it. Tell the mob who's sinned, and the mob will dance them to the scaffold. Forget your Rousseau. It's an animal, and animals bite.

Wait. *Enough* of this.

See it Danton's way, every mote and atom. . . . It's not a circus, even if it resembles one. The beast is composed of individuals. Of men and women, of children, babies—composed of hungry bellies and sore eyes, hands stretched out in a desperate instinct to save themselves from going under. As they go under.

Report them, then, sitting around the guillotine, mouths open, open palms clapping. Report the drunken laughter and the cruel mindless jibing *hating* wrath. But then follow them home. *Home!* Some sty, some hovel, to which, in this endless war upon the palaces of privilege, the benefice of peace has been accorded. Peace to starve, to sicken, and to despair. Remember, then, you who dare to give a voice to this multitude, that these you show in the deeds of beastliness and moronic violence also lie down on beds of rags, also crouch before a hearth with three sticks burning or fester in the stinking summer heat. Here, in these holes to which peace is extended, they give birth in pain and dirt, they grow up broken, the bugs crawl over them, they wither and suffer till they die. And the great eyes turn after the light, helplessly, as the shoot turns after it under the black soil, blindly. Though the light may be only Fata Morgana. Will we live to see it, the day of glory, the hour of freedom? Or will we see only this?

There isn't even anyone to pray to, now. They took them away, the Christ-god pierced, as they are pierced, and thin and pale as a hungry child, and the blue-mantled girl-woman who would intercede, and the splinter of the True Cross, and the rosary, and the sacred handkerchief once dipped in the tears of a saint. Pull down the belfries, so no tower can stand higher than another. (Even towers shall be equal.) The bells have gone for cannon. Nowhere to rest now, except on the bosom of Robespierre's hard calm God, Supreme Essence of the Universe.

Yes, then, give them their voice, but let it be a true one.

Let them cry out: Why does it never end? The worse for us that makes the worst *of* us. When will the torment stop, the betrayal finish?

Make your grand speeches and, having offered us bread and wine, put stones and snakes into our mouths. Then tell us what scum we are.

Teach us to find the dregs of ourselves, and we shall find them, never fear—and astonish you.

But when will you love us enough to keep your loving promises? When will you feed us, shelter us, see us safe, give us quiet sleep and hope on waking? When will you give us anything but lack or threat of lack, war or threat of war, suppression named law, ugliness for entertainment, lies instead of dreams.

When, then, will you teach us to be fine?

Tomorrow? The next day? *When?*

Danton's ill. The Seine department isn't far enough anymore. He wants to convalesce at the home province, by the Aube.

Too hot for him here, eh? Too exhausting, all that roaring? Too much suspicion flying around?

Well, let him go.

"What?" said Camille Desmoulins.

"The Convention's authorized a pass, and he's off. The apartment's locked up again."

"Fabre, if you're—"

"No, Camille. It's true," said Lacroix. "You're lucky you weren't there to hear him letting off steam about the lot of us. God, he looked terrible. He was lobster-red in the face one minute and pale mauve the next. There were three doctors finicking about. Louise was dissolved in tears."

Camille said something about Louise's tears that Lacroix and Fabre d'Églantine pretended to ignore.

Fabre seemed terrified. He gave the impression of a well-dressed mouse on an outing who has begun to realize the charming inn is just a touch like a mousetrap. He was into a number of deals speculative that Danton, at one point, had seemed to have the measure of. But then, so were they all.

It was a shame about Fabre, really. He had just had the opportunity to play God and had done it with the same slightly untidy romantic dash apparent in his clothing. A new calendar had been decreed for revolutionary France, and Fabre given the naming of these dispositions of ten-day weeks and totally equal months. The piece of fantasy (Fabre-titled for wine and flowers and winds) was now quite real. Everyone perforce adhered to it, if sometimes getting in a pretty awful muddle. (There were stories of gangs of Breechlesses who roamed the capital by night, catching lone travelers and pressing them to the brickwork with cries of: What's the date, citizen? And if the citizen was remiss enough to say it was October, there was trouble.)

Now, though, with no thought of dates or seasons, the three Revolutionaries stood and looked at each other for a lead.

Eventually Lacroix said, "Aside from anything else, Georges can't make his mind up on this Antoinette affair."

"He cn-can't make his mind up on nn-anything." Camille, stammering. Not so usual now. He must be in a state.

"Robespierre," muttered Fabre, also in one.

"What are you talking about?"

"Maxime Robespierre. I don't trust him. He makes snide remarks about speculators battening on the body of their country. He's taken against me—"

"Oh, *dear,*" said Camille.

Irritated with everything, and with each other, they expressed their disapproval by staring, unpremeditated, in three different directions. It seemed, in

that moment, very nearly symbolical, although they were in fact, all three,
already on the same road.

❊

So, what day is it today?

It's the something-or-other of the Mist Month.

But it isn't misty.

Never mind. It's the Mist Month – October to November. No, wait then. It's still the Wine Month. Of Year Two.

When was Year One?

Up until September this year. That is, up until this Wine Month. (September to October.) And it's the Wine Month now. Everything's backdated. You start with September 1792. The proclamation of a Republic after August. Although that would be the Hot Month, wouldn't it?

What hot month? There can't only be one.

Officially. I'm speaking of Thermidor – the Gift of Warmth – it's Greek.

It's all Greek to me. If they wanted to do this silly damn calendar, why couldn't they use French?

Some of it is French. (And I hate to say this, but some of it's Latin, too.)

And new weeks of ten days at a stretch. They should try working at *my* job nine days instead of six before they get a day off. And anyhow the damn thing doesn't fit the year.

How's that?

Well, look. There are three ten-day weeks for every month – thirty days for every month. Twelve months of thirty days makes three hundred and sixty days. Leaving five days over.

That's the Thirteenth Month, the Sans-Culottides. To be kept for festivals.

Who's going to want any festivals? We'll all be too worn out with this confounded ten-day week. Thirteenth Month. Don't they know thirteen is unlucky?

Anyhow, you should just hear what that Marcandier says about that Fabre d'Églantine in that paper, *Men of Prey.* . . .

❊

But Fabre's a poet. The calendar, even incomprehensible, has a lyrical sound.

The Wine Month, burgeoned grapes, brimming cups, giving way to visions of a Misty phantom wood, a pool veiled in silver. And then the Month of Frosts, thin lace on the windowpanes, and so the Snow Month, white fur thick in the streets, to be washed away by the lashes of the Rain Month (Drive home your pretty white sheep, shepherdess), and the whips of the Wind Month. After which, the buds open, its the Bud and Blossom Month, and then the Flower Month, and then the Picnic Month in the sunny meadows, and the Harvest Month all racked with heavy sheaves, and the Hot Month, and the Month of Fruit, before the wine bowls overbrim and silver breath clouds the pool once more.

Nature, the Revolution's formative muse. Will nature be obliging and do everything on cue?

Recollect now. No winds in the Rain Month. No rain when the buds break. Snow down for the Snow Month and no nonsense, if you please. And Thermidor must always be hot.

⚜

But *she* recalcitrantly dated her will, the witch in the prison, October 16, 1793.

⚜

Antoinette.

It has all been done, for a fact, in steps. First they took her power, and then they took her name. Then her liberty and her comforts were removed. Next her husband. This very summer her son was carried away into another tower. There, filled with brandy at eight years old, until he vomits, then filled with more, slapped about, choked with food he does not want, eternally threatened, there is little chance now for his health or his sanity. "If the king-licking émigrés want to make a king of this little prick," reportedly says Simon, the boy's guardian in jail, "I'll give them *this,* and see if they still want to." Sometimes the little drunkard has been paraded under his mother's windows. Simon has bashed into him some rather obscene songs. "Sing up!" says Simon, and clouts the boy. Who duly sings up. How very odd, the effect of the trembling genderless small voice, enunciating the dirty words it does not understand. Simon stands and gloats, like a villainous puppet. Surely he can't be real, or half the tales of what he has done. Certainly the royalists spread horror stories, and the Republicans deny them in rage, and information on the entire matter is extraordinary. Nobody would treat a child in such a way. Even a prince. No, no. Would they?

The mother meanwhile, like the child, has remained a potential focus for conspiracy. Her very existence is a danger. The word has been for some time that she will be sent before the Tribunal and as a result made into a parcel bound for Austria.

But she is guilty of a dreadful crime. She has been a king's wife, and not at all equal. If belfries must be leveled, surely queens must be laid low.

In August, a carriage took her south across the city to the River Womb. (Here, on their island, crouched the midnight buildings of Justice, with a few sour-lit, evil-eyed windows peering out over Paris through the dark.) And so to the courtyard of that prison fashioned from a palace gatehouse, the Conciergerie.

Over that cobbled court, in at a door, along a narrow passage thick with lantern fumes and tobacco smoke. The dogs of the jailers growl at her as she passes. Can it be even the dogs of Paris hate a queen? Or is it the look of her, poor ghost, with her black rags and her thin white hair.

Installed in her cell, she waits.

Guarded, insulted, stared at with an absorbed and crucial nosiness, her responses are few. Sometimes the women prisoners, who take exercise in the inner courtyard outside the barred window, shout curses in at her. Or, on occasion, encouragement.

There are still those who secretly revere royalty as a special element, just as there are still those who go secretly to some hidden mass or who harbor priests. Now and then, someone with a crush on the woman in the Gatehouse Prison will bring her a flower or a fruit. Even the Commune allows her books. But her eyesight is failing, through anemia and general malaise. And it is also possible to blind oneself with crying.

She used to be so afraid of boredom. Is she bored now, scratching phrases of prayers, like any vandal, into the walls of her cell?

But there are supposedly attempts to rescue her, even in this soot-black box.

It can't go on, the suspension of fate. With the war the way it is, the Vendée, dissension and plotters everywhere, *hélas,* madame—you're too perilous. Something must be done.

And in the second ten-day week of the Wine Month, Year Two (October 1793), the widow Capet is put on trial.

Welcome, citizeness, to the bottom of the staircase.

The trial is held at the Justiciary, and the courtroom is packed. Outside, the crowds palpitate and press close. The roadway, the bridges, everywhere people, and the blue and red of the National Guard, or the stripes of the Breechless Wonders, keeping order.

There are a great many women on the public benches of the court. There's a particular fascination in it, to watch her come to this, this other woman. (I could be pretty like her if I had what she has. But regard her now, all prettiness is gone. How can she still look down her nose at us, that scarecrow? She's no better than we are now. She knows she's human. We've shown her. She knows she can die, just like *us.*)

She sits on the hard chair they have put out for her. Fouquier-Tinville has arrived in his raven black and is sorting his papers. Hébert is present. (Prosecutors in plenty.) *He* wears a smart gray-green coat with high collar and winged lapels, and revolutionary boots. His hair is not revolutionary, but rolled and tied back in the normal Hébertian fusspot way. Clerks are sharpening their pens busily and calling for refills to their ink dishes. The judges sit under their nodding black plumes. The funeral cortège is all in position and ready to go.

Hébert stands up and squints at the woman.

"Name!"

She starts to speak. He interrupts. "None of your so-called titles. Who are you?"

She tells him who she is.

"Age?"

"I am thirty-nine."

They read aloud the list of accusations against her. It takes a long, long time.

Vampire, Plague—these are some of the names they give her now. She has preyed on France, devouring the money earned by French sweat and tears. She has sought counterrevolution. She has arranged orgies to corrupt the soldiers, and on August 10, 1792, she incited these men to murder the People, even helping herself to load the muskets. In captivity she has, through foreign agents, bought up the stocks of food in the capital to instigate riot and famine. It was she who planned the royal flight, aborted at Varennes. To the last, she has worked to destroy the rights of the Nation, holding it in utter contempt, willing to cause the death of every citizen as a man will swat gnats which trouble him.

Finally, it must be remembered that this corrupt woman is the modern Messalina, as lascivious and depraved in all her boudoir business as she was ruthless and bloody in her political intrigues.

Her lovers are reviewed. Beings of both sexes. The legitimacy of her children is, in passing, glanced upon. Alone in the Temple, has she not libidinously attempted to suborn her jailers and, deprived of amenable male company, taken her son into her bed, there tutoring him in the incestuous conceits of mutual masturbation?

Hébert is sure now he must have scored a hit that will tear some response out of her. When nothing happens, he shouts at her. "Answer! Come along, damn you, answer, Capette!"

"My lips could never repeat your words," she says. "Are there no mothers in this room who can understand my silence?"

And from somewhere a woman cries out in the affirmative and a pulse of sympathy moves there, a wild hysterical reaction apt, for a moment, to escalate. The mob is easily moved. Careful.

Fouquier-Tinville calls Hébert to him. "Don't go too far, you silly fool."

"Too far? The cow has done all of it."

Fork-Tongue pulls a slight face. "If you enjoy imagining so, that is your problem. Don't wreck this session." And it is Fouquier who rises, gives her a little bow, and politely says, "Be calm, Widow Capet. Things are said of you, but this is a court of justice, not morality."

Then the witnesses are brought in.

They offer various testimony. Yes, she's planned escapes, counterrevolutions, assassinations.

She put her handkerchief to her eyes. Is she crying? She asked for water. Will she faint?

The evidence is all botched. Some of her defamers seem to be honored to have known her. Others fall back on personal grievances and cause laughter from the public benches.

The jurors can't convict her on this. But she's culpable. They have to convict her.

"And you can hardly deny you have, all this while, considered your son the heir to the leadership of France."

"If France should ever require a king, I hope it will be my son who is chosen to be that king. But if France needs no king, I am happy for France not to have one."

Two advocates plead her innocence, as form dictates. They are both pale and ill at ease. Both have been threatened with what they can anticipate if they should succeed in getting her off.

Hermann, the president of the Tribunal, rises. He is still as a rock but for the quivering death plume on his hat. He directs the jury, which hardly needs, by this time, any direction. He suggests the magistrate jurors ask themselves if it has been proved that the Austrian, Marie-Antoinette, has sent money to foreign powers to facilitate their invasion of France and has attempted, in the interim, to foment civil unrest in the Republic's heart.

The jury goes out, comes back, and unanimously says that it's obvious she has.

"Death," proclaims Hermann.

And Fouquier-Tinville may be seen to gaze fawningly upon the woman, like some tradesman hoping he has got something in his wares that will please her.

But she, looking at and addressing no one, leaves the court.

They can humiliate and degrade and abuse and debase her, and they have; they can condemn and execute her, and they will. But nothing else. Nothing at all.

⚜

She writes her last letter in prison to the woman who has shared most of her captivity, her husband's sister. The document is full of unswerving pride and tenderness. It never reaches Élisabeth. It is taken to Fork-Tongue instead and doubtless provides him some interesting reading as he sips his nightly bottle of brandy.

In the morning the prisoner cuts her own hair. "But I'm supposed to do that," exclaims the executioner's son.

She says, with a spectral playfulness he will be at pains to forget, "I wished to spare you the task of performing the duties of my maid."

She is dressed. And by her dress, she has honored the old custom of royal widowhood, making of herself a *reine blanche* for the scaffold. Presumably her captors are too stupid, or indifferent, or uneducated to figure out the trick she has played on them, dressing all in white as the White Queen of French tradition. Only her stockings are black, and her shoes have uppers of magenta prunello—because she has been warned the floor of the cart, and indeed the platform of the guillotine itself, may be soiled.

How many brave women have passed and will pass along this route. Some, as she is, dressed elegantly, or even charmingly, for their death day.

The soldiers stand ten deep in spots beside the way. The drums beat and rumble. The crowds are mostly quiet.

David the artist, perched like a vulture in a window, sketches the White Queen as she goes by. He has been known to flatter his subjects. But not this time. He makes the lines cruelly, as if with a pin.

Curtius' protégée, Marie the waxworker, also at a window, collapses, unconscious, in an uncharacteristic display of emotion. (Later, though, she will take a cast of the head.)

Watching from a distance, then, the vast throng in Revolution Square sees the white shape go, rather haltingly, up the steps and lie down without hesitation. The angled cat's tooth waits between its uprights. There seems to be a minor difficulty, and some adjustments are being carried out.

Behind the scaffold, one notices, stands a plinth, and seated there a muscular and inappropriate female statue with all the revolutionary attributes: cap, pike, globe – Liberty.

And yet, this *is* the gate to liberty, is it not, the only true freedom, as in that drawing on the wall?

They've corrected whatever needed to be corrected. The men step away, all but one.

The flash of light comes, as it always does. And then the flash of red.

Adieu, Madame la Reine Blanche. Whatever your wickedness or error, you've paid for it. The blade dropped to your neck, a single shining tear. Can you doubt history will weep for you? And young girls press dried flowers between the pages which will tell them how you lived, and how you died.

⚜

And Hébert's *Father Duchesne* comments, "Behold my joy in witnessing the Veto bitch's bloody head chopped from her fucking useless neck."

⚜

THE REVOLUTIONARY TRIBUNAL
FOR CRIMINAL MATTERS

The Keeper of the Prison of the Gatehouse

To deliver to detention: Brissot, Vergniaud (and to be entered here twenty-one further names).

Prior to their appearance before the above Tribunal.

Year Two of the French Republic,

One and Indivisible.

Signed.
Sealed.

The wedding canopy: Third tableau

Danton had belatedly made some attempt to keep the Girondin faction from trial. When he couldn't, he ran. By which I mean he became so ill he was advised to get out of Paris till late autumn. It was apparent to almost everyone by the start of October that a visit to the Tribunal would amount to the Girondins' death sentence. Robespierre, approached by various persons, asked them, Why do you want to defend those men who, if the positions were reversed as they wish them to be, would already have condemned you to the guillotine? He is also supposed to have said there was no use in talking about it further. There were moments in a Revolution when it was sufficient crime to be alive. A man must be willing to be sacrificed for the People, as were the kings of antiquity, and, like them, to accept the hour of his death. He is also alleged to have said, when Danton was present, "No one can make an omelet without breaking eggs." To which Danton, deliberately missing the point of the phrase, disgustedly replied, "Christ, Maxime, who ever thought you *could?*" and stalked straight out and into a dangerously high fever.

I say it was apparent to everyone that the Tribunal would mean death for Brissot and his associates. Not to me. I willfully misunderstood and fretted about the waste of time it was, this hollow trial. They were clever lawyers, most of them, and would get off with a kiss and a bouquet. At first, it seemed I had been right, and what I felt was a rush of annoyance.

"They're going to make idiots of us," I said.

One of my companions asked what did I want for them. I think I said banishment. Something like that.

"You're mistaken, Camille," said someone else, I forget who. "Maximilien's Committee has brought in a new procedure. After three days of debate, the President of the court is enabled to ask the jury if they've had enough evidence and will they judge on that."

"They've had three days and to spare. And what do you mean, *Maximilien's* Committee? Does he own it?"

"He and Hébert. And they agree on this one."

"Rubbish," I said, off at a tangent. "Maxime practically pukes at the mention of Hébert—who ought to be shot, incidentally." Then I considered and added, "When is the jury due to go out?"

"Today."

"Oh. Today."

I seem to recall hanging about, creating jokes from it, but half an hour later I made up my mind and walked over to the Palais de Justice. Something forced me to do it. Mostly, I believe, the overwhelming theory that I was still right, everyone else wrong, and I should be there, in situ, to behold as much.

It was a cold day, and the building cold and dank from all the human breathing going on there. They had drawn a crowd.

I pushed my way through to the front and sat down on one of the public benches. "Père" Vilate was already in position, writing notes. Nothing much had started yet, they were running late.

"Well," he said. "You're here for the dessert."

"I have a bet on it," I said. My hands were cold, and I chafed them with a sort of eagerness, or an inability to stay still, like a dog waiting to be slipped its leash.

"Ah, yes?"

"They're going to get away with it, you know," I said.

Vilate shook his head.

"You don't think so? Well, that's a relief. There's some justice. They can put them in the galleys and delight me."

When they came in, the prisoners, I sat and looked at them. I knew them all, of course, fairly well. Very well. Sillery, Vergniaud. Brissot was there, with that long face of his gray and dreary but completely composed. Quite suddenly I began to have a kind of dread he would look at me and wondered how I should meet his eyes. Altogether they seemed not to see anyone, save now and then one of the witnesses, but then they only gazed at him in an indifferent, aimless way. They were like sick men whom nothing can interest anymore—men who know they are already dead.

Vilate went on scrawling his notes, infuriating me. Was he representing a writer? *I* was the writer, and here I sat empty-handed, with only my gloves to employ me in wringing and pulling at them. Rather than listen to the evidence, or whatever it was, I found myself trying to recapture my former aversion to Brissot. He had said enough to me to incense me. He had done enough, or I had said he had, to retain me as his enemy. That wretched composed gray face of his. Bastard, making a show of fortitude, innkeeper's brat, sniveling sniping creep. The jury got up and went out. I said acidly to Vilate, "Did they read the jury any of my pamphlet as evidence against them?"

He halted in his writing and peered at me, then patted my arm. "Why don't you go, Camille? You're obviously upset. You don't need to wait to hear what we already—"

"How am I upset?" I grinned at him. My face writhed. It felt as if I had shaved that morning too close to the bone beneath. I felt an urge to leap up on the bench and address the dully murmuring crowd, jolly it along. My eyes darted from face to face, bench to bench, wall to wall, over the prosecution's position, the vacant seats of the prisoners, the table where that plumed twit Fouquier groveled into his files. My eyes couldn't rest. They were inclined to spring from their sockets and whiz about the ceiling. What, after all, would it have mattered if he had looked at me, Brissot? Here I am. I found you out and showed you up for what you are. . . . Off with the mask, old unfriend. But the head may come off with it.

"The jury," muttered Vilate, as if I had gone blind and needed now to be told everything.

I had acquaintance with one of the jurors, so I got up and strolled across. I leaned on the wooden barrier. "So you've agreed to vote them all for king?"

The man grimaced at me, and my insides turned to lead.

"All right," I said. "You've got a rotten job."

I backed into Vilate, who grabbed hold of me. I was nauseated and think I said to him, "I'm getting out of here."

But they were asking the jury for its verdict and the verdict was death. What else? I'd known for months, just like everyone else.

You've killed him, Brune said to me, a year before.

And I had.

The accused were being herded back in, and stood up, and told what was to become of them. There was some shouting. Protests. Other Girondins were throwing money they could no longer need to the crowd, which scrabbled frantically all around us, trying to get to it.

Vilate was shaking me. "Be quiet, for God's sake, Camille. This isn't the place—"

It was true I was blind; I could no longer see him or any of them. Black lights came and went across my sight. The floor seemed to rock from the clatter of feet, and the president rattled his bell, and the noise soared upward through my head. I couldn't hear what I was saying. I must have said something un-Jacobin to scare Vilate so much.

"Control yourself," he bleated. "It doesn't look good. They'll twist any-thing, now."

"For God's sake let me get out of here!" I heard myself say, and I turned and walked through the crowd, shoving and heaving all about me, a river of flesh in spate. I am ashamed to say I was crying. Ashamed to say it since it seemed to me then I had brought it all about, and still seems so, and that being the case, to stand with their life's blood smoking on my sword and shed tears for them was an offensive act, horrible. Yet even Judas is permitted to weep. Permit me then also to do so.

I must have reached the door, but I no longer knew where I was. Tall arches seemed bathed in a green light as if under the sea. I wanted only to escape but could not discover the way. Someone had brought a chair and I was in it. Somebody else was rubbing the back of my neck—yards of unwound cravat linen—and again another trying to pour brandy—Fouquier's blood—down my throat. And it was all "Citizen Desmoulins has been taken ill" and "Get a carriage for Citizen Desmoulins." And I thought, Nobody insults me by calling me Windmill anymore. And I thought, I am not Windmill anymore, that boy with a sky bird rising for a heart, that stammering fire-worshiping Dionysian dreamer. This thing named Revolution has killed him too.

TEN

N OW HELL'S MOUTH has been opened wide and begins to spew demons and nightmares, fire and blood. While over all there stands the tall black upright, high as the sky, with its slanted pane of ice. Not distant now, not to be mistaken for anything—a tree, a tower—anything but itself. And miles off you may see the white flash and the flash of red. And again the white flash and the red. And again. Again.

The parks are full of brazen hammering and smoke, the anvils of the Republic, and the heartbeat of the streets is drums. And up and down run the clockwork things, the jolting carts with their loads of living animals due at the abattoir. White flash, red. There's another one seen to. White flash, red. And another.

Busy, the Tribunal. Guilty; the sentence is death. Down and across and out and up. Hair shorn, collar torn off, hands bound. The horses plod tirelessly on, and the crowds tirelessly call and stare and scream. And the tireless shape stands waiting, and the tireless blade comes down. White. Red.

Some, condemned, take poison smuggled to them in their cells. Others stab themselves with penknives. The carts go by with corpses to the guillotine. The dead are thrown on the plank and their dead necks severed.

Some of them go lively and singing the battle hymn, the "Marseillaise." The blade stops every song.

Who are the guilty ones?

We saw the Gironde carried to the place and shortened. It took only half an hour. They were all courageous, and the blade, though thick with blood, did not stick once. Circe, Manon Roland, went the same road after her court. To the statue she made some remark about crimes being committed in Liberty's name, which was far from popular, obviously.

Who, then, of the wicked came after?

Any, all. These enemies are in disguise.

That girl who whores, she's a spy for the English. As you groaned between her thighs, God knows what secrets you let slip. And that fellow there, he had a picture of the tyrant Louis. And that one, he made coats for Brissot.

Cattle, cattle for the slaughterhouse.

How many carts went by this morning?

Fifteen. And all full. Awful.

I'll tell you, though, that story about bitten baskets—they don't use a basket anymore. Can't, you see. Too much custom. Just straw now, and then into an old grain sack, with spent barley to soak up the wet.

(They moved the apparatus, once, twice, had to, so many complaints about the stench, the crowds, the injury to commerce. The first subsidiary site was near the demolished Bastille, the second on open ground near Overthrown-Throne Gate. But the complaints followed the scaffold like the flies. In the end it was reerected in the Place de la Révolution and some compensation offered, which was never paid.)

And life, you see, goes on. Look at it, swaggering past, swinging its hips or laughing loudly. Watch! I'm alive. (For how long, pray?) Dolled up in my folded fichu or my complicated winding of cravat—can there ever have been such a fashion for bandaging the head onto the neck and then protecting it at the back and sides by a high upstanding collar? As if the guillotine, like some gigantic bird of prey, would fly at you from behind on the street. But La Guillotine is spared this exertion. They take you to her and on the way strip off the armoring, the long curling hair, the collars and cravats. These things are only sartorial interruptions.

They say, though (just as in the villages they say now werewolves patter over roofs and wriggle down the chimneys, devouring the babies in their cradles), they say she does go hunting by night, Madame the Cat. In the darkest hour she leaves her station and she *walks*. She's searching for more blood, since she is insatiable now and must be fed ceaselessly. In the morning haven't there been found cadavers, with their heads *bitten* from their shoulders?

More than any human thing in Paris, *she* is alive. She *takes* life from all she puts to sleep. Every juddering downward blow brings a quickening. Madame of the many husbands.

There stands a new tree in the garden—
Tree of Death—and we go there like cattle.
It sheds its round fruit without pardon,
Just a sting of cold light, and a rattle.
Remember the hundreds this tree has kissed;
Do you think a few more will be missed?
(Even God is on Fouquier's list!)

1793: Winter

"I CAME back and didn't know the place," he said. "Cordeliers Street now being Marat Street—the blasted coachman got lost. I went to the Convention and

tried to find someone there I recognized. A lot of new faces and empty seats,
aren't there?"

"Yes."

It was bitterly cold and the sky was red. Every breath filled the lungs with knives. But he'd stopped on the bridge the way he always did, looking off toward the islands, where the raped cathedral flamed as if it burned in hell.

"Don't keep blaming yourself," said Danton. "It gets tiresome."

"I'm very sorry."

"All right. I blame myself too. I made a fool of myself when they told me: wept, shouted, swore oaths. Bloody useless. I should have stayed here, whatever it cost me, and pulled their Committee into line. Brissot was an imbecile. They needed a spanking with Manon's slipper. Not what they got."

"I hear she—heard she died like the heroine of a tragedy."

"She would, wouldn't she." He stared on at the sunset and the city. "And the old man," he said. He meant Roland.

"The old man stabbed himself in a muddy field."

He had been in hiding at Rouen but walked out there at first light to fall on his sword. They'd told him Manon was dead. She'd had men enough, but that didn't seem to concern him. There was supposedly a paper pinned to his coat, which read: *I will stay no longer in a world fouled by such enemies.*

"These maniacs," Danton now said, gathering up them all. "Nutty Roland. Honor-mad old Sillery, the dolt. And Hébert's ravening wolves. The thrice-putrid Collot, and that paralyzed ghoul Couthon. And Hérault languidly stifling a yawn in the middle of it all. And Maximilien making sure nobody comes in with dirty fingernails. God almighty. Do they think they can clean everything up by another wash in fresh blood?"

Smoke rose in pillars from the Tuileries Garden, and more palely across the river in the direction of the Luxembourg. The forges sizzled overtime, casting arms for France. After nightfall, the swag of the clouds would be underlit.

"This city looks like hell in a dream."

"It *is* hell. Nor are we out of it," he said.

The *tricoleurs* hung, deserted by gusts of wind, all along the bridge. As Paris lost the voice of her bells to the cannon, she began to speak more and more in sign language. Everywhere the slogans: FREEDOM OR DEATH! EQUALITY OR DEATH! COMRADESHIP, VICTORY, THE REPUBLIC—OR DEATH! And the blue, white, and red waterfalls dripped or roped, stretched taut as sails or flaccid as impotence.

I'd dreamed of those flags. The banner of Free France hanging down, the Bourbon white draining out of it, because we no longer had a Bourbon king, turning to a black stripe which mourned. A tricolor then of blue, black, and red. Then the red unraveled and it ran. Off the edge of the flag, over the square, along the gutters. Blood. The red stripe of our banner was made of it.

I'd told him. He had replied with another ghastly English pun—he began to call the *tricoleur* the *trickler*.

"Look at the sky," he now said. I looked into the west, at the opaque sunset. "And the river." I looked at the river. "Everything crimson. The Seine's turned into blood." I said something about God and leaned on the bridge with my head in my hands. He cuffed me lightly. "Stop that. Come and get a drink." I followed him, like a lost dog that thinks it recognizes a master.

Le coeur en hiver: The months of Frost and Snow

I suppose I had had no real valor at any time, only the nearsighted optimism of a drunk—or a madman. (Where did I see that written on a wall, to the last of my given names: *le Benoît Fou?*) But it seemed to me, looking back as if into another country, and at this stranger who had borne my name, that he was brave and full of a spirit and an energy alien to me. Truly now it was the winter of my courage.

Skulking from place to place through Fabre's November-December frosts, I would cross the street to avoid anything or anyone that might touch my heart or my mind too closely. And of course, being so fragile, was everywhere pursued by disturbance. Women, fighting over scraps of food or a reputation, tore at my coattails and screamed invective after me—not because they knew who I was but simply because I accepted no part in their distress. I came across the lifeless body of a girl in the roadway. She was being taken up, but not before her clothing had been rifled and every small item of use removed. Her shoes, if she had even had any, were gone too. The pathos of the small feet, blue with cold and death, would not leave my thoughts. Elsewhere, but not far off, the bloodbath went on. Red sunset followed red sunset. There was a fashion on many levels now for pretending nothing was happening out of the ordinary (it had become ordinary, anyway) over there in the Place de la Révolution. There were the dinner parties and the theater, still. You could dance and play cards and sing and laugh and fuck, and if anybody mentioned the Revolution, you drank a quick noisy toast to it and changed the subject. The sans-culottes were everywhere, like an infestation of striped bugs. When a civic upheaval occurred, they streamed to the spot and swarmed over it. At the Cordeliers, they stood like columns against the walls. Sometimes, if they knew you and still cared for you, one could be cheered or chaired. Others would step in your way and want an explanation of something. But the name *Robespierre* had become a magic password. Robespierre. . . . I'll tell him what you said. Have you spoken to Robespierre? He'll listen. Oh, yes, good old Maxime, incorruptible Maxime. He was the one, wasn't he, got the food prices fixed? And they would go to the Jacobins and attend on and to him, hour after hour, as he droned through his ideal of a cold white utopia. I had lost faith in it, as in everything else. Danton had, after all, described to me explicitly, once, what Robespierre's version entailed, that scrubbed, bleached heaven where nobody—

And Saint-Jewel had recently added his mite, putting all the desexed angels into uniform. Each must dress for his social stratum—the young as workmen, those in their twenties as freedom fighters or jurors, the old as decorous ancients. Fiancés who wished to end a betrothal must report the fact to a special committee. God knows how *they* were expected to dress for this event—one angelic wing at half-mast, perhaps. Saint-Just. Ice-blond and an ice-blond heart. He had taken exception to my remarks on his porcelain profile in the Dillon Letter. Allegedly he leaped up and threw his gloves into the fire, vowing he would kill me. But I'd met him since; he only turned his eyes of ice away from me and moved on about his master's business.

The other cry I had been hearing was, "How interesting, when the enemies of the Mountain were condemned, everyone cheered but for Camille, who, having burst into tears, cried, 'The drops of their blood fall on my hands, which have slain them and can never be cleansed'—and toppled in a dead faint at our feet." I retorted that this picture of me as Shakespeare's Lady Macbeth was an atrocious lie. But there had been witnesses to my downfall. (I'm sure that gossip, Vilate, did not hold his tongue.) I later excused myself on the grounds of bad wine. And later still went back on it all and demanded why I shouldn't lament for the corruption of men who had been my friends, and that corruption's punishment.

There were also days I stayed in the house, writing allegories and essays that I could get to make no sense, and so tearing them up. (Our hearth was busy.) Then I would go to look at the child, tottering in a gleeful prison of cushions, where Lucile played with him like a young cat with her kitten. I would have a minute's sensation of normalcy, safety, and ease. Then anything, the settling of wood in the fire, a shout in the street, even the striking of the clock, would put me back into my private land of darkness.

Besides, in the chimney corner, one could still read.

That glory Hébert, who wrote in his sparkling paper: "How well we recall the day when C. Desmoulins was flashing his chestnuts in the Palais-Royal, and the subsequent reaction which felled the Bastille. What a pity that Camille has lost the power of speech!"

Or the occasional letters, which arrived, unsigned, to warn of something, anything, everything. One observed, "You slighted the handsome head of Saint-Just—he swears he will have yours on a plate." And another, "Tell your friend Georges your other friend, M.R., has been heard to remark, *Some of us would be more comfortable dead.*"

Well, if Danton was right, it *would* be comfortable to be dead. A dreamless sleep, from which none could awaken you. Oh, you lazy bastard, Danton. To sleep forever, no more responsibility or guilt.

Orléans had gone to it, Philippe-Equality, led astray in a balloon of aspiring hot air. And all the girls who had been kind to Brunswick's soldiers along the frontiers. And Manon, who had praised my eyes and damned the rest of me, around whose waist I had once slipped my arm only to be dislodged by a feminine wriggle and a look as hard and masculine as any her elderly husband never managed. (How had he looked in the field, the sword through his vitals, the paper fluttering on his dingy old coat?) And Brissot, whose voice says to me even now, in a quiet, encouraging way, "The meal is on me—eat up, Camille. We can't let you starve."

Stop blaming yourself. You're tiresome.

And the motto of the Committee of Public Safety?

Esprit de Corpse.

❋

The way into the Café Flon was by means of an alley with one lamp-iron, having a globe of gray glass in which only a last ember of the sunset was alight. At the door no questions were asked or suggestions offered. It was merely, Ah, good *evening,* citizens. And up a turning stone stair, into the private rooms above. Danton never lost his taste for the furnishings of the aristocracy. The scrubbed tables and peeling shutters of the home estate, or the *pied-à-terre,* were only an almost Antoinettish pleasure in "rusticity." (Rousseau is responsible for so much.) Danton's apartments, domiciliary or hospitable, were always of the very best, this no exception. Crimson plush over the windows to hide the crimson afterglow of that terrible Avernal sunfall we had examined on the bridge. Tiers of candles dappled with stars of fire, held in the hands of nymphs in the dead-white "Roman fashion." A carpet with roses and urns and everything but the Bourbon lily mingled on it.

The meeting was less casual, more prearranged, if one took oneself to the Flon, but I hadn't known I was going there until maneuvered into the alley. "Ah, look," said Danton, of the lantern hook, as he generally did. "One you missed." Nobody had ever been hanged there. Tonight he made the crack with such bitter malignity I might have known the barb was not aimed at Camille. But Camille being Camille scowled and took off on some diatribe, cursing him, until I had eventually lowered myself to the pitch of inquiring if his hemorrhoids were troubling him, and so nearly got myself kicked all the way up the stair.

I remember who was there, most of them, and who walked in later. Fabre for one, who was continually pulling Danton aside and chittering at him in obvious unease about something or everything. I caught the name of the East India Company; Fabre even came to me with it. This fiddle was only one of a series run by elements of the Convention, boosting various merchant companies, then bringing them down, buying shares at this point—when the price was negligible—selling when the credit of the company had been caused again to soar. Advised to profit from fluctuations of the India, I'd made some money a while before but pulled out when I realized what actually went on. Now it was only one more revolting mess I had no patience with and wanted to push from my brain. I shrugged Fabre off, and he went over to Hérault, whom I presently had the sour amusement of seeing shrug also, and in rather the same manner.

Aside from Hérault, Fabre, Danton, Desmoulins, there was Lacroix, and Thibaut, I believe, and Souberbielle the well-known sawbones, now on the Tribunal jury and unhappy enough about the whole thing he treated us to a monologue on the matter through three courses of the dinner.

"Oh, come on, Sou'belle, what's the difference?" said Lacroix. "They get hacked up either way. Is it just that you miss doing it in person?"

"Don't you ever come to me," retaliated Souberbielle ominously, "with a broken leg."

"Careful," said Lacroix. "I'll set Roch-Marcandier on you."

"But there is too much of it," said Thibaut, flexing his thin hands.

"Too much what? Marcandier? Agreed. Or do you mean sauce? Pastry?" Lacroix, attempting to be that evening's jester.

"It's too easy to lose one's head. What's the latest count?"

"Sixty heads is the total for November."

"For *what?*" yipped Fabre, very cross.

"What? Oh, confound it, for Brumaire, Month of Mist. Forget your idiotic calendar a minute, d'Églantine, sixty is sixty."

"Or seventy, depending on who is keeping score."

"They bring them in," said Souberbielle in disgust, "twenty at a time—yes, I've sat and watched it. Like cattle at an auction. Before October, the trials were reasonably well conducted and the verdicts fair. Now we get a homily from Hermann, or Tinville, that adder, on the wickedness of generals and the licentious royalism of seamstresses. And the poor victims shift from foot to foot, or the girls faint, and the tribe on the public benches sets up a yowl that *there's* good practice for La Guillotine. Some of the prisoners even rub their necks, as if to be sure they're still attached. The verdict's guilty every time. My fellow juror magistrates are carried away with enthusiasm and righteous rage. I've seen Hébert's filthy paper circulating like a religious tract in church. All pity goes out the window."

"How do *you* vote, dear 'belle?" said Lacroix.

"With the rest, after some argument. I'm becoming unpopular, I'll have to be careful. No, they're all honest, trustworthy, and true. I'll write notes to that effect in case they raid my apartment."

"And then there's poor Hérault," said Lacroix, who had insisted on cutting up his fowl as if under the surgeon's direction.

"Poor me," said Hérault.

"Moderation's last agent on the Committee of Public Safety. Don't they listen to you at all?"

"No," said Hérault imperturbably.

"And you'll soon be booted out. Or do you swim with the tide?"

"Even Danton," said Hérault, in his musical lackadaisical way, "has demanded severed heads for the Republic."

Danton had only been lying in his chair, listening. Now he sat up and shot Hérault a blazing look that quelled him. "Of the *guilty*," Danton said, not very loudly, so the crockery quailed and the quails rocked in their gravy, but not a single candle plunged from its sconce or window plummeted to the street. "I said, the guilty. I stressed the preference. And the innocent to go free. Trials there will be. It's as lame to announce there are no villains in the world as it is to suggest all the world is a villain and all the world must be bitten to death by Sanson's quaint toy."

We were surprised. I was. Lacroix said, "Beware, my friends, we've woken him up."

"What made you think I was asleep?" said Danton.

"Little things—the closed eyelids, the snoring—"

Danton overrode the pleasantry, brusque and hard. "What I want for France now, I always wanted. This: Law and justice for every citizen, whatever his rank or lack of it. A constitution that will work and be seen to work. A truce with our enemies—yes, Thibaut, a truce, and peace thereafter. Good God, man, how long do you think we can keep this war going? Finally, a country with her seas open, a flourishing commerce, and a wealth of arts, a country able to lead every other in her institutions and her inventions, both scientific and aesthetic. A Republic whose citizenry is genuine, not a hoard of squealing rats who prove their humanity by showing an identity card or a club ticket. We wanted to change things, and we did it, but the job isn't finished. We can go down with this ship or refloat her. Which?"

There was some applause, between joke and earnest.

Danton, with the sword-light in his glance, waved it away like gadflies. He glowered at us. He lifted his glass of the red wine high and said, "The horrible imp which now impedes our progress is solely this—blood. Everything is awash with it. It's all I can think of. My wife ties a red sash on her dress and I see her cut in half and bleeding to death. The red leaves falling in the woods at home—the sunset on the river—and I said to Camille, the Seine is changed to blood." He moved the glass again. "Do we drink blood till it makes us sick? Or do we refuse to drink?" And he turned the glass so the wine ran on the tablecloth. I think we all drew back from the spreading stain as if it were the thing he told us of, not wine at all.

There was silence. Then Souberbielle began to mutter to me; I didn't hear what he said.

It was impossible not to respond to Danton as he was now. He had been saving this power. He opened wide the wings of it and we were borne upward. And yet? Yet. Some part of me, even at that moment, had begun to limp, to lag

behind. Could I no longer keep pace? Or is it that the great voice cried – not
lion – but wolf? (If I denigrate your spirit with the reflection, it is not meant. Even you, Danton, were only a man. But forgive me.)

Thibaut said abruptly, "The cause of the trouble is Hébert."

"Much more than Hébert," said Lacroix. "The Jacobin Left has split into two halves, and one of those is now so far to the left it's ruptured its bloody self."

"Hébert is the scum, but the strength of the vintage lies elsewhere," said Hérault. "I have had the luck to see the fermentation close at hand."

"He who calls for Pilate's washing water twenty times a session, to sluice his hands," said Lacroix. "And gives the clean lamb's bleat for mercy to be remembered, and always has the frozen eye for Hébert's lot. And then another pronouncement –"

"Let's make an omelet," mewed Fabre nervily.

"*Yes*," said Lacroix. "I wonder what he's doing tonight, dear Ro –"

Boots ran up the stairs and we all lurched to our feet.

Conspirators have this habit. We knew ourselves already, even without speaking it, or that other name.

But it was only a young man who urgently implored Souberbielle to come to the hospital: there had been another riot in the Markets, with Breechless pikes mixed in, and surgeons were needed. Souberbielle rose with a bad grace and left us.

Hérault sat down again, and Danton. The rest of us did not. Mildly, Thibaut said, "I met Legendre near the Tuileries. He asked for you, Georges, and I said I thought you'd be at the opera tonight."

Danton said nothing. Then there were more footfalls on the stairs and we all looked at the door. One of the café people opened it this time, with some formality, and in walked Joseph Chénier.

There was a jest in Paris: Don't walk out in a coat that hasn't a hole in it. Though few of us resorted to that, even the dandies among us had reduced our cravats to crumpled muslin, generally with a ghost of the tricolor shot through. But Chénier's linen was starched and perfect, and his revolutionary slovenliness of attire was that of a prince in exile. I must have stared at him, with everything in my face. I hadn't seen him to speak to, more than a word, for a year. He brought the Beginning in with him, trained to his poet's cue. The lodge on Iron Jar Street, the nights talking by the river. The one line I had written that his brother André had praised me for: *l'hiver est printemps*.

He came straight to me and shook my hand.

"I'm sorry," I said.

"No," said Chénier. "No, no, Camille." Sometimes, one detected a trace of the accent of Middle Europe, his origins. It was a giveaway, irritation or tiredness, or that his guard was down with you. "He's writing, in that God-cursed prison, some of the finest verse any man ever put pen to." We were speaking of his brother, who had admired one line of my own pen, now shut in

Saint-Lazare. It came freshly to me, with a dreadful shock, as if I hadn't known that this incarceration, one of thousands, had taken place. But naturally I had known. André had been disgusted with our antics, the mauling of the Dream. "Whatever happens, he's the genius of this century and will be remembered."

Remembered. Will be remembered. And which of us can say that he—

Danton came up to us.

"We must get him out. He'll write even more fascinatingly in the free air."

"Hmm," said Chénier. "Perhaps." Danton embraced him and, emerging from the depths, Chénier added, "You must come and see my latest play, *Timoléon*. It concerns a king who is a good man." Some laughter, although I didn't laugh. "I hear that Robespierre dislikes my play."

Ah, now. The name, spoken at last.

Robespierre: Stone-dressed-as-a-man.

"Maxime only likes declamatory tragedies," said Lacroix lightly.

"Not when they concern honest kings," said Chénier. He accepted nothing from the dinner table; he said, "I can't stay. But I'm here. That's enough?"

"Splendid," said Danton.

"Your friend," said Chénier to me. "Young de Polignac. Did you know he was arrested?"

"Gabriel de Polignac isn't any friend of mine. But I didn't know. When?"

"A few nights ago. He's now in the Luxembourg, which is the first step. It will be the Conciergerie next, and then—"

"But for Christ's sake, why? Blasted aristo faking Republican, he—"

"Our beloved Tribunal," Danton interposed, "the monster *I* birthed, God help me, got hold of his father and kindly ordered the old man the chop."

"I knew that."

"And you know Gabriel and his romantic odes. He wrote a eulogy on his father. One romantic ode too many."

"For that—?" I said, and faltered to a stop.

"For that."

"In the L-Luxembourg," I said stiffly. "Hn-he'll get out of that. Clodie will b-bribe sm-someone to get him out." (Clodie, the elegant mistress. I'm stammering. Shut up.) I drank down my wine and went back to the table to get more, in defiance of Danton's image of blood.

Thibaut had followed me. He filled our glasses and said, "Robespierre." As if, now it had been said, we had better keep on saying it.

"Why," I said, "are we talking about Maxime as if he is the prime cause of everything that's wrong, and has, besides, a knife fixed over the dr-d-door to get us all on the way out?"

"Because, my Camille, he is, and he does."

"Never."

"Who said we must rule through terror because without that threat our foes will triumph? Your Never-Robespierre."

"Rhetoric. Georges has said the same."

"But differently, differently." "This Law of Suspects, then; who do you suppose was behind that? Can't you detect Robespierre's incorruptible hand?"

"And then there's Camille's favorite," said Lacroix, grabbing the wine bottle. "The dearly beloved Saint-Just. Who has been pushed off to the war zone again, the German border—a wise move. He's sending the Convention furious letters demanding two thousand beds for the wounded. Better than slinking about here demanding two thousand heads for the basket."

"And do you suppose Saint-Just is Robespierre's altar boy for nothing? Who taught Saint-Just how to think?"

"And the high altar is the guillotine," I said. "But Maxime isn't the fount of all this. He's a clever, bigoted—"

"Oh, well, there's no convincing you, is there?"

"What is all this about?" I said.

Chénier was leaving again. He went out the door. There was manuscript paper sticking out of a pocket of his coat. Poets, writers. (Fabre stood quivering and gulping wine down his throat.)

Danton looked at us.

"Let me give you an extract from Robespierre's personal notebooks," said Danton. "And, in parenthesis, let me assure you, I have it on good authority. It says, *Writers must be watched. They are the most fearful enemies any country can have.* That is verbatim. It comes under a heading that recommends supervision of the press at all times, leading to a control of it as the means to influence, even to force, public opinion." Danton paused. Since he had poured the wine on the table, he had drunk nothing more. He said, airily, "This meeting of minds is becoming too heavy. I hope no one will object to a certain liberty I took, inviting some ladies to join us in a short while." As we stood gaping, he said, "By the way, Camille. In a day or so I'd imagine our friend, Maximilien Robespierre, will be asking to see you. He's got some idea into his head of starting up a newspaper again, I gather, for some odd reason one really *can't* fathom at all. . . . And since, as he found out from his sales on the last occasion he put pen to paper, he has the literary ability of a night pot, he'll need someone else to see to the business of writing. And there you'll be on the doorstep, Camille. Wondering what he wants you for."

I had felt myself going pale, the way it can sometimes happen, all the warmth of the blood sinking out of the heart.

"Well, I'll say—no."

"Say yes," said Danton.

Hérault was cutting fruit neatly. The gleam from a ring on his hand made me giddy. He said, "You see that if anyone else of note attempts it now, Maxime will stop it, or try to stop it. But if Maxime puts his own name behind it, he'll find it rather more difficult to stop."

"You're all mad," I said.

"Yes, yes. It's something in the wine. That's why dressed-stone Peter is sane, he never drinks."

"Robespierre—he's nothing," said Fabre, with utter inconsequence; he was shaking like a leaf. "A fig for Maxime, from the purple trees of the south. Let him stuff it."

Danton ignored this. "Robespierre may even approach you," he said to me, "as if he wants what we want."

"*What* is that?" I cried.

Fabre relapsed in a corner. Lacroix looked at his napkin and sometimes gave it an admonishing little twist.

Danton moved across space. He came between me and the lights, the candles, the recurring glint of Hérault's jewelry, between me and all of them, and the room, everything.

"What," he said softly to me, "do *you* want?"

"I? To en—to end this butchery, this—*carnage.*"

"Why?"

"Because I'm sick of this blood on our hands!" I shouted at him, my voice as high as a woman's, so I was ashamed of it.

"Good," he said. "Then there's no problem."

He pushed me, then caught me. He filled my glass and handed it to me.

"You can drink it. It's the blood of the sacrament now," he said. He put his hand on mine and got the glass to my lips as if I were an invalid. "Don't glare at me like that. Wait till you see the gorgeous girl I've selected just for you. What will you call it, your paper?"

And here I am no longer sure, those passages between then and now, between not knowing and knowing, and knowing and forgetfulness, the lies which obscure the other lies, and the truths which hide all. But either then to his face or after, in my heart, when he asked what I would call my new paper, I said, *Camille's Death.* And downed the wine just as we heard the women on the stairs coming up to us like flowers out of the dark earth of night, and the door opened on their smooth shoulders, grape-cluster hair, bright scent and sound, and the candlelight came back like morning.

❦

The girl who lay across my chest, whose warm hands moved ceaselessly along my sides, my ribs, the thin skin lit by their passage, and her breasts with all their flawless poreless melting beauty of youth, their buds brushing me sometimes in another sort of fondling all their own, and her mouth coming to mine and leaving it, her fair hair showering down on us—she was afraid of me. I knew she was afraid, the instant she came up to me. So, contrite, I had tried to be kind, to show her I was no monster. Her pink dress stripped off to show flesh of a paler, more succulent pinkness. She could have been no older than sixteen. The other was different. A trader, but more than willing, prepared to enjoy it all; they go one way or the other, love it or are cold and pretend. This second girl had fastened on me and was drawing the very soul out of me, flushed and wild and reared like a mare in her own pleasure, even as she had flung her arms around the neck of Lacroix.

(An orgy? Maybe. There had been many Dionysian proceedings the same.)

(They said Danton was always faithful, for once, to his current wife, but I could tell them a thing or two.)

But the girl who gave her mouth to me, the girl with her hands like warm waves—

While the other bucked and raved on my body, I wanted this first girl with me, lingered over her, drawing her in like a precious mermaid in the catch. My hands moved on a body as limpid as marble but so much softer. Only the tinsel down in her armpits, and fading to her groin, altered her texture; the velvet between her forehead and her chin was the same velvet that covered her from throat to ankles. In the crease of her she was scarcely more than dew and pulse, but deeper, a taut glove finger of heat. Yet I was wrapped in the cushiony amber of the other.

So I spoke to the girl who gave me her face to look at and kissed me with her breasts and hair. I tried to take her with me, with every invading caress to pass my rhythm into her, to close her cool eyes. I told her she was beautiful, and even that I loved her. Her eyes knew otherwise. She has lost a brother or a sister to the guillotine and blames me. Is that only a fancy? But she scratched at my breast with her round nails and put out my sight with her hair. The wave burst, the death struggle, under her wise uncompromising look. I dragged her down and stifled in her mouth, I made her writhe and shudder with my throes. And when she drew back and shook aside her hair, I saw I had bruised her mouth. I put up my fingers to touch her gently, and she giggled without mirth and slipped away. It was the second girl, gripped against Lacroix, who rolled against me, screaming in delight, both of them. Where in God's name did the other go? Vanished. Put out like a candle. Spilled and lost, the semen, petals, wax, the wine and blood.

❦

A man I crashed into took my arm, and I thrust him off.

"Camille?" he inquired, interested.

"Yes, Camille. Good night."

"Well, wait a minute. Where are you going?"

"If it's any of your business."

"Tsk." Laughter in the voice. I knew it. Whose? "If it's your home you're seeking, then you have the wrong bank of the river and the wrong direction, alas. Or perhaps you're bound elsewhere at three in the morning."

I halted. Drunk to the extent of having no ground underfoot and the picture of things a mosaic fairly removed and of no consequence. But I drew myself together and tried to take my bearings. The man laughed out loud.

"Let me offer you, for a temporary bivouac, the shelter of my lodgings. A jug of hot coffee. A camp bed if you wish, and in that case also a messenger so Madame Desmoulins need not be distressed."

I heeded; we were not alone. Swirling fragments of torchlit military uniforms, a small detail, topped by grins. No doubt very entertaining, a plastered Deputy Desmoulins spinning all over the road. But I had my clue. What other officer was going to accost me so affectionately, blast the fellow.

"Dillon," I said, after some effort.

"You can still see? I congratulate you, sir."

"I can still—see. I'm going nowhere with you. I've been called a royalist enough. Thanks, but no."

"Come along then," said confounded Arthur Dillon, and hoisted me around the corner, into a court, and up some outer and inner stairs.

I had once been taken to task by my wife for referring to Blue-eyed Dillon; Lucile assured me his eyes were brown. Now, at three in the morning, I was disinclined to make a fresh decision.

His lodgings, a haphazard billet in which, no doubt, he was still "surveyed," were modest. Only one of the soldierly detail came tramping up after us, deposited some boots without explanation, and went off again. The windows of the room looked out, by day, over the pigeon-colored roofs, to the paler, darker groupings of some church. The flags of the Nation hung between, and I saw a sentry go by once, twice, before the shutters were closed. Dillon lit a lamp, and I fell into an armchair. To begin with, I did not mind being there. The fire bubbled up brightly. There were a few woman's touches in the room, but no sign of her. It seemed to me he had a wife, but not in the city.

I began by insulting him, since I had rescued him earlier. And for the sake of that he bore it.

Why had he written to me from jail; why had I defended him? Countless reasons, most of them conditional and absurd. I said, "Raking up dust for you got me the worst name of my life."

He made a gracious gesture and bowed.

"That's a shame. But these are raw times."

"So my wife says. And there I was thinking the streets were pure gold."

"No one more cynical than an idealist," remarked Dillon. "But I'm sorry Madame Lucile has had to notice the grim days we're in."

We looked at the fire, but coldness had come to gnaw at me. I began to sober by his hearth, but the drink had loosened my tongue and my memory. In a few days I would embark upon a work—something—that would rise up black against the tide of red and roaring. Danton might tell me he was at my back, and Robespierre might be persuaded to condone my action, but I would stand alone, clinging to the brickwork. Yes, alone. I knew it then, in the ebbing hours before the winter sunrise. I, who always said what They (who were They?) wished to hear, was about to cry out in the patois of the damned. Turn back, then. Do nothing. Run, fly, bury awareness in a girl's body and a bottle of good wine. But orgasm is the finish of sex, and the splitting skull and furred mouth crawl after that delicious hag called drunkenness. And the reality, meanwhile, was always waiting. Remember me.

Dillon, of whom I knew nothing, offered me more coffee, or (with a caution) brandy. I put my head down on my arms and said to him, "Christ, I'm so afraid—I'm so *afraid*—what's going to become of me? Oh, God, what shall I do?"

He grew still as a rock then. I felt his serious attention, though I could not see it.

"What brings this?" (He could speak his French just like the language of Ireland.)

"They're everywhere around me, closing in."

"You're speaking like a fighting man, for sure. The enemy?"

"Yes, the enemy. Whoever, whatever the enemy truly is. My God, what's going to happen—I don't know what to do. Whatever I do will be wrong. It's going to kill me, this thing."

I heard him sigh.

My own tears fell like burning nails into my hands.

He said, "Half the city believes it's under sentence of death. You can't be certain anymore quite who or what does the choosing. Your faceless enemy. There you have it. Oh, yes, put a name to it. Say the Mob, the Safety Committee. Say Robespierre's Reign of Terror. But are we sure it's that? Or some other formless ambient thing that motivates and drives us all, downward. The goddess of death is in this place. The great beast of destruction."

"Be quiet," I said. "I don't need your bloody superstition."

"You feel it too," he said flatly. "Hardly one here who doesn't. Pardon me, Camille. I can't cheer you. Only say draw the sword against it, laugh in its face."

"All right, all right." I stumbled over words in indescribable confusion, trying to make him comprehend me. "But if they take me, then I'll die—Christ, I'll die—but Lucile, what about my wife—and my child? For God's sake, he can barely walk—so small—his hands are hardly larger than my c-coat buttons. I wn—I wanted to see him grow up, is that unreas-unreasonable? Doesn't any man want to see his son grow? He's worth ten of me, he'll have the best of any gift I have, but all her sense and looks and goodness. Jesus. What will become of them?"

"Hush, Camille," he said to me presently. "There's nothing to be done. We're caught in it." I looked at him, and saw him, as if far off along a tunnel of wavering blackness fringed by fire and water. "You're a brave man," he said to me.

"A sniveling coward," I said, wiping my eyes on my sleeves. I was still drunk enough to say that.

He smiled and said, "We all of us have the dead lights around us. But what man doesn't? In the field I've seen a score of times how I could go. And if it's peace, there's sickness and murder and the earthquake. Kick the thing in the backside, I say. Which calls me again to the subject of brandy." He stood up and abducted a bottle from a cupboard. "Take heart. We could all be wrong. We may dance on the grave of bad luck in twenty years' time."

And to that we drank, and at length believed it.

When I left I had forgotten most of it. I was making plans to dance on bad luck's grave with Lucile. To bring out a journal once more seemed a noble idea. I was angry enough to do it. And the River Womb flowed black as ink. And the stars were going out. And someone may have been following me.

※

That I had met Dillon and poured out my fear to him, this I did recall, and it became burdensome to me. Even by the time I woke out of next day's stupor, I was at odds with it and, in the days which followed, embarrassed by the whole scene, I avoided any chance meeting with him. Besides, I soon had other things to think of.

※

Almost a game, then, to be at the Jacobins and wait. And sure enough, one evening when the session ended early, before ten o'clock, Robespierre came over to me.

He took my arm. We strolled along the street toward the Duplays.

There had been the usual nightly run-in with Hébert, army officer Ronsin, Momoro, and other Duchesnian barbarians. Robespierre spoke lowly of them, tapping with his stick at the cobbles sharply, to emphasize points. Feeling that I was trembling, he took it for the cold weather and said we had neglected each other, I must take care, praised Betsi's chocolate, or it may have been Elie's, and lured me into the parlor.

There we sat, with an audience of all the little Robespierres, the busts and cameos and etchings—there were several more since I had been there last.

The chocolate came in, brought by a nervous smiling maid. It was tolerable, if I could have tasted it.

I thought, as he whittered on, What for God's sake am I scared of? I know this man. He likes me. Didn't I keep the pack off his back half the time at school? I've known him for two-thirds of my life. He's my son's godfather. All this talk is nonsense.

"My own poor newspaper," he said. "Do you remember that? I wish I had the time and skill at my disposal now. But I'm a speaker, I'm afraid, not a writer."

He means an orator, not a scribbler.

He means, Write for me, let me dip you in the ink. Direct public opinion, like the last time. The dog in the yard catching rats for him, and Camille barking Brissot all the way to the scaffold.

"Do drink that chocolate. You don't look well."

Danton has told me to do as you say, Maxime dear.

"And you're needed, Camille. Listen now," said Robespierre, "would you take up your pen—a new journal—a voice for the Jacobins, rather than these cawing fiends of Hébert's?"

"A Jacobin voice?" I said. "Why not take it back a little further. Not the Jacobins, the Cordeliers. Where the fight for freedom started."

You see, Danton. You've misjudged him. I mention the club you began, where you thundered and your slogan—Liberty, Equality, Brotherhood, now the watchwords of all France—was hammered in the wall. And Maxime only blinks. And says, cautiously, "The Cordeliers was well enough, but is now corrupted by those same evil fools of Hébert's, mindlessly howling for blood."

He may even approach you as if he wants what we want.

Be fair, Danton. Doesn't he?

"No secondhand mock Cordeliers, then," I said, playing my chess game so artlessly. "Our *first* Cordeliers. The old battalion. Those of us who founded the place."

"Danton," said Robespierre, fastidiously.

Yes, he *is* jealous. Always? Presumably. He was jealous of Marat's death. Even Antoinette, going bravely to the blade; he spoke of her with such uninterest: poor stupid wicked punished woman. What does he want? A white world under the snow of virtue, and for himself a sort of living martyrdom inside a hill of glass?

I said, "Surely Danton escapes the charge of mindlessly howling for blood."

"At least for some while," said Robespierre very dryly. Ponder September, Camille. Then, perhaps afraid of offending me, he said, "But as you know, I defended him quite vehemently the other night. You should take note of that, Camille. I'm no enemy to any man who has kept faith with our ideals." (No one more cynical than an idealist? Danton had sat down beside me after this particular defense, and said, "Well, that's one way. Drag out every bit of slander against me, make sure they all hear it, then say of course it can't be true.") Robespierre seemed aware of the drift. He began to praise my literary talents. This time it sounded false, and I was not flattered. "For such a long while we've wasted you. But now, with the power of your writing, and your honesty—And I won't deny it will be a great aid to me. They are beginning to look to me at last.

Oh, don't imagine I speak in pride. Do I even want the onus to rest on me—can I support the weight of it? God knows, I don't. But I can try. I can try to find the strength. I must. To lead them, these poor lost children of France, out into the light."

Christ, what is he saying?

He is saying *I will be king.*

"Will you stand beside me, Camille?"

A spasm of pure nausea went through me. I told him I would. He was draining the life from my veins. He wanted to be made the Dictator of France. Then he could lead us into the light. Let go of me, vampire. No. This isn't Robespierre. It's just the damn silly way he talks. But he clasped my hand and I was repelled by his touch, the curious galvanic quality of it.

A brief discussion of ethics and inclinations came next. Patently he was in favor of leniency to the blameless. Yes, Camille, a point worth stressing. Opposition to the Hébert faction. France must not sink to godless lawlessness. I meant what he meant, didn't I? He intimated that I should have financial assistance with the paper. Not a bribe, of course. But being so honest, I hadn't made myself a rich man on the back of the Revolution. Well, Maxime, I've profited by the decline of the East India Company. He must never hear about that. Why, what would he do—could he do?

"Also, Camille, if I might glance at the proofs."

"I'd be glad if you did. Help me check the galleys for printers' errors."

He cleared his throat, not having meant quite that, but never mind.

We parted with expressions of undying love.

My paper was a power. It breaks my heart to lay down my pen.

I was shivering and quaking, dithering like an old man, biting my nails to the quick, pacing up and down, horrified.

And yet, deep within myself, another was stirring: Let me cry out!

Danton meant to use me. Robespierre meant to use me. But I too had a voice. Damn the pair of them, and damn all fear. I would do this for myself.

❧

It occurs to me that when I began this, I made, and more than once, two statements. The first of these was to the effect that I took Robespierre as my hero and would have followed him to extremis, into hell itself, did so, and found I had been deserted. The second statement I set down frivolously, exclaiming that those whom the gods wish to destroy they first convince they can get away with anything. But since I have tried to find the truth in all this (though perhaps cannot always admit it), I must say here that what I said before is misleading and I have even allowed it to mislead me. Because of what happened, my perceptions are clouded, and were more clouded at the start, but have come clear in patches.

Though I had had moments of passionate loyalty and admiration for him, moments when I thought I would, and perhaps would, have followed Robespierre to the death, this last enterprise was not conceived, as is obvious, from any such motive. When I said, Yes, Maxime, as you tell me, you are Liberty's slave and the high priest of Virtue, and I will mount guard beside you and smite the unrighteous in your name, I was in the thrall of Danton, or of what was in my own self. So Robespierre is not to blame, as I later blamed him. Be sure of that.

While for the rest of it, my outcry in Dillon's room shows very plainly I knew, in my soul, I would not get away with *anything*. But as I pushed the embarrassment of that breakdown from my memory, so I chose to forget what I had said. Even with the example of the Gironde before me, I persisted in thinking, in my outer mind, that words never kill. Yet in the deeps of consciousness I was well aware they might. Hadn't I already sent bloody mad little Marcandier to such a fate?

I would give myself as much license as Roch would give himself.

I would say what was in me, shrieking to be said. And old wounds would be opened, new wounds tailored to fit every adversary. I would hold up a mirror and make them scorch and wail for what they had done to our Dream of Freedom.

Did I still think I could change the world?

Yes!

No. Even I was not such a fool.

There now. I absolve Robespierre, and even the gods. Mea culpa, after all. As someone yelled during the trial, at Danton, with a ghastly sportive misquote of Molière's famous line, *Tu l'as voulu, Georges Danton!* Just so with Camille, who also, himself, and very knowingly, *asked for it*.

But you will say I was a hedonist, a life-lover, and, additionally, a coward. Why, then, ask for death? Guilt, despair. Tiredness with this ocean of misery relieved only by mirages, or by islands of horror. Even Jesus Christ chose the scaffold, when he could stand no more of it.

15 Frimaire, 2nd Decade, Year Two of the Republic, One and Indivisible

The Cordelier Leader (Number 1)

L I V E   I N   F R E E D O M — O R   D I E

When those who rule come to be hated, their opponents
are not far from being admired.

— MACHIAVELLI

O Ministry of England! I render my homage to your genius. If you cannot destroy us through our royalists, you will do it by means of our extremists.

In 1789 we rose against the blades and banes of the aristocracy and founded our Republic. Are we now to behold its vanquishment? In his cradle I see our Hercules of Liberty in the grip of tricolored serpents and on the verge of being strangled. Danton has only to speak of moderation at the Jacobins to be shouted down—*Danton*, the Horatius who for so long alone held the bridge against our enemies. But, strengthened by that ground won under cover of Danton's illness and absence, the League for Blood and Violence feels mighty. It booed and jeered, smiling in pity as if this hero's speech had been condemned by every voter in the club.

Nevertheless, the band of the Old Order, the Ancient Cordeliers, the founder members, the Father Confessors of Freedom—ordained by the dust of a collapsing Bastille, the rain of bullets over Mars Field—*we* are not routed so swiftly.

Victory! Amid a landscape of so many ruined civic colossuses (reputations), that of Robespierre still towers. For he stretched out a brother's hand to his rival for the love of France, Danton. And sanity carried the day. Robespierre, whose talents increase in proportion to the perils about him. Once this orator had spoken, no man any longer dared raise his voice against Danton, for fear the speaker be thought in the pay of the English.

But what has brought us to this—that the word MERCY should require a lightning bolt in its defense?

It needs to be written. It is necessary to put away the slow pencil of a Revolutionary History, set down at one's fireside, to snatch up again the fast, breathless pen of the journalist. My colleagues, caught in the whirlwind of politics, away on military missions, working for the committees, have had no space, as I have, to collate events.

And I say that Paris, awash as she is with journals and news sheets, has no paper which speaks the truth, though a plethora that speak rather less than the truth. I reenter the theater of combat armed with all the honesty and the courage I can lay hand to.

And to this end of honesty, and truth, I say too the press must stay free, whatever excesses are committed in print. Better that than that every pen be a bought slave.

The upheaval of a Revolution provides no excuse for restraint. As I said five years back, it is the *wicked* who fear the light of the streetlamps. We have all heard of those who take it into their heads to spill forth every political secret they know, and so wreck their country's policy. Do not fear this from me. Though I will not keep silent, I shall betray nothing and no one, save those whose betrayal will save the Republic.

"Do I take it," said Danton, "Peter the Stone Rose saw most of the proofs but not all?"

"There were some amendments," I said.

"For example, the last several pages?"

I said nothing.

"But he'll have enjoyed being the lightning bolt which saved me."

"He thinks he was. The way you speak of him now, I assumed you thought so too."

"Robespierre?" Danton laughed.

"He isn't dangerous, then?"

"Very. But what am I?"

The second issue, due on the streets tomorrow, had been virtually dictated by Maximilien, who had looked at me sternly and said perhaps I would care to take some notes; he felt this and this needed saying. Certain men were to be targets, and Hébert ("bought by the English" – the bastard deserved that lie) and his cult of Reason, which Robespierre loathed. Powdered girls on cathedral altars were not for Robespierre. He had not mentioned my remarks on journalistic liberty. He had merely appended, "*All* the galleys, next time? I was a little surprised. Am I not to be trusted?" A last-minute inspiration. I know how busy – "Never too busy to discuss such a matter, Camille."

"The religion of Reason needs slamming," I said now, "You can't graft that atheistic claptrap onto superstition. We'll have another monster on our hands."

"Well, he'll like all that. You two hand in hand with your Supreme Being."

Danton had proposed a festival to celebrate this Supreme Being. Classical. Games and banquets, offering-smokes going up. Tongue so firmly in cheek it nearly protruded through one ear. Or do I misjudge?

Other festivals elsewhere. Out in the provinces, Good Old So-and-So with his portable guillotine and traveling show. Roll up and see the heads roll. In Lyons, retaken for the Republic, cannons turned on the condemned – condemned for supplying sour wine to the army. Condemned because the list was one short and you were handy, or because you happened to be in the line of fire. "Something odd here, captain. It says one hundred prisoners to be shot, but we've got one hundred and two bodies." "Oh, those two fellows were right, then, when they kept shouting at me they'd only come up here to sell ices." And it doesn't even kill cleanly, the cannon shock aimed so impromptu, and sometimes by gunners averting their eyes, the scoundrels, from young girls, children, babes at suck in the very instant before the blast, on milk poisoned by their mothers' fear; it's necessary to go and finish them off. The bits. But the guillotine's too slow for all these traitors, these traitor babies. Boats, then, by night – at Nantes – crowded with prisoners, sunk. Or they bound them together, a man with a woman, and flung them in – water-couplings, they call it. Or deportation *vertically.* Christ. These tales weren't true. True. True.

"You seem," I said to Danton, "less concerned with this venture of journalism than at the start. Didn't you buy my services at the Flon? Half a chicken, three bottles of claret, two girls—"

"Ha, Camille."

"Losing interest again?"

"Just watching you."

Watching me. You must have seen something dark and gloomy then, *noiraud* to its soul. And I was particularly dismal that night. I had heard on my way to the dinner party that Dillon was rearrested. They said the Luxembourg was his destination. So much for bad luck's grave. This time I could do nothing. It had become part of the case general. So I would write what Maximilien wanted, then revert to my cause. He had, as Danton was aware, said to me, "I, too, hate these excesses." He hated Hébert's influence more. And David, whom Danton called the Knave in the Cards, had pushed against me at the Cordeliers and said, "What are you trying to do? Lay down the sword, you say, then what? Sell ourselves to Prussia?" Go and play with your brushes. "Oh, yes. You don't like it when we ask for explanations." I had heard it said he followed Billaud around the prisons in September '92 and fashioned sketches of battered dying women lying between his knees, and now I told him so. He made voracious noises at me and was dragged off, shrieking over his shoulder that soon I would have to account for myself at the Jacobins. One guessed that such an event was possible. They would stand me up and demand my excuses. What then? "A matter of form," Robespierre said, when I mentioned the notion. But you'll save me, Maxime. Won't you? I'm writing this paper for you all night long. Who cares if I defended Dillon, and a man who is called Philippeaux and says the military tactics in the Vendée stink, and if I made a scene when the Gironde went down. Or used that vile obscenity: mercy.

"It may be," Danton said, "we'll need to pull our horns in after all. Wait."

"Yes," I said.

"Particularly since those beautiful well-chosen phrases of yours tend to hit below the belt. Tread a little more quietly, Camille, on the corns of your adversaries."

"Yes," I said. He patted my back. I took no notice of the gesture or the words.

Knowing myself, by now, utterly alone.

I lived from day to day, like a starving dog in the snow. There was no way out for me. Quite often I would find some place of hiding and go there to weep. At night, if I slept, my appalling dreams would wake me again and again. But I was learning, even asleep, to deceive. I would rouse in dumb terror, now. And so would not disturb the young woman who shared my bed, my wife, who when she found me in despair was at her wit's end to comfort me, but discovered half an hour later it was all to do again. I could argue myself to better humor, too, sometimes. But not for long. My companion of darkness was always with me, like the mark of sickness. I lay down to sleep by him, debated night-long, sleeping or waking, with his shadow, rose to find him in the morning, passed the day at his side.

Only when I wrote was there release. Some other spirit came then, and spoke in my ear, and moved the pen, and held my heart in his golden clasp, making me brave and strong for a little while.

Danton had already begun to refer to my paper jokingly, in public, as "Camille's pastime." He was saying, Oh, I approve, but it isn't serious. *Is* it? I had gone my own way as well as his, and he had no intention, if my ship foundered, of sailing onto the rocks with me. But I expected nothing else, at last. It is foolish to misremember and aver that I did. He gave me good dinners and comradely warnings. I ignored the latter. The former were the pleasure and suppliance of a minute. He took me aside, too, from time to time to tell me, Things are looking up. They had mooted another committee at the Convention, this one for review of those detained in jails—leniency for the slight offender. Robespierre, intent on checking Hébert's ascent, put his approval behind the scheme. But Camille said blackly to his acquaintances, "Here is an impossible sum. Committee of Public Safety equals Guillotine. Committee of General Security equals Guillotine. Committee of Mercy equals *no* Guillotine? That doesn't add up."

So you're fighting for what you believe can't happen.

Yes, I think it would be fair to say that.

And I went on limping through the starving snow, where spring would never break.

❁

Stop now, if you wish. Turn down the page and turn away. I would do it, if I could.

❁

After screaming at me in the Jacobins, they gave me the floor. They gave it me because Robespierre was there and offered one of his just perceptible signals that I should have it, so I stood, out in the open, the knife-edged wind of their disapproval whistling around me. I found it hard to catch my breath, but spoke up as I was invited to. I felt a duet of things: the uselessness of it all, and a strange fright and nervousness which astonished me—I was so pervasively afraid, I failed to understand such fear has itself many moods.

"Very well. I defended Arturius Dillon because I thought his courage and skill were precious to France. As for the Gironde—have none of you ever been mistaken in a friend?" Which earned me more howling. Naturally, they were never mistaken in anything. When the griping died down I said, in a rush, "I loved Mirabeau but renounced his friendship when I found him false to the Revolution." And then something which afterward shamed me, since it was personal and they did not deserve such a bone tossed to them, "Of the sixty Revolutionaries who signed my marriage contract, only two remain to me as friends—Danton and Robespierre. All the rest have left the country, by means of a boat or the guillotine."

Cunning to remind them who my friends were? Canny to crack a joke, however black? Well, some of them laughed. Others commiserated. The tune changed, though there was yet a bass accompaniment of grumbling. (The political noises would be funny, both at the Jacobins and in the Convention—if life and Liberty were not at stake.)

Then Robespierre (my friend) stood up, and I moved aside to give him the rostrum over the tombstones. He caught my arm, however, and kept me there, standing by him, while the elevation of the speaker's position now made him rather taller than I.

"We must pardon Camille his weaknesses," said Robespierre, as if I were some naughty child, caught stealing candy, or his dog that had misbehaved on the rug. He angered me, holding me there with his kind fingers on my shoulder, making me listen, and be seen to listen, an object lesson for them all. Yes, anger, even in fear—anger being, like the blasting grief, another of fear's components.

"Camille is easily led astray by strong emotion. Truly, he did worship Mirabeau—but he himself smashed the idol when he learned it was dross. In future, we would only ask him to be more discerning in his choice of whom to follow."

Follow you, you mean. I remember you bawling in a schoolyard corner because someone shoved a snowball down your back.

I said to him afterward, "Thank you, Maxime. You made me look a perfect fool."

"No, Camille," he said gravely, "I'm sorry to say you are responsible for that." He bore my look. He said, "I'm your friend, and I value you. But you persist in putting yourself in harm's way."

I am two men. One knows he is finished and has only to conclude the act. The other lives in the moment and loses his temper.

"We're all in harm's way. Or have you forgotten your Committee of Safety's nicest pronouncement—the Law of Suspects?"

"What has that to do with this?"

"Who does nothing for his country is as guilty as he who works against it. Do I have that right? If I sleep late in the morning I'm wounding France by my laziness. If I piss against the damn wall I'm pissing on the Republic."

"There's no talking to you when you're like this."

"I'm always like this. So I take it you'll prefer not to see any further galleys of the paper."

"This is a different subject."

"No. What I write is mine, therefore *me*. So you won't want to look at it. It might compromise you."

He gave me a long slow stare. "Then," he said, "it might." He touched his hand to his eyes, as if the sight of me hurt him.

One of me said to me, What's it matter? I can win him over later; he's still Robespierre. One of me said to me, Now go and do as you want. And I said nothing, but went and did it.

My *confusion*.

❊

> *Au clair de la lune,*
> *Mon ami, Pierre-Robes,*
> *Prêtez-moi ma plume,*
> *Pour écrire un mot. . . .*

❊

Ah, Maxime, poor Maxime. They all desert you. There in your Gethsemane, the only one awake, the rest asleep and locked in the toils of their unconscionable dreamings.

What is it you wanted? An end to bloodletting by a letting of blood. To keep the ultimate weapon of the guillotine in order to eradicate every plotter, expunge every blemish on the body of the Revolution. Hang death by the neck until it be alive.

Making your omelet.

Like the flawless knight in the legend, your strength and power sprang from your purity. Even the vision was pure. You wanted the best and most beautiful thing for your world, and would kill a world to get it.

And crazy impure corrupted Camille Desmoulins, whose visions were so muddled, so confused by human doubt and remorse, didn't show you the proofs of that third issue of the paper most of Paris, for its varied reasons, was rushing to buy. You saw it first when Collot d'Herbois, hot home from the killing in Lyons, put it in your hand with a scowling oath.

❊

The Cordelier Leader (Number 3)

Since the monarchy and the Republic are at war, which state of affairs must end in victory for one side or the other, let me promote the triumph of a Republic by detailing what one can expect from a monarchy.

To accomplish this, all I need to do is to go back to antique Rome and the Caesars and crib from Tacitus. Accept then, if you will, this hasty translation from the Latin.

Caesar Augustus was the first to make laws which revealed how even words and glances might be taken for state crimes.

Soon it was a crime for citizens to put up a statue in honor of their war dead. Augustus had been fighting on the opposing side.

A crime, too, to weep at the death of a son, or a close friend, who had offended the ruling regime. (Everything annoys tyrants.)

Were you popular? Then doubtless you would use your popularity to start a civil war: you were *suspect*.

On the other hand, if you sought obscurity out of the public eye, you might be plotting in the dark. *Suspect*.

Were you rich? Heavens above, you would be planning to suborn the people with gifts. *Suspect*.

Were you poor? For sure, mighty Emperor, watch this fellow closely. No one tries so hard to get something as one who has nothing. *Suspect*.

Were you downcast and slovenly? Doubtless you mourned the prosperity of the Emperor's reign. *Suspect*.

Were you in the habit of gorging yourself at supper parties? Then you must have been celebrating the Emperor's attack of gout. *Suspect*.

Were you a philosopher, public speaker, or poet? You might gain for yourself more good regard than those who governed. Could one permit more attention to be paid to an author in a garret than to the Emperor in his high-walled mansion? *Suspect*.

Last, if someone had gained a reputation in war, was he not most awkward of all? His soldiers would respect him and he would never stand alone. Better get rid of him. *Suspect*.

One might add that to be related to Augustus was not fortuitous either. Being of royal blood, you might aspire to the throne. *(Suspect.)*

Tacitus, I thank you for this alarming picture.

In fear of losing one's authority, it can be seen, men may go to extremes.

But I say this: The death of all who are innocent makes a human calamity no less awful than the escape of villains from justice.

What hope do we have, when a place of judgment becomes the Palace of Death?

I have not, in this number, aimed a hidden dart at anyone. Have I? It is not my fault if certain persons find resemblances between the conditions in Tacitus's Rome and these imperfect times of ours.

If I have taken up a sword for a pen, it is in order to eradicate all such resemblances once and for all.

How appalling that Liberty should be confused with despotism.

For we must never persuade ourselves that this portrait of a tyranny sixteen centuries old will pass today for freedom and the best of all possible worlds.

※

One afternoon when I came home, a woman was standing on the inner stair. I barely saw her in time to avoid collision; she had dressed like the shadows in dull black. I thought her nothing to do with me until she put her hand on my arm and said, "Monsieur . . . Desmoulins?"

Her voice was as pale as her face, hardly there, yet with a most beautiful diction. She used the outmoded and uncivic address "Monsieur." These two things gave her away. She was a woman of (previous) rank, and I stared at her I suppose very hard and very oddly. "Yes, I'm Camille Desmoulins. What do you want?" A few years ago, to stab me, probably. But now:

"Oh, monsieur," she said, "only to thank you."

Ungraciously, very ill at ease, I said, "I don't think you know me, citizeness."

"Oh, yes," she said. "Your voice crying out in the middle of this nightmare for reason and justice. You, one of their own, calling for an end to it. Of course I know you. My son and my husband are under sentence at La Force—"

"I can't do anything for them."

"But you are doing it," she said gently.

I said, "If you want to petition against the verdict you should approach me at the offices in the Tuileries."

"Many will," she said then. "Not to your unembarrassment, I perceive."

"Madame," I said, "excuse me. I don't want to distress or insult you, but I'm not fighting for the royalist position."

"For the cause of the innocent," she said. "That is enough. I won't trouble you further." She turned to go down the steps, and said, "You're in my prayers, monsieur. Half the city prays for you, I may tell you. Which must also discompose you a good deal."

My eyes filled with painful tears. I stood twisting my gloves, moved as I had once been moved by the plight of the slum dwellers of Saint-Antoine, upon whose kind this woman's kind had for centuries battened. But not this one, surely, so very mild in her voice and actions, her cloak threadbare as none of mine had been for years. "Wait," I said. "Allow me to take you up to my rooms. It's a cold day. My wife will want you to have coffee, or some wine—"

"Not at all," she said, looking back at me with a sad amusement. "I fear I've compromised you too much already."

And she was gone.

I staggered up the stair, reached the door, and getting inside almost fell. I clutched the wall, and Lucile came running with exclamations.

"I met—a ghost on the stairway."

She held me, and I her. Presently I was able to say, "It seems the aristos want to congratulate me for espousing their cause."

It was a fact, I had heard, even seen—I'd walked over there, drawn by a sort of frightened vanity—they were *fighting* to get possession of my journal, mouthpiece of the first and original Old Cordeliers, *The Leader.* The crowd around my printer's near Saint-Roch was in tumult. Later that unbound collection of papers, much pawed, would be sold, and resold.

Soon it would be the royalists who kissed and embraced me on the streets, and the Revolutionaries who spat on me. (Though I'd met a very drunk Fabre last night who crowed, "Hey! You called Robespierre a tyrant! Bravo! He had it coming.")

And had I? No, I'd spoken only of Caesar Augustus.

Yes, the sans-culottes would spit on me. What else could I expect? (I, the arch-traitor to the Republic. No. *No.*)

While all the velvet prayers of Madame-the-Aristo and her peers would not save me.

⚜

In the war zone, Saint-Just had done wonders. Rallying the men, seeing they got shoes and coats, digging their truant officers out of theaters, having conspirators shot. Louis Antoine—and Philippe Lebas, whom he had chosen to go "on campaign" with him—were even seen charging at the head of the armies against Austrian troops, in the wild heaven-inspired method Saint-Just had introduced—*ordre du choc*—shock tactics, prescription to collide (which Georges Danton once perversely called the *ordre du chocolat*). Lebas had written to his young pregnant wife, Betsi:

> Saint-Just is as anxious to get home as I am. I've promised him one of your special dinners—I'm so glad you've lost any ill-feeling you had for him. He's astonishing, a great man, I believe; every day I admire him more. The Republic has no more ardent or able crusader. We get on so well. We are always talking about you.

The French soldiers, climbing onward through the snows, sang:

> *So who is he fears victory*
> *Will shun a winter scene?*
> *All months are fine for glory's wine,*
> *And laurel crowns always green.*

Paris was a mirage behind them now, glittering, consolidated. Saint-Just was the living proof of it: handsome, dedicated, pale with exhaustion on their behalf, never giving up. A deputy who spoke of the high ideal of Liberty as a holy thing and would fight beside them for it, regardless of shot and shell.

Nothing much amiss with the heart of Paris, if it could produce a Saint-Just. The city, the Republican ethic, the crowns of evergreen, firm in unity at their backs.

❊

Like an eruption of boils, that damnable paper, it would keep coming out on the skin of the Revolution. The *Vieux Cordelier,* the *Cordelier Leader:* you saw it everywhere. The fourth issue was selling sixth-hand for one whole livre. They smuggled or bribed it into the prisons. In the black daylight under the gratings, the abject prisoners read it and shed tears. At those valiant last suppers of theirs, they drank to the health of Camille—and not without, perhaps, the pepper of irony to season that toast.

It was the fourth issue which raised shrill outcry into a flaming roar. It was the fourth issue which said: Who are these wrongdoers in the prisons? The feeble and the foolish. Take them and execute them? Why then how clever, you rid yourself of one enemy and gain ten more from among their family and friends. And the crowds who pack Revolution Square: do they go there to watch out of a wholesome love of the Republic? Or because this live show is so much better than the fakery of the theater?

I take a different stance from those who have told you that Terror must be the order of the day. I ask for *Clemency,* for a COMMITTEE OF CLEMENCY. Of all the measures of the Revolution this would be the soundest, for it would *end* Revolution—a state which is, in essence, that of one part of the civil body ranged against another, embattled with *itself.* Clemency—mercy—ideas surely not unworthy of the French Nation. Let us wipe out the mistakes of the past; let us create a new era from which to date our birth. Can our vaunted patriotism, the dream of the betterment of one's countrymen, even exist—where there is no humanity or care for one's fellows? Do such flowers blossom in a waterless desert, or in a heart which is like a desert?

"Camille Desmoulins is a bloody traitor!" one voice yelled at the Cordeliers, and was instantly blocked in by a hundred others yowling the same thing.

So the paper which had named itself for the Cordeliers Club found its editor-author expelled from said Cordeliers.

Late in December, as English-occupied, Republican-besieged Toulon was beginning to crack under wild assaults of artillery, and the Vendée giving at its knees, a light snow dampened news sheets in the outdoor hands of readers, who saw there in print the words: "Oh, my dear Robespierre! It is to you that I address this plea." (See, he's gone and named him again. Well, he names everybody, and then makes a monkey out of each of them, too, usually. Not Robespierre, though; no.)

Because I have seen how no one could overcome you, seen how, without you, the ship of our hopes would have perished, the Republic gone down in chaos, the Jacobins and the benches of the Mountain, both, become a tower of Babel—my old school friend, do you not recall those debates historical and philosophical by which we learned that love, and only that, is more mighty, and more lasting, than fear? This lesson is not unknown to you.

You wouldn't think he was afraid of anything, would you? What about the expulsion from the Cordeliers, he doesn't even seem to care about that. For by now Number Five of the irrepressible paper is on the street. And it says:

Brothers and friends—Having seen Daddy Duchesne and all his patriot sentries on the deck, holding their telescopes and preoccupied with shouting "Look out! Desmoulins is playing with royalism!" I, original Cordelier and veteran Jacobin, can only retort, "And *you* are playing with exaggeration." Excuse me if I continue to refer to myself as a "Senior Cordelier," even after being forbidden to do so. Frankly, what else *can* a grandfather do when his infant grandsons refuse him use of the family name?

And he had said, "Liberty is not a child who needs to grow up through an adolescence of gauche brutishness and tears. She springs forth like Athene, fully formed and fully armed."
And he would say:

Even if injustice is to triumph and bring me to the foot of the scaffold, I should not wish to change places with those who have screamed for murders and brought France to desolation, drunk on blood. What is a scaffold to the true lover of France—but martyrdom? In this time of war, when I have seen my brother savagely cut down for Liberty's sake, what is this guillotine more than a steel kiss, the most glorious accolade for one who dies in honor for his beliefs?

⚜

The day was so dark, Lucile had had the girl light an oil lamp for the breakfast table. I remember how the rosy light mirrored my wife that morning, against the chill dusk of the window at her back. She appeared no more than an alabaster seventeen, but so sad. Only when she played with our child, or looked across at me, did her eyes brighten. She was watching me carefully, I was conscious of being almost always under scrutiny. She wanted to make everything serene and pleasant about me, to soothe me. But I knew I wore her down. Lovely kind angel, beating your pretty wings around my eyes and ears so I shouldn't hear the shouts, see the lengthening shadow move across the floor. I tired you out. You tried so hard. Neither of us could help what we were.

When Danton arrived, unexpected and bleak as the morning, and heaved himself into a chair, Lucile flew up to see to everything—more bread, more chocolate, this, that. (Jeanette had left us long ago. Her splendid cooking and wretched coffee. I remembered her with bundle and box for the country and how she cried on Lucile's neck, drowning my wife in tears and flesh, so anxious at betraying her to other domestics and so mistrustful of me. Jeanette had liked me, once, but by the light of Lucile had come to see Camille's worthlessness. Like the replacing domestics, I was not good enough for this golden girl-goddess. Like them, I would let her down.)

"Give me that child," said Danton, taking Horace from her arms. Horace went willingly and began to climb the slopes of the new brown coat, planning doubtless to plant a flag of possession in Danton's mane. Reaching a protruding ledge of paper, however, the baby unearthed a sheaf of *Cordelier Leaders*. (How many arrived with these in tow, and sat down to say, What the hell are you *doing*, Camille?) Danton and I both regarded my son, as he opened wide a sheet with a smile of discovery.

"We're lucky he can't read it," said Danton.

"Have you? I've sent you every number."

"Yes, I've read them, like everyone else. Including Maxime, I gather."

"Yes."

"Yes. He said," said Danton, "open letters addressed to him were not what he favored. And that flattery left him untouched when the motive behind it was insincere."

"Damn and blast him," I said in a sudden fury. "It wasn't flattery, it was true—could be true of him—I tried to reach him through these walls of ice he's so busy building around himself. I went across to the Duplays and was told he was away. *Away.* I ask you. And this is to *me.*"

"He's sulking," said Danton. "You've trodden on his tail. Altogether, Camille, you're making a bit of a fucking mess of everything, aren't you?"

"*Am* I?"

My son glanced into the storm of my wrath. He was used to me of late. Unlike Lucile he paid not much attention. I think I had lost him already. Once my tears had fallen on his face, and he had stared at me and turned away with a petulant gesture that irrationally wounded me to the heart—poor little boy, he only thought it was raining and wanted to get into the dry.

"Control," said Danton. "You're going too fast."

"You've said that before."

"And been right."

"Then go away. Go back to Louise and have a nice time. And I'll—"

"You're writing yourself into prison."

"So I've been hearing since 1789."

"And from prison into one of those nasty dung carts we see so often on Saint-Honoré Street."

"Shut up for Christ's sake. Don't let Lucile hear you."

"Lucile knows. Do you think she's witless? When I came into the vestibule downstairs, someone had written on the wall, *To the lamppost with the lampposter.* The mud came off quite easily."

"Thanks. Yesterday it was something else. They'll get tired of it."

"Will they?"

"Hébert and Momoro—God, that fat bag of shit, when I think how he pushed my pamphlets back at me, too strong for him, the blood-gulping parasite—they pay men from the slums to write these slogans."

"If it makes you more comfortable to think so."

"I also have other things written to me. Letters of praise and entreaty by the coachload."

"From those whose names all begin *de,* or *la,* or *duc.*"

"And others. There was a deputation at the Convention the other evening— you saw them, shaking my hand—from the provinces all of them, with holes in their shoes."

"And knowing very little of the political climate of Paris."

"This was your idea."

"Was it? I begin to wonder. When it was discussed—"

"You told me, Write and stop the butchery."

"*Yes.* And I told you, Let Robespierre think it comes from him. But what do you do? You attack half his courtiers by name as monsters and then implicate him. You yell across the streets of Paris, Oh, dear Robespierre, remember how you used to talk of goodness, and lift your mitts out of the blood. Clumsy, Camille."

"Fine. You write it, then. You do it."

"Oh, come on. I'm not saying you're wrong. But you're precipitate. Haven't you learned yet to read the weathervane? You've seen what happened at the Jacobins when I spoke out for moderation. We've had a surfeit of *that* word, sang Robespierre's chorus in harmony, and the room applauded them. Oh, I'll still speak. I'll make them listen. It has to be sorted out and stopped. But you— you're like a man in flames throwing himself out of a fifth-story window. Rein in. Go more slowly. I need Praetorians, Camille, not berserkers. Hell, I should have known better than to touch your gunpowder off. And look at you, look what you're doing to yourself. Have you slept for a week? How much weight have you lost? You're a skeleton. Scared cockless, aren't you? Admit it. Look at your hands. How can you hold a pen if they shake like that?"

"They dn-don't shake when I—whn-when I write."

"Pity."

"An-nn-all right, Danton. I know now. I've heard you."

"You'd have paid attention, once."

"I *have. Always.* I'd have followed you through—but where are you? Do it, don't do it—oh, then, we'll do it tomorrow."

Danton did not thunder back at me.

My son frowned. Did he guess this meant something; his Uncle Georges and his father were always insulting each other, but was this altercation different? Suddenly the small physiognomy of the child started to pucker. Danton looked down at him. "Now, now, my best Horatius," he said. And Danton raised him high and held him, smiling up into the baby's face with such a glorious joy, such a willful, fire-filled ordinariness, he made me wither at the uncomplex force of life in him. Was it so easy? Wait, choose words, experiment; if needful, retreat, let slip, let slide.

"You're aware," said Danton, still smiling at him as Horace began to kick and coo in approval, "that Robespierre has decided the only way to save us all is to aim for a dictatorship."

Where had I had this conversation before?

"It seems so."

"So stop playing about with him, Camille. Stop trying to treat him as your dear old school chum from college who loved the philosophy lessons. He's gone over the edge. Let him alone."

I felt abruptly violently sick, as though everything in my stomach was about to leave me, one way or another. As I walked out of the room, Danton said nothing; Horace had begun the mountain-climbing again.

When I returned, calmer, very cold, they were drinking coffee at the mahogany table as if everything were everyday. The pages of the *Leader* had been pushed from sight. Horace was communing with the toy sheep on the floor.

Lucile was even laughing.

"Guess who is responsible for the English retreat from Toulon."

I shrugged, trying to smile.

"Some little artillery officer," said Danton.

"Whom I used to know," said Lucile. "The awesome Léon. He came to our house once or twice when I was about fifteen. So bossy. I'm not surprised at Toulon. Léon absolutely hated to lose at anything."

"He's a Corsican. What can you expect?" said Danton. "Like the English—an island the size of a cat's tit. They grow up inevitably wanting to conquer the world."

"Oh," I said. "That little kid, Bonaparte."

"He knows his cannon, it seems."

"All the drummers were dead," said Lucile softly, "and the hail came out of the sky to beat the drums."

"God is on our side! Twenty thousand conversions to the Supreme Being in one night," said Danton.

"Yes, splendid," I said. "Laugh. You don't believe in anything."

"I believe I must be going. I'll see you over at the Jacobins, since they won't let you in the other place."

He put his arm over my shoulders, as he passed me, and leaned down next across the sheep to Horace, with a fearsome falsetto *Baaa!*

Horace screamed with delight. Lucile ran to Danton and embraced him. Thank you, Marius, for five minutes of normal conversation.

Fréron had been at Toulon. As we listened to Danton going down to the street, I said Fréron must be written to (I'd defended him already in the paper from the rubbish-chucking Duchesnites). Lucile informed me she would write for us both. I left matters thus, knowing she would pour out her anxieties to him (he still wrote her love letters, carefully worded), and all her nervousness for me. I resented it, but how could I protest? She was my confessor, and must have a confessor for herself. We had seen Fréron briefly earlier in the month. He had said to me, "Lucile looks very pale." Inference: She would not have been pale in *my* care. Would she not? No. He had always managed his escapades better than I did mine. Later, he wrote to me, "Be cautious, Camille. Don't undo all the hard work by becoming sentimental over the slave masters now you see them on their knees. Give them back the whip, we'd hear another story." Clever Fréron. No doubt, a deputy representative of Paris, he would execute some harsh justice on Toulon, which had whored with the English.

Tonight there was a domestic engagement I wanted very much to get out of: Lucile and I were due to call on her parents. Instead, I would prefer to sit and write, Oh, *God,* until the walls fell around my ears. But I realized, after the slogans and certain badinage on the street, I could not let her go out alone, even in a carriage with the girl in attendance. They might encounter those who would throw dirt, or worse, because Lucile was married to me. My rich wife, as Hébert had informed the world, a girl I had come at via a liaison with her mother and thereafter seduced and dishonored so her dowry could be wed to no one but myself. *Control,* Danton had told me. My reply to all that had been controlled enough. ("My wife is my heaven-on-earth. Any money she brought me is all the unearned income I have. I have made nothing out of the Revolution. Can Hébert say as much?")

And could I, who said as much, say as much?

Oh, God, let me live through this. Let somebody take heed and help me, and the world alter. And let us escape, she and I, out of this filth, somewhere that is hidden from the glare of Fortune the Huntress.

I heard Lucile scolding the maid. She did not tell me why, but I had caught a word or two. It seems they had been discussing, some of our servants on the steps, whether persons who betrayed the Republic and got the downstairs walls smeared with offal and other muck should be allowed to go on living in a decent district.

Her father had never wanted me to have Lucile, and I believe he was never resigned to it, in his pudgy little heart. But he'd moved with the passions of the time, and I'd been grateful to him. When things had subsequently come my way, they had also come his. As his son-in-law he had nothing to reproach me with, except that I was as alien to him as if I had been born on the moon.

When our child arrived, Papa Duplessis found a new interest to paper over the cracks in his mistrust. He would jog Horace on his knees and tell us all what a likeness my son had to every one of the Duplessis male side. He was like Papa's papa, and grandpapa. Like the uncle who had gone off to be a soldier at a famous battle in Germany–whose name he always mispronounced. Or the other uncle who had discovered America–or could that merely be sailed over there? It was true: Horace had his mother's looks, thank God, and something of Demeter, also to his benefit. To my mind, only the infant sparseness of Horace's coiffeur gave him any resemblance to a masculine Duplessis.

Nevertheless, those afternoons and evenings we spent *en famille,* I used to think and drink myself into fellowship with the man. I would come away saying, Oh, he's not a bad sort. I can stand him. He listens, now. But every fresh visit it was, Damn it, *him* again.

With Demeter, of course, it was not the same. She was as naturally part of our family circle, Lucile's and mine, as once Lucile and she had permitted me to be a part of theirs. Often, if the old man was off somewhere on business or carouse, Demeter would drift gracefully into our apartment, displacing nothing, causing no difficulty. Practically, she was a bonus of rare accommodation. She would mind the child with an absolute, sensible, sensitive devotion. She would assist us in every matter of housekeeping, even to the selection of servants. When female friends, such as Louise Robert (and especially Danton's Gabi), had deserted Lucile on gusts of intrigue or political upset, the charming mother had fortunately been at hand, my love's earliest friend and consolation. Lacking Lucile, I could see her reflection in Demeter, as–in the utmost beginning–I think I had mistaken Demeter *for* Lucile.

We had not brought out the child with us: It was very cold. Which furnished an excellent excuse to leave him safely indoors. Lucile had been murmuring that she never left our rooms. Should we take a carriage? Oh, a foolish extravagance for such a short distance.

We stepped out boldly, as if lacking a care in the world; such actors we were. And the Cordeliers section, the sections Luxembourg and Julien around and about, seemed quiet. It might have been a winter night in any city of Europe. The cobbles ran straight, with nothing very terrible strewn on them. The familiar architecture of our district loomed up, with its angular Roman window places, and chimneys breathing faint plumes. Between the slats of shutters, slitted eyes of candle shine beamed down. The lamps along the theater's portico had been put out, but that was nothing much. Every streetlight was burning in position (a couple broken, but the wind could have done that), as if Paris were the most

412 orderly metropolis on earth. And high up were the untouched stars, who watch everything, indifferent and pitiless, like drops of diamond ice.

There was no unreasonable noise. There was even singing in one house — nor was it the Battle Hymn. (*Amour jadis de moi, ah, vous dis-je!*)

Let me pretend, then, that we are at peace.

Yet we hurried the slight distance, making out it was the temperature which spurred us.

Presently, a corner turned, and what I had taken for the sound of a carrier's cart was found not to be.

Lucile came to a standstill as if struck to marble. "Oh, God—what is it?" she whispered.

The door to the Duplessis residence stood wide. Men with lanterns grouped about the doorway, calling in up the stair, nudging each other, stamping their boots impatiently. A crowd had gathered across the road, and neighboring windows gave evidence of figures peering down, trying the while to conceal themselves in their curtains.

I moved Lucile back a pace.

"Stay here. Let me see what's going on."

She caught my hand to stay me, then let me go, torn between loyalties.

My blood had turned to water, but I thrust through the crowd. The bevy at the door was of Breechless Wonders, who turned to me with looks of ireful humor.

"Now, now. You can't go in yet."

"Either get out of my way or tell me just what's happening here."

"Out of his way. There's a fine gentleman. Look at his handsome coat."

"Oh, *pardon* us, but we've got a bit of business to attend to on the premises."

One of them, stinking of cheese and beer and dirt, dangled a lantern in my face. When I pushed it away, he said, "Well, look, boys, if it isn't Monsieur Lord Lantern-hook Desmoulins himself."

And they looked. Christ, how they looked.

What now? I stared them out, with my heart trying to burst my skull open and fly to Jupiter for refuge.

"How's the leading Cordelier tonight, then?" said another of them. "Going to write something natty for us? Kiss the aristos and dance in a ring, eh?"

"You bloody bugger," said his neighbor. "We ought to string you up. Duke Desmoulins on his own lamp-hook. That'd be pretty cozy."

At that moment, there was a clatter down the stair inside. Scarlet caps and loud mindless voices. Their arms were full of books and rolls of paper and, in one instance, beyond all reason, a clock.

The man who came out first made it a point of honor to thump into me, then ostentatiously beg my forgiveness. "Good evening, Citizen Camille. Just paying a quick visit to your wifey's dad."

"Why?"

"Well, the section has been hearing some funny things about him."

"For one, that he's *your* father-in-law."

"This will be taken up at the Convention," I said. But I stammered, and they liked that. Somehow I organized my tongue and shouted at the one with the clock, "Who sent you?"

"Section Superintendent."

"His name?" I demanded. I was deadly afraid, yet one more modulation of the Fear, acting out my theatrical there in the biting weather while the crowd stood gaping. These scum had loved me once. They said a name. Naturally it was no one I had ever heard of. "All right," I said. "The Committee of Public Safety will be inquiring into this abuse."

"Oh, will it?" The man who had barged into me joggled his fellow with the clock, and it gave off a tingling yammer, at which they all laughed.

"Victimization of a private citizen," I said, or tried to, but they shoved me aside and I could do nothing but let myself be shoved. I remembered, long ago, a million years away, how the royalists had slapped my face and brought ropes into the arcades of the Palais-Royal to hang me with.

The crowd, bored, was dispersing. If they knew me, I didn't much interest them, and I was thankful.

When Lucile and I, without a word exchanged, fled into the Duplessis house and the door was shut, we were met by an anticipated scene of riot.

The gallant marauders had been everywhere, upturning and vandalizing as much as they legitimately could in the lights of the "search." (They had been in pursuit of royalist giveaways, of course.)

Below, one of the maids was having distant hysterics. Lucile's father sat in a chair, running his hand over his face and head—as if to feel they were yet on his shoulders. It was Demeter, gray as ash, who came to Lucile and took her in her arms. "There, there," said Demeter. "What an interesting episode. Such stupid creatures, to make off with the clock because it had a lily-shaped hand and miss an entire cupboard of love letters between your father and Marie-Antoinette." At which Lucile burst into tears.

Her father looked up, yellow and sweating, breathing like a bellows with water in it. He pointed at me directly. "Your fault," he said. "It's you they're after. Don't quite dare do it yet. So they come after me. You wretched dolt, you damned maniac, bringing all this down on us."

Demeter shook her head at me quietly as she comforted my wife. Her scared face was full of pity for me.

I blustered, saying again what I had said to them outside. I would expose the act at the Jacobins. It was a disgrace. It would never happen again. Someone would pay for it.

Lucile's father looked at me in contempt.

"Oh, you just go on," he said. "Just keep it up. It might fool some people, but not this one. You're poison. You're a plague. I always knew it. May God excuse me for letting you ruin *her* life."

"No, Papa!" cried Lucile. "Don't speak to him in that way."

"How then? If I had any sense I'd get a pistol and shoot him. His old college friend Robespierre would probably give me a medal for it. Services to the Republic."

Tortured beyond endurance I think I would have hit him and, having started, might not have been able to stop. Demeter placed herself between us. She said, "No harm has been done. We've got rid of that monstrosity of a clock, which should be a cause of rejoicing. I'm sure the section is welcome to it. It can bong and rattle away in the superintendent's room for the next five years and most welcome. Meanwhile, things are being said that will be regretted. I forbid any of you to utter another word until we have had some wine."

We poised in tableau, with the dying firelight on us and the guttering ocher of candles knocked sideways in their holders. Lucile hung on my arm, till her father had shrunk by degrees into his chair, away from us. Then Demeter picked up a dainty bell and rang it decorously, so the maid in hysterics should bring us some wine.

1794: January
(Nivose, 2nd Decade)
Camille: Warrior without a shield

THEY CALLED the name of Fabre d'Églantine three times at the Jacobins, and then the name Desmoulins. Neither gentleman rose to acknowledge this summons. The Club looked to Robespierre, who said since the gladiators were not in the arena, any accusations against them should be deferred.

At this juncture, Louis Antoine Saint-Just, newly returned from the war zone (with a new secretary blessed by the name of Cake), touched Maximilien lightly on the shoulder and nodded toward the door.

Camille, garbed by a flurry of cloak and rain, was hurrying in.

"Someone warned him to be here," said Saint-Just. "Or, to keep away, and he chose to ignore it."

Elegant, couth, combed, Louis Antoine fixed the arrival with his most sculptured look. (Afraid my profile will be chipped? Let us see you try.) By contrast, inevitably, Camille looked like a lunatic. Black hair streaming water, black eyes glaring out of the sallow face. He had entered with an odd mixture of bravado flourish and shiftiness—a combination only such as Camille would be capable of. Now he stood twitching and was shouted at from every quarter.

Robespierre called the room to order.

He motioned Camille forward with a prim courtesy that displayed him as impartial and therefore no longer a friend. Whether Camille, in the state he had now reached, was able at all to read this message was itself illegible.

"Well?" came the shouted query, backed up by assent on all sides. "What's he got to say for himself?"

Camille stammered a moment, mastered the stammer with difficulty, was jeered. Seemed to lose his temper, regain it, grow frightened, arrogant, at a loss, finally still—all in a succession of instants. Eventually he flung out his arms. "For God's sake," he was heard to say. "Give me a chance. I don't know if I am on my head or my heels. If I've made mistakes, is that a crime? I'm slandered on every hand—"

"And can't speak!" came the cry.

And someone else: "*Write* us an answer in the *Cordelier Leader!*"

Which invoked much laughter.

Camille stood with his head hanging. His clenched fists gave evidence of rage, or only nerves. Obviously, he *could* find nothing to say. He was as much scared stiff as angry. Some club members squinted across to see what Georges Danton was doing. He sat massively, looking on. He had no expression. Hébert, meanwhile, had jumped up and was calling familiar charges. Who did not know the aristos paid Camille to take their side, and sent copies of his paper to the foremost adherents as a sign counterrevolution was well on its way; there would soon be a new king in France, and the river full of dead Republicans. Suddenly Camille whipped around and yelled back at him. Translated, Camille was informing Hébert that, conversely, *Father Duchesne* was quoted in every enemy journal in Europe, to illustrate the theory that the French were a foul-mouthed, unlettered, brainless, obscene troop of morons, Paris a garbage dump, the Seine a sewer, France a disease that should be cauterized from the earth. Quite effective in its virulence, except that Camille's stammer ruined the effect, and even Hébert could not make head or tail of it. As Camille ran out of breath, therefore, Hébert simply went on extemporizing, banging the rail with his open hand—until Robespierre requested him to be quiet.

"Oh, well, if *you* want it, I suppose I've no choice," snapped Hébert, and sat.

"I do not," said Robespierre, "think this is fitting."

Silence.

Robespierre waited in his pulpit, reviewing the assembly, pale and calm. He did not glance once at Camille. Camille, who had deserted him, was nothing to him now, only one more betrayal, only one more blow to the heart which Maximilien must bear. He did not hate Camille. But, as with something broken, there would now and then come an urge on Robespierre to throw away the failed liaisons of his life. Less hurtful, if one need not be constantly reminded. But, for that very reason, he, above all men, he, Robespierre, who set so much store by justice, *he* must be fair.

"I have defended this man before," he said now. "All I can say today is this. I respect all he has done for Liberty in the past. What he is doing currently—well. He has had success, and success has gone to his head. The aristocrats throw flowers dewed with tears at him, and he's led astray. As with this business of Philippeaux, whose own thoughtless pamphlets have so undermined—"

"Hn-phn—Philippeaux was right!" Camille had stuttered out again. Had interrupted Robespierre and contradicted him. Nobody had expected it. Perhaps Camille had not.

Robespierre still did not look at Camille. He paused, about to continue, as if a dog had yapped. But Camille himself seized the pause, to yap again.

"You're not going to stifle me. Philippeaux had the courage to tell this city what a diabolical farce was being directed in the Vendée."

"So you have asserted in your paper," said Robespierre. He looked straight toward the ceiling and the holy sky beyond it. "We don't need to hear your views again in this club. Your philippics over Philippeaux have been aired enough. He is himself under the gravest censure. Do you still wish to associate yourself with him?"

Oh, that voice now. Not reassuring to listen to. And the snarl of approval all about comes thick and fast.

Camille, whirling from one extreme to another, gives in to insecurity. He says, "All right. I don't know the man. Only his writings, which seemed to me—yes—all-ll right. I withdraw mn-my support on th-that—"

Maximilien's turn to interrupt. Which he does unsparingly.

"We know too well your weakness for supporting issues which appeal to your passions, regardless. As we know, perhaps also too well, your weakness for all things Roman. But this is not Rome, Camille. We are in Paris. The dreams of a willful child do not suit our needs. Though you may be pardoned, your writing must be condemned." Robespierre took in a deep breath. Why? Some uncertainty, or some satisfaction? Or only the instinct of the small animal which swells itself up in order to alarm adversaries. "To make this differentiation plain, I demand that all copies of the *Cordelier Leader* be burned."

"*No,* Robespierre!"

A transformation. Camille with his head flung back and his eyes shooting fires. And the voice coming strong and loud. "Burn my work? That's been done before. My God, have we had a Revolution or did I only imagine it? *Burn? Burn,* Robespierre? Let me remind you of your Rousseau, since you seem to have forgotten him. To burn is not to answer."

Only two actors on the stage. The theater hushed as death, gazing on in fascination.

And now Maximilien Robespierre does turn and look at Camille. It is the movement of a snake, and a snake's look, the coldest look in the world, the look which turns to stone. And Camille loses all his dramatic impetus before it, and all his composure.

"Do you dare," says Robespierre, "do you *dare* to uphold your paper to me? Do you dare to speak of the Revolution to me? You, who have tried to stab Freedom in the back with this self-same paper of yours? No, no more, Camille. I will tell you frankly, if you were any other, I would not have tried to defend you so far as I have. But now, I finish. *To burn is not to answer. To* dare to speak those words to me."

When he looked at me as he did, my very soul shriveled. I had no armoring against it, perhaps had not anticipated it, in my naïveté, from him. I was a fool. And though I had taken note of his unique power, some part of me had never assimilated it. Now it was as if he had knifed me. I almost dropped at his feet. In his sightless eyes I saw the walls of ice I had irritatedly alluded to before. They were real enough. I would never be able to scale them, let alone melt them, again.

But I drew myself together, the shreds of me. I thought I could be crafty and play my winning card. I said, and quite distinctly, "But Robespierre, you're saying all this about my paper. Yet didn't we talk the project over together? You read the galleys. I brought them to you and asked your advice."

There was quite a murmur all around.

And in his frigid eyes, a white shine: Fear? Good. I'm glad you feel it too.

But he said, "I saw only the first two numbers. As you perfectly recollect, I declined to read any more."

I started to say something to the effect that the policy of the paper had been demonstrated in those very first issues he had read. I still believed I was being Machiavellian, innocent that I was, in throwing salt at the tail of anything which ran.

But Danton suddenly called across the room, "This is going beyond itself." And that colossal voice silenced me, and all the rest of them. "Camille," said Danton encouragingly, "really will have to learn to take in good part an occasional tutelary rap on the knuckles. One must sometimes be cruel only to be kind. Robespierre's motives are of the best." I stared at him, and his eyes on me were heavy, angry. I could see he would have liked to wring my neck. Then he added, with a sprightly speciousness, "On the other hand, all this does raise one highly important question. However you judge Camille—and with cool heads, I trust—be careful you don't decapitate, at one blow, the freedom of the press."

I took my seat, and sat there, and let them decide they would read out to each other, today and tomorrow, all the editions of the *Leader*. It was only time, now, that stood between me and my expulsion from the Jacobins. The first step, as they said, toward downfall.

Danton did not approach me, or I him.

Next day Robespierre was to announce that Hébert and Camille were equally at fault.

And a few days after that, Fabre (falling foul of Robespierre at the club for preferring the opera to the end of a Robespierrean harangue), was prevented from leaving and accused, of all things, of aiding and abetting my paper. So Fabre was expelled from the Jacobins, and in the Third Decade of his own Snow Month, arrested and dumped in the Luxembourg. I heard the tidings, typically, not at the Convention, where it caused some noise, but in a coffeeshop near my printer's.

I was not, at the time, even shocked. It was merely one more pebble falling with a leaden plop into the well of horror all around.

For Danton, who essayed a defense of Fabre and got nowhere, was otherwise speaking out in all places at all opportunities. His oratory was strong, elaborate, *controlled,* and remarkable for its basic restraint. (The Lion's growling softly nowadays. Danton's no fun anymore.)

I wrote in my paper, "Yes, I have been guilty of conspiring — conspiring for the freedom, prosperity, and happiness of France. And was I bought? Yes. By love of the heroes of our day, who I believed would lead us all to glory."

It comes to me to wonder, if I had felt myself less alone, would I have found myself less so?

There came a morning when a note arrived, and Lucile, with a face of snow, told me her father had been taken to the Carmelite Prison.

Immediately a faked scenario of action. Camille leaping to his feet. Letters written and dispatched, persons sought, doors hammered on and doorbells rung. I rushed in all directions simultaneously, trying to do something because this one of all the hundreds was who he was: Papa Duplessis. I knew my efforts would be fruitless, which they duly were. But what closed portals I was met with, and what quantities of closed faces besides. Had I needed further evidence of my own position, it could not have been more generously rendered.

Going home with bad news in the misty murky dusk, the wolf-dog hour when all things change their shapes, I had an odd encounter near the river.

A cart had been overturned and pilfered, but here and there something lay in the icy mud and rubbish of the street. One of these items, a vague image of dark on pallor, was a miniature windmill. Or so it seemed. Spontaneously I had bent to look, and as I did so, my vision of the object was altered. In fact, some poor simpleton had been abroad trying to sell religious wares, of all hopeless things. His cart was promptly tipped over, naturally. God knew where he had gone. To prison too, or else he had been strung up to greet the night. What lay in the gray ice, then, was a toiling Jesus, with his cross tilted over his shoulder. The bowed hump of the figurine and the clod of mud it had lodged by, the angle of the four-pronged cross, the fading light, the winter haze, tired eyes — these things had combined to offer me the hallucination of a little conical mill with its sail arms lifted for the winds.

But the omen was dire and did not leave me. It is not every man who finds notice of his Calvary written so clearly on the way.

ELEVEN

❊ ❊ ❊

Paris 1770: Early Spring

EVERYTHING GRAY; EVERYTHING moving. What's this? It's not the warm static bed at home, with the vine and the last star in the window. Devils and miracles, no. It's the carriage, all the way from Noyon, which rumbled and bounced through the night with the rabbits flying before its wheels like fireworks, and you said to yourself, I shan't sleep. I'll look out of the window. But the window blurred and went away. Dreams came, of bouncing and rumbling and rabbits flying for their lives, and Mama in tears, and the little sisters in fits of giggles from bewilderment. And the father giving his gentle lecture, to which you listened, then, all eyes and ears. (Yes, Papa. I'll remember, Papa.) And the kitchen girl who crept out under cover of the cart's departure, to present sweets in a sticky little cloth. After that, the rattly journey to Saint-Quentin, and from here, another rattly journey, in another haphazard conveyance, to celebrated Noyon—where, in the shade of the cathedral, you were bundled into the stage. (What's this? Young gentleman for Paris? Well, I thought it was His Majesty himself.) Darkness closing fast. Stripped trees dipped in sugars of weather. Spring just a piercing nip in the air. Let the other passengers snore and roll from side to side amid the insulating straw. Lucie Simplice Camille Benoît Desmoulins, ten years of age and eager as an ermine, would stare out the night (yawn). Look, there go stars in long streamers. Every overhanging tree, hit by the carriage lamps, seems to catch alight. Owls' eyes yawn. (Yawn). And the Desmoulins's kitchen maid flies over. . . . But am I dreaming or waking—or waking up?

Somewhere a stop. Horses blowing like dragons in the cold. Hot bread in a napkin.

And a new sensation: a tightness in the throat, a tension in the spine. The stomach saying, Am I quite happy? For here we are, miles from our beginnings, adrift on the ocean of fortune. What lies before—the unknown life of school,

421

and the great strangeness of the city. All the warnings, all the forecasts for good or ill, begin to hurtle back and forth in the skull as the hoofs and the wheels hurtle inexorably onward.

So you stare out in anxiety now, afraid to miss a thing. But seeing only grayness, phantoms, motion, until—

Until a hint, a flicker far away, tinder struck on the horizon. And there, between the curve of the high road and the first gleam of sunrise, a lake of darkness like no other thing ever glimpsed before.

What can it be, a forest? Water? A cloud fallen on the land by mistake? No. Blearily stirring, the carriage's other occupants flap at the windows and tell each other, *Paris*.

Paris? That blank gray nothingness?

Then the light comes.

And then, and then, before the weary, blasé eyes of the adults, the clear visionary eyes of the child, beauty rises from its shadow. Every tower, every dome, every portico, terrace, and roof, is stitched in golden thread, against a sky half topaz-rose, half violet. Paris. She seems to cover the earth. She seems a heavenly city built by angels. She seems a wish come true and, better yet, a promise.

The little Picard boy with jet-black hair is consumed by excitement. He is standing on the seat of the coach, clinging to the window. Concerned he will be shaken down and damaged, his fellow passengers entreat him to desist.

How right they were.

Such hopes. Such symbols. That child on fire, on fire still even when the patchwork walls open wide and swallow him, the stink of sewers permeates the carriage, and the meaner tenements crane over—that child, blinded by love and optimism and innocence. How could he know he would come to this?

1794: Winter

THE LIGHT came in softly through the shutters.

"Why," she said, "you were smiling in your sleep. You looked like a little boy."

"I was a little boy. I was dreaming I was back at school again. At Louis-le-Grand. I'd won a prize for some vast work I'd written."

"What was the prize?"

"Oh, a book. I was very proud of it. I can't remember what it was. I was eleven. Or twelve. I was so *proud*. I remember the sunshine falling across the desk and on the book. I can see it all. But I don't remember what the book was. I was happy, then. What day is it today?" She told me, old calendar and new. (And Fabre's wretched conjuration hung in the room a moment, pleading for rescue.) "It's strange. Half the time when I wake up I can't recall—the day, the month—even sometimes where I am."

"You worry so much," she said to me. "When you sleep, your soul goes far away."

"Oh," I said. "My soul."

What use have I for that, that thing of smoke and desperation? This is real. The warmth of the bed and of your body, the scent of you and of the room, the city, the earth. *This* I can be sure of.

❊

Imagine then a black alley, one of hundreds, choked by filth, with here and there, in the black leaning hills of hovels, a cave entrance of reddish light—some murky wineshop, or cheap brothel of pathetic whores who spread their legs for the price of a fish head or a shred of tripe. (Oh, far from childhood's dreaming, this. Are they even able to dream? Do they have the energy for it in the deathly sleeps this locale gives rise to?) But offer even a sleepy one an assignat and she'll set on you, tear your hair out, or worse. This is the Faubourg Saint-Marcel, the Gobelins section. . . . Rat pie on sale here, so they say, and lucky to get it. And in the shop that sells this delicacy, they deal the greasy cards that show the queens now as Libertys, in red caps, and they read *Father Duchesne,* the ones who *can,* to all the ones who can't.

"The Revolution's legless, he says. They want to cuddle up to the aristos and put us back where we were in '89. And I mean *1689.*"

"Yeah. Hébert knows what he's saying, all right."

And in the corners of the shop, which may be taken as representing several others of its ilk all about the city, and taverns and bordellos and one-room hell dwellings besides, they mutter. Another revolt, against a faltering Revolution. That's what we need. Don't we?

Hébert's conscripts have been about, stirring with a sticky spoon. Hébert has begun to have his own dreams, of getting to the top of the heap, the ruined anthill of Paris. Hébert, with his paper's wide circulation in the army and his friends implanted in the Commune, and his fidgety wrath, even under that powdered nest of hair, against anything of the old order. . . .

And the slums, so stirrable, stir.

All through the first *décade* of the Rain Month, the Duchesnian grasshoppers leap hither and thither. What? That piece of crap, the *Senior Cordelier* or the *Cordelier Leader*—who'll lead you straight up the garden path—that thing has said Hébert has got money from the treasury for his journal far in excess of its production? Lies. It's Desmoulins who's paid and wants to be an aristocrat. He's gone soft, like the rest of them. Show him a king now, and he'd be on his face to adore.

And didn't the so-called "Incorruptible" Robespierre defend this traitor?

The Hébert party looks about them and feels strong. We can, they assume, rely on Collot d'Herbois: a former actor, he resents Robespierre's always getting the starring role. And Collot detests Camille (who has insulted him in print and out and made quite some play on the name "Collot" and the words *snare* and *collusion*.)

And the commander of the National Guard seems to have swung around to the idea of a spring cleaning at the Convention. Not Maximilien's man anymore.

If you leave the holes of the Saint-Marcel–Gobelins slum and head northwest, you'll get to the Cordeliers Club and see quite a change in it.

Not Georges Danton's anymore, this place. Blue-black, dingy white, and searing blood-red, the tricolors hang, and between them the slogans sprawl over each other, few of which concern brotherhood or equality. You get free wine if you shout loud enough. And though the rainy gusts blast through the glassless window (the sacking pinned there blows down), a black stove struggles to steep the area with fug and fumes and the perfume of dirty heated hating humanity.

Hébert's no hero. Why, he's got a rat's face, like those morsels in the faubourg pies. His eyes never flame like Camille's did when Camille was on our side, and his voice has no range like the operatic bellowing of Danton. Despite his pernickety coat, Hébert will hawk and let fly on the floor, if you mention, for example, God. He'll never say, like Robespierre, The hope of man which turns to an Infinite Possibility can only enoble him—even if he should be mistaken in his belief. "Fart God," says Hébert, and stokes his pipe. "Where was God when you needed Him?"

What does Hébert offer them? A bit of excitement? A change is as good as a rest? Pull down this lot and get a new bunch in the driver's seat. An insurance that blood will continue to flow.

Oh, God, can this worn-out powder keg explode again? Is it capable of another orgasm of violence?

Or is the wheel, already clogged by blood and its own ceaseless turning, sunk too deep in mire to do anything more than revolve on the spot? Come on, Hébert, whip the horses of discontent, and maybe the carriage of revolt will break free.

In the third *décade* of the Rain Month, Robespierre, walking out of the Jacobins after a politically volatile evening, collapses in the courtyard and is carried to the Duplays by loyal members, amid great exclamation.

Saint-Just: The cold priest

Maximilien Robespierre, lying on his back, five fathoms down in a swamp of fever, sees a blurred shape against the window and whispers uncertainly, "Camille?"

"Not quite."

Saint-Just is hygenically amused more than offended. His humor is usually of this type: dry, detrimental. And yet there have been witnesses who have sworn this exceptionally handsome young face has lit into laughter, that they have *heard* him laugh on a clear pale golden note — once or twice. Now only the earrings and the finger rings are gold. Cold gold in the gray February light, to match the cool splendor of his linen, his stockings, his hair and skin. Porcelain, yes. A tidy hit. The set of the jaw and the sculpture of the nose alone win him a place in the Panthéon of glamour. And inside it all, what?

Priest. Saint-Just the priest, altar boy to Robespierre, the priestly slave. Saint-Just has made the exaltation of a Republic his high altar and taken Robespierre as his bishop. So young, held back on one hand by a pragmatic caution in his nature, goaded forward on the other by a longing to learn and to uplift, Saint-Just is not yet disillusioned, either in the Dream or the one he has allowed to expound it to him. So he has brought — found somewhere — some silvery flowers which Élie has arranged in a glass vase. And so he has been arguing below with Philippe Lebas, the Duplays' son-in-law, who in turn worships him. No, Robespierre is not crushed, not going down. No. If they are steadfast to their goal, the weeds can be cut away and the garden made fair, as was always intended.

The weeds . . . cut away.

Louis Antoine, don't you see, those weeds are living men and women?

No. It's only the glory of the great altar of perfection in the colossal cathedral of eternity *you* see.

(Yet which of them, actually, has unimpaired vision?)

When he was imprisoned — it was for theft — the act, and the fount of retribution, both unexpected, if the story were true. (He had, in necessity, stolen from his widowed mother — disgraceful, and disgraceful cliché. She in her turn had him hunted and thrown in jail. Which itself sheds some light on why such a theft could take place at all.) There, in durance, he was not treated ill or well. A prison is exactly that, and even to one maintained, certain laws that owe nothing to the legal system will come into play. Flung in darkness literal and figurative, disgraced, humiliated, and sodomistically importuned, he had frozen in due course into this shell of ice. It made him sensitive to criticism and to ridicule, which scratched the frigid surface like needles. It had not been easy to endure the essential grossness of a jail. If anything he had been too adaptable. And now he wished to rise above it all, fly to the clean and organized heights. The depths had taught him to be insecure and so a grudge bearer. Had made him, also, seek redress, as did so many others, not merely for himself but for all flung-down, humiliated, importuned, wretchedly adaptable mankind. In the scrubbed world of utopia, where everyone was in pristine uniform, you would see from miles off who was coming at you. Who then could get close enough to defile?

He was exasperated by the slowness of progress but hid impatience, too, under a glaze of frost.

"Are you lucid?" he says now to Robespierre.

"I—think I am."

"Good. Then listen. Hébert is trying for the crown."

"What?" says Maximilien feebly.

"There are posters up, calling for the Convention to disband. New elections. The citizenry to rise in order to enforce the matter."

"Oh, God," says Robespierre.

"Lie back. You can't do anything in this state. But you must recover quickly."

"How? Tell me how—I try—"

"You must subdue yourself. You've done as much before. You're steel, Maxime. Will, and passion, can triumph over mere flesh."

"At least—Camille has no part in this."

"No. Camille is doing well for you. Calling the Hébertists by their true names. The *Vieux Cordelier* says, 'Can an Hébert repent? A miracle. There will be rejoicing in heaven, as heaven never needs to rejoice for the *original* Cordeliers who have never strayed.' Well, you know his style. Florid but occasionally effective."

"Camille."

"Yes, Camille. But we understand, don't we, that his war with Hébert's gang is not yours. Danton's followers want no one in power except—I wonder."

"Oh, Camille."

"Come now. Don't cry over him. You're remembering someone who has died. You've lost him; he's left you. Corrupted. I'd spit on him if I were anywhere but in your room."

"The fever makes me—regretful."

"Sentimental."

"We were at school together. You forget."

"Slight chance of that. You constantly tell me. *Camille*—Danton's cur. Leave him. We go on alone."

Robespierre gazes at Saint-Just, whom Paris calls *Ange-Mort*. Alone? When will *you* desert me?

There's nothing sexual between them. Danton would tell you, Robespierre, he never—But emotionally, idealistically, a sort of wedding. And in these realms where, even sexless, gender roles are adopted, Maximilien has become the "woman." He waits for his acolyte to instruct him again. And the command, communicated to every shuddering nerve (Take up thy bed and walk), makes him instantly relapse. He is almost delirious again by the time Saint-Just leaves him. (And passes, on his way, Souberbielle the surgeon doctor, hurrying to attend the patient.) Saint-Just himself steps across to the Jacobin Club, with Robespierre's mantle swinging from his straight shoulders.

First the Hébert gang will attack the purity of the altar. Then Danton's crowd will attack it. One could make bets on this, if one still made bets. (Once, on cockroach races over prison straw.) Beset by enemies, Antoine? How calm you seem. But then, you are above it all and ultimately cannot be touched. That element within you, which makes you, also, uncomfortable with yourself (so that any stab that seems to encapsulate the feeling—the chipping of a profile—is entered on your blacklist), that element must render you impervious.

At the debased Cordeliers they have hung a mourning veil over the panel inscribed with the Rights of Man. Saint-Just will hang a veil of shadow over Hébert.

The white priest, Robespierre's oracle, preaches rationally.

And later, Souberbielle, coming back with a box of happy, bloated leeches, exchanges cheery words with Saint-Just, during which the surgeon manages, pointedly, to slander Danton. And after that, a secretive message comes from the commander of the National Guard, to the effect that no one *he* knows has had a change of mind about anything.

Collot d'Herbois, meanwhile, declines a part in any new production.

And the slums? You can kick and tickle an exhausted starved hound. It may growl, it may try to get up. But it falls back down again.

In the end, only one section of Paris seems likely to move at the Duchesnean rallying cry.

And for the Convention? It is composed of men who are coming to be so nervous, they say whatever will please their current companions and something else to please the next batch. In a shaky landscape, one must applaud whoever crawls out of the ground as victor, and we are ready to do it.

On March 12, Robespierre, framed by striped bodyguard, totters into the Jacobins, looking like a corpse—which will *never* lie down. The club rises and cheers him. Helped to the speaker's position by Saint-Just, Maximilien, shivering, frail, indomitable, speaks for nearly an hour.

Almost simultaneously, National Guardsmen break into the Cordeliers over the river.

"I didn't do anything," wails Hébert, rounded up with his associates and escorted from the premises. "It's just my way. You needed waking up. That's all. Look! We've taken the veil off the Rights of Man—"

"Extremists who scream only for blood," says Saint-Jewel, gleaming on the assembled Convention, "and moderates who extend their weakening indulgences toward enemies who would smother the Republic—both are equally wrong, and must be eradicated. Our foes in England rejoice when we waver. Are we to tolerate such plots? There are devils among us. They sell their pens as they sell their consciences. They alter their hue like a chameleon. And when they do not write, they infiltrate. The workshop, the harbor, the farm, the field, the very battle lines. Go then, you monsters, and learn goodness and honor where you would defile—But no. There is no time for you to gain any virtues. You are late for the guillotine."

 Who is he speaking of—a *chameleon*—Hébert? Or is it a pun? Does he mean Camille?

In fact, it is Desmoulins in his paper who suggests, if the blood-mongering Hébert Society is to sample that scaffold they have so often recommended to others, the day should be proclaimed a festival, the journey to execution a cavalcade with banners and lights.

There is, of course, to be a trial.

It'll go . . . as expected.

⚜

Hérault de Sechelles, who was sophisticatedly to say, "Why is one always attacked when eating or drinking or in bed?" was actually reading a book when his manservant came to announce some gentlemen had arrived to arrest him.

"What is the charge?" Hérault inquired of them, as the manservant packed his bag.

"You're a damned spy."

"I see," said Hérault.

He walked out to the closed carriage looking immaculate and slightly bewildered, as though called suddenly to the bedside of a rich dying relative he had never heard of. His manservant faithfully accompanied him, as if on a country visit. Destination, the Luxembourg.

1794: 22 March (2 Germinal)

THE DINNER party was decorous. The rooms neat, the service circumspect, and since the waiters had been hired from the inn, no one could catch a whiff of aristocratic helotry. The food, too, was almost simple, of a pastoral wholesomeness, served with well-mannered wines and a pitcher of water. All this in deference to one of the guests. There was even, ironically, a sweet omelet. If that were somebody's joke, no one had the poor taste to comment.

As he came into the room, Robespierre had checked. There across the fireplace was Georges Danton. Bringing together a jilted bride with her erstwhile lover could hardly have seemed a more clumsy business, in those moments, to the gentlemen who had engineered it. But it was Danton, of course, who came forward. "Maxime, I'm glad to see you looking so much better. Come over to the fire." It was a forward spring. The public gardens of Paris were already turning green; but when the sun went, the dusk turned cold.

And Danton, ignoring the dusk-cold of Robespierre, went on sunnily beaming upon him, till charm dripped down the walls.

The other men kept watch. At table, Legendre, stuffing butcher's meat and gravy down his gullet, stayed nervy, got drunk, and received privately a kick under the cloth from Déforgues. About the time of the omelet, Danton sighed and said to Robespierre, "I'm very happy with my marriage, but I have to say my first wife was a paragon. When I lost her, my world fell apart. I remember you, Maxime, and how consoling you were to me in my distress. I kept the letter you wrote me then; I have it still. I retain it in my memory. Don't shut your heart, you said, to the voice of a friend who shares all your anguish. I've never forgotten your comfort to me in that hour, Maxime." Robespierre seems a little embarrassed. Before he can say anything, if he even intends to, Danton continues, "And now, think how wounded I am to find I've displeased such a friend as you. For I have, presumably, displeased you? Something's caused this rift. I wish you'd tell me what it is. Let me put it right."

Robespierre glances at Danton and away. Robespierre glances at each of them, making a note perhaps of who has got him into this uncomfortable position. Finally: "No rift, Georges. But we seem to have taken different paths."

"Different paths—which lead toward the same mansion: the health of the Nation. Shake hands, then, over the hedge which separates our paths." Robespierre smiles faintly, and spoons a fragment of the omelet between his lips. "I surmise," says Danton, "Saint-Just has been at work against me. I once said to him that if he was so bloodthirsty at such an early age, what would he be like when he was forty? You know him. Such a remark will make him my adversary for life. Which is unimportant, unless he then invents lies about me for your benefit. Then there's Billaud-Varenne—has he been on at you? The rascal owes me money. Don't let him poison you against me, Maxime. What's he said?"

"Really, Danton," says Robespierre, laying his spoon to rest.

"But I don't like this, Maxime. I don't like to fall out with you, a man I esteem, because of the tittle-tattle of a couple of intellectual halfwits."

"You esteem me," says Robespierre, fingering his formerly untouched wineglass, "but you dislike my policies."

"Who tells you so?"

"You yourself. With every tirade which calls for clemency."

"I have advocated a sensible moderation, as you have. I'm no Hébert, nor are you. Nevertheless, I couple indulgence to a strong arm that deals punishment to the guilty. And between us, we've defused Hébert's maniacs. Are you sorry for it?"

"I've read the *Cordelier*," says Maximilien.

"No, let's not quarrel over that. As you well know, Camille is a hotheaded child who rashly leaps every obstacle into every bed of briars on the other side. I neither claim nor make defense for the excesses of his journal. He has the right to speak—that is all I would say."

Across the table, Panis says, "Camille's Debate For and Against the Scaffold is a would-be indictment of Ro—of the Tribunal."

"I'm not discussing the Tribunal," says Danton.

"Of course not," says Robespierre. "With Danton's present penchant for compassion, a Tribunal is superfluous. No one can be convicted of anything."

"Oh, what a *shame,*" says Danton sarcastically.

Robespierre looks at him. "At the conclusion of Number Seven of the *Cordelier,*" says Robespierre, "there is an extraordinary passage. You've read it?"

"Yes. He calls Hébert the high priest of a temple of bones, I believe."

Robespierre pauses. "It's to be considered, the nickname 'high priest' is generally awarded only to a couple of men, and neither is Hébert." When Danton says nothing else, Robespierre says, "I'm sure we all await, with interest, the next number of Camille's paper." Then, dabbing with his napkin, he glances about again and says, "You must excuse me, I'm afraid. I have a great deal of work at home on my desk, and my doctors have advised me not to keep late hours."

When he stands, everyone stands, even Legendre, red in the face and swaying.

Danton is also on his feet. He puts his hand on Maximilien's shoulder. "I'm with you," Danton says. "You've only to ask me. We'll smash the royalist faction, you and I, and the Counterrevolution—anything they send." And, flirtatiously, "Your clear thought and my fists, eh, Maxime?"

Robespierre says, "Yes, Danton, we will smash the royalists."

"Come to Sèvres and dine with me," says Danton. "Let's get rid of all these rumors I'm rolling in luxury there. It's just a small house I bought my in-laws. You'll like it, and the country air will do you good. Yes?"

"Very well. Thank you."

At the doorway, Danton embraces Robespierre.

An hour later, with Déforgues in a carriage trundling toward the Theater-of-France section, Danton observes, "That little squirt wants to bring me down."

"He's said," said Déforgues, "not one innocent man has been sent to the guillotine."

"He's raving. He's a bloody lunatic."

"And lethal."

"I'll snap him in half if he tries any tricks with me."

"The Commune, vacated by Hébert's protégés, is about to be restaffed by Robespierre's supporters. The ministry is washed up. The Committee of Public Safety is pure Robespierrean—and you know where Hérault de Séchelles went. Saint-Just has made a fair bid to scare the pants off the Convention; there are English and Austrians under every bed. The National Guard is under Maximilien's thumb. The Breechlesses—"

"All right, all right." Danton is wide awake, it seems. "I'll tell you this. Anyone who wants to topple me, they won't need a lesson from Madame Cat. I'll bite off their heads myself; I'll eat their brains and shit them back in the skull."

"Yes, Georges."

"I want change, by God I do. And I thought I could hold the thing on the road—but look what I've got for horses. Drunk butchers, potty playwrights, Camille with his exploding inkwell—hysterics, wimps, imbeciles. I've been too quiet. It's time *I* made a little noise. *I, Danton.* Robespierre's got the Commune sewn up, has he? And the People's National Guard? Splendid! I've got the People. Let's see that little wet-fish-handed bat turd deal with *them.* I've only got to raise my voice. One roar from this throat, we'll have the roof down around his dinky little powdered ears."

"Danton as dictator?"

"If I have to. God forbid. But if I must."

Danton relapses. He breathes heavily and fast. The ultimate power, which always beckons him, always dismays him too. Coming to know ourselves, we fear what is in us, the stranger who wears our skin. Once before he has ruled. It was September.

Déforgues regards Danton in the shadowy interior, or when the sudden splash of streetlamps is thrown over them. Moment to moment, as with the light and dark, Danton's face alters. Now young, strong, brutal, filled by energy; now sunken and sick and tired. There is another look, too, a look Déforgues has seen on the face of the disordered Camille, who wanders in to supper now and then in a coat the charcoal color of dead wood ash. A Camille who tends to inquire who died today in Revolution Square, as if he asks about the weather. Who gloomily listens and has sometimes muttered such phrases as, "*He* died bravely. That's all there is left to you, I suppose, then, of self-respect. To go to it like a hero."

What is it? Terror of death, or practicing death wish?

If that sinister blade is to exculpate so much personal guilt (an English pun, Danton, a guilt-o-tine), then one by one how many of us must go to it, we shrieking, trembling, sobbing heroes.

"Look," says Danton abruptly. "A lamp still burning." It is his windows he sees. His eyes are full of tears. But he strides out into the street, huge, vital, a Titan. Attack Danton? Who would dare?

❉

For Maximilien, as he approaches the Duplays', with his now usual and voluntary escort of two or four sans-culottes, lamplight reveals a message left on the door.

Robespierre stops. Shortsightedly he peers. But he has read something like it before—yes, the last paragraph of Number Seven of the *Cordelier Leader*—

with one amendment. The names Hébert and Momoro have been cut out and two others pasted over.

"Royalists," says Robespierre, and his guard searches the night with eyes and pikes, dutiful terriers of the Terror. When he has shakily gone in, they burn the scrap of paper at a convenient brazier located a few paces up the street.

And the words burn too, as if by sympathetic magic, into Maximilien's brain.

Do you then relish this death rite, gasping for blood—for which the High Priests Robespierre, Saint-Just, and their like dare to demand a temple? A temple constructed on the lines of one that is to be found in Mexico, out of the bones of three million citizens. While they say incessantly, to the Jacobins, the Commune, the Cordeliers, that very thing which was said—by way of logical explanation—to Mexico's conquerors: *The gods are thirsty.*

Ah, Camille, ah, Judas. You sell your messiah to his enemies with a paper kiss. Up he goes then, into his Gethsemane, all grieving shattered ruthlessness. Your cross borne valiantly on his shoulder.

❋

They say the mob is going to organize another demonstration. Who says? Gossip—but it could be true. There have been a lot of placards over Paris walls lately. BREAD, NOT BLOOD! And one bright green sheet which says: BE CAREFUL WHEN THE LION WAKES. Danton? Could be.

Then there are excerpts from the *Vieux Cordelier* pinned up everywhere. That Number Seven—they tell you the printer was too scared to set it. Camille told him to get out of the shop, he would roll up his sleeves and do the work himself.

I maintain we were never such slaves as now, when we call ourselves free Republicans—that never have we so vigorously licked the boots of those in authority, even if we need not remove our caps as we do it.

Oh, yes, surely Robespierre liked that. Camille says the Mountain has given birth to mice. He says:

Liberty is humanity. Where is Liberty then? She does not prevent a mother saying farewell to her condemned son; she does not leave this mother, as the only recourse, to wait at the side of the road to watch the tumbril go by. No, I believe Liberty is generous. She does not torture and slander the condemned. She reckons death is enough.

Someone met Camille in the street and said, "Don't let those journals of yours you're carrying brush my sleeve! They'll set fire to me."

And have you heard, at the theater the other night (that new play, *Nero*), when the actor cries out "Kill the tyrant!" half the stalls stood up and yelled the words at Robespierre, who was sitting in a box. Danton's friends are supposed to have put that together. It certainly upset Robespierre.

Conversely, though, the Convention doesn't seem to be listening to Danton. They don't applaud his speeches anymore.

Where *is* Danton, by the way? In the forefront of it all, I suppose, if things are going to happen.

Well, actually, he's gone off to Sèvres with Louisette.

❦

On March 24, the cavalcade goes along Saint-Honoré Street, with Hébert and his pals.

If Camille asked questions about how fearlessly a man could die, he wouldn't want to know about Hébert, who fainted again and again. "Cheer up," said Ronsin. "We're all in the same cart. But I'll tell you this, the pack that put us on this road aren't far behind us."

Mother, Mother, come and see, cry the human fiends in the square. Can this be currant jam?

Szrrr-sltt goes the renowned apparatus.

Up and down, up and down, like a bucket from a well.

Well. We live in interesting times.

❦

By March 29 the lilacs are coming out in the Tuileries Garden and the gardens of the Luxembourg. It's the Blossom Month, of course. Poor old Fabre's sorcerous calendar has worked its spell again. Mauve scent. Mauve and white snow clusters of petals. Between the smoke of braziers still churning out weapons for the war. You hadn't forgotten the war, had you?

❦

"We have to get out," said Lacroix. "Goddammit, Georges. Run!"

"You forget we're at war with everybody, which could cause complications." Danton, leaning on the rose-red wall, gazing idly at Germinalian blossoms, a path, a kitchen garden with Louise in a gilded pannier of a hat.

"There are ways and means to get around that, as there are ways and means to get passes out of the city."

"You do it then, sweetheart," said Danton. "I've had my fill of running. This is my country and my fight. I stay."

"But you're not fighting."

"How do you know what I'm doing? Isn't it our own precious Camille who said, We are also working when we think?"

"That bastard Robespierre is thinking *and* working. And Louis Saint-Just is baying for your arrest."

"Bay on, Saint-Just, my Angel of the Privy."

Lacroix flung up his arms and relapsed on the wall. He said, "There's Camille."

"Oh, goody. Everyone's going to arrive bad-manneredly early."

Camille was picking his way through a horde of three dogs and at least two children. So thin in his dark coat, the sun shone around the edges of him and seemed to meet in the middle.

Lacroix got off the wall and went up to him. "When's Number Eight coming out? The one that'll kill us all?"

"Oh, go to hell."

"Yes, and you're sending me there. Christ! You stupid prick. You don't know when to—"

Camille pushed Lacroix away with some difficulty and the dogs barked, hoping it was a game.

Lacroix spat into a flower bed and stamped toward the house for a drink. One dog ran eagerly after him. The others sat panting, amazed.

Camille reached Danton. They scanned each other.

"I thought you'd be on the sea by now," said Camille.

"Did you?"

"Landing at England."

"Did you."

"When are you off?"

"Oh, first light tomorrow, I should think. Coming with me this time?"

"I'd love to."

"Right. We'll drive over to Paris after supper and get Lucile and your boy."

Camille sat down on the wall. "And what *are* you going to do, Danton?"

"The only thing you've left me any room to do. Duel to the death."

"*I?* Why *me?*"

"Not now. Robespierre will be driving up in about five minutes, in that ramshackle carriage the Duplays hire for him."

"You were serious, then. He *is* coming."

"Absolutely. Dine at Sèvres with me, Maxime, and let the nice air put some color in your cheeks."

"He must be out of his mind. Are you planning to sprinkle aconite in his soup?"

"What, and have to parley with fair Saint-Just? Maxime's safe with me. We'll talk. You'll shut up."

"Don't bank on it."

"I do bank on it."

"All right. Tell me what you'll say, or I may choke on something and wreck your effect."

"This and that. I'm going to point out that with me gone, it'll be rather drafty up there on the summit for him. Not that I think he's got the weight to pull me down. It takes more than a Robespierre. But his attempts could be irritating. I like a quiet existence now."

"Nothing can destroy Danton."

Danton laughed. "Do I look fragile? Do you know how alive I feel? How real and how permanent? Muscle, flesh—sheer *life*. That girl over there in muslin, she could tell you how much life there is in me. My God, and the world's a beautiful place, isn't it? No, I'm not leaving. Not France. Not the world."

Camille did not look at him. Danton glanced at Camille and said, "Why the hell are you crying? You're like a public fountain: eyes pissing tears. Pull yourself together."

There was a puff of dust on the Paris road. Danton spruced his cuffs and marched toward the lane. But the dust was only a wagon. Robespierre was late.

Late all evening, in fact. In fact, absent.

"So it's come to this," shouted Danton. "Very well. We're all going back to Paris tonight."

❦

It was about ten o'clock when we went over to the Duplays. They were frightened when they saw us, particularly since Danton had got around the sans-culottes lounging at the entrance to the yard, and they were guffawing and singing the "Marseillaise" fit to rouse the whole street. Duplay came out, with the son-in-law, and said Robespierre was asleep. "Not any more," said Danton, and we went through.

We were on his stair when the door to his room opened and there he was, Maximilien, in his shirtsleeves, staring at us. He thought we'd come to assassinate him probably.

"Forgive the intrusion," said Danton. "But we were worried about you."

"Yes, I . . . should have sent you a message. Such pressure of work."

"Yes, we'd have liked a message. My wife was very disappointed."

"Oh, dear. Please apologize for me. But you know, I've not been fit. Camille," he said to me. "Oh, Camille—" and his eyes implored me. "You know how I am when I'm ill. Things slip my mind."

He may not have been afraid of sudden death, even resigned to it. But he didn't like it in this shape, plainly. Where were his bold Breechlesses who should have kept us out? As he blinked and fluttered at me, the vicious schoolboy in me (pickled, too, as I always ended my social evenings now) shrugged smilingly at him and said, "I *know* you forget things, Maxime. You—"

At which Danton's hand glided on and off my arm. "May we come up for a moment?" Danton asked, with such polite and silken menace I almost laughed.

Robespierre drew back. "Not *all* of you."

"No, naturally not. Myself. Camille, if you like." Robespierre went on backing into his cave, and Danton sprang suddenly up the stair and into the room. I followed leisurely and closed the door on us. The others, and we had become a party since the carriage got us in at nine, stayed below.

"Well, Maxime, you do look pale. You were just about to retire. I won't keep you." The light was poor. Danton, and the colossal shadow he cast, seemed to overwhelm everything. I looked at it in vague wonderment. Danton stood gazing at Maximilien. Finally Danton said, "I'll speak frankly. I want peace between us."

Robespierre blinked. He was like a stunted child before a giant, but remember David and the pebble. No, there was no substance to Danton anymore. The mass—it was *all* shadow. And the dwarf twitching there at his feet—granite.

"We're not at war," said Robespierre, with every iota of the old infuriating primness.

"What are your terms?" said Danton, very quietly. I believe he had planned none of it. It was impulse. We broke into the stronghold, and Danton kneeled. "You see, Camille is here. Camille, as I do, wishes to be of service to France, no less, no more." He was promising my obedience. I put my head back on the plaster and shut my eyes and let the drunken room go swimming through my brain.

"There, Georges," Robespierre said. "We have no need of this. It can be discussed. But you mistake me. Now Camille"—I opened my eyes and looked at him—"we know each other, you and I." He came across to me and took my hand, patting me on the shoulder. He smiled. "All this is absurd, at this time of the night. Go home to your beds and leave me to mine."

He closed the door softly behind us.

Danton said nothing to me, and I said nothing to him.

Outside, our companions were singing the *Ça ira,* and the night went on with that, though once, I seem to recall, we sang Chénier's "Song of Farewell," the unpolished version.

It has been in my mind, my heart, all this while that Danton let us down. Our captain, he stood boasting nothing could harm him, while the sea washed in over our heads. He cast down the sword because it wearied him. If he had acted differently, he could have saved us. But the fatal seed, which the Greeks tell us we carry always within ourselves, had come to flower. His conviction of indestructibility was the only weapon his integrity had left to him, and it was a sham at that. We had heard him and almost believed—did believe. But the golden light we tried to say was dawn was the dying of a fire.

He was too exhausted for anything. He could, at last, no more summon the required mental and physical energy needed in organizing his escape than he could rally us for a pitched battle. So that was why he would not run. And that was why he did not fight. He sued for peace instead.

Oh, Danton, I have cried out, again and again, it seems to me, why did you fail us, why did you deceive and falter and go down? It was your stumble that murdered us. What were we—beside *you?* You could have made us—why stint the word?—you could have made us kings.

But I see it now; we hung on him and *pulled* him down. And I—I too—I dug your grave if ever you dug mine. My journal of courage, my shout for justice and mercy, that paper kiss of death. I would not heed, or wait, or curb my pen. Gallantly I fired the arrows in the air, and my friends fell with my enemies. Danton, Danton. In that room I would have settled for your truce. Yes, I would have—would I? But then I think we knew the banquet had already ended; the menu could hardly be changed.

And it comes at last that I must say, as Roman Horace said, *Lusisti satis, edisti satis atque bibisti: Tempus abire tibi est.* (You have sung and supped enough. It is time to depart.)

1794: March 30–31 (10–11 Germinal)

DURING THE day, a letter came from Guise. I took in the yellowish look of it and was distractedly aggravated. "Someone else my father wants me to find a choice position for in the Convention offices. Doesn't he know my name is mud there now?" But I opened the letter and read this:

> My dear son, I have lost the moiety of my heart. Your mother has gone from us. I have always trusted she might recover and so did not tell you of this worsening of her illness; she died today as the clocks struck for noon. She is worthy of being missed. She loved you so tenderly. . . .

"I can't bear this," I said. To whom? To God? Who knows.

I hadn't seen her for years, my mother, my poor, poor invalid mother, wasting away with the nuns in that gentle gray building circled by trees. But he had gone dutifully to wait on her, and sometimes she had come home. He had loved her. He had told me so, in that letter written me on the eve of my own wedding. Where in God's name was that letter? I must find it—quickly; it made a pair with this—let me drive the spike in deeper, let me feel it all, before it was too late.

Lucile found me on my knees turning out the bureau.

"I have to find that letter he wrote to me when we were married."

She knelt by me to help me search. We could not find it. I sat on the floor surrounded by papers, and then she read the new letter.

"Camille, you should go to him."

"Funny. Do you think they'd let me that far out of Paris now?"

"But—"

"Last night—something stupid. *Robespierre.* And Saint-Just is letting fly at us all over at the Tuileries, I gather. Calling for irons, no doubt."

She put her hands to her mouth. She was very white, and for a moment she looked only like a little bird seeking frantically for some means of escape. I thought, as I did a thousand times a week, Why do I say such things to her? Does it help me to distress her? But I wanted her comfort, even if I could not believe in it. And in her unselfish miraculous way, she never left me wanting. Now she lowered her beautiful hands and said quite calmly, "There are so many people on your side. And Marius will do something. They'll listen to him. This is a madness, but it will pass. Your motives are so good. You want to save your country, and they *know* it. Soon, there'll be a change for the better. Why, even next month—then you can leave for Guise. I'll even allow you to go."

After the bureau had been tidied again, I searched elsewhere for the first letter of love. It seemed very important. It was a fine afternoon, the spring already glittering in the air, and the light stayed a long while for late March. But then the sky faded. Candles were lit, and I went on looking, intermittently, by their uncertain overcast.

It was, in itself, a normal day. Lucile did not go out; her picture was being painted by an artist with a pretty style, but she had no sitting with him until tomorrow. A not unusual evening. We dined. We played a somber game of cards. But it was on my mind to work, to work. I had been writing some developments of and extrapolations from the seventh number—either a supplementary issue or the Number Eight in embryo. I returned to this constantly, in a sort of fevered determination.

My mother haunted me. She was at the back of my thoughts, continuously. Images of my guilty neglect would rise to torment me, and I would rigorously (what purpose could they serve?) push them down. It was something else, the feeling of utter horror which had begun to fix on me, underpinning every nuance of the afternoon, the meal, the card game, the darkness, and the candle murk. Her death—a symbol. The opening of a door.

My mother. What had I known of her? Those agonizing visits: my shame that I could give her nothing, only my strained filial concern; the ache of helplessness. *She loved you so tenderly.* No. I can't think of it. Oh, God, this damnable unfair parody of a world, this farce, this circus.

In the end I wept, because I wept now at everything: a nostalgic dream, a child with a top, the clamor from Blood Square. I meant to be silent, disturb no one. But the pain of it racked me. I wept for all of us, all, all. And my wife, who had ten years less of life than I, my wife, lover and mother both, held me in her arms till it finished and left me empty.

At two in the morning, Lucile stole exhausted to bed while I, also exhausted but wide awake, stayed at the table writing.

I remember I looked in on her once, and how she sweetly slept, and the baby curled in his cradle.

I remember the old candles guttering, and lighting fresh, the hard flame blazing on the ink so each word I wrote dazzled me. As I completed every frugal sentence, I had the urge to stop. To leave the page in order. Nothing— unfinished, *broken off.*

A little before six, I got up, stretched, and half considered I too might now go to bed. It seemed to me I had passed some meridian of the darkness and could now permit myself to relax. But even then I hesitated. If I slept, let go, what might occur beyond my vigilance?

Then I heard—it seems to me in retrospect a very special noise, but surely only footsteps—coming down the street, those many heavy ill-repaired boots, moving in unison, that meant a patrol was going by. The *tramp-tramp* came on until it reached our building. And halted.

Every stone, every windowpane listened.

Then two or three blows fell on the door, sharp and positive. I felt them through my soles.

I opened the window and looked out and saw them gathered there, guards- men in their toy-soldier uniforms, the lantern shining, and a fellow standing away, holding up a piece of paper for me to see.

"You Camille Desmoulins? No? Then better fetch him."

I said, perfectly clearly, "I'm the one you're looking for. What do you want?"

"What do you think? You're to come with us."

"Where?"

"Not a great way. Just up the hill."

"Wait," I said.

"You can have five minutes. Then we break in the door."

I stood back from the window, out of their sight, and my guts turned to water. I started to retch with terror. Then it went away. A leaden cold settled on me, a second terror less human than the first. I turned and walked into the bedroom. Lucile still slept. Somehow all the sounds and the shouted exchange had not woken her. But as I stood staring down at her, her eyes flew suddenly very wide. She sat up. I said, "They're here." She shook her head. I said, "They've come to arrest me." Unnecessarily. It was as if everything were prearranged, a scene in a play.

I don't remember anything else until I was in the street.

It was growing light, the cold eating through my greatcoat.

The guard formed up about me, saying perfunctorily, a sort of mumble, "In the name of the Republic!" I sensed a hundred awarenesses tensed, listening, all around. But we inhabited different universes, they and I. I recollect a yellow transparency on the cobbles—from our window. No other casement showe i lumination. We walked, a carriage having been reckoned unneedful for such a short distance. Soon we mounted the hill and were at the gates of the Luxembourg.

⚜

How curious it is. The window of my room looks out across the Luxembourg Gardens. Those green lawns and spilling frissons of water, where I spent so much of my time searching for a beautiful girl I could never think to have, and where later she came to me and told me I was loved, and where, thereafter, she and I wandered like two exiled souls, happy and unhappy, ecstatic, in despair. My Lucile. These misty morning walks under the leaves are full of the ghost of you. I feel, as I did then, that you are lost to me. How kind, how pitiless they are, to imprison me, of all places, here.

Yet it gives me, too, a sort of hope. I have won the impossible before—why not impossible deliverance now?

And truly, winter *is* spring, this forward spring like an early summer on the gardens . . . or is this spring my winter, the killing frost?

> *C'est l'hiver, mais pas le printemps,*
> *Du lilas—non,*
> *D'la neige qui tombe.*

1794: Spring

WHEN THEY first brought me in, they showed me the paper for my arrest, as a formality or to assure me the nightmare was real. I looked at it without amazement. Nothing about it startled me. Then we went through a long room, not uncomfortable, with even a fire burning in the grate. In five seconds I saw five men I knew, who had been beside me, so it seemed, on the Convention benches, at the very barricades of the Revolution—and there too was Hérault, who had been playing cards with someone at the fire, quickly standing up. My guard hustled me on. I was not permitted to hesitate and exchange a word with anyone. Hérault remained standing; he lifted his hands in that elegant way of his and shrugged. His look was all, Well, I see you can't stop, in such company.

They put me in a room alone, a cell. Bars on the windows. At first this
seemed quite normal, but as full light began to come (dawn was late, the
morning overcast), the bars grew blacker and more solid and more personal to
myself. They were *my* bars. For me. To nail me in and the day outside.

I paced about, up and down, expecting any moment to be taken out again
and questioned. Indignant answers to all their imagined demands and accusations flooded my head. Sometimes I even spoke aloud. I worked myself up to a
pitch of rage. Finally I was dizzy and sat down on the hard narrow couch, which
had blankets but nothing in the way of linen. I had brought some things with me
and laid them out on the bed. There were two books. It seems I thought reading
would be needful, consoling. But more than that, I required to write and began
to scribble on some paper I had brought with my writing case. Would the ink
last? Well, I had also a small quantity of black lead for the pencil. . . . Besides,
they would let me have ink. And sheets. Comforts. I must write to my wife, then
bribe someone to take the letter to her. This was what the prisoner did. It was all
perfectly simple. I, never before a prisoner, had heard enough of their lifestyle.
How long would I be kept here? It might be months. I would learn to cope with
the day-to-day event of it, even to endure the solitary condition they had
apparently thought necessary. Or maybe I would be moved into a larger room,
with companions. Please God that would happen. This place was too small.
The urge would come to call to be let out, to scrabble at and rattle those
bars. . . . No, they would move me. I would be reasonably situated. This was
the Luxembourg. There were worse places. Patience, patience.

After some hours, a red-cap jailer arrived with food I didn't want (anyway,
the vilest slop), and the first wriggle of bribery was performed, and soon
another man came and I bribed him, too, to take the letter I'd written to Lucile.
He pocketed the letter. I had a spasm of horror, thinking he would read it (if
he could), lose it, throw it away, make sport of me—and all this probably
showed in my face for he said, quite kindly, "Cheer up. You can rely on me."
And went off promising to return about midday (which he did, mission accomplished, so I shook uncontrollably at finding something had been done; I had
been able to reach out from hell, after all, and make contact with the world I had
once known). He swore he would return tomorrow morning, and thereafter at
sunset, too, for new messages. I became almost brisk in the afternoon, making
out a list of things I would need: spectacles, for one. I had been meaning to get a
new pair and put it off. Sleeplessness and strain reduced my reading matter to a
blur, though I managed to write, for to me writing was by now an instinct,
scarcely requiring vision. I even essayed some notes that I intended to publish
on my release; others I meant to deliver to my interrogators when they should
have the goodness to interview me. During this passage of optimism I began to
believe no sooner should I be sent for than let go. What? Camille Desmoulins
here? A mistake. My God, had I not been shown the signature on the warrant for
my arrest?

The idea sank in at length. Then a depression came over me that almost took away my reason. I can't describe it, any more than the blind can properly describe what their affliction is to them, beyond the obvious. It seemed to me I could not understand what had happened to me. I did not know how I could be there. Terror, like no terror I had felt at any time before, got hold of me. Looking back at it all, I almost wonder if I knew, until those moments, how afraid I was. It seemed a revelation, and past my scope to bear. (In retrospect, I look to myself to have been aware of my road, and its terminus, with all my mind. Was I? This awakening may indicate otherwise. Like history itself, I cannot help but sometimes mix afterknowledge with conception.) And these instants of thinking I would be released. These instants of anger, and the preparedness to rant and rave before my accusers. I'm reminded of the fable in which there runs this passage: "No sooner had the wolf allowed himself to fall into the hunters' trap than he howled in a loud voice, 'Help! Help! Someone get me out of this trap!' "

Supposedly I made some noise during this bout of mental agony. When I lapsed, I began to hear answering groans on the far side of the wall. Now comes a paragraph from a cheap adventurous romance. We have all read it many times. Usually it ends happily (in an escape).

I located a worn place in the wall and called through it. "Yes," he wailed in the muffle of the brickwork. "Who are you?" I gave my identity. A sort of floundering commotion ensued. I heard him staggering about and falling down on his bed. "Oh, Christ! Christ Jesus! Oh, my God!"

"Fabre?" I said, "For God's sake, is it you?"

"Yes, me—but *you*—why are you here? Are the Austrians in Paris?"

"Not quite," I said. "Only Robespierre."

He laughed, and the laughter turned to weeping. We each wept, either side of the wall, like two children punished in some ogre's castle. "And Danton?" he said after a time.

"I don't know. One of the bastards said he was here. Another one said he was on a ship heading for America."

"Here, then. He's here. Like you. Oh, Christ, Christ—if they've got Danton there's no chance for *me*." All this went on, respectively, awhile. Then suddenly he hissed through the wall, "Stop it! Stop talking. They'll hear us. They'll say we're plotting. Don't laugh. They will. I'm sick, I'm ill. They'll throw me in some rotten dungeon with rats tearing at my feet. Shut up, Camille. Don't speak to me."

So, our conversation ended.

I watched the gardens fade as the afternoon deepened toward sunset. There seemed to be a haze, or was it that my eyes were weaker? When the sun fell, the pleasure park would be shut. I could smell the fragrant drifts of scent from the spring trees. It made my heart ache.

Lucile had not sent me a letter in return for mine. Perhaps she had feared some other would read it. What was she doing? I wanted her to do nothing, I wanted her to leave Paris, to hide. No, I wanted her to fling herself, in all her loveliness, before the Committees and implore them to free me. No—no—for God's sake, *no,* Lucile.

Then another jailer came (if he was a jailer; they seemed to do it for pleasure, a hobby, waiting on us to see how we suffered). *"Your* wife loves *you,"* said he, putting down a pot under a napkin. "She's sent you this. And fruit— look. The others are green with envy. My old woman'd send me poison, I reckon." I did not believe the food came from Lucile. It was a sinister joke to pretend so. Or else poison, as he hinted. Then I recognized the napkin, the dish—it was from home. I didn't care, then, what might have been added to it. Once he left me, I ate some of the soup, which had a remembered taste of the herbs from Bourg-la-Reine—till my throat closed with tears.

They mean to drive me mad. It is itself a plot. I can trust nothing, be sure of no one. They mean to drive me mad and will succeed.

I paced about again, up and down, around and around, and the room grew tinier by the second. I went to the window as if I would die from lack of air. The westering shadows were folding down like fans on the lawns of the garden. At the end of the gravel walk, a woman stood. She wore dark clothes, as if in mourning. For a moment I took her for Lucile. But it was Demeter, looking up at me, one more shadow in the shadowland.

There had been a scene at the Gélys. That was after the scene at the Desmoulins's apartment. Papers scattered everywhere, those that had been discarded in the search for something incriminating. While the Committee agents rifled her home, Lucile stood bravely and Demeter stood beside her. Demeter had gone through this herself, once, twice, when her husband was carried off to the Carmelite Prison. At one point, a man rushed in and gave superfluous orders that nothing be overlooked. "Do please," said Demeter crisply, "search the baby's cradle. Heaven knows what may have been hidden there." The man gave her a type of frozen glare he had learned from his priestly sponsor—it was Saint-Just's secretary, no other, the pastry individual, Citizen Gâteau.

The mess they left, when they did leave, reminded Lucile of how she and Camille had searched yesterday for his father's letter. She cried her heart out in Demeter's arms.

Then Lucile decided to go over to Danton's, though they had already learned that Tribune Marius, too, had been arrested under cover of night. It was not quite an astonishment.

Sophie-Louise was upstairs with her parents. She lay on a divan, looking as white as if drained of blood, and breathing in dreadful gasps. Lucile entreated Louise to go with her to Robespierre's house and fall on her knees with her to the "monster," to sue for mercy. Louise said something faintly. Pressed for an audible reply she said, "No, no, don't ask me. No, I couldn't."

"But he won't dare to refuse us," said Lucile. "The shame of it will blast him. He's been misled. Or he's gone mad." She looked quite mad herself, with all madness' composure.

"No," said Sophie-Louise Danton. "See Robespierre? Oh, no."

Then Mama Gély intervened. She began to shrill at Lucile that it was Danton's friends, dissolutes, connivers, and idiots, who had landed him in this pickle. Her daughter, who perhaps should not have married so young, had been exposed to enough danger as it was.

"This is wickedness," said Lucile, and her own whiteness flamed. "I shall go, then, alone."

"I couldn't," said Louise. "Danton would never forgive me. To beg from his enemy." And she swooned, which she had been doing on and off since the boots of the National Guardsmen had come to her door and stopped. Danton's last sight of her had been of a pale doll collapsing into someone else's arms—the key signature to her future.

"I must do everything I can," Lucile then told her mother.

Camille's son was left in the scared attentive care of Demeter's maid. Lucile, who did not answer her husband's first letter, wrote six or seven to other persons. In Demeter's company she went calling on the sullen doors of several who would not let her in, or let her in only to wait and wait, until she despaired as intended and went away. Her husband could have told her, had done so. He had gone through much the same performance on behalf of her father.

They found out, the way one can find out these things, that a selection of Danton's accomplices had rooms which faced onto the Luxembourg Gardens. It was a perk of captivity there. Your relatives could sit on benches below and gaze at you, and the whole group of you thereby break your hearts into even smaller fragments.

"I can't," Lucile now said. "I'll cry, he'll see me crying. He mustn't see that. I have to give him hope."

Eventually, Demeter went alone, to keep vigil under the windows of the prison.

There was a bizarre new fence about the building, a barrier of tall peeled stakes, rather like bones. But it was possible to see over this, from a slight distance, to the upper stories.

She was there some while before anything happened. She was not sure of the window, for lies are also told at such times.

Behind her, among the trees, a distant hammer was plied in the park, though the Nation's armorers had fallen off at the war effort in the heat. Some children were—incredibly—playing somewhere, and Demeter, catching their high voices, was aware the prisoners, too, might hear them. This made her cry herself. She had many reasons for tears. She gazed at the line of casements ruled by bars, and she remembered how he had written her such frenetic poetry (Oh, goddess, let your worshiper draw near, no temple shuts its door against a prayer) a decade ago, and how he had looked then, so little altered now. And that she had only loved him in the safest of ways—no, not her son, her youthful brother, perhaps—not liking risk, not liking to be cut, but now the knife had sheared to the bone despite every precaution. And just then, with a blazing pang at her heart, she saw him appear like a lunatic at one of the windows.

So he did see a woman bitterly crying, if not Lucile.

As they looked at each other then, across the irreparable distance of lawn, gravel, wall, Demeter's daughter, Camille's wife, was writing to Maximilien Robespierre:

> You—have you no memory? His hand, which you have so often held in friendship, threw down the pen which could no longer write anything good of you. And you mean to kill him. Ah, yes, then—you comprehend the omission!

※

At the time I did not know, and it hardly concerned me, how it had been done. The unwondering wonder I felt, seeing Maximilien Robespierre had signed the warrant for my arrest: a jackal who betrayed his friends. But he had ceased to credit us, reckoned we had betrayed *him,* and his good angel, Antoine the magician priest, had furnished proof.

A man named Fouché had attended to it. Drinking companions, and those one goes rutting with, are not always the most reliable. One says things off guard and does them. And is seen to say and do. The words and deeds were gathered like flowers, the bouquet given to Fouché, by Fouché handed to Citizen Cake, and thence to Saint-Just, who left it with the roses for Robespierre. It is a simple thing to picture them about that table in the Justiciary Building, at three in the morning: Billaud, Barère, Saint-Just, Couthon, Collot—all our dearest foes. And Maximilien in the middle of it, behind that stack of papers, reading them. What Danton had said about him. All of it. And what I had said. Enough. Belittlings, jokes, insults. Set in the ornamental surround of our café discussions, junketings, dinner schemes, and wine dreams. Booze Maximilien didn't drink, whores he wouldn't have wanted, feral political debate which excluded him as a leper. Fouché's reporters had done most cleverly. And Fouché had the additional aid of disliking our "kind." He was known to have said, "There is no such animal as an Intellectual. The beast is an invention. I have also been told of a unicorn, but removing its paper horn, we all saw at once it was only another lame old horse."

"And this," said Robespierre, amid the dossiers Fouché had prepared, "is verbatim." *Yes,* Maxime, said the angel at his shoulder. "*All* of this?" *Yes.* And maybe he looked afraid, Maxime, sensing isolation on a high mountaintop. And Saint-Just would have said, We are with you. *I'm* with you. Danton had always taunted them. ("Virtue? What's that? Oh, do you mean that thing I do with my wife every night?") How could this licentious brigand save their Revolution? No, Danton would tousle everything, fuck the life out of the Lady Utopia, till her orgasmic shrieks brought the sky tumbling into the muddy barnyard. He didn't understand how to behave. The Supreme Being would frown and cast down Paris. And maybe Robespierre and Saint-Just were right, in their peculiar way, in thinking that. And I? Well, I was Danton's pet. Look at the stories he had told about me. (What, Danton? What did you say? Well, perhaps you did. What does any of that matter now?) And the others, of course, Danton's creatures, all in it: Lacroix, Philippeaux, Westermann, Hérault, Fabre — libertines and liars. Writers, talkers, parasites. Crush them.

So he signed the paper. With his usual slight flourish at the end, as if afraid the signature might otherwise be ripped away or eroded.

He had made up his mind. Or thought he had.

It was finished.

⚜

Luxembourg Prison. 12 Germinal: Five o'clock in the morning

Lucile . . .

Sleep the kind benefactor interrupted my misery: one is set free when sleeping; one has no sense of captivity. Heaven has had pity on me. For a brief moment I saw you in a dream, and held you, and in turn Horace, and Demeter — who was at the house. But our little boy had lost an eye, because of some ill which had been cast upon it. And the sadness of that woke me.

I rediscovered myself in my cell; there was beginning to be a little predawn light. Unable to see or hear you anymore — because you and your mother had both spoken to me (in the dream) — I got up, so I might at least talk to you by means of a pen and paper. But opening my shutters, the thought of my aloneness, the frightening bolts and bars which cut me off from you, have destroyed all my strength. I drowned in my tears, or else I sobbed out from my tomb, Lucile! Lucile! Oh, my darling Lucile, where are you?

Yesterday, near evening, there was another moment like this one, and my heart was similarly cracking into pieces — when I saw, in the gardens, your mother. With a movement I could no more resist than if I had been some machine, I found I had flung myself on my knees against the bars of the window. My gestures implored her; I knew she had shared your sorrow, I saw yesterday her grief. She hid her face in her veil, unable to bear the sight of my distress. When the two of you come, sit a little nearer — there is no danger in this, it seems to me — and my eyes make a poor telescope. I need you to get me another pair of glasses, not silver frames but steel. The dealer will know what you want if you ask for the number fifteen. But above all I beg you, my Lucile, by my ceaseless love for you, send me your portrait! Let that painter take pity on Camille, who would suffer nothing now if he had not taken pity on others — let your painter give you two sessions a day. In the horror of my prison, it will be for me a festival, a time of rapture, the day when I receive this portrait. While I wait, send me some of your hair (still warm from you), so that I can keep it against me, over my heart. Oh, my darling Lucile! Just look at me, returned to the time of our first love, when anyone fascinated me if he had only come from you. Yesterday, the citizen who carried my first letter to you, when he returned – Oh, God, you've seen her? I said to him (as I used to say to those who had seen you, in my stead, in the past). And I surprised myself looking him over carefully, to see if there might be, about his clothes or his person, some mystic element of you. He has a good heart, since he gave you my letter without delay. I'll see him when he comes to me twice a day: morning, dusk. This messenger of our sorrows will become for me as dear as, in some other hour, would be the messenger of our happiness.

But, my best love, you can't imagine what it is to be shut up, secluded, in this way, without being given a reason, without having been questioned, without access to a single piece of news. It is to be alive and to be dead, simultaneously. It is no existence, but a foretaste of being in the grave. They say that the innocent are calm and brave – oh, my dear Lucile, my beloved! Too often my innocence shudders, because it is the innocence of a husband, a father, a son! If it had been our English enemies who had so harshly betrayed me: But my colleagues – but *Robespierre* – who signed the order for my imprisonment, and our goddess the Republic looked on, after all I have done in her name! *This* is my reward for so many acts and sacrifices. (When I was brought here, I saw many I know, among them Hérault de Séchelles. They are not so woeful as I, they are not kept in solitary cells.) It is I who have so devoted myself through five years, through so much spiteful hate, so many dangers, for the Republic's sake, I who have stayed unbribable in the environment of the Revolution (!), I who have no need to ask forgiveness, no, not from anyone in the world but you, my darling, who have granted me that forgiveness, because you knew that my heart, despite all my weaknesses, isn't unworthy of you – it is I who these men, those who called themselves my friends, just as they call themselves "True Republicans" – I who have been flung into prison, hidden and alone, as though I were some intriguer. Socrates drank hemlock, but at least he was companioned in his cell by his friends and his wife. How much harder it is to be parted from you. The direst wrongdoer on earth would be punished too much if he were to be separated from a Lucile. Unless it were by death, which makes us taste, only for a moment, the pain of such separation. But a criminal would never have been your husband, you could never have loved me, except you knew I never drew breath save to work for the welfare of this city's multitude – *Someone is calling my name.*

❧

In the midst of my confessional, two guards bustled in and took me downstairs into a side chapel of the prison-cathedral, to be questioned properly.

As I had figured the jail-rat-messenger nicely in my letter, in case he could read, and read it, so I set out my sterling qualities before God by means of my angelic wife. And for all the bastards who might come on the letter after, perhaps some hundreds of years hence. See how blameless I am! Whatever have I done amiss? I have only worked for the good of my fellow citizens! I meant every word. I writhed in my martyrdom. It was my way of telling heaven, Look, I'm a saint. Free me. *Baa,baa,* Camille. Bleat loud, and see who'll hear the strayed lamb.

Downstairs they know different.

Oh, yes. Downstairs they know it all. Another world, my friend, my self. The real one.

They asked who I was. Where I had been born, where I lived now, my profession. In the real world, no one credits you till you speak and are written down.

A man sat there behind a table. He had a dark stupid face. But every face was growing dark and moronic, with the mindless evil in it one sees flicker in the eyes of a deadly snake. Seldom looking at me, but reading from his parchments, he asked me if I had conspired against the Nation, desiring to restore the rule of kings to France, thereby bringing down the Republic, sole representation of the People's will.

Thus, with all about my blackly blatant, silly, despicable sad crimes, this was the one, the one of which I stand forever *innocent,* they meant to saddle me with and so ride me to oblivion. Thus, the satirical reply of the gods to the bleating of the black sheep. Thus.

I stared at him, this human representative of the irony of God.

It was gibberish, the accusation. As I hadn't understood my special pleading, so I flinched aside from the cosmic jest. Missed it. Beheld only insanity, and the man across the table. Seeing I was at a loss, he had the idea to repeat his question. And I too went insane, then, and shouted at him. I forget what I said, only that it was a relief. They dragged me away, stammering, spluttering, screaming, and had the devil's own job to get me again into my room upstairs. Restored to it, I threw myself against the walls, slid down them in an uproar of rage and fear, as if the emotions were new to me. (No response now from Fabre. Unconscious, removed, cautiously deaf.)

The unfinished letter, my only means to express my frustrated anguish, or anything, finally drew me back to its unwarm soulless un-Lucilelike being.

As rage subsided, pain and fear grew worse. I was no fool; I raged as long as I had the stamina for it. I was alone. No one would help me. I knew all that, for certain now. But I must write it out still, *deny* it.

No overcast this morning. Day had filled the park beyond the bars. But day and light no longer had any meaning. I had lost my rights to them. They were nothing to do with me. Oh, Lucile.

In that moment the agents of the Revolutionary Tribunal had arrived to interrogate me. They asked me no more than this one question: Had I conspired against the Republic? This to *me,* the most dedicated of Republicans—how filthily *laughable!* I see the fate in store for me. Good-bye, my Lucile, my sweet wolfess; say my farewell for me to my father. You see in my treatment an example of the mindless barbarity, the thanklessness of mankind. My quietus shan't dishonor you. Oh, you see my dread had substance—our presentiments were genuine—I married a woman of a divine beauty and tenderness—I have been a loving husband, a not unreasonable son—I would have made a good father—I will be regretted by all sound Republicans, all who value true virtue, Liberty—I am only thirty-four when I die but it's a miracle that I've passed across five years of revolutionary precipices, not falling, and still live—I will rest once more, in confidence, upon the pillow of my writings, excessive in amount but which breathe, all of them, the same philanthropy, the same wish to make my fellowmen happy and free—and which the ax of a tyrant cannot dismember! I see very well that power makes a drunkard of nearly every man. They say, Tyranny is a handsome epitaph. But take consolation in this, my widow robbed of your husband, the epitaph of your wretched Camille is better: It reads KILLER OF TYRANTS.

Oh my darling Lucile, I was born to write poetry, to speak for the rights of the oppressed, to strive to make you happy, to assemble—with your mother, your father, and other people close to us—a colony of like minds. I have dreamed of a republican state that the whole earth would have worshiped. I could never have credited that men were so carnivorous, so unfair. Why should I think that some jokes I made, in my writings, against colleagues who had irritated me, could wipe out all memory of my services? I can never deceive myself; I die a victim of my *jokes.* And of my friendship with Danton. I thank my murderers for letting me die with him; nearly all our colleagues have grown sufficiently cowardly to be able to desert us, lending an ear to slanders I know nothing of, but which doubtless are of the worst. I see that we die the victims of our bravado in denouncing traitors and of our liking for truth! We can take with us this testament—that we who perish are the last Republicans!

Forgive me, sweet girl, you, my true life—which I lost at once when they parted us—forgive me that I employ myself with my memorial stone. I should do better trying to make you forget, my Lucile, my wolf-girl, little hen. I entreat you, don't dwell on how we are to be divided. Never name me when you lament; your cries will tear me apart even in the depths of the Pit. Live for my son, talk to him about me. You will tell him what he can never properly understand—how much I would have loved him.

Despite my execution, I believe there is a God—a god. My spilled blood will wash away my faults, the frailties of a human man—and I have done some good—my strength, my love for Freedom, will this god remember also these? I will see you again one day, Lucile. Oh, so sensitized as I am, is death, which delivers me from the sight of this plethora of guilty crimes—is it so terrible an unhappiness? Good-bye, Loulou. Good-bye, my life, my soul, my goddess. I leave you to kind friends, the few there are who are gentle and good. Good-bye, Lucile, my sweet Lucile. Good-bye, my son, my father. The shores of my life draw away from me. I see Lucile still. I see her. My arms reach out to encircle you tightly, my bound hands hold you—my severed head retains your image to the last second of life.

I am going to die.

⚜

I must have slept. It didn't seem to me I had done so. But the day was nearly over. Where was I? Still *here?* I stumbled to the window. Gardens all vacated. Had Lucile come to the bench by the walk and I hadn't woken? My God, surely that would be impossible—or had I woken and looked out and seen her there? Yes, I recalled her standing looking at me and holding up our child. But that was another woman I had seen earlier—Philippeaux's wife, maybe, or somebody's. Had Lucile been there? Had I seen her? Had I dreamed it?

For sure my messenger, who had so reassured me that he could be relied on, had not returned for the second letter. Prevented? Or would he come now?

No sound but the vaguest noises of the prison edifice. A bird sang in a tree. It had some cause, no one had caged it. Fabre, next door? Still afraid to signal, or gone.

Then footsteps along the corridor. The door opened. "Excuse *us, citizen.* You're wanted downstairs."

My heart leapt—and fell like a shot deer. Release? Rescue? Fool.

I put my hand on the wall to steady myself as we went down. "Drunk again," said my guard.

⚜

Danton was standing in the middle of the big room. He looked slightly amused, as if he had been persuaded to the opera against his inclination and did not much care for the singers. To his massive figure the rest had rallied, but no longer with any sense of a redoubt. Other prisoners sitting about the chamber gazed at us, glad not to be associated. The Luxembourg was stuffed with royalists. Some invective had been flying. Danton had apparently told them, "Chirp away. You may enjoy seeing us go down, but when the water smooths over, watch out for what's left on the surface."

Yes, by Christ, he was almost cheerful. As if something had been settled, and now he had only to polish it up with a theatrical stance and a witty footnote or two.

I went over to him and he clapped his arms around me with expressions of delight in finding me, a lost friend—finding me *there*. And when he saw my reddened eyes, he said, "Now, now. The way to the scaffold isn't a dead march, it's a dance."

Lacroix laughed. "Aren't you going to save our necks, Georges?"

"Of course I am." He stared up at the ornate ceiling. "Naturally."

"Your mincemeat man spoke up for us," said Lacroix. He meant Butcher Legendre.

"And Robespierre shut him up," said Philippeaux, who was sitting off to one side, reading a book. I didn't know him well. We didn't greet each other.

"There are lists compiled of all the loathsome things we've been doing, tsk, tsk."

They had all got more news than I had. No doubt by bribing the jailers to tell it. But how could one be sure what was a fact?

"The food here," said Hérault, "is revolting. You'd better get us freed soon, Danton, before we're slain by bad vegetables."

"Fabre's succumbed already. I told him not to touch the stew."

"I was told he swallowed poison."

"He did. The stew."

"*Fabre* take poison? (Oh, come, vial! What if this mixture do not work at all? Shall I be married, then, tomorrow morning?) Kill himself when he's writing a play?"

"Is he?"

"When isn't he? It's called the *Injured Orange*. It's about Robespierre."

I stood and looked at them. They were all strangers, no less so than Philippeaux. I knew none of them. I hung my head, listening drearily to the jolly banter, until someone started to call our names, one by one, with an odious, insolent formality. And like soldiers we stood to attention. Even Hérault turned his gilded head and looked.

"By order of the two Committees, of General Security and of Public Safety, the so-named are to be taken forthwith to the Gatehouse Prison."

"That's it," said Lacroix. He grimaced and put his hands over his face, and sang, "Good night, good night, sweet world, good night."

Someone shouted across at us out of the shadows, "Good luck then, Danton, with the Tribunal. Hope it's fun for you. It's your baby."

"God help me, that's true," said Danton. "Though the child's grown up into a freak."

But the men with the faces of snakes were bawling for silence, and silence came. Candles were being lit as the windows blackened. A smell of tallow and tinder and smoke. There was something else they wanted to read to us; they must be able to see to do so.

He had himself read it to the Convention in broad sunshine, so I had been wrong, that time I said villains feared light. He wore for the occasion the dark clothes that had become the mean fashion of our Republic, staid and virtuous and conscious of the threadbare mob. A dark coat, a waistcoat the color of cold stones, but his stockings ice-white as ever, a pale lavender cravat. And at his waist the *tricoleur* sash worn now only by committee members: stainless and pure, the very perfect knight Saint-Just. He had wanted to recite his thesis to Danton's face, but they'd panicked and told him no, he must wait till the ferocious lion-bull was safely picketed and penned in jail. Honey Saint-Just hadn't cared for that. He had lost his temper, I believe. He'd lavished so much time and effort on the item, embellishing it and making it pretty. Saint-Just— unjust Saint-Just, damn your soul and may you writhe in some Catholic hell of fire forever. Danton, yes, you wanted to dance your minuet across his broken body. And Camille—didn't you want him, too?—Camille who had made you look such a strutting ninny. Who didn't know you'd sworn to see me dead? I put you into a page of print and you put me into a written page of lying and deceit. I had mocked you; you would murder me.

Saint-Just . . .

Tolling it out before the Convention, every man cowed, using all the tricks you had learned from watching your Robespierre, borrowing that chilly power—and your arm going up and down like the blade in Revolution Square.

"—Danton, the servant of the People? Never. Of the aristocrats' regime. Does he dare deny it? That he has sold himself again and again? That he has compared the faith of the People to the favors of a harlot? Said that glory is a fever dream? Said that to be honorable is to be ridiculous? Let me cite his liaisons: Mirabeau—La Fayette—Dumouriez—the Prussians— Orléans. And his deeds: A coward's flight in times of insecurity (England knows him well), a plotter's contrivance that caused the massacre on Mars Field; that almost saved the genocide, Louis Capet, from retribution. And then this journal we have heard so much of, this *Cordelier Leader*—who led it out by the hand but Danton, that arch sower of strife? For who corrupted Desmoulins but Danton?

"Desmoulins, a dupe in his childishness, but finding himself in the river, he learned quickly how to swim. An accomplice. Like d'Églantine, Desmoulins weeps easily—but the crocodile also sheds tears. Swimming, then, and like the serpent following the stream, seeking for prey. Liberty has brought plunder and pockets lined with gold to a nonentity of a lawyer whose lack of talent provided him no work. And such as he need money. A list of his pleasures, which would shock this assembly both by its license and its extent—lesser merely than Danton's own, this despotic fornicator Danton the Corrupter— informs us how much need Desmoulins has had to bleed the Revolution, and how he has gulped its blood as eagerly as the aristocrats. Small wonder he pleads their cause."

Either vomit, sick to the stomach with rage, or cry out to drown it.

Danton tried to stop me. I think he said, as if interested, "Let me listen." The attorney, weighing up the prosecution's evidence, searching out its flaws.

But to me, vinegar dripped in open wounds. "Damned lies. Who'll believe him, for Christ's sake, that damned sodomite—they'll pay attention to *this?* God help France."

"All together now with the chorus," said Lacroix.

I pushed at him and went on shouting. But the Inexorable also went on reading itself out.

"There. Saint-Just hasn't forgotten even my humble self," said Hérault. "How kind. Praising my repartee, surely?"

"Camille, be quiet."

"What did I ever do," I howled, the wolf in the trap (*Au secours, au secours, quelqu'un m'aide!*), "but fight for freedom, justice—this rubbish—fucking Saint-Just with his—"

"*No!*" Danton roared at me. He turned his terrible face against me, raw with agony and anger, and I saw it and was silenced indeed. I choked and slunk back and waited, shivering, in the stink of tallow and smoke and hate and terror, every man's terror and my own, for it to finish.

It did, at length, finish. Saint-Just had said, "The sacred duty of the Patriot exceeds all others. It is greater than any other love, remorseless, unafraid, without respect for any life but its own." He had said, "The era of crime is at an end. Heed and beware, all you who would be criminals."

In the ghastly half-dark, Danton put his hand on my shoulder, then removed it, as if he could not bear contact with my utter demoralization. I heard him say very softly, hoarsely, "We'll see. It's not over yet."

They sent us to collect our personal effects. As the guardsmen waited rock-faced by the door, I spewed emptiness and acid bile in the cell's convenient receptacle. Then wiped my mouth and gathered up my belongings carefully, methodically. Empty in truth. Trembling far off, some note of passion and horror nothing to do with me. I placed the letter I had written her in my pocket. I must find someone I could give it to, who would take it to her. This was important. It was the last thing of mine she would ever receive.

We went out.

I walked straight and firmly, with no difficulty. We were all three in step, my guards and I. I remembered that with Mirabeau, how we had automatically walked in step, marched in it to the Revolution's drum—unknowingly—he to his death, I to mine.

Closed carriages. Black night. A breath of the sweet night gardens, gone. Hérault, in with me, gave me some brandy, or something his sedate domestic had handed him as they parted. Hemlock? Not.

We rattled across the city, over the river, seeing none of it till we reached the midnight buildings on their island, their few sour-lit snake-eyed windows peering over Paris through the dark. And so to the prison fashioned from a palace gatehouse, the Conciergerie.

Over the cobbled court, in at a door, along a narrow passage.

The first night they placed us all together in one cavern of a room. It was the cell the Girondins had shared in October.

❧

"Once," said Danton, "there was a poor fisherman, who had nothing but the clothes he stood up in, and a little boat, and a line to catch the fish. For a whole season he had taken very little and things were serious for him, when one day this fisherman caught on his line a fish so large that all he could do was struggle with it. And a terrible struggle it was, for neither side would give in. Then, in the midst of it all, the fish cried out to the fisherman in a human voice: Pay attention! I will give you your heart's desire. Then give me power, exclaimed the fisherman at once, power and riches, and let me be first among men. Look, said the fish, at my shining side; I will show you how that shall be. Then the fisherman looked at the gleaming scales of the fish, and every scale became a picture. He saw himself step ashore and come into a great inheritance. He saw himself in fine clothes and with a fine house and a fair wife, and servants by the score. He saw men bowing down to him and making him first a judge, then a minister, then an emperor over them. But here, blood from the fish's mouth had smeared its scales; the pictures grew more somber. The fisherman looked closely, and he saw how men began to be jealous of him and to hate him, how his friends left him or cheated him, his wife betrayed him, the people spat at him, and assassins lay in wait for him day and night, and he did not have a single second of peace or joy. He was old before his time, ill and wretched, and so he lived, and so he died. Having seen all this, the fisherman said to the fish, Take away this curse from me. I would rather be a poor fisherman than a ruler of men. Then let me go, said the fish. So the fisherman let go the fish, only saying to it, as it sprang away into the depths of the ocean, Tell me your name. And the fish, as it vanished, murmured, *Fortune.*"

TWELVE

O Fortune!
Fickle shape-changer
Like the moon,
Always increasing—
Till you fade.
Maker of life's cross!
Now the ground is firm—
Next it gives way.
Our dreams your game,
Kingship or beggary, both,
You melt like summer frost.

�֍ ✖ ✖

1794: The Last April

TAKE YOUR SEATS, ladies and gentlemen, citizens and citizenesses.

Lot Number One, a batch of variable quality. Fouquier put it together with his own infallible taste. A political gang assorted with lesser valuables. Here's a nice orator now, several previous owners: himself, the Revolution, two wives, two thousand trollops, and all the men who bought him. Bit on the large size. Never mind, we plan to cut him down a little to fit your requirements. And next, this item, skin and bone, fits in anywhere. Hardly decorative, but wind it up and it writes things. And which of you can pass up a smashing golden-haired hero like this one? Or we've got this brawny Alsace soldier (is Alsace, isn't he?), fresh from the front, still in uniform. The rest—a touch tarnished. Bankers up to no good and caught in the act. Swindlers and speculators. But there's a diplomat in here somewhere, and a poet-playwright—where's he got to? ah, yes, in a fever and a chair—juggles oranges and makes alterations in documents pertaining to the East India Company.

So take your seats for the auction, *mesdames et messieurs, citoyens et citoyennes.*

"Name?"

"Georges Jacques Danton."

"Your age."

"Thirty-four years."

"Profession."

"Lawyer. And deputy to the Convention."

"Place of residence."

"Shortly, I shall reside in Nothingness."

A murmur all around.

457

Irritated: "Where do you live?"

"Forever, conversely, in the temple of history."

A louder murmur, and somewhere from the public benches a voice yells, "Get 'em, Danton!" before being silenced.

The clerk pauses over his pen and paper. Fouquier signals and Hermann nods, both under their black plumage. Let it go. They know his address. And he's just told them, hasn't he; they've got him between two chunks of bread. He's bound for Nothingness and history.

And Danton steps back, looking grimly amused (still that look). And heroic Hérault is there, appearing brushed and laundered—a fraud, he's been cursing the lack of vanities provided all the way here.

"Name."

"A common one. Jean-Marie."

"The former Count Hérault de Séchelles."

"Who once sat not far from your own place and made enemies of royalist advocates."

(Well, we knew this bunch would be a bunch of smart alecks. Spoon the brew, quick, dip up a forger.)

"Name."

"François Chabot." (Speculator.)

"Name."

"Junius Frey." (*Notorious* speculator.)

Name. *Likewise.* Name. *Likewise.*

(Shows the company Danton's accomplices kept. Even if they didn't. And in this case, now, they did.)

"Name."

A swaying, half-unconscious mumble.

"*Name.*"

"Fabre—Philippe—d'Églantine" (unfortunately also *likewise*).

As Fabre collapses back in his chair, Camille Desmoulins is discovered at the front of the herd. He looks at Fouquier-Tinville, and there is a terrible sneer on Camille's face. (We expected Camille would look merely frightened, but we were in error.) Fork-Tongue, beloved cousin, takes no notice.

"Name."

Camille gives his name. He bites his thumbnail and glares.

"Age."

And Camille puts back his head and says in a loud clear voice, stammerless and pure, for it mustn't be missed, "My age is thirty-three. The same age as the well-known freedom fighter Jesus. A dangerous age for Revolutionaries."

Which causes a stir. Quite a stir. So the bell is rung for order from the judges' bench. (God, how did he do it? Must have been practicing it over and over all the way upstairs, to get it right.)

Danton is seen by some to be grinning.

Now, gentlemen. This isn't the theater. You are on trial for your lives.

No, actually, it *is* theater. Yet another farce.

And the rest of the dramatis personae—the jurors—are being reviewed.

"I object! I object to the inclusion of that man."

Camille again, slightly flushed from the spirit of camaraderie that seems to have broken out among the prisoners' benches, shaking his hair, pointing flamboyantly.

The objected-to juror looks back at Camille in a display of nervous, self-righteous venom.

"The nature of your objection?" (Hermann.)

"I knocked one of his teeth out at the Jacobins."

Laughter. Oh, wonderful, wonderful. Not just a farce, a farce with real *jokes*.

The bell.

The juror, Renaud the violin dealer, is asked if he recalls the incident. He "does not." The objection is overruled and Camille throws his arms up and damns them all. Lacroix calls, "Perhaps he's got a forgiving streak. Show us your teeth, Renaud. All there? How about a tune on your violin?"

The *bell*.

The whole jury is rigged, or looks to be. Not picked by lot but by the stern vermicelli eyes of Fouquier this very morning. One has a hearing problem, apparently. Another one seems to be drunk. Another has funny turns and adds up two and two as one and a quarter. For the others, aside from Camille's former sparring partner, you behold a gentleman fondly known as August Tenth, for his enthusiasm in the pike department, and who, when not doing jury service in the justice department, nips over to see the end product of justice in the guillotine department. There are some bemused types from the shoe, wig, and snuffbox trades who could teach you a fair amount about prunello, horsehair, and tobacco but who, when they sit here, only think over their accounts in their heads and pop up and go *Cuckoo!* when everyone else goes *Cuckoo!* And then, over here, what do we have but Doctor-Surgeon Souberbielle, dinner guest at the Café Flon, current leech applicator to committee members. And here's another friendly face. Why, if it isn't Maurice Duplay, whose upstairs room contains the slumbers—and whose downstairs parlor contains five million replicas—of Maximilien Robespierre. *Bon appetit!*

How can one not be charmed?

One thought it went out with the Borgias. But someone would seem to want to be sure of something or other. . . .

Do they still suppose they can be saved, any one of them, the fifteen ill-assorted men on trial today in the Palais d'Injustice, that house of death, that gateway to the guillotine?

Presumably the Freys can have no hope, the Austrian bankers and the Dane, none.

But Danton, with his epigrams, his towering aura—surely he's about to put up a fight? And Camille, who spoke his one line for posterity so beautifully one would like to give him a silver apple and send him out to play forever in the flowering fields. And poor Fabre, semi-slain prematurely by food poisoning. And gorgeous Hérault, and Westermann, stern of mouth: "Stripped, my soldier's body will show you several wounds, only one in the back—that which I receive today." Philippeaux, still reading, or trying to read, his little book (there is a miniature of his wife concealed between the covers). Lacroix, who once pulled the "de" off his name and now sees he might as well have left it on.

Fight? Ah, no.

When your clothes are burning, you continue, on a reflex, to beat at them, to try to put them out; even as the flesh is seared from the bone of you, you "*fight.*" Instinct. Just as you would struggle for breath in the depths of the sea. And strike over and over the bolted lid of a coffin in the hell of quickness, though you know, you *know,* you can never get out.

❧

And yet, it did seem he had rallied us. Passing from darkness, when he said, "Our revolutionary brothers are called, every one of them, *Cain.*" When he said, "Posterity, at least, will be just to me." When he said, "Better a fisherman—" When he said, "Camille, can you ever forget the way he was the night before the arrest—Robespierre, your *friend*—Nero couldn't have done better." Into the light to say, "If I go, they'll never get out of the mess. God, I'd better make a will. Leave Billaud my brains, and some of my blood for Saint-Just; poor bugger, he's got none of his own. My legs to Couthon, he'd like that. And for Robespierre, my balls." And shot out into a colossal mirth, adding, "But I may still have a use for those. I may not be leaving after all."

"It hangs by a hair," he said. "He'll have picked men on his jury, and that thing with a forked tongue, that'll be there. But the crowd gets let in, and the crowd loves me. Do you know what they were shouting over on Saint-Honoré yesterday, under his own landlord's window? Free Danton! Free Camille! You see, no need to be jealous. And there were even some ladies from some establishment screeching about Lacroix. Well, trade's going to be hit hard all over town if we go."

When they gave us our breakfast of mashed black paper bread, Danton had told us, "We need spirit and wisecracks. Bear that in mind. For example, they'll ask again for names, addresses. To me they'll say, Where are you living? *Soon, in oblivion.* Which shows the crowd on the public benches, if they had any doubts, that we know this business is fixed so high it stinks like month-old herring." He looked at me. He said, "You're thirty-three, that gives you a perfect comedy line. You're Christ's age, and you're innocent. How would it go? *Rebels get martyred at thirty-three.* Try it, improve it."

"I'm thirty-four."

"One month. Pretend it's February again. You're thirty-three."

Westermann was locked up elsewhere. I wondered if Danton passed him a message: All my scars are at the front, but for this trial, which has knifed me in the back.

"Object," he said, "to the jury. Not the obvious. Leave Robespierre's trooper alone. But anyone you can say has some personal quarrel — do I need to tell you? We're lawyers. We can rock the island."

Games and game players. We took the mood. I don't know how. We did.

When they conducted us up into the court, that sun-struck room of flesh-packed benches, platforms, tricolors, and crossed axes under the scornful red bonnet of — ha! — Liberty, to the funeral cortège of black feathers, the *waiting*, men came to their feet and someone jumped across the barrier, grasped Danton like a lover, and then fled. The bell rang for quiet. And the crowd quieted, as it does at the play.

Where do you live, they asked him, and he said his lines, and the human mass responded. Fouquier's fucking C-shaped hag's face winced inward on its brandy-sodden struts, and Hermann nearly twisted in a circle under his hat.

(Cousin Fouquier was so near me, I could have throttled him. Christ, Christ, ten seconds of happiness before obliteration, why didn't I?)

But Danton had made us think we'd get away with it. Or, he had made us into his legion again. We were together, shoulder to shoulder, and we were on the side of right, and he stood up and spoke and the room roused like his woman, his dog. Acquittal — be saved — why shouldn't it happen? Would they dare otherwise? Paris would rise for Danton. They'd come to our aid, those men and women of the teeming streets we had fought for. The ones who kissed us and clung to us, July fourteenth, August tenth, Red September, *Janvier de la mort du roi* — Liberty — and not for us, who had been their voice, their heart? The People loved us. We had begun it, and they recalled as much. And it was, ultimately, impossible to believe in Danton's death.

"Age," they said at me.

"Thirty-three. The same as Jesus. A dangerous age for Revolutionaries."

Only one month out. Last month to the day had been my birthday. One month into thirty-four. (My number on the sheet when I voted for the king's death: 134.)

After I protested at Renaud, the fox I'd violined onto his back at the Jacobin Club, Danton said to me, "They're wetting themselves. Are we supposed to be afraid? They're terrified."

The evidence began by skirting us entirely. And went on that way. They lapsed into a long, long harangue of the hapless Freys, and the other mercantile and administrative dregs they had plumped in with our batch of cakes, as they called it, to discredit us. Presently, Danton stood up and asked politely, in a gargantuan boom, why our case was being dealt with alongside that of thieves?

At first he was told his comment was noted; he sat, but about every twenty minutes, at some point of shadiness in the indictment, would stand, gravely and loudly, to make it once more. In the end, every time it happened, the crowd burst out laughing in delight. If he delayed, they would prompt him: Giddy-up, Danton! Rear! You tell 'em!

The bell was rung.

"Sit down."

"How do you expect me to go on sitting on these bloody hard benches?" (Laughter.)

"We are sorry," said Tinville, "that they displease you."

"Then," said Danton, "be *more* sorry for yourself."

Tinville flinched. He drank from his water glass—the water was unbashfully amber with liquor today. He was definitely scared of Danton. Oh, yes, Fouquier was of the kind that slithers and coils around your ankles, then gets a purchase to swing up and bite. Kick the brute in the jaws and it falls down to slither again.

"I *will* be heard," announced Danton, in a dulcet crescendo. "I require to know why I, and my colleagues, are here to be examined beside common felons."

"What sort of felons, then," said my cousin, "do you and your—*colleagues*—consider yourselves to be?"

"Felons," said Danton, "who have seeded and harvested a Revolution. Who will build a Republic, if allowed. Felons who stole privilege from despots and gave it to the People. Felons who killed the cruelty of kings—" Even his voice was overwhelmed by the acclaim of the stalls—I beg their pardon, the public benches. When the outcry died, that bell was heard effetely tinkling. Danton said over it, "Whereas the felons who are attempting to judge us—"

"You will show respect for this Tribunal," said Hermann.

And Danton roared, "I was the *father* of this Tribunal. *I!* If I stoop to whip the brat, then it's done something wrong!"

His voice seemed to crack the roof.

We were electrified, on the seat's edge like the whole audience. Lacroix called something. Even Fabre's eyes were shining, like a sick child's.

But the thunder sank.

They had heard him the other side of the river, the noise of the lion-bull's bellowing. The windows of the court were open, the hot day still; I've no doubt they did hear. Outside people packed the walk, the quais were pebbled by faces, the bridges impassable. *That's Danton, listen! Can't be anyone else.*

But when he sat back down, you could no longer hear Danton. Only the fly buzz of the indictment against swindlers, forgers, speculators.

It droned on. And the first spangles of light in the air went out. It grew stifling and sullen. And Fabre moaned, and slept, or fainted.

We looked at our elected defense counsels, given us though both Danton and I had told them we would conduct our own defense. Of course they were

Some clerk brought Fabre water. Danton got up (vague whoops) but only
went over and helped him get it down his throat. Danton said something to
Fabre no one else heard, a pleasing foil to the bellows; Fouquier nearly strained
himself trying to eavesdrop and go on as if not noting it. Fabre's name was in
with that of the forgers and speculators. He had falsified sections of the order
which closed the East India Company, they said. I pitied him. Ridiculous. Here
I sat at his side.

On and on, it dragged. They did not plan, it seemed, to do any Dantonian
business today.

I remember the smell of that room. Something intense and stale, more than
the odorous crowd, the dust of ledgers. Something that had gathered on the
walls, accretions of frustration, terror, anger, weariness.

I bowed my head. Sometimes I jotted notations, entire paragraphs, on the
paper I had brought with me, now and then with vehemence. But my body and
soul sank inward. Almost I forgot where I was, until some singular jolt of
alarm, triggered by some phrase of theirs or thought of my own and very like a
blade under the ribs, caused me to sit up. To stare about.

Lucile. . . . What was she doing? Far away. Go far away, Lucile.

And what would it be like now to stroll down the avenue of limes at Queen's
Market, to drink lemonade under the shade trees. To sleep, or to make love. To
lie on one's back in a field and try to fashion poetry out of the dip and gauzy
glimmer of a butterfly, a scarlet flower on heaven's blue?

Roar again, Danton, roar again and wake us up.

He did roar. In the afternoon (after we had been shunted out and back a
couple of times—the judges needed their refreshments), we found Couthon-the-
legless and a brace of his cronies from the Safety Committee sitting to one side
of the court. Danton thumped down, then rose.

The crowd, which had begun to get bored, made a frying noise.

And the judges gathered themselves against the blast of the tempest.

"No," said Danton. "This won't do."

They rang their bell. He ignored it. His voice grew louder. Across the
Seine, they said, *Uh* huh, *Danton.*

"I find the procedures of this court to be at variance with the law. I suspect
some unfavorable influence is being brought to bear. Look at that!" And he flung
suddenly around on the committee men, who jumped like crickets. "We dread
we are on the road to a dictatorship, but here's the proof. I demand—"

"No demands, Danton!" shouted Hermann, his voice a cracked reed in the
onslaught of the storm.

"I *demand* access to the National Convention, of which I am a member and
to which I have been illegally denied recourse. I *demand* that a commission be
set up, *forthwith,* to look into the exploits of the self-styled Committees for

 Public Safety and Security, who, having trumped up charges against us behind a mask of secrecy, false friendship, and lies, now send their henchmen over to watch the fiasco take place. Good *God,* who are we to be shoveled into this—I, Camille, Philippeaux, Lacroix, we watchmen of this city's honor—we, the elected representatives of the Nation? Where are those things we risked our lives for; *where are our rights?* I demand a commission of inquiry! I *demand* it. Liberty! Equality! Brotherhood! Who gave you those words?"

And the benches, galvanized, are screaming after him, A commission! Justice! Danton! Rights! Liberty! Brotherhood!

He turned, a live Colossus, and raised his arms to them in a sort of barbaric benediction. *Danton!* They screamed, and outside the cry was being taken up: *Danton! Danton!* His head touched the sky. All our enemies seemed swept away, like twigs in a hurricane.

He came back to us, smiling. He looked young, his eyes burning. I seized his hand and raised it to my lips, held it to my forehead as if I made him my king. He *was* my king. Lacroix was singing the "Marseillaise," and so were we all. Even the forgers squeaked it out, even the Dane. And all the crowd, standing on their benches. Vaudeville.

Tiny figures in black, somehow our judges concluded the session and darted away like rats into a hole.

Even the guardsmen, some of them, who must now take us below, were enthusiastically wringing Danton's hand.

His final remark as we left was, "Silly bastards didn't let me finish. No matter. The judges will be begging for mercy tomorrow. Perhaps I'll give it them."

Only Fabre was not elated. They carried him out and I was sorry for him again. But the rest—was pride and joy.

⚜

Pride comes before a tumble, spelled tumbril.

⚜

The scene in the court was not reported in the journals, or else misreported. What news of it got on the street was garbled. And though there had been quite an amount of shouting outside, it faded. Somewhere in the passages of the prison (that place I recall as soot-black, its walls, ceilings, floors, its shadows—light not admitted but, where it forced its way, through apertures and drained lanterns, nearly useless), somewhere in those passages the guards turned morose, and then there were new guards.

"Hey," said Lacroix, affronted. He was excited still, not ready to admit the first act had ended, the curtain down, another act about to begin.

They split us up. Two by two, the animals went into their cells. Or one by one. Word had gone ahead of us. We were perilous. We were conspirators. Together, we made plots against the sacred Tribunal. And I was one of the worst; I was to be, again, segregated. They gave me my luggage.

"In here."

"Damn you, there's no room in here. Christ, it's no bigger than a cupboard."

"*In.*"

A shove that threw me forward and across the cell and against the opposing wall immediately. I stood clutching my bag, my writing case, and my coat, while the door was slammed on me. No window. Some light squeezed through the door's grill. A lantern hung from a hook in the wall, with a fitful candle in it. I stood under the lantern hook. Appropriate, for the lawyer of the lamppost.

I thought, in a dull cold horror, Why did we sing? Danton—Danton has no power. Only *this* has power. In that moment there was no Danton, and neither any Saint-Just nor any Robespierre. Not even the Tribunal. Only some large superhuman force that pushed us on downward and shoveled the earth in over our heads. Dillon's words: the faceless enemy, a formless ambient thing, the goddess of death. Well, didn't they say La Guillotine stalked the darkness; you found men in alleys at sunrise, decapitated?

I groaned, and in that instant the door opened again and they said to me, "Not so vocal; come along orderly."

"Whn-where—?"

"Somewhere else," the guardsmen said, enthralled with their enigmatic abilities.

I stuttered at them. They waited. I walked out and let them take me again through the roping corridors of that rat warren, half underground, that earthly Avernus, the Gatehouse Prison—till they conducted me into a jailer's room, with a table and chairs, some wine left in a bottle, and someone's forgotten pipe reeking as it went out. Plenty of candles here. Shadow and light, disturbed by our arrival, their departure, lurched and swooped over the low ceiling. I shut my eyes not to see it; it made me seasick.

"Visitor for you," said the guard stationed in the doorway.

I opened my eyes in a kind of ecstatic dismay. Lucile? Could it be she had somehow—no, not Lucile. Dear God, not Lucile in this place—and yet—

I turned and then, the oddest of things. His shadow fell ahead of him on the wall outside the door. A little shadow, shorter than all the others, with a little barrel chest, and the head very neatly shaped into a rounded forehead and some powdered rolls of hair.

"No," I said loudly. And the shadow stopped where it lay, there on the wall, the shadow of my friend Maxime. "This prisoner doesn't want any visitors," I said, as loudly as before. "Put me back in sl-solitary confinement in that box you cl-call a cell. That would be what I'd like."

He had signed the warrant to bring me here. He knew what it meant. Yet there he stood, waiting to come in. I looked at the shadow with hate and sickness. Then the shadow gestured and I heard it murmur. His escort, even the guard by the door, reversed untidily and clomped away. Then he stood there by himself outside the room, and I by myself inside. He did not move forward. We both waited, and I laughed a little.

Robespierre: The slave with the knife

He stands there, then, in the foul-lit corridor, and he thinks what? Yes, indeed, why *is* he there? He wasn't going to come. Camille was lost to him, corrupted, ruined. Maximilien would never be able to forgive that betrayal and that fall. *Would* he? It must be duty, then. The duty to a friend of one's youth who, through his immature foolishness, has got himself into bad company and a pretty shocking scrape. Robespierre, entering on Camille, will say, Now listen to me. I will get you out of this if you will do exactly as I tell you. Forget Danton (well, he would have to say that), Danton is dead, has written his own order of execution with the blood of France. But you I can perhaps save. If you will let me.

But Camille, himself half-dead already of fear and mortified disillusion, won't even let the rescuer in the room.

Maximilien, when he hears the other man laughing softly, or sobbing, says quietly, "Camille?"

And the voice comes back at once, stammering, almost strangled with most of the direst emotions known to humanity. "*No,* your *mistake.* Camille? There's no such person. I'm only a felon, a conspirator, a traitor. Camille? No Camille. Christ, how could Camille be here?"

"I should like to—"

"Don't. Don't do anything. Don't come near me."

"Camille!" A whisper.

"Who?" carols the voice, blithe with its anguish. "He keeps talking, this fellow, about someone who doesn't exist."

The shadow shifts. It straightens. It says, "Then you're not to be reasoned with."

"Reason—reason and virtue. Go and roll in them."

The shadow shifts again, and now it shifts right away from the space beyond the door. It vanishes. And instead you can hear the dainty little *clip-clop* of the well-heeled shoes, like a tiny horse, trotting down the passageway. And then the shuffling and stamping of the guards at the passageway's end, coming alert and returning to accompany the prisoner to the cell he has told the world he prefers to the proximity of his old school friend.

When Robespierre was sixteen, one hears the story, he fell in love with a girl, yes, truly fell in love, no doubt most honorably. And she picnicked with him and danced with him, and he read her his political essays. And in the end she married someone else. And he cried, sitting alone—where Charlotte his sister, with a sort of sinister sympathy, found him and comforted him not at all by saying that no one was good enough for him, so there. Previously he had also cried when this same Charlotte left a pet pigeon of his out in the rain and it perished. As a little boy, he used to make small models, of farms and castles, inhabited by weeny pristine animals and weeny ultra-clean people: perfect Lilliputian utopias. One had to kill none of the inhabitants to bring them into line. If they got dirty or maimed, one simply cast them away. It didn't hurt. No one argued.

He tappety-taps through the prison, face not readable and mind no longer to be read. You might set him in antiquity, the slave in the legend who served peerlessly for several decades the needs of a great master but who, on the day that master performed a base act, came into his presence holding out to him a sharpened dagger for his instant use.

I am the slave of Liberty, a living martyr; that which I fight wounds also me. That which I destroy cuts me to the heart.

But oh, the knife, Robespierre, so polished and bright in your manicured hand. Oh, the pigeons, Robespierre, dying in the rain of blood.

Yet, be free of it. Now I can say, be free. I acquit you. We were guilty. We deserved your gift. Each in his turn held out the blade and in succession fell on it. Be free of my blood.

But not of hers.

⚜

The cell was a different one, somewhat larger and aboveground. There was an arched window high up, thickly barred, benighted now. To judge by various sounds it looked across the prison's inner yard. Sometimes, distantly, a woman's voice could be heard singing, of all weird melancholy accompaniments. One candle. I offered my bribe and asked for more. Astonishingly, they arrived. ("Scared of the dark?") I could only rest my writing case on my knees as I sat on the wretched pallet, which dully stank and was verminous, probably. The ubiquitous vegetable mush arrived, was ignored. Even a bribe did not elicit wine. I might get drunk and cause trouble. Later, earlier, about seven the next morning, I used the poisonous water to shave, a miserable affair with no means to heat it, and crumbs of soap. But I had let the nicety slip the day before in my debauch of unhappiness. Today, the debauch of unhappiness was almost businesslike. Since appearances mattered not at all, why not keep them up? And the scraping of the razor was a fair beginning.

It was all like that. Through the night I wrote. I was angry awhile and went on cobbling together that notation to the seventh number of the *Leader.* (Saved

468 from chains? Are you? Or is it only that you accept what passes for manumission. You flung out one tyrant and terrified all the kings of the earth. Do not make the blunder now of permitting other false kings to grow from the stem. For there are still those who will be kings if you let them, pretending all the time they are Republicans—just as the queen card in the revolutionary pack passes herself off as Liberty by her red cap.)

And I wrote my answer to Saint-Just's putrid "Report." I said there what I might be expected to say, and have already rendered scattered versions of it, as of so much before, over and over.

See, Maxime, the pigeon furiously pecks at the cage as it dies.

Through the dark, till the day's steel showed against the bars, I was this: sleeping and waking, in a rage, in a sweat of ghastly fear. Resigned, panic-stricken, grieving, ashamed, momentarily insanely *hopeful.* So, drowning, you rise and sink in the sea's grip. So life is, while there is life.

❦

And the morning of the second day. . . .

The farce goes on. I am two people, perhaps three. (Is each of us taken in this way?) One Camille is determined to speak, has even cried out to this effect. He makes notes, still. He is febrile yet resolved, quicksilver. Another Camille, sitting close by him in his skin, keeps leadenly telling him it is all useless. Sometimes this Camille makes himself heard, but there's another as well. He laughs a lot, having turned the high-strung tension into something which tickles. And Danton has been making jokes.

Danton seems to have lost none of his vigor, though he looks drawn under his stubble—so, valiant master, you chickened out over the cold water. Lacroix muttered something about Georges's Sophie having sent him a wretched desolate letter, but that's unlikely from her. What was Danton doing while I, the three of me, went mad together all last night? Prowling to and fro? Sleeping? Lusting and screwing with dreams? Planning his attack? (A letter? All she'd be capable of sending him would be one of her garters. Like a whore, and nobody could pin it down as *hers.*)

(I still had my own letter for my own wife. No chance to settle it with anyone "trustworthy." And then the moments of thinking, She doesn't need this; I'll be free soon, and with her. And the moments of thinking, I'll be rotting soon, and it's all of me she'll have. I'd engaged one of the guards in conversation and slipped him the last of my money. He said, "I'll take you the long way round tonight, when we go back. You may see someone in the big room who can keep it for her." He didn't speak coarsely or unkindly. He never met my eyes, I think from embarrassment, for he had an honest face—but what do I know, having always misjudged everyone. And why am I going over this now? I should be paying attention. Because, when they turn to me, I am going to read my defense — when they turn to me. Oh, yes. *If.* And Danton is demanding that Westermann be privately questioned, as is customary, before being exposed to the Tribunal. It seems this was not done. A point of law that is pedantic, says Hermann. We are all here on a *very* pedantic point of law, says Danton. And all of us in the dock burst out laughing. Camaraderie. For a moment it's there again, and the strength it brings — then, gone.)

❀

Cambon, the financier, sits before the jury in a chair. He is a witness, called for the prosecution.

As the man arrived, Danton rose.

"For the prosecution, Cambon, against us?" Cambon looked at him. "Do you really believe that we — *we* — are conspirators against the Nation?" And Cambon smiled, probably from nerves. "Look at him," said Danton, in a huge merry voice. "He's laughing. That's how absurd the idea is. Go on, Citizen Court Clerk, put it in the record that, when asked if he believed Danton was a conspirator, the prosecution's witness *laughed!*"

The public benches enjoyed this and went off themselves into guffawing cheers.

Hermann picked up that blasted bell and tinkled it again.

As the noise died, Hermann rapped out at Danton, "Don't you ever hear this bell?"

"*Bell?*" Danton stared at him with eyes on fire. Hermann waited uneasily. "A man fighting for his life," said Danton, "may hear a *bell,* but he won't let it stop him."

He sits down to noises of acclaim, from the benches and the dock. (Outside the walks and bridges are again packed, as far as the Mint, they say. And beyond the court's doors, the salon they call the Pacers' Waiting Room is jammed so full of people it's doubtful anyone can take a single step, let alone indulge in any pacing.) But.

They ask Cambon things about Lacroix and about Danton. About corruptions in Belgium and wagonloads of gold and fine linen. Lacroix sits swearing and is requested to be quiet. "Then I fucking will." Danton stands. He calls again to Cambon. "Aside from all this — how shall I put it? this *mythology* — I would ask this witness, once more, if I am a conspirator?"

Cambon grimaces. "It would seem to me you are not."

"You are out of order," says Hermann, to Danton.

Lacroix jumps up and shouts, "A man fighting for his life may be out of order, but he won't let it stop him!" And gets an ovation from the benches.

And then one of the Camilles jumps up and yells at Cambon, "And I? Am *I* a conspirator?"

Cambon looks at Camille now, licks his lips. Cambon frowns. He glares at Fouquier and says, "In my opinion neither Danton nor Desmoulins can be named conspirators. Rather they are patriots and good servants of the Republic."

"Oh, Fouquier, call another prosecution witness," says Danton. "Your prosecution is going to acquit us."

"Sit down, and we shall see," says Fouquier-Tinville coldly.

�֍

They started on the indictment in the afternoon. It had taken them long enough to come to it. By this point Cambon's evidence on the India Company had finished the forgers and profiteers, and so Fabre. (He was now so ill they allowed him to go out. As the boneless body was half carried from the chamber, a woman hissed from the benches, "One more corpse ready-made for the guillotine *there*." I'd heard that, at a play during which was depicted the death of a king—there had been an endless number for a while—the audience had every night complained mournfully since there was "no proper blood to speak of." To this conoisseur's opinion the sights of Revolution Square had trained them.) But Danton had told Fabre that if we escaped, he would get him off, or so Lacroix had informed me. I had also seen a little cartoon that had been passed us from the public rows. It showed, on one side of the paper, a black object of two uprights, holding in the crosspieces a movable part dependent on a handle, and with a table arrangement at front: a printer's press. The caption read, *How easily this becomes*—and one turned over and found the same object exactly drawn the other side, except the movable part had simplified into a single angled blade and the "table" to a plank that stuck out instead behind. *This!* said the caption. It was meant for Fabre or for me, presumably. Very amusing.

The indictment seemed put together from the wonderful report of the wonderful Saint-Just. Hermann had prefaced the reading by saying to Danton, "When you have heard the charges you will be permitted to speak."

"Try and stop him!" someone shouted from the benches. There was a mild scuffle there.

Danton though, abruptly etiquette conscious, nodded coolly and settled himself to attend.

I did nothing to hamper him. I heard it all out again.

The clerk of the court, reading the indictment, was a former friend of Danton's, and often the man's voice faltered.

It was very hot, and the world very still.

"Dumouriez," the friend said, clearing his throat, "abetting such schemes, which would involve marching on Paris with these troops—"

And all the rest of it. Danton, the secret monarchist, bought and paid for. Martian Meadow. August. England. (I remember Saint-Honoré Street, ten o'clock: What are you playing at, d'Anton?—I?—And later, that scorch of a morning with the dung from La Fayette's troop of horses down in the road: You know, things aren't going quite as I foresaw; we've gone too far—Better run, eh, Danton? And he cried in Gabi's arms. And bloody little David with his: The story is, Danton's bought the Prussians. *Lies.* Or, if it's true, not the way they're saying it now. There were reasons. Good reasons. No, it isn't true. I don't remember, after all.)

The metallic smell of human sweat hung raw in the air today. So alive we were, we sweated. And the smell of summer through the windows. It reminded me, of all things, of being at school. Except then Robespierre would have been there. "You've broken another pen, Camille. You always break them." Let me borrow yours, then. You've finished. "Here. That tall boy kicked me when I came in." Kick him back. "But I'd done nothing. Why did he?" He kicks everyone. Shut up, Maxime, and let me write.

Shut up, Maxime, and let me write. Go away, let me alone. You lent me your pen (*prêtez-moi ta plume*). For God's sake. How easily this becomes—*this.*

When the long, long indictment was coughed through to an end, there was thick silence. Did they believe it, our audience on the benches, who loved us? Did they believe all that of Danton?

(I remember. I remember nothing at all.)

"You may speak now, Georges Danton. Take your time. We will listen."

Danton got up. He walked into the center of the space. He bowed with enormous irony to Hermann, and next to Fouquier (they were exceedingly courtly bows), and to all the jurors (Souberbielle reddened, then blanched), which performance raised more than a hint of tittering from the public end. Then, turning to the People, he addressed them, and only them.

"You know my voice," he said, and the great roll of that voice was suddenly beautiful, controlled, nearly singing, the way Mirabeau's voice had been, but gold to Mirabeau's dark silver. "You know my voice because it has cried out, so often, on your behalf. Will you listen again, now it cries out for itself, for me and for my friends? Yes, you will. Because you alone are to be trusted. You alone are just. Not merely this little courtroom, but all Paris should hear me now. And not merely Paris, all France."

They responded. And hushed themselves for him.

From the tail of my eye I saw Hermann gesture and Fouquier shake his head. But I was mesmerized by Danton. Yes, even in my doubt, my despair. The tears filled my eyes and flames my heart. So he was. So I remember him, and will always remember him so. Damn the rest of it.

"You will see," he said, "that I am accused by *invisible* men. By masked and hooded priests who conceal their daggers in long robes. What do they say? They say I go out by night to conspire against the Republic. You know me, citizens. Would I be out when I could be home in a soft bed with my pretty wife?" (They laugh. They hush themselves.) "They say I have been bought. But I'm priceless—who could afford me?" (They *laugh*. They call vast sums, and he waves them down, laughing too.) "I am a monarchist, am I? I, who ringed the Capets in their palace with bayonets so they shouldn't escape. *I, who* on August tenth directed the storming of that palace. I, a royalist? I, who ran away in August, yes, all the way to my mother's house to kiss her good-bye and to make my will—I'm a good son—and then ran all the way *back?* I thought I might die in the upheaval. Was I to leave my family unprovided for? Yes, I thought I might die, that's how far I meant to risk myself. As for England, that was business. Even Marat went to England. We returned. By Christ, I'm no émigré who deserts France for the foreign English whore. Where am I now? Right here. I, the *royalist,* who said, The head of a king shall be our battle gage." (They laugh and roar, *Danton! Danton!* And hush themselves yet again.) "But the invisible men in the forefront of all our struggles—they dare not attack me in the open. I say, let them come *out!*" Oh, God, his voice fills the shell of the room, seems to lift it into the sky. "Out, you sons of Cain, and let me unveil you, let me tear off the masks and the flesh together. Let me trample you back into the dirty slime from which you should never have been allowed to ooze."

He has the crowd galloping at his heels. Everything is going up in cannonades again. Somewhere Hermann finds the power to shriek, "Quieter! This noise isn't the mark of innocence but the bluster of guilt."

And Danton rounds on him. Danton thunders. "Am I permitted to be human? This monstrous dish of lies that has been served me—I choke on it! *I am a Revolutionary!* Do you think we took the Bastille *quietly?*" (Cries of approval.) "Do you think the guns were *quiet* when the Tuileries fell? And I—I—stung to the very soul by what has been said, may I not call out in my agony? Expect no calm frigid *report* from *me.*" (The room is in paroxysm. It is Danton who smooths it down, the judges being unable.) In the new silence Danton says, more softly, so only the water glasses break, "There is no bell on earth that can check me, and no man. I've listened to you. Now you will listen to me."

And turning back to the people, he says, "I am about to refute every detail of these slanders." And commences to do it.

Fouquier-Tinville writes.

The note is passed to Hermann. It reads: *In half an hour I shall adjourn. We need some discussion here.*

But fortune is on their side, it would seem. The heat, the dusty air, emotion—the great golden voice begins to fray. And at last Danton pauses, and rubs his hand across his face to clear the sweat, and one of the jurors calls to him, "Tell us then, if you weren't bought with him, why Dumouriez never chased the Prussians when he had them in his hand after Valmy?"

Danton turns to regard this one who aims at his back. Danton looks tired. He is tired. Three years ago, this session would not, physically, have touched him, but now it does, it has. After all, it's not just an afternoon, it's exactly those three years – of bellowing. A man can't shout down the world his whole life and not, at some moment, find himself worn out.

"Dumouriez's tactics were his own. I'm a politician, not a soldier," Danton says to the juror.

He's sidestepped. There are many things he could have said. Hasn't Camille already said some of them in that fatal *History of the Brissites?* But no. Either he mislays the familiar answers or disdains them – or feels he cannot build on so shaky a foundation.

And Fouquier (infallibly sensing, like any beast of prey, the instant of surrender, however unconscious), signals to Hermann, and Hermann rises.

"Georges Danton," he says, "has been speaking for almost two hours. For his own sake, now, I advise an end to this sitting. The evidence of other prisoners must also be heard." Danton moves a little. He – the incendiary Revolutionary, the roaring lion – seems almost grateful to be prevented. "You may continue tomorrow, Danton. We hope, with greater calm."

"Never," Danton says. His face is scarlet, his eyes half shut. He holds his hand to his throat now, as if to contain the bulging pulse; long ago the cravat was dispensed with, the shirt pulled wide open at the neck. "But on your word I shall speak again, I will accept the ruling. And if you assure me I may call my own witnesses tomorrow, for the defense."

"Lawyers have been appointed to defend you."

"I am my own lawyer and will call my own witnesses. I have a list of them, which I'll give you now."

"This is not the hour –"

"When will the hour *be?*"

"This is an improper area –"

"Don't put me off! Christ blast you, I'll have my witnesses in on your bloody damnable life!" His voice cracks again, and the strong language, habitual to Danton as the jewelry of his intellect is habitual, causes Hermann to lilt into a little wince of triumph. Danton sees it. With no warning, Danton goes back to the prisoners' benches and sits down. He seems to be trembling.

He was trembling. He said to me, "I'm done." Then he added, a father anxious not to scare his children, "I'll be all right tomorrow. Tomorrow – witnesses. We'll make a thing of it. Interrupt the bastards. Jesus, I'm finished." And his head sank forward; he gave himself over to breathing.

Hérault said softly, "Don't worry, Georges. You've killed them. You can rest." It wasn't true. We knew it, but Hérault, such a gentleman – Well.

⚜

As he promised, when we went back my guard stuck by me, took me aside, and "around the long way," to the "big room."

It was black, like everywhere else in hell, but for a few slits of sky high up, and the rank torches blaring. Cells opened off it behind cages of bars, but everyone was out in the *grand salon*. And there was a racket—worse than in the court up above. My guard balked and stopped me at the gate. We both concluded it was a riot. But then he chuckled. "They're cheerful this evening!" They were singing, wildly as a bacchanal. Then it ended in a shout. A young man's voice called out, "And I'll give you a pledge to drink to—the Republic." A gap of nothing. And he said, "No, I don't mean the filthy thing His Revolutionary Majesty Robespierre plans, I mean the True Republic—the mirage, the song unsung—the paradise where no one is butchered or does the butchering, where no one dies in an open sewer named Revolution Square." And at that there were some cries of acclaim, some curses, and a glass or two smashed. I pushed by my guard, who let me, through into the blackened torchlight.

The room was full. They sat or stood, or leaned or lay, in their dead powderings and soiled lace and ragged coats. They seemed packed into their garments like stuffing into bolsters—everything was stained and nearly color-less, perhaps due only to the gloom—all but the revolutionary ornaments so many had about them; these had stayed bright. Who were they, such people, what station would they claim? All edges blurred. Prison, like Liberty's first mad fête in Mars Field, had made them equal. Aristos, tailors, usurers, gallants, whores. One distinguished a priest or two, robed and on his knees. A girl or two who had rubbed rouge into the jail-gray of her cheeks. But they were a grisly family at last, and it seemed they almost knew it. Though everywhere was movement—as they twisted or straightened themselves, altered the patterns of their hands in reading or speech or drinking—yet for a moment it was Curtius' waxworks, fallen into decay. And then and there, standing on a wooden stool— my God, my own image coming back to me—the young man whose voice I had thought I knew and did know: Gabriel. Gabriel de Polignac. And at that second he turned and saw me. I flinched—he could announce who I was, and that might provoke any number of reactions. But he did nothing like that, only jumped down lightly on his dancer's feet and came up to me with a glass of brandy in his hand. He said quietly, only to me, with very little viciousness, "Well, well. Deputy Desmoulins. Do join us for a drink. To what might have been."

"Give it to me," I said and grabbed the glass out of his hand and drained it. He laughed. The spirit rushed straight to my head, and suddenly, in the relief of that, I was ashamed. "I'm sorry."

"That's quite all right," he said. He retrieved the empty glass. "I've had my fill. And I want to be a little sober where I'm going tonight."

My eyes would not focus on him. I said, "Whuur-ere?"

"Where do you think, Camille? Where does one go from this place?" And he wasn't laughing now, he was furious. He could have killed me or anyone. He said, "Old Bloodless and his puppet show."

"What? When?"

"Now. Presently we go up to be barbered nicely for the cut." He tugged at his fair hair idly. The pearl was gone from his ear, leaving a perfect tiny hole there—some bribe, the brandy, maybe—that pearl.

"Gabriel," I said.

"Don't grieve," he said. "You didn't do it." He was flippant again. "Or, no more than I." I began to be able to see him. "Yes," he said, "you may note me, please, reasonably well turned out and freshly shaved for the final shave. But look at you. Tut, Camille. You were such a dandy once, as soon as you got any money. Haven't they told you the dodge for shaving here? It's quite the vogue." I gazed at him. He seemed now far off and now close. "Urine," said Gabriel. "Your own piss, you fool. It's hotter than cold water." There were shadowy fissures under his eyes, old and black as under my own. "All right, Camille," he said. "I'll probably see you in hell. We made a mess of all this, didn't we?"

"Yes." My guard had gone off to talk with another, where the brandy was.

Gabriel said, "Clodie's alive. She's shut up in the Pélagie. Her husband ran and left her in the mousetrap, Christ rot his soul. My God, I can't stop thinking about her, on and on, even here and even *now*. It tears me in pieces. When they do it, her face, her body—she was always so shy—the last image I'll see. I'll go into nothing with that. Oh, Christ damn them, damn them all. Don't cry," he said to me, almost absently, after a moment. "What? Oh, yes, your Lucile. What? I can't hear—a letter for her? Yes, I'll tell you who's a good bet, old Beau'garde over there. He may even get out alive. Give it to him. Tell him I told you. I'm not so popular, but he and I, we've played chess together." Then there came the echoing tramp of boots, approaching unseen as yet, phantoms, to the other doorway.

Not a figure in the place, not a moving waxwork that failed to stiffen. The attentive soundlessness of death's waiting room. It settled like a century's dust.

The detail of guardsmen walked in and looked about. They had no particular expression. Perhaps, at the start, there had been some eagerness to punish the wicked, but they had got tired of it. Duty. One stepped forward, a beefy jackass in a dirty uniform. You glimpsed his broken teeth as he began to read off the names of the dead.

And Gabriel, hearing his name, swore and threw his glass away and flung his arms around me, and I my arms around him.

"God give you peace, Camille. But I think there's no peace for any of us. We're damned for this." And then he drew away and sauntered across the long room, calling out as he did so to those who hung back, weeping, giving at the knees; "Come, children of your fatherland, the day of glory is at hand!"

When he was gone, when they were all of them gone, my guard, having had temporarily sufficient drink, came and ushered me over to the man called Beau'garde. I'd met him once before. I showed him the crumpled letter and he said he would, if he could, see to it. I had to remind him who I was, but he made nothing of that. "Please," I said. "On your life see she gets this."

"Yes," he said. "If I can. I swear I will. If I can."

My guard took me away then, in rather a hurry, perhaps realizing doing this for me was a risky business. I stumbled through the room. Some women, just now parted from their men, were screaming and crying. I looked back over my shoulder until we had passed through the door, keeping in sight the man who had my letter. He was precious to me. He would meet with Lucile. When I was carrion, he would put those papers in her hands.

In my cell, I lay and thought of Gabriel de Polignac.

It was the evening of April third, by the old calendar.

⚜

Those who heard, in the prison, toasted Gabriel that night, whatever their differences with him. He had stood, smart and bold and raging in the tumbril. The crowd had not liked his aristo name, his bearing, his brushed azure coat. Someone threw half a deliquescent cabbage at him. Reaching the scaffold, he mounted the wooden steps and, reaching Sanson, the executioner of Paris— Old Sans-sang the Blood-letter, posed up there with all the smugness of a professional—Gabriel truly lost his temper.

They said, even in extremis, be careful and polite. Though the blade does the work, it's best not to fall out with the crew.

But Gabriel de Polignac, against the red sky of his own personal sunset, in his beautiful brave finery marred by Malice's stinking cabbage, turned and spat on Sanson.

Yes, he spat on the bastard. Thank God someone did it.

(Manhandled for it, too; they nearly tore both his arms out of their sockets when they slung him on the plank and strapped him there. They liked to think of themselves as Sanson's "boys." Fellowship in all things. Though the blade, when it fell, was clean.)

Raise your glasses, then; tell beautiful Clodie languishing in the Sainte-Pélagie prison: Your friend died with style. Tell her since, in only a few days' time, she too will mount the scaffold and, as in life, lie down where he has lain. For the great tide is not content with killing only us, it must have our lovers, too, our wives; *our souls if it could.*

So much, Gabriel, for beauty, bravery, and love.

When the rain is heavy enough, flowers are smashed by rain.

15 Germinal (April 4, 1794)

AND THE morning of the third day. . . .

The curtain goes up late this morning.

The prisoners are brought in fretting; they haven't slept well in their lodgings. They seem shot full of random galvanics, twitching, getting up and slumping down, scribbling notes, twisting said notes, jerking around to chatter into each other's ears, or over their shoulders to those seated behind them. Their faces stay wooden, with glazed eyes, till suddenly all flickers into life and works frantically, as they gnaw their lips or frown convulsively. They look a disreputable lot. Fashion, as with cleanliness, suffers in the prisons. Lacroix and Camille Desmoulins seem to have given up shaving again; Danton would appear to be growing a beard. Though Hérault must have unearthed a barber and wooed him. Their shirts are yellow and gray, their stockings eye-catching. If there is a piece of decent linen or muslin among them, they have concealed it. Even Hérault has not been able to find a laundry and has left the ribbon off his hair, which falls around his neck in chains of gold that still contrive to shine.

No sooner was everybody in than Danton got up and marched out into the center space he had held, so rampantly, yesterday.

He can hardly have failed to notice the public end of the chamber is not so full as it has been. There are, also, an extra quantity of guards standing about and, more sinister yet, little groups who sit quiet and have no expression on their faces—creatures, surely, of the Tribunal, who'll keep mum till required to vociferate, at which juncture they will sound to the accused's detriment. Not good. Not good at all. But Danton only glances, then turns himself toward the judges' bench and toward Fouquier, fresh down from his hot bread and bottled spirits.

Danton—under the quills of tough stubble—pale this morning, his face heavy, all jowls, pouches, the searing eyes sunk in, with no flames alight behind them.

Fouquier quizzes the apparition. "Well?"

"Well," says Danton firmly. "I'm here to speak, as I was told I should."

"Oh. Later, Danton. There is other business that must be seen to first."

A sluggish flush is all the fire now that can be drawn up to Danton's face. But he turns and rumbles at the public benches, the room, the windows, the world outside. "I was told I might speak freely. These were the terms on which, last night, you adjourned your court."

"Terms? This is the Nation's Tribunal, Danton, and you are on trial before it. We don't make terms."

"Christ, you finicking little baboon," shouts Danton, turning back to him; it would not be unimpressive, if one didn't know of what Danton is capable. He is like a man running—hard and gamely—but with a load fastened on his back.

"Respect, Danton, for the court," says Fouquier.

Danton shudders. He realizes, plainly, with one disgusted survey, the crowd in the chamber is largely useless. Like everything else? He slams his fist against the empty air and says, doggedly, "And my witnesses? You were presented, I believe, with my written list. When are they to be called?"

"Do me the great favor," says Fouquier, "of sitting down. We shall come to all that in due course." And all at once, he smiles and makes a wriggling, fawning gesture toward Danton. Danton sees it, and knows infallibly what it means. It means Fouquier is sure of him, or begins to be. And Danton can do nothing, or can think of nothing he could do.

He turns, as yesterday he did, and retreats to the prisoners' benches. He sits carefully and well back, folding his arms. He sets himself to scrutinize Fouquier, but Danton's eyes are not quite focused.

Soon, a new prisoner was brought in. The charge against him, which was made much of, was the usual kill-all: Treason Against the Nation. But it seemed rather scrappily applied. The man stood looking sheepish, insecure, but not much horrified, and when finally motioned to the prisoners' rows, he sat down well away from the others.

"Ah," said Lacroix. "Do I spot the rose on the thorn?" He nudged Philippeaux. "What do you say?"

"Probably," said Philippeaux. He was not interested, lost in reading his book or reading the face of his wife in the cameo. But "What?" demanded Camille, like a nervous dog, anxious to miss no tidbit, however indigestible.

"That one," said Lacroix, "the new one down there, shunning us as if we've got some particularly irksome disease. *He'll* get off. Look at him. He knows, all right. They're going to find him guiltless, while the rest of us—"

"An old method," said Hérault. "It makes any trial look *so* much more fair—"

Just then, the name of Hérault was called.

He suffered the questions with implicit dignity and the aspect of a man called from some other, more pleasing pastime, who chooses to be polite and patient. Nevertheless, somehow the questions utterly condemned him, a profiteer, the agent of alien interests.

And now, the name called is Camille's.

Mine.

I stood, that cold-pudding audience on my left; there, the jurors at whom I could gape (I knew several; one had spent a lot of time consulting me on the answering of letters over at the Convention) or from whom I could avert my eyes. And *there,* the judgment of the ravens. The defense I had written was in my pocket. There was too much of it. I already knew they weren't going to let me read it. But I put my hand on the paper. I looked at Fouquier. I'm not afraid of you, you black flea, you squirming biting worm. But I *was* afraid. I shook. And my voice.

"You seem rather surprised, Citizen Desmoulins. Do you know why you're here?"

"Y-n-yes. I know quite well. Vindictive spite."

Fouquier pursed his lips.

"Not a unique defense," said Hermann.

"Hear some more," I said. "Hn-Sn-Saint-Just, with whom, as is common knowledge, I have had occasion to quarrel—he, before several people, who wll-well r-remember the event, swore to have my life."

"You are saying that because of some slander you made against Saint-Just—"

"I made a joke about Saint-Just. Saint-Just was one of the minority who didn't find it n-funny."

"So you tell us you're here for making jokes. Not because you are implicated in certain conspiracies: for one, the affair with Dumouriez."

"I denounced—I denounced Dumouriez—as Danton denounced him! The Gironde were the lovers of Dumouriez, not Danton or any one of us. Even before Marat spoke out, I—I and-d nn-n-not the first time I was before Mr-Marat—I warned France ag-against Mirabeau, and Orléans."

"Yes, yes. You've spoken out against several persons, when once their treason was apparent."

"*What?* I—"

"Another joke, perhaps?"

"You," I said, and my voice sprang into a shaking shout. "*You* sit there and represent revolutionary justice."

"You would like to see an end to the Revolution?"

"I *began* the Revolution. On July twelfth. I started it, and my murder will end it."

"Yet you befriend royalists."

"No. I never have. Whoever says that is a liar."

"Your own writings say it. We shall have them read out."

"I have asked for common *pity,* that's all."

"And printed, for example, a defense of a known monarchist, Arthur Dillon, now held at the Luxembourg for his crimes."

"His crimes—crimes—what crimes? My God, he was my friend. *One* dubious friendship—I never agreed with his views, but he loved France and he served France—he did nothing against the aims of a Republic that I knew of. What do you do in such a case? Turn a blind eye? In times like these, what man hasn't had a Dillon?"

"We return to your paper, the *Cordelier Leader.* You have used this vehicle to spread discontent. There is hardly a page that doesn't reek of wanton divisiveness. You jeer at the Committees, you ridicule the Convention. And over all, again and again, you call for the sword to be stripped from our hands, leaving France defenseless before her adversaries."

"Nr-*never.* Never, do you hear me? Can you *hear?* I called for an end to extremism. To wanton bloody slaughter. To stop that! Since Robespierre approached me—"

"Why bring in the name of Citizen Robespierre?"

Someone—Lacroix—shouted, "Why *not?* Is that blasphemy, now?"

"Robespierre de-disliked the format of the paper," I said. "I toned it down out of consideration for his views. I retracted—"

"Oh, come, Desmoulins. You *retracted?*"

"I've done nn-nothing but retract since the fourth issue."

"Ah, yes. And we shall see how you did it, when the paper is read."

"Read it all, then. Not just bits of it, to mislead, the bits Saint-Just has carefully underlined for you." (Lacroix laughing.) "Do you think all France wants to sit under the steps of the guillotine and lick blood?" My voice no longer shook. It was hoarse. It sounded desperate. "I've had hundreds of letters, begging me to go on, to cry out for a clemency committee—for mercy—*sanity.* Men who hide now came up and shook my hand and encouraged me."

"Royalists."

"*No!* Didn't you try Hébert and his faction? Well, didn't you—and sent them to death? Who gave them to your justice? I myself. It was thought necessary then for someone to speak out. It's to my credit that I did it. I was congratulated. I was the hero then. Now, for saying the same things, I am the villain. Is this the reason and morality of the Republic?"

"You are becoming incoherent, citizen."

"You want to crucify me on the accusations of an ice-blooded witless bastard who hates me."

"It would seem the sentiment is mutual."

And over there, a murmur of chilly laughter, from the court's creatures on the public benches.

I swallowed the bitter dryness in my throat and said, "I have prepared an answer to his so-called report. I have it here."

"So we see. But the Tribunal instructs you to retire for the moment, until the relevant sections of your paper have been read."

"You refuse me the—"

"You are refused nothing."

"Then let me read—"

"The journal will be read first."

"That's a refusal."

"A deferment."

I took in, as I must, their blank faces. Hermann looked nearly benign under his mask. Fouquier—I recalled him in my office that day: Could I help him? I was such a celebrity, such a shining example of revolutionary zeal. And my feet on my desk, and his sliding movements as he *crawled.* My hand fell from the papers in my pocket.

As Danton had done, I went back to the bench and sat and let them get on with it.

They read all Saint-Just had underlined. It was enough to incriminate me, by their lights. Three or four times I think I leaped up and shouted at them, but my words were lost. I couldn't marshal them or get them out; they wouldn't listen.

Our company sat now with its collective head hanging.

I felt as if I had run a hundred miles across a parched desert, to reach a place without water or shade. I struggled to find some way to rest and to be calm. My panic was their ally. But I could only writhe, and clasp my head in my hands, sometimes talking to the floor of the court in a mumble, telling it I should go mad.

❉

Are the black rats smug?

They sit and preen their blackness, and cheep.

What is left now to the doleful prisoners? They are dismissed from lengthy speech and seem to have obeyed the dismissal, giving up.

But there must be other devises. If nothing else, the sheer disruption of almost-mindless jeering, learned so ably at the Assembly, the Cordeliers, the Jacobins.

❉

Lacroix begins it.

The Belgium linen has been mentioned again, in the midst of the examination of Westermann, the soldier. And Lacroix stands up, coughs, and spits on the floor—an action he does not generally perform, its mannered intent fairly obvious—and shouts, "Damn these lies! I want my witnesses in. Justice!"

That bell they still have the nerve to ring—though less often, let it be said—is shaken at him. Lacroix hammers on over it. "Witnesses for the defense, as promised." (A look at Danton, who raises his brows. Lacroix turns to the public rows.) "Every man here to take note: we are denied our legal rights. Is this a trial?"

Some altercation ensues, between Lacroix and Hermann, during which Hermann is told that Lacroix spits on his bell. When he tires, Lacroix sits down, which seems prearranged. (Certainly, Lacroix has been exchanging words with Danton.)

The examination of Westermann continues.

Presently, Danton gets up. (Though the public benches are not as they were, still there is, at this, an evident frisson among them.)

"May I speak?"

"You have spoken, Danton. Sit down."

"I have partly spoken and been curtailed."

"This was discussed earlier."

"I demand," says Danton, "that our witnesses for the defense be called immediately."

"There will be no more talk of witnesses at this point in the proceedings."

"Oh, won't there?"

"Sit down."

"I demand my rights and the rights of my fellows."

"Sit."

Danton says, in English, which causes something of a reaction, particularly where it is not understood, "Do you think, sir, you're addressing your hound?"

The bell is rung. Danton indicates the bell, and somewhere, far back in the room, there is some laughter. After all, a coarse voice cries enthusiastically, "Don't you trust the buggers, Danton!"

Danton, sitting, has the hint of a smile on his face again. This is a game, and games he can handle.

The prosecution reassembles itself and resumes. "Men of your command," says Hermann to Westermann, "have been known to complain that—"

Danton is standing up again.

"This won't do. You're quoting hearsay. Is there a witness to prove it? Westermann has informed me he has witnesses who contradict this statement of yours. Let them be called at once."

Hermann is seriously ruffled. "You will recognize the ruling of this court, and sit."

"The ruling of this court, yesterday evening, assured us that our witnesses would be brought in today. I appeal to the Free People of France, who are in this room, to remember and to note how we are being misused."

Danton sits.

And, as in a flurry of evident haste, Hermann races to say, "There have been aspersions cast, General Westermann—"

Danton gets up again to exclaim, "All of which will be disproved if you will hear the witnesses!"

After which, the game takes off. It takes off with Lacroix bounding up and howling the sorcerous word (witnesses) at every break or pause for breath. And Camille, catching the rhythm, doing likewise, but with no taint of amusement, all crazy fury. And even Philippeaux deigns to stand and say, "I have witnesses too." And Danton, ever Danton, each upsurge ominous, and his disheveled power so great, even now, that they begin to fall silent, to *wait* for his inevitable interpolations, or to stutter like Camille as they try not to wait for them.

And now the rats no longer preen, for sure.

And, what is more, there is found to be an element of genuine populace in the court, right at the back, who are themselves prepared to join in the chorus again: Witnesses, witnesses, give them their witnesses!

At which, as is to be expected, the prisoners are fired to new heights and ceaselessly address the public rows, exhorting support and detailing their abuse by the Tribunal.

The avalanche escalates, predictably, into pandemonium.

Everyone is on his feet at last. In the body of the court a vague impulse to fight is coming to flower between the court's implants and the actual spectators.

In the dock they are all standing, Hérault too; the Freys — screaming tearfully — the Dane lapsing into Danish but yelling it. The decoy suspect, brought to trial to be "fairly" acquitted, has got up too and looks ready to abscond through a window. Finally the judges are up in a bevy of plumes, and Fouquier himself, who shouts back and back and *back* into the maelstrom, until he is heard. "Very well — very *well* — stop this brawl!"

And at length there comes a bemused, half-attentive lacuna, into which Danton says amiably, "You want it stopped? Then give us our witnesses."

Fouquier, out of breath with shouting, grabs the space of quiet breathlessly. "If you accord no respect to this Tribunal, will you listen to the National Convention?"

At which the quiet is held.

This is unprecedented. Nobody can go so high. Has Danton achieved this?

Danton glances around. "No disrespect was offered. You misunderstood the outcry of the blameless pleading for justice."

An apple has been thrown, small, uneatable, by someone on the public benches. Fouquier stoops and picks it up. He holds it to show Danton, then drops it on the table.

"This brawl," repeats Fouquier. "Have I stopped you now? Are you prepared to be sensible?"

"You mentioned, if I took your meaning correctly, that you would apply directly to the Convention on our behalf."

"I said I would apply to the Convention."

"Everyone hears you, Fouquier," says Danton. "Do you give your word, and will you keep your word?"

"I can do nothing else with you, since you and your *followers* insist on behaving like lunatics."

"There's a cold draft we feel on our necks. It addles the brain. Do pardon the outburst."

"I will," says Fouquier, "withdraw at once and write to the Convention."

"I've asked for nothing else," says Danton blandly.

"The Convention's wishes will be exact. Do you consent to abide by them?"

"The Convention," says Danton, "is the Convention. I bow my head to the supreme authority of France, which I myself, let it be remembered, helped to instigate, and of which I myself am a part."

Fouquier nods. The plumes of his death hat back him up. He salutes the judges and walks directly out.

Danton sits down. Lacroix cranes around to him. "*Well?*"

"Mm," says Danton. His eyes look drowsy and far away. What's he thinking about? Victory, release, Louise? Or only of sleep? Or of the dreamless comforting feather bed of Nothingness?

❀

Ha! The rats are running now.

The rats that squeak and nip, can think and read, and write and speak.

Saint-Just, a white rat of unusual intelligence, takes the note from Fouquier, a black rat of exceptional persistence. Saint-Just reads the note. It's true, it's come to the Convention offices, if not quite into the Convention.

In a short while Saint-Just is reading out Fouquier's note to the other members of the Committee for Public Safety, whose motto, we recall, is Esprit de Corpse.

A storm has raged here from the beginning of the session. The accused are clamoring that defense witnesses be called. These include many who are their personal friends, for example Stanislas Fréron and Legendre. They appeal constantly to the public benches to take note of how this "rightful claim" is being refused them. (As you know, the outer chambers and streets are also thronged.) Although the President and the entire Tribunal have stood firm, these continual protestations disorganize the session. They also declare furiously that they will not desist until the witnesses appear. We must therefore request from you a direct ruling as to how we shall proceed, for legally we have no formula for denying their demand. We postulate that the only way to shut them up is by direct order of the Convention. Can such a thing be managed?

❖

It was Fouché again, Fouché the *gray* rat, who supplied the key.

The prisons were full of prisoners but also full of his little lost sheep—the dear little sheep who wandered about among the rest, pretending, themselves, to be prisoners. But who, on this word or that whisper, bleated to the ratly shepherd. *Baa, baa, le mouton narre.*

The wicked monarchist Arturius Dillon, who had a not inadequate income, had been living neither too ill at the Luxembourg, courtesy of a host of very bribable jailers. On April 1, enriched by a bottle of good burgundy, Citizen Irish Dillon had been heard to remark to his dinner companions, "Those creeping bastards have got Camille Desmoulins, on some untrue lying idiot's falsehood of a charge. Poor devil. He was trying to put things right. My God, if I were out of this place—" Well, what? asked one of the loitering sheep.

And Dillon, too drunk and too fed up to care, told him, "I'd get my men back off the borders and take this God-cursed city by its throat. The People'd soon sling them out, Satan and all his bloody silly works: Committee of this, Committee of that, Committee of Murder and Mayhem." The People would kill you. They won't rise for Desmoulins any more, or Danton. "Forgetfulness, the unction of crowds. Ah, but one look at Camille's beautiful wife with tears in her eyes—the men of France can see sense when a lovely woman represents it, for

all you threw out your Madonna." You *always* liked Camille's wife, one hears.
"Yes, and I can tear your ears off your head, too." Sorry, sorry.

"Sorry? Yes, this country will be sorry, one day, when it's too late. He knew they'd do this to him. But still, he went on. He couldn't help himself. Poor Camille. God damn them, if they weren't damned already. If I weren't shut up in here—"

And this interesting sample of burgundaria was soon retailed to Citizen Fouché and so came, in due course, to snuggle against the lavender cravat of Saint-Just, inside his coat.

It was meaningless. Dillon was cooped, and his bad wishes impotent. *He* could do nothing. But armed with the idea, Saint-Just, his mind a nimble cabinet full of files, duly arrived at the Convention in the late afternoon of April 4, when a sudden overcast had caused the lamps to be lit.

There was some consternation. Saint-Just had demanded an immediate opportunity to address the assembly. What could this hurry be about save the Danton faction, currently fighting for their lives a mile or so northeast along the river? And everyone had been so cautious, the past day or so, trying not to bring up the awkward topic.

Saint-Just mounted the tribune and spoke, or rather he read his latest report. The gist of it was as follows:

The prisoners over at the Palais de Justice have been causing an unlawful upheaval. Their purpose in this is to delay and to undermine the progress of justice. They have good reasons. Meanwhile, we have unearthed a diabolical plot. Camille Desmoulins's wife, who, as is known, has a long-established association with Arthur Dillon, has made plans to have him escape from the Luxembourg. He is to rally his troops and assault this Convention, killing all deputies reckoned to be unfriendly. To ensure the further success of the venture, the Desmoulins woman and her accomplices are in the process of paying insurgent elements among the people, who will then rise against the existing authorities. The whole is, demonstrably, part of a larger royalist plot. Its end result will see not merely the scurrilous Danton gang released, and the Convention slaughtered, but the Republic overthrown and the Capet child reinstated on the throne of a monarchist France.

"In order to save your country from this ghastly peril, I ask this Convention to give the order that, warned of the conspiracy of Desmoulins, Danton, Lacroix, and others, the Revolutionary Tribunal shall employ every and any means at its disposal to contain the revolt of the prisoners in the dock. I require from you a decree that all those accused of conspiracy shall be outlawed on the spot and receive the summary justice which is all an outlaw merits."

Who will believe it? Anyone?

Oh, yes. Plenty. The world's a weird place right now, royalists under every bed and table, up every chimney with the baby-biting werewolves. Walking a tightrope, which one of you likes to look down? They've heard it all before, and they've condemned on such hearings before.

The grapy, thunder-color light, the flicker of the lamps, Saint-Just's marble figure, so unearthly in its youthful and supreme composure—these things have their effect. Elected in the teeth of laws which, having held society together for centuries, were overthrown in a handful of months, of course the deputies of this assembly are insecure. If it happened once, it can happen again.

Is Dillon's army already marching on the capital?

Is the blond witch Lucile already flying over Paris throwing gold, wine, and white bread into the mouths of the mob's gargoyles?

God help us all. Vote, vote for the decree. Cast them out and shut them up. Cauterize the infection at its root.

Here you are, Saint-Just, our Savior.

❅

When Fouquier-Tinville reentered the Tribunal, his movements were slow, his face slightly contorted, head tilted to one side, more than ever like a bird of prey, but one which, partly with masochistic pleasure, anticipates a blow.

They knew, intuitively, every one of the prisoners, in those seconds.

The examination of Westermann, which had gone quietly since Fouquier's declaration, had just been concluded.

The judges looked at Fouquier. All eyes were on him.

He stole forward and opened a sheet of paper. It bore the seal of the Convention.

"In the name of the Republic," said Fouquier, "One and Indivisible. I have here, and will now read to this court, the answer made by the National Convention, both to the Tribunal and to those who stand accused before it." His voice was obsequious. Obsequiously, he read from the paper, glancing up from time to time, at Danton particularly, as if trying to win his favor.

" 'A perilous discovery has been made. A prison plot has been uncovered. The monarchist Dillon has planned to escape the Luxembourg and to dispatch his troops against the city in an attempt to rescue the prisoners Danton and Desmoulins and their co-conspirators. To abet this end, the prisoners have themselves sought to damage the authority of the Tribunal, and to confuse the People, by scenes of riot. Meanwhile their accomplices have set out, with money stolen from the Nation, to suborn ignorant citizens and incite them to revolt.

" 'In the light of these findings, the Convention hereby empowers the Revolutionary Tribunal to proceed with its investigations in closed session. The prisoners are placed outside the law, as traitors, and will henceforth be excluded from the court.' "

Fouquier has ended.

For a moment nothing. Then the wit calls from the public benches, that misquote of Molière, "You asked for it, Georges Danton, you asked for it!"

And Danton cries out, "I asked for justice, not the diseased emptyings of their chamber pots!"

And then, predictably, they are all shouting, while the spectators— shocked, bought, confused, predatory—buzz.

Hermann does not go for his bell. He stands portentously. "No more," he says, and motions to the National Guard, of whom vast quantities seem to be in the room; they begin to move in on the ranting prisoners. "Your noise is finished."

Danton's roar breaks through. "Finished? We never began. Scenes of riot? What have we done? Tried to defend ourselves from your fucking lies—you turds passing for men. Look at them!" he thunders at the world. "Look at this human shit that dares to pass judgment on us. But this is how a tyrant works. He sends in his regiments of shitheads to gag you when you would cry out. We're to be condemned to death—without a word spoken for our defense, without a single witness called." And back to Hermann, the thunder, pouring round that little indoor sky. "Make haste, then. Do it. Butcher us. Christ, I've lived too long if I see France come to *this*. Run to the scaffold, Danton. *Run!*"

The guard are in position all around them, but there's a looseness to the formation. The blasting cacophony of Danton still forms a barrier, while Lacroix, the first on whom they lay hands, lashes out with his fists and feet. It takes two of the uniformed men to get hold of him, and then two more as he goes on punching and kicking.

Hermann, like a schoolmaster, is tidying the papers on his table. Some of the jury seem in disarray. Fouquier, who had paused at the end of his reading, a student meekly awaiting praise for his essay, now turns and speaks privately with two of the jurors.

Through the general hubbub, Danton is heard roaring again. "Look! The place is full of committee agents. Look at the stinking scum, come to hunt us down."

"Robespierre's tyranny! Slaves of tyrants!" screams Lacroix. "You cunts, licking the dongs of your pox-ridden revolutionary *kings!*"

In the midst of the mêlée, elbowing guardsmen off him, Camille, with insane eyes and a snarling insane mouth, is ripping his written defense into long strips, telling it, as he does so, why he does so. And then, shouldering through the mess, he throws the paper at Fouquier. Who turns and steps back. "Killed by cousins," says Camille, or tries to.

Fouquier says, "And you involved your wife in the plot."

"Lr-l-*liar.*" Camille barely responds. This nonsense, even in the mad-house, is too mad to take in.

Fouquier says loudly, "Lucile Desmoulins is known to have intrigued with Dillon. She's been going the rounds, trying to buy an uprising in Paris. A fact."

The words have been generally heard, by some fluke of the rhythms of outburst or acoustics. A hush falls. It would seem the climax of the scene has, itself, a climax.

Camille is still. His hands, raised as if for Fouquier's throat, fall to his sides. "Whose fact?"

"The Convention's."

"No."

"I have it here, in writing."

"Let me see."

"You heard me read it, I believe. Your 'accomplices.' These include your foolish wife, who has been meddling in politics, which she doesn't understand. A fault she no doubt caught from her husband."

And Fouquier smiles, fawningly.

"Oh, Christ," says Camille. "Oh, Christ, oh, Christ!" And then, spinning away from Fouquier, he hurls himself across the muddled space, evading the arms of the guards as if in some catcher's game, and springs almost into the public rows. "My wife!" he cries out to them. "Oh, God, my wife! The bastards are going to kill my wife as well!"

But the guards surge up on him again, bored now with the struggle and so prepared to be brutal.

Like a drowning animal he clings to the bench he has collided with, by hand and arm and foot and body, and perhaps, almost, by his teeth, and threateningly and dangerously he strikes out, rabid with horror (horrifying), so they are afraid to touch him, but eventually they prize and cuff and tear him from his anchorage and haul him away, still shrieking in that appalling masculine shriek, as if he is being tortured (isn't he?), the beautiful name "Lucile" mixed with every foul obscene imprecation known to man.

❦

Oh, Lucile—oh, Lucile—what have I done to you? No, it isn't true. It can't be true. *It's true.* One more life. What do they care? One more doll for the guillotine. It isn't real, it's only play. After the blade comes down, we get up, entirely in one piece, and walk off.

Oh, Lucile, Lucile, Lucile.

God in heaven help me—if there's a God, help me. Oh, my love, my Lucile. Oh, someone hear me and help me! Help me!

What have I done? How did this happen?

No. Be calm. Be calm and think. I must find the answer. There must be an answer.

No, there's no answer.

They'll kill me. They'll kill her. And the child will be left—our little child— left stranded on this empty beach by the sea of blood I brought to Paris.

I remember that dream—the baby, my son, losing one eye—symbol: He would lose me. Killed by my cousins (*Ah! le coup des cousins*). But

Robespierre—he couldn't hurt her—it isn't possible. My death, but not her's too.

Oh, Lucile, Lucile!

(*"Quiet in there, damn you."*)

Someone outside. Will he help me? No money left. What can I offer? Nonexistent spoils of the Revolution. Bribed—was I bribed? Of course. Never. Oh, God, let me think.

She's innocent. They'll know it. They'll look at her, and they won't be able—

But that doesn't matter to them. They don't have feelings, can't pity, can't love. They're not men. No hearts, no genitals, no minds, no souls—

Souls—who has? They don't exist. Danton's right. There's nothing. Nothing for me, and nothing for her.

Just—the flash of the blade. The pain. Is there pain? Will I feel it? She? It's too quick. You don't feel the pain till you're dead, and by then—by then, you can't feel anything.

I knew I'd die. I sentenced myself. But now I know it's true. It's real. It will happen.

No, it isn't going to happen. It's a mistake.

And Lucile is at home. She's wearing a pink dress, or the silky gray. The gleam of it, over her soft full bosom, and her warm silken waist, and her hair dusted by sunlight—is there sunlight there? Yes—and she's holding the child. He's laughing and playing with a ribbon she's given him. His hands always amaze me, so small, but already able to do so much. This July he'll be two years old; I won't see that. But nothing will happen to her. She'll grieve. My darling, she'll cry for me—but it will ease. She'll live, and she'll tell my son about me. All the best things, none of the flaws. Sweet deception, silly girl. *Your father,* she'll say. His second name is Camille—she's going to forget to call him Horatius. She's going to call him by my name; she'll make me out a hero. Handsome and good and a genius. *He died for his country.*

I don't want to die, Lucile. I don't want to face that ride, that open place, that thin black thing on the sky. I don't want death. I want to come home and live with you.

(Screech of a lock, door slamming; you feel the vibration through every stone and bone. Earlier, you could hear the women washing their clothes at the trough in the yard, chattering. But they weren't real women, they didn't exist.)

The jury may find for us. The verdict hasn't been decided. But someone said they were already setting up the type for the printers: *Guilty.*

Fouquier lied.

He lied.

They can't touch her.

Christ, but they will—they have to—everything innocent has to be cut down. I've poisoned her with my death. And she won't even try to fight them. She'll say, No matter. It's day-clear. They've killed my Camille, and I don't want to stay here alone. She's so beautiful. So tender and sweet and lovely. Her skin, that holds the light inside it, and her eyes that make the light—all that can't be ended in a second. Live, Lucile. Live.

Don't touch her. Don't touch her! Christ, let me get out—let me escape and kill them all—help me, Oh, God, help me. Nothing exists but this prison. There's no escape, no help, no miracle.

Only this.

❊

The boat draws out.
The shores of my life recede before me,
And the echoing dock
That holds forever one loud changeless note.
The Ferryman, in his black cloak,
Leaning on the great oar, which
So resembles, in the water's depth,
An ax,
Takes life's coin; how thin his hand.

The boat draws out,
The shores of my life recede before me,
And one pale figure on that shore
Stands powerless in the mist.
I have no passport back to land.

Farewell, my love, my only life,
My soul, my song, my day, my evening's star.
Farewell, and think of me.
But only that black sea,
Sailless, empty of anything, the void,
Is here about me and on every side.

Death's consolation is:
I shall forget the sun,
And love, and light.
I shall forget that shore
Which fades into night.

The boat draws out.

THIRTEEN

❊ ❊ ❊

April 5, 1794 (16 Germinal): The Last Day

AS I ASLEEP? No, I can't have been asleep. Yet there's light imploring at the bars — fine crystal day. Another beautiful spring morning.

It's Saturday, isn't it? Day Sixteen of the Second Décade of Germinal (by Fabre's damn calendar), Year Two. Fabre . . . I wonder if he's still alive. It doesn't much matter, does it.

But Lucile was here, I saw her; I remember now. She was standing — *there*. Oh, my God, I do remember: her hands were bound and they'd cut her hair — she looked like a little girl going to church — but the church is the machine in the square, the Red Mass.

My watch has stopped. It got some knocks yesterday. Yes, the case is dented.

What time is it?

❊

At about eight o'clock, the prisoners were conducted to the Conciergerie waiting room. Here, they were informed that they had been found guilty and were therefore sentenced to the ultimate penalty. These sentences were read out to them. Danton said, with a loud toneless leaden violence, "You can refrain from spewing this rubbish. We're assassinated, that's enough." But the Conciergerie clerk, aware of protocol, went on reading. "My wife," Desmoulins called out to him. "Tell me what they've done to her." The clerk only went on droning, and Desmoulins's almost involuntary shift forward was checked by the guards, as was any exaggerated physical action of any of the prisoners.

In the corridors, on the way back to their cells, Camille began struggling, throwing himself to and fro, shouting aloud the names of his wife and his son. Danton halted and refused to move, blocking the way like a refractory elephant. He started to go back to Camille, and when the guards tried to prevent this, pushed them aside with a terrible, "Come on, what are you, men or *things?*" So he reached Camille, grasped him by the shoulders, and shook him. Camille, who was crying like a child, looked up at him and said, "Georges, they'll kill her—my Lucile—my Lucile—"

And Danton took the other man into his arms, the way a father does with a child who cries. And holding him, Danton said firmly, and rather dryly, "This won't help. Come on now, no weakness. You have to face the facts. We can't do a thing—for ourselves, for anyone. Steady, now. Yes?" And the voice and the touch and the unutterable reason of this deadly philosophy seemed to quiet Camille, at least sufficiently that the grim procession was able to go on, and every man was presently deposited back in his cell, there to sip the last hours of life.

❖

Such men—no one could expect them to die in bed. It must, almost mathematically, be a death by violence. A firework which traces the sky can hardly disappoint by falling unnoticed, with a hint of smoke, into the trees. It must go out in an explosion of sparks that make the night a sunrise.

❖

I have said I would try to speak the truth. And so I must go on with this, having no wish to. And, what is more, I must no longer draw back, conceal myself in the wings, say "he" instead of "I"; Camille—I, he—we're one, and have been throughout, and who did not know it? You knew. In your heart, you knew. For I told you I was a coward and a fool and, worse, *a writer.* So, no longer Camille, but "I." I, guilty of everything. I.

The light in the window was warming. It was the afternoon. The resolve to be stoical soon vanished. I began by sitting on the bed, next lying on it, then rushed about the tiny space, beating sometimes at the walls. And finally I found a corner and sat there, with my head on my knees. The agony in me, in my nonexistent soul, was so great it could only find release in tears and cries. Not that they did me good, but I could no more have held this misery in than blood from a gaping wound. Poor Camille, you see him as he is, naked before the contempt of your bravery. I was not brave. I howled like a dog in my anguish of terror and lament. Nor did I any longer know how I had reached this state. It

simply *was*. These dreadful conditions had become the substance of my life.
The recurring images were only these: Lucile in a sort of limbo of light which I knew was death; that cart ride before me; the moment when I must climb toward the guillotine. The sound the blade makes, which I had had described to me but never heard for myself, when it falls.

All the while, time passed. The light altered, the reflection of the bars on the wall. And then they came for me and unlocked the door. I got up, when requested to do so, and went out to them. It's true, I can see myself quite clearly. My frightened unshaven face, tear-blind eyes, the way I moved, stooping a little because I was stiff from my vigil on the floor. One of them took up my coat and draped it over my shoulders. We went to the room where they "dress" you for the guillotine.

And here there is demonstrated another interesting facet in the plight of one condemned. Though you fill the earth with the sound of your grief and fear, still you do not utterly believe in it. No, you don't believe you can die. Who does? Who could live a moment if he did? And so, every fresh reminder brings you to the verge of a new abyss.

Such a reminder was this small room. One by one we were hurried inside. There was a chair, three men, one with barber's scissors. The blades took off each man's hair with great ease. And you heard the exclamation of each collar as it was snipped, then ripped away. And when it came to my turn, I wouldn't go in. I fought with them. I fought for my life — mindlessly — as you fight with a river that drowns you, or a wolf. But they bundled me through and crushed me into the chair and held me there, and one of them said with a laugh, "*This* one's got a lot of energy, *this* one's going to jerk about a lot." I didn't know what he meant. The second man made a face as if annoyed by his companion's behavior. He said, "Pay no heed," to me. But when I went on struggling he helped them bind me into the chair with some thin harsh cord — it seemed others had made a fuss before me; they were not unprepared. The cord burned through to my skin, as I struggled on. "Keep still now, citizen. I don't want to do the job premature." The man with the scissors came for my collar first and tore it away. Finding the chain of the locket, he pulled that too, off my neck, snapping the links, and passed it to his assistant. "*Give me that!*" I shouted at them. "This?" He who had it was inclined to be flirtatious.

But Danton walked through into the room and took the locket from his grip. "You cretinous pig," Danton said to him. He turned and said to me, "Look, here. Where's your hand? Good. Now sit this out. It'll be over in a moment." They pulled my hair up in a hank and cut through it, and then hacked at the sides. The back of my neck seemed covered by ants which ran in circles. The scissors hadn't touched my flesh. They undid the cords and pushed me out of the chair and swung me around to tie my hands. I held the locket closed in my fist. The locket with her hair, the hair she had sent me those years ago, dulled now and no longer quite hers, but all of her I had. I'd said once it was a charm which could protect me from anything. *By your safeguard bound, here in my hand, no ill can find, no sword can—*

They took longer over Danton, though he sat like a statue. They didn't dare nick him, and the shaggy mane required some shearing.

"Well, we meet again," said Hérault in the adjoining room. "But not for long."

But I couldn't exchange pleasantries with him. No.

Fabre had been brought, so feeble he could hardly stand up for more than three or four seconds. The others came in. The Freys were praying and slobbering. Westermann had already cursed the barber roundly—it seemed the scissors had slipped after all. Lacroix and Hérault laughed. "You realize we're one man short?" "The expected one. Found innocent, and set free." "I should have had a bet on it. I'm going to miss this," said Lacroix. "Oh? What?" "Being alive." Lacroix wiped his eyes on his sleeve and afterward controlled himself. God knows how. It was beyond me.

Fabre wept. But he was only partly conscious. Delirious, he kept saying that Billaud-Varenne had sent him to death only in order to steal his unfinished play.

Eventually we hardly recognized each other, I think, our clothes torn by the butcher's boys and our hair lopped to our ears. We had done many things in each other's company, quite a few of them intimate. But this, the crowning intimacy, to *die* together, made us uneasy, even if we were not abject. It seemed only I was that.

How is it they were not afraid—or not afraid as I knew fear to be? Hadn't these fine imaginations stretched to the preview of death a thousand times, as had mine, giving more cause for horror with every showing? Or were they only able to accept the unacceptable? To comprehend nothing might be done.

I forget so much. Doubtless because it is preferable.

I don't remember. It would be easier, again, to say "he," or to say "Camille." But no. Let me not hide behind my own shadow. Let me not do it. Let me put down every disjointed, wretched, harrowed fragment. They were so precious then, those fragments.

So they took us up and we saw daylight again, in the courtyard. Sunny luminescence rose from the cobbles like a haze, and the tall black doors looked flat and far away. The sky above the walls and roofs was exquisitely blue. It was so warm, a wonderful day. Beyond the wrought-iron gates, the crowd, staring. There was quite a crowd in the yard, too. Around the carts.

"Why," asked Lacroix, reasonably, "are the carts painted red?"

"We're parricides," said Danton. "Traitors to our country—red for parricides. They want to be sure everyone knows. A nice cheerful color."

"*Christ, Robespierre.* I hope the little shit dies of his own insides, dies vomiting his own putrid guts."

The guards thrust me toward the carts. I hung back, I couldn't move. Some of the crowd (they'd been pointing and jostling since we emerged, blinking like daylight owls), began to shout; "Buck up! No stragglers. Not scared, are you?"

Hérault had remarked to Danton, "I suppose the crowd will have been fixed, too: an agitator to blacken your name on every corner. What do you think?" But they only looked the way the mob always does, in any era or place—avid, *hungry.*

We reached the carts, and I, with the rest, was shoved up into them. Two of Sanson's "boys" helped load us in—our hands were tied and we were clumsy—and then stood forward in the cart, dumb-faced. One of them had a ruined cheek, from a fight or an accident, his left eye almost sealed over. The other gawped and turned from me, bold but uninterested.

The carts seemed very high off the ground; it made your head swim. I slumped on the bench, by Danton. He looked thoughtful—but elsewhere.

"Oh, God, Camille," said Hérault. "Be quiet. Stop crying. Let's die with some dignity."

You die with dignity, Hérault. You do it.

Lacroix laughed nervously.

Fabre lay like something broken, on the bench.

Our mounted guard hemmed us in; the gates were opening. We were going out.

The tumbrils jolted, rolling forward, drawing up with a wrench that came up through the teeth.

"Out of the way!"

They were forcing the crowd back. But the crowd wanted to be close, to see, to watch. Did they know, any of them, who we were?

They don't know. How can they know, and let this happen to us, when all the while we've fought for them—for *them?* Of course, our enemies have used the methods the lodges taught us: the agents who whisper now here, now there; the Bastille cracked at such whispers—but no; it took a shout to bring it down.

So blue, the sky. Barely a cloud. Except westward, where we're going, a few little flecks, little islands with long tails and camel humps, that same warm color, from the westering sun.

Over the bridge, the river, so peaceful. I've seen it nearly all my life. Will I never see it again? How can it be my heart, beating so hard, can stop, everything extinguished, hearing, vision, speech, thought—oh, God, the river, it's almost out of sight. I'll never see it again.

The crowd. Vile, stupid. Don't you know, you clods, you milling beasts, don't you *know* what's happening?

Something hits the second cart, behind ours. Eggs. How can they find eggs to spare? The egg's rotten. The guardsmen shout at the crowd; they don't want stinking eggs on their uniforms.

I'm standing up at the side of the cart. I don't recollect rising. I'm shouting down into that mass of faces. But they pass by; they're so far off, miles below on the ground. And so mean, the faces, so devoid of intelligence or response—they look like masks made from human skin. Not even skin, not even masks—wet dough with eyes and lips dropped into it. But no brain. Do they hear?

One of the executioner's assistants makes a move to come toward me, but the other (with the collapsed cheek) holds him back, saying something I don't catch.

The terror has become a raging terror—rage itself. There comes with it such a surge of power in me, suddenly, that I feel I can move them, this sodden crowd. Didn't I do it before? After the whispers, the great shout. It was I, I who called them to arms—

"—I, on July twelfth in 1789—Camille—do you forget your own history so soon? They've lied to you, they've told you lies. If we die, your only hope dies with us."

The tumbril bumps, jolts, grinds forward. The faces change but scarcely alter. Some grin at the show. Black teeth and white. Men with raddled scars, missing an arm, an eye—veterans of our wars—women with red scarves, or spring flowers tucked in their hair. Even children being held up to see. *While my child—*

"Don't let this happen—justice is all we ask. *Listen* to me, *listen!*"

"Where's your lantern hook, Camille?" someone yells at me.

"I called for mercy," I shouted. "That's my crime: I pleaded for an end to the slaughter! Paris is an abattoir—do you want that? You're starving; you need bread, not blood."

"The blood's all right," someone answers, "if it's yours."

"They've lied to you. The villains who should fill these carts are sitting in the committee offices, laughing at you. *Change it!* Save us and set yourselves free."

"Oh, dry up!"

Another egg lands, on our cart now. They rock with mirth. Mindless sabbat, they dance and cackle, not human; how could I think they were? And they won't let me speak. They're singing now, to smother my voice—oh, that bloody song, the Ça ira. "Damn you, you brainless gawks, up to your eyes in blood. Can't you see anymore?" Oh, he's getting personal now.

"Listen to me!" Oh, it'll be, it'll be, more work for the guillotine—"Damn you, you stupid fools, why don't you listen before it's too late?"

"Sit down, Camille," Danton says.

But I can't stop shouting. I go on and on. To shout is life to me. And to their bestial curses I hurl back my own. How can I stop? I must make them grasp the truth. My voice is a blazing wire in my throat, almost crumbled to nothing. I can't believe they won't listen. I can't believe they won't understand. It was all for them. I risked my life for them. I would have died for them—but not this way, not this.

"Sit down, for Christ's sake. Camille!" And then his hand on my arm, a gargantuan tug, so I almost fall. "Shut up, for God's sake." And then I see his face, Danton's face. He looks at me with anger and allergy. I am nothing to him but a joke gone sour, one which will make more horrible for him the last minutes of this horror. "This bloody row you're making. You're inappropriate. Leave them, let them get on with it. Verminous rabble. Shut up, Christ blast you."

And so I am silenced, and I sit down, and nothing is left to me. Drained of all agony, all rage, all hurt. He had struck me, the heart of me. The blow numbed me. Perhaps there was kindness in that.

I sat by him on the road to annihilation, and I thought of how I had followed him and been his soldier, and of where it had gone, and that here, in the loneliness of death, a further loneliness was added.

Some of our fellowship were singing the "Marseillaise." The crowd, the *verminous rabble*—how right he was, at last, Danton. No more; There is no such thing as a mob. We are a part of it; they are men. It joined in, jeering and waving its arms.

Sometimes one of us spoke, generally to himself. We were in the narrower streets. From the close stories overhead, eyes burned down on us. Occasional rubbish, even offal, was flung in the cart. The executioner's boys, when they disliked it, threw it out. (Once Danton said a woman's name. Not "Louise." It was "Gabriella.") And we passed somewhere a group of artists—David and some of his adherents, seated at a café table to sketch the condemned as we went by. Danton roused. "The vultures are gathering early." He roared at David, "Fucking vulture, who'll make a picture of *you* on *your* fucking way to the scaffold?" And the crowd seemed to enjoy the outburst in its unhuman fashion. But David only cupped his warty cheek and went on drawing. Danton sank back and swore again, but his voice had become disanimate, as if the subject had no interest anymore.

The sky was deeper as we came along Saint-Honoré, and the sun began to glance in our faces.

We had passed so many familiar scenes. Every one looked different, as if distorted, not physically but in some more subtle way. And yet, it was the tumbril which was the phantom. Each thing we passed would remain, and only we—

The tricolors hung down. Weather-stained and withered rags, their edges torn; they had lost their freshness. At the end of the curve of tall pointing roofs and soaring chimneys, the clouds were stretching out and rosy.

Beyond the musty stench of live things, there was too the evening smell of Paris, her dust and bricks, her stone, her very glass and tiling tuned and dry in the bright air. Wood burned somewhere, and spicy food was cooking, and there came, from the Tuileries, the honey smell of lilac.

"Look," said Danton. He said it to me. We were coming to the Duplays' house. It was all shuttered, locked in as if for a siege. Blue shadow hung down it in a stripe, one band of a tricolor. Inside me, there was a sensation like a tight string breaking. I had no voice left, but I croaked, "Robespierre—Robespierre."

And then Danton was standing, and his colossal voice crashed against every wall and window of the street, so even the hell crowd was stunned to speechlessness.

"You'll be next, Robespierre!" Danton shouted. "Our death—it's yours!" And he regarded the crowd and shook his arms, smiling, as if with satisfaction, though his eyes were lead. "The strong man topples—*and my weight pulls down Robespierre.*

"It's so," he said to me, as he sat down again, conversational, as if in some café. "He can't last without me. The cup they give us to drink today will be his tomorrow." Then he looked briefly at me and said, "You're calm now. That's good. The other—wasted effort."

And then he stretched himself. That was all. He had finished.

I recall their faces, like the faces of ghosts. Lacroix looked melancholy, Hérault also. Fabre slept in a fever sleep, wet-eyed, shuddering with the shudders of the cart. Danton—an enigma. No expression. Not regret, never fear. His eyes were intent and somber. *Wasted effort.* He would expend no more energy. He spoke of Louise only at the last instant; perhaps it then seemed needful. Etiquette. You note, I am still trying to fathom how he was. He had lived so much, and now, did he lift life off over his head like a soiled shirt. . . . Let it go, then. Splendid Danton. You're calm now, he congratulated me, as if I had come to see sense, and logic had made me so. He put his curse on Robespierre's windows, but that was for posterity, was it not? He believed what he shouted; he supposed, when it came to pass, they would say; Remember how the Lion roared?

Well, what do I know—I knew nothing.

Forgive me, Danton. In the ultimate hour of life, neither of us understood the other.

❧

And so we came to la Place de la Révolution, all gilded by light under the blue sky and the pink bubbles of the April clouds.

❧

The cart stops. Down, now, and line up for death. No one speaks anymore. Nothing to say.

The crowd is also thick in the square. Mostly silent too, as we are. They don't want to miss anything. The light everywhere, a benediction. This is all there is. No, impossible. I believe in the immortality of the soul—something persists; something *must* persist—to be and then *not* to be. But then, the teachings of my childhood, angels, and purgatory, and the basement of flame? No. Never. I reject it. Oh, God, I can't think. This is all there is. This is all I have left.

La Guillotine. . . .

She doesn't look, after all, the way I had pictured her. She looks—ordinary, mundane. All around, architecture, open land, trees going to the river. And the graceless Liberty statue, in its breasts and cap, like the flags, already muddied

and blurred. These things, a frame for an item of no great drama or importance.
Is that all, then: the uprights, the crosspiece, the razor's blade, somewhere to
lie, the little round "O"? No aura even of all the lives she has had? No, la
Guillotine's nothing special. It's only that she kills you.

But I turn my back. I don't want to see. I look at the ground, every pore and
texture of it. Exhaustion makes it easier to bear. Does it? I wish I had a drink. I
wish—Lucile. . . .

They've come for Hérault, the guards. He's to be the first. He moves to
Danton to embrace him, and the guards manhandle them apart. Danton swears
at them. Hérault has that look, Oh, what can you expect from such types? He
touches me on the shoulder as he goes by; I seem to feel the pressure of his hand
long after. He walks steadily up onto the platform, I hear the sound of his shoes.
Then other sounds. What? No. I won't look at it.

How silent the crowd in the golden glaze of light. Every golden eye is on
the platform.

Then I hear the blade. The slick rasp of it as it travels, and I hold my breath
like every other human thing in the square. And then I hear the blade thud
home. And they make a noise, a sort of groan that is also a cry. (They tell you,
the mob always cheers. Perhaps they'll cheer later.)

It's done.

No—how can it—?

Done. Over.

Hérault, who was alive, is dead.

Ridiculous. I can still feel the pressure of his hand on my shoulder. If I turn,
I'll see they haven't yet—Jean. Ah, Jean.

So simple. So irretrievable. Where now, Jean? Nothingness.

And the ministers of oblivion, they come for us one by one. Hérault—and
now they take another, and another. One by one the feet go up the stair, and the
sounds of wood and metal are made, and then comes the sound of the blade,
rather different, after the first—blood has oiled it—and the curious unlikely
thudding home—and then sometimes a thudding, rattling coda—and I see the
heads of the crowd move like snakes, trying to follow something: the after
spasms of the headless corpse. No. I won't look at it.

One by one.

Hérault. Lacroix, walking briskly. Fabre half carried up, moaning.

Alive. Dead.

Alive. Dead.

And soon it will be the same for me.

And it is now.

I catch at Danton's hand and he at mine—ritual—he doesn't look at me. The
stair is before me, open behind the treads, so my eyes mislead me and I am
dizzied between steps and step over the gap, and almost stumble but keep on, for
if I hesitate now—

The platform is bloody. You put your feet in it, do what you will, slip, and are steadied by one of Sanson's men.

This close, now, to the machine. The smell of blood and drink—they've been drinking, every one of them. I say to the boy, "In my hands—a locket—take it—find someone to give it to my wife."

He peers at me; then his fingers take the locket from my grip, and though I have said, take it, it's hard for him to make me let go. "Will she pay?" he inquires. Yes. I pant the word at him. I don't even hate him or wish him in fires for asking it. "All right. I'll do it. You're Camille." Something to say, in case it's remembered. Say it now. My tongue, paper.

"Camille," I say, "the first apostle of Liberty." Is that what I meant to say? Is there more? But another of them says,

"First apostle of Liberty, and here you are." And they lift me and sling me down on the plank, and a low cry comes out of me, unplanned, for no one—"Oh, Lucile."

They're busy. They're fastening the straps by their buckles, tight. The plank—they've washed it over with brandy. It stinks of brandy, blood, and urine, and the damp wood's rough, the splinters driving in through my shirt. Then the apparatus runs forward and settles with a jar. My head stuck out, into space, the bottom of the wooden "O" choking into my throat, and suddenly the rest of it slams down, is fastened shut. My God—this is the moment. It's truly here.

A noise, something squeaking; below, waiting, a mound of straw, scarlet. What else? What else?

Give me time. Only a minute. My brain is full of jostling confusion. A second more, only half—

It comes from the sky. From high high up. It comes and it comes on—shall I hear—

A *flash,* as if cleaving water, an indescribable meeting in the throat, cold and stinging-sweet, nose full of blood, ears roaring, the whole body tingling, itching, unraveled in a stream of lights, but th   ligh   go   g   t .

⚜

It's over then. They're dead.

They saved the giant till the last. He went up onto that stage of blood, white as a corpse already, and said, in his huge voice, to Sanson; "You. Show my head to the People. Let them get a good look."

And when the Lion's head, maned with blood, plummeted into the straw, they did pick it up and show it, the way they had shown the head of Louis Capet. The head of a king.

And, as then, the vast crowd stood silent and, maybe, wondered what had been done in its name.

But then they pushed the head in the grain sack, like the other heads, flung it in the wagon with the others, the heads and the bodies. They took them away into the gathering darkness. In an obscure cemetery, in one pit, by the light of lanterns, they poured together bloody flesh, quicklime, and earth.

And so it is, those passionate, those flaming lives, lost in the dark of earth and night and time.

❧

They who have been most famous, for the greatest glory or ill luck, or for quarrels or fortunes of whatever sort: Then consider, where are they now?
Ashes and smoke, and a story imperfectly remembered.
Of what worth, then, these things after which men ferociously strive?

❧

The executioner's apprentice, bearing the locket Camille Desmoulins had given him, trudged to the apartment in the Theater-of-France (once Cordeliers) section. But on the stair, even outside the door, he heard the sound of women crying. It was a high and dreadful sound, a symphony of despair, like wild birds adrift above a shoreless winter sea, into which they know they must descend. In a strange way, it frightened him.

And so, after a slight hesitation, during which he did lift his hand to find a bell, he withdrew his hand, turned, and went away again. It was more than he wished to be involved in.

He sold the locket for the price of a long drink.

And years after, haunted by the breathless terror and urgency of a man whose face he had forgotten, the voices of weeping women whose faces he had never seen, he told his story differently, in various other ways.

❧

But as they will tell you also, she hadn't long to weep, beautiful Lucile.
But who's that they've got now?
Don't you know?
But what did she do?
Haven't you heard—that plot to raze Paris?
But she's so charming and gentle.
You can never trust the quiet ones.
Her mother writes to Robespierre.

Not content to have assassinated your best friend, you will have the blood of his wife too. Your creatures of the Tribunal have just now condemned

Lucile to the scaffold. In less than two hours *she will be dead.* But what is this to you? Camille's blood has not sent you insane. You have forgotten quite the evenings you spent as part of our family, my daughter's year-old son on your knees. What, you *do* remember? Then set free my innocent Lucile! Or if you are truly some wild beast disguised as a man, in your lion's rage—then quickly! Take us all: Horace, my other daughter, Adèle (you will not remember her either), and myself. Yes, be quick and claw us in pieces with your talons that run with Camille's life blood. Be as swift as you can. Let us find the peace—which you will never have—together in one grave.

But Lucile has said, "Your sentence on me is a gift of joy. You're sending me to my husband."

And like a bride, she sits in the tumbril. She is dressed in white (like Antoinette? *La reine blanche*). She's not afraid. Anyone can see that. And they stand in awe: the throng along the streets, the men who have "judged" her and those who will murder her, and her fellow victims.

She has, besides, Arthur Dillon to talk to. He is all gallantry and absurd courage. His eyes shine with malign humor. He shouts sometimes into the crowd: *God save the king!* Which the crowd dislikes.

"Have we brought you to this?" Lucile asks him, politely apologizing on behalf of herself and Camille.

"Lovely lady, you have not. The Revolution has brought us all to it. Our stars. The will of God."

"Is it a great sin," she murmurs, "that I should be so glad to die?" Or perhaps she only thinks it, for a moment, and then the cloud lifts from her.

We see her face, so fair, a cameo, so young—she might be only sixteen—so certain, the face of the priestess who offers herself in sacrifice to the gods: consent, submission, tranquillity. Happiness.

We see her walk lightly, and with much grace, up the steps of the scaffold and lie down for the stroke. But turn away from the stroke. The pale flower falling. The burning of the rose—

Lucile. . . .

There are no words.

It's too late for words.

Lucile.

1794: Summer

HE SAID, "Placed as we are, if we show mercy too soon, we are lost." Is it necessary to explain who said this? Yes, Robespierre.

The trial of the Danton faction had set a precedent. No longer did the Tribunal have recourse to proofs or to witnesses. Moral justice prevailed. Whoever is delivered to the Tribunal must be guilty. Where suspicion glances, there crime shall be found. The New Commandments, brought down from Mount Sinai, in tablets of *ice.*

And they say, too, Fork-Tongue muttered, Next week I should be able to prune four hundred. Heads flew off like tiles in a tempest. Hundreds, thousands left for—for Nothingness, by way of Revolution Square.

He *is* a monster, then, our Robespierre, our Little Pierre, our Maxime? Yes, for sure, a monster. The saint and the genocide are both extremists. The disparity is only in *what* they do. Sometimes the border lines melt. Robespierre has given himself to the god, and the god has taken him.

Atheism, he proclaims, is the illness of the aristocrats. And a great novelty Dionysia is held, to honor Robespierre's Supreme Being (Man makes God in his own image). There's a bonfire on which atheistic Selfishness and Discord are duly crisped. But when Wisdom rises from the soot, her face is dirty. Some amusement then mingles with the bad moods of the deputies. It's becoming noticeable, even Robespierre's sans-culottes, they who provide him constant bodyguard, are beginning, en masse, to look disillusioned. There's no other scapegoat now. Under the blue sky, in a sky-blue coat, he picks up such phrases as, "Look at him. He wants to be God, next."

"Oh, yes, he wants to be God all right," says Stanislas Fréron, summoned back from Toulon by a Robespierrean decree. There have been some goings-on in the provinces, at Toulon not least of all. Traitors, herded by hundreds into boats and drowned, or traitors herded into squares in hundreds and shot, little things like that. Or is it the other matters that offend Robespierre? The selection, and reprieve, of pretty women from the jails, or the money appropriated?

Well, everyone's getting sick of Robespierre. He won't let you have any fun. Even the whores are in hiding. And if you go to the theater and someone says a line in the play—like, Let the guiltless throw the first stone, or, Those who forgive are the ones who are forgivable—they stop the performance and arrest all the actors. Molière plays are of course banned; didn't *he* say, after all, "Virtue should be tractable" and "Only a first-class nitwit tries to improve the world"? Not to mention, "As is well known, in Paris, they hang you *before* they try you." My dear Molière, you were a prophet, and a prophet, of course, has no honor, et cetera, et cetera.

Life is very serious. And he, the gentleman in the blue coat, is a touch prickly. If you sneeze quietly, he glares. What did you just say about him in that sneeze? And if you do it while he's making a speech (isn't he always making a speech?), he gives you a look: Are you trying to interrupt him? That's treason. A sneeze of treason. And treason is—

"We know what treason is," says Fréron, but voicelessly. "It's being twenty-three and your friend's widow. This is what treason is."

He has sneaked—and let it be said, to do anything *but* sneak would have been most inadvisable—over to some dismal lodgings near the Luxembourg Gardens. There stood a shadow which he managed to recognize, with difficulty. "Madame—"

"Oh, do I look so old to you?"

"Annette, excuse me—"

"I suppose," she said, "There's no one left to call me 'Demeter' ever again." But she doesn't cry. She gives him a glass of wine, and when he mentions her husband, she says, "Yes, naturally. Thank you for your condolences. But I'm not alone in losing most of my family to the guillotine." Later, he sees the little boy playing with the toy rabbit, which Fréron himself (who orders men and women shot in droves), long ago sent him. Horace doesn't know he is an orphan. Probably he misses something, someone—perhaps. Now and then he pauses and looks about with a perplexed air, but it lasts only a second. Soon, even that will be gone.

When Demeter gathers him up, her eyes do fill abruptly with tears. Fréron is afraid and takes his leave.

One summer day, Fréron goes also, contrastingly boldly, to visit Maximilien. "Now you know you can trust me," says Fréron. Robespierre's answer is utter silence. Out in the road again, Fréron says to the friend who went with him, "A *demi*-god, at least, it seems."

"He's turning against everyone. Even Fouché, who was so *useful*."

"He should watch Fouché. Clever, that bastard." Fréron thinks of the carts pounding down Saint-Honoré. (The guillotine has been temporarily moved again, back to Overthrown Throne Street; it's improved this neighborhood; you see roses in the windowboxes again. Doubtless all those wheels grinding along under the windows got on Maximilien's nerves.) *Lucile,* Fréron thinks, with a dull reverberation of fury, and bites his knuckles. If the tyrant had let her alone, here she would have been, husbandless, helpless, and in need of comforting. But when he thinks of Camille, too, there is a twisting in Fréron's guts. Carried to it, ranting and shivering—and the great Danton, for once, dumb. "My neck," says Fréron, "aches all the time. We'll be next. King Robespierre wants to guillotine the whole Convention."

They go on a way; then the friend says, "Did you ever come across a man called Roch-Marcandier?" *Oh,* yes, says Fréron. "Well, you'll have seen his journal—there was a story at one time Camille was behind it, but Camille never wrote that peculiar sort of prose, and it attacked Camille too—Marcandier brought an issue out after Danton went down. He headed it: 'We want the real People's Friend, not a hypocritical fucker like Robespierre." Which Robespierre enjoyed. "Marcandier attacked everyone. He was mad as a nit. He seems to have started that wonderful tale the celibate Maxime beheads ladies who won't accommodate his rampant lust. Maxime did for Marcandier, certainly. Got chopped on July twelfth."

"It's still," says Fréron blackly, "July."

And meanwhile Robespierre has said, "Save the Revolution without me!" (I *dare* you to.)

But Robespierre, all we said was that some of the harshness of your strictures might be—smoothed a fraction. We are, for example, no longer quite so hopelessly embattled. Toulon is safe. The Austrians have been overwhelmed at Fleurus—where a hot-air balloon spied on them in the sky like a great French eye on wings. And Brussels is occupied by our troops. The Vendée, too, stays under control. Lyons doesn't even growl beneath the lash. So now, must we still keep searching out agitators? Must terror remain our daily bread?

You miss the point.

Yes, Robespierre? Which point?

We have won all we have won by our unswerving remorselessness. Falter now—

But it is Robespierre who falters. Deserted so often, he can always tell when desertion is on the wind. He whispers to Saint-Just, I see only darkness before me and about me.

Gnawed by his cares, sloughing off his bodyguard, Robespierre walks in the country where everything is hot Thermidor green, and the flowers grow and the birds sing. He breaks his heart over it all, so lovely nature is, and men so vile. It was quite another way, when he made the model. Born free, man is found everywhere in irons. To arms, citizens! You have nothing to lose but your lives.

But then, justice for Robespierre too. He, like everyone else, will pay his fee.

He is so tired and full of his betrayals, and it is real enough for him. Why condemn him for his wicked cruelty, when he doesn't know he is wicked or cruel? He is not an aristo of the Old Regime, who, by right of those laws which such as Robespierre have vanquished, might disembowel a serf in order to soothe his feet in the entrails. Robespierre takes no pleasure in killing. He doesn't do it for himself. (Far worse, it is done for the rest of us.) But when you blame him for his orders and his actions, consider this. Do you blame the cripple because he limps or the blind man because he cannot see? Robespierre, crippled and blind, has yet to be healed to the knowledge that service—his desire—is a deed of savage-speaking gentleness, not soft-spoken savagery.

In fact, he suffers the added burden of a genuine hatred of violence. Every execution appalls him—with its necessity. He's come to resent those who have forced him to such measures: the Dantons, the Desmoulins, the political Mountaineers, the entire Convention.

In the end, the Gethsemane of summery paths leads him back, in his skylike coat, to stand alone in the Tuileries and—venting his disillusion, horror, and paranoia—to condemn them all, since he doubts them all. Pale and dreadful, he is aureoled by godhead and nearly brings it off. They cower. They are afraid of this midget in majesty. They have seen what he can do with them, and to them. He will not be the last small short man to rein their Revolution with a bridle of fire.

But then, somehow, it comes to them that he is one and they are many and this is all nonsense.

The undercurrents of fear he has engendered in everyone suddenly erupt like poison from a boil.

A deputy defies him. And then another. So, another. And on and on.

Saint-Just, striding forward, is swept away. His attempts to speak are obliterated. Robespierre himself is refused the tribune, shooed from it. His enemies, as he has always predicted, rise up on every side with daggers in their eyes and mouths.

He runs to and fro before the tribune, squeaking to be heard, like a frantic mouse. And they laugh and curse him. And when his voice fails, a stronger voice calls from the tiers; "Oh? So Danton's blood finally sticks in your throat."

And then he is still and he says, "I see. It is for that you want vengeance."

They push him away from them when he tries to sit down. "Not here. Patriots have sat here."

Then they vote for his arrest, and for that of his acolytes with him.

"Take me too then," says Robespierre's hedonist brother, surprisingly. But they agree. "And I'll go with them!" shouts Duplay's son-in-law, fighting his way free of friends who would detain him, forgetting wife and child, gazing at Saint-Just with dilated eyes. But Saint-Just doesn't appear to notice. He gives his written defense, which nobody has allowed him to read, quietly to a Convention secretary. *Cold priest.* Why not tear it into shreds and throw it in their faces? No, better leave it for posterity. Elsewhere, you have written, *Nothing we have said will be lost to this world.* He has written, *I am part of no faction; I will fight them all.* But, quite recently, in a private notebook: *I despise the dust I am made of. It can be debased, brought low, slain. But I defy you to take from me that element of me which is eternal.* And he wrote, too, *Well, I am going to get myself killed.*

David, however, who has so frequently shrieked he will drink hemlock with Robespierre whenever so required, is mysteriously unavailable. *David!* You ugly wretch. Only your undeniable genius excuses you.

After which, the last extravaganza is scheduled to begin.

⁂

The National Convention and both Revolutionary Committees have condemned Robespierre. But the Commune, with the core of the Jacobin Club, is pure Robespierrean and comes out on his side. And now are we set for internecine strife which will carve up Paris like a fowl?

Trundled to the Luxembourg, Robespierre is refused admittance—he is not to be accepted as a prisoner. "I will remain in custody, I will obey the law," says Robespierre. "Since it is the law which will reinstate me. I'm blameless."

He is borne in an agitated clatter to the office of the mayor, which receives him with open arms and sobs of loyalty. "We are your friends."

The National Guard is called out by the Commune. Its commander, Robespierre's man as everyone knows, gallops amok through the Saint-Antoine slum, calling for supporters. In the end, about half the guard turn out. For Robespierre—or is it for the intoxicant rush of action? There are quarters already where they drink to the tyrant's quietus. Others where one hears the mumble, He cared for us. He wanted us to be free. (Free and starved, eh?) I don't know about starved. He doesn't carry on like a lord. (No. He's *above* it.)

Whatever, however, the military venture is a mite ramshackle. The doors of the houses, hotels, and shops are shut. Only the red eyes of taverns look out. The Nationals go by on their horses, dragging a score of cannon. Where are they heading? To the Tuileries. The Convention's still sitting, and petrified, handing out the muskets.

Robespierre is escorted to City Hall, and squadrons of the out-turned guard assemble in the square below, the Place de Grève of the famous Empress of Lantern Hooks. Ill-omened, maybe, for a last stand, Robespierre. But they're rallying to your banner.

Night arrives, too, to mount a watch outside the Hôtel de Ville. And as the wind rises, the ghosts of hanged bakers swing with the torchlight.

Robespierre makes a speech or two. All his lieutenants (Saint-Just, Couthon), his brother, have been sprung from their various captivities and conducted to him here. They are temporarily secure. Cannons sit in the square. Cannons also sit around the Tuileries. Some twenty thousand men are at your disposal, Maximilien. Now is the time to jump. *Now.*

But he's the Slave of Liberty, the slave with the knife, no strategist, no warrior. He stands and makes speeches, and outside the guardsmen fall asleep on their horses, and the crowd in the hall begins to say, There's a decree passed by the Convention: whoever assembles here is proscribed, an outlaw. We've come to him, but what's he going to do?

And then, and then, as it always did, it always does.

A stroke of velveteen lightning and *Il pleut, il pleut.* The rain comes splashing down: through the stone tunnels of the city, through the flags and plumes, across the shoulders of the guard, shining on the cannons. Ah, glory, it will face fire and steel, but it doesn't stand wet through.

The hall empties. And in the square the torches, men and horses, smoke. The lights flutter down like birds and vanish, and the battalions steal away.

At the Tuileries, orderless, they hear the rain say *March!* And having no alternative orders from Robespierre, they obey the order of the rain.

Look forth, valiant deputies, trembling with your muskets; see how the night men steal away, and heed the sliding, fading rumble of the cannons' wheels along the paths.

Robespierre, do you hear the rain on the windows? Rain, your fate. Can it be the gods of Danton and Camille are ranged against you, primitive entities of thunder and tears? Or does your Supreme One spit at you? Ah, Maxime, you knelt in the rain by the carriage of a king and told him, in faultless Latin, he was good, so he believed you. And later you killed him for that belief. Oh, the rain: remember it running in the fields of home, the corn bending at its silver arrows? *Where is Mama? Be quiet. You know Mama is with God.* The rain, the rain, the curtain of nature itself falling upon the final act, the pigeon dashed in its cage.

He was writing to the once Vendôme, now Pikes section, his own. (Take heart, Freedom is on the road to victory.) He has begun to sign his name when he breaks off. There is a noise of horsemen returning fast into the square. And presently the noise of guardsmen, some of the fifty thousand who had not risen for Robespierre, forcing their way into the undefended building.

When they charge into the room, these soldiers of the Convention, Robespierre gets to his feet.

He makes, in his pale blue coat, a perfect target. There is always some insignificant fellow who wants fame badly enough to suppose he will get it by picking off a celebrity. The pistol detonates. The fame-seeker's also a rotten shot. Robespierre lies on the floor. The fighting continues around him. Men, grappling with each other, stumble across his legs; their feet drum into his sides. Perhaps he doesn't notice. The bullet has entered and been expelled from the right side of his face, deflected by his jaw and smashing it like a mirror.

⚜

"Do you want him here?" the Convention is asked.

The Convention replies, The honor of this chamber would be defiled by admittance of such a traitor.

So they carry him, along with Couthon the legless and Maximilien's brother, now broken-legged to match, and, walking, the captured Robespierrean guard commander with a freshly disfigured face, and Saint-Just, pristine and unharmed in all but heart and mind, to the committee offices. (Lebas, the Duplay in-law, has shot himself and expired on the floor by Saint-Just's feet. There were other casualties.)

Robespierre is put into the anteroom. He lies on a table in the midst of high-ceilinged space. Someone has pushed a bread box under his head to mitigate the hemorrhage. They give him paper to stanch the blood.

A wounded chimera, no longer dangerous, he has become a freak show for anyone who cares to drop in. They come and stare. Nobody loves him anymore, and that's a fact. A Breechless One slaps Robespierre's ankle. "Oh, in *pain,* sire?"

Of course he's in pain, you barbaric evil bloody fool.

"Hey, don't muck him about," one of the clerks says. (Sitting at the periphery of the table, do they dip their busily writing pens in his blood?) "We want him spry for the guillotine, don't we?"

What are you thinking, Robespierre? Your eyes are shut. Sometimes you mop up the fountain of blood with the inadequate mockery of the paper. When someone loosened your collar you said, reverting to twenty years ago, "Thank you, monsieur." Is that where you are, then, back in the promise of your youth? A child again, a student, or a young lawyer making your name? *There must be no death penalty,* you decidedly wrote. *It debases both the condemned and his judges.*

Just before sunrise, a surgeon arrives. (Not Souberbielle, whose head today, doubtless, is well down.) This one cleans the wound, pulls out several teeth and shattered bone segments, sets a rough splint, and applies a bandage to hold the mess intact. No point in doing too much, the whole job'll be off in a bag inside twenty-four hours. Through all this unrecountable agony, the Monster makes no sound. It even moves a little, to help the surgeon's efforts. When it is all over, astonishingly, the Monster sits up. It draws itself slowly off the table and goes instead to a chair. Monster. Of course, every crime in the universe will now attach itself to him. Oh, the savor of the burnt offering. Go thou, with all our sins on thy head.

His timing is excellent, nevertheless, for at this moment they bring in his court, and the guardsmen urge the sightseers aside from Robespierre. "Let *them* get a look at him, see how they like their master *now.*"

Saint-Just stares at the wreckage of Robespierre, then turns away. (Shouldn't the sacrifice be unblemished?)

They are taken to the Conciergerie.

Robespierre asks for ink and paper and is refused. "Wanted to write a note of complaint to his Supreme Being, I expect."

The trial follows the procedure Robespierre himself has established. Fouquier attends to everything just as Robespierre would have wished. (Well, Fork-Tongue, you have seen a good many of them out. How much longer do you think *you* have left? Something less than a year later, you'll stand where they have stood and say, But I was only following orders—and a few hours after that, you too, you bastard, will wend your way toward darkness.)

At a quarter to five in the evening, the tumbrils go out of the prison yard.

In honor of this occasion, the guillotine, which during the Festival of the Supreme One had been draped in purple-blue velvet, has been moved back to Revolution Square.

And so you take the route you sent us, Maxime.

At the Duplays' they pause. A bucket of pig's blood is flung against the door, and in the slops they write on the wall TRAÎTRE, but it runs and soon might be a word written in Greek as well as gore.

You sit in that cart, your eyes half closed. As it jolts, halts, rumbles on, your body moves only with its movements. Saint-Just, your saint, is standing, immaculate, noticing nothing, his porcelain about to be broken into two bits.

As the carts come around Nation's Road toward the square, a girl with red hair and a child in one arm forces her way forward and walks along beside Robespierre, staring at him. She is prettily if rather garishly dressed and the child–it's about a year old–snowy clean. But *her* face is dirtied by hatred. She says, after a long while of walking by the cart, "Yes, you're going back to hell, where you came from. You'll weigh heavy in your pit with all the curses of the women and the mothers." And she smiles and says, "The thought of your blood makes me *drunk.*" Then she stops walking and lets the carts go on, glaring after them, though still smiling, and holding the child tight.

He can no longer support himself and must be lifted to the guillotine. Sanson's man, wantonly rough-handed, tears the bandage from the victim's head and throat to free it for the cut–and Robespierre gives a kind of groaning scream, his first. His last.

The sun shines on the blade. What else is there to be said, save that it comes down?

⚜

"Hush," says Betsi to the dog Brount. She is crying and frightened. She wants the dog to lie down. To oblige her, it does.

But every time there is a footstep or movement in the house, the dog starts up, whining, ears lifted, face anxious. It's waiting for Robespierre to come home.

The Balance

The Egyptians of antiquity would tell you that, after death, you must face judgment–a widely held belief, it seems, in many orders and nations. The Tribunal consisted of gods who had the heads of jackals or hawks. . . . A great balance was put out, and into one scale of it went every mistake and every wrong deed of one's life. In the other scale was placed–a feather. And if the wrongs of your life weighed more than the feather's weight, you could expect no leniency.

So into the balance with it, that life. And into the other scale throw the feather, the quill of a writer's pen. Does it waver? Which side sinks down?

There had been written, to Fouquier-Tinville, a letter, which began:

> 'Camille Desmoulins (who is my son); you should know that he has always aspired to the truth. Almost from the cradle, it has been his god.

And he has sought only to serve this truth and his country. How can it be that you would send him to his death for this?'

My dear, my good father. You left your ledgers and your books, you left your reticence and your caution, to plead for me. I think I never knew you loved me so well as that. Your censure had stayed with me, your affection too. But to speak of me in this way: had I pulled the wool over your eyes too? Or is it that you truly saw me, as, in my heart, my mortal soul, I yearned and strove – and bled, and died – to be. For I never knew myself. I was a stranger. Even, an enemy passing for a friend.

Let me tell you, here and now, by the heaviness of my sins or of a quill pen, not *one* of you can judge me more harshly than I will judge myself.

But you are beginning to be outraged.

You say (of course), How can he speak to us *now?* He's dead. Didn't we watch the goddess in the square do for him? Didn't we see the body, in two installments, rolled in a grave, and the quicklime, and the earth? How then can I go on shouting, from my chair precariously balanced on a table in the Palais-Infini?

Why, because there is something left of me to shout, voiceless, maybe, but vocal for all that. No, not my soul, not my ghost. That is theosophy. What, then? Ah, but it's hard to describe. Let me say – and conceivably you, who live, will understand me – let me say I can go on speaking because I *have spoken.* I can live still because I *have lived.* No atom ever lost. Each of us will leave an undying echo behind him. One needs only to listen; you will hear. And so you have.

And so you have heard me out, all this great way. Followed my search, my cross-examination of self, with all its evasions, lapses of memory, and all its biases I could not, try as I would, correct, and my affiliations of the heart, some too personal, that filled this space with ecstasy, tribulation, and ridiculousness. And wretchedness.

Such discoveries made! I had forgotten, for example, how well I loved Robespierre, despite – despite. I had not bargained on the force of hate still lingering, poignantly surprised at itself, or the debts accrued by hate (Marcandier, who died out of my sight on the anniversary of the day I had called Paris to arms) or supposed, reasonable debts which somehow have been canceled – Brissot, Pétion. I *had* reckoned on the falseness of remembered things, the traps they set. Into several snares I have plunged and in the end was content to lie there, telling not quite the truth, or truth *out of order* – since oddly, by the very juxtaposition, I found I had reached another truth, which was, of the alternatives, more true.

I would have tried to betray, or misfigure, no one but have doubtless done it – yet again. Where I have spoken ill of them, it springs from pain (oh, yes, pain also lingers). I can't retract, would not. I think by now you know me, and make allowance for the libels of immaturity and of despair.

For what I did, you have heard enough of my guilt. You have the facts at your disposal, all the facts I could summon.

It comes to me—too late, naturally, and there is a rationale, too, in that lateness—that any man who tries to change the world, unless he is God or all the gods together, can manage much—but much of that much will be a nightmare and, worse, chaos. Those who attempt the feat, the idealists and dreamers, are too drunk on their ideals and dreams to see the errors in their modus operandi. They end to the neck in blood as we did, all of us. The deity we created devoured its own fathers. (The name Camille derives from the Etruscan. It means Attendant at the Sacrifice. Fortune must have had a hand in that.)

Nevertheless, I will not relinquish the Dream. It remains before mankind, of which sacred brotherhood I have been a member, like a flaming beacon. If passion cannot reach it, hope may. Still I cry out, even with all my sins to thrust down the balance and send me to hell—still I cry out, Bring the sea to Paris, seek the unbelievably beautiful girl—though the city beach stays empty and she—she is too lovely to exist. The facility to hope and to dream is the birthright of men, by which they sustain themselves in the cold and darkness of the cosmos and of the heart. And, as we learn, who knows but in the end we shall be wise enough to reach the distant light, and to live as gods live, but with the goodness of which felonious man alone, and never the gods, is capable. For man is the wingless one who has learned to fly, high as birds, in the golden balloon of aspiration. Oh, believe in this child that we are.

Truly, so much beyond myself, I wanted that glittering freedom and that beauty—not merely for myself, not merely for France—it was some incoherent vision of the whole earth, set free from chains, in the heaven of some morning far away, that I had dreamed of, forgotten, yet *remembered.*

But I too was a baby. Phaëthon-like, I tried to touch the sun, and burned the world, and burnt my hands.

I don't ask for pity. If I have seemed to ask for it, you mistook me—perhaps small wonder. A margin to collect myself. But that is all Camille now asks. I have told you why he did as he did, which is not to excuse it. Now he rests his case, lest you tire of all the oratory of the pen, the feather thrown to weigh against his educated ignorance, thoughtless capacity for love, thoughtless ability to be cruel, his clever foolishness, every ash and ember of his fire, which we call Life. The feather the pen that, with each joke and jibe, wrote his very soul, also, across the page.

Without pride or shame, now, I must accept that I too have helped to make the future. The future will judge me.

And I stand before that ultimate verdict, my head bowed, my hands tied, finally silent. Judge me, then.

I am at your mercy.

Non omnis moriar.